I0760524

Lottie's Luck

A Novel of Frontier West Texas

By Preston Lewis

Bariso Press ★ San Angelo, Texas

San Angelo, Texas

ISBN: 978-1-964830-01-8

Cover design by: Preston Lewis
Edited by: Harriet Kocher Lewis

Library of Congress Control Number: 2024910770
Printed in the United States of America

In Memory
of
Jeanne Williams

Who Provided
Hope
and
Encouragement Early
in My
Writing Career

Bariso Press
Harriet Kocher Lewis, Editor & Publisher

Lottie's Luck

Fall
1876

Chapter 1

Into his clenched fist he coughed once, twice, three times, each throbbing convulsion gouging at his lungs. Today, the excruciating attack had started sooner than usual, but he was up earlier than normal. The Fort Griffin stage left Jacksboro at seven o'clock on Saturdays, and John Henry Holliday planned to catch it.

His cough hacked through the cool stillness as light chased away the faint stars in the western sky. A stinging scorpion, seeking a hiding place from the emerging daylight, scurried from a crack in the gray clapboard sidewalk toward the leather medical satchel and maroon carpetbag on the weathered planks outside Dan Brown's General Merchandise. With the toe of his boot, Holliday crushed the arachnid, grinding it into the splintery wood well beyond the lethal requirement. As he slid his right hand inside his black broadcloth frock coat, his nimble fingers brushed against the .38-caliber Smith and Wesson pocket revolver in the clip-spring shoulder harness, then skirted the sheathed dagger in the breast pocket before pinching a splotched handkerchief free. After wiping his hand, he jammed the blue cloth to his mouth to shut off another spasm, or at least catch consumption's debris.

Over the cloth in his balled fist, his blue eyes, deep and foreboding like an unfilled grave, focused on a cavalry officer marching toward him with army-precise steps, uniform new and crisp, face handsomely chiseled beneath a brown mane and matching eyes that were curious but pleasant.

John Henry Holliday wondered if he should kill the captain.

If he must, Holliday could blame only himself. He had violated his rule for survival: Never return somewhere you are unwelcomed but wanted. Just fifteen months ago, in a Jacksboro saloon, Holliday had wagered a token of lead against an identical bet from a cocky Fort Richardson lieutenant no luckier at gunplay than at cards. The bullet, which had rearranged the lieutenant's chest cavity, could have hurt no more than the tuberculosis in his own lungs. But Holliday had not lingered that night to inquire. He had grabbed the disputed pot and, by the time the white smoke of black powder had cleared, so had Holliday.

Jacksboro had numbered one less gambler among its population that night—and would have still, except for Lottie.

Some faro dealers were better; none were prettier. Lottie Deno, she called herself, was a lady, no saloon harlot available for the taking. The same dark auburn hair, gray eyes, down-turned lips and sexual aloofness attracting Fort Richardson soldiers and Jack County cowboys to her faro table in swarms had drawn Holliday back to Jacksboro, like a bee to honey.

As Holliday fought the recurring cough, the captain sidestepped a puddle spotting the street from last night's shower and preserved the shine on his new boots. If this officer asked about the lieutenant's murder, he would die wearing fine footwear, Holliday thought. Turning away from the officer and switching the handkerchief to his left hand, Holliday unbuttoned his frock coat and hooked it behind the 1851 Colt Navy revolver holstered at his waist. His empty gun hand tensing for business, Holliday twisted to meet the soldier. He noted the captain lacked a sidearm, but wore the insignia of the Tenth Cavalry. His deceased poker victim had ridden with the Sixth Cavalry. Holliday's fingers relaxed.

The captain marched toward him with the martial precision of a soldier who remembered what it was to be a lieutenant. His step crisp, his uniform fitted to his lean frame like bark on a tree, he betrayed neither fear nor recognized danger. Holliday's thin lips, fringed by the bottom of his handlebar moustache, twitched at the corners into a sinister scowl.

Perversely amused that this inscrutable captain might spoil his clandestine return to Jacksboro, Holliday remembered his precautions, faultless except for this chance encounter. He had timed his arrival for Friday afternoon and his departure for Saturday morning. Between the two, he had scoured the saloons where Lottie once dealt faro. Holliday had stabled his horse at Harrell and McLeod's Livery at the northwest corner of the courthouse square and paid three days in advance. As long as the mount remained in the livery yard, Sheriff Crutchfield or Marshal Bingham, should they learn of his arrival, might not so soon discover his departure. Holliday would buy time with his horse and saddle, for both were well worn. At the Horton House, he had rented a ground-floor room for three days. Then this morning, while it was still dark, he had climbed out the room window with his medical satchel and carpetbag. Clinging to the back of buildings, he had walked to the store of Dan C. Brown, general merchandiser and agent for C. Bain and Co. stage lines, and paid his Fort Griffin fare to a spindly, bespectacled clerk more interested in reading the paper than waiting on customers.

Now as he stood anxiously, his fingers curving to fit the ivory grip and trigger of his nickel-plated revolver, Holliday tilted his head toward the street. The cavalryman approached the clapboard sidewalk and stopped. Holliday ruptured into a coughing spasm, covering his mouth with the handkerchief in his left hand. Despite the cough's quiver, his steady right hand froze on the Colt's ivory grips.

"Good morning," the captain said, his voice no more threatening than the call of a quail.

"Depends on what kind of night you had."

"Sounds like you've had better."

"They're all the same these days." Holliday relaxed his fingers. Talkers weren't fighters. He unhooked his coat from behind his revolver and shoved his dirty handkerchief back into his pocket.

The captain extended his hand. "Heading for Griffin?"

"If that's where the stage is going." Holliday bent and unlatched his carpetbag. From among the spare change of clothes and the fresh decks of cards, he extracted a half-full quart bottle. Uncorking it as he straightened, he paused, then drowned a budding cough with two cheek-bulging gulps of bourbon. "Medicine," he sneered and dropped the re-corked bottle in the valise. Turning before the captain could reply, he stalked inside Dan Brown's store and shoved the door shut, its windows rattling as he advanced past the valise on the dark varnished plank flooring and down the slick, whitened path between mounds of darkened merchandise. As Holliday moved toward the lone clerk standing in the halo of a single lamp on the far counter, his step fell softly on a floor that usually creaked with weight.

The spindly clerk glanced up indifferently from behind yesterday's edition of *The Frontier Echo*, advertising Brown's wares purchased in New York, Philadelphia, and other eastern cities, then turned to the last page.

"When's the stage leaving?" Holliday demanded.

Frowning, the clerk cocked his head and eyed Holliday through the smudged lenses of his spectacles. "On time."

Holliday admired the economy with words, unless he wanted information. He leaned his arms on the counter's glass case and drummed his fingers. "Any other passengers?"

Grimacing at the smudges Holliday tapped on the glass, the clerk folded the paper in half. "The captain out there. His fare's paid. His bag's by the door."

Holliday shrugged. "He talks too much for me."

"Next stage departs for Griffin in three days. Same time of day," the clerk offered, placing the newspaper on the neat rolltop desk against the back wall.

"How about your paper?" Holliday asked. "Reading beats talking."

"Only one I got," the clerk replied, his shoulders drooping with boredom.

"Fellow like you shouldn't have trouble getting another. Easier than me trying to find one between here and Griffin."

"This one's Mr. Brown's, not mine. He likes to see his advertisements in print."

A commotion outside closed the subject. A bottle-green Concord stage rumbled to a stop, its four dry wheels screeching with thirst, its trace chains jingling from each bump remembered, its six mules bawling at tight harnesses and the driver's curses.

The attendant bolted through the swinging counter gate for the front door. "If you're going to Griffin, better be fast about it," he snorted. "Chuck cares more for his mules than his passengers, and his mules are impatient." The clerk grabbed the officer's valise and flung the door open. "Got one more coming, Chuck," he yelled.

"He'd best hurry," Chuck shot back, spitting a muddy stream of tobacco over his scuffed boot on the brake lever.

Holliday tugged the wide lapel on his tailored frock coat and stepped past the batwing gate and around the counter to the rolltop desk. Picking up Mr. Brown's paper from the neatly organized documents, Holliday folded it twice more and stuck it inside his coat. His unhurried gait carried him outside, where the braying mules complained as much as they broke wind.

"Decided to go after all?" the attendant taunted as he bent over Holliday's satchel and carpetbag. "Want your bags in the boot?"

Lottie's Luck

"I carry my own," Holliday said, grabbing them from the clerk and sliding to the stage. He planted his foot on the folding step and leaned inside the coach, tossing his bags on the rear bench. The captain lounged in the preferred seat, his back to the front of the conveyance. Holliday skirted him and the middle bench, sliding onto the cushioned leather of the back seat. As the clerk slammed the door, Holliday poked his elbow out the window and jerked from his coat the purloined paper.

The mules pulled against their harnesses, tugging the coach against the brake, as the clerk lifted the folding step. "Let 'em loose, Chuck," he shouted.

The stage lurched forward. Holliday stuck his head and the unfolded paper out the window. "Tell Mr. Brown thanks for the reading material," Holliday called, grinning as the clerk kicked at the street and shouted epithets. A laugh tumbled out of Holliday's throat, which erupted into an uncontrolled cough that he spit outside.

The stage rumbled down the street, accompanied by the noise of clinking trace chains, rattling double-trees, creaking harness leather, and the popping of the driver's whip—like firecrackers celebrating the departure. Skirting the courthouse square and turning wide around the corner, the coach leaned heavy into the thoroughbrace support, rocked gently as the team gathered speed in front of the crumbling sandstone courthouse, then passed the row of lesser stores and saloons and headed out of town toward Fort Richardson.

A half mile south of town, Holliday spotted the oak, cottonwood, and pecan trees growing in clumps along Lost Creek. Across the pathetic creek stood the buildings of the army post. The fort awoke slowly this morning, as it did most days now that the Comanche and Kiowa threats had diminished. The soldiers moved singly or in pairs between breakfast and their tasks. By the stream a laundress built a fire beneath a black wash pot. And farther upstream, two soldiers filled the post's water wagon. The soldiers, once in numbers great enough to make twenty-seven saloons profitable between the Jacksboro square and the edge of government property, were gradually being decimated by War Department reassignment rather than Indians. Extinct or soon to be were the Island, First National, Union Headquarters, Little Shamrock, and Last Chance saloons.

The road, still damp from yesterday's shower, pulled away from Lost Creek and Fort Richardson toward Belknap and Graham. An economical landscape—not given to the frills of mountains or tall trees—stretched westward in rolling, grass-covered swells that waved with the dry breeze at the ever distant horizon. Holliday stared at the vista, then picked up the paper from his lap as a shield from the captain, who dozed. Gradually, though, the pain returned to Holliday's lungs. Dropping the news sheet, he opened his carpetbag for another boost from his bottle. He popped the bottle's cork, startling the officer, whose eyelids fluttered open for an instant, before drooping shut.

The Frontier Echo slipped from his lap to the floor. As he picked it up, his gaze fell across a bold black headline over two paragraphs at the bottom of the first page. He snapped the paper to his face and, despite the bouncing of the coach, read the dispatch quickly:

> *"Wild Bill (James B. Hickok) was murdered in a mad cowardly manner by one Jack McCall shooting him in the back of the head while he was playing cards.*
>
> *"McCall claimed that Bill murdered his brother several years ago. McCall, after standing a sort of mock trial by the miners, was acquitted."*

Occupational hazard, Holliday thought. A gambler created his own justice in the west, and if the deck was stacked against him in one town, he'd best clear out and stay out. Holliday had violated that credo but once, and that single time for Lottie.

He studied another story about the luckless cavalry still chasing Sitting Bull and the Sioux across the northern plains. Almost three months had passed since Sitting Bull had made news of George Armstrong Custer and his Seventh Cavalry command. Sitting Bull, evidently pessimistic about his own future, had kindly conveyed to the *Boston Transcript* his "last words" now reprinted in *The Frontier Echo*. "Wah-wah, munkgooro, nix-any," reported the account, "which freely translated means 'Don't let 'em write any dime novels about me.'"

Holliday grinned as he threw the paper on the middle bench seat, braced himself with another swig of whiskey, and watched the west Texas countryside wither as it passed before his eyes at eight miles an hour. Now and then he spotted the bleaching bones left by the buffalo hunters. Fortunes had accrued off those skeletons, and Holliday had collected a cut of his own from them at Jacksboro's faro tables. But the buffalo slaughter and the killings at the gaming tables had moved west to Griffin, the roughest town in west Texas before El Paso.

The officer stirred, stretched, and yawned his eyes open. Holliday, sensing the captain's gaze sizing him up, returned the favor. The captain was a precisely made fellow, lean and tightly muscled on a medium frame the way General Sherman, who on this very road four years earlier had avoided an Indian ambush only by the whim of a Kiowa medicine man, liked his cavalry troopers. His wavy brown hair, parted down the middle, matched his brown eyes, squint-wrinkled at the corners from too many months in the field searching for water and Indians but finding little of either. He was narrow-jawed, broad-nosed and thin-mouthed, but his features lacked a military hardness, as if he were more at ease following orders than giving them.

"Conversation bother you?" he asked.

"I prefer cards."

The captain's eyes narrowed. "You sound southern."

"Georgian! General Sherman's locusts devastated my state," Holliday answered.

"I wasn't there."

"But you're still a Yankee. Every blue uniform I see reminds me of the stench the Yankees left behind after they torched Georgia." He reached into his valise and extracted a pack of Hart's Linen Eagle cards. Pulling the pasteboards from the box, he manipulated them adroitly between his nimble fingers. "Care for a friendly game?" he offered.

"I don't gamble."

"Sure you do. That's all life is. Soldiering on the edge of the Texas frontier is a gamble as well." Holliday slipped the cards into his carpetbag, pulled his revolver from his shoulder holster and aimed the weapon at the officer's heart. "Right now you're gambling my trigger finger doesn't slip."

The captain never flinched. "You, my Georgia friend, will be gambling not only with cards in Griffin but with your life. Vigilantes take your type straight to Judge Lynch, instead of court."

Holliday smirked and returned the pistol to his shoulder holster.

The captain motioned toward *The Frontier Echo* on the bench seat between them. "Mind if I read your paper for a spell?"

"As long as it'll keep you from gabbing."

The soldier retrieved the news sheet and settled back into his corner. For several miles they rode without words, hearing only the coach sounds, Chuck's affectionate blasphemy for his mules, and Holliday's monotonous cough until the captain whistled.

Bending down the corner of the paper, he stared at Holliday. "Somebody killed Wild Bill Hickok. Been a rough year for gamblers, wouldn't you say?"

"A worse year for blue-belly soldiers. Just ask General Custer."

The captain shook his borrowed paper and said nothing more until Belknap, where a gate salesman with a squeaky voice and jittery eyes climbed aboard the stage and began a conversation with the officer, returning often to the merits of the gates he was willing to sell the army.

****

A heavy stench drifted across the prairie. Before Holliday could see the town, he could smell it. The fetor discomforted him, so he jerked the bottle from his carpetbag and drained it. Instantly, he felt better. Bourbon solved many problems.

The Flat, as the place was called, rested in a broad valley carved by the waters of the Clear Fork of the Brazos, a river traversing Texas from the High Plains to the Gulf of Mexico. Beside the Clear Fork, Fort Griffin the town had sprung up as a parasite at the foot of Government Hill, the terraced plateau where the military post had preceded the thriving community. Now both the post and the settlement shared a name and a deathly odor, the breeze reeking of rotting flesh still clinging to thousands of buffalo hides. For Holliday, it was the perfume of money.

The gate drummer squirmed in his seat, wrinkling his narrow nose. The captain sensed his perplexity. "First time to Griffin?"

"Yeah," the drummer replied, covering his nose.

"You're smelling it."

"Bad as a gut wagon!" The drummer shifted uneasily in his place.

"Now that the weather's cooled, it's not bad, not like it was. Fewer hides now. You'll grow used to it."

"I don't plan on staying long."

"Just as well," the captain said, staring at Holliday. "Griffin's hard to like. More vagabonds and temporary trash in the Flat than any town I've ever seen. Maybe five or six hundred permanent residents and twice that number of thieves, gamblers, prostitutes and other vermin hang around Griffin." As his words tumbled past a West Point smile, the captain's eyes locked on Holliday's.

Holliday glared back. "The stench comes from the blue bellies at the fort."

Slowly, the captain leaned forward and pointed out the window. "Judge Lynch must've held court for a gambler."

Toward a bend in the Clear Fork a hundred yards distant, Holliday spotted the distorted body of a man hanging from a pecan tree. The drummer saw the corpse as well and sank deeper into his seat, his face crumpling with a grimace.

Holliday scoffed. "He didn't play his cards right, Captain, but you should never bet against a gambler."

"I hold gamblers with the same contempt you hold Union soldiers. Nothing you have said has changed my estimation. I may be a fool, but I'm no coward or liar."

Holliday's lips curled into a cynical smile. "You're no fool, Captain." He leaned out his stage window. On the plateau ahead, he spied the Stars and Stripes waving atop a fifty-foot flagpole at the military post. The coach lurched down, then up a smooth gully, the driver cursing the tired mules for their awkward footing. Slipping forward in his seat, Holliday grabbed the strap handhold and studied the countryside just in case he should need to leave Griffin, as he had Jacksboro, on the run.

The valley was broad and long. The Clear Fork twisted like a huge, shimmering serpent in the late afternoon sunlight. Beside the river rose stands of oak, cottonwood, and pecan trees, their leaves tinging yellow with fall. Cradled in one giant curve of the river was a fine grove of trees surrounding a gigantic cottonwood with no competitor growing in its shade. Sharp green grama grass still thriving on the moisture of a summer flood tinted the stream banks as far as the eye could see. Beyond that ribbon of green all the way to the slope of Government Hill, the Flat melded in with the gray of the distant grass, the tan of the ground, and the dark brown splotches of buffalo hides piled as high as a strong man could throw them from the bed of a freight wagon. Holliday noted a strand of thirty tepees strung out along the creek a half mile upstream from town.

"Looks like Sitting Bull's found you, Captain," Holliday scowled.

"Tonkawa. They're harmless," the officer offered. "They scout for the army."

Holliday nodded. "Between the buffalo hides, the Tonkawas and the blue bellies, no wonder Fort Griffin stinks."

"Don't forget the other vermin, mister."

"Yeah," Holliday grinned. "We discussed them earlier." He twisted in his seat to better view the Flat. More tents than buildings sprouted from the soil, but even so, some sixty structures lay scattered up and down the creek. Outnumbering the buildings and tents, great bundles of deep brown buffalo hides stood stacked in piles behind the merchant houses and in less imposing but more numerous stacks beside many tents. Baled and ready for shipment like cotton on a Galveston wharf, the hides welcomed the coach with their rancid odor.

As the stage drew closer to the creek, Holliday observed the flotsam of a summer flood. Brush and debris hung like Christmas decorations on the low branches of trees rooted in the bank; bundles of grayed grass queued up behind every stump or rock that poked from the earth; and pieces of driftwood, like bloated corpses, lay half submerged where they had snagged along the shore.

When the stage hit the water crossing, the shouts of the driver flushed a trio of turkey buzzards from atop the naked limbs of a dead cottonwood. Emerging from the water, the stage attracted a buzzing swarm of insects, big ugly blow flies sensing in the autumn air the end to a prosperous summer feasting on rotting buffalo flesh. Holliday swatted at the pesky insects, spitting one from his mouth. "Damn flies," he sputtered, jerking his whiskey bottle to his lips, then remembering he had drained it half an hour ago at the first whiff of Griffin. He tossed the empty out the window and watched it cartwheel by the roadside, startling a mangy hound scrounging about for a meal. The dog snarled at the glass intruder, sniffed at it, then turned toward the creek and a string of cribs where harlots on cornhusk mattresses allowed men to spend their money and themselves on female companionship.

The road, hard-packed from the tons of hides it had carried, led straight through the Flat and up Government Hill to the post. Flanking the road, widely spaced buildings were laced together with a myriad of footpaths and wagon trails among the ricks of buffalo hides. A few buildings wore false fronts, and even fewer boasted chiseled native stone walls. Most stood as an unpretentious cross between the functional and the intolerable, the illegitimate offspring of adobe and pickets, chinked and painted with sand and lime.

In the late afternoon sunlight, the street boiled with Saturday activity, the horses, wagons, and pedestrians parting for the stage to pass. Holliday, more interested in spotting old enemies than in making friendly acquaintances, searched for familiar faces. Seeing none among the stew of human leftovers mixing on Griffin Avenue, he looked next for saloons which might hire a good faro dealer, or serve good liquor. He preferred the latter, but there were eight or ten, saloons that could suit either need.

Ahead a knot of cheering men blocked the road. The stage stopped shy of the Bee Hive saloon, which spewed patrons into the street to see the finish of fisticuffs started inside. Holliday opened the stage door and leaned outside to see the commotion. The shouting spectators jeered as one pugilist, ducking too late to avoid an iron right hand, dropped like a ball of lead in front of the stage's mules.

Chuck popped his whip at the dispersing crowd. "Damn you all, somebody jerk his tail out of the street before I decorate him with muleshoe and wagon tracks."

"Do it yourself, you old coot," yelled a cowhand grown eloquent from liquor.

Glimpsing the insolent spectator before he could meld into the throng, Chuck snapped his twenty-foot whip. The drunk's hat flew off like a felt duck.

"If you don't want me to pick your nose with this bullwhip, you'd better move your friend," Chuck threatened.

The cowboy ran his fingers through his exposed auburn hair. "He ain't my friend," he answered, bending to grab his hat. The whip flashed like lightning through the air and cracked thunder at the cowhand's ear, drawing blood. The lanky cowpuncher slapped his ear and shot straight up.

"Unless you want your other one to match, move that jackass out of my way."

Convinced of both the driver's sincerity and his skill with a whip, the hatless spectator struggled to drag away the defeated fighter, twice tripping over his unconscious load. The instant the wobbly but humbled cowhand cleared the mules, the driver urged the animals forward, right over the cowhand's hat. Holliday drew himself back inside the stage, but before he could settle in, the coach stopped at the building beside the Bee Hive.

Instantly, an agent opened the door and welcomed the three passengers to Griffin, even calling the captain by name. Holliday grabbed his medical satchel and grip, emerging from the stage first, his thin frame aching from every jolt between Jacksboro and the Flat. He tramped to the back of the coach, working loose the knots in his legs and shaking the kinks from his arms, then stepped to the plank walk, where the aroma of food piqued his nose.

He felt icy stares upon himself and looked beyond the passing faces toward a lanky man wearing a badge and a broad-shouldered fellow leaning casually against a hitching rack, rolling a smoke in his massive hands and returning Holliday's stare. Depositing his cigarette fixings in a tobacco tin under the sleeve garter on his left arm, the man straightened from the hitching rack and shoved the smoke into his harelipped mouth, his thumbnail flicking a flame from the match in his hand. His eyes were deep-set and dark. Even the flame tipped to his cigarette failed to penetrate the intent of his brooding eyes. As the big man inhaled, the cheeks of his broad face deflated, then regained their normal shape as a stream of smoke flowed out of his flat nose over the ragged moustache which could not hide his harelip. Holliday eyed the stranger's brawny frame, taking in his starched white shirt with sleeve garters, his bulky gabardine britches tucked in Napoleon leg boots, his wool hat and, most importantly, his suspenders. Without a belt, the stranger lacked a sidearm. The lawman seemed less interested in Holliday than the big fellow in suspenders.

From among the passing throng, a woman jumped off the plank walk and rushed past the smoker toward the stage. Holliday admired the fair cut of her narrow-waisted figure, the bounce of her freshly washed blond hair, the glimmer of emeralds in her eyes. As the captain pulled his grip from the stage's boot and stood erect, she threw her arms around him and planted her lips upon his, bringing a cheer from an envious buffalo hunter.

She came close to being a widow today, Holliday thought.

The captain, breaking from his wife's kiss, seemed to sense Holliday's thoughts. Turning from the wetness of his woman's lips, the officer squinted at Holliday, his narrow jaw and thin lips tight like his hand on his wife's arm.

Holliday laughed. "Enjoyed our conversation."

"You're among your kind here," the officer replied, his voice tight with sarcasm.

"I'll bet." Holliday stepped on the dilapidated walk, turning from the big fellow and the badge-toter just as another guy approached, extending his hand with a business card between his fingers.

"Should you need a horse or rig, I run the best livery stable in town. Pete Haverty's my name."

Holliday took the card and studied it: HAVERTY'S LIVERY STABLE/HORSES FOR RENT & SALE/WILL RACE HORSES. PETE HAVERTY, PROPRIETOR.

"No better horseflesh in town than my stable," Haverty offered.

Holliday slipped the card in his coat pocket. "I need a steak, not a horse."

"Try Uncle Billy's Eatery," Haverty said, pointing down the street, "but remember me, if you need a horse." Haverty tipped his hat and ambled off in the opposite direction.

As he neared the café and the aroma of food tickled his nose, Holliday stared through the smudged window at Uncle Billy's Eatery, then shoved his way inside. The long, narrow, frill-less room smelled of fresh food and stale men, and its unlit lamps and low ceiling accentuated the dwindling afternoon light. Roughhewn benches carried the weight of two dozen appetites. Hunters, cowhands, a couple soldiers and two women of uncertain virtue, shared the seats and a common like for the cooking. The mob attacked a huge buffalo roast in the middle of a long table. Platters of fried salt pork and sweet potatoes and bowls of canned tomatoes and corn cakes populated either side of the meat or circled the table as patrons spooned out extra helpings. A chorus of spoons and forks hitting the tin plates rang out over the conversation subdued by stuffed mouths.

The slight meaty aroma wafting toward him stirred his stomach, and he moved to the closest end of the table where the bench was less crowded. As he dropped the carpetbag by his feet and placed his medicine satchel atop the plank, a fellow talking with an Irish brogue approached, wiping his hands on his ankle-length, stain-splattered apron, smiling through his unkempt beard like he'd just won a poker hand or found a new customer.

"Me name's Billy Wilson, Uncle Billy mos' folks call me, and I run this place. Just off the stage, are ya, mister?" The words rolled off his tongue like the alphabet in an avalanche. "'Tis a far ride from Belknap, maybe e'en Jacksboro, eh? 'Tweren't President Grant on the stage with ya 'twas he?"

Hell, no, thought Holliday, but he only shook his head.

"Okay, boys," Billy Wilson boomed across the room, "the president didn't arrive today, so ya table manners ain't so importan' now 'cause if ya be spilling somethin' on me tablecloth, I'll 'ave time to wash and iron it 'fore the next stage. Jus' don't spill somethin' I can't wash out."

The other customers ignored Wilson, who confided to Holliday that President Ulysses S. Grant wasn't actually coming to Fort Griffin, the lie being perpetrated only to preserve among these ravenous men the virtue of his only white tablecloth.

"I can serve ya the bes' meal on the Texas frontier or regale ya with true tales of what 'twas like to pan for gold on the Yuba River in the Rush of Forty-Nine out in Californy." He unhooked his wire-rimmed glasses and dabbed at the lenses with a patch of his dirty apron.

"A plate and fork'll do, along with a cup of coffee. I've got my own knife," Holliday answered. He reached inside his coat and pulled out his dagger, placing it on the table cloth.

"I'd be rich today 'ad I gone prospectin' up the middle fork of the Yuba River instead of the north fork," Wilson continued, replacing his spectacles and squinting his eyes back into correct focus. "Why, I'd live in a gingerbread mansion on Nob Hill in San Francisco and spend a couple months a year back in Ireland, showin' me distant cousins how a gentleman lives. And, I'd have—"

"Stop your palavering," ordered a stern woman who waddled up beside Wilson. Her eyes were bloodshot and sweat-rimmed from her work in the kitchen, and her shoulders drooped from bending too much over a hot stove. "Only one gentleman in this conversation, and he's a customer. Fetch him some grub," she scolded.

"If I'd gone up the middle fork," Wilson murmured, "I'd a 'ad me a wife that'd let me finish a conversation." He strode off, swatting at a fly like it was his wife.

"Don't mind my husband none," Mrs. Wilson apologized. "He always is a talking when others just want a bit of grub, not gab. Uncle Billy'll get you a plate. Help yourself. There's plenty, or I can fix you an omelet for a nickel more. We got fresh eggs."

"That'll do," Holliday said, pointing at the roast, "if I can get a plate."

"Uncle Billy," she yelled, spying her husband halted in conversation, "hurry up with that plate 'fore you lose a customer or your wife. I slave back in that hot kitchen, and all you do is talk and collect their money."

A sheepish grin crossed Wilson's face, and he moved on, but too slowly to satisfy his wife, who waddled after him. From any angle, both looked like they enjoyed her cooking. Shortly, Wilson returned with a plate and eating utensils, collected a quarter, and promised he'd return with coffee.

Holliday removed the medicine bag from the bench and sat down, leaving plenty of space between himself and a buffalo hunter in need of a bath. Reaching for the meat platter, he took his dagger and cut off a generous portion of the buffalo roast. After serving himself with fried sweet potatoes, runny canned tomatoes and a pair of corn cakes, he took an occasional bite, toying with the food. The meal wasn't bad as vittles went, but the realization failed to match the expectation. Holliday figured most of life was like that, except for bourbon, good or bad. It never let him down. He wondered if Lottie would have been like bourbon or like everything else.

After a while, he gave up on ever getting coffee, as Uncle Billy tied himself up in another conversation, reliving the Gold Rush. Holliday stared at his plate, feeling the bench sag as a big man claimed a berth uncomfortably close. An uneasiness grated down Holliday's back like chalk on a slate. Out of the corner of his eye, he recognized the harelipped man who had eyed him off the stage. Behind his shoulder stood the lawman. The table trembled when the stranger dropped his clenched fists, one holding a smoldering cigarette, on the white cloth. Holliday reached with his right hand inside his coat toward his shoulder holster, then twisted his neck to study the man with the unhealthy curiosity. Their gazes met, Holliday detecting caution but not fear in this stranger's deep-set eyes. The man turned his face away and stared across the table.

"Not meaning to spook you, mister," he whispered, as if revealing a secret.

"Then why's that law dog shadowing you?"

"Sheriff Larn helps me out in a pinch."

"You might tell him there's a dead man hanging from a pecan tree a couple miles out of town."

The fellow snickered. "He knows. Now, we just watched you off the stage. Usually, I meet the stages looking for fools to part from their money. I don't take you for such as that, but you look like a man that might know of a good card mechanic, say a fellow that's skilled at squeezing the pips."

Holliday's tight muscles loosened, and he pulled his hand from the butt of the revolver under his coat. He didn't speak at first, just stared at the big man's clenched paws, rough with scarred knuckles. Holliday took a bite, in no hurry to respond. He wanted to consider the angles and if he were being set up. The big man betrayed no impatience as Holliday chewed his food. Holliday liked that. Patience was a virtue among swindlers.

"By gosh and by golly, 'tis Shawn Chancey," Uncle Billy Wilson said, stepping up beside Holliday. "As good an Irishman as ever to dirty a boot in Fort Griffin. What brings ya to me eatery on a Saturday evenin'? The slop ya serve in ya saloon not as good as Mrs. Wilson's cookin'?"

Chancey glanced over his shoulder. "Uncle Billy, sometimes I like to visit the other establishments in Griffin and steal their business. Take, for instance, this gentleman by my side. I'll have no trouble persuading him to eat a bite down at the Cattle Exchange. Granted my food's not as good as Mrs. Wilson's, but he's almost finished, and you've yet to set a cup of coffee before him."

Uncle Billy shrugged, turning around to see if Mrs. Wilson had discovered his forgetfulness. "Me apologies, mister. "Ya should've reminded me. I'll be back with a cup of mud for ya."

"Obliged," Holliday said as Wilson paused and looked at the peace officer.

"Shouldn't ya be out chasin' vigilantes, Sheriff Larn? Ma Wilson and the rest of Shackelford County would sleep better if ya was lookin' for the brigands."

Larn snarled his reply. "I can only tote this badge one place at a time. Saturday nights always mean trouble in the Flat, so I'll stay in town for a spell.

"Uncle Billy," said Chancey, "bring me a cup, too. We don't serve much coffee in my saloon." Then to Holliday he whispered again, "Wilson's a good man, talks too much, but he's trustworthy. Can't say that about a lot in Griffin."

"Can you say it about a fellow that has the sheriff stuck to his shoulder?" Holliday asked, lifting his fork at Larn.

Chancey took his time about answering. Holliday liked a man that chose his words carefully and didn't lower their value by flooding the market with them. Wilson returned with two cups of hot coffee, the heat clouding up around the edges of the tinware, then retreated to find another conversation.

"I run a saloon, but I'm no gambler, not with cards at least, though I do use gamblers to improve my take. Not sure you can say I'm trustworthy. If I were, I wouldn't watch the stage arrivals or be here with you now."

Holliday pushed his plate toward the middle of the table, answering softly. "It's hard to trust a guy with the law trailing him like a lost orphan." He smothered the cup with both hands for a sip of the burning coffee, swallowing it hard, like bad liquor. At least it was real coffee, not one of those poor imitations they tried to sell in some places. But real coffee wasn't bourbon, good or bad. Holliday decided to hear Chancey out, as long as he sent the sheriff along.

Chancey nodded slowly, looking over his shoulder at Sheriff Larn. "Take a walk, Jay, and I'll catch up with you later." The saloon owner waited until Larn exited the eatery before speaking again. "Now, do you know a good card mechanic?"

"I might," he offered, "if I can find him. What's the best hotel in town? That's where he would be."

"Planters House's better than most. It's away from the saloons and a little quieter than the others. It's the only hotel in town with locks on the doors."

"If I find this gentleman, what should I tell him?"

"Ask if he has enough money to get in a fifty-dollar house stakes poker game—"

"He does."

"—tell him to come to the Cattle Exchange Saloon around ten o'clock. Sit at the poker table farthest from the door. The dealer will be tooled. Your friend will win, splitting the proceeds thirty-seventy, with me getting the big end, of course."

Holliday mused over the offer. "Double the average take at thirty percent. Generous terms for a man you don't even know."

Chancey drained his coffee, then spoke. "You must take risks to make money. I need someone not recognized in the Flat. Several cattlemen returning from Kansas with full pockets think they can fatten their money rolls at my tables and at my expense. Looks funny if the house dealer wins it all."

"I'll pass along the message," Holliday said. "Anything else I should tell my friend?"

Chancey stood up, crushing his cigarette stub in the empty coffee cup. "Tell him to stay out of the Bee Hive. At least for now."

Chapter 2

From the frameless poster tacked into the stark adobe wall, a Bengal tiger silently snarled, its paws upraised to fend off the clouds of cigar and coal oil smoke. The large cat, its comic orange and black stripes as gaudy as its circus broadside kin, hawked the Bee Hive's faro tables. Except for the splattered remnants of spittoons missed and the pockmarks of bullets gone awry, only the paper animal decorated the wall. Faro was the lord among games of chance; the tiger, faro's deity.

Only in the great cat's green eyes smoldered a semblance of life, but they were forever stilled in ink, staring down upon a dealer beginning another shift in the Bee Hive. This cardsharp shuffled the deck from hand to hand in the fashion of the day, three dozen sets of eyes joining the tiger's, all transfixed on the swift hands. Back and forth, the dealer pitched alternate portions of the deck between soft, agile fingers. Bee Hive proprietor Mike Fogle, rearranging the house's orderly stacks of chips on the check tray, admired the faro dealer's fluid grace almost as much as the dealer's luck. Faro was more than just a game in the west, it was a religion. And this table was the most popular—and profitable—altar in his house of worship. After a final shuffle, the dealer squeezed the cards into a neat stack and placed them on the green felt.

Lottie Deno was ready for work.

"Gentlemen," she purred, the word floating like a downy cottonwood seed on a spring breeze, "and you are gentlemen for I allow only gentlemen to take my money—" She paused, a delicate smile lingering like a kiss upon her lips, "—if they can."

Her customers laughed, and she with them, an auburn ringlet shaking free from under the brim of her ribbon-spangled Parisian hat. She brushed the curl back in place.

Fogle felt the corner of his lips quivering against a smile. That damn curl. He'd seen it fall a hundred times, as if on cue, and a thousand times more he had watched her beguile her customers and dislodge the money from their pockets.

With Lottie behind the faro layout, the nobility and the serfdom of the west Texas lined up to buck the tiger. They gawked at her silky white hands, her refined neck, and her attractive face—the only flesh save for her delicate hands peeking from her long-sleeved, high-necked, floor-length dresses. Her pale skin captivated the men, all more accustomed to the wind-chapped, reddened faces of their wives and sweethearts or the thick skins of the prostitutes. Lottie's alluring gray eyes suggested liaisons that would never be. Her lips, down-turned at the corners, always said "no" more sensually than the downstairs calico queens could say "yes." And her soft auburn hair, slipping from under her broad yellow hat, invigorated fellows attuned to the drab colors of the fall prairie.

Lottie's beauty and charm, Fogle realized, deceived her customers, who sensed a vulnerability existing only in their minds. He knew within the folds of Lottie's delicate lemon dress, she packed a revolver, and in her hat she wore a hatpin as dangerous as any stiletto.

"Gentlemen," she said softly, "let us begin." Picking up the pasteboards, Lottie inserted them face up in the dealing box, a metal rectangle with a framed top exposing the identity of the top card. On one side, the box was open to admit the cards between the spring-fed tray, which kept the deck tight against the top frame. The opposite side was covered, except for a narrow lengthwise slit just wide enough for a single card to pass.

Lottie surveyed her domain, a rectangular table swathed with a green billiard cloth worn from activity. Thirteen spades were acid stained into the felt in two rows of six, the odd seventh card offset between the adjacent rows. She leaned over the dealing box and the discard squares tattooed into the cloth and rested one hand on the nearest row—the ace running from the left to the six on the right. With her other hand, she flicked tobacco ashes from the upper row, extending from the king on the left to the eight on the right. Looking up, she smiled. "I see some new faces at my table. A couple of you look a little too young for my game. You, in particular, cowboy," she said, pointing to a blushing youth, embarrassed further by his guffawing companions. "Promise me you won't bawl to mother when I take all your money."

The cowboy shrugged sheepishly. She was setting up another cow hand for a fall, Fogle thought as he unfolded an abacus-like device in front of the chips. From the kid's wide-eyed looks, he was no match for Lottie, the saloon owner guessed.

"Ma'am, I—," the young cattle herder struggled to complete his sentence, taking off his hat and running his fingers through his stringy auburn mop as if feeling for the words.

"He'd be pleased," shouted one of the red-faced cowboy's companions, "to tell his mother about this instead of what he plans to spend his money on downstairs later."

Everyone laughed, except Lottie. "If this is your first time, cowboy, good luck. What's your name?"

"Jimmy," he answered with a gulp.

"Let me explain how we play, Jimmy."

"Somebody should've explained to Jimmy how to play with that saloon gal downstairs," interrupted the youth's companion. Again, everyone but Lottie chuckled.

"It's a simple game, Jimmy." She pointed at the faro box. "The first card is soda, which doesn't count for anything. You place your bets on the cards you think will come up. You beginners just bet on one card at a time by placing your money atop it on the felt. When I pull the soda from the box, the card that shows is a loser. I take everything on that card. The next card is a winner, and I pay those who've backed it. Every two cards after soda is a turn, and we repeat the procedure until we get down to the final three pasteboards. The last card, hock, is dead. But, if you can pick the order of the final trio, I pay you four to one for calling the turn. Say you're better at picking losers than winners, then put your money on a card and drop one of these coppers atop it," she said, pointing to a stack of hexagonal tokens. "If that card comes up, I lose and reward you for coppering it. Of course, if you bet to lose and the card shows second, I win. Any questions?"

The bettors crowded closer to the table, shaking their heads and chattering for luck.

"Now, place your bets." She paused a moment as the men smelling of the prairie dropped their money all over the board. "One more thing for those still wet behind the ears at this. If on any turn two cards of the same denomination show up, I take half of all bets." She smiled. "That's how I win money for the house. And," she added, "for myself."

The gamblers chuckled.

"I know you gentlemen are good at counting buffalo hides and cattle, but remembering the cards is not so easy. To help you out," she said, motioning to her boss and his abacus-like device, "each game uses a casekeeper. Tonight, we are lucky to have Mike Fogle keeping case for us. He owns the Bee Hive and usually avoids such chores." She winked and leaned across the table. "But he thinks I cheat the house." She tilted her head closer to her customers and, in a mock whisper, continued. "I'd rather monkey with the house's take than swindle you gentlemen."

The bettors laughed as Lottie straightened, and Fogle held up the abacus. "Like on the layout, we have a set of thirteen cards and four beads opposite each one. As a card is played, the casekeeper moves a bead by that denomination. A glance can tell you what cards remain. But it won't do you any good because Lady Luck will always outsmart you. Let's play."

The men, including Jimmy, placed their bets on the layout.

"Okay." Lottie pulled the soda from the dealing box, exposing a seven of clubs, the house winner. Then she pushed the seven through the slot, revealing a queen of hearts.

"Whoopee," exulted Jimmy, lifting his sweat-stained felt hat and running his fingers through his red hair. "A winner."

A narrow smile broke across Lottie's lips, like a crack in ice. "Evidently, the ladies have all been good to you tonight," the words rolled provocatively off her tongue. "But I never knew a first bet to lose. It's the way Lady Luck ensnares you."

It wasn't just Lady Luck setting this cowboy up. Fogle nodded as he drew in the house's share and paid the lucky cowhand from his check tray. The Bee Hive owner settled back for a long night. The yellow light of naked kerosene lamps swinging from the ceiling beams cast an unhealthy glow through the smoky haze above him. Tobacco odors and the stench of men who worked more than they bathed mingled with the aroma of the high-priced cheap liquors his barkeeps hauled from the bar downstairs to quench the thirsts and deplete the money rolls of his customers. Fogle called a barkeep to bring a glass of iced lemonade for Lottie—she drank nothing stronger—and a whiskey for himself.

With the drinks from downstairs came the strains of music. A piano, fiddle and horn struggled to be heard over voluble drunks, brazen dance hall girls, and braggarts seeking a Saturday night's refuge from their hard lives. The music making it up the stairs arrived in fragments, choruses severed from stanzas, stanzas dismembered from songs. As Lottie paused her deal to sip the lemonade, Fogle stood and stretched his legs, surveying the room. Two competing faro tables, a half dozen poker games and a keno operation in the corner attracted respectable business, but garnered neither the crowd nor the profits that centered on Lottie's table. He glanced at the check tray now overflowing with chips and bills that ninety minutes earlier had resided in the pockets of the surrounding men. The Bee Hive, thanks to Lottie, drew more customers and made more money than any of the nine other saloons or three dance halls in the Flat. Fogle needed the cash to cover his own gambling debts. Thank God for Lottie, he thought, as slipped back into his chair.

"Shall we resume, gentlemen?" After a final sip of the cold lemonade, Lottie inserted the cards in the dealing box and pointed at Jimmy. "Maybe some of his luck will rub off on the rest of you."

Unlikely, Fogle thought. Had it been a man, Fogle might have called it cheating—the turns falling too often against her opponents, the splits coming too frequently to be mere chance—but with her he simply named it "Lottie's Luck" and enjoyed his share of the profits. Her finesse at blind shuffles, jogging cards and blind cuts made the manipulations hard to detect. And with her, no man tried.

"Hot damn," the innocent cowboy celebrated another winner. Then a blushing smile drifted across his reddening face. "Sorry, ma'am, my language, I mean, not about winning."

Lottie nodded her acknowledgement.

Fogle estimated the kid had increased his roll by a hundred and fifty dollars at the house's expense, but still he figured the youth would leave this game disappointed. He detected a glint of mischief in Lottie's gray eyes each time he won.

As Fogle pulled the knot from his string tie and unbuttoned the stiff paper collar around his sweat-moistened neck, he glanced about the gaming room. Business downstairs must be slowing because he observed two nymphs du prairie defying house rules by wandering among the gamblers, drumming up their trade. Fogle stared at the pair until they gazed his way. With a jerk of his head toward the stairs, he flushed them away. Their frivolous trade should never interfere with gambling's more serious calling. He yanked in the losing bets on Lottie's next hand, then looked back at staircase, thinking for a moment he had also glimpsed Big Nose Kate, ducking behind a pot-bellied stove. If it were Kate, it would take more than a glance to send her scurrying downstairs.

Lottie remained oblivious to everything but the game and the bettors. Her concentration, Fogle guessed, might be a large part of her success. Just as Lottie inserted the cards in the dealing box for another game, a strident harlot voice grated over the cacophony in the room. Dammit, Fogle thought. It had indeed been Kate dodging behind the stove. As he watched, Kate elbowed herself through the knot of spectators watching Lottie.

"Get out of my way, you varmints," Kate cried, holding the skirt of her scarlet dress in her hands. "Jimmy, where are you? Heard he was having a run of luck. Where is he?" The young cowhand winced at her voice. Big Nose Kate, well-endowed at both places men tended to notice and pay for, bulled herself nearer to the table. "Hey," she shouted, turning to slap an offender, "who pinched my fanny? You pay to play with this merchandise." With too many potential perpetrators, all looking equally guilty and amused, she lowered her hand to her face and pampered her rouged cheek. "Don't anyone here know how to treat a lady?"

"When we see one," answered a buffalo hunter behind her.

"You boys've spent too long herding cattle or chasing buffaloes to recognize a lady. It's affecting your manners. If you want a night with a woman instead of a few heifers, you best behave." Kate fluffed the black satin bow at her belt and then plowed through the crowd to the betting edge of the table. "So, there you are, Jimmy. You said you'd be back in an hour so I could teach you a few things. You're late. Let's go."

Lottie slammed the dealing box into the layout, knocking over two tall stacks of chips by Fogle's check tray. The spectators turned from the amusing spectacle of Kate to the simmering Lottie.

"Mike," she said to Fogle, all the time cutting her icy eyes straight at Kate, "you make the rules, now enforce them. The wag-tails belong downstairs, not in the gaming room."

Kate lifted her hooked nose, rolled her green eyes, and gave a sweeping gesture with her arms. "Pardon me, milady, but this young man and I have business to attend," she said, bringing one arm around his reddened neck and brushing her free hand across the front of his work pants. Jimmy grimaced and shifted away, but Kate stuck to him like a leech.

"As long as he stands at my table, you'll not pester or embarrass him with your loose ways. Conduct your business downstairs, or I'll find your crib and interrupt your customers with an offer to play cards."

Fogle stood up. "You know the rules, Kate. Now move."

Kate jerked her arm from around the cowboy's neck. "Jimmy, all she'll do is take your money. I'll give you something to remember."

"Yes, sir," Lottie said, "something the doctor will remember, too."

Kate's eyes flared like sap in a burning pine knot. Screaming like a wounded mountain lioness, she lunged across the betting layout, scattering the chips and money. Three men grabbed her flailing arms before she reached Lottie with her claw-like nails. Lottie's steady hand flew to a waist-high fold in her dress. Seeing the fellows had restrained Kate, she returned her empty right hand to the table.

"You boys that's got a hold of Kate," shouted the saloon owner, "throw her down the stairs."

"You horse's ass, Mike Fogle, I can well make my own way."

"But Kate, this is probably more hands than you've had on you in a week. I'd hate to deprive you of the sensation. After you fellows deliver her where she belongs, tell the barkeep to set you up with a couple of free drinks."

The three men jerked her from the table. Kate struggled against them, her flailing legs clearing a wide path through the spectators. "Jimmy," she called as they dragged her away, "don't forget our agreement."

"How can I?" he said meekly.

"I'll see you later," she smiled. "Bet you can't wait!"

"I guess," he replied, his eyes downcast, his face a deeper red than before.

Lottie picked up the cards and resumed shuffling. "Please excuse the interruption, gentlemen. It was a most inopportune display. Despite what that vile woman may have said, I have never dealt faro with more mannered gentlemen. My sincerest apology if you were offended by my response. Shall we continue?"

The men grunted their approval as they picked up the scattered chips and money.

"Perhaps I should reshuffle," Lottie announced, taking the cards from the dealing box and remixing them.

As Lottie inserted the deck in the faro box, Fogle spotted the soda card, a three of hearts, the card the fortune teller would read as sorrow or poverty. Fogle watched Lottie's eyes; the glint of mischief for Jimmy was gone.

"Okay, gentlemen, place your bets," Lottie said. "I hope the woman's intrusion ruined no one's luck." She looked at Jimmy without smiling.

By hock, Jimmy had lost his winnings plus the bankroll he had started with. Now he couldn't afford Kate, cheap though her price may have been.

Lottie's Luck, Fogle thought.

Chapter 3

Refreshed by a bath and by the aroma of shaving tonic, John Henry Holliday snapped the corners of his four-ply linen collar over a black silk cravat pierced by a gold stickpin. Staring into the cracked mirror nailed over the washstand, he adjusted the band with his nimble fingers, invigorated by the feel of a fresh shirt. He paused for a moment to gaze at the tintype of Lottie Deno he had propped against the back of the washstand.

With a quick catlike motion, he spun around and plucked the pocket Smith and Wesson from its clip-spring shoulder harness, aiming at the furniture. After dispatching the bed, the chair, the lamp table and the plain bureau, he sighted in on the seam of the mail-order-house wallpaper puckered from washbasin spills, squeezing off a final imaginary round, then checking the load. He repeated the process with the Colt sidearm. A man could never practice too much with cards or guns.

From the iron bedstead opposite the washstand, he lifted his vest, slipping it on and immediately covering it with his frock coat. He glanced again in the mirror, nodding his approval and tugging on his lapels. The suit had cost him plenty, but fine clothes made even a lunger feel better.

He patted in his pants pocket a money roll that was down to three hundred and fifty dollars and then slid his hand inside his coat. As his gaze fell on the wallpaper blister above the washbasin, his fingers flashed free of his attire, the thud of steel striking wood following instantly upon the motion. Holliday's dagger, dead center of the paper bubble, still vibrated as he grabbed the hilt and jerked it from the wall. Bending over as he returned the gleaming weapon back into its sheath, he blew out the lamp and stepped out the door.

When Holliday emerged from the Planters House, it was past ten o'clock, but he was in no hurry to keep Chancey's schedule. Patience was a virtue among gamblers, and Holliday avoided partnerships with men so eager to take a pot that they became careless. He would test Chancey's gambling mettle.

Holliday noted the convenience of Pete Haverty's Livery Stable across the street, should he need to steal a horse, then strolled north toward the Cattle Exchange. The cool air carried a stench that smothered the shaving tonic's aroma. Nearing Griffin Avenue, Holliday joined the throng of boisterous men and loud women wandering from sin to sin or watching a drunken Tonkawa, who squatted in the middle of the road, chanting incomprehensible songs, and trying to start a fire with a handful of twigs.

Holliday spat at the boots of three approaching soldiers, linked arm in arm and singing a bawdy tune. "Damn blue bellies," he called, his curse drowning in their rendition. Holliday crossed Griffin Avenue just ahead of two racing horsemen, one brushing by the Tonkawa pyromaniac. Wobbling to his feet, the Indian shook his fist and yelled, "Eat dung, white man!"

Holliday agreed with the sentiment and chuckled, then spied the Cattle Exchange and sidled up to a saloon window, the imperfect glass swarming with flies drawn by the seepage of a jaundiced light. Swiping away the flies, he peered inside. Chancey towered behind the bar, serving drinks and glancing often at a back table. Holliday's gaze fell on that spot. A dozen spectators gathered around it like the flies circling his head. Swatting at the buzzing pests a final time, Holliday, plenty tardy to gauge Chancey, surrendered the window to the insects. As he straightened his coat, a drunken teamster, one jigger shy of spending his night on the clapboard sidewalk, bumped into him. Holliday swung about, his hand darting for the Colt riding on his hip.

Staggering backward a step, the whiskey-addled teamster slurred a warning. "Watch where you're standing, fellow." The drunk raised his fist, holding an empty bottle.

"Watch it! Behind You!" Holliday called, pointing to the chanting Tonkawa in the street. "Comanche! Run!"

Screaming "Charge," the befuddled fellow broke toward the Indian, misjudging the step from the walk. The empty bottle, like the teamster, tumbled to the ground to stay awhile.

Letting his fingers slide off the ivory grip of his Colt, Holliday readjusted his coat and pushed through the saloon's swinging doors into a long, narrow room with a bar running along the entire wall to his right. From the back, a roulette wheel telegraphed its invitation to suckers. Money lay on three poker tables, a faro layout, and the rail of a billiard table rooted before a rear office door. Beneath the drooping horns of a mounted steer head—the taxidermic masterpiece among six longhorn heads hanging on the opposite wall—spectators clumped around the money game. A pot-bellied stove mid-room and a silent piano against the far wall divided the gaming tables from the front tables dedicated to drinkers. As he eased up to the bar, Holliday observed a dozen tables with customers and, weaving among them, a pair of prostitutes and a banjo player who overvalued his talent.

Chancey operated an orderly saloon, except for the banjo musician. Behind the bar the owner stood half a foot over six feet, his bullish shoulders the breadth of an ax handle, his powerful arms protruding from his rolled sleeves as threatening as a bear trap, and his thick fingers, when clenched, more sledge than fist. Set deep beneath his forehead, his black eyes were dull, like twin caves in a mountain too great to climb. From the harelip his jagged moustache failed to hide, Holliday guessed a few unwise men had tried besting that mountain. Except for Samuel Colt's invention, Chancey might have had few equals in all of Texas, but damn if his size didn't make him a better target, he thought.

Chancey glanced toward Holliday, offering no sign of recognition. Without emotion, he pulled his cigarette makings from the tin strapped around his left arm and constructed a smoke. Chancey was plenty patient, Holliday decided. Holliday propped his boot on the bar's brass footrail and rested his arms on the walnut top, noting in the backbar mirror reflected paintings of bulls, their testicles a prominent testament to their virility. He coughed into his fist, then wiped his hands on the soiled towel in the nearest handhold as Chancey, his cigarette smoldering, advanced.

"Mind handing me that towel when you're done?" Chancey asked through a cloud of smoke. After Holliday obliged, the owner tossed the used towel into the corner and offered Holliday a fresh one from under the bar. "What'll it be, a beer?"

"Whiskey," Holliday replied. "Good whiskey. Jigger first, then the bottle if it's good. No barreled house liquors."

"Ever try Silver Star sour mash whiskey?" he queried, reaching to the backbar for an amber bottle and the glass atop a pyramid of its mates.

Holliday shook his head.

"Many around these parts like it. Comes from Clark and Tollant, the liquor dealers in Weatherford."

"Yeah, Weatherford's known for great whiskeys."

Uncorking the fresh bottle, Chancey shrugged, then poured.

The gambler grabbed the brimming jigger, gauging the vile color of the liquid against the lantern light, then drained it. He grimaced. "This the best you got?"

"Didn't say it was the best. Just many folks like it."

"Your neighbors've never had good whiskey."

Chancey offered a harelipped grin. "I keep some quality liquor for special occasions." He bent over the backbar, slid a door open, and pulled out a virgin bottle. "Monarch Bourbon. Best I can get in these parts." He uncorked it and refilled the jigger.

Lifting the glass slowly to his lips, the gambler sniffed, then emptied its amber contents, savoring the taste before swallowing hard. "Don't give any of this to the locals. They won't appreciate it. I'll take the bottle."

Chancey shoved it at him. "Two dollars."

Holliday pulled the wad of bills from his pants pocket, dropping his payment on the counter.

"Mister, you look well heeled for the card game going on in back," he offered, wiping the bar.

"From the observers, I'd say it's the money table," Holliday said, his eyes aimed straight at Chancey's. "Only problem is, I don't feel too lucky tonight."

For an instant, Chancey's eyes, flaring like a powder flash in those dark caves, betrayed his stake in the game. But that sign passed so soon, Holliday wondered whether he had imagined it.

Holliday leaned closer. "With a fifty-fifty split of the winnings, I'd feel luckier," he said, tucking his money roll back in his pants pocket.

Chancey nodded with a narrow smile. "Well, sir, it's a pleasure serving you. Remember, next time you get thirsty, I'm the only one in the Flat who carries Monarch," he said, picking up his rag and Holliday's two dollars.

Holliday grabbed the owner's wrist, feeling the strength in Chancey's coiled muscles. "Thirty percent's fine," he whispered. "I prefer playing for a man that doesn't bluff easy."

When Holliday loosened his clasp, Chancey spit his cigarette to the floor, crushing it with his boot. "You won't need luck tonight," he quietly answered as he polished the bar. "First hand after the dealer calls for a new deck, run up the biggest pot you can. It'll be ours."

Chancey retreated up the bar, and Holliday lingered, letting the bourbon dull the pain rising in his chest. A cough died in his throat. He jerked the bottle to his lips and gulped at the liquid, swilling the last mouthful to deaden the taste of sickness. With the clean towel beside him, he wiped his face, beading with sweat. Damn consumption. A rigor convulsed through his slight frame as the liquor settled. Holliday shook it off, tossed the cloth over his shoulder and ambled toward the money table, carrying his bottle.

Past the clicking roulette wheel and the faro game, he squeezed between the observers and stared across the chip- and bill-littered table at the dealer, flat-nosed, broad-mouthed, and wide-jawed like a frog. His fleshy face melted into a short, bulging neck, which lapped his stained and frayed collar like dough rising out of a bread pan. His moldy shirt, a virgin to the washtub and soap, strained at the buttons against his paunch, which peeked at his cards through the bowed gaps in the placket. As dirty as his top, his coat may once have corralled his girth, but no longer. A gambler who ignored his clothes, Holliday believed, ignored his craft. He coughed in disgust.

The dealer, sensing the disdain, lifted his bushy brown eyebrows and stared through muddy eyes at Holliday. Baring his yellowed teeth, stained from smoking the silver-inlaid pipe he clenched between them, the sporting man tossed his cards on the deadwood—the discards—and grunted his distaste for them and for Holliday.

A lanky cowman won the hand. "Keep giving me hands like that, Ed," he said, raking in a modest pot. While the dealer gathered the cards, Holliday's eyes focused on his stubby fingers protruding from small, plump hands. The best card manipulators had broad hands, long supple fingers. Ed was no card mechanic.

Holliday watched Ed place his smoldering pipe beside his money on the table, then toss the cards from hand to hand, his movements jerky, uncertain. Then Ed passed the pasteboards to his right for the cut, waited for the slice, then stacked the bottom half on top. No blind cut there. The players anteed, then Ed. Fifty dollar floor. Bailey dealt five cards around the table, too slow Holliday decided for bottom dealing or dealing seconds. The gamblers picked up their blue-backed cards emblazoned with an anemic eagle and fanned them out. The cowman in front of Holliday glanced over his shoulder at the spectators behind him. After tossing their rejects into the pile of deadwood, the gamblers took their replacements, and Ed picked up his pipe, drawing upon the silver mouthpiece, smoke boiling from the pipe's shiny bowl.

The pipe. The damn pipe, it dawned on Holliday, was a reflector, the laziest way to cheat. These cowmen had stared at longhorn butts too long to catch Ed watching the reflection as he pulled each card over his pipe. A dealer relying on so simple a ruse lacked the skills Holliday preferred in a partner. He shrugged. You never knew how deep the water was until you waded into the creek. Holliday dug into his pants for his money roll. As Ed was gathering the deck for another hand, Holliday tossed the wad on the table. "Room for one more?"

Ed glanced at Holliday, jabbing a finger in his tight collar for relief. From his neck, Ed's hand went for Holliday's money.

Holliday bent over the table and plopped his liquor bottle atop his cash, nicking Ed's stubby fingers as they retreated.

"This is a fifty-dollar floor game, mister," the dealer spit out. "Your roll of greenbacks looks a little thin for our stakes?"

A cocky one, Holliday mused. "Enough to last awhile. Just how much, I keep to myself," he said, lifting the bottle and using it to sweep the money his way.

The card sharp licked his tingling finger tips. "What do you boys think? Is present company adequate? Walt?"

"If he's got the money, let him play a while," the man answered from under the brim of a sweat-stained hat.

"Hell, we've been at it more than an hour with nobody doing much damage," another added. "Your thoughts, Blackie?"

"No matter," Blackie said, his words caustic as acid, "as long as there's more card playing and less jawbone diarrhea."

"Okay, mister," said Ed, "we'll be glad to take your money."

Holliday settled into the vacant chair, placing his bottle and towel at his side on the table.

"Ed Bailey's the name," the dealer said. "Yours?"

"John," Holliday replied.

Bailey waited for the rest, but Holliday just coughed. A gambler's name, like bad news, traveled fast.

"Okay, John," said Bailey. "To my left here is Blackie; on your other side is Beck; and between him and me is Walt."

"Shuffle, Ed, this ain't a social," Blackie growled.

Holliday liked Blackie's attitude. Bailey mixed the deck, passed to Walt for the cut, deposited his pipe on the table, then dealt out five around as the others anteed their fifty dollars.

"Make the pot right, Ed," Holliday said as the dealer finished. Their eyes met and clashed until Bailey tossed in his entry fee. The scowl embedded on Bailey's face offered no favors, and Holliday knew he was on his own until the Ed called for a new deck. His three hundred and fifty dollars wouldn't go far against these stakes.

Holliday gathered his cards, drew them to his chest, and fanned them enough to read the corners. A pair of kings and three throwaways. Holliday glanced across the table at Bailey and his pipe resting beside the deck. Walt raised the pot fifty dollars, Bailey dropping out, everyone else staying. Out of the corner of his eye, Holliday watched the taciturn Blackie separating three discards from his keepers. Holliday pulled two cards from his hands, then squeezed three back together. As Blackie tossed his rejects to the middle of the table, Holliday pitched his castoffs —two cards—beneath them.

Blackie took three. So did Holliday. He added the new trio to the three cards in his hand. His nimble fingers stacked and re-stacked them twice, his left wrist twitching when he finished. Then he pulled the cards to himself, slowly exposing the corners of an ace, king, ten, eight and seven. A sixth card—the king of diamonds—had disappeared up his sleeve.

Holliday, feeling Bailey's icy gaze upon him, hesitated a moment after Blackie upped the pot another fifty dollars. Did Bailey suspect the card under his cuff? If he did, Bailey would draw in the deadwood next and count the discards before anyone else threw in a hand. Bailey leaned forward, but only to pick up his pipe. Puffing on it, he leaned back in his wooden chair, as ignorant as the others. Holliday pondered the raise, stacking and re-stacking the cards between his nimble fingers.

"Too much for me." Holliday shook his head.

"Thought this might be a little out of your reach, John," Bailey said, the satisfaction warming his eyes.

You arrogant son of a bitch, Holliday thought, a sinister smile slithering across his thin lips. He examined his cards again, shaking his head. His agile fingers snapped together, the cards disappearing in his palm for an instant. His left wrist twitched as he tossed the cards—one shy of five—onto the deadwood. Now he had a pair of kings up his sleeve, but his money roll was skinnier by a hundred dollars. Could he last?

With three deuces, Walt claimed the seven hundred bucks in the pot. As Bailey put down his pipe and pulled in the deadwood, everyone anteed another fifty, Bailey remembering to add his promptly this time. He dealt Holliday a sorry hand, an ace high, but nothing else above a nine. Holliday, with only two hundred dollars remaining, folded and watched.

Blackie laid his cards on the table and tugged at his waxed moustache. "I'll go fifty dollars," he said.

Beck tossed his cards on Holliday's. "No sense wasting any more money on this hand," he said, digging in his shirt pocket for his cigarette papers and tobacco pouch. As Beck rolled his smoke, both Walt and Bailey sweetened the pot.

Blackie took one. Holliday watched a glint of a smile, as out of place as snow in July, speed across his face. His hand dropping to his money pile, Blackie had received the card he wanted. Walt took two, revealing no emotion. Bailey took one, then picked up his pipe.

If the dealer stayed long, Holliday knew the pot was Ed's. Blackie bet a hundred, Walt and Bailey following, but the dealer upped it two hundred. Walt was frightened, but not Blackie. He matched Bailey's raise, then revealed a queen-high straight.

The dealer shook his head. "Close, Blackie, but mine's a full house." Bailey revealed three eights over kings, the two kings Holliday lusted for.

Blackie's smile soured. "Damn, Ed, you always seem to know when to stay in. How is that?"

Bailey swallowed hard, then acknowledged the god of gambling. "Just good luck."

"I've heard of Lottie's Luck, but you're not in that class."

Holliday felt his throat tighten at the mention of Lottie. Could she be in Griffin? But he must forget her for now.

"Just lucky," Bailey repeated, dragging deep on his silver good-luck piece and pulling in his take. The dealer left his pipe beside the fresh winnings, then mixed the discards with the rest of the deck. With Blackie suspicious, the dealer was stupid to leave the pipe on the table, Holliday thought. If Bailey blundered again, Chancey's plans might fall apart before the first hand of a new deck.

Adding fifty dollars to the pot, Holliday's fingers slid over the next cards Bailey had tossed his way. Slowly, he spread them, his fingers tacky from perspiration. Damn. No king. He stared at a pair of nines over an ace. The two kings not up his sleeve hid somewhere else. Three kings would be hard to beat, if only he had a third sovereign, but his money was shrinking fast. He must make a move soon or he'd be broke. Perhaps he should risk it with two pairs.

No one upped the pot until the bid reached Bailey. "Doesn't appear anyone's too certain of their cards, does it?" Bailey asked, poking his finger between his neck and the noose of his collar. "I'll go fifty dollars to keep it interesting."

Damn him, Holliday thought. If Bailey's raising, he's setting everyone up. Holliday, joining the others in the pot, was down to a hundred dollars. He followed the deal around the table, guessing at each hand. Blackie took three cards, a good sign he only had a pair. Holliday asked for three and, when they came, stacked them unseen atop his keepers as the deal went to Beck, who raised a mug of hot beer, pondering his play. He discarded one and picked up its replacement without emotion. Both Walt and Bailey took three. They were staring at a pair themselves, but what about Beck?

Holliday's pulse quickened as he lifted his cards and spread their corners. Nine of spades, nine of hearts, he knew of them. Then came the six of spades, ace of diamonds and six of diamonds. Damn. Two pairs with no chance of three of a kind. It would be risky, especially if Bailey stayed in. Blackie passed the bid. For bluff, Holliday added fifty dollars, half his remaining funds. Each opponent, including Bailey, matched him.

"First time we all stayed in after the draw," Bailey noted.

With Bailey meeting the raise, Holliday knew the dealer figured to win. With more money, Holliday could bluff the cowmen, but Bailey and his damn pipe would never fold. Holliday exploded with a cough as Blackie passed the bid again. Looking at Bailey as he wiped his mouth, Holliday spoke. "I'm fine."

Bailey grinned as the bid went to Beck. "Well, John, I'll go up another fifty." Blackie folded, but Bailey and Walt contributed to the growing puddle of money.

Holliday, his wrist twitching twice, stacked and re-stacked his cards, then eyed them coldly, nodding his satisfaction as nines over sixes had become kings over nines with the diamond ace throwaway. The creek was getting deeper, Holliday thought, pushing the last of his roll to the middle of the table.

Bailey chuckled at Holliday. "I'll raise you two hundred and fifty."

Beck and Walt folded. Holliday stared hard at his cards, but he was broke. The others knew it and, most galling, Bailey could take the pot without showing his hand. Now all Holliday could afford was a lie. "I've got a fine horse in Haverty's Livery Stable. What's he good for?"

"He's good for getting you out of town," Bailey laughed. "This game is cash or gold. Your damn horse ain't worth a bucket of spit at this table. Same goes for any pigs or chickens you got." The crowd laughed.

Holliday squeezed his cards together, considering how delighted he would be to kill Ed Bailey.

The dealer reached for the pot, his hands freezing at the sound of two icy words.

"John's in!"

Everyone turned to Blackie as he tossed two hundred and fifty dollars onto the growing pile and then made a return trip with more. "He'll raise you five hundred dollars."

Holliday nodded at Blackie. "Obliged."

The spectators shuffled their feet and moved closer to the table as Bailey grated his teeth against the stem of his pipe. A toothy, yellow grin formed around the pipe. "Blackie, you don't want to lose your money on a hand you can't even see."

Blackie clenched his fist. "Tired of seeing you win every time you stay in, Ed."

"I'll see your five hundred and raise you two-fifty," Bailey spit back, counting the money from his dwindling pile.

Holliday looked to Blackie, who pitched another two hundred and fifty dollars into the pot. "We call you," Blackie said.

"Two pairs," Bailey said. "Queens over jacks." The dealer reached for the pot.

Holliday nodded, and the crowd groaned. "Two pairs here," he said, "and the pot's mine."

Bailey's hands flinched as Holliday exposed kings over nines. Bailey's eyes widened. As he yanked his pipe from his lips, his broad mouth gaped. "But, you—," he stammered.

"But I what?" Holliday asked, leaning forward, his elbows on the table, his right hand draped over the edge near the gun under his coat.

"You didn't have, I mean—," Bailey caught himself.

"Surprised your luck soured?" Holliday goaded him. "Why's that? You care to explain. Maybe you best suck your pipe this next deal and think about it."

The dealer's eyes burned with rage, the fire flaring his nostrils and reddening his cheeks with defeat. Bailey was stumped, and Holliday knew it. To accuse Holliday of cheating would expose the dealer's own artifice. Bailey had been outwitted at cheating on a crooked hand. He shoved his pipe back in his mouth.

Holliday spoke. "Blackie drag in the pot for me. Take your money and an extra hundred for the stake."

Blackie retrieved his contributions. "I'll take what I risked. You keep the hundred. Seeing Bailey's face fall was worth it."

Bailey ignored the comment. Twisting in his chair toward the bar, he called, "Chancey, bring us a fresh deck."

Instantly, the owner of the Cattle Exchange towered over Bailey's shoulder and tossed an unopened deck on the table. "Things not going your way, Ed?"

"Luck frowned at me on the last hand," Bailey offered, the pipe still clenched between his teeth.

Holliday felt the hard edge in Bailey's voice and saw in Chancey's deep-set eyes growing doubts that his plan would succeed. A coughing spasm attacked Holliday's spare frame. He grabbed the towel and covered his mouth, wondering if his infirmity might tempt Bailey to pull a weapon, now that he was distracted. The thought soon strangled the cough.

Instead, Bailey gathered the old deck and handed it to Chancey. "Save those cards for me, Chancey. I'll count them later. Perhaps I can learn a little about John's skill." Bailey nodded his froglike face at Holliday. Then Bailey broke the seal on, to all appearances, a virgin set of cards, but Holliday knew better. It was a cold deck, altered or stacked to the dealer's advantage, then repacked to appear unmolested. Extracting the cards, Bailey crushed the box, dropping it on the floor.

Chancey, doubts clouding his face, fumbled for his cigarette makings in the tin on his sleeve. "Don't let one bad hand ruin your night, Ed," the saloon owner said. "If the house dealer bellyaches each time he loses a big pot, it'll cost me customers."

Holliday stacked his winnings and eyed Bailey, the tiny red veins visible in the dealer's fleshy cheeks. He toyed with the money, annoying Ed, then took the whiskey bottle to soothe the recurring pain in his chest. Bailey split the new cards to shuffle.

"Just a minute," Holliday said. "Let me inspect the cards."

"What?" yelled Bailey, leaning back in his chair like he might go for a weapon.

Chancey clamped a hand on the dealer's shoulder. "Easy, Ed."

"Give me the deck," Holliday said, extending his left hand, his other hand gun ready. "Just to make sure it's not marked."

"Dammit, Chancey," shouted Bailey, shaking his shoulder against Chancey's iron grip. "We've got a troublemaker accusing us of cheating. Thinks you brought in a marked deck."

Holliday slapped his hand on the felt table. "No accusations now and no reason for any later—if I see the deck." Holliday lifted his palm at the dealer. "The cards."

"Do what he says, Ed," Chancey ordered, his knuckles whitening on Bailey's fleshy shoulder. "We've nothing to hide, and we don't want trouble, not tonight."

Bailey slapped the pack into Holliday's hand, and Holliday studied the red ink splattered in triangles on the card backs. He examined them for markings, but if the cards were coded, Holliday knew he was unlikely to decipher them. Instead, he wanted a feel of the deck, his fingers stroking the deck's edge, pressing the pasteboards together from side to side. Just as he suspected, the cards had been stripped, the edges of some—the bottom four especially—shaved so that practiced hands could discern what calloused hands could not. Holliday tilted the deck enough to see the bottom card, an ace. He nodded his head, offering the cards to Blackie.

"Looks good to me," Holliday said. "You fellows care to inspect them?" When everyone declined, he dropped the cards on the table. "I'm ready to play."

"The rest of us were ready a long time ago," Bailey answered.

"Ease up, Ed," Chancey commanded, loosening his hand on Bailey's shoulder. "An angry dealer doesn't pay attention like he should. Don't lose a hand because you weren't thinking."

Bailey shuffled the deck as Holliday, finishing a drink, banged the bourbon bottle on the table, drawing the stares of the cowmen and distracting them from Bailey's inept blind shuffles. Finishing, Bailey crimped the deck at the spot he wanted the cut and shoved the cards to Walt. Taking the pipe from his mouth, Bailey started to the table with it, then, thinking better of it, returned it to his lips. He crossed his hands, picking up Walt's cut, which had fallen at the bent spot, uncrossed them and stacked the cards in their original position, a blind cut.

"Is anybody going to ante before I pass out cards?" Bailey griped, tossing fifty dollars on the table to make his point. The others followed suit.

This was it, Holliday thought as he studied Bailey's moves. He observed three faultless rounds of the deal. No tricks so far. Then, on the fourth round, Ed's fingers paused a fraction of an instant as they came to Holliday and then continued at normal speed. Again, on the fifth round, the dealer's fingers stilled for the blink of an eye. Holliday hoped the cowmen missed Bailey's pauses—and the two cards he'd dealt from the bottom. As Bailey finished, Holliday gathered his pasteboards in a single stack, running his fingers along their edges, discerning two strippers by their slighted widths. Perhaps the ploy would work after all.

Holliday fanned his cards. Two aces, a king, a four and a five. The aces were shaved. They were keepers. The king perplexed Holliday. How was the cold deck stacked? For four aces? Full house, aces over kings or kings over aces? If he kept the king and called for two, he might worry away a cowman. If he discarded the king, he might wreck the prepared hand. Safer to keep the king, he decided.

To his right, Blackie twisted his moustache and stared at his cards. Beck lit a cigarette, but it smoldered between his fingers like wet timber afire, and Walt glanced from player to player, trying to read his opponents' cards as he would the pages of a closed book—by guessing. No one offered any clues. Only one man wasn't guessing. Bailey sat simmering behind his cards, his eyes glowing hot like the fire in his pipe. He drummed his fingers on the table and glared at Blackie, who pondered for a moment, then moved a hundred dollars from his funds to the pot.

"Cost you a hundred to stay in," he said. Everyone anteed.

"Raise you a hundred fifty," Walt challenged, and again, no one backed down.

"Damn," Bailey said, grabbing the deck, "someone's gonna put in a fine night's work when this hand's done. You ready for cards, or will you price me out of this hand?"

"I'll take one," Blackie snapped, his words as taut and prickly as stretched barbed wire.

Could be trouble, Holliday thought. The cattleman might have two pairs, four of a kind or even a shot at a straight flush. Blackie snagged his new card the instant it hit the felt, inserted it among the others, and let his left hand fall to his money. Blackie, Holliday figured, was ready to back up his hand.

Holliday tossed his two rejects on the deadwood. "Two," he said, studying Bailey's fingers as the cards flew from the deck and across the table. Two more from the bottom. Sliding them in with his three keepers, Holliday knew he had two more strippers. When he spread them out, he stared at four aces and a king. Bailey had played straight, provided Blackie didn't have a straight flush.

Then Beck asked for two. Maybe three of a kind, Holliday thought. Walt took three cards. A pair to begin with and maybe a full house at best, Holliday figured. Bailey took three.

Without waiting for Bailey to look at his hand, Blackie fattened the pot. "Five hundred," he called, the bet echoing from mouth to mouth among the encircled spectators. Holliday matched Blackie before the murmur subsided. Without hesitating, Beck added his five hundred dollars. Walt was a little slower, but stayed in.

Bailey eyed his opponent. "I think you're bluffing, Blackie. I'll match you and raise you five hundred." Bailey counted out more sweetening for the pot.

All matched the raise. Then Blackie spoke. "I'll see you another five hundred bucks," he said, staring at the dealer.

Bailey sputtered a moment, sucking hard on his pipe, and counted his bills. As Holliday and Beck matched Blackie, Walt folded, then Bailey tossed his cards to the table in defeat.

"Now who was bluffing, Bailey?" Blackie laughed. "You can't buffalo me."

Unwisely, Bailey reached for his coat pocket. Before he could withdraw his hand, he stared at the gaping mouth of Blackie's Colt .45. Bailey's trembling hand emerged snail-like from his pocket, clamping between his thumb and forefinger a tobacco pouch like he would hold a dead rat by the tail.

"Wasn't a smart move," Blackie said, re-holstering his gun.

"All I'm after is more tobacco," Bailey answered. "You're a mite jumpy tonight, Blackie."

"Just suspicious, Bailey, of you monkeying with the deck."

"I'll call you," Beck challenged in a friendly way that cut the tension like sunshine cuts a fog.

Blackie grinned. "Queens over tens, full house."

Beck nodded. "Four nines."

"But it doesn't beat four aces," Holliday said, showing his cards.

Beck sat stunned, disbelief etched on his face, as if carved out of stone. Blackie picked up his cards and tossed them on the deadwood. Turning to Holliday, he shook his head. "Mister, how do you do it, winning the night's biggest hands?"

"Bailey," Holliday said, staring across the table, "deals me rigged cards."

The dealer's eyes flared like a flame doused with cheap liquor, doubt and uncertainty racing across his face like a prairie fire.

Blackie glanced from Holliday to Bailey, then slapped the table, his mouth erupting with laughter. "Like hell he does," he gasped. "Bailey wouldn't do favors for anyone but himself. I like your humor, mister, but I'd prefer to see how funny you are when your luck is as sour as seven-day milk."

Chancey bent his colossal frame over the table, leaning on his doubled fists. "Gentlemen, I think there's been enough for one night," he said. "We're tempting trouble. Free drinks for the lot of you."

Shortly, the cattlemen stood and stretched their cramped muscles, then ambled to the bar. Holliday lingered, wrapping his winnings in his handkerchief and stuffing the wad in his pocket, making sure that those watching saw the gun hanging from his hip, just in case any had ideas about waylaying him. As Bailey slipped away, Holliday corked his liquor bottle, picked up the towel and marched to a vacant section of the counter.

"Another bottle of Monarch," he called to Chancey.

Chancey obliged. "Anything else?"

"Yeah," Holliday said, shoving the towel to Chancey. "Under there, you'll find a pair of sixes. Add them to Bailey's deck before he counts them. I'll settle with you tomorrow afternoon in my room, the last door on the left down the hall at Planters House.

Chancey nodded. "Just one more thing."

"What?"

"Stay out of the Bee Hive."

Holliday shrugged, his left hand grabbing the necks of the two liquor bottles, his right falling to the ivory grip of his Colt. In the wash of the jealous stares of the less lucky, he strode from the Cattle Exchange.

Then he evaporated in the darkness of the Flat and in his single thought. Was Lottie in Griffin?

Chapter 4

The light of an afternoon sun bounced off the Clear Fork's rippled waters like reflections from a million shards of broken crystal. Like a mirror flawed, the ribbon of water distorted the forms of the giant pecan trees, which gathered in clusters along the stream. A soft wind came from the north, the tall prairie grass waving as it passed, the leaves murmuring among themselves about the winter not long away. Husks of pecans a thousand fold had darkened, dried, and split open, many dropping their nuts like scattered jewels on the grassy carpet lining the creek.

Under a sky stained with meandering white wisps of clouds, the animals rested during the heat of the day, reserving their strength for winter's stealthy approach. The long-eared jackrabbits hunkered in the sweep of grass, nibbling at the plants within reach. Squirrels, lords over more nuts than they could ever collect, sunned themselves on the highest branches of the pecan trees. Quail huddled in coveys under squatty bushes; prairie dogs—except for the sporadic lookout—reclined in their dens; and turkeys hid behind the brush scattered in patches along the river. Overhead, a solitary orange-breasted hawk circled effortlessly, floating on unseen air currents, surveying the land below and spotting an occasional fish leaping from the creek and defying gravity before disappearing in a splash.

It was Sunday, and it was peaceful, the countryside at ease with itself. Even the dead man hanging from a pecan limb seemed grotesquely tranquil, his suspended presence no longer concerning the animals at rest. Screened from distant eyes by the surrounding trees, the dangling body attracted only flies. As lifeless as another husk-sheathed pecan, the corpse waited to fall to the ground, the harvest of a savage reaper.

The ears of a jackrabbit twitched, then stood at attention. A prairie dog sentinel squeaked an alarm that brought the heads of a hundred chattering rodents peeking above the mounded ramparts of their earthen burrows. The quail sent up their whistling call to warn others, then darted headlong through the grass. From up the river came disconcerting human sounds, peals of laughter tumbling across the still land. Man was dangerous. He killed his own kind.

****

Stretching the full reach of her lithe frame, Rachel drew back the whip and snapped it at the pecan cluster clinging to a twisted branch. The lash cracked, but missed its target, and Rachel lost her balance, the slick bottoms of her button-up shoes slipping on the thick grass growing along the sloping stream bank. She slid toward the water. Like windmill blades in a stiff breeze, her arms spun for equilibrium, but still she skated nearer the creek, too slow to fall, too fast to stop. "Help me!" she giggled.

Dropping her basket of pecans, Lottie lunged for Rachel's whipping limbs, but stumbled over the container and plopped down on her seat, her hat at a rakish tilt. "Oh my," she laughed as Rachel threshed her arms against gravity and an unscheduled bath. Gathering her full skirt in her hands, Lottie hurried to stand, but Rachel was beyond reach and help.

Then Rachel's thick heels dug into the mud at the stream's edge, her legs braking quicker than her upper torso. For a moment she teetered over the water, but her flailing arms pushed against the sky and she, too, settled roughly on her rear, dropping the buggy whip half in the creek. At the jolt, a startled laugh wrenched itself from Rachel's slender throat, followed by an embarrassed cackle at her awkwardness.

"Some help you are, Lottie," Rachel said, twisting her head to look at her companion. Then she laughed in torrents and lay back on the grass, her hair touching Lottie's shoes.

Lottie snickered, then leaned forward until her eyes met the green of Rachel's. "You're laughing at me, Rachel?"

"Such an elegant hat you wear, Miss Deno," Rachel started, then broke into more laughter. "But it's not as pretty on the side of your face."

Lottie's nimble fingers raced to her auburn hair and the broad-brimmed hat that dangled limply by her ear. In the fall, her tresses and her hat had shifted—like her balance—downward. She patted her mane, mussing it further, drawing bursts of giggles from Rachel. Exasperated, Lottie extracted two giant hat pins and tossed the sunhat toward the rented buggy. Her joy, like her long auburn locks, fell loose and free. "Such grace befits ladies of the plains like ourselves," Lottie said.

"If you can call an army wife and a gambler ladies," Rachel shot back.

"Indeed we are, madam," intoned Lottie. "Have we both, in our younger days, not read *Miss Leslie's Behavior Book*?"

"It's true, but I confess I've forgotten so much."

"Me, too," answered Lottie, "especially the chapter on falling on your fanny."

"Perhaps we could borrow a copy of Miss Leslie's book from a harlot in the Flat."

"Indeed, my dear Rachel, they might have neglected other chapters, but they'd certainly be familiar with reclining on their fannies."

Both ladies giggled like schoolgirls, unconcerned that others could hear their silliness for they were five miles from Griffin. Lottie enjoyed these Sunday afternoons with Rachel as if they were sisters. She spent too much of her life among gambling men and the wrong kind of women.

Lottie grabbed the upturned basket, then the buggy whip. "Care to knock down any more pecans from that top branch?" she asked, adding the scattered nuts within reach to her container.

Rachel tossed one pecan at the basket, a second at Lottie, then stood brushing the seat of her sky blue muslin dress. When she bent to attend the splattered hem, she groaned. "Grass and mud stains! Can't afford this, not on an army captain's pay."

"Rachel, my dear, I shall buy you a new skirt."

"I could never allow that," she answered, releasing the folds of stained cloth from her fingers and grabbing the whip.

"Then perhaps you should take up gambling and enhance Richard's meager earnings," Lottie teased as she stood.

"At the cost of my marriage?" Rachel questioned without offense. "No, Lottie, I should never do that. Richard is a fuss body. He even worries about me seeing you. Fears I might get the gaming urge."

"You could get worse urges, Rachel."

"That's what concerns my husband. Anyway, he thinks I should see you married to someone who'll take you away from those saloons." She moved up the incline toward the buggy, Lottie walking with her. "Why," asked Rachel, "have you never found a husband? You could have your pick of many a decent man."

Lottie stiffened, her lips tightening, her knuckles blanching tight around the basket handle. She failed to answer because the words were buried too deep within her to uncover.

"Why haven't you married? The war?"

Lottie coughed, but the knot lingered in her throat. "Sometimes, you show your hand. Other times you don't." Lottie smiled. "Do we have enough pecans or should we try to knock a few more down."

"Lord knows Richard will put away plenty, so if I want any for myself or for baking I need to bring home a bunch. We both love pecan pie. And the pecans are so full this year. Must've been the summer flood."

Lottie gathered another handful. "Then perhaps, Rachel, we shall be fortunate enough this afternoon to meet a teamster with an empty wagon we can fill for your husband. A teamster I can marry, of course."

Now Rachel cleared her throat. "Lottie, forgive me for prying. I would hate for my curiosity to harm our friendship."

"My dear, Rachel," Lottie said, "promise me but one thing."

"Anything?"

"At the next pecan tree, I'll handle the whip."

Rachel laughed and nodded. "Race you to the buggy." She darted up the creek bank, bending over to scoop Lottie's hat from the grass.

"You're crazy," Lottie called after her. "I'm saving my energy to gather all the pecans you and Richard can eat."

At the top of the embankment, Rachel waited for Lottie. "Just one more stop, Lottie. There must be bountiful pecans in those trees," Rachel said, pointing to a copse downstream. "We'll get what we can there and head home."

They walked together toward the buggy, its black piano box body glistening in the sun, Rachel shading her face with Lottie's hat. At the rig, Lottie dumped the nuts into the tubs in the back as Rachel untied the reins to the grazing bay mare.

Lottie leveled the new pecans over those they had gathered earlier, the nuts filling three of the four casks.

"We may wish later we had run into a teamster with an empty wagon, Rachel. I'll bet we've a hundred pounds here. Your Richard can't eat that much, can he?"

"Not in a single sitting," Rachel answered, tossing Lottie's hat on the green body cloth seat and climbing into the buggy beneath its three-bow top. She fluffed the folds of her skirt, knocking a layer of mire from the bottom flounce. "More mud and would you look at my shoes?" she said, disgust distorting her voice. "And the grass stains! They'll never come out."

"But," replied Lottie, approaching the other side of the buggy, "at least Richard will have plenty of pecans."

"And a wife that dresses like a field hand."

After handing Rachel the whip, Lottie lifted her skirt to her calf—a sight that men at the Bee Hive would have paid a lot to see—and placed her foot on the wagon's Brewster green step. Taking Rachel's fingers, Lottie stepped up into the rig and settled in beside Rachel on the cushioned tufts of upholstery, adding the hat to her lap.

At the snap of the whip, the horse pulled the conveyance toward the copse of trees downstream. The buggy plowed through the grass, which bowed down behind it. Game skirted ahead, with an occasional jackrabbit popping its head from the vegetation to watch. The mare pranced in the sunshine as if she knew she was pulling the best rig from Pete Haverty's Livery.

Then, unexpectedly, the horse stopped, jarring both women forward in their seat. Rachel cracked her whip, but the horse reared on its hind legs and whinnied, coming down hard on its front hooves at a buzzing patch of grass.

"Rattlesnake," Lottie shouted, grabbing the reins and yanking them to the right, her hat tumbling to the floorboard. The mare fought against its harness just as the rattler darted for her legs. "Hold the animal, Rachel," Lottie commanded, tossing the lines to Rachel's lap, jumping from the buggy and landing as gracefully as a cat in full stride. She circled behind the wagon and, while out of Rachel's sight, pulled from the folds of her blouse a revolver. Gun in hand, she moved cautiously forward until she spied the serpent.

The coiled snake uplifted its tail, which buzzed ominously. Beady eyes stared at Lottie, and a slithering tongue darted out at her. Inching ahead, ever careful to stay out of striking distance, Lottie lifted her hand, and the gun exploded in an angry fit of lead and smoke. And then the prairie was hushed, except for Rachel's sobs. The reptile convulsed in the grass, its white belly turning to the sun, its rattle flopping limply on the ground.

"Oh, Lottie," cried Rachel, "are you okay?"

With her back still to Rachel, Lottie nodded, straightening her blouse. When Lottie turned around, neither hand carried a gun, but Rachel never noticed the difference. Lottie walked to the mare, patted the animal on the neck to calm her, then bent to examine her forelegs. Lottie lifted each leg and ran her hand over the short hair perfumed with perspiration.

"No bites," Lottie called to Rachel. "We're lucky."

"Lucky to have you, Lottie."

Lottie skirted around the rattlesnake, still writhing in death, and estimated it was more than five feet long with an impressive rattle. "You want the rattle for Richard? Or maybe for your future children to play with?"

"Oh no, Lottie, I wouldn't touch that disgusting thing. Never!"

"Suits me, because you'd have to get it yourself. I'm not touching it either."

They enjoyed the sound of each other's nervous laugh as Lottie climbed back in the buggy, retrieving her headgear from the floorboard. "My hat won't survive this outing." Lottie punched the trampled crown in place.

"Your hat and my dress, I might add. Maybe we should head for the Flat, Lottie?"

"And let the day end on such an unpleasantry? No ma'am, my dear Rachel. You want more pecans for Richard, so we'll make one more stop to fill our final tub."

Rachel slapped the reins against the jittery mare's flank and pointed her toward the trees ahead. "Lottie," Rachel asked softly, "where'd the gun come from?"

"In my business, Rachel, I always carry one."

"That's why I worry about you so, wishing you would end that life. It's dangerous. Why, just yesterday when Richard returned from Jacksboro, another stage passenger, a fellow he took to be a gambler, pulled a pistol on him for no good reason. I saw the man—thin, evil-looking man—when I met Richard. You're not safe around that type of people."

"You worry too much, my dear Rachel. There's no more danger there than, say, a Sunday afternoon ride through a rattler-infested prairie. Everything's chance or happenstance in life. I just happen to make money off chance."

"Precarious living, though."

"Beats working in a harlot's crib, rutting like hogs."

"But it's not like having a husband." Rachel stopped and shook her head. "There I go preaching another sermon. Forgive me, Lottie. I'm concerned, nothing more."

"Forget it." Lottie reached over and squeezed Rachel's hand. "Someday I'll give it up. That's a ways off, though. Now we've got pecans to gather."

The buggy neared the clump of pecan trees, flushing a flock of turkeys from the nearby brush. Rachel flinched. "Oh, me, that rattler sure left me jumpy."

"It made both of us nervous." Lottie patted Rachel's knee.

At the trees, Rachel tugged the mare to a halt and tied the reins around the brake lever, but the animal seemed skittish, pawing at the ground instead of eating the tall grass. "What's a matter, girl?" Rachel asked. "Please, not another rattler."

A faint odor drifted on the slight breeze, the festering smell of death. Lottie caught the aroma, but its source was screened behind the enormous trunk of the nearest pecan tree. "Dead animal must be near. Makes the mare nervous," Lottie said, adjusting her hat. "Let's be quick. I'll knock the pecans down this time, and maybe you won't fall on your fanny, Rachel."

Both laughed as they climbed from the buggy. "Oh, look, Lottie," Rachel said, pointing at the grassy carpet beyond the nearest tree. "Many pecans have fallen here. Our best find today." Handing Lottie the whip, she said, "We may not need it here." Rachel raced down the sloping earth, which bled into the creek and fell upon her knees, scooping handfuls of nuts into her skirt for a temporary basket. "Hurry, Lottie, with the basket."

Lottie tossed the lash on the seat, grabbed the basket, and followed Rachel's trail until she passed the massive tree trunk. She stopped cold, her mouth gaping. "Ahhh—," she caught herself before her surprise turned into a scream. Hanging not six feet behind the kneeling Rachel was a corpse.

"Just look at all these pecans," Rachel called, glancing back toward Lottie. "Unlike anything we've found before."

And Lottie knew why. As he had struggled for a foothold in mid air, as he had fought for his last gasp of air, as he had thrashed in death's throes, the dead man had shaken the pecans to the ground. Lottie held her breath a moment, fearful her voice might break, then called. "Come, Rachel, we've got enough now."

"Oh, Lottie," she replied, "I've just started. There are so many, but it won't take long, not like this."

"Rachel," Lottie implored, a tinge of panic in her intonation, "suddenly I feel sickly."

Rachel stood, holding in the lap of her skirt a mound of pecans. Almost within reach behind her, the corpse swayed toward Rachel as if she were death's magnet. "I'm sorry, Lottie, you feel faint. Then we must go, but I should remember this place so I can bring Richard." She turned around.

"No," cried Lottie, but too late.

Rachel screamed, both hands flying from her skirt to her mouth, the pecans tumbling to the ground, some rolling into a sticky stain of body fluids beneath the dead man. Rachel stared in horror, too disgusted to look, too fascinated to turn her face from the hideous corpse with bulging eyes like glassy walnut shells, bloated tongue twisted like driftwood between two rows of teeth tombstone white, the flesh puffy and purple, nose strangely contorted, and neck decorated with torn skin and dried blood on either side of a hemp rope.

Then Rachel's thin frame went limp. Lottie dashed for her, discarding the basket, grabbing Rachel under the arms and easing her upright. Lottie's touch seemed to revive Rachel.

"It's okay, Rachel. Let's go." Lottie's words flowed calmly. She patted Rachel's pale cheeks and looked into innocent eyes that had seldom seen death this close. "We'll leave."

Rachel nodded. "Please, let's do," she said, her voice brimming with desperation, her face swathed in terror's paleness. She broke from Lottie's grasp and trudged toward the buggy. Lottie started behind her, turning a second to retrieve the dropped basket, then deciding to leave it. They must depart and now. For Rachel's sake.

At the rig, Lottie caught up with Rachel, her cheeks regaining their color, but her eyes still vacant. Rachel's hands shook as she jumped on the seat and untied the reins. As Lottie fought against her skirt to get in, Rachel grabbed the buggy whip. Lottie had just lifted her leg over the sideboard when Rachel popped the flank of the nervous mare. The wagon lurched ahead. As the horse turned a sharp circle back toward the Flat, Lottie struggled to pull her other leg in. Then she collapsed onto the bench beside Rachel, who whipped the frightened animal. Lottie wrenched the whip from Rachel's white-knuckle grasp. Rachel slapped the mare with the lines, hollering at the animal, as the buggy bounced over the terrain, scattering in its wake dozens of pecans.

"It's okay, Rachel. No matter how fast we get back to Griffin, it won't do him any good."

Rachel seemed neither to hear nor to comprehend, as if her mind had been seared by naked death's terrible torch. She screamed at the horse again and drove harder until Lottie held onto her seat. Fearing that Rachel would overturn the rig, Lottie lunged for the reins. Rachel fought against her. "No," she shrieked, but Lottie's resolve outweighed Rachel's terror, and her friend let go. Rachel burst into uncontrollable sobs as Lottie slowed the mare to a lope.

"I can still see him, Lottie. Even when I shut my eyes," she struggled with her words. "He's … oh … he's still there, his eyes bulging, his tongue sticking out at me. I will have nightmares forever. I still see him, Lottie. He won't go away."

The contorted face lingered, too, with Lottie, but she had seen other men dead. Their faces had all dissolved hazily in her memory except the first. Though it had been over twenty years earlier, she remembered a trip with her father on a steamboat. Just up from Cairo on the Ohio River, there had been an altercation over a card game. A handsome man, fashionably dressed, was sitting in a chair, but the chair had fallen backward on the floor from the impact of the bullet, which had turned the back of his skull into a bloody pulp. She recalled a single drop of blood crawling down the slain man's face from the hole in the forehead. She remembered the blue eyes empty of life, glaring at her, asking why. She could still see a paleness on his lips, which grinned into eternity at a fatal card hand. "Sure, you'll forget it," Lottie assured Rachel, knowing it was all a lie. "One day you'll have a story to tell your grandchildren."

Rachel gasped, her sobs louder. Lottie regretted her well-meant words. Nothing could change them now, just like they could never erase what Rachel had seen. Not now, not ever.

"I'd never tell my grandchildren something that horrible. I couldn't. I doubt that I can even face Richard."

"You'll forget it, Rachel," Lottie said, the sincerity in her voice as lacking as prairie mountains around them.

The somber music of Rachel's sobs accompanied them for better than a mile, their minds dulled to their surroundings until a rider was almost upon them.

"Someone's coming, Rachel."

With the edge of her sleeve, Rachel dabbed at her eyes.

Straight and lean, the horseman carried himself like one accustomed to miles in the saddle. As he drew nearer, Lottie recognized the set of his head, even though the broad brim of his

Stetson cast a shadow over his face. Coming closer, he removed his headgear, and Lottie smiled. She patted her hair and pushed the stray curls she could under her hat.

"It's Jack Jacobs, Rachel."

"The sheriff?"

"Not now. He was until April when Jay Larn replaced him. Jack's a fine man, too good a man for this wicked county to keep long as sheriff. He's someone we can trust."

Lottie stopped the buggy, as Jacobs met them, his hat over his heart, a genuine smile across his broad face. "Afternoon, Lottie, ma'am. Fine day for a Sunday ride."

Rachel sniffed twice, as if she might cry again. Jacobs, his grin evaporating into a mask of concern, dismounted.

"Jack, there's been trouble back down the river." Lottie said, handing the reins to Rachel. "Hold on to these."

Lottie stood in the buggy, lifting her skirt enough for the paleness of her calf to show. Taking his extended hand, she smiled as Jacobs turned his blushing head away from her leg's exposed flesh. "Pardon my looks, Jack." She stepped onto the ground. "My hair's a mess."

"You look fine, Lottie, I promise you."

"Let's take a walk, Jack." She nodded toward Rachel.

Jacobs replaced his hat, took his mount's reins, and walked with Lottie twenty yards behind the buggy. "There's been a lynching back down the river."

"Vigilance committee?"

"Don't know. Didn't linger. Finding him shook up Rachel too much."

"That's a half dozen or more lynchings since spring."

"I preferred it when you were the law."

"Thanks, Lottie. If more folks had been like you, I might still be sheriff, but a man here has enough troubles of his own without taking on those of everyone else's making. I'll ride down river and bury the fellow. Did you recognize him?"

"No, not with his face like it was. When you go, Jack, would you do me a favor?"

"Name it."

"We left a basket there near him. Bring it in the next time you're in town?"

"Sure. Now get your friend back to Griffin," Jacobs said, mounting his horse and turning him away from the dead man.

Lottie pointed downstream. “He’s that way.”

Jacobs pulled his reins and nodded. “I’ll need a shovel to bury him. There’s a ranch house a half mile away. I’ll borrow one there. You two just forget about this.”

“I wish we could.”

Chapter 5

Holliday doubled over the bed's edge, convulsed with coughing. Fumbling for the whiskey bottle on the plank floor, he squeezed the glass neck between trembling fingers and lifted the muzzle to his parched lips. He spit out curses as he drew air from the bottle's dryness. The empty slid from his grip, clattering on the floor, useless against the pain raging deep in his chest. Where was his extra bourbon?

As he stood, the ache settled deeper in his lungs, and he kicked the empty aside. His watery eyes struggled to focus. Shaking his head to clear sleep's cobwebs, he batted his eyelids against the afternoon sunlight bursting through the open window and stumbled around the bed to draw the curtains. Dropping to his knees, he searched beneath the bed, his quivering fingers following his gaze, touching the cold glass and grabbing his liquor.

Twisting on the floor, he sat back against the bedframe, stretching his legs until he could feel the wooden coolness prickling his flesh through the long johns. As he jerked the stopper free from the bottle, his arm brushed against his holstered Colt hanging from the bedpost. He swallowed his medicine in quick gulps, the alcohol numbing the agony in his lungs. In damning consumption for another night without rest, he began this day like most, with a drink and a curse.

Above the consumptive gurgle of liquor in his throat, he heard heavy footsteps halting outside his door. He slid his Colt from its holster and cocked the hammer at the slight rap on the entry. Pointing the barrel just above the chair wedged under the doorknob, he held onto the bottle. "What do you want?" he called, his weak lungs mustering but a whisper.

"It's Chancey."

Holliday pushed himself up and ambled to the entry. He twisted the key in the lock as his bare foot nudged at the chair until it came free. The door slid open enough for Holliday to confirm Chancey. Holliday yanked the doorknob, then released the hammer on his gun.

"You look like warmed over death. Gambler's disease?"

Nodding, Holliday coughed in his fist, retreated across the room, tossing his pistol on the bed, then falling onto the mattress and wadding the sheet at his mouth. Tears moistened his eyes as the cough shuddered through his frame. "You came for the money, not to check on my health," he said, his words muffled by the sheet. He pointed limply to the overturned washbasin. "Money's there, two stacks."

In four strides, Chancey reached the washbasin, uncovering the bills, thumbing through the thicker stack.

"It's all there," Holliday said, his voice squeezing through the tightness in his throat, "split like we agreed, though I figure I deserve a bigger cut for putting up with that bastard you call a dealer."

Chancey, counting the winnings, shrugged. "Most folks get along with Bailey."

"I'm not most folks. If I hadn't swapped kings for sixes, he'd skinned me of my money and everything you had hoped to win. I don't like being double-crossed."

"Nor do I."

Holliday's thin lips curled into a smile that was not reflected in his steely eyes. "Less my stake, I had seventy-six-fifty when play ended. My cut comes to a little over nineteen hundred dollars. You keep the difference for cutting me in."

The saloon owner nodded, tucking his share in his britches pocket, then extracting his cigarette makings from his tin. "You ever thought of owning a share of a saloon?" He sprinkled tobacco onto a slice of paper, then lifted the result to his mouth, closing the cigarette with his tongue.

"I like to take my assets with me if I have to skedaddle out of town."

Chancey exchanged his tin for a match, scratched it to life on the washstand and stuck the flame to the devil stick, blurring behind the cloud of smoke. "Another deal for you. If you win, I'll give you a table in the Cattle Exchange."

"Bailey's?"

Chancey drew hard on his cigarette. "Local folks like him. Bailey brings in a regular clientele. What if I say no?"

"If that's the case, the conversation's over."

"Then, Bailey's it is. I want a share of the Bee Hive. Mike Fogle runs the place, makes the best profit in the Flat. I can't get a run at him, but a stranger with my money can."

"Let me think about it a day or so."

"No time for that. It's tonight or never, with you anyway."

"Don't like to be rushed," he answered, raising the whiskey bottle to his lips.

"You're new and unknown here, but word's getting around after your winnings last night. And, today's Sunday."

"Tomorrow's Monday," Holliday shot back. "So what?"

"There's a dealer at the Bee Hive I intend to avoid," Chancey started slowly, wrapping his words in a ribbon of smoke. "This dealer doesn't work Sundays."

"Religious fellow?"

"It's not a fellow, either."

Holliday noticed tightness in his throat. He swallowed hard. He had found her.

"Ever hear of Lottie Deno?" Chancey asked.

Holliday nodded, thinking how much simpler his life might be if he hadn't.

"I don't want her involved in a turn of the cards," Chancey said matter-of-factly. "I don't plan to buck Lottie's Luck. Her luck's too queer. You gonna play my hand or not?"

"Bailey's table if I win?"

Chancey nodded, drawing the cigarette fire down to his lips as he inhaled.

"I deal faro, and that's what I'll play."

Chancey dug into his pocket for last night's winnings and tossed the wad on the bed. "I can come up with two thousand more if you need it."

"Be a shame to lose all your money." Holliday grinned.

****

"Mr. Fogle," the dealer called across the subdued Sunday afternoon gaming room, "I need you a moment."

Fogle felt a sinking in his stomach and glanced from behind three sevens. Benson was in trouble.

"Damn, Benson," Fogle shouted. "I'm in the middle of a winning streak."

"Not at my table, you're not," Benson replied, a wash of panic rising like floodwaters in his voice. "There's a gentleman here who wants to remove the house limit on bets."

Fogle wondered why every time he hit a lucky run, something went awry. Now the trouble was a thin fellow with ash brown hair, a walrus moustache, hollow cheeks, thin lips, pasty complexion and an unhealthy cough. Fogle slammed his cards onto the table. "Excuse me, gentlemen," he apologized as he shoved his chair away from the game. He could feel anger's flame heating within him, stoked by the narrowed stare from the slender wisp of a man standing at the faro layout opposite his dealer. By the gambler's natty dress, Fogle took him for a professional, a leech who sucked blood wherever he landed. "What's the problem, Benson?" Fogle asked as he stepped to beside his dealer, all the time staring at Holliday.

"I'm the problem," the emaciated fellow responded, his words ringing of the South, his insolent eyes watering with insult.

Fogle nodded, observing the gray frock coat hooked behind the gambler's sidearm, knowing another gun would be under the man's lapels. Fogle noted the bottle of Monarch Bourbon in the man's left hand. Only Chancey at the Cattle Exchange sold the Monarch brand in the Flat. Was Chancey behind this? "Now, what is it, Benson?"

The dealer pointed across the table. "He wants to lift the house betting limit."

"That true, mister?"

Holliday nodded, "I'm here to gamble, not shoot the breeze."

Fogle leaned over the table toward Holliday and rested his weight on his hands. "Then maybe you'd just better live with a hundred dollar limit."

Holliday nodded, stacking his winnings. "I'll take my business elsewhere, someplace more accommodating."

"You do that," Fogle said. "Go to Chancey's, since he likely sent you."

Benson pointed at Holliday's winnings. "He's more than five hundred ahead."

"What?" Fogle straightened to face his dealer. "You should've called me before now."

"Thought my luck would change."

Now Holliday leaned across the table toward Fogle. "I *will* take my winnings elsewhere, if you can even cover them."

"I can pay." Fogle clenched his fists. "I want a chance at you. You want to play no limit, then let's play. I'll deal the box." Benson backed away, and Fogle took his seat.

Holliday grinned, though his eyes remained as emotionless as a rattlesnake's. "Who's dealing doesn't matter as long as we continue the deck as is."

"The deal will continue as is, mister," Fogle said loudly, "once you place your bets."

Holliday took his time, surveying the casekeeper, dropping a dozen chips from palm to palm.

Fogle drummed his fingers on the table and tapped his booted foot on the floor. He wished for Lottie to play his hand, as she would never let this tinhorn cardsharp anger her. Fogle studied the casekeeper. Twelve turns had passed, thirteen turns remaining until hock. The cards had split evenly between the highs, eights through kings and the lows, aces through sixes. Already three aces, three kings and three sixes had fallen. No splits were possible on those three denominations when play resumed. A knowledgeable gambler would bet big on those, unless he was superstitious, Fogle thought. Three fives, three sevens, three eights and three nines remained in the dealing box, plenty of chances for splits, if the stranger was fool enough to bet on them.

The gambler pushed a stack of chips—Fogle counted five hundred dollars' worth—onto the ten. Fogle, his hands growing clammy, hoped his luck had accompanied him from the last table.

"That all?" Fogle sneered. He pulled back the exposed card to reveal a ten, a loser. Fogle laughed. "All that thought on a loser." As he revealed the next card, his smile evaporated. A split. Instead of taking all of the gambler's money, he'd draw only half. Fogle divided the stack of chips, raking his share to the check tray. Before Fogle had stacked his winnings, Holliday doubled his own two hundred and fifty dollars on the ten and moved the stack between the queen and jack, so either card would win or lose. After a turn without result, Fogle exposed a losing five over a winning jack.

"You owe me five hundred," Holliday said under his breath, his thin lips quivering beneath his moustache.

Anger boiled inside Fogle. He knew what he owed without being reminded. As Fogle slapped a matching set of chips beside the gambler's bet, Holliday pushed the entire stack across the queen until it rested between the lady and her man; either a king or a lady would win. Fogle pulled two turns without a result, then uncovered a losing four and a winning king.

"Add another thousand dollars," Holliday commanded.

Steam rising in him like the pressure in an overheated boiler, Fogle reached across the table, but his hand froze when Holliday's slipped inside his frock coat. The saloon owner sighed as the gambler extracted a handkerchief. Fogle's outstretched hand dropped to the table and counted out the loss as his opponent coughed into the cloth. "Damn luck," he said, dropping his loss in front of Holliday's chips.

"Or, damn unlucky," Holliday challenged.

Fogle winced and stared at the casekeeper, trying to calm himself. He could do little to change the tide of misfortune seeping across his table. The stranger must make a mistake. Though only a single queen, jack, seven, five, four, deuce and ace remained uncovered, three nines and three eights were still to be exposed. It might not matter until the final turn, as his opponent would avoid eights and nines in fear of splits. But on the last turn, if the gambler could call the order of the final three cards, the house paid greater odds. If the cards were all different, the odds were four to one. But if two of the last three were the same, odds were only two to one. That might be meaningless should his antagonist stumble before then, but offered Fogle a glimmer of hope in case he didn't.

Holliday pushed his chips back across the face of the queen and stopped between her and the jack for either to win. Fogle slid the top card out of the box, revealing an eight to lose. Then came a nine to win. Fogle cursed to himself. The next turn revealed the same two cards, only in the opposite order. Damn. Now only nine cards remained, all of them singles. Fogle shook his head and stared at the casekeeper to confirm he hadn't miscounted. He hadn't. When Fogle turned back to the layout, the gambler was moving his hand away from his bet. Fogle's own hand trembled as he extracted the top pasteboard. His eyes widened, and he slapped the table at the sight of a losing jack. Both hands reached out to drag the pot in as a mother would pull a child to her bosom. But his fingers hesitated just inches shy of their target. A copper token rested atop each stack. Had the gambler placed a token there before the turn? Fogle's eyes blinked twice. Was he mistaken? He now spotted what he had missed while studying the casekeeper. The gambler indeed had coppered his bets, played the queen and jack to lose which they had.

"Two thousand dollars," the gambler declared softly.

"Benson," Fogle said, "did he copper them before the turn?"

"You're damn right I did," Holliday responded in a low, menacing voice. "Now pay up. You're not playing with a dumb schoolboy, so don't think you'll sucker me." Holliday stared at Benson, who was slow to respond.

"Well, Benson, did he?"

"Yes," Benson nodded. "I warned you he was lucky."

"Shut up," Fogle ordered as he emptied the check tray of money. Lacking some nine hundred dollars to square his loss, Fogle shoved chips and money across the layout toward Holliday's stack. "There's eleven hundred. That clears out my check tray."

"Where's the rest?" Holliday demanded, his hands counting the saloon owner's settlement against being shorted further.

"When the deal's over, you'll get all that's yours," Fogle answered. "You gonna let that ride the next turn?"

"All of it, plus the nine hundred you still owe me," Holliday replied. "Four thousand total on this turn. The money'll stay where it is, less the coppers." Holliday removed the tokens.

Fogle stared at the casekeeper, as the plinky piano music drifting from downstairs grated on his nerves. Another win by this emaciated gambler would break him. And if that weren't enough, the saloon girls were slipping upstairs to test his rules again. A queen, nine, eight, seven, and four were the final five cards, yet this gambler left his bet between the queen and jack. Damn insulting, Fogle thought. With no jacks remaining, the gambler was betting on the queen alone, yet he had not pushed his bet atop the black lady on the layout. Fogle's neck burned at the contemptuous gesture.

"We gonna play?" The thin man challenged.

Fogle slapped the dealing box and pulled away the top card, revealing a losing seven, then a winning eight, resulting in no action on that turn. Three cards remained hidden—a queen, nine and four. Fogle felt his jaw tighten and the blood pulse from his neck to his temples. He knew the odds, four to one if the gambler named the order of the final three cards. If the gambler succeeded, Fogle had lost the Bee Hive. Six possible combinations meant the odds stayed with the dealer, but Fogle's intuition suggested odds no longer mattered with this foe.

The gambler gulped a mouthful of bourbon, then wiped his lips on the back of his hand. "Odds, four to one on the turn?"

Fogle nodded.

"I'm going the entire four thousand," Holliday said, "Four, queen, nine."

Fogle swallowed hard, but his throat was dry, and he almost gagged. He slid his hand over the dealing box, delaying the pull of a card and spotting Big Nose Kate making her way to the table. His luck had turned even worse.

With his free hand, Fogle wiped the sweat from his forehead. A four, queen, and nine hid beneath the top card. He just prayed not in that order.

Sliding the top card from the box, Fogle's breath hung in his throat. It was the four. If the next were a queen, he'd lose the Bee Hive. Fogle looked across at Holliday and despised the man for his imperturbable face, his contemptuous manner, his damnable luck.

Fogle pulled away the four, exposing a queen. The gambler had called the turn. The Bee Hive was under new ownership.

He stared at the queen with glazed eyes, then slid it out of the dealing box. As should be, a nine came up hock.

"Sixteen thousand dollars," Holliday smiled coldly.

Fogle nodded at the vagaries of luck, then turned the dealing box on its side, a gesture akin to a defeated general surrendering his sword to the victor. "I'll bring what money I have. There's not sixteen thousand."

"Plus the nine hundred you already owe me."

"There's not sixteen nine, either."

"The saloon will make up the difference." Holliday grinned.

"You're Chancey's man, aren't you?"

Holliday nodded.

"I figured as much, though it didn't change my luck," Fogle replied, watching Big Nose Kate move up to the faro table. "Kate, peddle your wares downstairs, not up here."

She strode forward, her hands on her hips. "Way I figure it, Mike, you no longer own the Bee Hive, so I don't take your orders now." She winked as she stopped behind Holliday. "I want to be on good acquaintance with the new proprietor of the Bee Hive," she said, placing her hand on Holliday's shoulder.

The gambler twisted toward her, his own hand reaching for the gun under his left shoulder, then relaxing.

Her fingers fell away. "Jumpy one, isn't he, boys?"

"A lady keeps her hands to herself," Holliday scolded.

"Mister, you and me aren't gonna fool anyone here into believing you're a gentleman, much less me a lady. All I care about is you're the new owner of the Bee Hive, and I want to get to know you better."

She touched his shoulder again and ran her hand down the front of his shirt.

Disgusted, Fogle backed away from the table. "I'll return to settle up."

"If you can," Holliday answered, his words salt in Fogle's open wound.

"I'll settle one way or the other," Fogle said, turning his back on Holliday and Kate, then walking slowly down the stairs. The music still played downstairs, but it lacked jauntiness to Fogle's ears. Tomorrow, the saloon owner thought, he might be tending bar, if someone would hire him.

At the foot of the stairs, Fogle, lost in his thoughts, bumped into a perfumed woman. "Watch it, you whore," he called. Then he glanced into the soft gray eyes of Lottie Deno. He shook his head, but could not rid the flush from his face. "I'm sorry, Lottie, I didn't expect to see you on a Sunday."

"Had an unsettling experience on my afternoon ride, Mike. Found a man hanging from a pecan tree. Thought I'd come in and play a little to ease my mind. What's troubling you?"

"I've lost the Bee Hive."

"Oh, no."

"Chancey put up a lucky fellow to make a run for it. Never seen luck run that deep except at your table."

"You can't cover the losses?"

"Sixteen thousand dollars."

Lottie whistled. "I can help!"

****

Holliday swigged on his bourbon to cut the edginess tingling through his body. The tubercular pains had subsided, and now he drank out of impatience with Fogle and the harlot hovering over his shoulder. As he put the bottle on the table, Kate grabbed it and poured a mouthful into herself.

"Woman, you don't drink with me unless you're invited," Holliday said, jerking the flask from her lips and spilling some of the amber liquid across her dress.

"My favorite perfume," she answered, rubbing the wetness from her dress onto her fingers and daintily transferring it behind her ears. "Well, well," Kate mocked, "don't think you can have me without an invitation." She primped her hair and moved to his other side.

"I want no part of you."

"Sure you do," she answered, licking her bourboned lips. "I won't even charge you."

"I can find better free."

Kate laughed. "But will it have you?" She turned and walked away, the scarlet hem of her dress sweeping a clean trail through the sawdust on the floor.

Holliday strode around the table to the dealer's chair.

Benson made a tentative gesture to stop him, then held back. "Customers don't sit in the dealer's place," Benson started, then reconsidered, "but I guess you're the owner now."

Holliday took the seat, wondering if the dealing box were rigged. Crooked dealing boxes were easy to come by, if you had the money. Holliday remembered ordering one out of San Francisco, but after killing the Fort Richardson soldier, he had escaped Jacksboro before it had arrived. Holliday pushed the box back and forth on the felt-covered table. With some rigged boxes, such a movement would release a spring, allowing two cards instead of one to slide out of the slot. On other rigged boxes, one pin holding the metal frame together was a dummy. By pushing the tiny rivet, the slot would widen enough for two cards. Without success, Holliday tried each rivet. Maybe the box was honest after all.

A crooked box worked in tandem with rigged cards. Unless a cold deck was used after a blind shuffle and blind cut, the cards had to be altered in some manner, to give the dealer an edge. Holliday reached for the pasteboards, then inspected them by sight and touch. Some gamblers punched tiny holes in the cards to see what followed the top card. Others roughed the backs and the fronts of selected "tell" cards so their perceptive fingers could read whether the next one was high or low, for instance. The game was only as honest as the dealers it attracted, and the gambling fraternity seldom earned honors for its integrity. Holliday shuffled the cards from hand to hand, scrutinizing them, his soft fingers detecting nothing. Damned if he hadn't stumbled into an honest faro game, Holliday thought. Best, though, to always assume and play otherwise.

Lottie's Luck

Waiting for Fogle to return, Holliday dealt out a hand of solitaire, turning over to begin with the three of hearts, a card he loathed. By legend, it foretold sorrow or poverty arising from indiscretion. Holliday thought himself no more superstitious than any other gambler, but still the trey bothered him. He continued the game to kill time. At least no money was riding on the solitaire, Holliday thought.

As he dealt himself another game, he heard a commotion of several men coming up the stairs, Fogle's voice among them. Holliday tossed the cards on the table, his hand slipping to his belt, nearer to his sidearm. He tensed as Fogle marched opposite him, throwing a money bag on the faro layout.

"Is sixteen thousand there?"

"I'm six and a half shy."

Holliday's moustache lifted atop a smug smile. "Then the Bee Hive ought to make up the difference."

"If I don't get a chance to win it back."

"Brash talk for someone that can't match his losses."

"I've found someone to cover my debt. You'll get full pay. Are you a sporting man or should I pass the word that you and Chancey don't give a man a chance to recoup his losses? Won't be good for you reputation or Chancey's business."

"One time through the deck, no more," Holliday offered.

"Agreed. No limit?"

"I'll return the favor."

"Someone else is playing for me," Fogle stated.

"Benson wasn't any luckier than you."

"Not Benson, someone else."

"Seems you want to be nurse-maided, if you can't call your own turn."

"Agreed or not," Fogle demanded.

"Okay, let's get on with it."

Fogle smiled broadly for a man with sour luck. "Lottie," he called.

Holliday could feel the heat rising in his face. He had wanted to find her, but not like this, not across a gambling table. He watched the stairs and saw her appear, step by step from under the broad brim of a yellow hat covering her auburn curls. Her face was as soft as he remembered. She was beautiful. As she stepped before him and walked across the floor, the hem of her pale yellow dress obliterated the trail made by Kate's skirt. He watched her gray eyes sweep across him, and he hoped for some glimmer of pleasure, but there was none. Several men tipped their hats as she passed, but she ignored everyone until she reached Fogle. To him she extended her delicate hand, and Fogle bent to kiss it. She never missed a trick, Holliday thought, his blood boiling with envy. She rattled an opponent any way she could. Before Holliday, she stopped with a modest curtsey.

"John Henry Holliday," she said softly. "How long's it been since Jacksboro? Ten or eleven months?"

"A long time, Lottie, too long." He removed his hat.

"It's never too long, John Henry. Not among thieves."

"But among admirers, yes."

"No, John Henry, not even among admirers."

"Guess there's no sense in discussing old times, huh?"

Lottie nodded, a curl falling across her forehead.

"I suppose you're here to play for the former proprietor of the Bee Hive."

She nodded again.

"You got enough to cover sixteen thousand?"

"Not with me, but I can cover it. My word's good. You know that."

"I do," Holliday said as he shuffled the cards from hand to hand several times. He inserted them in the box as he looked at the circle of men gathering around. A nine showed as the soda card.

"Place your bets, Lottie, unless you've changed your mind."

"I owe it to Mike for keeping me on at the Bee Hive."

Holliday laughed. "Everyone knows he owes you for the crowd you bring in." Holliday glanced at Fogle, who nodded at the one thing both men agreed on.

"Eight thousand," Lottie said, "on the low cards. I'm betting to win."

Holliday thumbed the nine soda card from the dealing box and stared at a naked jack, the loser. Slowly he pulled the jack from the box and grimaced at the sight—the trey of hearts. He pitched Fogle's unopened money bag to Lottie. "The money should be there, if your man's honest."

"He's more so than most," Lottie answered, leaving the sack where Holliday tossed it. "Now I'm playing the low cards to lose."

As Holliday pulled the winning three of hearts out of the way, the crowd cheered. A six of clubs had taken its place. Lottie had triumphed. Holliday's only chance to hang on now was a split, but the next card turned up a ten. The Bee Hive had changed hands again. Holliday turned the faro box on its side. "How do you do it, Lottie?" he asked.

"I work at it."

"You must," Holliday answered, standing up and turning toward the stairs. He heard Fogle's laughter following him downstairs.

"God bless Lottie's Luck," Fogle kept yelling.

Chapter 6

At the poker table, underneath the stuffed head of a mottled longhorn with a twisted horn that threatened its eyes, Holliday sat, idly fiddling with a tin plate of salt pork, red beans too salty, and dark bread too stale. The food's saltiness lingered in his mouth like the bitterness of last night's defeat by Lottie. The thought of her opened in him an emptiness he could not fill. Perhaps she offered him a chance at respectability, rather than the life he lived. Failing to hold the Bee Hive was Chancey's loss, Lottie his.

Since killing the Fort Richardson soldier and escaping Jacksboro, Holliday had wondered if she shared his desires. Many times he had imagined finding her, perhaps in a hotel lobby, maybe on the street or during one of the Sunday excursions she relished so. Always in his mind she had welcomed him with a smile that overflowed into the depths of her gray eyes. But last night, her shallow smile never reached her eyes. Herding a bite of beans onto this fork, Holliday wished faro and money had not passed between them. It was foolish, this schoolboy fixation on her, but not he could shake it. He could manipulate the cards and his luck at the poker table, but never this.

Holliday jabbed a piece of salt pork and sopped up a puddle of bean juice with a hunk of bread. Glancing up from his plate, he scanned the bored room calmed by the midafternoon doldrums, the dozen customers as silent at their tables as the mounted longhorns on the wall. A pair of buffalo hunters shot pool nearby, but they played without talking. A lethargic, barrel-shaped bartender squeezed between the empty chairs as he followed a broom around the floor. Behind the counter a thinner barkeep emptied and polished the Cattle Exchange's spittoons, stopping occasionally to dump the fetid black liquid into a battered bucket or to pour another round of liquor for the lone patron bellied up to the bar. Holliday wondered if Chancey cut his house whiskey with those chaw fixings in the dented container.

He shuddered and mopped up a last bite that turned sour in his mouth when the saloon doors swung inward with Ed Bailey behind them.

"Howdy, Ed," said a pair of men leaning back in their seats near the door.

"Afternoon, boys," Bailey answered, then greeted the barkeeper dancing with the sweeper and the one riding herd over the spittoons. Bailey approached the counter, taking off his bowler with both hands and aiming for the opposite wall. "Free drink if I make it," he called to the bartender wrist deep in a spittoon. "I buy a round if I don't." As the barkeep grunted approval, Bailey flung his hat at the nearest mounted longhorn. The dust-discolored hat twirled twice around the horn's point, almost hanging on, then falling away, the bartender with the broom catching it before it littered the floor.

"Well, gentlemen," Bailey bellowed, "looks like I buy a round of drinks." The patrons nodded as Bailey twisted his kettle belly in a full sweep around the room and glanced from face to face. "Pleasure to buy my friends a—," he started, but stopped, his eyes burning toward Holliday.

Holliday glared back.

"—a good drink," Bailey continued, "including you in the back." He nodded at Holliday.

Holding up his bottle of Monarch Bourbon, Holliday shrugged. "I'll stick to my own," he said. "It's better than the cheap stuff you'd buy." He watched Bailey's fleshy cheeks redden and his eyes bulge with more hatred.

"You should try my liquor before you insult it." Bailey accepted his bowler from the rotund sweeper.

"Way you play poker," Holliday answered, "I doubt you can afford anything but that bucket of spittoon juice."

Bailey clenched his fists, turned to the counter and slammed them on the bar. "The best in the house." The saloon's patrons cheered. "On me." His voice quivered with rage. Turning back to Holliday, Bailey leaned an elbow on the counter, his tight coat puckering between buttons until he undid them and freed his abundant stomach. His hand inched inside his lapel and just as slowly reappeared with the silver inlaid pipe in his fingers. "From what I hear, John, Lottie Deno stripped you of your winnings last night in five turns of the cards."

"Three," he corrected, "and she didn't use a shiny pipe."

Bailey, straightening from the bar into a more defiant stance, pointed the pipe stem at Holliday. "You misread me," he answered. "One day, I'll teach you a few things about cards."

"You couldn't teach hog droppings to stink." His words sliced through the humorless air like the clink of unsheathed swords.

"One day, John, one day," Bailey replied, shaking the cold pipe at Holliday.

"What's wrong with today?" With catlike quickness Holliday stood, his hand by his waist, his fingers curled to fit the ivory grip of his Colt, his every muscle tensed with the exhilarating expectation of conflict. Bailey drew his pipe back to his chest with startled suddenness, and the two pool players, quitting their game, backed away from the pair. In the rounds of Bailey's eyes, Holliday could see a thread of fear unraveling. "One day, what, Bailey?" Holliday challenged.

His eyes widening above fleshy cheeks that quivered like spilled jelly, Bailey swiveled around on his heels and stared blankly in the backbar mirror at Holliday. "Drinks around the house," Bailey repeated, his voice breaking into heavy panting. "The good stuff."

"Bailey," Holliday spat out the name, "don't load your mouth with more than you can back up." Ed's mirrored eyes averted Holliday's, so Holliday slid into his chair, disappointed there would be no fight.

The bartender quit his spittoons long enough to offer a jigger of Monarch Bourbon to everyone but Holliday. Bailey downed several jiggers, one after the other, until his courage recovered. Then he asked the barkeeper for a deck of cards and led three customers to a table in the corner opposite Holliday's perch.

The two pool players chalked their cue sticks and picked up their game. Holliday watched Bailey open the fresh pack, fire up his pipe, and draw deeply on his larcenous companion until his face disappeared in a veil of smoke. Damn brazen of him to still use the pipe, Holliday thought.

With time, the saloon filled. The piano player came in, and his music drew customers like flies to a gut wagon. A few prostitutes straggled in to lasso the randy ones from the herd while the cadre of drinking men grew with those desiring to cut the dust from their throat or the monotony from their day. With the company of his bourbon, Holliday waited at his table for Chancey. When his glass companion went dry, he motioned for the bartender to bring him another bottle.

Lottie's Luck

Midway through the second bottle, Holliday saw Chancey scurrying through the swinging doors, a scowl on his face. Big Nose Kate tailed him. Holliday groaned. Chancey marched brusquely through the room, Kate jabbering at him every step of the way. The pool players stepped aside as Chancey strode to his office door, jerked a throng of keys from his britches pocket and fumbled for a moment against the lock. "Woman," he blurted out, "give my ears a break."

"Then let me work your place." Her voice screeched like chalk on slate.

"Okay, okay," he said, shoving the door open and entering.

Kate trailed as close as his shadow, then backed out, her ungainly step quickened by a sound shove.

"Don't damage the goods," she cried with the compassion of a wounded mountain lioness. As customers twisted their heads to watch, Kate smoothed a ruffle on her black blouse and dusted an unseen speck from her matching skirt. After fingering the kinks of her mussed brown curls when only a brush could help, she surveyed the room. "Kate's here and ready for business," she called with a swagger.

Holliday glanced away, pulling his hat lower over his head, but too late. She had seen him. He could tell by the broad, toothy grin that chilled him. Marching with big steps, Kate stood over him before he could move.

"Well, well," she said, "remember me?"

"How could I forget?"

"My looks, they do that to men."

"Not your appearance, darling, but your crass manners."

"Such a nice thing to say, mister, because most fellows like my crass."

"Crass, darling, means lacking refinement, sensitivity or even intelligence."

"Buster, my manners are no worse than your gambling, as I recall from last night."

"My luck was running right well until you showed up."

"Lottie changed your luck. Your eyes were as big as twin moons, the way you were staring at her. And it wasn't the big pot you were gaping at, but her bosom. Don't think you or anybody else is gonna get a piece of Lottie Deno. You may fondle her cards, but that's all of hers you'll ever touch. She's colder than a block of ice, unlike me." With her foot, Kate shoved a chair closer to Holliday, brushing her skirt from around her full hips as she plopped down beside him.

Holliday retreated to his bottle.

"I'm not here to discuss Lottie or to accept your compliments on my manners. You owe me an apology!"

Holliday stared blankly across the room at Bailey's table.

"I said, you owe me an apology." She smoothed more wrinkles from her skirt, pulling the hem to her knee, as she waited for a response. She grinned at his indifference. "Mister, I can be loud, and it don't embarrass me to call attention to myself. It's how I make my living. Now, are you gonna apologize or not?"

"Apologize for what?"

"You got me run off from the Bee Hive!"

"Just how did I manage that?"

Kate cleared her throat and straightened her back like a schoolgirl about to recite in class. "It seemed you were the new owner of the Bee Hive," she started. "Mike Fogle didn't like me sassing him when he ordered me downstairs. Of course, he wasn't the owner when I got sassy, but by the time Lottie finished whipping your tail, he was back in charge. Way I see it, if you hadn't fouled up, I'd still have roaming rights in the busiest saloon in Griffin."

"More curves in your thinking than in a ball of rattlesnakes and likely as much venom." Rubbing his chin as he spoke, Holliday felt his cheek twitch, and he could not stop the grin that pried at his lips. Kate's pose lost its stiffness like a corpse coming back to life, and Holliday, for the first time, took in her features. She had weathered the storms of many men's lusts well. In her silence reposed a spirit unusual among women in her trade. When she was quiet, her doe-like brown eyes hid behind the flutter of her long lashes; her patrician nose, slightly hooked, stood guard over full, inviting lips; her rouged cheeks melted into a defiant chin; and her brown hair, though mussed, hung soft and shiny around her head like an expensive curtain. But when she spoke, the red lips uncaged a biting tongue, the eyes flared with sparks, her nose drew deep masculine breaths, and her hair seemed like a low flame over the glowing coals of a nasty disposition. Whether speaking or quiet, she could appeal to men with her breasts pressing tight against her blouse, her midriff funneling in on a narrow waist, the waist blossoming into broad hips that swayed invitingly when she walked.

"I'm waiting for your apology."

"Did I just hear you'll be working the Cattle Exchange now?" He pushed his empty plate to the middle of the table.

She nodded. "Chancey doesn't do the land office business like the Bee Hive, but there's enough pickings here to keep me busy." Kate leaned toward him, resting her forearms on the worn felt, her hand tentatively reaching for his. When he did not retreat, she clasped it gently. "My offer last night still stands, if you ever get the itch."

"No charge, the best I recollect." He pursed his lips, then pulled his hand from hers.

"You know how, don't you?" She grinned.

Amused at Kate, Holliday leaned back in his chair, the front two legs rising off the floor, and rocked gently, scratching his moustache and tugging at the corners. "What you lack in manners you make up for in gall, woman."

"Kate's the name, Big Nose Kate," she answered. "And what I lack in manners, I make up in other ways. You've just got to let me show you."

"Lots of things I may need to be shown, but that's not one of them." Holliday stretched his arms, then massaged a leg cramp.

"Let me rub it for you." She reached for him.

"Woman—Kate—what's it take to get through that thick skull of yours?"

"The way to get to me isn't through my skull."

"You want to do something for me? I've got something you can do," Holliday said as he eased his chair down.

"Name it."

Reaching toward the table, he pushed his half-full whiskey bottle aside, then leaned forward like a man bracing against a strong headwind. He shoved his dirty plate and empty bottle toward her. "Return that to the counter."

A cloud of disappointment fleeted across her face and left in its wake a smile, like the sunshine following a thunderstorm. Her grin surprised him. He relaxed.

"My pleasure," she answered, arising from her chair like a gentle dowager at a tea. Picking up the tin and the bottle by the neck, she spun around and sailed the plate through a crack between two customers at the bar, the tinware clattering from the counter against a freshly polished spittoon.

Holliday realized he was dealing with nitroglycerin.

Kate twisted around at Holliday, striking the empty bourbon bottle on the edge of the table, shattering the container into a hundred noisy pieces. "I'm not your maid," she screamed, waving the jagged shard at Holliday's nose.

Chancey's office door flung open, and he lunged into the gaming area, dropping behind the pool table and leveling the business end of a double-barreled shotgun across the room. Customers dove to the floor.

"Easy, Chancey," called the thin bartender. "No trouble, just that hussy throwed a plate and broke a bottle." He pointed to Kate.

Chancey glared at her, while customers picked up themselves and their conversations. "Kate, if you cause any more trouble in my saloon, you won't have a place to peddle your goods short of Haverty's Livery." Chancey broke the breech of the shotgun with a loud click.

"Just an accident, Chancey," she said, her hand holding the bottle shard hidden behind her hips. "I dropped them."

"You're not smart enough to drop anything but your drawers." A cackle of laughter spread across the room.

Holliday stood, cursing at the glass fragments that dotted his new suit like crystal insects. As he brushed them off, Kate stepped toward him, pointing a crooked finger at his nose and cutting loose with that stinger of a tongue. "His fault, Chancey. He's soured my luck. And for some of yours."

Holliday clenched his fists and wondered the penalty for strangling a woman. If the jury knew Kate, Holliday suspected they'd reward him handsomely for his service to humanity.

"I'm telling you, Chancey," she said, flinging the bottle neck at Holliday's boots. "He cost me my job at the Bee Hive, and now he's ordering me around like I'm his servant."

Chancey glanced at Holliday, a glint of recognition flashing across his eyes for a brief instant, then shook his head. "Kate, you're like a jackass. You bray too much."

A wave of laughter lapped across the saloon, but Kate turned to face the gaiety. Her back to Chancey, she bent forward and flipped her skirt up over her hips.

"Now, that's an ass in case you didn't know." The patrons roared, a couple clapping. As Kate straightened and herded her skirt into place, she whispered at Holliday. "I'll still do you any time." Kate marched away, proper as a virgin at a Sunday meeting.

Lottie's Luck

Holliday didn't know what to think about Kate Elder. Annoying as she was, he found her feisty spirit intriguing. He picked up his bottle, spotting the flush of amusement in Bailey's face, and followed Chancey into his office. The room was small and windowless. On a rolltop desk to one side, a single lamp with a low flame pushed a ball of light against the dimness. Chancey laid the shotgun atop the desk's clutter and adjusted the lamp for a higher flame. "Close the door," he ordered.

The thick plank door shut with the lock's metallic firmness, and in the growing light Holliday noticed a peephole. He turned and took in the room, observing the strongbox bolted to the floor by the desk and chair, the many cases of liquor stacked along the side wall, three barrels of beer hugging the back wall, and two outdated calendars tacked above them.

Pointing to three rawhide-bottomed chairs, Chancey settled into his seat, propped his feet atop the desk corner, and started fixing a cigarette. "I ought to shoot you for taking up with Kate."

"Seems she's taken up with me. I had little say in the matter," Holliday said as he sat in the middle chair.

"Whatever she wants, you best give her, or she'll pester you until hell freezes over."

"I can't explain last night," Holliday started.

Chancey grimaced. "I can, Lottie's Luck. Yes, sir, I came close to owning the Bee Hive. A month of Sundays and Lottie Deno wouldn't show her pretty face inside a saloon. Then some damn peckerwood gets his neck stretched when my luck's running good, and she's there in time to change it. There's something to Lottie's Luck, but I intend to beat it one day."

Holliday nodded as he arose from his chair. "I'm not so confident I ever will," he said, turning to depart.

"Wait a minute," Chancey called. Standing, he leaned over the lamp chimney until his cigarette took to flame. "Don't you want a table at the Cattle Exchange?"

"The deal was if I won the Bee Hive. I didn't," Holliday answered.

"After the last two nights, word's gotten around you're a gambler, so you won't be surprising anyone anymore. I need a faro dealer. Lottie'd be my preference, but you'll do. I'll give you seventeen percent of the winnings, more than I pay the others."

Holliday stroked his moustache. "Good money, but working in the same saloon with Bailey don't appeal to me. I'd spend as much time looking out for him as I would for your money. That'd be unhealthy for both of us."

Chancey scratched his head, drew hard on his cigarette, then exhaled a heavy ribbon of smoke. "Bailey's got a lot of friends, local men that give me a steady business between cattle drovers and buffalo hunters. Can't say I want to get rid of him. Had we hung on to the Bee Hive last night, I'd a had two saloons to keep you apart. I don't favor Bailey much, too loud, too careless sometimes, but he draws customers. I more than make up in drinks what he loses at poker."

"There are other saloons, by my count," Holliday answered. "I'll make out."

"That's for certain, and that's why I want you here."

"I'll remember that, but I've got money to last awhile."

Chancey grinned. "If you work at another saloon, take Kate and her charms with you."

Holliday walked out the door, scanning the room for Kate, but she had disappeared. He breathed easier. Skirting the pool table, Holliday eyed Bailey's game, the reflecting pipe at his side as he dealt. He felt a cough rising in his chest and took a quick swallow from the bourbon bottle he still carried. Drawing about as much air as whiskey, Holliday stopped at the bar, bought another flask to last the night, then exited.

The sun burned low in the west, like a candle about to die, and the street dozed in the supper-time quiet. He marched down Griffin Avenue toward the Clear Fork and stopped to lean against the false-fronted wall of Shifflet's Tannery. Resting there, he could smell the bittersweet odor of unpleasant chemicals mingling with the aroma of raw and finished leather. He stared at the adobe front of the Bee Hive, awaiting another frenetic night.

The biggest and gaudiest saloon in Griffin, the Bee Hive stood two stories high, the tallest structure between Fort Worth and El Paso. On the Bee Hive's plastered and whitewashed front was the most famous sign on the Texas frontier. Painted in natural colors on that wall, two prominent hives trailed streams of bees flitting among the honeysuckle branches in bloom and lettered in the fresco was the crude poetry of a frontier muse:

Within this hive, we are all alive,

Lottie's Luck

Good whiskey makes us funny,
And if you are dry, step in and try
The flavor of our honey.

As the long shadows merged between buildings and distant stacks of buffalo hides, Holliday waited, swigging on his bottle, swatting at the buzzing flies. He lost track of time before he glimpsed Lottie approaching the Bee Hive. She carried a small carpet bag, empty now, but by night's end it would hold her winnings, a couple hundred dollars or more. He admired the cut of her frame as he pulled his pocket watch from his vest and held it close to his eyes. Lottie was a beautiful creature, nonetheless, one of habit. She would begin her turn at the table each night at the same time. It was eight o'clock. Holliday turned and walked toward the Planters House, wishing she were beside him, her arm in his.

****

Damned if he wasn't a noisy customer, Kate thought. Lying atop her, he moaned and grunted like a rooting hog, and he smelled just as bad. Buffalo skinners stank as if they had bathed in a cesspool, and this one was a credit to that reputation. Kate rubbed his chapped back and forced perfunctory moans, a professional courtesy. But he kept snorting and grunting and ughing and gasping and groaning and whooping. Kate struggled to disguise the guffaw building within her. Kate wondered if her paying pal had taken his lessons from copulating buffaloes. The idea tickled her, and she snickered, softly at first, then almost maniacally, as the spent buffalo skinner collapsed around her in a sweaty embrace. He grabbed her head and turned it to kiss her. Running his fingers through her hair, he pressed his rough lips against hers. Kate returned his lust with the passion of a corpse. His breath reeked of cheap liquor and his mouth of strong chewing tobacco. Kissing a buffalo's behind couldn't be much worse, Kate decided, then sniggered, wrenching her lips loose from his.

"Let me breathe, fellow, I need air," she gasped, disguising the laughs, each growing harder and harder to control. Finally, with too much to restrain, she cackled in his ear.

"Funny, is it?" he scowled.

Kate unwrapped her arms from around his back and spread them until they drooped over the head of the cornhusk mattress and her bosom pressed even tighter against the man's scaly chest. "Don't tell me you didn't enjoy it 'cause you howled more than a pack of coyotes."

"It wasn't worth the cost."

"You haven't paid me yet. Next time, though, do me a favor and sit in the creek for a week so you don't smell like a buffalo's behind. Hard enough to keep my sheets clean without a walking slop jar rubbing off on them."

The buffalo skinner pushed away from her, as if he were picking himself up from a dung heap, and tweaked her breast. "Won't be a next time with you."

"No matter, just do a favor to whatever girl you rent and use something other than buffalo innards for tonic water."

Her customer stood bedside in the darkness, groping for his clothes. "My pants? Where'd you throw them?"

"I don't know, and when I took 'em off, you didn't care what I did with them. You were too eager to get out of them and into bed."

"Light a lamp."

"Lamp? Fellow, you don't need light. Crawl around and sniff 'em out. A dead hound could smell them at half a mile."

The skinner kicked around the floor for a moment. "I can't find them. Light the lamp."

"Either your nose is broke or the pants rats carried them off."

"I don't have lice."

"Can't they stand the stink?"

"You gonna light the lamp?"

"You need it, you light it."

The hunter eased along the bed to the wall and the small table within reach of Kate's pillow. He fumbled for a tin of matches, knocking over the lamp's dome. It clattered on the table.

"You break my lamp, you're gonna owe me more than for a poke."

"Woman, don't you ever give a guy any peace?"

"Not until I get paid."

"Oh, hell." The skinner found the match tin, opened the container lid and spilled several matches into his hand. He pinched one between his fingers and let the rest fall with the tin to the table. Cursing, he flicked it against the rough adobe wall. The flaring match bled sulphur fumes as the hide man lit the wick and adjusted the lamp until a jaundiced light contaminated the room.

The crib was small and dominated by a bed, Kate demurely pulling the sheet over her naked body. Besides the bedside table, the enclosure contained a washstand at the foot of the bed, an eating table and two chairs near the door, a trunk for her clothes, and a small stove, all crammed inside. A stack of newspapers littered the dirt floor by the woodbox, and a dozen books stood on a rough shelf resting on two pegs protruding from the wall over her bed. The room functioned well for her occupation, but for little else, including ease of movement.

Finding his britches under the washstand at the end of the bed, the buffalo hunter worked them quickly up his legs. He glared at Kate for covering herself. Angering at her false modesty, the buffalo skinner spat on the hard-packed dirt floor as he buttoned his pants. He pulled his shirt over his head, wrestling his arms through the sleeves. After hitching his suspenders over his shoulders, he bent to retrieve his boots, then sat on the bed, almost on Kate's leg.

"Use a chair."

The skinner ignored her, pulling worn boots over dirtied socks. He stood up, slapped at Kate's leg and walked to the chair where he had hung his holster and hat.

"Say, fellow." Kate sat up, holding the sheet around her neck. "Aren't you forgetting something? Like my pay?"

The skinner whirled around, a grin flashing across his face. "Now it's my turn to laugh. This was on the house."

"No, it wasn't," she shot back. Kate let the sheet fall down from her neck, exposing her rounded breasts and a .35-caliber revolver in her right hand. "Don't move for your gun, fellow," she ordered, pointing her pistol toward his crotch, "or I'll plug your manhood or what there is of it. Then you'll have no cause to pay a woman for anything but sympathy. Now fork it over. Three dollars like we agreed."

The buffalo skinner stood frozen, the grin exposing his tobacco-rotted teeth like dirty icicles. Kate pulled back the hammer on the revolver. The smile disappeared like melting snow. The skinner reached cautiously for his right pants pocket. Now Kate smiled. He was going for his money. She knew it was in the right pocket because she had already stripped the roll of two bills while pulling down his pants. The skinner jerked three soiled bills from the others and stepped toward her.

"Just drop 'em on the floor and stay where you are," she commanded. He obliged, then backed to his hat and holster. "Pick up your hat first." He obeyed. "Now with your right arm, take up your gun belt by the buckle. If I even think you're gonna try something funny, I'll start shooting."

His eyes rolled in anger, and the pink flush of liquor reddened his cheeks. Perhaps raged boiled within him, but he was not too drunk to let it overflow. The gun barrel pointing at his privates promised more excitement than he had bargained for. Holding his hat at his waist, as if the greasy felt shield might save his manhood, he inched backward to the door, lifted the handle, and slipped out into the darkness, leaving the entry ajar. Kate jumped from the bed, blew out the light, and stumbled naked for the door. Sticking her hand through the doorway, she squeezed a shot into the ground to hasten his retreat. From somewhere down the creek, another gunshot answered hers, but that was all. She stepped across the opening and shoved the plank door shut, barring it for the evening.

It was midnight, maybe later. Though time remained to find another customer, she had amused four already, skinning two of them of a few bucks more than they thought. That was enough for the night. Through the narrow darkness, she made her way to her bed, relit the table lamp. From the box of cartridges beneath the mattress, she replaced the wasted hull, then slipped the revolver into the holster nailed into the wall inches below the mattress top at the head of her bed. Holding the lamp close to the bed, she satisfied herself no lice escaped from the skinner, then sponged herself with the cold water from the washbasin. The water sent a pimply chill over her body and muted the smell of the men who had used her. She dried with the towel hanging over the bedstead and picked up the money the buffalo skinner had dropped on the floor. Like him, the bills smelled, and she tossed them in the wash basin's murky water. "Wish I could do that to all of them that come in before we got down to business," she said to herself.

Though she had had four men in as many hours, she thought about another as she pulled the newest book from the shelf over her bed. As she tugged the sheet to her chin, she wished she were drawing the covers over the new gambler, the one they called Holliday. She knew he wouldn't smell. He dressed well and shaved daily, unlike most of her professional acquaintances. She would like to feel his slender fingers in hers. Kate wanted to run her hands through his ash blond hair and look into his blue-gray eyes, which glinted danger like the edge of a finely honed saber. Behind those eyes, Kate sensed a vulnerability which drew her to him like a mother to a hurt child. She fluffed the cover at her neck and opened her book, Mark Twain's latest, a volume called *The Adventures of Tom Sawyer*. Kate had enjoyed it so far, its story of young and innocent love, a kind she could never have, if she ever had love at all. She settled into her bed and read ponderously but steadily until her eyelids grew too heavy. After dropping the book on the floor and blowing out the light, she dreamed peacefully. In her sleep, she was Becky Thatcher, but rather than Tom Sawyer, she preferred the mischievous Huckleberry Finn. Huckleberry reminded her of the new gambler in town, the one with blue-gray eyes of tempered steel.

Chapter 7

A naked ace of spades fell boldly onto the hemstitched white linen tablecloth covering the gate-leg breakfast table. In rapid order, its nearest relatives in black dropped by rank—king, queen, jack, and ten—in a perfect deal. Lottie smiled, amused by her manipulations. Every time she touched the pasteboards, she remembered her father and herself, a girl in lace and bows, nestling in his lap during the gentlemanly poker games he enjoyed with other wealthy planters. Oh, how he had loved gambling. She, too, had been infected with its permutations, never thinking it would become her living. But that was before Fort Sumter led to Appomattox. Before the war, little seemed more secure than being the eldest daughter of a Kentucky legislator. After Appomattox, little was more useless than her kinship to a dead man. Lottie had had nowhere to turn but to cards.

Except Sundays, Lottie practiced daily an hour or more on card table artifice—runs, dealing seconds, palming, bottom dealing, blind shuffles, blind cuts. Like other gamblers, she practiced more tricks than she used, but when Lady Luck needed a boost, Lottie assisted. Satisfied with the day's effort, she placed the cards in a tiny drawer in the table's side. Yawning and stretching in her chintz robe and muslin nightgown, she stood and walked to an imposing walnut bureau that somehow had squeezed through the adobe cabin's small door. She pulled a tortoise-shell brush from her vanity and attacked a tangle of auburn hair.

Standing in a window-squared shaft of western sunlight, she stroked her shimmering red hair and hummed a gentle ballad—her father's favorite—about love gone awry. Outside, the mockingbird she fed each day took up its grating cry as a pack of taunting school kids passed on their way home from class on Government Hill. Such a beautiful creature, the mockingbird, to squawk such horrid music, she thought. As she acknowledged her fine looks in the bureau mirror, she knew the song of her own life—at least since the war—was no prettier.

Finishing her mane, she opened the bottom bureau drawer and extracted a small maroon carpet bag, placing it on the adjacent bed. Sitting on the mattress and unhooking the latch, she freed a revolver, then dumped out the carpetbag's remaining contents, last night's winnings scattering upon the quilted cover. As she always practiced cards before combing her hair, so too she always slept before counting the previous evening's take. Perhaps it was superstition, but impatience bred bad luck. Wait long enough and Lady Luck would treat you kindly. Now, though, she quickly counted her take, totaling only forty-seven dollars and some assorted change. Not a good haul, even for a weeknight, but still she had come out ahead. Things would slow with the buffalo hunters refitting for another winter season, when the hides were thickest and most valuable. Most cattle outfits had already passed Fort Griffin with their trail drive profits. It would be spring before they returned and late summer before they came back from Kansas with any money.

Gathering her cash, she slipped into the back room, dark from the shuttered windows, depositing the roll of bills on the cold cookstove. A rough-hewn table with a box of groceries and a stack of dishes atop it, a washtub, and a woodbox also hid in the shadows. Standing sentry by the door was a loaded double-barreled shotgun. After checking the latches on the window shutters, Lottie bent over the woodbox and removed its kindling. With the box emptied, her index finger slipped knowingly into a small knot hole, lifting the false bottom. Even in the dimness she could make out the stacks of bills and coins. With her other hand, she reached atop the stove, but a loud rap at the front door startled her.

She shoved the money into hiding, fitting the fake bottom in place and tossing kindling over it, the wood clattering around the lip of the box. The kindling still rattled as she grabbed the double-barreled shotgun and cocked both hammers, the dual triggers going deadly stiff. Slipping into the adjacent room, she addressed the door. "Your name and business?" Her throat tightened.

"Jack Jacobs," answered a welcomed voice. "This a bad time, Lottie?"

Easing the hammers down on the weapon, Lottie released her breath. "No, Jack, just a moment." She raced to the bed, threw the revolver in the carpetbag, then shoved it and the shotgun under the bed. She smoothed the slight ruffle in the quilted spread, glancing as she did in the mirror. Retrieving her brush, she ran it through her hair a couple times, pinched her cheeks to give them color and retied her loose robe to cover her nightgown. She unbarred and unlatched the door, swinging it open.

Jack Jacobs stood before her, a hat in one hand, a container of pecans in the other. "I came to return your basket."

Lottie smiled, giving a toss of her head, her auburn hair rippling with pleasure. "Come in, Jack, won't you, but forgive my appearance?"

Shuffling his feet, Jacobs cast his blue eyes downward. "You look fine, Lottie, just fine." Jacobs was tall and lean, without an ounce of nonsense on his frame. He wore working clothes—denim pants and flannel shirt, old but clean—without shame, for he had frayed the cuffs and frazzled the knees through honest labor. When he smiled, his grin came narrow under a broad nose, but his eyes danced under arched eyebrows. By the set of his jaw and the challenge in his eyes, he feared no man and respected all women, though around the young and pretty ones he might bite his lower lip.

"Come on in, Jack, and quit biting your lip. It's always a pleasure to have a gentleman visit me."

His tanned face colored, gratifying Lottie that she could still make a decent man blush. Jacobs extended the basket awkwardly. As Lottie's hand touched his on the handle, her robe parted, exposing a sliver of her gown. His gaze passed by without lingering.

As he stepped inside, Lottie carried the pecans to the back room. "You shouldn't have filled the basket."

Shifting his hat from hand to hand, Jacobs took in the precise neatness of the room. A walnut bedstead, bureau with mirror, and dress cabinet spoke well of Lottie's gambling success. An eight-day clock in an enameled case with gilt designs ticked its displeasure at sharing the dresser top with a lamp. At the end of the bed she shared with no one reposed a huge traveling trunk on a rag carpet that covered most of the wooden floor. The quilted bed cover was as free of wrinkles as the sky and so, too, the linen cloth on the gate-leg table. Two walnut chairs by the table, a store-bought cane-bottom rocker and a small divan offered more seats than Lottie ever had visitors. For a moment, the heavy silence was broken only by the irksome clock.

"I'd offer you some coffee, but my stove is cold," Lottie said, emerging from the back room.

Jacobs waved her apology away with his hat. "No matter, Lottie."

She motioned to the divan, and he settled down on its edge, dropping his hat at his side and leaning toward her. Lottie sat down in the rocker opposite him. "Thanks for returning the basket, filled with pecans at that. I doubt that Rachel has any appetite for pecans just yet."

Jacobs rubbed his calloused hands together. "Shame she had to see that," he answered, biting his lip after he spoke. "You, too, for that matter, Lottie." His face flushed again.

His embarrassment was contagious. "I know what you meant, Jack," she reassured. "I've seen unpleasantries before. It wasn't a pretty sight, but it hasn't haunted me. Did the sheriff know who he was?"

"Sheriff Larn never saw him. I buried him with a borrowed shovel and without a prayer. Then I let Larn know, but he'd rather polish his badge than find the killers. I suspect he knew more about the lynching than he let on. Hell, Larn—" Jacobs looked up full into Lottie's eyes, "Pardon my language, Lottie."

"I've heard worse."

"But you shouldn't in your own home."

"Your apology's accepted, though unnecessary. Go on."

"Sheriff Larn may be a member of the vigilance committee, maybe not. Many ranchers and merchants around the Flat aren't above stretching a neck to civilize Shackelford County."

"This is a hard country, Jack, but it'll change. My kind won't be around then, but yours will, and things'll settle down."

Jacobs appeared lost in a tangle of his own thoughts, and Lottie, sharing his discomfort, shifted in the rocker. "Your kind?" He bit his lip. "Lottie, a lot of men around here would favor your kind for a wife."

She felt a blushing heat in her cheeks and stood. "My kind?" she said, walking to the unshuttered west window. "My kind is no different from the girls selling themselves in the back of the saloons or in their cribs. I just take men's money by another method." She stared out the window, spotting a mockingbird hopping through the grass and pecking at insects.

Jacobs cleared his throat. "Not a man in Shackelford County and maybe in all of Texas would think you that type."

"The less men know of me, the more they flock to my table. They come to see this female outcast with the mysterious face and past, but it's an illusion, like a card trick. They don't know my past, and I tell no one of it." Lottie, smiling slightly, turned to Jacobs. "Except maybe you." She watched him bite his lip. "At San Antonio," she laughed, "they called me 'Mystic Maude' when I dealt faro there. Now Maude's an ugly name, isn't it?"

Jacobs nodded. "It's several steps down from Lottie, or even Charlotte, I'd guess. But here they call you '*Lotta Deniro*.'"

Puzzled, Lottie shrugged.

"Spanish. Means lots of money."

She giggled.

"Don't know that it's that funny, Lottie. Seems a lot of men, men I'd trust with my life about as far as I could throw my horse, have been noticing that you tote away more money from the Bee Hive than you lose. Word's going around you were covering Fogle's losses on Sunday against Chancey's man. Some men might be tempted to look around here for your cash."

Lottie stepped to the rocking chair. "Nobody knows where I keep my money."

"But they know it's here somewhere. They know you don't spend much, so you're bound to stash it here," he said, tapping his boot on the rag carpet, "or there in the kitchen."

She glanced away from Jacobs to the woodbox. If an honest man like Jacobs could figure it out, no doubt a lot of men with fewer scruples could, too. Her lips tightened.

Jacobs stood, reaching for Lottie's hand. "Everyone in the Flat knows you can take care of yourself. But someday some fool might want to test his luck at finding your cache. A storekeeper in town, Frank Conrad, has a new safe, the only one this side of Jacksboro, I hear. He's putting up valuables for a lot of people with less to worry about than you. Don't know that you should keep your money there, but you ought to put something in for show."

Lottie stirred, her hand squeezing his. "How's that, Jack?"

"Cut some wedges from a catalog or newspaper the size of bills, wrap them in paper, tie it up with twine to leave in the safe. Carry a bundle like that to Conrad now and then. Make sure people see you, so they think your money's there, even if it's not."

Lottie laughed. "You've got it all figured out, don't you, Jack?"

"Everything but what your kind is," he grinned, his smile unable to hide the burning curiosity in his eyes.

"Just a wayward woman in an untamed town, making my living at the expense of a lot of foolish men. I wish I were your kind." Her lips lifted in a smile of remorse, but her eyes avoided his.

"You make it sound worse than it is, Lottie." Jacobs released her hand and bent over the divan for his hat. "But why the gambling? And what do you save the money for?"

"To bury a past and buy a future, a better life, Jack. One day, I'll get away from this, not in shame, nor in pride. That day'll come when what few looks I've got will survive only in a tintype or two, and the men will no longer pay attention to me."

His Adam's apple bobbed deep when he swallowed. "You're most becoming, Lottie." Pausing, he bit on his lip. "A man can't help but see that and maybe even want to court you."

Lottie reached for his free hand and lifted it to her lips. Such a good man, she thought, as she kissed the back of his hand, then looked up into his eyes, which held onto hers. "I know I can depend on you, but we must remain just friends."

"I'm not your type?" he asked.

"Oh, Jack," she stepped toward him and closed her arms around him, resting her head on his hard chest. "I'm not your kind."

"I would do anything for you."

Lottie nodded against his chest, and she felt his arms tightening as her eyes moistened. A single tear rolled down her cheek. There was something he could do, but would he misunderstand? Perhaps she should do it herself.

"What's the matter, Lottie?"

"Jack, there is one thing."

"Name it."

"There's a man in town I should see."

His grip loosened, and he backed gently from Lottie's embrace. Dabbing at her wet eyes, she looked into his face, wreathed in hurt. "It's nothing like you think," she said.

Jacobs nodded. "I'm not thinking, Lottie. It's too hard to figure."

"Would you deliver a message for me? His name is John Henry Holliday. He's a gambler you'll find at the Cattle Exchange. Slender man, walrus moustache, handsome in a subtle way."

"The one you beat at the Bee Hive? He your kind?" He asked without malice.

"Ask him to visit me tomorrow at five."
"Nothing else?"
"That's all."
"What if he won't come?"
"He will. Wouldn't you?"
Jacobs nodded without emotion, then left.

****

The stiffness in his fresh shirt crinkled as he straightened his string tie, then tugged on his freshly ironed frock coat. Holliday coughed, a dry, empty hack borne less of consumption than nervousness. Though a betting man, he didn't care to make odds on what Lottie wanted. Holliday rubbed his smooth-shaven chin, then twisted the bottom of his waxed moustache as he stepped to the door of a modest adobe dwelling in front of several enormous cottonwood trees near the Clear Fork of the Brazos. As he knocked on the doorjamb, he felt the warm rays of the sun seeping through the black wool of his coat and into his back, heating his flesh and blood not nearly as much as thoughts of this meeting had. Receiving no reply, Holliday rapped again, louder, the noise provoking a mockingbird resting in a cottonwood rooted just beyond the house. The bird's shrill cry taunted Holliday, ridiculed his infatuation, tested his patience. The cardsharp vilely cursed the bird just as the door opened.

The world, including the mockingbird, quieted as Holliday looked into the puzzled gray eyes of Lottie Deno, a flush of color rising in her cheeks.

Folding her arms across her breast, she shook her head. "John Henry Holliday, never have I had a caller greet me with a more vulgar word." She spoke softly, her Kentucky accent lifting the words seductively from her lips. "Was that meant for me?" she asked, the trace of a smile softening the corners of her mouth.

"That, ah, mockingbird—," Holliday stumbled over his words like a blind man over scattered firewood, "—I mean, not you."

"What mockingbird?" Lottie cupped a hand to her ear.

Damn bird, he thought. Instead of roping himself tighter in his bind, he stared silently at Lottie. Never had he seen her with her hair down, a soft auburn river flowing from the top of her rounded face, falling down her shoulders, and lapping across the full breast of her blue silk taffeta dress. She tossed her head with a laugh, which rippled down her hair. Holliday smiled at the sound, as flawless as a crystal bell.

Lottie's Luck

"Come in, John Henry," she said with a sweep of her hand, her dress rustling as she stepped aside. "That mockingbird serenades me all the time."

"I'd call it noise," he answered, his hand going for his hat. "Maybe I should use him for target practice when I leave." Fear flashed through Lottie's eyes, and he regretted his words, his fingers dropping empty from his head.

"Oh not," she cried, a trace of panic in her voice. "He keeps me company. I feed him scraps and even got him to take a few from my hand last week. Please don't harm him."

Holliday nodded as he lowered himself onto the small divan. He wished she would join him, but she brushed a wrinkle from her pale blue dress—a becoming color on her—and paused in front of the cane-bottom rocking chair opposite him.

"A gentleman takes off his hat indoors, John Henry." She smiled and extended her hand.

Cursing to himself, Holliday removed the derby, thinking she enjoyed his vexations. Why did things never go right with Lottie? Was it her own roguish temperament, or was he so taken with her that he was as foolish as a schoolboy carving his beloved's initials in a favorite tree? He wondered if he would ever know because he could never read her. He presented his hat to Lottie, who deposited it on the gate-leg table beside a small wooden box.

"Care for coffee?" she offered. As Holliday shook his head, she gathered the pleats of her dress and sat in the rocker. "Thank you for coming, John Henry."

"The invitation surprised me after our game, quick though it was, at the Bee Hive."

"Professional encounter there," she smiled, her perfect teeth sparkling like gems in a jewel case.

"I was perplexed, though, by your messenger."

"A good man, Jack Jacobs," Lottie said, brushing her hair behind her shoulder and tossing her head like a frisky filly. "He doesn't frequent saloons like some of us." Her crystal laugh followed on the tail of the self-deprecating words.

"The way he eyed me before extending your invitation worried me, like he was the law."

"Intuition, John Henry. He was sheriff until this spring, but he was too honest for the job, at least in Shackelford County."

"Never met an honest sheriff before, like I never met an honest gambler," Holliday continued. "This Jacobs, though, should be more careful about how he approaches people, or he'll be with a few honest saints. By the time he came up to me in the Cattle Exchange, I had my pistol out under the table, pointing at his gut." For a moment, Holliday thought he saw a flush of paleness sweep across Lottie's face. "This Jacobs special to you, Lottie?"

"He is, John Henry, he is. Nobody else in the Flat I can trust, like Jack Jacobs."

"Then tell him to be careful around me. The law makes me nervous since the killing in Jacksboro."

"If I'd known I'd endanger Jack, I'd never sent him after you, John Henry. The reason I sent for you—"

"I'll take that cup of coffee now," he interrupted. He coughed nervously, stalling for extra time. He knew what he wanted to ask, but not how. And, he had to inquire before she explained her invitation.

Lottie excused herself, returning shortly with a single coffee cup and saucer. Holliday accepted the steaming drink from her soft hands, then swallowed hard, a gulp of hot liquid burning no less within him than the words he wanted to speak. As she seated herself, he spoke before she could resume. "Lottie," he began, "there's something I would like to know about you." He watched her eyes narrow and her brow furrow. "Your name. What's your name?"

"Why, Lottie Deno? You know that, John Henry." The words came as cold and pointed as icicles.

"No, your real name." Holliday's confidence withered under her cool response. "Not your saloon name."

Lottie stood and walked behind her rocking chair, folding her hands across the rocker headpiece, building a wall between herself and Holliday. "You wouldn't ask that of a man in these parts. Too many with an unflattering past to hide, or a recent reputation they prefer not to get back to their families. Why ask me?"

"I thought if you told me you might—" Holliday faltered, his voice fading.

"Might what?"

"Might consider—" Holliday stumbled again over his speech, the words being lost between his brain and his tongue.

"Consider what?"

"Marrying me," he blurted out. The words exploded across the room like a cannon up on Government Hill, and the moment he had said them Holliday felt foolish instead of relieved. An ashen look clouded Lottie's face. Holliday thought he saw a glistening veil drop over her gray eyes. "If you thought enough of me to reveal your name, I thought you might consider matrimony."

Lottie caught her breath and walked around the rocking chair to the table, picking up the small wooden box beside his hat. She tossed it from hand to hand, shaking her head.

"John Henry, I'm surprised and flattered." Her words came deliberately and even sympathetically, he thought, but for whom he could not tell. "Marriage is impossible. You or anyone else." Then she laughed. "Two gamblers marrying. Nothing could be any unluckier."

"We could give it up," Holliday answered. "I've had training as a dentist, even practiced in Dallas. I could start over."

Lottie carried the wooden box to the rocking chair, falling into the seat without gathering her skirt. "You're like me, John Henry. You might know other occupations, but gambling's in your blood. You might give it up, but it won't be for another occupation or a woman. It's an evil neither of us can root out until our blood runs thin with age or bullet lead."

"Then you won't tell me your name?"

"No, John Henry, neither you nor most anyone else."

"When I got your message, I hoped we shared the same feelings for each other."

Lottie stared at the floor. "John Henry, I'm surprised you're letting your emotions get the better of you. That's not healthy among gamblers." She held up the wooden box. "This is why I asked you here. It came after you left Jacksboro. I thought I might run into you later, seeing how flies like us always find the busiest dung heap, so I kept it for you."

Holliday sipped at the coffee, but it was bitter in his mouth as he remembered the crooked dealing box he'd ordered.

Reading the peeling address label on the box, Lottie smiled, a hint of larceny in her eyes. "From Will and Finck, Leading Cutlers and Bell Hangers," she said, then clucked her tongue. "John Henry, I never realized you liked fine knives—or is it bells?—so well." She laughed. "Will and Finck, I swear John Henry." She extended the box to him. "These purveyors of cutlery and bells sure go to great lengths to hide they are a sporting house dealing in crooked gambling equipment. Please pardon me for having opened it, but I was curious if its contents were square."

Exchanging his half-full coffee cup for the carton, Holliday nodded. "You should have known I'd bought a crooked box. Helps on days like this when I'm short on luck. Cost me a hundred dollars." He pried the lid from the container, the tiny nails giving way easily. It was just as he had ordered. He replaced the top and stood. "Your name, Lottie?"

"No, John Henry, though it flatters me that you should ask." Her words came softer now. She placed his coffee cup on the gate-leg table.

His thin lips curled into a defeated smile beneath his moustache. "Just one more thing."

"Yes, John Henry."

"Not a word of this to anyone."

"You have my word," she said, extending her hand.

Holliday held her fingers as she arose, then lifted them to his mouth as if for a kiss, but released them instead and picked up his derby. Hat in hand, he edged toward the exit, before turning to look at her a final time. "Should you ever—," he began, then stopped and nodded. He saw Lottie's lips tighten at the unfinished sentence. Stepping outside, he heard her close the door behind him.

The mockingbird picked up its taunting call as Holliday strode from the house. Holliday paused, scanning the cottonwoods beyond Lottie's dwelling. Spotting the bird on a low branch, Holliday drew back his arm and heaved the faro box at the feathered pest. Neither his aim nor his strength threatened the bird, though the missile did flush him, grousing, from the tree before it landed in the creek.

Holliday tramped away from Lottie's place, losing track of time and place. Realizing the lateness of the day, he walked through the Flat with fast, exaggerated steps until his lungs screamed from the exertion. In minutes, he shoved through the swinging doors of the Cattle Exchange and headed for the bar, buying two bottles of Monarch Bourbon as Big Nose Kate swaggered by. She smiled as she passed, then Holliday spun about and grabbed her arm.

"So you want to play, do you?" she asked, loud enough for others to hear. "I told you you'd come around, now didn't I?"

"I'm not in the mood for talking," he answered. "Are you going with me?"

Before she could answer, Holliday jerked her toward the door as many in the Cattle Exchange watched. At the door, Kate shook herself free, turning her back to Holliday to straighten her dress and to wink at Chancey's customers. Then, with proper decorum, she linked her arm in Holliday's and stepped with him outside.

"Where's your crib, Kate?"

She pointed toward the creek, and the two walked silently into the night.

Winter

Chapter 8

Outside, a December norther beat its fury against the thin wooden walls of the Kate's crib, the chill whining and whistling into the room. It was cold, and Kate was warm. Nothing else mattered. She wasn't Lottie, but she was accessible and free, at least to him, and her spirit amused him.

His body rocked from a riveting cough, which echoed off the walls and seemed, for a moment, to drive away the winter winds. Holiday felt her hands massaging his back, trying to help him expel his troublesome cough, but her touch failed. He sat up on the side of the bed, trying to strangle his annoying hack. When the spasm passed, he fell back on the mattress and watched the flickers from the coal oil lamp's feeble flame cavort on the ceiling.

The bed shivered as Kate tugged the covers up to his neck and snuggled closer to him, her face resting on his shoulder. A racking spasm vibrated from his body to hers before he jerked from beneath her head and twisted on to his side to fight the seizure. Kate inched over the sheet into his vacated warmth and molded the front of her body to the back of his. Her fingers toyed with a button on his long johns.

"You ever thought about marriage?" Her words fell as softly as her hand button.

Holliday offered no reply. The silence stretched taut.

"Don't play possum on me." Her rigid words passed through clenched teeth. "Would you ever consider getting hitched?"

"No!"

"Not even after all the time we've spent together?"

"You bringing it up is one thing." He struggled to breathe. "Me thinking about it is another."

"You enjoy my company," she said, wriggling her fingers between two buttons.

"At times!"

"Like now?"

"Not when you talk about marriage."

"You're about as romantic as Huckleberry Finn." Her nails dug like fangs into his chest.

He swatted at the pointed pain beneath her nails. "Who the hell is Finn, buffalo hunter?"

"Tom Sawyer's friend, that's who. You got any friends here but me?"

"None, so marry this Finn or Tom Sawyer and make us both happy."

"They ain't anybody, just a couple of Mississippi River boys I've been reading about. Tom's got a girl, Becky Thatcher, but Huckleberry's as vinegary as you toward females."

"Kate, you're educating the wrong end with all your book reading. If you'd spent less time behind books and more time under customers, you'd have enough stashed away to quit frequenting saloons and seedy men like me, maybe find a decent husband."

"That so?" As she spoke, Holliday felt her knee in his back and before he could brace himself, he was grabbing for the covers on the way to the cold floor. Shivering, he scrambled up for the mattress. Her words, icy as the floor, noted his return. "If I'd charged you for all my free favors," she yelled, "I'd own every damn saloon in this town, and I'd kick your tail out every time you walked through the door."

Holliday playfully swatted at her cheek, but Kate's upthrust pillow deflected the blow onto the mattress. In an instant, she rolled upon his arm, harmlessly, Holliday thought, until he felt her teeth sinking into his flesh through the sleeve of his long johns. "Whoa, woman!" He grimaced, then rubbed the wound as she broke free. "Your mouth is lethal. Between your words and teeth, I can't decide which is worse."

Kate fluffed her pillow, then straightened the covers over them both. "And, I'd hire Ed Bailey just to spite you."

Holliday shook his arm to ease the pain, then rearranged the blankets to his satisfaction. "He's a cheat."

"You're a gambler, not a circuit-riding preacher, so don't tell me you've never cheated."

"When I arrived in the Flat, Chancey brought me in to win a cold hand and skin a trio of cattlemen of their money belts. I won the big hand, but had to out cheat Bailey and his reflecting pipe. When he cheated against me, he was defrauding the house."

"Then why'd Chancey wait until last week to cut him loose?"

A growl gathered in Holiday's throat. "Chancey's loyal to the dollar, nothing more. As long as he figured Bailey was bringing in more business than he was costing, he let him stay. But then he caught Bailey cheating the house, losing too much to his friends and taking better care of them than the Cattle Exchange."

"He's gone. It's done." Kate slipped her hand in his. "But that's not our worry."

Holliday laughed. "Maybe not yours, but it's mine. Chancey told Bailey I'd offered him five hundred dollars so I could take over his table. Even said I'd volunteered to take a lesser cut of the winnings. Chancey promised to let Bailey keep his table if he matched my deal that wasn't." Holliday settled deeper under the covers and rolled onto his side. "It'll be the death of one of us."

Kate answered with a sigh and the soft touch of her hand along his back. He squirmed closer to her warmth and felt her moist lips and her warm breath upon the nape of his neck. What an abominable name, that Huckleberry Finn, whoever the hell he was, Holliday thought before he sank into the haze of sleep. And outside it was cold, and she was warm, and nothing else mattered.

****

Kate hummed a saloon song as Holliday fell asleep beside her, his breath wheezing like bellows worn from overwork. She massaged his back gently at first, then harder, as if she could exorcise the demon disease within him. As her hand tired, she rested her ear to his back, her saloon melody exhausting itself, and listened to each breath drawn like a dull saw through dried wood, rasping and grating. Maybe he was more Huckleberry Finn than Tom Sawyer, but it was the tuberculosis that put the vinegar in his veins. She felt a tear roll down her cheek. Damn him, why did he have to have consumption? And, why did she have to fall for him? What was the cure for him? And for her? She remembered reading of patent medicines in the *Frontier Echo*. Perhaps she could get him well, and one day they could marry. She dreamed one day that he would invite her to his room in the Planters House.

A sharp gust of wind rattled the single window pane in her crib and whistled its fury at the impediment, the wicked melody sending a chill down her spine. She pressed tighter against Holliday, wondering if any woman could ever win him, and then, remembering Lottie Deno, Kate stiffened and her face soured. Lottie could, if she wanted. Kate had seen a flame deep in Holliday's steely eyes for Lottie, and she felt as helpless to extinguish it as a waterless woman at a fire. Holliday was like the other men, all enamored of her beauty and the virginal vestige she made out to be among a horde of local prostitutes. But pure though Lottie pretended, she still slopped at the same trough as the dirtiest whore in the Flat; she still wallowed in men's wallets for money and gave less in return. Fearing that the coals burning behind Holliday's blue eyes could only be stoked by Lottie, Kate drew herself closer to him, her arm around his chest, as if by proximity she could change his heart. Only the wind moved until Kate worried herself asleep, without releasing him.

Time dissolved in her sleep, the minutes passing as a mist into hazy hours untotaled. How long she had dozed, she could only guess. At first she believed herself caught in some inexplicable dream, a trance alternating between heated shivers and cold sweats. Slowly, her mind cut through the fog of drowsiness. It was Holliday. She shook the haze from her head, moaning at the cramp in her arm still locked around his body. Perspiration's dew drenched his nightclothes, and through them she could feel a fevered heat fueling his shivers. He was dying. "No don't," she heard herself say, her trembling hand sliding to his simmering forehead, then stroking his cheek. His breaths came as dying whispers instead of great gasps, and Kate nudged him for a spark of life, the flame within him burning low like the bedside lamp. He groaned, his head shifting, then falling limp again. "I'll take care of you," she whispered. She parted from him, pulled him over onto his back, tossed her covers away, careful not to expose him to the chill, then stepped onto the floor, her feet arching from the cold wood.

Kate scurried to her washstand and grabbed the clean towel, folding it into a sponge. She slipped beside Holliday and held the towel above the lamp chimney to absorb heat from the feeble flame. With the warmed towel, she knelt bedside and planted a kiss upon his cheek, then wiped away each bead of sweat glistening on his leathery skin. Alternately, she mopped his head and then, to evaporate the absorbed sweat, held the towel over the lamp. His breath gathered sickly strength and exploded in a horrid hack. Kate's eyes misted at the cough, and a dozen times more, she swabbed his face. Though she shivered on the floor, his sickness bothered her more than the cold.

Never moving from his side, she lost track of time until she could see through the window layers of darkness peeling away from the sky. Her body was numbed with the cold, and still she could not pull herself away from Holliday in his helplessness. Leaning her head against the mattress, she almost dozed off until she was jarred from her rest by a hammering hack that pried Holliday's eyelids open for an instant. He rolled toward Kate, and she wiped the phlegm from his chin.

Fighting her exhaustion, she struggled to her feet and staggered around the bed, crawling in beside him, her teeth chattering. She felt a scratchiness in her tight throat and wondered if that was how consumption began. She hoped not. Even her bone-deep weariness failed to lessen her worry for him. Turning on her side, she propped her head up on one hand and rubbed Holliday's bony chest. So strained was his breath, she lifted her hand as he inhaled and pressed down on his chest as he exhaled. How could he live with himself each night if consumption meant this?

Finally, her body forced upon her the sleep her mind tried to refuse. Kate rested her head beside his and dozed as Holliday's fever drained away with the lingering shadows. The room was fully lit when she awoke to a gurgling noise. Holliday was strangling, she thought, spinning over toward him. Holliday held a bottle to his lips and drained it like he hadn't had a drink of anything for a month.

"Slow down," she chided. "You've been too sick to polish it away that fast."

Holliday broke for air. "It's like that most nights," he answered, then kissed the bottle until it was empty.

Kate watched him drain the liquor into his anemic frame. "That much liquor that fast can't be good for you. You need medicine."

Holliday laughed and coughed at once. "Nothing but death cures consumption."

"But I've read about cure-alls in the *Frontier Echo*."

Holliday ignored her. "The whiskey eases the pain. It's worst when I wake." He reached for a handkerchief in the frock coat hanging on the bedpost at his head, but started coughing before he could retrieve it, his spare hand flying to his mouth. Wresting the handkerchief free, he wiped pink mucus from his palm. "See that," he said, holding the stained handkerchief to her grimacing face, "that is my lung. Every day, I lose a bit more, and I'll keep losing it until I can't breathe."

Kate sighed when he folded the cloth over consumption's litter. "Every night you fever and sweat so, how do you sleep?"

"This strong body," he mocked, "tires easily. Exhaustion," he coughed, "overcomes distractions like pain."

His body shook with a paroxysm of coughing. "Damn it all."

Kate withdrew her hand from his chest. "I never realized it was this bad."

Holliday controlled his cough for a moment. "It's like this most days. Damn, it's cold."

"I'll put some more wood in the stove." She arose. "You sure all that liquor helps?"

He nodded. "I'll tend the stove. The liquor doesn't help my lungs, but it gets the rest of me through the day. I may drink a lot, but you'll never see me drunk."

"That's what worries me. That much liquor's unhealthy for you."

"Consumption isn't?"

"There are medicines. I've read about them in the *Frontier Echo*."

"Kate, you believe too much of what you read, like that damn Cuckleberry Ben."

"Huckleberry Finn," she corrected.

"Whatever! You'll find about as much truth in the damn newspaper as you will in your books. None!"

"But the medicine, the advertisements say, will cure consumption. It'd beat all that whiskey."

"Kate, you've been drunk before, so get off of me about the liquor."

"But the medicine?"

"It's all alcohol, nothing more, just not as good as bourbon. A keg of beer or a case of whiskey has as many curative powers as those fake cure-alls and wonder tonics."

"They say, though–"

"I don't care what they say. Woman, I'm not accustomed to arguing my way out of bed each day, and I don't want to start now."

"Here I am trying to take care of you during the night, and all you do is fuss at me."

"I've cared for myself many a night worse than this. I don't need you pawing over me like a mother hen. If that's what you have in mind, find somebody else to warm your bed." Holliday threw back the covers and slid off the mattress, heading for the stove.

She grabbed for the covers and yanked them to her head. "This was the last night I'll ever freeze my tail off for you."

"I'd been better off dealing faro until dawn than coming to your place last night," Holliday answered.

"Your room was closer. Why don't you ever invite me to the Planters House? I'd like that."

He ignored her as he struggled into his pants, then stumbled toward the stove.

"You son of a bitch," Kate called.

Holliday lunged at the bed and slapped Kate full force across the cheek. "Don't ever call me that again."

Kate rubbed her cheek. Holliday's snake-quick motion had startled her, but his palm had only stung her face. She laughed. "That as hard as you can slap?"

Holliday nodded on his way to the stove, opening the grate and shoving a log in. "The disease eats away at my lungs and withers my shoulder strength. You'd been a man, I'd a shot you. Doesn't take too much strength to pull a trigger."

"I've been hit by breezes harder than that." She shook her head. "Now I know why you got the scrawniest chest and arms I ever did see. All these fellows about town fear you, and you're not strong enough to knock a poot out of a bean-eating schoolboy."

"Don't ever call me that again," Holliday replied.

"Then don't treat me like a wicked woman, even if I am one."

Holliday turned away and finished dressing.

"You know your problem, Mister John Henry Holliday? You don't like yourself enough to let anybody take a shine to you, and you're too proud to let it bother you."

"Not another proposal, Kate."

"You have any friends in Griffin? No, just me, and you won't claim me. I'd be your wife, but who else is there? Tell me, who?"

"Ed Bailey," Holliday scowled.

"I wouldn't marry Bailey," Kate said, then paused. "But I would marry you."

Holliday spun around, half grinning. "Woman, do you ever give up?"

"Not when I'm after something I want and intend to get, John Henry Holliday."

Chapter 9

Standing in front of the only safe in Shackelford County and rocking on the heels of his polished shoes, Frank Conrad wore the look of prosperity, his thumbs hooked in his suspenders. Like the hair on his head, the buffalo of the Great Southern Herd were thinning out, and no man contributed more to or profited more from the decimation than the merchant Frank Conrad. His eyes as sharp as his business sense, Conrad bought lead and gunpowder by the ton at the Kansas railheads, freighted it to Fort Griffin, and sold it by the pound in the Flat.

With the best selection in town, his mercantile would prosper this season. In one day alone during the fall, hide men and townsmen doing four thousand dollars in business—guns and ammunition accounting for almost two-thirds of that—had passed under the sign: CONRAD AND RATH, GENERAL MERCHANDISE. Just ten days away, 1877 held equal promise when the buffalo stalkers returned with their hides, and the freight wagons lined up by the hundreds to take the bales to the railroads in Kansas.

The arrival of his chest-high, chilled-steel safe earlier in the year had all but made Conrad the acknowledged banker of the Flat. Behind the back counter in the main room jammed with goods and provisions and smelling of newness and coal oil, he displayed the safe as a symbol of security in an insecure town. Like Conrad's reputation for honest dealing, the safe's visibility was good for business. With a proud flick of the wrist, he would twirl the combination dial, grab the handles, pull the heavy twin doors apart, swing open the inner metal plate, and deposit or retrieve a customer's money or gold from among the stacked tobacco sacks, envelopes or wooden boxes filled with valuables.

Though Conrad insisted on knowing the contents and value of each addition in case a shortage was later claimed, Lottie Deno always refused. And today she had done so again when the merchant added her sixth deposit—another saloon brand cigar box wrapped in newspaper and tied with twine—to the safe. Lottie knew Conrad suspected money in each, paper bills in the four light ones, gold pieces in the two heavier boxes. She had only smiled in the face of his request, saying the risk was entirely hers. His curiosity thwarted again, he shrugged, then rocked proudly on his feet, his close-trimmed beard jutting confidently forward. "It's been a good year, Miss Deno. As long as the buffalo hold out, a man can't ask for more."

"Good years, like good cards, come in streaks, but I've had a fine run of luck here," Lottie said, loosening her heavy wool cloak in the stifling warmth of Conrad's store, his stoves always burning the hottest in Fort Griffin because he had the money to haul in abundant firewood, the local quantity being scarce.

Conrad popped his suspenders with his thumbs and glanced over his shoulder at the locked safe. "Yes, Miss Deno, I'd say you've done very well for yourself." His lips pursed like a pair of fallen question marks.

"Since the War ended in sixty-five, odd-numbered years have been unlucky for me, Mister Conrad. Of course, being a merchant, you wouldn't believe luck blows like the wind—sometimes with you and sometimes against you. You never know when it's about to change, until it's too late!"

"You're too superstitious, Miss Deno. It doesn't take luck to make money, but it sure does to hang on to it. I'd say you've managed right well, guessing by our few dealings."

Frowning, Lottie folded her arms across her bosom. "Have you been peeping?"

"No, no," he said, waving his hands. "I didn't mean that, just that everyone in these parts has heard of Lottie's Luck. No, your deposits are safe. My business is based on square dealing, and I shall never misplace the trust of my customers, especially one as pretty as yourself." He smiled, proud of his compliment.

Lottie lowered her hands and mirrored his smile. "There is one thing more," she said, stepping to him. "Should something ever happen to me—"

"Well, your fears seem—," Conrad started.

"If it does," she continued, waving aside his interruption, "give all my packages to Jack Jacobs. He'll know what to do with them. And if he ever asks for my deposits, do what he says and hand them over to him. Remember, the risk is mine."

"I shall abide by your wishes," Conrad intoned, "but I worry you fear 1877 without reason."

"Perhaps, but I am a gambler. Not quite the same as running a respectable business, now is it?"

Conrad anchored an arm across his chest, rested the other on it, and swept his steady hand through his beard. He grimaced like a judge pondering the arguments of a starch-shirted lawyer, but his pronouncement was interrupted by the approach of clerk George Wilhelm, who each week delivered to Lottie's cabin a standing order of provisions, always throwing in an extra apple, bag of nuts or some other gratuity for which Lottie insisted on tipping him well.

"Miss Deno," greeted Wilhelm with a wide smile. "Pleased to see you, I am. I didn't by accident forget anything in this week's order, did I?"

"Absolutely not, George. In fact, I was just telling Mister Conrad what fine service you've provided me these past months."

"You were?" Conrad's lips said without the words passing between them. Then he recovered and spoke. "Yes, she was, George, as a matter of fact."

George grinned. "Why thank you, Miss Deno. The pleasure is always mine. Nobody around here gives a better tip than you. Those that are moneyed enough are too mean, and those that are nice enough are too poor, except you."

Wilhelm bent over and tucked one leg of his ducking overalls back into his boot. Tall and lanky, George appeared almost too gangly to navigate the crowded aisles of Conrad's store.

"Besides that, I've suggested that Mister Conrad up your pay so you won't have to deliver the provisions yourself just for the tip."

Conrad shrugged.

"Oh, I don't do it for the tip, Miss Deno," George said, then wiped the sleeve of his blue flannel shirt across his lips, too late to cover an embarrassed grin. "Is there something I can get you?"

"Thank you, George, but I've business today with Mister Conrad. If I decide otherwise, I'll call."

"Then I best attend some others." George retreated to a grizzled patron.

Lottie's Luck

Lottie tied her cloak and braced herself for the walk back to her cabin. "Always a pleasure doing business with a gentleman, Mister Conrad," she said, extending her right hand.

Taking it, he bowed his head toward her. "The honor is mine."

As she turned to the door and wove her way to the front, Lottie could feel every man's gaze upon her. She was glad to emerge into the cold. The icy breeze slapped at her face and pricked her bare hands like a thousand pins as she stepped off Conrad's boardwalk. A wintery haze shrouded the town like a gray garment. Except for a knot of men outside the Bee Hive and the horses shivering at the hitching posts, the late afternoon street stood empty. Lottie heard the men down the street laughing and jeering, probably at an overflow fight Fogle had swept out of the saloon or maybe a drunken Tonkawa. Those fools were outside by choice, so Lottie pitied the animals that had no say in the matter. They whinnied and nickered, sympathizing among themselves over the misery wrought by the norther.

The only person in town profiting from this bitter cold spell that had frozen the creek was Uncle Billy Wilson. Lottie detected the grating bite of his hired men sawing through the ice. Wilson would stock his substantial ice house near the stream with now worthless chunks of ice. When summer came, he would turn that frozen water into money, gambling being the only thing closer to alchemy than that, Lottie believed. Carried by the chilly gusts, the sawing noises arrived as plain as the shouts of the crowd down the street.

Drawing nearer the Bee Hive, she ignored the taunting circle of men and would have passed, one fight or drunk being the same as another, except for a high-pitched plea as desperate as the wind. "Come on, Pa," cried the girlish voice. "You've got to get up and make it home. I can't carry you, and you'll freeze."

Other voices deep and male mocked the plaintive cry. "Get up, Pa. Get on home. You can't carry your liquor, and your girl can't carry you." Laughter followed.

Lottie darted from the windbreak of the buildings toward the throng of men. She reached the tight knot and shoved her way through. A couple of men raised their fists to swing at the intruder until they realized it was a woman. Their hoots trailed off as Lottie elbowed into the center of the circle and saw a coatless girl no more than seven bent over as drunk a man as ever tried to walk, his legs stretched straight out, and his torso propped up by his elbows behind him. His hands slid more and more from under him each time the girl tugged at his coat. An empty bottle lay beside him. Near the bottle, a bleached buffalo skull stared with ghostly eyes at the spectators.

"Please, Pa, come on. Ma, will switch me if I don't get you home soon."

The girl glanced up at Lottie. Her big blue eyes met the gambler's and conveyed her silent frustration more eloquently than words. Understanding that Lottie now dominated the quieted crowd, the girl hung her head, toeing the dirt with her scuffed shoe and kicking a few pebbles toward the buffalo skull. "He's not a bad man, ma'am. Just sometimes takes a drink. Ma can't do nothing about it. Me neither." Then her father collapsed backward, his head slamming into the street. One man, himself reeking of liquor, laughed, "Beddy bye." Lottie cut her icy eyes at him and untied her cloak. From beneath her covering, Lottie pulled her revolver.

"That funny, fellow?" she said, aiming the revolver at his head. His laughter evaporated like the color in his face. "If my finger was to twitch, you'd go straight to hell. That's where you belong. That's where all of you men belong for not helping this poor child. God have mercy on a place as callous as this. What do you have to say for yourselves?"

She waited, but only the rasping ice saws on the creek and the moaning of the stiff wind answered.

"That's what I thought. None of you have enough gumption to apologize to this child." Two fellows with downcast eyes mumbled embarrassed words, directed more at her than the girl. "What's your name, child?"

"Sophie."

Two men were inching away from the circle when Lottie looked up. She raised her gun and fired it into the air. "I'll shoot the next snake that tries to slither off." The retreaters froze in place. "Now, Sophie, where do you live?"

She pointed toward Government Hill. "Cabin on the creek side of the far slope, ma'am. It's a good walk from here. Pa's horse being lame, we all walk, my Ma and sisters."

"How many sisters?"

"Three, ma'am, all younger." Sophie's voice rang with girlish pride. "I'm oldest. That's why Ma sent me."

Slipping her gun back under her cloak, Lottie looked from Sophie to the men. "Anyone know where her cabin is?" Two men nodded and stepped forward. "You two and a couple more take him home.

Walk him if you can, carry him if you can't. I'll be there later with Sophie. You tell her mother that. When I get there, I'd better find you've tucked him in bed, or I'll come after you." Lottie revolved slowly around, studying downcast faces and averted eyes. Four men bent over Sophie's unconscious father and lifted him, groaning from the ground. "All of you should help," she shrugged, "but four's enough." Most wagged their chins as they retreated for the warmth of the Bee Hive.

"Thank you, ma'am," Sophie said as the volunteers stood up her father, then draped his arms around two of them and started him toward home, his feet dragging on the cold ground.

Sophie picked up the empty liquor bottle and flung it at the Bee Hive, watching it bounce, then skitter between the legs of two nervous horses and break against a hitching post.

"Come with me, Sophie," Lottie said, trying to put her arm around the girl, but Sophie dodged her embrace and stepped beside the buffalo skull. Taking a deep breath, she grabbed it, a hand on each horn, jerking it to her waist.

"Okay," she answered, the skull's weight pulling her off balance until she stepped forward into Lottie's skirt.

"My goodness, child, is that awful thing yours?"

"It is, ma'am. Sometimes I find 'em, or they'll fall off a wagon along the road." She huffed under the load.

"Pray tell, you collect them?"

"Oh, no ma'am, I sell 'em. One this big might bring a penny, enough to buy my sisters candy for Christmas. Pa says plenty of nothing is all we'll get for Christmas."

Lottie dropped her arm around the girl's shoulder and drew her tight to her side, then rubbed her hand through her muddy brown hair, its tangles plentiful from infrequent brushing. Lottie felt a shiver race through Sophie and the cold pimpling her flesh. "My, what are you doing without a coat is beyond me, Sophie? I'll carry the skull. You wrap this around yourself." Lottie removed her heavy cloak and draped it over Sophie's trembling shoulders. "You and I are going to Conrad's store."

"I've never been there," she squealed. "Pa says there's too many things in that big store that we might want and could never have."

Lottie, taking the prickly skull and aiming Sophie toward Conrad and Rath's, walked rapidly, but could not outdistance the cold piercing her blouse. Sophie, her legs churning with excitement, kept pace despite the cloak dragging on the ground. At Conrad's, Lottie shoved open the door, Sophie darting in under her arm, then stepped into the warmth. Lottie slammed the door in the face of the cold, then dropped the skull at her feet, the clattering noise bringing hushed stares from Conrad's customers.

George Wilhelm, looking up from a grizzled buffalo hunter, excused himself and strode to Lottie. "What brings you back, Miss Deno?" Shaking his head as he studied Sophie, half-hidden within the cloak, he grinned as he spotted the buffalo skull on the floor. "Been buffalo hunting and brought us a Comanche child prisoner?"

Sophie's back arched and her head jutted forward, the cloak sliding to the floor. "I may be poor, but I ain't no stinking Tonkawa or any other injun," she challenged.

"By goodness you're not, are you?" George said, rubbing his chin. "Have you come to bring us your trade?" With a sweep of his arm, he bowed before her.

Sophie giggled at the theatrics. "I've got trading goods."

Lottie toed at the buffalo skull and winked at George. "We're trading that for all she needs."

"So we are," George mused as he straightened up. "Tell you what, princess, you go look around and see what you want. Holler for me, George, when you need help."

Sophie grabbed the cloak from the floor, half tossed it to Lottie, then scooted among the merchandise until she disappeared behind the stacks.

George laughed. "Excited little booger, isn't she? How'd you hook up with her?"

"It doesn't matter, George," she said, pointing to the buffalo skull. "Do you ever buy these?"

"Bones? Not here, though some stores in town do. Not enough money in it for Mister Conrad. What little money's in it is by the wagon load, not by the bone. Factories up north grind the bones into bone china or something."

"Whatever the girl wants, let her have it. I'll pay. And for sure, I want you to include a big coat she can grow into." Lottie draped her cloak over her shoulders.

George snickered as he watched Sophie dash through the store, then grabbed the skull and tossed it in the woodbox of the nearest pot-bellied stove.

Sophie darted from the back counter toward Lottie. "I found some," she announced. "The candy for my sisters. They'll have some Christmas now."

"Is candy all you want, Sophie?"

She nodded. "One skull just brings candy money."

Lottie smiled. "That was a special skull, though. George tells me it's the biggest he's ever seen and worth a lot more than others. We'll get the sweets later, but now you go find something else for your sisters, your mother and yourself."

"Really!" Her eyes widened into twin blue moons. "Thank you, ma'am."

Sophie stumbled in her haste and almost fell into a crate of canned tomatoes. She caught her balance, glanced at Lottie with an embarrassed smile, then disappeared again among the tables.

George turned to Lottie. "I haven't seen a little girl that excited in a long time."

"She ought to be. Her father's been having a run of bad luck and didn't expect to have any Christmas."

"A lot like that in this town, and I'm not just talking about kids, either. Men and women with no family and no place to go. A lot wind up drunk as a cat in a barrel of cut whiskey."

Lottie shuddered, remembering Sophie's father, stretched out on the street in drunken oblivion, unable to realize the surrounding mockery, the cold about him, much less his daughter's pleas.

Sophie raced up to Lottie. "Look, ma'am," she said, sticking out her upturned palm to display a rosy ceramic turtle with a padded back. "It's a pin cushion, but watch." Sophie tapped the cushion and laughed as the turtle's head and tail wiggled. "Ma could use this—see the pink diamond eyes glitter?—and some pins and needles."

Lottie extended her hand. "I'll hold it, Sophie, while you find something for your sisters." Sophie dashed away once more.

George snickered. "She'll enjoy that turtle as much as her momma. Shame many kids around won't have much of a Christmas. It does me good to see a child get excited like that. Some of these old buzzards may build a town, but it takes little ones like her to keep it going."

Lottie nodded. "George, what you said about a lot of folks not having much Christmas, do you really believe that?"

"Without a doubt! They're not always the best folks you'll find, but they're still people."

"How many days until Christmas, George? I've lost track."

"Today's the twenty-first. Four days."

"George, maybe four days wouldn't be much time, but if you'd help arrange it, we could have a party for anybody that came."

"That's a fine idea."

Lottie pointed toward the ecstatic Sophie. "Maybe a few more people could share her joy."

Chapter 10

Rubbing his hands together for warmth, Holliday leaned to the frosted window, then scrubbed a peephole in the frozen condensation and stared. Snow covered the Flat like a new sheet, white and unwrinkled, and the cold slipped inside around the window and through the plank walls. He shuddered, then coughed into his fist while retreating to the stove. There Chancey rocked on the back legs of his chair, having abandoned his office's seclusion for the stove's warm embrace. On either side of him sat his two bartenders, the stocky one whittling on small sticks of firewood before condemning them to the hell inside cast-iron pot belly. The thinner barkeep chewed a wad of tobacco, occasionally spitting the results onto the stove and listening to it crackle and sputter. A cowboy who had ridden through the winter storm to spend his Christmas in a saloon minded his own business and his newly purchased bottle at a nearby table.

"It still snowing?" Chancey asked, without seeming to care.

"It's stopped. The clouds are breaking up." Holliday yawned as he pulled up a chair by the stove. He straddled it backwards, propped his elbows on the backrest and dropped his chin in the saddle made by his palms.

"How much have we had the last two days? Six inches?" Chancey fluttered his eyelids in Holliday's direction, then snapped them shut.

"That or more," Holliday answered. "It'll be cold tonight if those clouds move on out."

The whittler grunted, and the other bartender spat more tobacco juice on the stove.

"A little moonlight would sure put the place to shining," Chancey said. The spittle on the hot metal sizzled the only answer. "This has been the worst Christmas ever. Usually, we have a better business, but the weather scared away all but one." Chancey motioned toward the lone customer. "And, he don't appear too sociable."

"Christmas's no different from any other slow day," Holliday said, pushing his palms at the glowing stove.

The saloon owner laughed. "Then why'd you come in two hours 'fore you usually do, dressed in clean clothes? It don't matter how big a man you are, Christmas is still a lonely day without family. Do any of you remember your best Christmas?" Opening his eyes, Chancey glanced from face to silent face, waiting and thinking, his memory's reflection shining in his dark eyes. "I must've been eight. We didn't have much, expected little. Father came home from work Christmas Day and gathered us kids at the table with Momma. He pulled from his coat an orange ball, least that's what I thought it was."

Pausing, Chancey rubbed at the corner of his eye. "Momma started crying. It was an orange. She'd always wanted to taste an orange, and Father had found her one, somehow. She passed it around the table, each of us holding and smelling it. Father wasn't sure how to peel it, so he took his knife and started real easy, but he wasn't getting anything other than a few flakes of peel. We'd never seen anything with a peel like that. Momma stopped him, taking and squeezing the orange. A squirt of juice wet her fingertips, and she licked them. Momma gave the biggest smile I ever remember. Then she figured out how to peel the thing. As she tore chunks of the peel away, she'd hand a piece to each of us kids. We rubbed that peel, put it up our noses to smell the sweetness and then stuck it in our mouth. We had a grand time, everybody giggling at the silliness and clapping when Momma finished peeling it.

"Then she passed the naked orange around again for us to hold and to feel. When it reached Father, he split it apart and handed a wedge to every one of us. There were two extra pieces. One he sat in front of Momma and told her to think of a number between one and twenty. Then Father and us kids picked numbers. I took thirteen, and that was the number, so I got the extra slice. Then we just sat staring at our slices, all of us afraid to take the first bite. We sat awhile before Momma bit into hers. Then we nibbled at those orange slices for half an hour before they were gone. I was the last one finished. Us kids pooled our seeds for planting in the spring so we'd have oranges every Christmas. Mice got the seeds, but not my memory of that Christmas."

Chancey reached over and tapped the whittler's shoulder. The fellow grinned, holding up the worn knife. "My Pa gave me this when I was a kid, best gift I ever got. He must've known it'd be his last present to me. He left Ma before the next Christmas and just disappeared. Never heard another thing from him. I might not even of remembered him, except for this knife." He smiled, then attacked another stick.

The saloon owner looked at his other bartender, but the fellow lifted a leg atop his knee and leaned forward, ignoring him. Chancey sat forward in his chair, and with his foot, nudged the bartender's leg off his knee.

"That's uncalled for," the man challenged.

"Tell us about the Christmas you'll never forget."

The bartender seemed more sullen. "When I was fourteen, my mother died of cholera on Christmas, late in the day, about this time.

"I'm sorry," Chancey said. "Didn't mean to open an old wound."

The barkeep nodded his understanding and punctuated it with a muddy stream of tobacco juice at the stove. Chancey turned to Holliday. "And you."

"The year I got a suit just like Father's. Guess I was prouder than a new father and twice as cocky."

Shaking his head, Chancey grinned. "I should have known it'd be clothes with you. You always do dress like you're going to court, Lottie."

"Who doesn't want to court Lottie?"

"Kate wants nothing to do with her," Chancey leaned back in his chair and closed his eyes, "though she's taken quite a liking to you."

"That woman talks more than she thinks."

"Seems there's one thing else she does every day," Chancey mocked. "You're the only one, though, that gets it free."

"It's not bad," Holliday said, his wafer lips curling into an understated grin, "if you can stand the jabbering."

"Marry the woman, John Henry, and make her happy," Chancey said.

"She'd want me to turn to something respectable," Holliday said.

"She's a dreamer," Chancey said.

"Gets it from that novel she's always reading."

Chancey's eyelids batted open like sheets flapping in the wind. The front legs of his chair thudded on the floor. "She's a reader? Do wonders never cease? Thought she spent all her time talking or flirting, though not in that order, though. Hard to consider brains behind a bosom her size."

"She's smarter than she appears," Holliday admitted.

"Anyway, where's she been the last few days? I haven't seen her working the saloon for a spell. Is she working someplace else or have you made her retire from the profession?"

"I can't make that woman do anything," Holliday grinned. "Don't know where she's hiding herself. It's been three days since I saw her. I've enjoyed the peace and quiet."

The whittler opened the door grate on the stove and tossed in a couple pieces of wood, including his latest carving. He slammed the metal shut and secured the handle in the latch. "I heard from one of the gals she's taken sick. Figured you'd know that." He stared at Holliday.

"I'm not her husband."

"Not yet, at least," Chancey interjected.

"Kate'll be around when she wants," Holliday said, as he stood up. "I don't owe her anything, and this is the sorriest Christmas I ever had." He stared at the cowboy sprawled over the adjacent table. He had finished his bottle, and the liquor had returned the favor on him. He was out. "Don't think you'll need a faro dealer tonight. I'm going to stare at my ceiling."

"This talk about Kate giving you the urge, is it?" Chancey crossed his thick arms across his broad chest.

"The three of you can sit here until you fall asleep in your chairs, but I'll do it in my bed."

"Or Kate's," Chancey laughed again.

"Could be," replied Holliday. "Why don't you get off your lazy tail and fetch me a bottle of Monarch?"

"Get it yourself," Chancey ordered. "You drink so much of it I'm regretting ever letting you know I stocked it."

"I'll leave your money on the bar."

"This one's on the house, John Henry, Merry Christmas."

"Good night, gentlemen," Holliday said, retrieving a bottle from behind the bar and walking toward the coat rack by the door. From a worn peg, he pulled a new overcoat and jerked it over his arms as he looked out the peephole in the frosted window.

"Say, Chancey, a few more people are out and about now. Maybe business will pick up," Holliday paused. "There are a lot of folks out there, wagons, horses and all." He opened the door for an instant and stuck his head outside. "Big crowd down at the Bee Hive," he said, pulling his face back inside. "What's Fogle doing this evening?"

"Hadn't you heard?" Chancey punched his palm with a wadded fist. "He rented the saloon to Lottie Deno, and she's throwing a Christmas gathering for anybody that didn't have any place else to go tonight. Whores, hunters, families, soldiers, even us, I guess, though I didn't receive a personal invite."

"Now, why would Fogle let her do a thing like that?"

"Way I hear it, Fogle's run into a little bad luck, and he's got some debts he don't know how to pay. He gave Lottie the saloon today for a couple hundred dollars, from what I hear."

"A Christmas social in the Bee Hive. Doesn't quite seem proper, now does it?" Holliday rubbed his chin.

"Tonight the Bee Hive's gonna be as pure as a sober Baptist. No drinking, no gambling, no whoring. Women, good and bad, I suppose, with mean men and mischievous young ones. As I heard it, Lottie had Jack Jacobs out in this weather, finding a splendid tree and shooting some turkeys for grub. Uncle Billy's been cooking them and everything else, and the ladies are bringing their own foods. Over at Conrad's, George Wilhelm's been gathering gifts for the kids. Supposed to be several musicians there this evening, too"

Holliday took his hat from a peg and pulled it down over his head. He looked at the bourbon bottle in his hand and returned it to Chancey. "Save this for me while I check out Lottie's festivities. Stepping out into the cold, he caught Chancey's final words.

"Hell, Kate might even be there."

****

Her breath labored so that each gasp was more a conscious effort that a natural reflex. Wracked with fever, Kate shivered beneath every quilt in the small crib. She had even unfolded some of the stacked newspapers she kept and layered them between the quilts for additional warmth. Still, she trembled, her teeth chattering.

She could no longer comprehend if the cold pulsing through her body stemmed from the fever or the weather. It had been hard to keep a fire going in the small corner stove, and she had given up.

Big Nose Kate could not remember ever feeling so miserable. Her throat burned like it held hot sand. She longed for a sip of water, but the water pail had frozen. She hungered for a warm meal, but she had just as well wished to be a virgin again, her will for food unable to muster the strength to fix a modest plate, much less walk through the snow to an eating house in the Flat. For two or maybe three days, she had subsisted on dry soda crackers, a flask of whiskey, and a bottle Allen's Lung Balsam. After last spending the night with Holliday, she'd purchased the balsam at Conrad and Rath's for him. She'd seen it advertised in the *Frontier Echo* and figured it might ease his pain, but she'd not seen him since then. Instead, she'd used it to treat her infirmity by rubbing it on her chest, but the cure-all hadn't helped. It smelled like coal oil. She despised it.

Damn him, she thought. She'd stayed up with him in the cold that night, planting within her body the seeds of her own malady, and he'd yet to come by to check on her. She could be dead for all he cared. The son of a bitch. Only one sympathetic harlot had stopped to check on Kate, stoking the fire in the stove and helping her attend her to bodily functions before tucking her back in bed. Twice she'd come by—at least that was all that Kate remembered. Something nagged in Kate's mind. The visitor had said she wouldn't be by on Christmas day. Was this Christmas? Kate strained her mind to recall the chronology of her illness. Her sister in sin hadn't been by today, at least not that Kate recollected through her feverish haze. Maybe it was Christmas.

Another thought lingered in her mind. A party at the Bee Hive. It seemed out of character for Fogle. But hadn't her visitor said Lottie Deno was throwing a social? Maybe she had said that, but then Kate had been delirious for several hours. Lottie Deno, confound her. Christmas day, confound it. John Henry Holiday, damn him most of all. If it were Christmas Day, he could have called on her, maybe even given her a small remembrance. She'd do so for him. He was probably flattering Lottie Deno or fawning over her charming manners. Kate wished she were beside him and in his Planters House room. That way, she could plunge a knife deep in his puny chest without messing up her crib. Her anger fevered with her.

Maybe she was just imagining about Holliday and Lottie. After all, her thinking had gone awry for the last few days. Seems she recalled at some point drifting down the Mississippi River on a raft. She wore a bonnet and a full petticoat dress while listening to the lies of a skinny Huckleberry Finn, who looked like a young Holliday without the moustache. Nothing made sense any more.

Kate tossed about in her bed, trying to escape her thoughts and to find relief from the pain. She reached for the whiskey bottle on the floor and sat up long enough to swallow a mouthful. She smacked her parched lips and fell back on her pillow, staring at the ceiling. The room glowed in an unnatural, ghostly light. It was neither day nor night. Then she heard the crunch of a horse approaching the cabin. It must have snowed, and the white powder was reflecting the moon's spectral glow.

For a moment she smiled, thinking, hoping, that Holliday had rented the mount to come and rescue her and take her to his Planters House room. That's how he could prove his affection. If he just visited her, however briefly, it would be the best Christmas she could ever hope to have. Or, if he would take her to his room for their liaison, that would warm her heart even more. But the noise of the horse crunching through the snow grew louder, only to fade away into the distance. Kate felt the tears gather in her eyes, then slide down her cheeks. She dropped her arm off the side of the bed for the whiskey. She felt alone and sick, hungry and morose and, most of all, unloved. What a pitiful Christmas. Perhaps the remnants of the bottle would ease the pain of her tears, which hurt more than her sickness. And then she arose, wrapping herself in the quilts and walking to the frosty window.

She knew she must find help.

John Henry Holliday was not coming for her.

Kate flung open the door and stumbled into the cold.

Chapter 11

At first they gathered quietly, almost reverently, the women talking in whispers, the men staring at sanitized surroundings devoid of liquor bottles, painted nudes, and splattered spittoons. The children fidgeted at their parents' feet or gazed with mouths agape at the cedar tree alight with candles and tapers and crowned with a tin star. The gents, freshly bathed, scrubbed, shaved, oiled, combed, waxed, and splashed with tonic, stood stiffly in newly washed, starched, ironed, and brushed clothes. Fellows with reason to fear anything snug around their necks wore ties, and others who never went unarmed came without visible weapons. The single men, lacking wives to poke them in the ribs when they misbehaved, snickered at one another's cleanliness and at the saloon's transformation.

Two breeds of women—those who had worked at the Bee Hive, and those who hadn't—mingled with their own kind, sharing only the female instinct to bring food. Each carried a kettle or a pan or a platter and added a pie, a cake, fresh bread, pickles, canned fruits, a sausage, or a dish of deviled eggs to the bar where Uncle Billy hovered over his own vittles.

The decent ladies clumped together, discussing babies, recipes, sewing, and their husbands' bad habits. Laced in their best dresses, the powdered, rouged, and perfumed women of the lesser breed tittered at the sober lunacy of celebrating Christmas in the Bee Hive.

So many had come. Through an ice-blurred window pane, Lottie watched dozens more converging on the saloon across a fairy-tale landscape. Outside on the clapboard walk, she could hear the sounds of people stomping their shoes of snow and laughing despite the cold. The loud merriment outside softened inside as the visitors shed their gaiety like their coats at the door and conversed in hushed tones, uncertain what to do or how to act. Sensing their discomfort, Lottie gathered the skirt of her yellow dress and marched to Uncle Billy, who was arranging dishes of food on the bar.

"Uncle Billy, do something!"

"What in tarnation do ya think I be doin', Lottie Deno, takin' an afternoon snooze?"

"No, no, tell folks it's okay to talk aloud, to have fun. Tell them anything that'll loosen them up. Anything!"

Wilson took a pot of beans from a new arrival, placed it on the bar, then backed away from the food. Wiping his hands on his stained apron, he thrust out his chest. "Okay, Lottie Deno," he said. Stepping to the room's center, he raised his hands above his head, waiting for every whisper to die, then he lowered his arms. "Those of ya that don't know me, I'm Billy Wilson, Uncle Billy to me friends, and all of ya are me friends, even if I don't know ya." He arched his bushy eyebrows as he unhooked his glasses to wipe them on his apron. "Now those of ya that don't know me won't know that I'm not much of a talker."

Those that knew Billy Wilson laughed, and he raised his arms again for silence. "I've been asked by Miss Lottie Deno, whose generosity has brought us together this Christmas evenin', to say a few words." He inhaled. "She says ya can talk."

Everyone laughed, and Lottie, regretting her garbled request, joined them.

Wilson refitted his glasses over his ears. "Let's everybody warm up by the stoves and get acquainted. We've pitchers of hot apple cider for those of ya that wanna warm up your innards. That's as strong a liquid refreshment as we're gonna have tonight, fellows, so don't go expectin' anythin' else."

A couple of male groans drew stern stares from the women.

"Shortly, we'll sing Christmas songs, then have treats for the children and dance a while. When me and me wife finish preparin' dinner, we'll eat. So, ya start talkin'."

The guests applauded Wilson, and a rising tide of voices drowned the quiet. Now, Lottie thought as she looked around the room, the holiday celebration was as it should be with people visiting and laughing. Spotting Sophie and her family by the tree, Lottie started that way until she felt a tap on her shoulder.

"Miss Deno." The voice was familiar. Spinning about, she stared into the uniform of a U.S. Cavalry captain and lifted her eyes until they met Richard's.

Lottie giggled. "I'm glad to see you, Richard, but Rachel?"

He smiled, offering his hand. "By the food."

Lottie clasped his fingers and pulled him through the mingling crowd. By the counter, she spotted Rachel. She released Richard's hand and hugged Rachel. "You've made me so happy by coming. I feared you might not."

Rachel nodded. "I had doubts about a saloon. Oh, Lottie, I've been such a fool after the hanging and all. I've so missed our Sunday afternoon rides."

"It takes a while to get over those things." Lottie's voice was soothing. "No, child, let's not talk about that day."

"I can manage it now, Lottie. Look what I brought." She stepped to the bar and lifted a towel from two round pans.

"Pecan pies. And I've been wondering if you'd ever look at another pecan." Lottie stared at Rachel, noting the sparkle in her eyes, the roundness in her face, and the fullness of her breasts. Perhaps her friend had gained a few pounds, her waist not as narrow as it once was, but she looked better, happier than Lottie remembered. Richard must be good to her, for there was a joyful lilt in Rachel's voice. "I'm glad for you both," Lottie said.

Lottie turned to her friend's husband. "Thank you for bringing her tonight. Except for a little girl and her family, you two were the only ones I invited by name."

"Looks like somebody did some inviting," Rachel observed.

"It's nice, isn't it?" Lottie answered, scanning the room.

"It is indeed, Miss Deno," Richard said, offering an arm to both his wife and Lottie, then escorting them to the tree. "Rachel was dying to see inside the Bee Hive."

"Richard," Rachel cried, jerking her arm from his and stopping with both hands on her hips. She held her head at a rakish angle, her chin defiant. Then a quiver she could not control broke her wholesome lips into a slight grin. "He's right." She shrugged, inserting her arm back in Richard's. "Oh, I wanted to see you tonight, but I'll admit I was curious."

"It's not as fancy as the Cattle Exchange, but the Bee Hive's the biggest saloon in the Flat," Lottie explained. "The liquor and the spittoons have been put away, and the floor swept for the first time I can remember." She tapped her toe on the plank flooring. "And we brought in extra lamps to brighten it."

"I expected," Rachel started, her cheeks tinting pink, "naughty pictures and such."

Lottie covered a grin with her hand. "Are you disappointed? The pictures, there are some, but I had them taken down and locked upstairs with the gaming tables." Lottie pointed to the staircase. "Care to go upstairs, Rachel?"

Blushing deeper, Rachel stumbled over her tongue to say no. "I fear not, just being inside the Bee Hive is more than I should do in my—" The words blurred incomprehensible, and Rachel turned away, dabbing at her eyes.

Pretending not to notice, Lottie pointed to a trio of men edging toward the piano, two picking up guitars, the third dragging out his fiddle. The players tuned the strings of their instruments long enough for a man, rain-barrel squat, to raise the piano stool and take up his perch behind them.

Uncle Billy Wilson climbed atop a rickety chair that trembled under his weight. He lifted his arms high and pious like a circuit preacher. "Will ya listen to me?" The noise continued. "If ya wanna eat, ya bes' hear what I say." Slowly, quiet settled into the room. "We'll sing Christmas songs first, then ya children'll get a toy from Miss Lottie Deno, and after a few dances, we eat. Play the music," Wilson commanded.

Everyone sang "O Come All Ye Faithful," "Silent Night," and "Oh, Tannenbaum," and then each again. And when it was done, the people gathered around the tree while Lottie passed out wooden tops, tin air wheels, magnets, or little tin trumpets to the boys and rag dolls or little tin dishes to the girls. Lottie handed the biggest doll of all to Sophie, who reached up for Lottie and hugged her.

By the time she had finished handing out gifts, Lottie had lost Rachel and Richard. She stepped from the tree, studying the room until she spotted them at a table along the opposite wall. Though she planned to join them, George Wilhelm intercepted her midway across the room and asked for a dance. Although she preferred otherwise, she accepted his invitation in gratitude for all he had done to make this night possible. Together, they moved to the dance floor as the musicians called out a waltz. When they struck up the song, George stepped awkwardly toward her, his timing off a half count. This improvisation he managed was not the waltz she had learned as a young lady courted by some of Kentucky's finest gentlemen. Step, step, close—she could do it from the memory of a hundred dances.

But George danced step, close, step, pausing on the wrong beat and several times trampling her feet.

The days she had danced a true waltz seemed like another life. Once she had waltzed on grassy lawns beneath Chinese lanterns and on the mahogany floors of Kentucky's finest hotels instead of on the roughhewn planks of a dingy gambling establishment. Once her partners had been the well-groomed sons of senators, prominent merchants, vast property holders, steamboat owners, and generals. Now she danced with a merchant clerk who still wore his hat. If the War Between the States had not come, she wondered how different her life might have been. Perhaps she might have borne the son of a senator or even a president; the ambitions of those who had courted her made it seem possible. But maybe the war changed nothing. Like her father, she had loved gambling on cards and horses. Perhaps every road she could have taken would have led to this dirty saloon in Fort Griffin. But like the cards of an opponent's discarded hand, she would never know.

When the music stopped, she danced a step more, grazing George's boot. She asked his pardon, though he had sought no forgiveness when he had trespassed on her toes, and thanked him profusely for the waltz. She thought George pleased by her words and excused herself to join Richard and Rachel, vowing not to dance again. The three watched and talked while the children played all about them with their new toys, and the adults careened across the dance floor doing their versions of waltzes and the schottische. People around her laughed, and she beamed. Several times she refused dances and was prepared to say no yet again when she looked up at the latest man standing beside her. Jack Jacobs, his hat over his heart, his upper teeth nicking his lower lip, offered her his calloused hand. Without a word, she lifted her fingers to his. He dropped his hat on the table and accompanied Lottie to the dance floor.

As the musicians began another tune, his hand fell gently upon her waist, and she saw the softness in his blue eyes. "I'm a poor dancer, Lottie, though I'll risk the embarrassment to dance with you." He stepped to the music, an unadorned two-step, his motions unpolished but their simplicity covering his shortcomings.

"Thank you for coming, Jack," Lottie answered, once she'd picked up the rhythm of his step. "I must pay you for fetching the tree. You should have seen the children's eyes widen at it. And the turkeys, how many did you get?"

"Six, one about as big as I ever saw. Uncle Billy says he's cooked many a gobbler, but never one that size."

"Then I shall pay you a good price, Jack."

"You're paying me now with this dance. That'll be plenty."

"Now, Jack, this is not your payment. I'd dance with you, no matter." She pleaded without convincing Jacobs of her debt. "No shame in a woman paying you for what you've done."

"And there's no shame in doing a friend a favor. Now, you are returning the favor." A barrage of applause ended the dance. Jacobs smiled. "You've repaid me."

"But I must owe you another dance," Lottie protested, as Jacobs steered her back to the table.

"One dance'll do. More, and I might forget what a poor dancer I am, and what a fine lady you are," he answered.

"Thank you, Jack," Lottie squeezed his hand. "This has been a magnificent evening for me, and I think for many others, too."

When they reached the table, Jacobs pulled Lottie's chair out for her as Richard stood to assist. She took her seat, and Jacobs picked up his hat just as Uncle Billy's voice called out above the chatter.

"Listen up," he said, moving into the dance area. As he walked, he sharpened a carving knife on a whetstone, the rasping of metal against stone sounding like the whispers of old maids. "One more dance, everybody. I'm about to carve up the biggest turkey ya ever saw. Then it's time for eats." Everyone clapped as Wilson retreated to the bar to attack the bird.

Lottie twisted in her chair. "Jack, will you join us for ... Jack, Jack Jacobs," she called, but he had disappeared. She looked from Rachel to Richard. "Where'd he go?" They shrugged. "He should've stayed because he shot the turkeys. Jack's a good man, too."

"The kind that would make a good husband," Rachel suggested.

Lottie ignored Rachel's remark. She stood, taking in the crowd, but Jacobs had disappeared. As she inspected the throng, she saw John Henry Holliday standing by the door, his gaze immediately locking on hers. So much for Lottie's Luck, she thought. "Perhaps we should start for the food line," Lottie suggested to her tablemates. Still, Holliday stared like a predator stalking prey.

Without waiting for an answer, Lottie marched toward the piles of food, Richard and Rachel joining her just as the music ended. Lottie grabbed a tin plate and eating utensils and worked her way along the line, helping herself to modest portions of boiled potatoes, hominy, red beans and a deviled egg. Using the carving knife and a serving fork, Uncle Billy dropped a thick slice of white turkey meat on her plate. After picking up a sourdough biscuit, a slice of Rachel's pecan pie, and a cup of hot apple cider, she angled back to her table and waited until Rachel and Richard rejoined her. She nibbled silently at her supper.

"I'm sorry for meddling about a husband," Rachel said. "I should be more gracious."

"Please, Rachel, let's forget that and enjoy the evening."

They talked between bites, Lottie learning about Richard's duties at the fort, the latest Comanche troubles, and the fun Rachel had shared on their Sunday afternoon rides. Lottie relished the conversation until she felt the awkward presence of someone beside her, an eavesdropper, an intruder. She frowned.

"Pardon me, ladies, sir," John Henry Holliday said. "Might I join you. Chairs are scarce now that most have been served." Holliday placed his plate on the table.

Lottie could smell liquor on his breath and could see the disgust in Rachel's eyes, but she smiled at Holliday. "It's Christmas. Certainly, you may join us." Lottie glanced from Holliday to Rachel, her face flushed with fear. "This is John Henry Holliday. John Henry, this is Mr. and Mrs.—"

"We've met," Richard interrupted her. "We rode the stage from Jacksboro to Griffin back in the fall."

"A good memory, sir. I recollected the face, but not the occasion." Holliday slid into the chair and up to the table.

"I don't forget people who pull a gun on me."

A sinister scowl worked its way snakelike across Holliday's lips, and he turned to Rachel, his voice harsh as a winter wind. "Yes, ma'am, that's true. You don't realize how close you came to being a widow that day."

Rachel dropped her fork, her hand flying to her mouth. "Perhaps we best be going, Richard."

"On no, ma'am," Holliday's voice turned soothing. "I promise you no harm, nor your husband. I wasn't much for talking that day, especially with a blue belly cavalry officer. No offense, sir. But this is Christmas, and I will ignore my prejudices against the U.S. Army."

"John Henry is a dentist," Lottie interjected to change the subject. "And, in his way, a gentleman, though ruined by the gambling urge in his blood."

Holliday took a bite from his meager plate, chewing it like a kid taking medicine. "It's something Lottie and I have in common."

"I'd say it's all you and Lottie have in common," Rachel answered.

"A noble heritage, ma'am," Holliday corrected, "is something we also share. Our blood may be tainted by gambling, but it is a noble Southern blood. Nothing personal against you, ma'am, or your husband, but the sight of his uniform brings back unfortunate days and events in Georgia." His voice had hardened.

"John Henry, this is Christmas, so show your upbringing and put aside these unpleasantries," Lottie said.

"Accept my invitation to dance, then, not just any dance, but a waltz." Holliday's voice was soothing again.

"I am growing tired."

"I understand your reluctance. Your toes must still ache from your two previous turns on the dance floor."

"They were decent men, John Henry."

"Not decent dancers," he replied. "Say yes, and I'll excuse myself so not to offend your friends." He stared coldly at the couple. "I'll behave as a choir boy until I collect my dance."

"Then we shall dance. A waltz. And now, will you allow us to finish our meal?"

Holliday nodded, then turned to Rachel. "Ma'am, it's been a pleasure to converse with you. And sir, you have a charming wife." Rachel grimaced at the compliment, and Lottie watched her cheeks color. Standing, Holliday gathered his plate and eating utensils, then left.

Rachel wrinkled her nose. "That man upsets me. How can you dance with him?"

"There are many things a gracious hostess must do, Rachel. You should know that."

"You continue to surprise me, Lottie," Rachel said.

Lottie laughed at Rachel's awkward smile. "And you never let me forget it."

They talked an hour away while the guests finished their first helpings, their seconds, and their deserts. At length, Rachel's shoulders drooped, and her eyelids grew heavy. "What time is it, Richard?" she asked, stifling a yawn.

Her husband pulled his watch and snapped it open. "Eleven fifteen," he said, closing the cover.

Rachel raised her hand to her lips and tried to shake the next yawn away, but her mouth contorted to let it pass. "It's well past my bedtime, Lottie. In the Army, men get up early, and their wives rise with them. At least this wife does."

"In saloons," Lottie replied, "we stay late without worry of the bugler. Perhaps you should stay long enough to watch me dance with Mister Holliday. Then you will see why I accepted his invitation."

"I'll never understand you, Lottie. You could have any decent man here, but why you choose to dance with him is beyond me. I'm too tired to figure it out," she said, rising from her chair. "Richard, I need my rest."

Arising with her, Lottie realized something about Rachel had changed. Lottie studied her a moment, the roundness in Rachel's breasts and the slight tightness of her dress around her stomach making sense. Rachel had not taken a dance all evening, and Richard had been most attentive.

"Lottie, thank you for a most pleasant evening," Richard offered.

"Except for Mister Holliday?"

Rachel nodded. "I hope you have an enjoyable dance," she said, turning to her husband. "Would you find my coat, sweetheart?" He smiled and excused himself.

"Rachel," Lottie whispered as Richard moved away, "are you with child?"

The startled grin, mixed with equal doses of joy and concern, answered Lottie's question. Her eyes lit up with a maternal glow which she could not hide. Rachel nodded. "I told Richard this morning. The news was my Christmas gift to him."

Lottie hugged Rachel.

"Oh, Lottie, how I wanted to tell you, too, tonight, but not in a saloon, not with news this holy and joyous."

"Yes, Rachel, but this day celebrates a birth, not in a saloon, but in a stable. I'd prefer a saloon, but no matter. You have made good my Christmas, by your news and your presence."

Rachel squeezed Lottie tightly. "This has been my best Christmas ever, Lottie, and I am glad I shared it with you, even in a saloon." Rachel snickered against her tears.

Richard returned wearing his coat, Rachel's over his arm. "Rachel, I told you that Miss Deno would figure it out."

"Well, Richard, just how do you know what we've been discussing?" his wife shot back, dabbing at a stray tear.

"You can't think, much less talk about it, without your eyes misting over," he replied. "And I detect a mist about them."

Rachel stepped into Richard's open arms and hugged him. "We must go, Richard, before I make a complete fool of myself around Lottie's guests. Good night, Lottie." Rachel started for the door without looking back. Richard followed her, draping her coat around her shoulders, then glancing back at Lottie and smiling.

"Good night," Lottie called after them as they meandered through the crowd to the exit.

"A touching sight, a man and his wife, Lottie."

Turning around to the voice, Lottie stared at John Henry Holliday. "They make a fine couple. You should be ashamed for scaring them so."

"I came to collect my dance, not discuss my manners."

"Seems I am repaying everyone with a dance tonight," she said, hooking her arm in his and moving toward the dancers. "I prefer a waltz."

"And I as well," Holliday answered, an unusual note of jauntiness in his consumptive throat.

"But that's not what they're playing."

"Just wait," Holliday said, as he maneuvered Lottie among the dancers. He released her arm, faced her and bowed, the music stopping instantly.

Lottie curtsied. "How'd you do that, John Henry Holliday?"

"Bribery. I passed a few dollars among the musicians, Miss Deno, gold dollars, not those foolish greenbacks."

Then the music began again, a new tune, a waltz. "The song reminds me of Kentucky." Lottie smiled as Holliday put his hand upon her waist, and she placed her hand upon his shoulder. Their free hands united, and at once they stepped to the music.

"I thought perhaps it would make you sentimental, and you'd tell me your name."

"And marry you here tonight?" Lottie said, smiling at his gliding step. "You may be an excellent dancer, but you're not that good."

They circled the floor, like one agile figure, molded at the hands and moving precisely in an ever-widening ring, like ripples from a stone thrown upon a pond. Step, step, close; step, step, close. Holliday performed the way a waltz should be danced. Except where they held each other, their bodies never touched; only the hem of Lottie's dress ever brushed Holliday as she twirled about in his arms.

He was wonderful on his feet, light and quick, like a cat. Lottie relished the vigor that pulsed through her body as her feet obeyed Holliday's, both dancers moving as naturally as branches in a breeze. Lottie saw in his blue eyes a smile unnoticed before, like a gold coin at the bottom of a clear blue pond, invisible in the sand except in a perfect light. About them, other dancers stopped to watch. When they alone waltzed, Holliday nodded his head to Lottie, acknowledging her skill.

Circling about the floor as easily as skaters on ice, she lost track of time and of people, as if she lived only to waltz, like a tiny figurine atop a spring-wound music box. Lottie savored his precise and fluid steps, recalling not a single man his better. Through several refrains, they continued, and when the music ended, they waltzed to the applause twice more around the floor, as if they could dance forever. Then they stopped as they had danced—in perfect harmony, Holliday stepping back and bowing to Lottie, she responding with a curtsy, then both acknowledging their audience. The spectators clapped louder and cheered in a simultaneous convulsion of approval. Lottie could see admiration etched in the faces of the matrons and jealously trapped in the smiles of the young women. The spectators called, "More, more, once more" and applauded harder.

Holliday took Lottie's hand and looked into her eyes. "Shall we?"

"I promised you but one."

"But this one is for them. Agreed, Miss Deno?"

"Agreed, Mr. Holliday."

The spectators cheered as Lottie curtsied in the four directions. She could see joy in their faces, and she could not hold back her smile. It had been a long time since she had enjoyed such a dance.

And then, as she curtsied the final time, she saw Big Nose Kate. Lottie's grin stiffened.

Kate stood on a chair by the bar, blindly stuffing handfuls of turkey in her mouth. She was eating like a savage, and she looked like one, her hair matted and uncombed, her eyes wild and distant, her skin splotched red, her shoulders sloped and trembling. Beneath the quilts she used as a coat, she wore a chemise instead of a dress. Though something was wrong with her, Lottie could find no sympathy in her soul for the harlot.

To Lottie's back the musicians cranked up another waltz. Holliday slid around to face Lottie and glided across the floor with her. He moved like before, but Lottie knew she was a fraction of a beat behind him, not enough for others to notice but plenty for Holliday to seek the reason in her eyes. Now, her gaze avoided his, and every twirl around the floor she glanced at the bar, Kate towering sinisterly above it, stuffing her mouth with food. Kate appeared bewildered or lost, staring blankly ahead, even when she wielded the carving knife to slice another chunk of meat from the turkey carcass.

This dance lasted and lasted almost endlessly for Lottie, and when it stopped, she glanced immediately at where Kate had stood. But she was gone. The crowd applauded again, louder, but Lottie felt no enthusiasm.

Holliday turned Lottie to face the musicians, and he gave a deep and long bow, disguising a rugged cough. Lottie curtsied beside him. Everyone cheered.

A blood-curdling scream cut like a saber through the merriment. The applause disintegrated into a terrified outcry. Lottie twisted around, jerking her hand from the coughing Holliday. She froze at the gleam of a carving knife drawn high in the air and starting toward her. She saw Kate's contorted face as the knife neared her. Lottie screamed. Then she was knocked to the floor as men from all sides rushed in like water after a splash.

****

Stumbling forward as the men surged around him, Holliday crashed into the piano, a discordant chord announcing his arrival at the worn keys. The noise, though, drowned in the confusion of heavy boots, husky shouts, and horrified women screaming for their children. Holliday bounced off the piano with a gun in his hand and swung around in a tight arc to face the attackers. His sweaty finger quivered with uncertainty on the trigger, and his mind raced with the memory of a dozen enemies, Ed Bailey foremost among them. Everyone else stared at the knot of men writhing on the floor like a ball of snakes, Lottie sitting just beyond the flailing legs, holding her hands over her mouth and shaking her head. Whoever started the commotion, Holliday thought, was under control at the bottom of that pile. He shoved the Smith and Wesson back into the holster riding under his sweaty armpit. As he stepped to Lottie, a straining voice from the floor called out, "I've got the knife. Get up easy."

Assisting Lottie up, Holliday felt her arm tremble. Her lips quivered, and her face had whitened. Holliday led her to the piano, shoving the piano player off his stool. Lottie sank down on the seat. Her gray eyes hardened like granite. She glowered at the fellows unraveling from the floor as she strained for each breath, her bosom heaving from fear. Then she spoke in phrases. Lottie pointed, "She tried—" a deep breath "—to kill me."

Holliday stared as the men peeled themselves away. One came up holding a carving knife, another sucking the blood from a slight cut on his hand. Then Holliday recognized Kate, pinned by the last two men. Damn her.

"What do we do with her now?" called one of her captors. Kate lay motionless, her eyes closed. "Something's wrong. She's burning with fever. It must've addled her mind." He looked around the room, his gaze stopping at Lottie and Holliday. "Miss Deno, you want us to save her for the sheriff?"

"Just get her out of here," Lottie answered, her voice composed now, as calm as water in a rain barrel, but Holliday noticed a tremble in her fingers.

The two men holding Kate nodded. "Anyone know where she lives?" one asked, but drew no reply. "Surely somebody has an idea where she sleeps." He shrugged at the quiet.

Holliday looked around the room, recognizing several men who had paid for Kate's favors, but not a single one would admit knowing her.

"Dump her in the street," Lottie spat. "Just get her out of here."

Holliday swallowed hard, a bitterness stinging in his throat. He watched Lottie's gray eyes. "I know her place." He felt Lottie's stony stare as her lips puckered with distaste. She looked from him to Kate, then shook her head, an auburn curl falling across her forehead. "Thank you, Miss Deno," Holliday said, "for the pleasure of your dance." He backed away.

Lottie nodded, brushing the curl back in place. "You're quite a man on your feet and, evidently, off them as well," she said without looking at him. "Good night, Mister Holliday."

Coughing away his nervousness, Holliday looked at Kate. She lay as limp and lifeless as an empty flour sack on the floor. "I can't carry her home. Somebody with a wagon give me a hand," he ordered. Another fallen woman and a fellow in a plaid shirt joined him as a path parted through the crowd toward the door. As the woman pulled Kate's chemise to cover her legs, another soiled dove tossed the blankets she had worn atop her. Holliday and the volunteer lifted her and toted her to the exit. The helpful harlot opened the door, and the men carried Kate out into the bitter cold as Holliday heard another waltz begin. Damn it all.

They placed Kate in a wagon bed beside a pile of firewood. Holliday crawled in beside her and felt her forehead, hot to his touch. As his two helpers climbed into the wagon seat, Holliday decided he should take her to his room. "Head to the Planters House. It's closer than her crib. Hurry!" Kate's moans and the crunching noise of horse hooves and wagon wheels breaking through the frozen glaze of the snow drowned out the music from the Bee Hive. The landscape in its shroud of white reflected the beaming moonlight, casting a sickly pallor over everything.

On the brief ride to the hotel, the cold pricked at Holliday's face like a thousand icy needles, and he rubbed his hands together to keep the stiffness from setting in. When the wagon stopped in front of the hotel, the woman jumped down to open the door as Holliday and the man unloaded Kate. They hurried her past the clerk's desk, down the hallway to Holliday's room. He let the helper hold her while he fished out his key and unlocked the door, kicking it open and carrying Kate to his bed. The female turned back the covers for Holliday and his helper to place Kate on the mattress. As soon as they did, she tucked her in, placing the quilts Kate had worn atop the others.

"Thank you both," Holliday said, reaching into his pants pocket and extracting a double eagle for each. He pressed the gold coin into the hand of each. "Merry Christmas," he said as they walked out of the room.

Holliday returned to Kate and felt her scalding forehead. She shivered at his touch, his hand coming away wet with feverish perspiration. Holliday stepped to his washbasin and moistened a hand towel. After squeezing the rag of its excess moisture, he moved to Kate's side, humbled by her sickness. Gently, he wiped away the fevered beads of sweat, cringing as he rubbed the cloth across her dried, cracked, and bleeding lips. Her tongue darted from behind her parched lips and lapped at the slight wetness left by the cloth. Then her eyes fluttered open, the little slits gradually widening, then blinking.

"Water," she whispered, her voice as faint and dry as a desert breeze. Her eyelids batted away the confusion as she focused on Holliday. "You came." She sighed. "Water."

"You've been delirious, Kate. Just rest."

"What happened?" she asked again. "I dreamed of walking through the snow and seeing you dancing with some woman."

"Don't talk, just rest."

Kate's parched lips strained to smile. "I knew you'd come for me." She twisted her head in the pillow and reached for his hand, holding it against her cheek. Holliday sat beside her on the bed until her fingers fell away from his, and she sank into sleep.

Though exhausted, Holliday decided not to crawl into bed with Kate, going instead to the vacant lobby, where he grabbed a rocking chair and carried it back to his room. He spent the night in the rocker so not to disturb her.

Chapter 12

Dawn arrived in a haze to John Henry Holliday, still in his rocking chair. A slight moan roused him, and he remembered Kate rested in his bed just inches away. Her breath was labored, while his came easier than on other mornings. He got up and parted the curtains to let the soft morning light reflecting off the snow lighten the room. Holliday then moved to the washstand and poured water from the pitcher into the tin cup and carried it bedside. Gently, he slipped his hand beneath Kate's neck and lifted her head as he placed the tin vessel against her parched lips. He let a little liquid wash over her lips and her eyes fluttered open.

For a moment, she seemed lost and dazed. Then she accepted the drink as Holliday tipped it toward her mouth. The liquid revived her enough that she looked around and offered a feeble smile.

"Is this heaven," she asked in a scratchy voice, "or your room?"

He grinned. "Just my room."

She smiled. "One and the same to me, John Henry Holliday."

"You've been fevering and delirious, Kate."

Still, she smiled and glanced slowly about. "You came for me and brought me to your room. You do care for me."

"You've been out-of-your-mind sick, Kate. Rest and I'll fetch clothes from your place."

"I knew you cared for me."

"You needed help, Kate. That's all."

"That's enough." She closed her eyes and sighed.

Holliday patted her forehead, relieved that the fever had broken. "I'm going to your crib to gather some of your things. I'll be back, Kate, with some food for you as well."

Doc left the tin cup on the washstand, then grabbed his coat and hat, putting them on as he exited, locking the door behind him. As he walked past the front desk, he told the clerk he had borrowed a rocking chair last night and would return it later, then exited the building, stepping from the porch into the snow. Every step resounded with the crunch of his boots into the frozen layer.

It was a hundred yards to Kate's crib, and the going was tiresome, slower than he had expected. The icy air, though, seemed to invigorate each breath and helped him reach his destination. He shivered when he entered her place. Anticipating at least the warmth of a low burning fire, Holliday discovered the inside as frigid as the outside. At her washbasin, he found a cloth half submerged in the container of frozen water. How long was it like this? He wondered, then admitted he should have checked on her those three days she was absent.

That was the past, but at least he could make it up to her now. He came across a satchel and shoved a couple of dresses, some undergarments, and some stockings inside. Then he realized when they had placed Kate in his bed, she had not been wearing shoes. She had walked barefooted in the snow and ice on Christmas night. He found her footwear beside her bed and glanced around for anything else she might need, his gaze landing on a small bookshelf with a dozen books on it, one resting atop the others. Picking it up, he read the title, *The Adventures of Tom Sawyer*. He stuffed it in the bag with her other things, grabbed her coat and exited, closing the door behind him and plodding back toward Planters House.

****

Kate dozed in and out of consciousness, awaking enough to know she was in Holliday's room as she had always hoped. She smiled and hugged herself, a tear of happiness rolling down her cheek. She looked for him, but he was gone. Now, though, she knew he would return to her. She sat up and glanced around, then eased out of bed and stepped to the washstand where she spotted the tin cup and the water pitcher. Her lips were cracked and her throat parched, so she picked up the pitcher with both hands and held it to her mouth, consuming every remaining drop.

As she lowered the container back in place, she saw her reflection in the mirror over the washstand. She looked terrible with her purple and cracked lips, her bloodshot eyes, and her disheveled hair. Though she couldn't change her lips or her eyes, she could make her tresses more presentable.

"A brush? Where's a brush?" Kate examined his room.

She moved the pitcher, tin cup, and wash basin on the stand, discovering a card from Haverty's Livery and a tintype of Lottie propped up against the wall. Kate turned the tintype face down by Holliday's razor, then scanned around the room, spotting a carpetbag and what looked like a doctor's bag. She opened the carpetbag, digging under a bottle of bourbon, two decks of cards and some clean long johns and socks, but finding no brush. Next she examined the satchel, discovering peculiar implements she could not explain—metal probes with small, round mirrors on the end, odd-shaped pliers or extractors, tiny picks, and other unusual instruments for which she had no explanation. Finding no brush or even a comb, she returned to bed and bundled up, dozing off for the rest of the morning.

When she awoke, Holliday was beside her with water and some stew he had purchased from Uncle Billy's Eatery. He gave her water, then fed her the lukewarm stew a spoonful at a time. Kate thought the concoction the best she had ever eaten, though she remained undecided if it was because she was famished or because Holliday was spooning it to her.

"You're looking better, Kate."

She ran her fingers through her mussed hair.

"Are you feeling better?"

Kate nodded.

"When you're finished eating, I got something that will help you feel better yet."

"What is it?" she rasped.

"You'll see."

"I can't wait."

After the last bite, Holliday carried the soup dish away and returned with a book. He handed her *The Adventures of Tom Sawyer*. "Here's your Chuckleberry Hen book."

Kate smiled as she took the tome and rested it on her bosom, her eyes misting over. "Thank you. Can I ask you something?"

Holliday nodded.

"I know I've been delirious, but I was looking for a brush or a comb while you were gone and found your satchel with the odd silverware inside. What are they?"

"Dental tools."

"Who'd you steal them from?"

"No one. I'm a trained dentist."

"A dentist? Dr. John Henry Holliday?"

He nodded. "I was until I discovered it was easier to pull money out of a sucker's wallet than teeth out of his mouth."

"Dr. John Henry Holliday," she said. "Dr. and Mrs. John Henry Holliday. I like the ring of that as much as I would like a ring on my finger."

Holliday patted her hand atop her reading material. "You're delirious again. You best get some rest."

She wagged her head from side to side.

"No ring, Kate, but I'll get you a key to my room. It'll simplify things from now on."

****

Kate flitted around Holliday's faro table, pesky as a fly, too nervous to alight. Humming to the tune of the barroom piano, she circled behind Holliday, strode by him, running her fingers along the spine of his frock coat, then slid away. With just four customers, Holliday dealt a leisurely game, but how Kate grated on his nerves, like a wheel on an ungreased wooden axle.

Since her recovery, Kate had pestered him with her foolish favors like a virgin after her first kiss. Holliday knew few dangers the equal of a woman with marriage on her mind. He grimaced as Kate traipsed by, dragging her hand across his back. He twisted his head to curse her, but she was beyond him. His customers snickered until Holliday's jaw tightened. He slapped a card atop the discard stack, glaring from customer to customer until he spotted Chancey ambling toward him, his crooked nose contorted by the wide grin beneath it.

"You think it's funny, don't you?" Holliday growled. "That woman's gonna cost the Cattle Exchange money distracting your dealers, and you're laughing about it!"

Chancey clapped his two massive hands and cocked his head. "She's not costing me anything tonight, business being poorest since Christmas. It's you she's causing the pain, Doc."

"Doc? Where'd you come up with that?" Holliday slid a card out of the dealing box and exposed a winning seven that no one had backed.

"That's what Kate's been calling you lately, says you're a doctor of dentistry. It's a lot easier to say than John Henry. Is it true? Why'd you quit?"

"Patients don't like a lunger breathing in their faces."

Cracking his knuckles one by one along a balled fist, Chancey pursed his lips, as if cogitating the mysteries of dental care or womanhood. "Since she took a shining to you, Doc, she hasn't given me any trouble. I keep you on just to keep her out of my hair." He laughed.

"Chancey, I earn you more money than she does."

The saloon owner tugged at his sagging ear lobe. "Why don't you just shoot her?"

"Because I'd never hear the end of it if I missed." Holliday drew another card from the dealing box. A red queen came into view, losing the Cattle Exchange two dollars to a customer. "Chancey, you've soured my luck."

The saloon owner reached for his smoke fixings in his tobacco tin and watched Kate, now dancing with a lame partner. "Yes, sir, she puts an edge on you like a double bit ax." He turned toward his office.

Doc slapped the table as Kate, her arms around a club-footed buffalo hunter, winked at him from across the saloon. Holliday nodded to his customers. "Twenty dollars for the one of you that'll occupy her the rest of the night. She's not bad." In unison, the four heads twisted about to judge if the prize matched their needs.

Kate stopped in her tracks, the cripple almost falling to the floor. "You best quit your staring, fellows," she yelled over the piano music. "It's bad manners, and you're ruining my partner's concentration." She jerked the bewildered hunter's arm, and as suddenly as she had stopped, she resumed her dance, the cripple lurching after her around the floor as fast as his lame foot could follow.

The faro players turned back to Holliday. "The offer still stands." Doc dug into the pocket of his frock coat and flipped a double eagle onto the table, the gold piece spinning, then settling on the green felt. "There's twenty dollars. Enough there for all of you to line up outside her door at five dollars a turn."

Reconsidering the offer, each man took a second look, then one by one, turned to Holliday, three shaking their heads, the fourth pausing, then glancing back over his shoulder at Kate. "Twenty dollars," he mused, spitting a stream of tobacco toward a spittoon and missing by a foot. "Does she have to get it all?"

Doc tugged on the stiff cuffs of his ruffled white shirt. "If you can keep her from pestering me for less than twenty dollars, the difference is yours."

Nudging the brim of his hat high enough to peek at Holliday, the cowhand nodded. "I reckon I've got a better chance making a profit in her bed than at your table."

"Don't count on it," Holliday answered.

The ruddy faced fellow grabbed the double eagle, tucked the gold coin in his britches pocket, then watched Kate until the music stopped. After she shoved her partner aside, the cowboy stepped toward her. Taking off his hat with one hand, he offered Kate the other.

"If you wanna dance," she yelled, "it's gonna cost you extra. That cripple stomped my toes into mush." The cowhand cleared his throat and half announced, half coughed out his intentions. Kate clapped her hands. "That's safer than dancing with you heifer herders and buffalo bangers." She grabbed his still proffered hand and, looking at Doc, shouted across the room. "At least somebody here appreciates good companionship." She jerked her client's hand toward the door. With each step her shapely behind twitched from side to side as if saying, "So there, so there, so there."

Kate grabbed her coat from a peg near the door and slipped it on without help from her customer. Then she scurried outside and headlong into an entering customer. The new patron shoved her back, but Kate swung her fist at his head. Though he ducked, the glancing blow knocked his hat to the floor. "I'm a lady, so watch out, you ill-mannered oaf," she screamed.

To a chorus of laughter, Kate disappeared into the darkness as her victim bent over his deformed hat and mumbled under his breath. Brushing the dust off his derby and molding it back into shape, Ed Bailey threw back his shoulders like he had been the victor in the encounter and scowled at Holliday's table. Doc's eyes locked on Bailey's, and sparks of hate flew between the men. Bailey muttered words too low for Holliday to make out, then spit on the floor as he turned to the bar. Bailey slapped his thigh and whistled at the bored bartender. Grabbing a towel and wiping the chill from his fleshy jowls, Bailey ordered a drink.

Holliday eyed Bailey's reflected glare in the backbar mirror. When he reached hock in the dealing box, he slipped his hand off the table and unbuttoned his frock coat before reshuffling the deck. As Doc slid the mixed cards back into the dealing box, he heard his name mingled among Bailey's curses. Holliday stretched, then wiggled his fingers of their stiffness, just in case. The portly customer downed another glass of whiskey, and Holliday wondered how many it would take to fortify his courage.

Twice more, Holliday made it through the deck before Bailey slammed his glass on the bar, looked at himself in the mirror and wiped his puffy lips on the towel. Watching the reflection, Holliday eased his chair back from the table, then slipped another card from the dealing box. One player laughed that he'd finally picked a winner, and Holliday shot a quick glance his way, before seeing Bailey unbutton the coat covering his sidearm. Holliday paid off the player. Across the room, Ed twisted from the counter, hiked his gun belt up his watermelon gut. With exaggerated steps, he marched to Holliday's faro layout and elbowed his way between two bettors.

"Learn some manners, Bailey, before you step up to my table."

"Teach some manners to that woman of yours," Bailey answered.

Holliday shoved himself away from the table, his chair legs screeching an alarm across the room. The piano music died away to be replaced by the thud of boots retreating from the faro table. Pulling his frock apart at the waist without taking his eyes off Bailey, Holliday hooked the coat behind the holster on his hip.

"You best apologize to my customers for interrupting their game or your only friend will be the undertaker," Holliday said, his words coming sharp like the retort of a gun.

Bailey's eyes darted from side to side.

"Give them an apology," Doc challenged, "or go for your gun, you S-O-B."

The words hit Bailey like a boulder, his watery eyes batting at the insult, which seemed to echo through the room's stillness. Doc watched Bailey, certain the challenge would remain unanswered.

Bailey swallowed hard. "Pardon me, boys." He shrugged in their direction. "Didn't aim to offend your sensibilities."

"Then just what did you aim to do, Bailey? Display the manners of a rooting hog?"

Bailey's fleshy hand flinched over his sidearm, his face growing white with uncertainty.

"Go for your gun, you S-O-B," Holliday baited him. "And when you pull the trigger, make sure you aim well because I don't make a third the target you do."

Bailey caught his breath. "You cost me my table here. No other saloon'll take me after the Cattle Exchange cut me loose. You'll pay for that."

Doc sneered. "If I'm gonna pay, then call in your debt right now."

Ed considered the challenge. "I lost my work because of you."

"Way I hear it, Bailey," Holliday answered, "you were cheating the house. No wonder you can't get work."

"That's a lie you started."

Holliday jerked his Colt free, a glint of terror flashing across Bailey's face. "You calling me a liar?" He thumbed back the hammer on his Colt, then heard the click of twin hammers nearby.

Chancey stood in his office doorway, shotgun in hand. "Back off, both of you."

Holliday ignored the saloon owner. "You calling me a liar, Bailey?"

"What you said was a lie." Bailey stepped back.

"Is it? You've cheated with that reflecting pipe for sure. You'd tried to cheat me the first night I ever put eyes on your pathetic face."

"I was good for Chancey." Bailey backed away from Holliday. "Brought him a lot of business, I did."

"Both of you cool off." Chancey's deep voice bellowed across the room. "Now let's everybody keep our heads. I've got a load of shot here that'll put an end to both your complaints. Ed, you just let your coat fall over your gun there and, Doc, you ease that revolver to its holster." Chancey stepped toward them, the shotgun at belt level.

For a moment the only noise in the room came from the slamming of the front door and a squeal Holliday recognized as Kate's. What in the devil was she doing back? As Bailey let his coat fall over his gun, Holliday eased his Colt into its scabbard.

"That's better," Chancey told them, releasing the hammers on the shotgun. "No killing in my place. It's bad enough to sweep up the floor without having to mop up your blood. Now, Ed, you know I don't like anyone disturbing my dealers. Why'd you come?"

"A drink, Chancey. That's all."

"Like hell, you've got a thorn in your butt about something. What do you want other than Holliday's hide?"

"My table back, that's all. I don't want any trouble," he said, eyeing Chancey for a moment, then turning to Holliday, "though I'm not running away if it comes."

"You could've come to me. You didn't have to cause Doc any trouble, now did you?"

"He's the one that cost me my table, taking a lesser split. You told me that yourself."

Chancey nodded, then grinned at Holliday. "That's what I said, but it was a business decision."

"Still cost me my job. And Holliday's been spreading stories I cheat."

Chancey paused a moment to weigh his next words. "Perhaps I can get you a table."

Holliday slammed his fist into his palm. "Now wait a minute, Chancey. Giving him a table will lead to trouble. Me and him in the same room? Or are you letting me go this time?"

"Neither," Chancey answered. "You fellows don't do something that'll cause anybody grief. I may acquire another saloon."

Bailey whistled. "Another saloon? Which one, Chancey?"

"When the time's right, you'll know, Ed. Until then, you stay away from here. If you cause any trouble, you'll never work for me again. Think you can hold up your end of that proposition?"

"You know I can, Chancey," Bailey said, backing farther away from Holliday's faro layout. "For sure I will."

"See to it or you won't pass through the door of any saloon I own."

Bailey nodded.

"Doc," Chancey said, "you'll get an explanation later."

"You're the boss, Chancey."

"Okay, Ed, step to the bar for one on the house. Then I'll see you out the door," Chancey ordered. "Doc, you settle with your customers, and we'll close the table for the night. Not enough business to merit a shooting. Maybe tempers will calm." Chancey turned to the idle piano player. "Get your hands out of your pockets and tickle the ivory, something easy."

The pianist jumped to his stool and started clacking out a popular tune. Bailey cast a malevolent gaze toward Holliday, then stepped to the bar. Their grudge wasn't settled, just postponed, Doc thought as he made right the bets of his customers. When Bailey leaned into the bar, Holliday's taut body relaxed until he saw Kate at the counter, a bottle of whiskey tilted to her lips. His twenty-dollar gold piece didn't buy him much time. Kate lowered the bottle, staring across the room at Doc, then swaggered toward him, choking the bottle by its neck.

"Chancey saved your hide, Doc," she smirked, then swigged at the liquor.

Holliday wiped his lips with the back of his hand. "I can take care of myself."

Kate slid up to the table and slapped her bottle hard on it.

Doc smelled the heavy odor of whiskey upon her breath.

"Why'd you pay that cowhand to keep me the night, Doc? That's what I wormed out of him." From behind her full lips, her voice sputtered like a lit fuse before it reached the charge. "And don't deny it. He told me you did."

Holliday ignored the question, staring beyond her at Bailey.

"Let's dance, Doc," Kate said, walking around the table to his side. "I hear you're a good one to waltz." She grasped his fingers.

He jerked his hand free. "You tire me, Kate."

She retreated around the table to her bottle. Holliday could see the hurt flooding in her eyes and could feel his own anger rising. Kate lifted the bottle as gently as she would a newborn child and sipped it. She looked at him with pleading eyes. "Please, Doc, just one dance?" Her voice was still soft.

"As long as Bailey's here, I'm keeping an eye on him."

"Then when he leaves?"

Holliday waved her aside, waiting for Bailey to slake his thirst. Kate slinked to the nearest table and nursed her hurt feelings with the bottle. Ed seemed to enjoy prolonging his free drink, but finally he eased away from the bar, Chancey walking step for step with him and then opening the door like a jail guard. After both men stepped outside, Holliday took a deep breath that scoured his lungs. He leaned back in his chair, rocking on the rear legs.

And then Kate was beside him. "Now the dance you promised, Doc." Her voice reaffirmed the invitation of her extended hand.

"I didn't promise anything, I'm tired."

"Tired? You lying polecat. I'm not good enough to be your dancing partner?" Her voice rose with her temper.

Holliday rocked in his chair, offering Kate the smug smile of a fat man after an enormous meal. "I made no promises. You thought that up yourself."

"That's not right, is it?" She looked around with widening eyes, as if someone might come to her defense, second her story of his unfulfilled promise. But no one paid her any mind.

"Dance, please," she yelled.

"Not tonight, Kate."

"What's the matter? I'm not good enough for you? You snake! You'll dance with that Deno woman, won't you? But not me," she screamed. "I don't remember what happened Christmas night at the Bee Hive, but I heard tell. You were carrying on with that woman, you and her dancing around the room. The hell with her! She's a card trollop, and she's no better than me, but I'm only good enough to sleep with, not dance with."

Kate kicked at Holliday's legs, striking the seat of his chair, knocking him off balance. His chair teetered a moment, as Doc's flailing arms and legs almost regained his equilibrium, then toppled backward, crashing onto the floor and ending the piano music.

"Damn you, Kate," Holliday sputtered, rolling over from the chair and crawling onto his hands and knees.

"And you, too, Doc Holliday," she shouted with a spray of spit. She darted to the door. By her hand, the door swung full open and banged against the wall, rattling the windows. "Nobody's gonna come between us anymore," she screeched. "Nobody."

She disappeared into the night, screaming indecipherable profanity into the pit of darkness. Good riddance, Holliday thought as he picked himself up and dusted the sawdust off his fresh suit. Kate was as unpredictable as a wounded wildcat and twice as dangerous. He was as glad to be rid of her as he would be to lose tuberculosis. As Holliday righted his chair, Chancey burst through the door, his eyes wild and his lips agape.

"Doc," he yelled, gesturing with his arms. "Kate's gone to kill Lottie."

****

Her hands moved deftly over the cards, cradling them, then tossing them from palm to palm, her customers transfixed by her motions as if they were watching a coiled rattler. Lottie wore a pale blue dress with ballooning sleeves, which narrowed into frilly laced cuffs, plenty adequate to hide a card or two. As she shuffled the pasteboards, they would disappear into a haze of lace and reappear again before passing under the shadow of her hand. Lottie mixed the deck without looking at her fingers, glancing instead at the faces surrounding her table. They were a modest assembly of bashful cowhands between jobs, unbathed buffalo hunters back from the plains, and tipsy merchants whose wives thought them attending a lodge meeting. Among them, there wasn't enough money to cover the bottom of a narrow-headed stump preacher's hat at collection time.

After inserting the shuffled deck into the dealing box, she fluffed her lace cuffs. "A fresh deck and a fresh start for you gentlemen." She smiled, and they grinned back, dropping their meager bets all over the layout.

As Lottie slid soda from the box and uncovered the first card, a shriek like a panther's cry cut through the downstairs noise. A stream of profanity rolled off a female tongue. Another jealous wag-tail, Lottie thought, as she listened to the footfall of someone running up the stairs. A second rabid scream echoed off the staircase wall. Lottie glanced up from her dealing box as Big Nose Kate stepped into view, her eyes thick with savagery, her nostrils flared from the hate in her heavy breath. Slowly, Kate lifted her hand. In it she carried a gun, pointed straight at Lottie's table.

"Lottie Deno," Kate screamed, "I'll kill you." Lottie's customers scattered.

The dealer arose from her chair, her right hand brushing the folds in her dress. Pulling her hand away from her bodice, Lottie steadied her own revolver at Kate's heart. "You know your kind isn't allowed upstairs, Kate."

Kate advanced, her gait deliberate and menacing. Two men with outstretched arms inched toward her, but she swung her hand at them, the gun exploding and a bullet splintering the plank floor at their feet. "Come closer, and I'll plug you." Then she looked at Lottie. "I'll kill you," Kate said, waving the gun around the room before pointing it at Lottie, "if you don't stay away from my man."

"Which one, Kate? You've had so many," Lottie replied at the sound of heavy footsteps on the stairs. Chancey, Holliday, and Fogle appeared at the top of the steps behind Kate.

"Doc Holliday's my man, and you stay away from him." Kate steadied her gun with her left hand and thumbed the hammer back. Holliday lunged for her arms, striking her hands as the gun roared, then coughed smoke. Another bullet plowed into the floor. Kate screamed like a wounded panther, her arms flailing at Holliday, striking him on the cheek with her gun. Doc wrestled with her. The acrid powder smoke from a bullet meant for her burned in Lottie's eyes as she watched Chancey grab for Kate's arms. Kate's wrath turned to him and his powerful hands long enough for Holliday to wrench the gun from her grip. Kate screamed profanities at Lottie. "Leave him be, you card trollop."

"If I stepped in cow dung, I wouldn't clean my shoe on him."

"He not good enough for you, you faro whore?" Kate struggled against Chancey.

"I'll show you," Lottie said, stepping around the table toward Kate.

"Grab her, Fogle," Holliday called, and the owner of the Bee Hive lunged at her, wrapping his arms around her. Lottie struggled against his manacle hold, then saw the futility of it. "Mike Fogle," Lottie shouted in his ear, "you make sure that she stays out of this place, or she'll be sleeping with the worms and maggots instead of every two-legged skunk that'll lower himself to her bed."

Kate lifted her knee into Chancey's groin. Gasping, he released his grip. Kate slid free and broke for Lottie. Holliday shoved her to the floor as she darted by.

Chancey recovered enough to pounce upon her, squeezing her wrists and dragging her to the stairs. "A couple of you fellows take her down before I kill her myself." Three helped tote the screaming Kate away.

"Trouble's over," Holliday told Fogle. The owner of the Bee Hive spit at the sound of Kate's curses. "Damndest woman in the Flat."

Fogle released Lottie. "Get back to your game." He turned to Chancey. "Obliged for your help. Kate's a troublemaker," he said, then paused for a moment, running his hand through his disheveled hair. "Chancey, I've been needing to talk to you. You have time to visit on the way out."

Lottie looked at Fogle, but his eyes avoided hers. She slipped her gun into her bodice, wondering why her boss needed to visit with Chancey? She walked to her table, smiling at her customers. "Okay, gentlemen, our interruption is over. Please excuse my language, but it was the only type that vile woman would understand," Lottie said, perplexed by the joint departure of Fogle and Chancey.

Chapter 13

Two horsemen raced along Griffin Avenue, shooting holes in the night sky. Their tongues and revolvers loosened by too much rye, they galloped up and down the deserted street, shouting obscene verses of "Don't Drink Tonight, Boys," the latest temperance song popular among sober women.

Inside the Cattle Exchange by a window stood Chancey, his double-barreled shotgun broken at the breech and hanging in the crook of his left arm as he watched the troublemakers. "What do they think this is, the Fourth of July?" Chancey's boot tapped on the floor. He had rolled a cigarette but had forgotten to light it. Now it hung from his drawn lips, darkening from soaked spit until it would never take to flame.

On a break from his faro table, Holliday leaned into the bar with his elbow and watched Chancey. To attract the bartender, he slapped the counter with his palm, the pop resounding inside the saloon. The saloon owner slammed the hinged barrel against the breech block and spun around behind the menacing stare of the shotgun's gaping black eyes. Realizing the danger only imagined, Chancey stared at Holliday, and then turned back toward the street. Chancey was as nervous as a bull at steering time, Doc thought.

Would their horses ever wear out? Or would the riders exhaust their ammunition? Holliday wondered. Kate was somewhere out there with her latest customer. Doc estimated the odds of her taking a bullet and feared for the two rowdies if they encountered her and her acid tongue. Holliday knew no man the equal to that task, one of Kate's traits that amused him. He grinned and motioned for some Monarch Bourbon. The bartender, conditioned by habit, obeyed his wordless command.

With his liquor, Holliday strolled to the window beside Chancey. Holliday turned the container to his lips, threw back his head, and gulped hard swallows. Finished, he held the bottle by the neck in front of the glass. "Wonder if they can hit this at a full gallop?"

Chancey shoved Holliday's hand away as the racing hooves neared, then passed. Accepting Chancey's rebuff as an invitation to drink, Holliday sipped again at the bourbon. When the bottle slid from his lips, he took a big breath. "You're too edgy tonight, Chancey. Those boys are having a good time. They'll end their celebration in the Bee Hive, not here."

"That's what's bothering me, Doc."

"Hell, Chancey, you've never cared what happened in Fogle's place."

"It ain't just Fogle's place anymore," he whispered. "It's half mine now."

Holliday whistled. "I pick up conversation at my table, but your winning the Bee Hive is the best kept secret in the Flat."

"Didn't win it, Doc," Chancey said, as the cowboys' winded mounts galloped past the Cattle Exchange again.

"Fogle didn't just give it to you."

"True," Chancey answered without elaboration.

Holliday leaned against the wall and unbuttoned his frock coat. "I've got all night."

Chancey stepped in front of the window, then pressed his cheek against the glass, looking for the riders. The firing had stopped. "Damn, Doc, I don't know where they went. Where in the hell has Sheriff Larn been? I may have to bribe him just to protect this damn town." The saloon owner slipped to the door, opened it and eased his head outside, glancing both ways down the street. "Looks clear, Doc, come on back to my office." He turned and walked away.

Waiting at his office door for Holliday, Chancey groped at a match in his tobacco tin, then tried without success to light the drool-soaked cigarette disintegrating in his mouth. Cursing, he spat the soggy mess on the floor, extracted his tobacco pouch and papers from his tin, and started a new smoke. Doc entered the office as a match flamed in Chancey's hand. Chancey touched the fire to his cigarette, and the ball of match light illuminated the trouble etched in his face. He shook the match out and stared into the low burning flame of his kerosene lamp. He drew deeply, then exhaled twin serpentine clouds of smoke from his nostrils as Holliday closed the door.

"Doc," he started, "I figured I'd own the Bee Hive one day, win it from Fogle in a game of cards. Hell, you made a run at it for me and would've had it if Lottie hadn't scrambled your card sense like broken eggs."

"She had a lucky run at cards."

A strained grunt escaped Chancey's lips with another ribbon of smoke. "Didn't think you believed in Lottie's Luck, Doc. I wanted that saloon so bad I'd challenge Lottie's Luck, so bad I could've whipped every man in town and the troops up on the hill to boot. Now, I own fifty percent without ever turning a card."

"So you've got half a sack now, what's the problem, Chancey?"

"It's the way I got it, Doc. The money I'd been saving to make another run at it, I used to buy a half stake. Since I paid Fogle, my flesh's been crawling like a barrel full of snakes."

For a moment, Holliday jiggled the bottle, staring at its turbulent amber contents. "What's the difference? You got what you wanted. He didn't sell 'cause he's your buddy."

"He got in debt over his head—it's hard to figure as much money as the Bee Hive brings in—and needed some quick cash for his debts."

Holliday scowled at the saloon owner. "So this is how you'll put Ed Bailey back to work for you and against me? Seems your luck is running better than mine."

Chancey's dark eyes narrowed. "I wanted to whip Fogle for the Bee Hive. In my younger days, I did a little prize-fighting. One time I'd readied for a match against a fellow I sure wanted to beat, but wasn't so sure I could. Night before the fight, he got wise with a skinny little runt that packed this peashooter of a derringer. Dang, if that pipsqueak didn't tattoo him with one of the smallest bullet holes you've ever seen, but when the smoke cleared, my opponent was one of the deadest men alive. I'd just as soon he whipped me around the ring the next day than never know how I would've stood up against him. Same way with Fogle. I don't know if I could've beaten him. That bothered me, so I told Fogle when he was back on his feet we'd play for each other's half."

"That's a fool thing to do, Chancey, splitting the pot with a man you've beaten. What about Bailey?"

"I heard you the first time, Doc. Bailey'll start tomorrow at the Bee Hive."

"That's what should worry you. He'll bring you bad luck. What about Lottie?"

"She stays where she is, though she's none too fond of me."

"As long as she deals for you, you'll do okay." Holliday wiped his lips.

"Can't explain it, Doc, just a feeling that this has come too easy to bring anything but bad luck."

"Your rotten luck'll rub off on me," Holliday said, holding up his bottle. "Just talking about it has run me half dry."

"My luck has nothing to do with it. You're always running dry. How you put away that much liquor and still stay on your feet is beyond me."

"Like cards, it takes practice."

"Then you ought to be as fine a bottle sharp as found anywhere," Chancey drew on his smoke until the fire reached his fingers. He crushed the cigarette between his fingertips and dropped it on the floor. "If you could just play cards as well as you can drink."

"If you drank a little more, maybe you wouldn't be as worried." Holliday stroked his moustache, pulling a grin across his lips.

Chancey's lips parted to speak, then froze at a shout in the saloon. The piano music died, chairs screeched to life, and fleeing boots pounded outside. At the sharp rap on the door, Chancey reached for his shotgun, and Holliday jerked his Colt from its holster.

"Open easy," Chancey said, as the head of a bartender slid through the widening crack.

"There's been a shooting at the Bee Hive," the bartender started. "A couple dead."

Holliday glanced at Chancey, a grimace clouding the saloon owner's face like he'd expected the news. Swallowing hard, Holliday stared at the bartender. "Was Lottie hurt?"

****

Trouble was coming as sure as lightning on the horizon foretold a thunderstorm's approach. Lottie could feel it in the air. And then the firing had started outside, a couple of cowhands from the Millett Ranch catching up on their entertainment by shooting the darkness along Griffin Avenue. In her customers she sensed the tension, saw it in their tight-lipped faces as their bets came slowly and sometimes on cards the casekeeper showed had all been played.

Finally, the gunfire outside died away, and she watched the faces of her gamblers relax at the quiet, then stiffen at the yelling and screaming downstairs. Lottie could feel her fingers growing tacky from perspiration. Trouble had entered the Bee Hive with the two cowboys. For an instant, the first-floor noises died away, then the shooting started. Eleven, maybe twelve shots, exploded below and echoed up the staircase, followed by the heavy odor of gunpowder. Then a moment of total silence was shattered by the wails of a saloon girl, the cries of the wounded, and the shouts for help. Lottie's patrons broke for the stairs.

"Don't let a little shooting scare you gentlemen away," she called. "If someone's hurt, there's nothing you can do about it. If it's just a cowboy showing off, he might not enjoy you interrupting him."

Her effort was as futile as a school marm trying to round up schoolboys after the last bell. Even the fascination of Lottie Deno, she thought, could not bring them back to the faro table tonight, not with the sound of groaning wounded and a harlot who wailed like every potential customer in Texas had been killed.

Lottie counted her winnings, seventy-nine dollars and some change. Awful night and it wouldn't get any better with the shooting, she thought, dividing out her twenty-five percent of the take. Twenty dollars beat a loss, but not by much. Maybe Griffin was nearing the end of its string. If the prices on prime buffalo hides this spring dropped much below a dollar, as had been rumored, business might not even improve when the buffalo hunters returned. Then, hiding behind a new name, she would move on. She didn't know where, but a town like Griffin would sprout up in the middle of nowhere, grow like a weed, and wither away like one, too.

After depositing the money in her small carpetbag, she headed for the stairway, the odor of acrid gunsmoke growing stronger with each step, stinging her nose and misting her eyes. Descending halfway down the stairs into a ghostly haze, she saw men and women kneeling over four blood-stained forms. One wore a cavalry uniform and twitched as people attended him. Another—a cowboy by his garb—writhed in the sawdust, struggling for each breath. A circle of men backed away from yet another downed man, leaving a towel over his face as the darkening stain from his forehead showed he would never arise. Against the far wall a fourth victim sat propped up, patrons tearing off his coat and pressed shirt.

From the foot of the stairs, she waded into the edgy crowd and angled for Fogle's office behind the bar. Elbowing against the human tide, she reached Fogle's door, her path converging with that of a big man who towered over her. Glancing up, she looked into Chancey's dark eyes. Beside him stood John Henry Holliday.

"You okay, Lottie?" Holliday asked.

"Be better if these yahoos hadn't shot up what little business I had. You come to laugh at Fogle's misfortune?"

"Don't you know, Lottie?" Chancey interrupted, folding his broad arms across his chest. "His bad luck is mine from now on."

She felt her stomach tighten at Chancey's words and at the insincere smile spreading across his face. "What are you talking about?"

Chancey just laughed, walked past Lottie, and shoved open Fogle's door.

Holliday coughed. "Chancey is Fogle's new partner. He's half owner of the Bee Hive."

Lottie's heart pounded like an angry hammer against an anvil. She stared from Doc to Fogle's open door. Holliday extended his arm, but she spurned his offer, her anger burning white. She strode into the office, past Chancey to Fogle, and slammed her satchel on his desk, rattling a lamp. Fogle caught it before it tipped over. Lottie saw the surprise in his blinking eyes as he righted the lamp, stood straight, and shook his fingers from the burn. She aimed her finger like a gun at his chest. "Is it true Chancey's got half interest in the Bee Hive now?"

Fogle threw up his arms. "Damn killings outside," his voice trembled, "and now this. Did my new partner break the news to you? I'd planned to tell you tonight, Lottie." Fogle dropped his hands and walked behind his chair.

Lottie's finger fell, and her chin slipped down, her fury receding because she believed him. He had never lied to her before. "How'd you lose? I'd played your hand."

Fogle pried his paper collar away from his neck and cleared his throat. "I sold him half. I had debts and needed the money. My gambling luck's not as good as yours."

Glancing at Chancey, she felt her face flame with anger at his smug grin. "I'd loaned you money, Mike."

"I just couldn't ask that of a lady, Lottie, not even you. Later, I'll have a chance to win it back, and you'll play my hand when that day comes."

"If I'm still around," Lottie answered.

Chancey stepped beside her, his devious grin straining his cheeks. "I want you to stay on at whatever your present arrangement is. Whatever differences we've had in the past are forgotten."

"Perhaps by you," Lottie started. "If I stay, I work for Mike, not for you." Lottie unhooked her satchel and dropped Fogle's take of the night's winnings on his desk. Taking the carpetbag, she frowned at Fogle. "I'm sorry for you, Mike." She drifted toward the door, slipping her hand through Holliday's proffered arm. "My luck just turned bad, John Henry," Lottie said as he accompanied her through the saloon. Gazing around at the carnage on the floor, Lottie felt a queasiness in her stomach and knew it wasn't from the blood. "I don't like the way the cards fell this time. It can't lead to anything good."

"Chancey said the same thing." Holliday steered her through the throng. "Called it bad luck, him buying the Bee Hive instead of winning it."

"Hah," Lottie retorted. "As long as I was in Griffin, he'd never won it. Neither he nor you would ever have beaten me."

They squeezed their way to the front door and emerged into the cold winter wind, which pricked at Lottie's face. She shivered and felt Holliday pull her closer to him.

"You've never cared much for Chancey?"

"He didn't take me for a lady when I came to the Flat. He offered to let me whore in his saloon, even offered to be my first customer."

"A lot of men take a fancy to you, Lottie."

"The answer's still no, John Henry. I'll not tell you my name, but at least you've been a gentleman about it. Chancey wasn't."

"Ashamed of your past?" Holliday asked as they walked deeper into the darkness toward her cabin.

"Most people in this country don't dwell on what they left behind. I don't either," Lottie answered.

"Those folks have something to hide."

"We all run from our past. It's called aging."

"I keep thinking maybe there was more in common between us than gambling."

"We're from the south, John Henry, and that's it, nothing more."

Holliday coughed, once, twice, three times hard, wrenching his arm loose from Lottie's. He was a sick man, she thought. He might have a past, but not much of a future. Holliday caught a fresh breath.

"I'll keep trying," he said. "You're too pretty to forget."

"Gamblers never give up, John Henry; they just go broke. Don't bet on me. You're better off wagering on Kate."

"You hold her against me? I'm not saying I'm a pure man."

"Nor am I a pure woman. I just don't take to Kate. What looks I have, I want to keep without her altering them with a knife or a bullet."

"She was delirious."

"Delirious, John Henry? She was jealous. Still is. She cares more for you than you'd ever admit. Marry her, if you want to become a husband. A lot of saloon women have turned respectable. Marry her, if you can walk away from your gambling table and hang out your shingle." Lottie was glad when they reached her cabin. She opened the door and left it ajar long enough to light a lamp, the glow of the yellow light filling the room. It was cold, and the night had been a bad one. "Come in for a moment, John Henry."

He obliged as she moved into the back room and put kindling into the stove, building a slow flame that she fed more wood. Looking over her shoulder, she saw Holliday standing just inside the door, his hat in his hand. Maybe she shouldn't have invited him inside. When the fire took hold, she searched for the whiskey bottle she kept for medicine. After finding it, she joined Holliday in the front room. "Maybe this will warm you up enough for the return trip, cut into that cough."

"Bad isn't it." He accepted the bottle.

Lottie nodded.

Holliday gulped the liquid down. Lottie flinched. Nobody could take liquor like him. He was like a horse at a water trough after a long, hot ride. He eased the bottle down and looked at Lottie. "I won't last many years. Maybe if it weren't for this consumption, things might be different between us." He took another swig.

"You're persistent, John Henry, I'll give you that."

"I'm a gambler. I took a gamble I could change your mind, but I lost. Most men do when they come up against you."

"I don't beat them. They beat themselves."

"You give them every opportunity to lose. Maybe that's the way it should be with a woman running a gambling table."

"I'm no different from a man running a table."

"Are you staying at the Bee Hive? I've lost track of whether you gave me an answer on that one."

"I don't like working for Chancey."

"You'd still be working as much for Fogle as for Chancey."

"It's not the same."

"Maybe not, but Griffin's still good place for our type, and the Bee Hive is the best spot in Griffin."

"There are other towns on the rise. The Flat may go down."

Holliday nodded and offered the bottle to Lottie.

"You keep it, John Henry. You need it more than I do."

Holliday nodded.

"Good night, John Henry, and good luck until we play again."

Chapter 14

The pounding on the door cut through the haze of his sleep. Holliday turned over once, as if it were a bad dream, then shot up from the mattress and grabbed for his holstered pistol hanging on the bedpost.

"Open up, you stinkin' polecat," screeched an unwelcomed voice. It was Kate, beating the entry like a bass drum. "Unlock this door."

Holliday coughed, then shouted back. "I gave you a key. Use it."

"I can't find it. Open up."

Doc crawled out of bed, his bare foot brushing against the bottle, now empty, that Lottie had given him. He returned his Colt to its scabbard and walked across the room.

Kate screamed. "Unlock this door 'fore I knock it down, you varmint. I gotta talk, and I'm not waiting. Do you hear me?"

Doc nodded to himself. Half the hotel heard her, and boarders cursed from adjacent rooms, the thuds of boots thrown against the walls punctuating their demands for quiet.

Shaking his head of sleep's rust, Doc whispered through the door. "You alone, Kate?"

"I am," she screamed. "Are you?"

"Not so loud, Kate."

"You sick fool, telling me to hold my voice. You don't own me."

Holliday unlatched the door and eased it open a hair, then wider until he stared at Kate in the dim hall light, her brown hair disheveled as if a West Texas wind had combed it, her breath strong enough of cheap liquor to light a match. She swayed like a tree in a strong breeze. Holliday parted the door long enough for her to stumble in. After closing and latching the entry, he stared at her walking to his bed.

"Thank you, Doc," Kate said meekly, then plopped onto the mattress in a shaft of moonlight that angled in through the window. For a moment, she glanced around the room as if trying to locate Doc.

Then she propped her elbows on her thighs and dropped her head into the palm of her hands. "You've been to visit her again, haven't you?"

"So, I have. No concern of yours, is it? You see other men all the time."

Kate sobbed and lifted her face to Holliday, standing impassively over her. "I keep thinking one day you might care for me for more than they do."

"Like a wife?" He spit the word out. "I play cards, and I travel light." Holliday walked around the bed and slid under the covers opposite Kate. "When I leave town, there's no time for extra baggage."

"Baggage! Is that all I am? You'd marry that Lottie if she'd let you." Kate's voice turned hard, her crying ceased. "Why not me? I'd take care of you, Doc. She never would. Did she ever get a patent medicine for your sickness? Why won't you give me a chance? I'm not ugly. Maybe she is prettier, but I'm not bad. Enough men pay for me, so I know I've still got some looks about me."

"Gamblers and consumptives don't need wives, Kate. Men of chance can't afford to be tied down, and lungers are headed to an early grave."

"You'd marry her. That's what I've heard people say. You paid her plenty of attention, dancing with her while I was dying in my cabin. You'd marry her, if she'd let you. She's not right for you, Doc, but I am."

"Marriage is not right for me, Kate. Can't you get it through your head?"

Kate wriggled off the bed and into the shaft of moonlight where Holliday watched her unbutton her coat and let it fall to the floor. She undid the back buttons of her dress, and it joined the wrap at her feet. Holliday shook his head when he saw the key to his room dangling from a leather thong around her neck.

"I thought you said you lost my room key, Kate."

She shook her head. "I said I couldn't find it."

"It's around your neck."

She grinned. "I forgot to look there." Kate slipped out of her undergarments and into bed with Holliday. She ran her hand over him. "I'm what you need."

"What I need, Kate, is to be left alone to gamble and to die when the day comes. Nothing more, nothing less."

"Then turn me down, like Lottie's done you all these times," Kate said, rubbing his chest. "You are warm."

He flinched at her touch. "Your hands are icy," Doc answered.

"Not as frigid as Lottie's heart. All she's ever held was a deck of cards."

"Don't bring her up again."

"You can't turn me down, can you?"

"I could."

"But you won't. You want me. You won't admit it, but you want me and need me."

Holliday tried to turn away, his mind willing, but his body under Kate's control.

"I'd do more for you than Lottie ever could, if you'd just let me prove it to you."

"No more talking, Kate," Holliday said, putting his arm around her and drawing her closer to him.

****

Mike Fogle jumped from his office chair and extended his hand to Lottie. "I'm glad you came, Lottie. You worried me that you might leave when you learned about Chancey."

"For the time being, I'm working for you, Mike." Lottie shook Fogle's hand.

Fogle threw back his head and stood akimbo, reminding Lottie of a rooster announcing sunrise. "I'm delighted you're staying with us."

"I'll stay until I win the Bee Hive back for you. After that, I can't say."

"I'd appreciate the favor."

"It'll be another chance to even a grudge with Chancey."

Fogle nodded. "And with Holliday?"

She smiled. "No, he's too good a dancer."

"He might die dancing, at the end of a rope some day, temper like his. At least Chancey doesn't fancy moving him over here from the Cattle Exchange, though I'm not sure I don't prefer him to Ed Bailey."

"What about Bailey, Mike?"

"He's working upstairs. Chancey made me take him on. He's a cheat, damn poor one at that, and he shorts the house more than his friends, and he has plenty of them."

"Except John Henry Holliday," Lottie said.

"That's why Chancey sent him over. Chancey promised Bailey a job, but Holliday didn't cotton to them working in the same saloon. Holliday doesn't forget a grudge."

"Nor a card trick," Lottie answered. "Chancey'll have Doc play for him when we make our move to regain the Bee Hive."

"We'll be ready, won't we?"

Lottie nodded. "But don't underestimate John Henry. He's a money player, and he'll be a hard one to hoodwink, unlike a lot of the men that play at my table. John Henry may be a gentleman, but he's a gambler first."

"That day is a good spell away, Lottie. Now let me escort you to your table. I've put Bailey on the opposite side of the room to lessen the distractions." Lottie nodded and followed him into the saloon. "Lottie's staying," he called to the bartender. "Our luck is on the way up."

The stairs creaked, and Fogle hummed beside Lottie as they climbed toward the gambling room. At the top of the stairs, Fogle cleared his throat, and most patrons turned to stare. "Gentlemen, Lottie's back!"

The men cheered, and Lottie smiled, grabbing the folds of her dress and curtsying.

"Now you fellows, can lose your money without feeling so bad." Fogle laughed.

Lottie glanced about the room. Bailey held court for a pair of patrons at his seat in the far corner. Good place for him, she thought. As the patrons finished acknowledging Lottie's presence, they returned to their business, several gathering around a table in the center of the room. As Lottie moved to her layout with Fogle by her side, she stared at the bunch.

"What's the attraction there, Mike?"

"Pair of gamblers trying to prove whose best. You ever heard of Smokey Joe from central Texas? He's one of them. Other fellow calls himself Monte Bill, says he's out of Arizona."

"Too many observers for it to be a friendly game, Mike. Could lead to trouble."

"They took an immediate dislike to one another. Decided cards should settle their differences."

At her table, Lottie sat down behind the layout, and Fogle cleared the casekeeper. "Gentlemen," he called, "Lottie is back in business. See if you can buck the tiger and this pretty lady as well."

Lottie's Luck

Beneath the tiger gazing from the wall poster over her shoulder, Lottie shuffled the deck from hand to hand, a careless nonchalance about her. Some men abandoned other tables to join Lottie, but many remained at the central table where the simmering words between Monte Bill and Smokey Joe drifted with the smoke above the other noise.

"Maybe you should cool that game off, Mike. Doesn't sound too good to me."

"They're big boys, Lottie."

"You're the boss, Mike." Lottie smiled at the men scattered around her. "Please don't win my money, or Mike may run me off." She inserted the cards in the dealing box. "Place your bets."

The game moved fast, the bets stayed small, the distraction remained the poker match between Monte Bill and Smokey Joe. Gradually, the crowd around the table backed away, giving a wider berth to the gambling antagonists. Lottie saw between the spectators, the two men, their postures stiff, their faces drawn with hate.

"You better break that game up, Mike," Lottie said. "It'll get out of hand when one loses a big pot."

"Last night was our run of bad luck for the month, Lottie. With you back, things'll go better. It's called Lottie's Luck."

Lottie gathered the discarded deck from the layout and reshuffled the cards. "My instincts tell me we're not over our sour spell yet. This is eighteen seventy-seven, isn't it?"

"What's the year got to do with it?"

"Odd-numbered years have always been unlucky for me."

"You're too superstitious, Lottie."

"Name me a gambler that isn't?"

"Ed Bailey, for one."

"He's not a gambler." She inserted the cards in the dealing box.

"Thinks he is, Lottie."

"Thinking's one thing. Being's another," she said, then started through her deck as the noise from the nearby table turned to shouts. Lottie paused as the voices grew louder, hotter.

"Go on, Lottie, don't let them annoy you," Fogle offered, re-stacking a pile of chips on the table.

"Raise that," Monte Bill shouted.

"I'm betting every last dollar to my name," Smokey Joe challenged.

The spectators backed away, and Lottie could see several hundred dollars in the pot.

"Full house, aces over queens! Beat that." Monte Bill threw his cards on the green felt.

Smokey Joe flung his cards on the money. "Cheated by a sneaking coyote that brings in a cold deck and marked cards. I'll take this pot." Smokey Joe reached with his left hand for the pot, his right hand dropping off the table.

"You're not bluffing me out of my fair winnings," Monte Bill yelled. His hand fell for his revolver.

Both men jerked their guns above the table. Spectators scrambled backward over each other and chairs. Simultaneous bolts of Colt lightning flashed across the table. Gamblers throughout the room dropped to the floor. The thunder of the pistols reverberated off the walls. Some spectators scrambled on hands and knees for the stairs. Two clouds of white smoke mingled together, like the blood of Smokey Joe and Monte Bill.

For a moment, only Lottie stood. Then others picked themselves up from the floor, Fogle among them. "Looks like you were right, Lottie."

Lottie stared at Monte Bill slumped along the edge of the table, his lifeless head leaking onto the floor. Smokey Joe had fallen beside the table, a chest wound gushing blood into the growing puddle from Monte Bill. In a moment, even the blood stopped. "They'll never make that mistake again, Mike."

Fogle pushed himself away from Lottie's layout and inched toward the disputed table. He picked up Bill's wrist and dropped it, then bent over Joe. "They're both dead." Other men eased over to look at death's work, one man reaching for the disputed pot.

"Back away, all of you," Fogle commanded. "Clear the room until Sheriff Larn can get here. Somebody fetch him." The men lingered a moment too long. "Move, dammit!"

Lottie gathered her cards. "Game's over, fellows. Go downstairs like he said."

Mike herded them to the staircase. "You don't want to be here when the sheriff arrives. Let him figure it out. Drinks are on the house until we get the mess cleaned up."

Lottie put her deck of cards in her satchel. When the room cleared, she walked to the table with the deceased. She counted and stacked their final bets. More than five hundred dollars. Still, not a pot worth dying over. She folded the paper money and gathered the double eagles, adding all to the satchel.

Fogle returned up the stairs and stood at the head, staring from the cleared table to Lottie.

"My price for staying on," Lottie said before being asked.

Fogle nodded, then turned around at the sound of heavy boots behind him. "Had a shooting, Sheriff."

"You've had a spate of bad luck here the last two nights," answered Sheriff Jay Larn, coming into Lottie's view, his badge freshly shined. His clothes were oversized, fitting his estimation of himself more than his narrow frame. His chin jutted forward with so much authority that his arrogant eyes looked down at everyone. He wore the responsibility of the job as poorly as he sported his duck britches and hickory shirt, but his sidearm glistened with the same pride as his tin star. You couldn't buy justice from Larn, but money always lined his pockets from those who had tried.

Lottie backed away from the table, catching a glint in the sheriff's haughty eyes as he stared at the table. Larn stopped beside her, toeing both bodies with his scuffed boots. "Shame to die over a card game without a pot, wouldn't you say, Lottie? Why didn't you get out like the rest when these two peckerwoods started shooting?"

"By then, it was too late."

"Downstairs, they say you stood like a tree. That so?"

"They weren't aiming my way. No sense in dirtying a dress in that case."

"You have nerve, old girl, and savvy, waiting until everybody left, then lifting the pot. It's something I wouldn't expect from Lottie Deno."

"Perhaps not, Sheriff, but you are not a desperate woman."

Confident that both men would not arise to challenge him, the sheriff grew bolder, kicking both bodies, Monte Bill's toppling over like a rag doll onto the floor beside Smokey Joe. "If they don't groan, they ain't living." Larn looked up from the table at Lottie, extending his hand, palm up. "Lot of vinegar over a game with no pot."

Lottie shook her satchel, giving the heavy gold coins a chance to slip further to the bottom. "I put the money in here for safekeeping."

Larn smiled. "That's the job of the law. A couple hundred dollars, I heard." His hand reached toward the satchel as Lottie unhooked it.

She slipped her hand in the narrow opening and pulled a wad of bills from inside, his hand relieving hers of the load.

"That all?"

Lottie dipped inside for a few more bills to feed the sheriff's greedy palm. "That's better." He spoke to the money more than Lottie. "If there was more, keep it," he sneered. "Just call it Lottie's Luck." He grinned, his smile as ill fitting as his clothes and his badge. "Maybe you'd better clear out, Lottie, 'fore someone other than me starts asking questions."

"Certainly, Sheriff. You're the law."

Chapter 15

The tall stranger stood flagpole straight, his blue eyes missing nothing in the saloon, not even the slight movement of Holliday's hand to brush his coat away from the ivory grip on his Colt sidearm. Holliday could feel this individual's icy stare upon his flesh, and once as he glanced over his poker cards, Holliday's eyes met the flint of the stranger's. Neither man flinched. The man's unbuttoned overcoat, dusted from a long ride, was swept behind his sidearm. A handlebar moustache anchored his square face. His defiant nose dared to be challenged. The stranger stood beside the bar without leaning against it. When his hands weren't lifting a drink to his lips, the fellow flexed his fingers, not in a nervous way, but in the calm, professional manner of a gambler. Or worse, a lawman.

This individual sought neither a card game nor a woman. He was looking for a man. Holliday wondered if the law was catching up with him for killing the Jacksboro soldier.

As Holliday took two cards, Chancey strode by the bar, glanced at the stranger, stopping instantly. Chancey and the lawman stared at each other until the stranger's lips twitched into a slight smile, and he stopped flexing his fingers long enough to extend his hand to Chancey. The saloon owner grabbed it with his own massive paw and slapped the man's back, neither saying a word. Chancey motioned toward his office door. The stranger, with a backward glance over his shoulder, disappeared with Holliday's boss into the room.

Distracted from his poker hand, Holliday tossed his cards on the deadwood and blamed his weak luck for withdrawing from the game. Coughing as he rose from the table, he moved to an empty table, wondering if it were time to abandon Fort Griffin and Lottie, maybe taking Kate in her place. Shortly, the office door cracked open long enough for Chancey to stick his head out, scan the room, then call to a bartender. Holliday watched as both men stared at him. Then the bartender nodded and started for Holliday's table as Chancey retreated behind the door. Drawing up beside Doc, the bartender whispered, "Boss wants to see you."

Holliday stood up slowly, slipping his hand inside his coat pocket for a handkerchief. He wiped perspiration from his moustache and returned the cloth, his hand brushing against the Smith and Wesson in his shoulder holster. Doc ambled across the room to Chancey's office, rapped on the wood, and pushed open the door. Entering, he slipped his hand inside his coat as his eyes adjusted to the dim light and to the stranger standing in the corner shadows by the stacked liquor crates.

"Doc," said Chancey, arising from his chair, "got an old friend here I'd like you to meet."

The stranger leaned forward out of the shadows, brushing his jittery fingers through his light brown hair, then offered Holliday a gaunt smile with his broad hand.

"Wyatt Earp meet John Henry Holliday, most folks around these parts just call him Doc."

Holliday pulled his fingers from his coat and grabbed Earp's powerful hand.

"On July Fourth of sixty-eight," Chancey said, "Wyatt refereed a fight in Cheyenne, me and Mike Donovan, who beat the hell out of me and might've killed me except for Wyatt."

"Good to meet you, Holliday," Earp said. "Chancey wasn't bad for a kid his age. Donovan just had several years of ring experience on him."

"Donovan gave me all the experience I wanted that day," Chancey said. "He pounded some sense into this thick skull. There had to be easier ways to make a living."

"How you earn your keep, Wyatt?" Holliday interrupted.

"A little gambling, a little star toting."

Holliday broke off their grip and backed away. "You carrying a badge now?"

"Nothing to worry about, Doc," Chancey intervened. "Wyatt needs some help. I thought you'd be able to assist."

"Not the first time the law's come after me," Holliday grinned, "but the first for help."

Earp sat on a pair of wooden liquor crates and crossed a leg over his knee. Holliday's tense muscles softened. A man looking for a fight didn't take a seat.

"I'm working for the Santa Fe Railway," Earp started. "I'm looking for a man named Dave Rudabaugh. He's been robbing Santa Fe trains. Chancey says you might recognize someone on the run or odd comings and goings here in Griffin? You heard of Rudabaugh?"

"I'm not accustomed to working with the law."

Chancey interrupted. "You can trust Wyatt, and you'd be doing me a favor, Doc. I owe Wyatt a chip or two."

Holliday nodded.

"Don't consider this anything to do with the law," Earp said, standing again. "It'd be a personal favor to me. And I won't forget it."

Doc nodded. "Give me three days. Don't come to me unless you're willing to throw a couple of dollars bucking the tiger at my table. I don't want my customers knowing I'm working for the law."

"You're working for me, not the law," Earp reminded.

"Won't look much different either way if word gets out, now will it?"

Earp nodded.

"Do you know anything else about this fellow?"

"The trail's a couple of weeks old. Rudabaugh rides with a man named Mike Roarke and a handful of other ruffians. They've taken a liking to robbing railroad construction camps and pay trains. They'll be carrying money, some gold, but mostly paper with a lot of it Santa Fe scrip. If you see any floating around, chances are those boys dropped it."

"What's keeping me from earning a few dollars pointing you out to them, if I find them?"

"I can do more for you than they can," Earp said.

"But they'd pay more."

"You're a man that weighs the odds, Holliday. The odds are always with me."

"Just don't spoil those odds by hanging around me for a few days."

"You do your job, and I'll do mine."

"Then I'll be leaving," Holliday answered. "Best we not spend enough time together for anyone to get suspicious. Good day, gentlemen." Doc turned and grabbed the door knob.

"And good luck," Earp called.

"Won't need any luck, if the odds are always with you, now will we, Earp?"

****

Kate traced the bony ridges of Holliday's back. He lay on his side motionless, his heavy breath puffing in the cold room. As Kate snuggled closer to him, pressing herself against his back, Holliday spurned her. Kate hated this mood, which came over him from time to time. His flashes of anger and even his rebuffs, she could tolerate because the reasons were clear. But his moods of indifference were borne somewhere within, somewhere beyond her reach, deep in his consumption-wracked body. He would brood for days, despite her efforts, until he resolved the problem himself. Given a choice, she'd have preferred him angry, but Doc rarely gave her a choice.

Kate flopped back over on the bed and stared at the ceiling lit by the flickering lamp on the bedside table. It was no use, she thought, jerking the blankets around her neck. "If I bother you, I'll leave."

"You're not pestering me. Now." Holliday sighed.

"Something's bothering you."

"It's not you, at least now."

"Meaning it was me a moment ago." Kate reached for Doc and pulled him on his back without a struggle. "Look at me," she said, and for once he obeyed. "It's her again, isn't it? You're still mooning over Lottie and can't accept she's too good for you."

"Don't insult me or her, Kate. It's times like these when I wish consumption would finish me so I wouldn't have put up with your ravings."

"It's her, isn't it?"

"No. I'm trying to do a favor for a friend, and I haven't had any luck."

"I'm the only friend you've got, Doc. Can't you ever understand that? Nobody here, not even Chancey, cares for you. If you get in trouble, you'll see who your friends are—me."

"This isn't Chancey or Lottie. He isn't from around here. Comes from Kansas."

"Doc, you're not the type that people take to, except for a fool like me."

"A whore like you, right Kate?"

Kate shot up from her pillow and twisted around in bed. She slapped him. Doc sat up, rubbing his cheek. "You dare to call me a whore? Maybe that's what I am, but don't you ever call me that when I'm in bed with you! You can go to hell." Kate flung the covers away. "Let your new friend tend you, and let him keep you warm. I've had it with you."

Doc scrambled for the blankets. "You walk out on me, Kate, and you'll never walk back in."

"And if I leave, you'll never get another woman, at least in the Flat. They think you'll spread your disease. Just try to get one of them to sleep with you."

Kate jumped out of bed onto the cold floor and pulled on her garments. "You've had me for the last time, Doc Holliday, unless you're willing to pay!"

"I can afford better than you!"

"Then pay for it." Kate pulled her dress over her head and buttoned the back. "I'll even pay for your first time. You've cost me money every time I've been with you, so this won't be any different. Where's my shoes?"

"No telling."

Walking around the bed, Kate scanned the floor. In the dimness, she spotted her shoes hiding under Holliday's boots. As she bent to put them on, Holliday slapped her rear. "I hope you wither away, all of you," she cried.

"I'll manage."

"Then you'll do so without me."

"But you'll be back, Kate. You always return."

"Come tomorrow or the next day when you get the urge, don't come crawling to my crib unless you've got cash to spend, say three hundred dollars."

"A hundred times your going rate? You won't get that kind of money from me. Even a buffalo hunter without a female for a year wouldn't pay that much. No, sir."

Kate yanked the room key from around her neck and threw it at Holliday. "I won't need this anymore." She jerked her coat on and shoved her hand inside the pocket, pulling out a fist full of bills. "In fact, I'll give you some of this funny money to buy you a woman. It's probably worthless, anyway." She flung the paper at his bed, and it fluttered about the room. Holliday snatched at the air for one which landed on the covers at his chest.

"Take this," he said, wadding the bill up, "and—" He drew back to toss it at her, then stopped. "Just a moment, Kate." Quickly, he unwadded the money.

Kate stepped toward the door and twisted the handle. "Bye, Doc, it was good for a time." She turned for a last glimpse, but he stared at paper like he'd never seen funny money before. "Bye," she repeated, and against her will, she opened the door and stepped into the hall.

"Wait. Come back, Kate," he called.

He must do more, Kate thought, than just call her back. Now Holliday must come after her. When she was half way down the hall, she heard the door open behind her.

"Kate, don't leave," his voice pleaded. She felt a tear sliding down her cheek, but she fought the impulse to run to him as she twisted about, hoping, praying for his arms to be outstretched. He held up a bill. "Where'd you get this?"

Another tear dropped from her watery eyes. Her voice came as a whisper. "Do you want me or that funny money?"

"Both." Holliday gestured for Kate to return.

"Then you come to me, Doc." She dabbed at her eyes as she waited. Holliday, wearing but his long johns, looked both ways down the hall, then stepped to her. When she felt his hand on her arm, she started to say how she felt about him.

But he spoke first. "I must know where you got this." He held the bill before her flooding eyes.

"What is it?" She walked with him to the room, but only after shutting and latching the door did he answer.

"It's Atchison, Topeka and Santa Fe Railway scrip—what the railroad uses to pay its people."

"No railway around here."

"Just where'd you get it?"

"A man, tall, scraggly beard. Smelled like he hadn't taken a bath since the war."

"You get a name?"

"None, though I heard some others call him Dave."

"How many?" Holliday crawled back in bed under the covers.

"Are answers all you want, or are you going to apologize?"

Holliday threw back the covers for her. "Answer my questions. How many men? When?"

"Three, maybe four of them, two or so weeks ago. How come you're so interested in my customers all of a sudden?"

"Now the men, are they still around?"

"Pals of yours?"

"They still in town?"

"No."

Holliday grimaced.

"But I know where they are."

"Well, where are they?"

"At least I know where they said they were going."

"Their destination?" Holliday asked, as he picked up her key on the leather thong and offered back it to her. "Where were they headed?"

"Doc Holliday, if you want your pals' destination—they looked about your ilk—then you treat me like a lady, not a trollop. No matter what I am; you can act like you don't know. Stay civil or you'll never get another night out of me or the location of your friends."

He jiggled the key toward her. "I want you to keep this."

"Then treat me like a lady for a change."

He dropped the key on her pillow, then rolled on his back and stared at the ceiling as she stood bedside. "Tell me about the book you've been reading, that Chuckleberry Ben, was it?"

"It's *The Adventures of Tom Sawyer*. "Huckleberry Finn. He's a character, just like you and just as impatient."

"He sounds fascinating."

"Just like you," Kate laughed.

Doc patted the mattress at his side for Kate to join him.

Kate hesitated, then picked up the room key and hung it around her neck. "Overheard them say they'd lay low around Fort Davis."

"Thank you, Kate."

"Now, will you marry me?"

Holliday shook his head. "Not today."

"Perhaps another day?"

"Let's sleep on it, Kate."

****

Holliday slipped the cards into the dealing box. "Place your bet, mister."

Wyatt Earp slid a double eagle on the black lady. "I always trust the lady when a gentleman is dealing."

Doc touched the brim of his derby, acknowledging the compliment, then turned to his casekeeper. "Take a break. I can keep up with a single customer for a while." When they were alone, Holliday spoke to Earp in a normal voice. "This cousin you're looking for, would he happen to have a shaggy beard and maybe stink like a gut wagon?"

Earp nodded. "With a better nose, I could smell him out."

Holliday reached slowly into his coat pocket and extracted a half dozen paper bills. "You ever see any of this before?"

Reaching across the table, Earp pinched the paper with his long nimble fingers. "Santa Fe scrip. Seems cousin Dave's been leaving his earnings along the way."

"Railroad men have lots of money."

"Sure would like to find cousin Dave," Earp answered. "To settle a debt."

"My source may not be the most reliable," Holliday paused as another midafternoon customer strolled by, "but from what I hear, he headed for Fort Davis, out in far West Texas toward El Paso."

Holliday pulled a pair of cards out with no result. Earp left his coin on the queen. "Any idea how much lead time my cousin has on me?"

"A couple weeks, maybe three."

"Not a good sign." Earp shoved the Santa Fe scrip back across the table. "At least I know I'm on his trail."

"Keep it to show your cousin, if you catch up with him."

"Obliged."

Holliday pulled another pair of cards from the box without result. "Staying with the lady?"

Earp nodded. "I always stay with a good lady."

"If they decide to stay with you, though, they're sure hard to get rid of," Holliday answered. "I can't guarantee the information about your cousin, remember?"

"Better than what I'd been getting. I'm not one to complain when a man delivers what he promises."

Holliday nodded. "Me neither."

Earp pulled his bet from the lady about the middle of the deck. "I feel my luck's changing. You can only trust the ladies for so long."

"My dealing getting that bad, or have you played a game for more than just fun?"

"When I don't have more pressing matters, I do from time to time deal a hand of poker or rub a faro box."

"Then we both know the face cards are stacked heavy toward the bottom of this deck."

Earp nodded. "You handle the pasteboards pretty well. Maybe we can sit down in an honest game sometime."

"Professional courtesy."

Earp pushed his chair back from the table and stood. "We should try that sometime, but this is not the place, not with the Santa Fe paying me."

"If you pass back through, look me up."

"I'll do it, Holliday. If you're ever up Dodge City way, I'll cheat you at my own table."

"Sounds like a good promise."

"In Dodge City, you'll have a friend.

****

In a bed never shared, Lottie lay on a feather pillow moistened from her tears. For two days now, ever since George Wilhelm had delivered with her supplies a letter from San Antonio, rest had been as scarce as blossoms in January. Without opening it, she knew the letter's author by his ostentatious handwriting. She had asked George to get a message to the one man she could trust—Jack Jacobs. Jack was a decent man, and now she needed a good man. She would have lingered in bed except that Jack might arrive, so she dressed without enthusiasm, waiting in the cool dimness of the house, staring at the missive left on the table where her tears had stained it. The letter's words haunted her every thought, its unexpectedness shaking her, though she knew it had been inevitable. Finally, she lost track of time, understanding only that the hazy light of an ashen gray day came from a western sun. A knock on the door startled her.

She stood and glanced in the mirror over her dresser, wincing at what she saw. Her face was drawn tight around her cheeks and lips, her eyes bloodshot, her hair mussed. A pitiful excuse for a woman, desired by so many and available to no one, she thought. Then she remembered the letter. Almost no one. Lottie stood inspecting herself, knowing it was too late to redeem her appearance.

A second, harder knock sounded at the door. "Lottie, are you home?"

It was Jack Jacobs. She grabbed a brush from her dresser and rushed it through her hair. "Just a moment, Jack," she answered, moving to the door and shaking her auburn tresses until they hung past her shoulders. Opening the door, she spoke. "I'm not much to look at, Jack, but thank you for coming."

Jacobs smiled as he came into her view. Taking off his hat, he stared at her, and Lottie saw the smile sliding away as the shock rose in his eyes. He bit his lip.

"I've aged these last few days, Jack." She smiled. "I'm plain when I'm not fixed up."

He shifted his weight from foot to foot as he rolled up the brim of his hat with his hands. "I've never seen you," he stammered for the right words, "with your hair down."

Lottie remembered differently. Jacobs was too decent a man to make a good liar, she thought. She motioned for him to enter. "Thank you for coming."

"Have you been ill?" He stepped inside, shutting the door behind.

She turned away from Jacobs and walked to the table. Picking up the letter, she folded it and inserted it back in the envelope. "I've not been sick."

Jacobs eased beside Lottie as she faced him. "Something's troubling you. Even in the poor light, I can see you've been crying."

"I'll not light a lamp, or you'll see how bad I look, Jack, but I've received this letter." She offered it to him.

Perplexed, Jacobs took it.

"Jack, I must tell someone I can trust of my problem."

"Nothing you'll say will change my opinion of you, Lottie. There's not a finer woman in these parts."

"A gambling woman?" Lottie broke away from Jacobs so he would not see the tears. "What I tell you, Jack, must remain secret as long as I am around Griffin."

Jacobs nodded as she turned around to face him.

"My real name is Charlotte—" She hesitated. "This you must tell no one ever."

He nodded again.

"My name is Charlotte ...," she began her story. For an hour she told him of her father, her mother and her sister, their life in Kentucky before the war. It had been a prosperous life, a good life. Trips throughout the South and even to the hated northeast. Long riverboat rides with her sitting in her father's lap while he gambled. Dances and balls and young men wooing her. It had been a magnificent life, as the daughter of a prosperous landowner, a state senator, a man known across the state. And a slave owner. Then came the war. Everything changed. Kentucky stayed in the union, but her father aligned himself with the South, even though he was too old to fight.

Lottie was just coming to the age when she was taking young men seriously, yet so many of her beaus were dying on both sides of the dispute.

When the war ended, nothing was left of that life. The land no longer belonged to southern sympathizers. The boys who had marched off to war hobbled back crippled of body or mind, if they returned at all. And, she told Jacobs, when she had needed her father's advice the most, she had refused to heed it. She had made a grave mistake going against his wishes. How it had broken her father's heart. And how she had missed his burial. Her mother and sister were without support then, and she'd taken up gambling, with good intentions, and supported them, her sister in an eastern boarding school and her mother in Kentucky until her death. And then when her sister had finished her education, she had abandoned her older sister, ashamed of her occupation. Then the letter reopened past wounds.

"Read the letter, Jack. It explains the rest."

Jacobs pulled folded paper from the envelope, holding it up to catch what light seeped in the window. He read slowly and shook his head when he finished. "I'm sorry, Lottie."

Lottie walked around the table, her hand clutching her neck. "I must win the Bee Hive for Mike, and then leave the Flat before he finds me, Jack."

"He'll just catch up with you somewhere else. Women gamblers rare. He'd just find out wherever you went. Could be he's bluffing. Sometimes it's best to quit your running."

"But I can't trust him to stop chasing me. I found out too late. It could be tomorrow, or he could already be in town. Who can say?"

"Or never?" he added.

She shrugged.

Jacobs stood. "I best be going before this starts tongues a wagging. Some think you entertain men here."

"Rumors likely started by that evil woman John Henry Holliday consorts with."

"Something's been bothering me, Lottie. I know it's not my place to ask, but are you fond of Holliday?"

"In a way, Jack." Lottie brushed the hair back over her shoulder. "He reminds me of men before the war and the days before my life changed. He can be a gentleman, but there is no one in Griffin I am as fond of as you, Jack." She reached for his calloused hands and clenched them. "Maybe it could have been different, Jack, but people like me aren't always what they seem."

"I'm sorry, Lottie, I truly am." He released her hands and put on his hat. "But you shouldn't run away this time. Promise me you'll not leave without telling me."

"I'll stay, Jack," she answered, raising on her toes and kissing him gently upon the cheek. "And I'll tell you before I depart."

Spring

Chapter 16

Pete Haverty flung a horseshoe at a rafter near the stable door. "Damn rat." He spat the words out with a stream of tobacco juice that splattered against the wall. Haverty, his shirt sleeves rolled up, scratched his elbow, then snatched a currycomb from a nail. His impatient jaw worked over his chaw, and his watery eyes, as brown as the tobacco drooling from both corners of his mouth, stared at Holliday. "What was it you wanted?" he asked, then hobbled on a gimpy leg to a rear stall.

Removing his derby, Doc fanned his face to drive away the beading sweat as he followed Haverty through the stable among horses sleek from good feedings. Haverty slipped into the last stall by the rear door and attacked the splotched coat of a frisky pinto with the currycomb. Drawing up beside him, Holliday took in the horse, the stall floor covered with straw, and the nearby water trough. Leaning against a post brushed by the slight breeze wafting in from the back door, Holliday refitted his hat. "Special horse?"

"I like him. Now, what was it you wanted, fellow?"

Holliday pulled a business card from his frock coat pocket and handed to Haverty. "You gave me this card last fall when I stepped off the stage. I want to know if you rented a buggy to Lottie Deno."

Pausing in his chore, Haverty scratched his elbow as he stared uneasily at Holliday over the paint's back. Running his calloused fingers through a mop of hair the color of rotting straw, Haverty cocked his jaw and fired a squirt of tobacco through his brown-stained teeth. "I ain't telling what nobody rents of mine unless they say to. It's bad business."

"I like a cautious man," Holliday said, stepping away from the post into Haverty's full view. He unbuttoned his frock coat and swept the right side behind his gun holster. "Yes, sir, I appreciate a careful fellow, but nobody's gonna get hurt if you answer me. I can't make any promise, if you don't." Holliday dropped his fingers over his Colt's ivory grip.

Haverty choked on his tobacco, then jumped when the pinto blew into the water trough. "Yeah, I rented her a buggy just like I do most Sunday afternoons when the weather's good."

Stroking his moustache, Holliday leaned back into the post and pulled his frock coat over his holstered revolver. "Where'd she go?"

"Up Government Hill to get that pregnant woman, the officer's wife. They cut off the road this side of town like they were heading toward the river bend. Ballgame's in progress there." Haverty hung the currycomb on a nail and crossed his arms over his chest.

Holliday nodded. "Now rent me a good mount and saddle. This paint'll do."

Haverty stammered, shifting his weight from foot to foot, scratching harder at his elbow. "This horse is my runner. I—uh—don't rent him. He's saved for races."

"You're saying I can't have him for the afternoon?"

The stable owner nodded. "I don't let the paint out of the stable without me. The paint's won a lot of money off folks." He slapped the pony on the rump. "Some might want to harm him or doctor him up and try to beat me in a race."

"I admire a cautious man," Holliday said, "but I—"

"Fellow, I'll tell you what. Pick any other mount in the stable, and I'll loan him for the afternoon. No charge. Deal?"

Holliday grinned at Haverty. "This deal's not helping your business any."

"But it's not hurting my racing. Sporting is more fun than livery work. I'll just take a loss here so it don't endanger my racer."

Slapping the horse solidly on the rump, Holliday nodded. "Fine, I'm not too fond of paints, anyway. They're ugly."

"This one gets prettier each time he races. He ought to be gold as much money as he's won. Now, which horse you want?"

Holliday shook his head. "No matter, as long as it looks decent with a good saddle on it. I'll wait outside."

After Haverty brought him a saddled bay, Holliday mounted and rode into the wind, away from the Flat and toward the cheers and laughter drifting on the breeze from downstream. From the sound, many Griffin residents were spending Sunday afternoon away from the smell of town, the buzzing flies, and the dusty streets. Holliday rode beyond thousands of buffalo hides from the winter kill. Like festering sores on the face of the land, the baled hides reeked of rotting flesh singed by the spring sun.

Riding easily in the saddle, Holliday scanned a distant copse of cottonwoods that fanned out in a vee from a broad crook of the Clear Fork. Two lines of buggies and wagons intersected at right angles under the shade of the trees, where spectators rooted for the local team against the boys from Albany, seventeen miles to the south.

The land had infected the observers with a spring laziness. Men and women sat leisurely in their wagons or reclined on quilts in the thick grass, their children running about, disappearing behind the steep bank and moments later coming back in sight a distance away. Holliday rode by the spectators and down the embankment to water his horse. Twisting in his saddle, he studied the river, noting where last year's serpentine summer flood waters had bitten a wagon-sized chunk of bank from under a great cottonwood tree anchoring the river bend. Though the ground at its base appeared solid, the undermined tree tilted toward the river, its exposed roots straining against gravity to carry the load. A handful of boys used the convenient, if dangerous, hiding place to sneak a smoke away from their parents.

When the horse finished watering and blowing, Holliday directed the animal up the bank and among the town folks. The mount shied away from the darting kids playing tag. Holliday's nose perked to the aroma of fried chicken, and he coveted a wishbone as he passed one wagon. Holliday heard from the roughhewn baseball diamond a thud drawing cheers from those around him. He turned in the saddle to see a local favorite racing from one towsack base to another. Holliday glanced at the crowd and shook his head. The game's fascination escaping him, though it seemed popular among merchants and cowhands, gamblers and wives, husbands and whores, hunters and children, soldiers and teamsters. Maybe they had bet money on the outcome.

On the far side of the field, Holliday spotted Lottie, seated elegantly on a pallet beside her buggy. Rachel, now very pregnant, reposed near her. As Holliday aimed his mount toward Lottie, he saw Rachel point her finger at him, her back going as stiff as her expression. He could see Lottie nodding, then looking toward him and back to the game. Holliday guided his horse to her buggy and stopped, twisting in the saddle and lifting one leg over the saddle horn.

"Afternoon, ladies."

"Good day, John Henry Holliday." Lottie smiled and brushed an auburn curl back in place. "You remember Rachel?"

Holliday nodded at Rachel's forced smile, which disappeared behind a cloudy brow. "You look well," he told her.

"John Henry," Lottie said, "I did not realize you enjoyed baseball so. Did you bet on the outcome?"

"I don't wager on child's play." Holliday slid off his horse and, after tying the reins to a buggy wheel, walked to the quilt and squatted in front of Lottie.

Lottie touched her index finger to her chin. "Does your lady friend know about this?"

"You're the only lady I know, Lottie," Holliday said, "excepting Miss Rachel, of course." He tipped his hat toward her. "Spring, being what it is, Lottie, I thought you might reconsider my offer." He looked at Rachel. "In private."

"John Henry has asked for my hand," Lottie said to her companion. Rachel gasped, then flushed in embarrassment. "The seasons have changed, John Henry. My answer has not."

"My run of bad luck with you will change one day, Lottie."

"If your luck changes, Mister Holliday," Rachel interrupted, "then surely Lottie's will have worsened."

Holliday tipped his hat to Rachel again. "Perhaps I am in the company of only one lady after all." He enjoyed the flush of Rachel's cheeks.

"The two of you are acting like children," Lottie scolded. "Let's behave like ladies and gentlemen. John Henry, you may join us, if you avoid a sharp tongue." Lottie gathered her skirt and made more room on the quilt.

As Holliday stepped to the pallet, Rachel struggled against her enlarged stomach to get up. Holliday extended his hand to her. Rachel refused it, but despite her effort, she could not arise. Her shoulders drooping from exertion, she sighed and surrendered to Holliday's still proffered hand. "I think I shall walk while you two visit."

"Don't stray far, nor strain yourself, Rachel." Lottie ordered. "Don't take chances with that baby." As Rachel walked away, Lottie turned to Holliday. "She's a good woman."

"Marriage does her well," Holliday said, sitting in Rachel's vacated spot. "Perhaps you should consider it."

Lottie's Luck

Lottie tossed her head, a soft laugh slipping between her lips and a curl of auburn hair dropping over her ear. She patted the wayward curl and ushered it back in place. "I'm not cut out to be a wife, John Henry."

"It's Charlotte, isn't it? Your name? You're a gambling lady, so some evening let's play a hand of cards. I win, you tell me your full name. You win, I'll never ask or bother you again."

She batted her eyes. "I'm not bothered, John Henry. I'm flattered, me well past my youth and receiving enough attention to make me giddy."

Holliday plucked a pair of wild flowers within reach and handed them to Lottie, enjoying her smile.

She studied the orange, red and yellow petals. "Thank you, John Henry. It has been years since anyone's given me flowers." She twirled the plant stems between the tips of her fingers. "They call these Indian blankets or firewheels."

Holliday leaned over and plucked another to examine.

"They're pretty," Lottie continued. "If I could only make a living picking them instead of men's pockets, I'd be happy."

Holliday nodded. "Seven groups of petals, three petals each cluster, twenty-one total, a flower even a gambler can like."

"Some of the petals have fallen off." Lottie lifted her hands to a blue ribbon in her hair and slipped the two flowers under it. "Always thinking of business, John Henry. You'll never marry or give up gambling."

"Care to bet?" He laughed.

Lottie covered a chuckle with her hand. "See what I mean? You'd bet on anything."

"Not this infernal game," Holliday answered, gazing at the playing field. "What people get from this escapes me, Lottie."

"They get away from Griffin."

Holliday tossed his flower in the Flat's direction and stood up. "It doesn't bother all of us. Every town has its smell, but I could take you away from this one."

"And I could take myself away, if I desired to go."

"Tell me your name." He stepped to his bay.

"I'll not dishonor my family name by disclosing it. Once it was a proud name in Kentucky before the war and before I became a gambler."

Holliday untied the bay's reins. "It's still a proud name!"

"But the answer would still be no."

Holliday spotted Rachel staring at him from behind a nearby wagon. "I should go. Your friend is tiring herself."

"You worry her, John Henry, but she's a good woman."

"You're a good woman, too, Lottie. If you ever walk away from the game, I'll walk with you." He shoved his boot in the stirrup.

"There you go, John Henry, though I'm not sure if all this flattery is for my hand or if you're trying to distract me."

He swung into the saddle. "Distract you from what?"

"Fogle's asked for his shot to win back the Bee Hive. I figured Chancey would've mentioned it to you by now."

"First word I've had of it. Maybe you're trying to distract me, Lottie." Holliday smiled. "Make me question Chancey's faith in handling his play."

"For a man who has all but proposed, you are most suspicious of the woman you would take for a wife."

"When it comes to gambling, Lottie, I can't take too many precautions."

"Nor can I when it comes to marriage, John Henry."

Holliday tipped his hat. "Good day, Lottie. I hope your friend Rachel does not find your quilt too soiled by my touch to take the load off her feet."

Holliday nudged his bay across the baseball field, instead of around it. Spectators jeered, and Holliday enjoyed their catcalls, tipping his hat as he passed.

He rode the horse straight for Griffin, leaving the animal at Haverty's and hurrying to the Cattle Exchange. He barged into Chancey's office without knocking and found the proprietor hunkered over his strong box, counting Saturday's take. "Has Fogle hit you up for a game?"

"Not yet, Doc, but I've heard rumors he plans to. I put little stock in that gossip."

****

His legs crossed on the bed, a bottle of Monarch Bourbon between them, Holliday shuffled the cards and dealt around the bed four hands, bottom dealing some cards, second dealing others, and occasionally taking the top card. In turn, he uncovered each hand, a pair in the first he expected, three of a kind in the second he didn't, and nothing in the third. His own hand was two pair. Discarding as an opponent might, he then dealt replacements, his hand becoming a full house, which topped the hands of his imaginary partners. Five-card draw, he practiced it again and again against three imaginary opponents. In his mind, they all were Lottie. He worked to take the chance out of chance. But how to set her up? She would be too shrewd to take a set hand. It would be too obvious. Then again, it just might fool her. Maybe the most blatant way would be the safest. Just deal her a pat hand and draw to his own hand, a higher one. Lottie could be taken, no gambler being unbeatable, but she would be no pushover. Holliday dealt two hands, himself against Lottie, manipulating the cards to his advantage, thinking out a ploy for the game that would count, a game that he anticipated would come sooner than Chancey expected.

At a knock on his door, Holliday set the bottle on the floor and reached for the pistol in his shoulder holster. Then he heard the key in the lock.

"What do you want, Kate?"

The door flung open and Kate barged in. "I want to talk to you, Doc."

Why did she always interrupt? He reached for his bourbon again. "Shut the door."

Kate slammed the door behind her. "What were you doing with Lottie yesterday?" She crossed her arms over her bosom.

"Talking, that's all we did."

"You could've come to me. I'd a talked to you."

"I went to the baseball game to get away from the stink of this place."

"You don't like foolishness like ball games. You like cards and whiskey and Lottie."

"There was better than two hundred people there. What of it, if our paths crossed?"

"You're still seeing her, that's what, and after all I've done for you."

He dealt a practice hand of cards on the bed. "No concern of yours, Kate."

"You'll walk away from me one too many times, Doc?"

He glanced up from the deal. "Every road heads two directions."

"Maybe I should just leave, make something of myself instead of throwing my life away with you."

"Stages leave Tuesdays and Saturdays, Kate. I'll buy your fare. I still owe you for the funny money you gave me."

"I was in town before you. Why don't *you* leave?"

"Same reason you don't. There's money here for the taking. I'm not through taking."

"You only take, Doc. You never give."

"Sure I give," Holliday said, squeezing the cards in his hands together. "Take this." He threw the deck at her.

Kate jumped back, but several cards hit her. She drew her arm to slap him and rushed for the bed. Before she reached him, he coughed hard and his face reddened. He fell back on the mattress, grimacing as another cough assaulted his body. Her hand flew to her mouth, then fell limp at her side as she bent over him. "I'm sorry, Doc. I didn't mean for this to happen." She handed him his bourbon.

Holliday grabbed the bottle, but was coughing too hard to take a swig. He sat up, his eyes wild and uncertain. Kate pounded him on the back.

"Don't die on me, Doc," Kate whispered. "You're all I've got in Griffin. You might not be much, but you're all I got. Let me take care of you, Doc."

"Nothing you can do. Nothing anybody can do."

"Maybe I could give you a little happiness." She ran her fingers through his hair, then rubbed his back. "We could marry and become respectable."

"If you want marriage, then maybe there are some other things you should give up."

"I gotta make a living, Doc, no different from you."

He sighed and hugged her. Holliday was running his fingers through her hair when someone pounded on the door.

"Doc, you there?"

Holliday recognized Chancey's voice. "What's bothering you, Chancey?"

"Need to talk."

"The door's unlocked."

Chancey barged in. "You were late coming in, and I wondered if something was—" He stopped when he saw Kate. "I should've known Kate delayed you."

"I've been late before, Chancey."

"Not when Fogle's called in his chips. Tomorrow night we play."

Lottie wasn't bluffing after all, Holliday thought.

Chapter 17

The water rippled through a rock-bottomed shallow where Holliday nudged his horse into the Clear Fork. He saw downstream an orange-hued blanket of flowers hugging the bank in the afternoon shade of a cottonwood. A twist of his wrist on the reins sent the bay in that direction, prancing as briskly as the breeze. Here, away from the Flat, the air smelled of spring sweetness. The land promised more green than scanty summer rains would fulfill, and a rainbow of wildflowers lay trapped between earth and sky, waving their violet, yellow, blue, red, and orange petals as if they could fly, were they freed from stem and root.

As Holliday anticipated, the firewheels Lottie had admired at the baseball game dominated the flower patch that was his destination. Dismounting, Holliday pulled a towel from under a leather saddle strap and carried it to the creek. Stepping along the water's muddy fringe, he bent and soaked the towel, then wrung it as he retreated to the blooms. Looking first to see that no one spied him, he then searched for firewheels with twenty-one petals. He plucked over four dozen and swathed them in the moist cloth to preserve the bouquet until nightfall when he and Lottie would play for the Bee Hive.

Though he suspected a wagonload of bouquets would never change her feelings for him, perhaps these few would fluster her concentration tonight. He wished the flowers were more than a gambling ploy. Standing by the bay as it nibbled green strands of fresh grass, Holliday enjoyed the shade's coolness. The breeze through the cottonwood blew snowy wisps down from the trees, coating the ground in places with a carpet of white, the color of a virgin's bed. Ironic, he thought, that he had such emotions for a woman he planned to cheat in a few hours.

Holliday the flowers in the crook of his arm, he mounted the bay and rode a half mile downstream to the bend where the baseball game had occurred. For a while, he let his horse graze as he stared at the giant cottonwood somehow suspended above the creek despite the bank undercut beneath it. Then, riding on beyond the majestic tree, Holliday saw in the distance a cloud of dust marking another cow herd following the trail north toward Dodge City. Thousands of cattle had passed over the route, leaving no grass but plenty of fertilizer. Holliday heard the balky cattle's faint bellows carrying across the land like a haunting lullaby.

By the lengthening shadows, Holliday knew he must return soon or Chancey would fret. He rode away from the creek, hitting the road for Griffin and riding toward the Flat. Checking his pocket watch, he noted three hours of leeway, plenty of time for a hot bath, a good shave, and a change of clothes before the game.

Nearing the Flat, he watched a rider approaching from the creek crossing. The horseman rode tall in the saddle, his shoulders thrown back and his head erect, his chin jutting forward. Holliday recognized Wyatt Earp, the Santa Fe railway operative.

Coming within talking distance, Holliday waited for Earp to acknowledge their acquaintance. Earp rode silently toward him, Holliday detecting a glint of recognition in his eye. As their horses met, Earp drew back on the reins.

"How you doing, Doc?" Earp smiled, extending his hand. "

"Still winning more than I'm losing," he replied, grasping Earp's hand firmly, then feeling a flush of foolishness at the bouquet he carried. "You find your lost cousin?"

Earp eyed the flowers. "Missed him, though your information was good. He stayed in Fort Davis for a spell, then cut out for New Mexico Territory. I'm not chasing him there, but maybe this'll get him out of the Santa Fe's hair for good." Pointing to the rough bouquet, Earp cocked his head. "Wedding or funeral?"

"Poker game."

Earp chuckled. "You must play cards with fancier fellows than I run into."

"It's not a fellow. It's Lottie Deno."

"Heard she's a looker."

Holliday reddened. "Quiet a looker, but an even better card player. Let's move to the shade of the trees, Wyatt, and talk a little more."

"The cottonwoods spook me. Found a man hanging in one west of town."

"I hadn't heard."

"Seems there was a shooting last night. Sheriff took this fellow into custody and kept him over night in one of the hotels, for some reason. Sheriff Larn was to take him to the Albany jail today, but the vigilantes broke in and relieved him of his charge. I found him, air dancing from a cottonwood. The sheriff didn't seem a mite upset when I reported the body. He just shrugged and said maybe it would discourage troublemakers from coming to Griffin."

"Vigilantes were active last spring hanging horse thieves, I hear," Holliday said. "Another fellow was lynched in the fall about the time I arrived."

Earp nudged his mount on along the trail, and Holliday turned his bay around to accompany him. "Take care of yourself. Don't overturn a barrel of trouble with those folks."

"I keep the odds on my side, Wyatt."

"Can't always depend on the odds, Holliday, not in a town like Griffin. It's been around long enough now that the upstanding folks want to get rid of the seedy types that made them and the town prosper. Griffin's at its peak, maybe on the downslide, and when the fine local citizens get nervous about our kind, they organize as vigilantes to make their town respectable."

Holliday coughed. "This consumption'll kill me before the vigilantes do."

Earp stuck his hand out to Holliday. "If you ever get in trouble or need a friend, look me up in Dodge City."

"I'll do it, and I'll hello Chancey for you."

Earp laughed. "Chancey's a good one, except in a tight. He looks after himself first."

"Maybe I'll look you up someday when business slacks off around here."

Earp slapped his horse's flank and rode into the distance.

****

"I don't like it," Chancey said with a sigh that bloomed into a cloud of cigarette smoke. The stairs groaned at his heavy steps. "The killing last night, the vigilantes, the hanging. That's not a good sign."

"You worry too much," Holliday said, following him up the stairs of the Bee Hive. Holliday smelled of soap and tonic water; his shirt new; his suit laundered; and his derby brushed. Walking at Chancey's side, Doc shielded the bouquet of firewheels behind Chancey's broad back.

"Maybe I'd worry less if you'd ever beaten Lottie's Luck, Doc! It's my saloon and money you'll be playing for."

"You want to play the hand yourself? I remember you groaning over buying half the Bee Hive instead of winning it outright. By evening's end, you'll own the whole thing. Lottie's Luck or not."

"If you don't believe in Lottie's Luck, Doc, then why in hell are you gussied up and carrying her flowers?" His voice was as pointed as stretched barbed wire.

Holliday angered at his tone. "Are you behind me or not?"

The question hung in the air until they reached the top of the stairs. Chancey drew deep on his cigarette, then flicked it at a spittoon by the landing. "I am, as long as you cheat her," he exhaled smoke with his words.

Holliday touched his freshly waxed moustache. "Then you're behind me." As Chancey laughed, Doc spotted Lottie across the room. She never looked better. Beneath the tiger snarling out of a gaudy broadside on the wall, she stood near her faro table, wearing a pale yellow dress with a high neck that buttoned up the front and set off her auburn hair like the flame from a candle. Her face was powdered, her cheeks rouged, her lips tinted pink. When his eyes met hers, Holliday tipped his hat, then pulled the bouquet from behind Chancey's back. Seeing the flowers, Lottie smiled.

"Just remember your betting my money, Doc."

"You're welcome to play your own hand, Chancey."

Lottie moved as softly as a yellow cloud from her table toward Holliday, raising her hand as she neared. Doc took it, lifting her fingers to his lips and kissing them. Then he wrapped her fingers around the bouquet of firewheels. "For the lady," he said, tipping his hat.

"Every lady loves flowers, John Henry. I must credit your persistence." Lottie spoke with a coolness as she lifted the flowers to her nose. "You forget that tonight I am no lady."

"Others should determine that."

"Tonight," Lottie said, "the cards will be the judge of everything." She released the flowers, and they tumbled to the floor as useless as broken promises.

Chancey stepped beside Holliday. "You dropped your flowers, Lottie."

Lottie's soft features turned hard, her jaw like chiseled granite until she spoke. "Mike was a fool to get tied up with you, Chancey."

Pointing his finger at her breast, Chancey matched the venom in her words. "You just be sure, Lottie Deno, that your partner Fogle has enough to cover his losses."

"I'll back him with every cent I've got against you or any other man that takes me for a common wag-tail."

"Good women don't frequent saloons." Chancey wadded his fingers into a fist and pounded his hand.

"And good men respect women," she said, her words simmering. She glanced at Holliday. "You are in the employ of a low man, John Henry. It'll bring you bad luck." She offered Doc her arm, and together they walked to a vacant table.

As Holliday pulled out a chair for Lottie, Chancey turned to Holliday. "Make this quick, Doc. Show her it's a man's game."

"Enough chatter," Holliday said, taking his seat and waving Chancey away. In his coat pocket, Holliday carried a rigged deck and an honest pack. "Five-card draw, my cards," he told Lottie. She would ask to inspect the cards, so he withdrew the straight deck from his pocket, broke the seal on the box, removed the pasteboards, then unwrapped them from their brown paper shroud. "Your money?" he asked Lottie, and Mike Fogle stepped to her side, dropping a packet of bills on the table.

Chancey slapped an envelope of his own in front of Holliday. "There's more where that came from."

Holliday shuffled the cards, tossing them from hand to hand, slowly at first, waiting for Lottie to ask to inspect the deck, then faster and harder when he realized she had forgotten the precaution. The argument with Chancey had distracted her. Disgust knotted in Holliday's stomach for not risking the rigged deck. Unknowingly, she had already outwitted him.

A ring of observers pressed around the table as Holliday left the cards for Lottie to cut. Holliday glanced at the faces as Lottie split the deck, his gaze stopping at a fleshy mug that made his own face tighten into a scowl. Behind her stood Ed Bailey. Damn! Now he must keep up with Bailey as well as the cards. Holliday picked up the two stacks from Lottie's cut. "No betting ceiling. Five-card draw. Ante a hundred dollars."

Lottie nodded and tossed her wager on the table, Holliday matching it. With the fresh deck, the deal didn't matter, so Holliday dealt straight, then placed the deck on the green felt and corralled his cards, lifting them to his chest, fanning the corners, an ace and two deuces appearing. Holliday would spar with these early hands, stacking the deck and setting Lottie up for the big hand. The ace would come in handy later. He rearranged his cards, the ace with the two discards, then looked into Lottie's impenetrable gray eyes, her emotionless face.

"I'll go another hundred. Two cards," she said, tossing a pair to the middle of the table.

Holliday matched her bet and replenished her cards. "Lady takes two," he called. Perhaps she had three of a kind with her luck. "Dealer wants three," he said, collapsing his three discards into a pile—the ace on top—and dropping them diagonally across the deadwood. He dealt himself a trio. A pair of fives appeared to reinforce his weak deuces. Still, they would be useless against her matching triplets, Holliday guessed.

Lottie bumped the pot another hundred. "You staying?"

Holliday rearranged his cards, deuces and fives, until the deuce and five of clubs were together. "Dealer folds," he said. As he closed his cards, his hands screened them for an instant, just long enough for the two clubs to slide up his sleeve. His other discards he placed atop the deck, not the deadwood.

Lottie smiled and threw her cards into the deadwood with enough force to scatter Holliday's neat stacks. Damn, Holliday thought. Now he couldn't be sure which one was the ace he had hoped to save. When she reached for the pot, Holliday nicked with his thumbnail the corner of the suspected ace of hearts. As he straightened the deadwood, Holliday slid the marked card to the bottom of the deck. Lottie stacked her winnings, oblivious to the cheating. She was growing careless.

So was Ed Bailey with his boisterous talk, saying how quickly Lottie would clean out Holliday. Doc felt the anger roiling in his throat, and his breath whistling between his teeth. He must control his temper, Holliday thought, or Lottie would thrash him.

"Chancey," he called, "see that I get a bottle of whiskey and a jigger." Chancey grunted and snapped his finger at one of the roving Bee Hive barkeeps. The bottle and glass arrived as Holliday finished shuffling. Putting the deck down, he poured a drink, spilling a puddle the size of a quarter eagle on the table, then downed the liquid. As he reclaimed the deck, he angled it in his hand as he dealt. From the reflection in the spilled bourbon, he confirmed the ace of hearts was on the bottom. Holliday manipulated the cards through three more hands, claiming two pots and Lottie winning the third. All were puny pots. So far, he and she were running even—except for the ace on the bottom of the deck and the two clubs up his sleeve. Holliday tossed another hand across the table to Lottie.

"You're forgetting your ante." Lottie smiled.

Holliday matched Lottie's bet, then poured himself another drink before picking up his cards and fanning them out. "Maybe this is my hand, Lottie."

"Three cards." She tossed an unwanted trio onto the table.

Holliday ignored her.

"Three," she repeated.

She was getting edgy. Holliday could feel it. Would she make a play before he dealt her the rigged hand? Holliday stared at two kings, two worthless cards, and the seven of clubs. He needed the seven to build the straight flush he was saving up his sleeve. He separated his cards, stacking two on the deadwood and leaving the seven of clubs on the bottom of his three keepers. After picking up the deck, he tossed three cards to Lottie. "Dealer takes three," Holliday said, and dropped three more on his keepers. He straightened the cards between his fingers, then laid them in his palm, coughing as he pushed the extra card, the seven of clubs, into his cuff. Holliday studied Lottie, and her eyes seemed oblivious to the swindle. Then he spread his cards. He had lucked out on the draw, the pair of kings being joined by two nines. Doc nodded toward Lottie. "You in?"

Lottie upped the pot two hundred dollars. "I'm with you."

Holliday grinned. "I'll raise you another hundred and call your hand." He shoved the money toward the middle of the table.

Lottie matched him, then revealed her cards. "Aces and fours."

"You beat my kings and nines, Lottie." Shaking his head, Holliday tossed his cards on the pile, sorry to have lost, but glad two more aces had turned up.

As Lottie pulled in the pot, Holliday heard Ed Bailey laughing loudest among all the spectators. Holliday glared from the table to Bailey's puffy face. Their eyes met, and Bailey's laugh strangled in his throat. When Doc glanced back at the cards, she had already added hers to the deadwood. Holliday damned Ed Bailey for distracting him long enough to lose her two aces in the discards. Doc bit his lip. The aces? He should have forgotten Bailey and kept his eyes on them. He must find them. His hand reached for the discards, his fingers picking them up just as a cough ripped out of his lungs, three cards falling from his fingers and overturning on the felt. Two were the aces of spades and clubs. His cough improved. He mixed the cards, manipulating the pair of aces to join their mate on the bottom of the deck. Now he needed the ace of diamonds.

He shuffled the cards, tossing them from hand to hand. "Ante, Lottie." Around her, the crowd seemed restless. Holliday shared their impatience, needing the ace of diamonds and three more clubs. He dealt another hand, finding in his the diamond ace and two clubs—the three and six—he needed. Lottie called for two cards without raising the pot. He obliged her, then she folded without comment. Damn her! Though he had won the pot, she had made it harder for him to sleeve the clubs. Instead, he slid them with the ace to the bottom of the deck.

"You're giving up too easily, Lottie."

"I'm ahead in the play."

"But Chancey still owns half the Bee Hive."

"We're still playing," she said matter-of-factly.

Holliday finagled the cards again, but too many were accumulating on the bottom. Six keepers there. He held the deck in the palm of his left hand as a cough screamed out of his lungs, then another, and he raised his right hand to Lottie. "May I get—," he coughed again, "—my handkerchief?"

Lottie nodded. Holliday shook his head, trying to throw the cough. Then, in one fluid motion, he screened the cards from Lottie by twisting his left palm toward his chest. With his right hand, he extracted the deck—except for the bottom two cards—and placed it on the table. As Lottie watched his right hand disappear into his coat for the handkerchief, his left hand flicked the two additional clubs up his sleeve. Now only the four of clubs was lacking, he thought as he coughed into the clean handkerchief.

"Your cough, John Henry, strikes at the oddest times."

She knew something was amiss. "Way it is with consumption," he answered.

Holliday, growing impatient for the four of clubs, split the next two hands with Lottie. He took the subsequent hand with a full house over Lottie's three fours, including the four of clubs. He pulled the pot in, then the deadwood. As he drew the discards to the deck, his thumbnail nicked the edge of the four. Rearranging the deck, Holliday slipped the four to the bottom of the stack with the four aces.

He evened the deck and, as he placed it on the table, he palmed the top three cards in his right hand. His left hand moved catlike from his money stack to the table's center for the ante. "Your ante," he told Lottie. When he jerked his left hand away from the pot, the sleeved cards slid into his palm. As he picked up the deck, he dropped those cards on top, then covered them with the three palmed cards in his right hand. He began his series of false shuffles, tossing the cards in batches from hand to hand, but always preserving the order at the top and bottom. As he shuffled, Lottie asked Mike Fogle to send for an iced glass of lemonade.

Finally, Holliday sat the deck on the table. "Cut?"

Lottie tapped the cards with her finger and, for a moment, Holliday sat disbelieving. She had declined a cut and instead sipped at the just arrived lemonade. Could she know more than he had figured out? Holliday picked up the cards, looked at Lottie, then shook his head.

He dealt her the top card from the deck. He didn't know what it was; it didn't matter. From the bottom, he dealt himself the four of clubs. Next, he passed her an ace from the bottom. From the top, he took an unknown card for himself. Another ace from the bottom for her hand and another unknown from the top for him. Another ace for her from the bottom. He studied her, but she betrayed no emotion. Then, from the top, he took the first of the stacked clubs. From the bottom he passed her a final ace and from the top he gave himself his third club.

Holliday dropped the deck and watched Lottie spread her cards apart. Her face never quivered, but behind her, Ed Bailey craned his neck for a glimpse of her cards. His mouth widened. Bailey's eyes glanced to Holliday, and his lips spread into a knowing grin.

Studying his own cards—four, five and seven of clubs along with a ten of spades and queen of hearts—Holliday realized a mistake. Damn, he hadn't placed the clubs in good order! Without the six of clubs, he might not draw into his straight flush. He might lose the saloon yet. Damn it all, the three of clubs would ruin him, too, if he didn't get it. He must get both the three and six, not the two of clubs to beat her. His throat went dry and tight. He grabbed for the bottle, this time unintentionally spilling liquor as he filled the jigger.

Lottie closed her cards and exchanged them for a stack of bills in front of her. Thumbing through the money, she spoke. "I'll up the pot five hundred, John Henry. You in?"

"I'll see you and raise you another five hundred."

"I'm in." She sipped at the lemonade, then spoke again. "And I'll bet Fogle's half of the Bee Hive against Chancey's."

The trap was sprung, Holliday thought, as Fogle edged toward Lottie. She leaned forward over the table, waiting for an answer. Reaching to her neck, she undid the top two buttons on her high collar.

"A lady shouldn't undress in the presence of gentlemen." Holliday nodded.

Lottie cleared her throat. "I make no claims to be a lady tonight. Are you in or not?"

"I'm in with Chancey's half of the Bee Hive. How many cards?"

Now Lottie stalled, re-examining her cards. Holliday knew she didn't want to appear too anxious. With four aces, you have little to consider except whether to discard for a higher off.

"Having second thoughts about your bet, Lottie?"

Her gray eyes stared over the top of her cards. "Might I ask a favor of you, John Henry, before I take my cards?"

"Ask."

"Pass the cards without picking up the deck this time."

Damn, he thought. He couldn't say no without being accused of cheating. If he said yes and Lottie got the three or six of clubs, his straight flush was ruined. She had a two out of three chance of beating him. Damn it, now he believed in Lottie's Luck. He hoisted the jigger to his lips and savored the liquor's taste as he figured his chances. "Odd request, Lottie! You suggesting I'm cheating?"

Lottie's eyes fluttered, and she answered. "Certainly not, John Henry. Just wanted to make sure you wouldn't try something that foolish now that the saloon's on the line."

He swallowed hard. "On one condition, I will agree, Lottie."

Lottie closed her cards. "That being?"

"We have a side bet—between you and me—on this hand."

She hesitated a moment, lifted her hand to her chin, and tapped her lips with her index finger. "Okay, how much?"

"Not money, Lottie," he answered. "I win, you tell me your name, your full name."

"And if I win, John Henry?"

"I'll never ask again, nor think you would ever tell me."

Lottie picked up her cards, fanned them out again, then collapsed them into a single pile. "It's a bet, John Henry, but a hand of cards will not mean a change of heart."

"Fair enough. How many cards do you want?"

She raised her hand to her chin again and tapped her lips with her fingers.

"How many cards, Lottie?"

She fanned her cards out. "Three, John Henry, three."

****

Maybe Holliday was one step ahead of her, Lottie thought. But his jaw went slack, and his eyelids blinked when she said three cards. He sat in motionless disbelief. "Three cards, John Henry. Three cards," she repeated. Behind her, Ed Bailey gasped, and she realized he had been watching her cards. At least she could be sure he wasn't in cahoots with Holliday.

Four aces and a nine. Wasn't much room to improve upon that, but John Henry had been manipulating the cards since the game started, false shuffles, false cuts, and maybe even slipping cards up his sleeve when he coughed. Consumption allowed a gambler at a card table some liberties for which a healthy man might be shot. Holliday had been playing to set her up. Only a straight flush would beat four aces. Holliday wouldn't dare deal her and himself set hands. He must draw for cards, otherwise it would be too obvious a setup. He would take two, maybe three cards. Two, most likely. He would be playing her to hold her four aces and maybe discard the fifth card for a higher one. If she ruined his straight, she could win with a lesser hand than she received. Taking two cards would leave her three aces, but if Holliday had stacked enough on the deck, he might still pull out a straight flush. If she discarded the nine and two aces, she'd still have a pair, and it would beat any pair Holliday could come up with.

Then perhaps Holliday had figured she'd suspect a pat hand and was playing her to think just as she was, then he'd pull in three of a kind to win over her pair of aces. Maybe he had even stacked both sides of the deck so he could play either way. So, she had asked him to leave the deck on the table. If he had two options then, now he would have but one. She hoped he wasn't a step ahead of her.

Holliday reached for the deck.

"Remember our bet, John Henry. Leave them on the table."

Holliday's scowl surprised Lottie, and she knew by his emotion that she had beaten him. He snapped each card from the deck and tossed it across the table as she threw her three discards to the center and gathered the new cards. Slowly, she fanned them open. Ace of spades, ace of hearts, six of clubs, three of clubs, two of clubs. Holliday had been going for a straight flush of low clubs. Unless he had lucked into three of a kind or two pair from the unrigged cards, she had beaten him.

"Dealer takes three," Holliday called. He eased them off the deck on the table and added them to his good cards. His stony face reflected defeat. Then he folded his cards together and stared blankly at Lottie.

"I'll raise you two thousand," Lottie said, rubbing it in. She counted out the bills. "Are you in, John Henry?"

Holliday squeezed the cards between his fingers, then threw them atop Lottie's discards. He touched his finger to the brim of his derby. "Dealer folds, Lottie."

Fogle shouted, "God bless, Lottie's Luck." The spectators applauded.

Ed Bailey laughed, a smirk of hatred not pleasure, of mockery, not admiration on his face. Bailey then pushed his way to the table's edge, leaned over and grabbed Holliday's discards from the deadwood. He flipped them face up, back atop the discards and hooted. "Lottie's Luck had nothing to do with it," he called. "Doc's stupidity lost the hand."

Lottie heard the words, and she knew by the flash in Holliday's eyes he had, too.

Chapter 18

Holliday shoved open the door and strode into Uncle Billy Wilson's Eatery, deserted except for the owner. Wilson sat on a stool beside a side window, fanning away the scorching mid-afternoon sun with a folded copy of last week's *Frontier Echo*. As Holliday seated himself at the table running the length of the room, Wilson inched off his seat and started toward the gambler, stopping to catch his breath and stare into the kitchen. "Hot weather be rough on a big man," he said as he wiped the sweat from his brow with his apron. "Wish't I was a thin man like ya. Heat don't bother ya?"

"Take up gambling for a living, Uncle Billy," Holliday replied. "You'd sweat even more and eat less." He glanced across the table set with tin plates and utensils, but barren of food.

Wilson chuckled as he drew up opposite Holliday, lifting a ham of a leg upon the bench, leaning forward, and resting his arms on his knee. "Mrs. Wilson wouldn't like me bein' near the saloon girls. I'm not the best lookin' husband in Shackelford County, but I'm hers, and she doesn't plan on sharing me."

"Food, Uncle Billy, what you got?"

Wilson lifted his hands from his leg and recited what would be ready in another hour. "Buffalo stew left from lunch is all I can offer now. This is me slowest time between dinner and supper. Fresh food'll be ready in an hour, maybe."

"A bowl of that stew will do, if it won't poison me."

Wilson grinned and retreated to the kitchen, where Holliday heard him giving orders to his wife. Shortly, he returned with a bowl of stew and a mug of coffee, his sweat dripping into both. He placed them before Holliday, then took a seat.

Doc dipped his spoon in the steaming concoction and shoved it in his mouth, grimacing at the saltiness. The pasty conglomeration had simmered too long on a hot stove, and his scalded portion had been scraped from the bottom of a burnt pot. Holliday could see specks of char in the second bite that went down his gullet. As bad as it was, he ate it in the hope Wilson wouldn't jaw at him so much. But Wilson let no customer eat in peace.

"Ya read the *Frontier Echo*?" he queried, fanning himself with the folded copy.

Holliday shook his head.

"Pete Haverty got a reply to his advertisement. Yes, sir, all the way from San Antone, the answer came."

Enduring another bite of stew, Holliday grunted. If the conversation was coming anyway, why force himself to eat more? He lingered over the meal, not caring to head for the Cattle Exchange this early, not after losing the Bee Hive last night.

Wilson adjusted his spectacles, then unfolded the paper and pointed to a small box on the front page. "'Pete Haverty of only Livery, Feed and Stage Stable in town will swap or run horses.'" Wilson refolded the paper and fanned himself with it. "Fellow all the way down in San Antone wrote challengin' Haverty to race horses, sight unseen. Crazy fool that Haverty is; he's gonna run his pinto against this fellow, come Saturday. Be a lot of cash thrown around the Flat on that one, eh? Haverty's pinto's never been beaten around here. Darn fools in the Flat will bet on anything, but I can't understan' them throwing their money away on an animal as dumb as a horse."

"Horses ain't as dumb as you think, Uncle Billy." Holliday washed the stew's salty sediment down with a sip of coffee. "You don't see any of them betting on people."

Wilson laughed, then noticed Holliday's dwindling coffee. "Let me bring a pot over." He waddled to the kitchen.

Enjoying the quiet in Wilson's absence, Holliday toyed with the spoon in his stew. He tried another bite, his tongue rebelling against the taste, and gave up on eating.

Wilson shuffled back to the table, a steaming coffee pot in his mitted hand. "Yes, sir," he said as he filled Holliday's cup, "I'd place me money on the pinto most times, but I'd sure like to see what he's runnin' against, if it's comin' all the way from San Antone." He set the coffee pot on the table near Holliday.

"An ugly horse like that pinto deserves to be beaten." Holliday spit the words out as if they were the stew.

Lottie's Luck

Wilson lifted his foot and dropped it on the bench beside his customer. "No, sir, it's not a pretty horse, but it's got a good heart. Reminds me of an animal I saw in Californy durin' the spring of fifty, durin' the rush, I tell ya. This horse was the scrawniest, ugliest critter I ever seen with less than six legs. Blind in one eye, walked with a limp. At least that's what he'd been trained to do we figured out later, but darn if he didn't outrun by six lengths the best looking horseflesh I ever seen. Taught me a lesson about horses, it did. Ya can't judge a horse by his color. Same way with a woman. Ya gotta see the heart to know what it's like. Take Mrs. Wilson. She's not much to look at compared to some of those saloon girls I see walkin' around bringin' outlandish notions to me mind, but she's got a good heart, and she's a good worker, and she'd do any man proud. Only one other woman in these parts with as good a heart, and that's Lottie Deno. Course, ya'd know that, Mister Holliday, 'cause every man in these parts has taken a fancy to her."

Holliday nodded, staring into his empty cup, remembering last night.

"A fine woman that Lottie is. She don't put on no airs over everybody. And I hear she's as good a judge at pickin' winnin' horses as she is at playin' cards," Wilson said, leaning forward and slapping his hand on his knee. "Like last night, I hear."

Holliday said nothing.

Wilson continued. "Lottie splittin' up four aces and beatin' ya. At least that's what Ed Bailey's been saying, but ya know 'bout that." His voice lowered to a whisper. "What 'bout the latest hanging, Mister Holliday?"

Holliday gazed from the bowl of stew. He shook his head, and it seemed to rattle like trace chains on a runaway wagon.

Wilson nodded. "Vigilantes are puttin' a scare in the bad element botherin' this town."

The words settled on Holliday as poorly as the stew on his stomach. He shoved his bowl to the center of the table. "Weren't for the bad element, Uncle Billy, you'd be a lot poorer. The better element wouldn't put up with this slop. Even a hog wouldn't eat it." Holliday pitched the coffee cup after the bowl, then reached in his pocket and pulled out two bits, which he slapped on the table.

"Didn't mean no harm, Mister Holliday?"

"You one of 'em, Uncle Billy?" Holliday asked, pushing himself away from the table?

"Huh?"

"One of the vigilantes that's making the laws as they see fit? You make this town respectable, Uncle Billy, and you'll kill it as sure as you bleed a hog at butchering time." Holliday bounced up and walked out, Wilson's sputtering apologies trailing in his wake.

****

Chancey took quick puffs on his cigarette as he glanced through the open door of his office into the saloon. He walked around Holliday and slammed the door.

"Not Bailey, not here." Holliday pounded his fist in his palm.

"I heard you the first time, Doc." Chancey returned to his desk. "If you'd just won the Bee Hive, Doc."

Holliday felt his face pucker. "Would you have broken up four aces on the chance of ruining a straight flush? You'd have to be crazy!"

"Or maybe shrewd, Doc. You ever think she outsmarted you?"

"Luck, Chancey, Lottie's Luck."

"Ha!" Chancey took a final drag on his cigarette, then dropped it on the floor and crushed it with his boot. "You laughed at Lottie's Luck heading into the game. Now you're blaming your losses on it. Seems you want it both ways."

Holliday clenched both fists, the rage throbbing in his temples. "And you can't have it both ways, Chancey. Me and Bailey here'll mean trouble."

"You're a decent dealer, Doc, among the best." Chancey paused, pulling the makings of another cigarette, his eyes avoiding Holliday's. "But the fact is, Bailey has more friends in this town than you do. Some come in to play that wouldn't bet a dollar against any other dealer. You may make me more profit, but Bailey adds the extra that nobody else gets."

"He'll treat his pals better than you, Chancey. Fact is, he enjoyed me losing the Bee Hive. He's too dumb to figure it might mean his job."

Chancey licked the tobacco-loaded cigarette paper and looked down at Holliday. He jammed his cigarette into his mouth, and from his shirt pocket jerked a match, which he flicked into a flame with his thumbnail. He touched the cigarette until he breathed smoke, then shook the match to death. "There's no loyalty in gambling, just money."

"Then cut him loose, or you'll lose money."

"I did once, and it cost me business. I keep telling you, he's got too many friends. Lottie's such a draw at the Bee Hive that I need the men he'll bring in. You rile too many people, Doc, for your own good and mine. People play you for spite. They play Bailey for fun."

"You know he's too spineless to stand up for the house's share."

"The answer is no, Doc. I'm not getting rid of Bailey this time, and you're welcome to stay as long as you forget your differences with him."

"We're heading for trouble, Chancey." Holliday turned away.

The saloon owner exhaled a dejected cloud of smoke. "If only you'd won the Bee Hive. Damn Lottie's Luck, Doc."

"Would you've broken up four aces?"

"Doc, you're the better dealer, but this town may not last many more years. I plan to suck all the money out of it I can. Maybe have something for my old age. If I chose my own company, I'd take you over him any day."

"You can have him tonight, Chancey, as I won't be in." Holliday strode out of the office. For a moment, he surveyed the revelers until he spotted Kate in the playful grasp of a buffalo hunter. Holliday marched over, grabbed Kate's hand, and pulled her away.

The hunter jumped up, his lean, six-foot frame rising over Holliday. "I was playing with her."

"Find yourself another whore," Holliday told him.

Kate yanked her hand free from his, her eyes flashing. "Don't call me that."

The buffalo hunter stepped toward Holliday. "Show some more manners, you slick-eared gambler."

Before the hunter could react, Doc jerked his gun and pointed it at the buffalo hunter's face. "Take another step, big man, and you can wipe your nose off the back wall."

The hunter halted as Holliday backed away.

"Come on, Kate."

Kate crossed her arms over her chest. "I need a customer."

"I'll pay," Holliday answered. "Now get moving before your acquaintance here tries something foolish, and there's one less customer for you later."

Kate stormed past Holliday and out the swinging doors. Holliday eased back toward the exit. "No offense, big man," he said, reaching with his free hand into his pocket. He pulled out a ten-dollar gold piece and flipped it at the hunter's muddied boots. "That'll buy you another woman and a round of drinks. Enjoy them both."

As Holliday stepped outside and re-holstered his pistol, Kate greeted him. With a gun pointed at his head. "Now, Doc, if *you* don't want to wipe your nose off the street, you apologize for insulting me."

"I told him to buy another whore. I didn't call you one."

"Then don't even insinuate it," she said, slipping her pistol under her blouse.

Holliday slid his hand in his pocket and extracted a twenty-dollar gold piece. "Professional deal, no blabbering about anything, especially marriage. Agreed?"

Kate started down the walk without taking the gold coin.

"Agreed, Kate?"

"I should've shot you."

"Agreed?"

"You could've saved your money, Doc, if you'd just brought me flowers like you did Lottie. I wouldn't have thrown them on the saloon floor."

"It was a gambling ploy. Thought it might ruin her concentration."

"Doc, you're the one that can't think straight when the two of you are together." Dejection rang in her voice.

"It was just a distraction."

"No, Doc, you've always had an eye out for her. You even bet to learn her name. You've never once asked about my name. You've never cared about mine, never asked. I've got a real name. I'd of told you. I'd of told you anything you wanted to know. And if she'd told you her name, what would you have done then? Asked her to marry you? I've heard talk that you'd proposed to her. Doc, why don't you care about me? Sure, Lottie's pretty, but am I that bad to look at?"

Holliday left the question unanswered. He held up his hand again. "Here's twenty dollars. That's more than you'd make in one night. No more blabbering. Understand?"

"I'm glad she beat you, Doc, 'cause it's made you miserable. Means you and Ed Bailey are almost partners. You deserve each other. One day Lottie's own luck will sour as bad as week-old milk."

"Twenty dollars, Kate."

She took the coin from him.

Chapter 19

"Where the hell you going, fellow?"

Holliday backed away from the barn door, gauging the stable hand standing there with a shotgun across his arm. Doc eased his frock coat clear of his holstered revolver. "Lift that scatter gun an inch, and you're a dead man," he said softly, his fingers drifting to the ivory grip on his Colt.

"Who is it?" Pete Haverty's familiar voice stammered from inside the structure.

"Don't know," answered the shotgun-wielding guard as Haverty limped from the shadowy depths of the stable.

"Afternoon, Pete," Holliday said. "Business so good you're chasing customers away?"

Haverty cleared his throat, cast a quick glance toward the back, then looked his worker. "It's okay."

"I've never seen this fellow before," said the hand, tapping his fingers on the breech of the shotgun.

"He's a gambler. Doc Holliday's the name. He works at the Cattle Exchange."

"I don't frequent those dens of iniquity."

Haverty stepped between the two men. "Go on back inside," he instructed his guard. "Mister Holliday, we've all been edgy since we flushed someone out of the stables last night tampering with the pinto. Lot of money's been bet, and somebody was trying to better his chances in the race today. We're just jumpy."

"Your guard may jump to an early grave if he pulls down on me again," Holliday said.

Haverty nodded. "We're all nervous. My opponent came into Griffin yesterday, all alone. Usually, there's more than one, if they're serious about horses, so this fellow may have had a partner slip in ahead of him. Crafty bunch these horse racers."

"Like gamblers?"

Haverty nodded, then grinned. "Now, what is it you want?"

"Rent me your best buggy and animal. I plan to bring a guest to the race."

"I'll give you the rig Lottie always hires out. It's best."

Holliday stepped toward the door and the narrow shade the stable offered from the mid-afternoon sun, but Haverty raised his hand. "I'd feel better if you stayed out here, Mister Holliday. With the start just an hour away, too many people inside make the pinto nervous."

"Remind me never to give you a break in a card game, if you're ever fool enough to visit my table." Holliday grinned.

"My foolishness is horses, not cards. I'll have your buggy fixed up."

"Do that. Just don't send your shotgun friend back out."

Haverty disappeared, and Holliday paced in front of the stable. Toward Griffin Avenue he could see the Saturday crowd gathering, already jockeying for good positions along the race course from the Clear Fork to the edge of Government Hill. While some men cleared the streets of wagons and animals, others blocked off the main paths converging on Griffin Avenue. Two men drained a sack of flour across the street for a finish line. The town pulsed with the rapid movement of excited people. A horse race always attracted a throng. Even the pious bunch that shunned saloons wagered on horseflesh. After all, it was quite different to bet on one of God's noblest creatures, the horse, instead of one of man's lowest inventions, the deck of cards.

Shortly, the stable door swung open, and a different fellow led the buggy outside. "Haverty said you could have this rig for the day with his compliments."

Taking the reins, Holliday grunted, "Tell him I hope his ugly horse loses."

He climbed in the buggy, which shone black from a recent cleaning, then slapped the reins against the bay's flanks. After making a U-turn in front of the stable, he guided the rig around the outskirts of town and toward the creek and a lonely cabin beneath a giant cottonwood. As the buggy neared his destination, the rattling trace chains signaled his approach. For an instant, Holliday thought he saw the flash of a face behind briefly parted curtains. Drawing to a halt outside the dwelling, he shouted. "Lottie Deno, I know you're home."

Lottie's Luck

The door opened slowly, Lottie coming behind it, her hair falling across the shoulders of her blue cambric dress, her arms folded over her bosom, her lips lifting at the corners with amusement. "John Henry Holliday, I am surprised."

"Good day, ma'am, I have come to escort you to the event of the year in Griffin." Holliday tipped his hat, then jumped from the buggy. "Everyone in the Flat plans to see Pete Haverty's horse lose today, and I thought you should, too."

"John Henry Holliday," Lottie shrugged, "you are worse than a schoolboy."

"My motives are not so innocent, ma'am. I need to beat you at something for my reputation."

Lottie walked out beside Holliday. "I'm not sure you'll help my reputation," she said, a smile in her eyes.

"Name your wager and your odds, and you can have Haverty's pinto," Holliday offered. "I'll take whatever he's racing against, sight unseen."

"But can you be trusted?"

"I can. No question about it, Lottie."

"As long as you're betting on horses instead of cards, is that not correct, John Henry?" She smiled again. "But we've played our last card game."

"The Bee Hive should be Chancey's, Lottie. Nobody breaks up four aces."

"And nobody should deal me a pat hand."

"I had to. I was keeping up with too many cards to risk going around on the draw. I wanted to beat you."

"And to learn my real name?"

"I lost, so I'll forget that. I bet you're not as good a judge of horses as cards."

Lottie frowned. "Thank you, John Henry, but I really shouldn't."

"I almost got shot renting this rig for you," Holliday complained.

"And both of us could get killed if Kate finds out you're here." She stared at the buggy. "Looks like Haverty's rig to me?"

"It is. They're mighty jumpy at the stable, carrying shotguns and not letting anyone in. They say someone tried to tamper with the pinto during the night."

"Odd, John Henry. Last night I could have sworn I heard someone prying around my place here. Must've been a drunk, but he was sure a quiet one, if it was."

Holliday extended his hand toward Lottie. "Come with me. No questions about anything but horses and gambling, I promise."

She nodded. "But let me put my hair up and change."

Shaking his head, Holliday spoke. "Your hair looks fine, just as is. Your dress too. If we want a place near the finish line, we better go."

"Okay, John Henry, I'll take the pinto, and you the other horse. Just give me a moment." She retreated into her cabin and emerged moments later, tying the blue ribbon of a broad-brimmed white hat under her chin. Holliday helped her into the buggy, then brushed against her as he climbed in and took the reins. They dashed away to the Flat.

The murmur of an excited crowd drifted out to them as they neared town and parked the buggy behind the Cattle Exchange. Other latecomers scurried like busy ants for places along the dusty street, and Holliday navigated Lottie through them, stopping under the shade of a pecan tree as a cheer rose from both sides of the street.

The spectators had seen Haverty's pinto stepping out into the middle of the road, Haverty beside it, a smaller man astride the bareback paint. As the animal skittered at the crowd noise, Haverty patted its neck. The jockey rode Indian style, without a saddle's extra weight, his legs hooked in a rawhide loop tied around the horse's middle. Jutting his chin forward, a scowl upon his face, the rider slapped the pinto's flank, and the animal danced away from Haverty. The crowd cheered again, and the horse seemed to understand, lifting its legs higher and tossing its head up. When the jockey nudged the animal with his heels, the pinto lurched ahead in a lope, almost stumbling before regaining its balance. As the horse ran by, the spectators cheered or booed by betting preference. Holliday studied the ugly animal, then turned to Lottie beside him. "I'm glad my money's on another mount."

Lottie moved forward for a better glimpse of the pinto. "Doesn't look like a speed horse, but Haverty keeps him well fed and exercises him daily."

A clamor came from down the street, and Holliday turned to the noise. A chestnut horse pranced forward, as confident as the rider on his back, a monkey of a man in a gaudy red silk shirt, a riding cap, and baggy white britches. As the jockey neared, Holliday could see him sitting astride an English riding saddle. "I like the looks of my horse," Holliday pointed out, "but I can't say I favor the dude riding him." Holliday watched the animal, waiting for an answer from Lottie, but none came. Even her breath seemed lost. He looked at her, taking in a paleness he had not noticed before, a frightened wideness in her eyes transfixed on the rider approaching on the chestnut.

"I don't like that rider's looks," Holliday announced, still without receiving an answer.

As the horse and rider drew opposite them, Lottie spoke. "You say someone tried to tamper with the pinto last night, John Henry?"

"That's what I hear."

Lottie shook her head. "It figures."

"What figures?"

"No matter, John Henry."

Holliday stared at the horse and rider as they passed. Blond tufts of hair tumbled from his cap over his face's tanned complexion, his eyes shifting from side to side as he alternately loped and walked the animal toward the finish line. A pointed nose gave him the look of a predator, and he sat in the saddle like a hawk in a tree, ready to swoop down upon innocent prey. Even so, his face was cut from a handsome cloth that must appeal to women. By his fancy clothes, some folks would take him for a dandy, but the steeliness in his eyes seemed brittle with experience. In the set of his shoulders rode an unconquered cockiness. Though not imposing, Holliday figured him dangerous anyway.

"Wish I could trade riders with you, Lottie," he said, glancing to his side, but Lottie had slipped behind him, her head lowering so the hat shielded her face. Holliday lifted her chin with his finger and stared into her gray eyes, spotting something he had never seen there—fear. "You're too worried over this race, Lottie. What are we betting? Fifty dollars?"

Holliday watched her, noting her eyes glazed with the morbid fascination of a woman watching a snake, her face still ashen, her breath irregular and heavy. The rider passed, reached the finish line and turned around, loping down the side of the street where Holliday stood. As he passed again, the rider stared into the spectators under the pecan tree, and Holliday felt Lottie draw closer into him, like a chick under its mother's wing. The rider stopped and twisted in his saddle, looking toward Holliday, then circling his horse back around in Doc's direction.

The frisky animal pranced at them until the rider jerked hard on the reins, stopping an arm's length away. Grinning, the jockey lifted his hat with a hand that carried a quirt, then ran the fingers of his other hand through his curly blond locks. He nodded toward Holliday. "Good day, sir," he said, then stared at Lottie. "Not a woman's hat I've passed the last eight years without looking under it for you, Lottie. It's been a long time."

"Not long enough, Johnny." Regret tinged her words.

"Your hair is as long and pretty as I remember, though you still cover it too often with your hats. Did you get my letter?"

"I did."

Holliday felt the discomfort in her terse admission.

Johnny replaced his cap. "Surprised you're still around here, but I would have found you, anyway."

Holliday released Lottie and stepped between her and the rider, the horse moving forward from the flinch of the rider's heel. "I'm escorting Lottie," Holliday challenged, "and she doesn't want your company."

"May not matter what she wants." The jockey laughed.

Doc threw back the frock coat and hooked it over his pistol. "Nothing funny to my way of thinking, mister."

"Johnny Golden's the name. Lottie could've told you that." He glared at Lottie. "A lot of things she could tell people. Her past would surprise them, wouldn't it, Lottie? There was a time when she wanted my company, right, Lottie?"

Lottie's voice came with renewed strength. "Like you said, Johnny, that was a long time ago."

"Not that long, Lottie."

Holliday lifted his arm with a snake-like motion and slapped the chestnut on the nose. The horse reared and Johnny grappled for a saddle hold. "You bastard," Johnny shouted as he rode out two bucks of the horse, then struck its neck with the quirt, drawing a bead of blood. The horse settled down, backing away from Holliday. Golden pulled his hat down low over his brow. "Damn you, mister," Golden called to Holliday.

"Step off that horse," Holliday dared, "and you'll have so many bullet holes you'll whistle when the wind blows."

"Mister, I don't know your name but—"

"John Henry Holliday. Some folks call me Doc. You want to look me up after this is over? I'll be waiting."

"It's Lottie. I want to look up after this race." The rider jerked the reins of the horse and aimed him toward the starting line at the creek. "I got no problem with you, Doc. But don't come between me and Lottie again. I won't stand for it." The rider hit the horse's flank with the quirt, and the chestnut galloped down the street to the spectators' cheers.

Doc turned to Lottie. "Who's your friend?"

"Just a man I knew once," she answered.

"Wish I had bet on another man," Holliday offered.

Lottie nodded. "Me, too."

Holliday strained to hear her over the spectators cheering as the pinto raced by. All around them, people made bets with one another, and the crowd thickened under the pecan tree. The local favorite pinto pleased the crowd, but the lines of the chestnut looked stronger, faster. Those who cherished their wallets more than their local chauvinism backed the visiting racehorse and Johnny Golden. The others favored the pinto. The crowd lining the street fanned out from the walks to watch the contestants line up at the creek for the start. Holliday craned at the starter, who held a gun in the air. A white puff of smoke followed by the muffled retort of the pistol sent the horses lurching forward and the crowd retreating to the walk.

The pinto stumbled, and the chestnut shot forward. For the split second it took the bareback rider to control the pinto, the chestnut had leaped ahead two lengths. Golden flailed at the chestnut with the quirt, and the horse's nostrils flared, and its eyes widened with fear. The animals lunged forward, the chestnut's big strides slinging dust and clods at the pinto. The smaller animal churned at the street like a dust devil darting across the distance. At the midpoint along the race course, the pinto had pulled within a length of the leader, and Johnny Golden, glancing over his shoulder at the gaining rider, beat his mount's flank savagely.

All around, the people yelled in a frenzy. The pinto was gaining, though the chestnut still commanded the race. Reaching the three-quarter mark on the course, the pinto made up another stride on the chestnut and was only a neck behind as they neared Holliday.

"Come on, pinto," Holliday shouted, "beat that arrogant cuss!"

His eyes as wild as his mount's, Golden looked to his side, where the pinto came within reach. Golden struck the chestnut with the quirt and, as Haverty's racer drew even, lashed out at the other rider. The bareback jockey ducked, and the whip's sting drained into the air. The pinto stuck its nose even with the chestnut, its stride faltering as Golden reached out to swing again at the pinto's rider.

"Did you see that?" Holliday shouted at Lottie. "Your friend's a mean one." Holliday moved into the street as the animals shot by, only twenty yards from the finish line. Other spectators surged around him like waves around a shore rock. At the finish, the two crossed together, the rider on the pinto drawing his animal to a walk at the same pace as Golden. When the animals halted, the pinto rider leaped from his horse to the chestnut, knocking Golden to the ground, then falling atop him. The two started rolling in the dirt, tossing punches at one another as Sheriff Jay Larn raced to them. If there was anything better than a good horse race, it was a fight, and the crowd pressed forward around the combatants.

"Your friend deserves a beating, Lottie," Holliday said, turning about. She was gone. He looked around, then pushed his way through the throng back to the pecan tree. The crowd was thick, and he did not see her.

While he searched for Lottie, the crowd murmured and waited for Sheriff Larn to break up the fight so the winner could be announced. Finally, Uncle Billy Wilson mounted the water wagon and held his hands out for quiet. Gradually, the muttering dwindled until Wilson's voice carried across the throng.

"Folks," he called, "we had quite a race here today."

The crowd mumbled agreement.

"Best us on the finish line could see, it be a dead heat."

The spectators groaned.

"But a winner has been declared. Pete Haverty's pinto will remain undefeated because of the other rider's foul in lashing out at our rider."

The crowd responded with a mixture of cheers and boos. Wilson held up his hands and signaled for silence. "A rematch is planned for next Saturday. Give all of ya a chance to look the horses over and decide if ya wanna change your bets." Wilson kept jabbering, but Holliday weaved his way through the crowd and jogged to the buggy behind the Cattle Exchange.

Lottie was gone. Holliday climbed in and slapped the reins against the animal. Making a big swing behind the saloon, the buggy turned toward the street, still crowded with spectators. It would take too long to get through, so Holliday circled the cart around again and headed behind the buildings lining Griffin Avenue, turning toward the creek and Lottie's cabin. As he passed the structures and stacks of buffalo hides, he saw Lottie in the distance, holding her skirt and running toward her cabin. When she spotted Holliday, she lifted her skirt higher and raced the final fifty yards to her door. Her white hat flew off, but she left it and slammed the door behind her.

Holliday reached the cabin too late. "Lottie, what's wrong?"

"Just go away, John Henry. I don't feel well," she gasped with winded breath.

"I owe you fifty dollars. The horses finished in a dead heat, but my rider was disqualified. I'm here to pay up."

Lottie did not answer again. After five minutes of waiting, Holliday turned the buggy around and started back to town, leaving her white hat where it had fallen on the grass.

Chapter 20

Across the room Ed Bailey, a jigger shy of drunk, dealt cards. Holliday shrugged.

It was Chancey's money Bailey was squandering—and doing it loudly. He blubbered for another bottle, then giggled from the effects of its predecessors. Circled at his table like a pack of hungry wolves around a wounded buffalo, his card players feasted on Bailey's dwindling stack of cash, Cattle Exchange money.

Holliday played solitaire at his faro layout, his customers long drained away by the easier takings at Bailey's table. In the yellow light diffused by smoke, Doc pulled his watch from a vest pocket and opened the cover. "One-forty," he said to himself, returning the timepiece to his pocket, then gathering his cards for another round of solitaire.

When a bartender suggested Bailey had had too much to drink, glass shattered at Bailey's table. Holliday leaped to his feet, his Colt cocked and ready to fire. He watched Bailey wave a broken bottle at the barkeep.

"Dammit," Bailey yelled, wobbling up from his chair, "bring me another bottle, quick."

Chancey's office door flew open, and the saloon owner emerged, accompanied by his shotgun trained at the noisemaker.

"No trouble, boss," Bailey stammered, "just dropped my bottle." He placed the jagged bottleneck on the table.

"Busted it is more like it," Doc said.

Bailey leaned forward, propping his teetering frame on the table with his hands. His eyes blinked at Holliday. One hand inched along the green felt toward his sidearm, then fell away as Bailey's eyes focused on Holliday's malevolent gun pointed at his gut. Bailey aimed his index finger at the threat. "You stay out of this, Holliday. The bottle slipped out of my hand." Bailey swept his arm over the tabletop. "This is my table, so don't interfere with my dealing."

"You're so drunk, you're costing the Cattle Exchange money I have to make up. What about it, Chancey?"

"Put your gun up, Doc. I don't want my dealers killing each other, sorry lot though they may be."

"You're gonna push me too far, Holliday," Bailey shouted. "I'll remember your interference."

"Shut up, Bailey, and holster your sidearm, Holliday," Chancey ordered, twisting the shotgun in Doc's direction.

Holliday eased his Colt back in its holster.

"Where's my, whiskey?" Bailey shouted. "I need a drink to get my mind back on the cards. Holliday better not fool with me!"

Doc's hand dropped back to his gun.

"Don't do it, Doc," Chancey called. "Come into my office."

Holliday marched across the room, his eyes locked on Bailey, who still insisted on a fresh bottle.

"Get in there and sit down, Doc." Chancey pointed to the door.

"I told you, he'd bring you trouble. That's all it's been. My winnings can't cover his losses forever."

"Shut up for a minute and let me think this one out, Doc. This is a powder keg you two jackasses are intent on blowing up." Chancey stepped inside, closing the door.

Holliday faced Chancey. "Put the shotgun away." When Chancey obliged, Holliday resumed. "It's either me or him."

Chancey scratched his chin, then fidgeted for the cigarette fixings in his tobacco tin. He put one together, flared a match and sucked the flame down into his tobacco. He exhaled a heavy breath. "There'll be less trouble if I get rid of you."

"Then do it!"

"But less money." Chancey paced across the room, stopping in front of his strongbox. "If I don't cut him loose, I may not need this." He kicked the iron coffer.

"You should've never hired him back, Chancey."

A knock came at the door.

"Go away," the saloon owner ordered.

A bartender replied. "Someone here to see you."

"Tell him I'll see him later."

"You'll want to see this lady."

Chancey grunted and strode to the door, his massive frame blocking Doc's view outside as he swung the panel open. Chancey drew deep on his cigarette. "President Grant himself couldn't have surprised me more," he said, then backed away.

Into the room walked Lottie Deno.

"Lottie!" Doc failed to hide the surprise in his voice.

"John Henry, I—" She started, then paused.

Holliday moved to her, and in the flickering lamplight could see her gray eyes glistening with tears. Her hair was mussed, and her dress seemed oddly wrinkled and ill-fitting. Holliday sensed her discomfort before his boss. She rubbed her hands together, staring more through than at the saloon owner.

"I've come to ask a favor of you, Chancey."

He crossed his arms. "I thought you were too much of a lady to ask me for any favors, Lottie, not after I sought one from you."

Lottie stared blankly at Chancey. "Me too. But things change. I—I—," the words seemed trapped in her, "—I want to deal for you. I'm through at the Bee Hive."

Chancey laughed. "Did your luck sour or did Fogle proposition you?"

"Go easy on her," Doc said, stepping between them. "This have anything to do with that fellow, Johnny Golden?"

Lottie nodded. "He started pestering me at work. My luck went down. He was spending enough money that Fogle wouldn't throw him out."

"And now," Chancey gloated, "you're scared and want protection in the Cattle Exchange?"

Lottie's nostrils flared, and she shoved past Holliday. "You've insulted me before." She drew back her arm and swatted at him, but his quick hand caught her wrist. "You know I can draw business without wagging my tail. Like you would say, it's a business deal. Nothing more."

"If a whore'd tried to slap me, I'd throw her ass out on the street."

"I'm no whore, Chancey, and you're no gentleman. We both know that from past experience, don't we?"

Holliday pulled Lottie's hand from Chancey's grip. "Give her an answer, Chancey."

He spit his cigarette to the floor. "Maybe you can solve a problem of mine, Lottie." He rubbed his chin. "I don't have an opening," he said, "but I'll make one for you."

"My cut of the winnings?"

"Same as Doc's," Chancey answered.

"That's acceptable. When do I start?"

"Sundown tonight. That'll give me time to spread word around town you're working at the Cattle Exchange."

Lottie shook her head. "No—please—he'll just find me sooner."

Chancey shot back, "No sense in hiring you, Lottie, if I have to keep it secret. I want the business you'll draw, or you can go back to the Bee Hive."

"But—," Lottie started.

Holliday interrupted. "If it's Johnny Golden that's got you buffaloed, we'll watch out for you, Lottie." Holliday stared at the saloon owner. "At least I'll look out for you."

"You'll be safe in my saloon, Lottie," Chancey reassured her. "Of course, Doc is gonna have to watch out for himself."

"I always do."

"You'll have more cause to now, Doc." Chancey checked the load in his shotgun. "Lottie, tonight you can have Ed Bailey's table."

Holliday's thin lips twisted into a malevolent smile beneath his moustache. He tipped his derby to Lottie. "You just helped rid this saloon of a skunk."

Chancey started for the door. "Doc, Bailey's gonna blame you." He stepped out of his office and into the saloon.

"Bailey," he called, "you've had enough to drink tonight. End your game. I'm cutting you loose." When Bailey didn't seem to understand, Chancey repeated his decision.

When it soaked in, Bailey exploded from his chair toward Chancey. He stopped cold when he saw the shotgun aimed at his chest. "It's Holliday, isn't it?" Bailey screamed at Doc, "I'll get you for this, you tinhorn gambler."

Holliday grabbed for his gun, but Lottie caught his hand, then shoved the door shut.

"I'll get you, Holliday, I'll get you yet," he heard Bailey shouting at the door.

****

Business was slow for Holliday, but across the room, a table was buzzing with activity. Word of Lottie's new roost had spread through the Flat, and men had come out in numbers to play at her table. Around midnight, Holliday pulled his last card from the dealing box and quit his layout. As he counted his earnings, Kate strode up and sat down opposite him. Holliday glanced at her, noticing her misbuttoned blouse and the whiskey bottle she carried.

"Well, Doc, you happy now that you can keep Lottie under your eye? Seems she cost you more business tonight than Ed Bailey might have." Kate guzzled the liquor.

"She's brought you so much business, Kate, that you can't button your blouse straight."

Kate looked down at her blouse, undid the top three buttons, and spread her top apart far enough for Holliday to see the pale flesh converging at her breasts. "Seven men've had their hands inside here tonight, Doc. I've made close to thirty-five dollars honest, and half that again picking their pockets."

"Then you've no reason to trouble Lottie, Kate, since she's brought you more business." He studied her for a moment. "What I see in you, I'll never know."

"I amuse you, Doc. I'm free entertainment," she said matter-of-factly.

Holliday scraped the remaining change from the table into his hand. "Free? That's a laugh. You cost me my peace and quiet."

Kate's lips pouted. "All this sweet talk's making me swoon, Doc. Do you ever talk to *her* like that?"

Picking up his cards and faro tools, Holliday stood. "She's a lady."

"Maybe she's a lady," Kate shot back, "but is she a woman?"

Without answering, Holliday turned away toward the bar, depositing his cards, the dealing box, and the casekeeper behind it, then carrying his money into Chancey's office.

Hunched over his desk, Chancey was counting the evening's early winnings. He glanced over his shoulder at Holliday, then shifted back to the money stacked before him.

"Here's my take for the night, Chancey," Holliday said, dropping the cash beside him. "Not much. Lottie's getting all the business."

Chancey huffed. "You wanted me to shuck Bailey, and I did, so don't bellyache about your take dropping off. Lottie's on a streak now. Few of her customers are winning anything, and even the big losers aren't complaining. How's she do it?"

"She cheats, Chancey."

The saloon owner held up a fistful of paper and coin. "She does it well. You ought to watch her and learn something."

"Chancey, you have a habit of becoming a burr under a fellow's saddle."

"And a way of making money, Doc. Yes, sir, I do my best."

Lottie's Luck

Holliday left Chancey to his profits, returning to the bar for a bottle of Monarch. Then he slipped behind Lottie. He watched her lithe movements and her grace over the cards. She played quickly, bantering with the men. Doc moved into her view, and her smile widened to acknowledge him. For half an hour, Holliday stood transfixed between her beauty and her gambling skills. He nursed on his bottle and was about to leave when a man in a green bowler elbowed his way among Lottie's customers to the edge of the table. Johnny Golden, the sneer of a hungry wolf across his face, had arrived. He carried a cane with a golden stag's head and slapped it on the table. Lottie jumped with a start, looked at Golden and lost her concentration.

"I'm placing a hundred dollars on the knave, the man that never gets the lady, Miss Deno." Johnny sneered, "It is Miss Deno, is it not, Lottie?" He pulled coins from his pocket and stacked five gold double eagles atop one another. With his cane, he pushed the pile over the jack.

"House limit is fifty dollars, Johnny." Her eyes avoided his. "I play by the rules here."

Johnny laughed like a coyote, then slammed his cane into the table, scattering his money along with the bets of others. Holliday elbowed between the grousing gamblers at her layout.

"Leave the lady alone," Holliday commanded.

Golden twisted his head, his teeth barred in a snarl of contempt. "Well, look-a-here, if it isn't Miss Deno's escort to the races." Golden's words, like his eyes, brimmed with contempt. "Lottie's always been fond of gamblers and their easy money."

As Holliday unbuttoned his frock coat, Golden laid his cane across the playing board on the table and dropped his hands to his own waist. Warily, he opened the front of his jacket to expose his hips. "I'm unarmed, mister."

Lottie shot up from her seat. "Don't believe him, John Henry," she said. "He carries a derringer in his pocket and a bigger gun under his arm."

"Make a move either place, and it'll be your last, Golden," Holliday said, putting his bottle on the table. Lottie's patrons backed away as a hush filled the room. Doc watched Golden's hawkish eyes and planned his play until he heard Chancey.

The saloon owner exploded. "What's the problem, Lottie?"

She pointed to Golden. "This man interrupted my game."

Golden laughed. "Pretending you don't know me, Lottie? Such a shameful woman."

"Shut up," Holliday ordered.

Golden stared back. "You keep butting in where you have no business, mister. I don't take kindly to meddling."

Chancey grabbed Golden's arm. "Now, mister, you must understand this is my saloon, and Lottie and Doc are my dealers. I don't want trouble, so why don't you just slip out the door, and we'll all forget this ever happened."

Golden spat on Lottie's table. "Some things a person just can't forget. That's true, isn't it, Lottie?"

Pale and her lips quivering, Lottie nodded. "It's true, Johnny, no matter how hard I've tried."

"Now, mister," Chancey said, "before I send for the sheriff, perhaps you should just leave." With his free hand, the proprietor picked up the cane from the table, admiring the golden stag at the end. "This belong to you?"

Golden nodded.

"Good looking walking stick, yes sir," Chancey said, holding the cane in the middle and staring at the heavy knob. As Golden started to speak, Chancey drew his hand back and slammed the thick end of the rod against the side of Golden's head. The powerful blow resounded with a sickening thud.

For an instant, Golden's eyes stared vacantly ahead, then his eyelids collapsed over them, and he tumbled onto the table, atop his spittle and his unwanted wager.

"Get him out of here," Chancey ordered a bartender.

Holliday stepped beside Lottie. "You okay?"

She nodded.

As two men pulled Golden from the table, Holliday reached for the five double eagles Golden had wagered on the jack. "He won't be needing these, will he?"

Chancey stared at Lottie. "You up to continuing?"

She affirmed she was.

Throwing out his chest, Chancey took a step toward her. "See how much better we take care of you than Fogle ever did? Who is this guy?"

"He's Johnny Golden," Holliday answered, "the one that tried to horsewhip Haverty's rider in the race on Sunday."

Chancey whistled and stared at his female dealer. "You know this fellow?"

"A long time ago," Lottie whispered, turning away from her boss to her patrons. "Okay, gentlemen, straighten your bets, and let's see if we can pick up where we left off."

Holliday eased from the table and felt a hard tap on his shoulder. Turning around, he saw Kate, fire in her eyes, a bottle in her hand, and too much liquor in her belly.

"You'd never stand up for me like that, Doc Holliday." She turned around and marched for the door.

Holliday watched Kate depart, amused as always by her feistiness, and then settled in at the bar with his bottle and studied Lottie as she finished a run through the deck. She lost heavily. Her luck had changed, and Holliday wondered if perhaps his had too.

Chapter 21

"You gonna take me, Doc Holliday?"

He stood at the washbasin, shaving his cheeks with his straight razor.

"Are you taking me or not, Doc?"

Holliday growled. "I'm not interested in seeing a damn puppet show."

She turned over and reached for the floor. Retrieving a spread-eagled copy of the *Frontier Echo*, she said, "Let me read this to you again, Doc."

"The answer's no, no matter how many times you recite it."

"It's not like I'm asking you to take me to church." She shook the paper for emphasis. "Now listen to this, 'Thursday and Friday Nights, June 4-5. Great Carnival of Fun! Grand Opening of the Fashionable Drawing Room Soirees of Signor Silvano, Aided by the Wonderful Royal Marionettes (17 in Number) from the Theater Royal and Princess Theatre, London.'"

"Wonderful," Holliday said.

"But there's more," Kate continued. "'Best Combination Traveling, a Large Stage will be erected handsomely fitted with appropriate scenery, curtains, carpets, and the room will be brilliantly lit by thirty patent safety illuminators.' Now, doesn't that sound exciting?"

"A horse race is exciting."

Kate threw the paper at Doc. "You can't forget her, can you?" Kate sat up, bending her knees and resting her chin on them. "It'll cost you a dollar for the both of us to see the marionettes. That's cheaper than renting a buggy for Lottie. A lot cheaper."

Doc wiped the lather from his face with a damp cloth. "You never give up, do you, Kate?" He stared at the tintype of Lottie on the washstand, thinking how much quieter her company would be than Kate's.

Lottie's Luck

"Fifty cents, that's all I'm asking you to spend on me, Doc. If Lottie asked you to take her, you'd go."

"She didn't ask."

"And she won't," Kate said. "I hear Jack Jacobs is taking her. That should kill any notion you had about getting her to accompany you."

Holliday wrestled his shirt on and then struck the bedpost for his sidearm. "I'll be out thirty minutes, Kate. When I come back, you be gone."

"Mean talk over fifty cents of your money and a couple hours of your time. I've given you more than that."

Holliday coughed. "Okay, Kate, you win. I'll take you to the marionettes. Just leave me alone for some peace and quiet."

"I knew you'd do it, Doc. You won't admit it, but you care for me." She arose from the bed, her sweat-stained gown clinging to her body, and walked to Holliday. She threw her arms around him. "You're my Huckleberry Finn."

"You've been reading that book again." Holliday broke from her grasp and backed toward the door, grabbing his boots. "You just be gone when I return, Kate, and take your book with you."

"Like I said, Doc, you *do* care for me, but are too proud to admit it, just like Huckleberry Finn."

As Holliday slipped into the hall, he turned to her. "Don't forget your book. It's giving you too many ideas."

Kate nodded to herself. "One day, Doc Holliday, you'll admit I'm right for you." She gathered her clothes, dressed hurriedly, grabbed *The Adventures of Tom Sawyer* and was gone before Holliday returned.

****

The line stretched from the locked doors of the Southern Hotel east along the street almost to the Cattle Exchange. Holliday shook his head as he emerged from the saloon, Kate's arm interlocked in his.

"I knew there were a lot of fools in the Flat, Kate, but not this many." Holliday motioned with his free hand toward the end of the line. "All those folks won't fit into the Southern. Too many of them. Too many fools."

Kate smirked and brushed an imaginary speck from the waist of her new yellow dress. "Too many fools and one weasel, Doc Holliday."

"What?"

"I knew you'd try to weasel out of this. You waited until the line got too long before coming over here. Ain't it a fact, Doc?"

Holliday felt his face flush. "Wish I'd thought of it." Holliday stopped at the end of the line. "I'll wait with you, but the Southern can't handle this many folks in one sitting."

For a moment, Kate stood motionless except for full red lips, which quivered into a smile. Then she tugged at his arm. "Come with me, Doc."

Along the heat-warped planks, Kate pulled Holliday.

"I knew you'd find your senses, Kate, when you saw the long line."

Better than halfway to the hotel door, they passed Lottie, standing with Jack Jacobs. Like Kate, she wore yellow, but the color seemed more becoming on Lottie. Doc tipped his hat as he marched by. Looking over his shoulder, he noticed Lottie's smile, but he felt Kate's pace quicken and her fingernails dig into his arm.

Pulling up within a dozen folks at the door, Kate turned to Doc. "We'll wait in line here," she said, pointing to two youths. Behind the boys, several people grumbled.

Doc took off his derby, then addressed Kate. "I'm not about to step ahead of these fine folks."

Laughing, Kate pulled her arm from Holliday's and stepped up to the pair. "Thank you, boys. I told you this skunk would try to renege on me."

Both sniggered, then swaggered from the line. "The pleasure was all ours," the taller one said.

Kate tugged Doc into line. "I paid them to hold our places for us."

The boys laughed, one looking back at Kate and winking.

Kate leaned toward Doc and rested her head on his shoulder as he replaced his derby. "Don't take it wrong, Doc, I just wanted us to get good seats near the front."

Holliday broke away from Kate's grip long enough to extract a flask from his coat. After fumbling with the cap, Holliday touched the flask to his lips and eased his head back. The warm liquid dulled the fire in his chest. He wished he had brought more to lessen the shame of standing in line to see a damn marionette show. The afternoon heat heightened his discomfort, and he shifted his weight from foot to foot, his obvious boredom displeasing Kate.

She jerked at his arm. "You're jumpier than a kid in church, Doc. You promised you'd go with me, but you're acting like you're under sentence to be hanged."

Holliday turned to Kate, lowering the flask from his lips and returning it to his pocket. "I promised I'd accompany you. I didn't promise to enjoy it."

For a moment, she stared blankly at Holliday as a gauze of betrayal covered her face. Clasping her hands around the sash of her dress, she turned to the street to watch the passing parade of people and horses. Holliday leaned his back against the wall of the Southern Hotel and waited, tapping his boot against the plank walk to annoy Kate.

At length the door to the hotel opened, and Holliday stepped away from the wall, motioning for Kate to step ahead of him. Grabbing her skirt and lifting it enough to expose the white of her calf, she marched sullenly ahead, never looking his way. Holliday lingered a moment, spawning impatient murmurs from those behind him in line. Kate waited at the entry long enough for Holliday to catch up and pay the overweight puppeteer with rouged cheeks, a spotless white shirt, and broad, red suspenders. "The show will begin in thirty minutes," he told Holliday. Lingering a moment, Holliday lost Kate among the people scurrying ahead of him toward the front seats. More than a hundred and fifty chairs were crammed into the room around a narrow aisle leading up to a brightly lit miniature stage. People pushed past Holliday as he searched for Kate. Finally, he spotted her in the third row, second seat from the aisle. Approaching the empty aisle chair beside her, he pointed to the seat. "For me?"

"Sit down, if you care about me," she said, her voice rising in anger. "If not, leave now."

Grimacing at her indelicate scene, Holliday sank to his seat, placing his hand on Kate's leg. "You're taking this all wrong."

Kate shoved his hand from her knee and twisted her legs as far away from Holliday as she could. "Don't touch me," she said, her words carrying the chill from her lips.

Holliday fumbled for the flask in his coat pocket, almost dropping it on the floor. His knuckles turned white as he twisted the stopper loose. Before this night was over, he thought, he'd need a case of bourbon. The flask at his lips, he drained all the amber liquid it offered. Though the bourbon's wetness helped douse the growing anger within him, it could do nothing to abate the sweltering heat building in the crowded room. Holliday looked at the open windows, but the breeze was too little to go around. While all about women fanned at the flush of their faces, Kate sat motionless, sweat running like tears down her face. Another sip at the flask drew air only, so he stoppered the container, shoved it in his coat, and removed his derby, placing it in his lap. He pulled his watch from his vest, popping the cover and squirming at the twenty-five minutes remaining until show time. He glanced at Kate as she looked at him. Her eyes glistened.

"You can go on, Doc." She spoke softly, the anger dissipating as occasional tears mixed with the sweat birthing on her face. "I've read too many books, wanted something I could never have. I just wanted to love you and be loved a little, not much, just a little. But you're no good. You don't like yourself, so you make it impossible for anyone else to love you. I want you, you want Lottie and she, who could have any man in this town, wants no one. Just go on, Doc, don't stay for me."

She buried her head in her hands and cried softly while around her women fanned themselves, men discussed politics, and the children fidgeted for the show to start. Holliday draped his arm on her chair-back and dropped his hand to her back, patting her gently. She flinched at his touch, then flung her head up and turned to Holliday. "Don't get any ideas unless you intend to pay again."

Holliday's arm retreated. "You're more perplexing than a deck with fifty-three cards."

A wave of laughter washed through the audience as a puppet stuck its head out from the maroon curtains of a miniature stage and called, "Just minutes from showtime," then darted back inside. The children giggled or stood in their chairs for a better glimpse of what they missed. A girl behind Holliday lost her balance and fell into Holliday's back. "Tell the man you're sorry," her dour mother ordered. The girl stepped around beside Holliday and offered a shy apology, holding her skirt with her hands. Holliday scowled at her, and she jumped back for her chair. "He's a mean man," she told her mother.

"Don't talk about strangers that way," her mother scolded. The girl cried.

Kate twisted around in her seat. "That's okay, darling, you're right about him."

Shocked by Kate's comments, the girl's mother gasped, then caught her breath. "You don't talk to my daughter, you—you hussy."

"Momma, what's a hussy?" the girl asked between her tears.

Holliday would have laughed, except for a commotion at the back of the room.

"Let me in. I'm not staying. Now where is she?"

Holliday recognized the voice and slapped his hat to his head. Turning around in his seat he saw Johnny Golden shove the money taker into the back row of chairs. Women screamed and gathered their children together like hens brooding over their chicks.

"Lottie, where are you?" Golden called.

Holliday felt Kate's hand grab his as he stood and glanced around the crowd for the yellow dress that would be Lottie. He missed her until the Jack Jacobs rose from a seat. Kate's hand squeezed tighter against his as Holliday slid into the aisle.

"Someone's with her. It's not your worry, Doc. Stay with me." Her voice broke.

Shaking free from the grasp that could never hold him, Holliday unbuttoned his coat and moved toward Johnny Golden.

Lottie stood up beside Jack Jacobs, looking from Golden to Holliday, her eyes rimmed with fear. "Please, Jack, stop them or they'll fight. They both have tempers."

"So there you are," yelled Golden, his speech slurred from too little thought and too much whiskey. "It's time you came with me. Have you told folks in these parts about me? About us?" He staggered for a moment, stopped to regain his equilibrium, and then stepped from row to row, holding onto the back of chairs for support.

Jacobs moved toward the aisle, tripping over feet and legs. "Hurry, Jack," Lottie called after him.

"Golden," Holliday shouted, "stop where you are."

The slight man halted and looked around until his eyes met Holliday's. "It's you again, is it?" Golden challenged. "By damn if you haven't taken too much of a liking to my Lottie."

"Hurry, Jack," Lottie pleaded, urgency growing in her voice.

Holliday pulled his gun from his holster, Golden too drunk to notice or to care.

"Don't shoot him, John Henry. He's drunk and out of his mind." Lottie's hand flew to her face as Holliday pointed the gun at Golden. "Hurry," she implored Jack Jacobs.

Jacobs stumbled past the cowering spectators and lunged into the aisle, holding his hand up toward Holliday. "No shooting, Holliday. There's women and children present." He stepped between the men.

"Who the hell are you?" Golden lunged toward Jacobs, releasing his grip on a chair-back and tumbling forward.

Jacobs reached out for him.

"Get your dirty hands off me," Golden shouted.

Jacobs stood him up straight and drew back his fist.

"Now get out of my—"

Jacobs plowed his bunched knuckles into Golden's nose, and he crashed to the floor.

Sprawled across the aisle, Golden struggled to raise himself, then his eyes rolled upwards, and he tumbled backward onto the floor, his arms twitching, then turning limp.

Jacobs spun around to Holliday. "Put up your gun and help me get him out of here so decent people can see the show."

Holliday holstered his pistol as the crowd applauded Jacobs.

Lottie stepped into the aisle and bent over Golden. "Why?"

She could say no more before Jacobs motioned her away. "Back to your seat, Lottie. We'll remove him."

For a moment, Lottie stared at Holliday. Fear pooled in her eyes. "Your gun can't solve everything, John Henry."

"It'll keep him from bothering you, Lottie." She turned toward her seat, and Holliday bent to grab a booted leg. "You helping, Jacobs, or not?"

When Lottie took her place, Jacobs answered. "You're too puny to drag him out of here yourself."

Holliday scowled. "That's why I carry a pistol."

"Or two?"

"Brother Colt," Holliday continued, "made all men equal."

Jacobs grabbed Golden's other leg, and the two men dragged him past the spectators, now crowding into the aisle, and out the door into the street. They left Golden by a horse trough amid a circle of the curious.

"Roughest puppet show I ever saw," Holliday growled, then kicked Golden's leg. "What's Golden's acquaintance with Lottie?"

"Can't say," Jacobs answered. "I best get back to Lottie."

"What's his connection?" Holliday persisted. "How does he know her?"

Jacobs started back for the hotel, and Holliday grabbed his arm, feeling the muscles go taut and dangerous.

"What Lottie told me, I promised to keep to myself. If she wants you to know, it'll be up to her to tell." Jacobs broke from Holliday's grasp and headed back inside.

Holliday pulled the flask from his pocket, then remembered it was empty. He took a step toward the hotel, then halted. The Cattle Exchange was just down the street, and as long as he was this close, he'd get his flask refilled. He'd need it before the puppet show was over or before Kate was through yapping and crying for the night.

Quickly, he was at the saloon, staring over the batwing doors, noting the dearth of patrons. The puppet show had cut into the crowd. Chancey was behind the bar polishing glasses. Holliday pushed inside to the bar and placed his flask solidly in front of Chancey.

"Why're you working the bar?"

"One of my barkeeps is out sick and the other wanted to see the puppet show. Hell, that damn Signor Silva, or whatever his name is, is stealing my customers and my workers. I thought you were escorting Kate to the show?"

"Give me a refill," Holliday shoved the flask at Chancey. "I got sidetracked by Golden, bothering Lottie again."

"Golden?"

"Yeah, he's out there by a horse trough. Jack Jacobs cold-cocked him."

Chancey pulled a fresh bottle of Monarch Bourbon from the backbar and uncorked it. "Somebody needs to take care of Golden. Lottie was a hell of a dealer until he broke up her game the other night. Since then I've been lucky if she's broke even. Damn Lottie's Luck! It's that Golden that's ruined her." Chancey stuck a flask funnel in Holliday's container and poured the liquor inside.

"Somebody needs to do something about him, Chancey."

The saloon owner wiped the lip of the bourbon bottle, then Doc's container. "I've been considering the same thing."

"If Jacobs hadn't interfered, I might have shot him at the puppet show. He was so drunk he would've gone to hell with a blank look on his face until Jacobs unloaded on him."

Shaking his head, Chancey shoved the corked flask toward Holliday. "You wouldn't have killed him in front of the decent folk, women, and children, would you?"

"Makes no difference to me."

"Maybe not, but it would to the vigilantes. They'd give you a good necktie party for that."

"You got any better ideas, Chancey."

Chancey began building a cigarette, lit it, propped his elbows on the bar, and leaned toward Holliday. "Sheriff Larn owes me a favor. Maybe I could get him to put enough of a scare into Golden that he'd leave town for good. When's he racing Haverty's horse again?"

"Saturday."

"You can always find something about horse racers that'll concern the law." Chancey grinned.

Holliday smiled back. "I'd take pleasure in killing him,"

Chancey leaned closer to Holliday. "Don't be a fool, Doc. The vigilantes won't tolerate that anymore. This town's changing."

"Maybe I should change towns."

"I've thought the same thing for myself. Buffalo can't last forever the way they're carting hides in by wagon trains. And the cattle drives will end when the railroad arrives."

"Then what's keeping you here, Chancey?"

"It's hard to move a saloon, but what's keeping you around, Doc? Is it Lottie or Kate?"

Holliday grabbed the flask and tucked it in his pocket. "There's money to be made."

"Lottie or Kate?"

"Lottie, dammit."

Chancey drew away from Holliday and grabbed a towel to wipe the bar. "You're a loner, Doc, not the type for a wife and a home."

Holliday headed for the door, calling over his shoulder at the bar. "Chancey, you're better at dispensing drinks than advice."

He made his way back to the hotel. The line once outside the hotel had jammed inside, and Holliday squeezed through the packed bodies toward his seat. After Holliday cleared the clump of people standing at the back, he squeezed down the aisle cluttered with spectators, ignoring the grumbles of those he tripped past. When he reached the third row, he found a man in his chair.

"You're in my seat, fellow," Holliday said with disdain.

The man glanced up at Holliday and shrugged.

"I escorted this woman." Holliday pointed to the next seat, then stopped. Kate was gone. Another woman sat in her place. He shook his head and stared at the woman again. She was old and matronly.

He looked up and down the adjacent rows for her yellow dress. Kate wasn't there. She had abandoned him. Holliday retreated.

"Down in front," someone yelled at him.

"Hold your horses, fellow," Holliday mumbled. He groped back down the aisle, wanting to strike out at the aggravated spectators he stepped on.

Reaching the door, he burst out into the evening heat. He walked straight to Kate's crib, but she was not there. Nor was she in his room when he returned to the Planters House.

Chapter 22

Holliday unfastened his sweat-softened paper collar and dropped it to the floor by the tub of ice. In the smoke and heat of the Cattle Exchange the garrote of a collar had distracted him from his poker hand. The cards, tacky from the sweat of gambling fingers, clung together like a stain to cloth. Manipulating sticky cards marked a fool, so Holliday played five card draw as an equal with his opponents. It was a low stakes game, maybe earning Chancey enough money to buy another tub of ice but never enough to cool the Cattle Exchange. There wasn't that much money—much less ice—in all of Griffin. Holliday had heard that three women passed out from the heat at the puppet show the night before. Maybe one was Kate. He had not seen her since then, nor inquired about her.

Holliday played five card draw because Lottie had siphoned all his faro business away. But Lottie's Luck, to Chancey's chagrin, had indeed soured since Johnny Golden had interrupted her game in the Cattle Exchange. The ante at his table was so small, Holliday would have given up for the night, but there was only the hotel to go to and his room would be as hot as the saloon.

At the cackle of Lottie's laugh, Holliday glanced up from his cards. All he saw of Lottie among her customers was a bobbing, beribboned leghorn hat of lavender, hazy through the smoke. After an opponent raised the pot, Holliday evaluated the measly merit of his own cards, then matched the dollar raise and called the hand. Grinning, the customer exposed a full house. Holliday grimaced. He should pay more attention to the game and less to Lottie. Holliday folded his cards and nodded for the winner to claim the pot. On a cooler night with a good deck of cards, the player smiling across the table from him would have been cleaned out by the sixth hand.

Collecting the cards without enthusiasm, Holliday looked around the room for a bartender, but all had disappeared just when he needed a fresh bottle. Holliday's head felt listless from the oppressive heat, and his mouth tasted of cotton. He needed more bourbon. Out of boredom he tossed the cards from hand to hand more times than required for an honest deal. Still searching for a bartender as he dealt the cards around the table, Holliday saw Kate swagger into the saloon, a man on her arm. Holliday swallowed hard against the dryness in his throat and felt a burning rage singe his cheeks. Kate walked arm-in-arm with the mangy mongrel Ed Bailey.

Kate stared back, smiling as smugly as the winning card-player across the table. Holliday folded his hand without examining his fresh cards. Kate, puckering her mocking lips at him, strolled to the bar. Bailey let his fleshy hand slip from her arm and down her thigh as he ordered drinks.

Damn Kate, Holliday thought, shoving the cards to the middle of the table. "Somebody deal for me," he commanded.

Kate and Bailey lifted their drinks, tilted their heads and drained the liquor. Finishing, Kate dropped her jigger on the counter and bent over, lifting her skirt above her knees and adjusting the garter halfway up her thigh, then letting the cloth fall over her leg again. As she straightened her frame, suddenly quite appealing to Holliday, she waved at him. Holliday's hands tightened into fists and slammed into the table.

Kate snapped her fingers at the barkeep, who lifted a whiskey bottle to refill her glass. She snatched the bottle by the neck, then grabbed Bailey's hand from her thigh and pulled him toward Holliday's table. Holliday felt his muscles tighten like an overwound spring. Kate was unpredictable, and Bailey shared his mutual grudge.

Kate stomped to a halt across the table from him and hoisted the bottle of Monarch bourbon above her head. "I drink the best when I celebrate, Doctor John Henry Holliday."

"Kate, you're bothering my customers."

Kate nodded. "But not them as much as I'm annoying you. I'm celebrating, Doc Holliday. Care to know why?"

Holliday unfolded himself from his chair, his fingers wiggling with trigger anticipation as he stood. "Not particularly."

"I've found someone to replace you, Doc Holliday. I ran into him after you left the puppet show. He showed me what a man could be."

Holliday answered, "I came back for you, Kate."

"You shouldn't have left me, Doc. You know Ed Bailey?"

"Get away, you slut," Holliday answered.

"Just a minute." Bailey stepped beside Kate. "Apologize to the lady or answer to me."

Holliday laughed, his fingers touching the ivory grip of his Colt. "Make me apologize, big man. See if you're as big as your mouth."

The gamblers at the table scrambled from their seats and toward the walls. A stifling silence filled the room.

"Go ahead," Holliday dared, "prove what a big man you are!"

Bailey backed away. "Okay, I'll—," he started.

"Stop it, both of you." It was Chancey. "There'll be no shooting in my saloon tonight."

Kate swung around to Chancey. "Holliday started it."

Chancey moved his shotgun in a slow arc from Bailey to Kate. "You brought Bailey in here for no good."

Holliday eyed Bailey with venom. "Bailey and I just as well settle our differences, Chancey. It'll come one day. Today's just as good as another."

"No day's a good day in my saloon, Doc," Chancey replied. "I don't want any gunplay here. Now back away, Bailey, and you with him, Kate." He waved the shotgun at them.

The pair retreated from the table like it was rabid.

"Another thing, Kate, you're through working my saloon. You can drag up your customers from somewhere else, Kate."

"You'll be sorry you kicked me out, Chancey," Kate said, waving the whiskey bottle at him. "You'll lose business because I draw customers."

Chancey laughed. "Kate, all you draw is flies."

"You'll be sorry, Chancey." She stormed toward the door. Suddenly, she stopped and turned around. "Doctor John Henry Holliday," she shouted, "you're a Georgia S-O-B." She hurled the bottle at him.

Doc dodged the glass shattering at his feet like a broken romance.

Chancey clucked his tongue. "Maybe you should take a break, Doc. I'll have someone else finish up your table."

****

The breeze was warm and gentle and agonizing. Holliday coughed up the staleness of the saloon into the darkness of night. Just in case Bailey was waiting to ambush him, he avoided the puddles of light which seeped out the windows around the Flat. But he suspected Kate had snared Bailey in her crib. Holliday wondered if she were charging him for the opportunity.

Lottie's Luck

Without a moon, the night sky was sharply punctuated with a smattering of stars, more stars than Holliday could ever remember seeing. A meteor trailed across the sky and disappeared in a shower of flaring sparks that glimmered in the heavens for an instant then disappeared forever. Down Griffin Avenue toward Government Hill more sparks were flying; a cowboy with more liquor in his gut than sense in his head was firing his pistol at the stars and missing. Between his shots, a bawdy woman bawled from somewhere about a missed lover; the strains of a harmonica carried from up wind; and the people hurried down the street, seeking refuge from the stink of festering buffalo hides.

For half an hour, Holliday walked cautiously from building to building along the street, his right hand riding easily on the butt of his sidearm. Returning to the Cattle Exchange, he clung to the darkness away from the rectangles of light bleeding out windows, then stopped to reconnoiter the men lingering in the street. His eyes strained to penetrate the darkness where sudden assassins might be poised. By a front window he saw a slight figure staring into the Cattle Exchange and swigging on a bottle of liquor. Holliday recognized him and smiled. Johnny Golden was surveying the saloon. Suddenly, Golden flung the bottle beneath the horses at the hitching rack and strode boldly to the Cattle Exchange door.

Holliday jerked his revolver. If he hurried, he could kill Golden. He pointed the Colt, pulling the hammer back and aiming for Golden's heart. His finger tightened on the trigger, but two men stepped between Holliday and his target. By the time they moved, Golden had disappeared into the Cattle Exchange. Slowly, Holliday lowered the gun and eased the hammer down, angered he had missed this opportunity. As Holliday slipped to the door, one of Chancey's bartenders scurried out, running down the street. In the bartender's wake, Holliday stepped inside.

Golden stood at Lottie's table, his hands on his hips. "You're coming with me this time, Lottie. I got the right to make you do it."

Lottie shook her head. "I'm never leaving with you."

By Lottie's side stood Chancey, puffing on a cigarette. As Holliday lifted his revolver, he felt Chancey's hard gaze upon him. Chancey shook his head. "Put it away, Doc. I told him he could speak to Lottie, if he made no trouble."

"Last time you saw him, you told him to stay out of your saloon. You're going soft, Chancey?"

"This will be taken care of in due time. Like about now," Chancey said, nodding toward the door.

Holliday turned around.

Chancey's bartender had returned with the Sheriff Jay Larn and two deputies at his side. The huffing barkeep pointed toward Golden, still arguing with Lottie. The sheriff drew his pistol and stepped toward Lottie's table.

"Johnny Golden," Sheriff Larn called out, "turn around slow and easy."

Golden lifted his hand from his waist toward his armpit.

"Don't try anything, Johnny, you're dealing with the law, and I've got two deputies with me."

Golden's hands relaxed. "Did you do this, Lottie?"

"No, Johnny." She sighed.

Golden turned slowly around to face the sheriff. "What's the problem, sheriff? This some scheme of Haverty's so I can't race my horse against his tomorrow?"

The sheriff laughed. "I've received word from San Antone that the chestnut you've been racing was stolen."

Golden stepped hard toward the sheriff. "That's a lie, dammit! Haverty put you up to this, but it won't work, sheriff, 'cause I've got the papers on that horse."

"Maybe you'd best come with me, Johnny. We'll inspect your papers and see if your story matches San Antone's." The sheriff waved his gun at Golden, as the deputies circled him.

"He carries a gun under his shoulder, a knife in his boot and a derringer in his coat pocket, sheriff," Lottie said softly.

As he raised his arms, Golden snarled at Lottie. "That's no way for a man's—"

Larn struck him across the side of the head with his gun barrel. "Shut up."

Staggering backward, Golden almost fell, but caught himself against Lottie's table. He spat at her. Instantly, Chancey lunged past the circling deputies, grabbing Golden's arm and twisting it behind his back. Golden screamed from the pain. Larn moved in and slipped his hand inside Golden's coat, removing a revolver, then the derringer from his pocket while a deputy searched his boot for the dagger.

"Now back away, Chancey," Larn called. "Let the law handle this."

Chancey wrenched Golden's arm upward a final time, then shoved the arm down free. "Don't spit at my dealers, you skunk."

Golden's eyes watered from the pain in his arm and shoulder. "You're all against me," he stammered. "There isn't any law in this stinkhole."

"You're talking to the law, Johnny. Word's gotten around you've been treating Lottie poorly, so you won't find many friends here," Trickus answered.

"But she's—"

"Oh, Johnny," cried Lottie. "I'll never be again."

Trickus grabbed Golden's limp arm and jerked him toward the door. "Until our jail's finished, we detain our prisoners in the Southern Hotel. It's better than you deserve."

"No," Golden grimaced, jerking his arm free, his eyes flaring with pain and hate. "I'll get even with you all. Lottie," he sneered, "see how much longer I keep our little secret."

"Shut up and move along." Larn pushed him toward the door. "You try anything with these folks, and you'll have the law to deal with."

The two deputies grabbed Golden by each arm and tugged him out the door. Holliday followed the sheriff outside, watching the law officers and their prisoner disappear into the darkness toward the hotel down the street.

When Holliday re-entered the saloon, he marched to Lottie's table. She was counting her money to split with Chancey.

"There's still a couple hours good playing time, Lottie," Chancey implored her.

Lottie kept counting.

"Must be quite a secret he has on you, Lottie. What is it?" Chancey asked without response. "I daresay he won't be bothering you again in the Cattle Exchange after tonight."

Dropping a handful of money on the table, Lottie looked up for the first time. "What do you mean, Chancey?"

Now Chancey ignored, Lottie.

Lottie stepped around the table. "What have you done, Chancey? Answer me, or I'll never turn another card for you."

"When you left the Bee Hive and started for me, Lottie, you sure didn't do it because you liked me. You've made that plenty plain," Chancey said. "You did it because this Golden was pestering you.

You figured me and Holliday offered better protection against him than Mike Fogle did."

Lottie drew back her arm, but Chancey's hand flew to her wrist before she could slap him. "Did you arrange for the sheriff to arrest him?" she asked.

"I sure did. The sheriff owed me a favor, and I told him to persuade Golden it'd be healthier to leave the Flat and never return." He squeezed her wrist until she grimaced, then he pushed her away.

"You polecat."

"That's what you wanted wasn't it? Now, it's done. If you're dissatisfied, it's because you misplayed your hand, Lottie."

For a moment, Lottie stood with her hands on her hips, her eyes laced with anger.

Holliday stepped between them. "Calm down, both of you. Let the dust settle."

Neither answered, but both heard two muffled gun retorts from down the street. Lottie's hand flew to her mouth. "Oh, my God, what have they done?"

Holliday took Lottie's hand. "I was out earlier, and it's probably the same cowboy shooting off a drinking bout."

Then came the clatter of boots on the plank walk outside, and Sheriff Larn burst through the door. "Need some men quick to find Golden."

"What happened?"

"He made a break for it. We fired at him? Deputy thinks he hit him. May have, from the sound of whatever the bullet hit."

"Come on," Chancey called to his customers, "let's find the body."

Lottie whimpered, tears rolling down her cheek. Then she cried softly.

"Hurry," the sheriff said.

A dozen men answered the call, Chancey among them, and headed out the door behind the sheriff.

"Why," Lottie sobbed, "did Chancey have him shot, for God's sake?"

Holliday helped Lottie to her chair, and she almost fell into it. "Chancey wouldn't have a man killed," he answered. "Like he told you, he just wanted to scare a little sense into Golden, make him leave you alone."

"I should never have come to the Cattle Exchange."

"Lottie, that's why you need a husband. Someone to look out for you."

She laughed, her mirth mingled with sobs. "It's that simple, is it John Henry?" She reached for his hand. "Husband'll take care of everything, will he?"

"He'd be by your side when you needed him."

Dropping Holliday's hand, she cackled like a mad woman until her laughter turned into an almost uncontrollable coughing fit.

"You need a drink, Lottie." Holliday motioned for a barkeep to brink a bottle to the table. When bottle and glass arrived, Holliday poured her a shot. "Why let a gambling tinhorn like Golden upset you so?"

Lottie downed the drink in a single gulp. "He's my husband."

"Damn Lottie's Luck," Holliday mumbled.

Chapter 23

Lottie's hand trembled against the door latch, the hinge moaning as morning's brightness rushed in. If only she had left the Flat when she had received Johnny's letter. But now, it was too late; she had tested her luck once too often. Jack Jacobs stood at the entry, straight as a soldier, his hat over his heart, his gentle blue eyes suggesting the worst.

"They found him."

"Dead?"

Jacobs nodded. "I'm sorry."

Lottie looked beyond him to the Flat. "Why all night to find him?"

He reached out for her hand. "You don't want to know?"

"Maybe not, but I should hear it."

Jacobs pointed with his hat to the couch. "Then sit down." She clung to his arm as he walked her to the divan. "He hid in the buffalo ricks. Though hit hard, he bled little and didn't leave a trail. Come midmorning someone noticed a pack of dogs gathered around a stack of hides. That's when they found him."

Lottie looked up into Jacobs' eyes, discomforted with sympathy. "Was he mauled?"

"He wasn't a wholesome sight, but he was beyond pain by that time."

Dropping her face to her hands, Lottie sobbed. She felt his tentative arm around her shoulder, the awkward pat of his fingers.

"I should have left when I got his letter." She spoke through her fingers as he pried them from her face.

"You couldn't run forever, Lottie. He would have caught up with you someplace else. Cry for him, but not for yourself." His fingers squeezed hers.

Hot tears streamed down her cheeks. "I'm crying for Father," she replied. "He told me nothing good would come of this marriage, but I was young and foolish and knew everything, and Johnny was adventuresome and monied and handsome and—"

"And a cheat," Jacobs interjected.

"The war was ending. Father was broke, landless. Our betrothal seemed to ease so many problems, but it only created more, breaking Father's heart and, by Appomattox, his will to live." She shook her head. "Father was right, and I was a fool."

Jacobs released her hand and stood. "I'm not much good at this, Lottie, and nothing I can say will change things."

She pulled a handkerchief from her sleeve and dabbed her eyes. "It was foolish to marry him. I never loved him, so why should I be upset? But you don't care to hear about that. There is something you can do."

Wiping her eyes, she stood up and walked to the window. "I owe Johnny a decent burial, at least. Buy a good suit of clothes and coffin. See that he gets a gravestone. Have the hearse stop by here on the way to the graveyard. Dispose of what belongings he had. If that chestnut horse was his, sell him to Haverty."

Nodding, Jack Jacobs tugged on his hat. "Certainly, Lottie."

"I need a new trunk for my belongings and my money," she continued. "Have Frank Conrad give you all my winnings and buy a trunk from him."

"Let me give you mine, Lottie. It might look obvious that you were leaving if I get your money and a new trunk. Somebody might try to jump you before you left. Anything else?"

"Jack, speak to no one of these arrangements. I have paid my rent through Saturday. Tell the sheriff nobody is to disturb my place until six o'clock Saturday afternoon."

"If there is more I can do, Lottie—"

She snickered through her tears a moment. "I keep thinking of things. Yes, later I'll give you something to take to my friend Rachel at the fort."

****

The curtains blocked the midmorning light. Lottie sat on her bed. Dressed in black, a veil covering her face, she counted the money and restacked it in the leather trunk with Jack Jacob's initials carved over the latch. She took five hundred dollars in paper and looked for something to put it in. She had but one envelope, the one addressed to her in Johnny Golden's ostentatious handwriting. Finding a pencil, she obliterated her name and replaced it with Rachel's. She removed Golden's letter and read it aloud.

"My Charlotte,"—the word "my" was underlined—"so you go by the name Lottie Deno now. Shouldn't it be Lottie Golden? Running out on me wasn't the smartest thing you ever did because I will find you, and we will live together as man and wife. That's my right. My luck was running mediocre until I overheard a saloon conversation about a red-headed woman gambler in Fort Griffin. I knew they meant MY Lottie. Do not run away from me again because I will find you, and you will be most sorry you ran out on me more than once. Johnny."

No mention of love. Johnny had never loved her, she thought. He just wanted to possess her, to own her, to control her like he did the chestnut racehorse. She wadded up the letter and dropped it on the table. Tears moistened her eyes. She lifted the veil and dabbed at them with a silk handkerchief, a gift from her father when she was but a girl. Why hadn't she listened to him? She might be living a decent life now, not working as a gambler in a festering Texas frontier town.

Outside she heard a wagon and the monotone of low male voices. She stepped to the window and cracked the curtains with her black-gloved hand. A somber hearse was approaching, the sunlight glistening off its polished wood and brass fittings. She felt her throat tighten as she stared at the dark coffin, peeking, like her, from behind curtained windows. She dropped the curtain and walked to the table, picking up the wadded letter and the envelope she had addressed to Rachel.

A horse nickered as the hearse stopped opposite her door. Lottie gritted her teeth and stepped outside. The men removed their hats. Jack Jacobs nudged his horse toward her, and she looked behind him. There sat the sheriff, John Henry Holliday, Mike Fogle, Pete Haverty, George Wilhelm, and the undertaker.

"I didn't know," Lottie said, forcing a smile, "that Johnny had so many friends here."

"They're your friends, Lottie, not his."

Sheriff Larn eased his horse up beside Jacobs. "Ma'am, we're terribly sorry. We didn't know he was your husband."

Lottie nodded. "He wasn't much of a husband."

"Even so, we didn't intend for it to turn out this way." Larn reined his horse toward the hearse.

"You've made fine arrangements, Jack," Lottie offered. "It's better than he deserved."

"I did it for you, Lottie, not him."

Lottie stepped to his horse and extended the envelope. "Give this to Rachel up at the fort in two days." Then she handed him the crumpled letter from Golden. Throw this on his coffin as they cover it up. I don't want to keep it, but something won't let me burn it."

"Sure, Lottie."

She moved closer to his horse and motioned for him to lean over. "Come by in the morning about six in a buggy," she whispered. Lifting the veil from her hat and standing on her toes, she kissed his cheek. "Thank you, Jack, for everything." Beyond him, she could see Holliday's stare, and she pitied him. "Goodbye, until tomorrow morning, Jack."

Jacobs nodded to the undertaker, and the hearse inched somberly away. As the riders passed, Holliday tipped his hat. Lottie watched the procession move upstream to the cemetery. Then, for the last time in her life, she turned her back on Johnny Golden.

****

Holliday grinned. "Business has been down since the shooting."

"Hell," Chancey answered, "it'd help if she came back to work. She can't stay in her cabin and mourn his passing forever. She'd be better off dealing faro and forgetting it. Hell, she must not of loved him, running out on him like that. Reckon she left town?"

Holliday closed the office door and ambled to Chancey's desk. Lifting his booted foot atop two stacked beer crates, he grinned. "I thought about that, Chancey and watched the stage yesterday. She wasn't on it, and she hasn't bought a rig from the stables, even Golden's chestnut is still in Haverty's."

Chancey coughed up a laugh with his cigarette smoke. "Doc, you beat all. Now that her husband's out of the way, you think you've got a chance with her?"

Tapping his boot against the crate, Holliday shrugged. "Worth a try."

"Doc, "I thought you had more sense than that. Lottie thinks she's too damn good for our type."

A sharp rapping on the door spared Holliday from answering. "Boss," called a bartender.

"Yeah," Chancey answered.

"Kate's outside with Ed Bailey," the barkeeper replied. "You want me to get rid of them?"

Chancey rose from his chair. "I'll get my shotgun."

Holliday moved toward the door.

"Stay in here, Doc," Chancey ordered. "You'd just flame the fire." He checked his shotgun's load. "Now Kate, she's the one for you. She'd give you more than most women."

Holliday growled. "If she wasn't sharing it with everybody else in the county."

The shotgun's twin barrels clicked into place. "If you'd marry her, Doc, it'd save me a lot of problems."

"Always thinking about yourself," Holliday answered as he fell in line behind Chancey, the bartender backing out of his boss's way.

Glancing over his shoulder, the saloon owner stopped in the door and scowled at Doc. "I thought I told you to stay in here."

"You did, Chancey."

"Well, do it. I don't want you shooting anybody in my place."

"I'll just watch," Holliday replied.

"Make sure that's all you do, Doc." Chancey barged ahead into the saloon. "Kate, I told you to keep your butt out of my place. Do you understand English, woman?"

Ed Bailey stepped toward the proprietor. "Just a minute, Chancey, she's with me. She's causing no harm, and she's not luring away your business." Bailey glanced behind Chancey toward the office. Holliday saw Bailey's eyes explode with hate. "She's better than some people you let work here."

Holliday emerged from the room.

Without looking around, Chancey issued orders. "Back in the office, Doc. You two jackasses can't leave well enough alone, now can you?"

Kate eased to Bailey's side, slipping her hand in his. "Let's leave, Ed. I've got better things for us to do." She ran her free hand up the front of his thigh.

The movement of her fingers stimulated a grin across Bailey's face. "I'm taking Kate with me, Chancey, and I'll keep her out of this place. But am I welcome here on occasion?"

"I'll take any fool's money as long as he doesn't cause me any trouble. Leave her behind when you visit."

"Come on, Kate, let's head to your place." Baily took her hand

Kate winked at Holliday, and he could feel his blood heating. "I always enjoyed men that make a woman feel wanted," she said.

"Get going, Bailey." Chancey waved the shotgun at the pair. "Remember, Kate, you're not welcome in the Cattle Exchange."

She cackled, her laugh exploding in short bursts. Waving her arm around the room, she spoke. "Looks like your business is down since I left. If you had a brain, you'd be begging me to return and attract a few more customers."

"It's Lottie, Kate. She was the Cattle Exchange's biggest draw, not you. It'll pick up when she gets back."

Bailey tugged on Kate's arm. "Let's go."

She shook free. "Maybe Lottie's out looking for another husband she can run out on. And her calling me a wag-tail when she was no better." She cupped her hands to her mouth and yelled. "Did you hear that, Doc? Lottie's no better than a wag-tail, leaving her husband, dancing with you and whatever else you did. Show your hide, you runt of man."

Holliday seethed from her words. He stepped from the shadow of the office, his lips drawn across his face and his eyes narrowed.

"Doc Holliday," she said as he moved into view. "You're a worse than a skunk in heat." Kate spun around and grabbed Bailey's hand. "Let's get out of here."

Holliday pulled his pistol from his holster. He took careful aim, his trigger finger drawing tight against metal.

Chancey yelled, "No, Doc, not in here."

The gun exploded in a cloud of white smoke. The bullet thudded into its target. Ed Bailey dropped to the floor. Kate stopped, looked down at Bailey, then at the door jamb beside her where the bullet had struck. She turned about to face Holliday.

"You're a fool if you think any woman better than me could fall for you."

Bailey got on his knees, his hand slipping toward his holster.

"Don't try it, Ed." Chancey waved the shotgun at him.

"Get off the floor," Kate scolded Bailey, her hands on her hips. "If he'd meant to kill you, you'd be deader than business in this saloon."

Bailey picked himself up like he would a bit of trash, disgusted and reluctantly.

"Hurry up about it before he plugs you." She tapped her foot on the floor.

"Shut up, Kate," Bailey said, dusting his britches off and staring at Holliday.

Doc waved his Colt. "Just try something, Bailey, and give me the excuse I've wanted to settle our differences."

Though he said nothing, Bailey's message was clear from the hardness in his eyes. He backed out of the saloon, a shrugging Kate marching after him. Once they were outside, she shouted, "You fool," but her ensuing words were lost in the street noises.

Chancey cursed Holliday. "No cause for that."

As he holstered his revolver, Doc nodded. "It proves Kate's got more grit in her craw than Ed Bailey."

"I'm tired of both of them. I should have told Ed to stay away, too."

"You'd never do that," Holliday smirked. "It'd be bad for business." He marched to the bar, the bartender setting out a bottle of Monarch Bourbon for him. "Thanks."

Chancey headed for his office, pausing by Holliday. "Don't shoot Bailey in my saloon."

"I won't shoot him here!" Holliday picked up the liquor. "On the house?"

"Sure," Chancey said, "business ain't worth a damn, and you're downing more free whiskey than ever here."

Nodding, Holliday stepped for the front door.

"Where you going?"

Holliday didn't answer.

Chancey marched stride for stride with Holliday, grabbing his arm at the door. The saloon owner's grip was vise-like until Doc's fingers fell on the ivory butt of his Colt. Chancey's hand dropped away. "Don't cause any trouble or it'll make business worse here. Where are you going?"

"To see Lottie."

****

A man knocked at Lottie's door. Holliday recognized, but could not place him. The tall, lean fellow wore overalls. He shifted back and forth on his feet, toeing at a wooden crate beside the door. He saw Holliday approaching, and a wave of relief seemed to wash over him.

"You coming to see Miss Deno?"

Holliday nodded.

"I can't get her to answer. It's not like her. She's too much of a lady not to answer."

Holliday rubbed his chin, looking at the grocery-filled box, then back at the bibbed fellow beside it. "Remind me of your name."

"George Wilhelm, Mister Holliday. I remember you from Miss Deno's Christmas party. You danced so well with her until, you know, that crazy woman came in." Wilhelm stepped aside.

Holliday knocked four times on the door. "Why're you here?"

"I bring Miss Deno supplies every week," the clerk answered. "I work at Conrad's store."

"Lottie, are you in there? George has your supplies. Don't worry us by hiding." Holliday waited for an answer. None came.

George took off his slouch hat and fanned himself with it. "Hot afternoon, isn't it?"

Nodding without caring, Holliday moved to a window. "Did you try looking inside for anything amiss?"

"Well, no sir. I hadn't been here long until you came up."

Holliday walked around the cabin, stopping at each window, peering into the tightly drawn curtains. "She'll roast in there without fresh air. Lottie, you okay?"

"Maybe she's staying in a hotel a few days," George offered. "Word I hear is she had Jack Jacobs take all her money from Mister Conrad's safe. Some say it's as much as twenty thousand dollars. You think that's possible?"

Holliday stopped. "You say she took her winnings out?"

Wilhelm nodded.

"Damn!" Holliday beat on the entry again. He tried the handle. The door was locked. He fought the urge to kick it open. "If you knew, other folks knew, too."

For a moment, Wilhelm caught his breath, then stammered. "You don't—you mean she could —you don't think someone harmed her, do you?"

"Fetch the sheriff so he'll be here in case there's been trouble," Holliday commanded.

Wilhelm's face darkened. "Why would anyone want to hurt her?"

"Twenty thousand is a lot of money. Now be quick." Wilhelm moved to pick up the supplies until Holliday propped his boot on the crate's edge. "I'll keep an eye on them." Then Wilhelm nodded and scampered away.

Behind the cabin, Holliday leaned into the wall's narrow shade. Had Lottie left? The possibility tore hard at his stomach. He feared more that she had departed than that she might be hurt or dead. He wondered if he would ever again find her. Mired in his thoughts, he lost track of time until he heard the noise of approaching men. Walking around to the cabin front, he saw Wilhelm gesturing wildly at Sheriff Larn. When they came within speaking distance, Holliday overheard Wilhelm. "He won't believe me. That's why you must tell him."

Holliday, waiting at the cabin door, nodded at the pair, then spoke. "Sheriff, I figured you'd need to be here before we opened up Lottie's place."

"We won't be interfering with her cabin."

Holliday stepped toward Larn, pointing his finger at the sheriff's badge. "She could be in trouble. Word's around she had all her money on her."

"I've heard the rumors, Holliday, but I've had instructions from Lottie by way of Jack Jacobs. Her place is not to be disturbed until Saturday afternoon at six o'clock. Her rent's paid through Saturday, and that's how she wanted it. I'll oblige her. It's the least I can do since the shooting."

"You did her a favor, Sheriff."

"Way I hear it, it may have been you I favored."

Holliday stepped to Larn. "How's that?"

"Just gossip I heard about you being soft on her, throwing card games to her."

"Don't you ever believe that I threw a card game to her," Holliday scowled.

"Didn't say I believed it, Holliday, just that I'd heard it. But you can believe that Jack Jacobs told me at Golden's burial that Lottie had asked not to be disturbed until Saturday. That's the way it's going to be."

Holliday shrugged and marched past the sheriff toward town. Until dusk, he checked the hotels and the livery stables for clues on Lottie. After dark, he watched her cabin for two hours hoping to see a light or smoke from her cookstove. He saw nothing but a crescent moon and the stars.

****

As he knocked on the door, Jack Jacobs enjoyed the cool of the evening shade on the long porch which faced out across the vast parade ground separating the officer's quarters from the enlisted men's hovels at Fort Griffin. He patted his shirt pocket, assuring himself the envelope was still there, then he took off his hat and wiped the sweat from his brow just as a tall officer wearing a captain's uniform opened the door.

"My name's Jack Jacobs," he introduced himself. "I'm here to see your wife. Lottie Deno sent me."

The officer nodded and invited him in. As he stepped inside, Jacobs recognized Rachel's voice coming from the same direction as the aroma of freshly baked bread. "Who is it, Richard." Her flour-smudged face peeked out from the kitchen door. "Oh, Mister Jacobs, what a pleasant surprise."

"I wasn't sure you'd remember me, ma'am, us meeting only at the Christmas party and at the—" Jacobs stopped.

"The lynching," she finished his sentence and smiled. "You are one of the pleasant memories I have of that day." She wiped her hands on an apron that hung like a shroud over her belly bloated with child. "I am always glad to see a true friend of Lottie's." She stepped toward him.

Richard spoke. "Mister Jacobs says Miss Deno sent him."

Rachel lowered her head. "I am so sorry, Mister Jacobs, if what I heard about Lottie is true. Was it her husband that was killed Saturday, the one that was racing those horses?"

"Ma'am, I fear it's true."

"Please have a seat," she said, motioning to a new rocker.

She sat down and reached for Richard's hand. "I am most sorry for Lottie, Mister Jacobs."

"And she was most ashamed, too, for fear you'd think less of her, so she sent me to apologize and say you were her only woman friend in Griffin."

"I wanted to see her when I heard, Mister Jacobs, but—," she paused, patting her enlarged abdomen, "—in my condition I must not travel, even so short a distance. But she is always welcome in my home. Tell her that, please."

Jacobs swallowed hard. "I wish I could, ma'am, but Lottie's gone. She left town on the first stage after the burial."

"I wish she'd come to see me."

"She wanted to, but her shame was too great, you being a decent woman and all. She asked that I give you this, though." Jacobs pulled the envelope out of his pocket. He stared at Lottie's handwriting and the blotches obliterating Golden's hand. The captain retrieved the packet for his wife. "She was fond of you and hoped to see the baby, but she just couldn't show her face in Fort Griffin anymore. Not with what happened."

Rachel took the envelope from her husband. As she lifted the flap, her eyes widened. She gasped. "It's money, Richard." She counted it. "Five hundred dollars in all. It's more money than I ever held at once. Did she have any left for her needs?"

Jacobs smiled. "Enough. She just thought a mother-to-be living on Army pay could find a good use for a little extra."

"Since I can't thank her in person, Mister Jacobs, I'll write her instead."

"I wish you could, ma'am. She'd have liked that, but she told no one, not even me, where she was going."

Chapter 24

Holliday arrived at Lottie's cabin a half hour ahead of the others and checked the door still locked and the windows still curtained. Then he walked to the cottonwood tree behind the dwelling and paced in the lengthy shade of late afternoon. Had Lottie left the Flat? She hadn't ridden the stage or bought a rig from the stables. Perplexed, he kicked at a dull gray patch half hidden in the grass and a receptacle tumbled on the turf.

Bending to pick up his find, he recognized it instantly. It was a dealing box, the rigged faro box Lottie had saved for him. Holliday brushed off the small ants scurrying upon it, then knocked the box against the heel of his boot, the collected dirt and plant matter tumbling to the ground. He remembered how Lottie had sent for him to give him the dealing box, how she had spurned his proposal, and how in anger he had tossed the dealing box away. He tried to rub away the decay of the box, but it had been too long ignored to give in to such caresses now.

Hearing the approach of others, Holliday ambled around the side of the cabin, carrying the corroded dealing box with him. He watched Sheriff Larn, George Wilhelm, Jack Jacobs and a half dozen others, curious of Lottie's fate, walk up to the cabin. Their voices lowering reverently the closer they came, they gathered in a clump at the door. Without a word, Jacobs handed a key to Sheriff Larn, who inserted it in the lock and opened the door, the stuffy heat escaping.

Larn stepped inside. "Give me a minute."

The men crowded at the door until he returned. "She's not here," he said.

Holliday pushed with the other men inside, one calling, "Lookahere, a note on her bed." He handed it to the sheriff.

"Read it," several called.

Larn cleared his throat. "It says 'Sell these belongings and give the money to someone in need.' That's all," Trickus scratched his chin. "Well, who's in need?"

Jack Jacobs spoke first. "The family of the little girl, Sophie, could use the money. Her father's taken too much a liking to the bottle to work."

Several nodded, and the sheriff gave his assent. "But what happened to Lottie?"

"She caught the stage Tuesday," Jacobs answered.

"That's not right." Holliday stepped forward. "I watched the stage, and she didn't get on."

Jack Jacobs nodded. "I carried her outside town, and we stopped it there. The driver'll confirm it on his next trip."

"Well, boys," said the sheriff, "I reckon we've seen the last of Lottie's Luck."

****

Collapsing into a chair, Holliday slammed the corroded dealing box on the table. As a cough ripped through his body, he lifted his hand for the bartender. "A bottle of bourbon," he demanded. The bottle and Chancey arrived the same time.

Chancey hitched his britches up, then leaned over the table, picking up the dealing box, running his fingers over its pitted surface, then toying with the ruined springs inside. "Not in very good shape, Doc. Reminds me of you. You don't look too good yourself."

Holliday dropped his derby on the table and ran his fingers through his hair. "Put it down, Chancey."

For a moment longer, Chancey held the rigged box.

"Maybe you didn't understand me, Chancey," Doc said slowly, his words buzzing like a coiled rattlesnake. "Leave it be."

Chancey let the box slide from his fingers and crash into the table. Holliday flinched, his tongue flicking across his lips.

"You're jumpy tonight, Doc, and late."

Holliday uncorked his bourbon bottle and drank heavily from it. "Lottie's left."

"It's just as well. Her luck had gone to hell," Chancey replied. "Are you dealing tonight, Doc, or just drinking?"

"I can hold my liquor."

"Better than any I ever saw, Doc." Chancey leaned forward, staring into Holliday's eyes. "But can you hold onto my money with your mind on her? You're a powder keg ready to explode."

"You're the match that's gonna touch me go off, Chancey." Holliday coughed into his fist, then snapped his palm at the floor. He lifted the bottle, but Chancey grabbed his wrist.

"No trouble or shooting, Doc? It's bad for business."

"My word, I won't shoot anyone."

The manacle of Chancey's grip loosened, and Holliday completed the bottle's trip to his lips. After several swallows, he came up for air. "I'll deal poker, but not faro, Chancey."

"It would never have worked, you and Lottie," Chancey said with as little compassion as if he paid for it by the ounce. "Forget her, Doc. No woman's worth that much."

"Lottie was a lady, my last chance at respectability," Holliday said softly. He brushed the weather-beaten dealing box aside. "Bring me a fresh deck and pass the word I'm dealing draw, Chancey." Slowly after Chancey returned with cards and chips, the table filled with Saturday night gamblers. Holliday played card after monotonous card, too bored to cheat, too indifferent to win big, too accomplished to lose much. The deck may have been readers, but Holliday never looked for markings. Occasionally, he would glance at an empty table nearby. Until Golden died, Lottie had dealt there.

As he raked in his nicest pot of the evening, Holliday spotted Ed Bailey, making his way from the door to the bar. For maybe thirty minutes, Bailey downed his liquor and stared back at Holliday. Finally, Bailey gulped a jiggerful down hard and broke away from the bar toward Holliday. Holliday eased his chair back from the table to meet Bailey's approach.

Bailey stood by the table, his bloodshot eyes wide over dough-like cheeks. "Deal me in, Holliday," he commanded.

"Go rut with Kate. No matter how bad you are, you're bound to be better at it than at cards."

Bailey's fleshy fingers curled into fists, and he planted them on his wide hips. "I left her satisfied back at her shack. Way she tells it, that's more than you ever did."

"She's got a short memory."

Smirking, Bailey unwadded his hands and clapped. "Memory's not what she told me you were short on."

"You wanna play, Bailey? Then sit down and shut up," Holliday answered, just as Chancey stormed to the table.

"Just a minute, you two," he called. "No trouble, tonight."

Bailey's face bloated like a toad frog. "I'm not looking for trouble, Chancey, just a little game. You're not throwing me out, Chancey. I didn't bring Kate, like you said."

Chancey rubbed his chin. "You gave me your word, no shooting, Doc? Bailey, I don't like this."

"You afraid I'll break your dealer, Chancey?"

"Oh, the heck with you both," Chancey shrugged.

"If you're playing, Bailey, take a seat." Holliday scowled as two customers gathered their chips and pushed away from the table. "If you're jabbering, take it someplace else." Holliday pointed at a chair on the opposite side of the table. "Sit and shut up."

Bailey frowned. "I pick my own chair." He pointed to the just vacated seat at Holliday's right. "That's my seat."

Chancey growled. "You two bastards are picking a fight. I'm getting my shotgun." He turned toward his office.

Bailey moved tentatively first, then boldly toward the chair beside the dealer. Holliday's two remaining customers shook their heads and stood up.

"You're running off my business."

Bailey threw a stack of bills on the table. "I came to play, not listen to you bellyache. You gonna deal?"

Holliday grabbed the cards and shuffled them from hand to hand, leaning slightly back and twisting his chair around for a better angle at Bailey. Holliday didn't like his position to the left of Bailey. If he drew his sidearm, Bailey could deflect the barrel with his left hand while drawing his own gun. Holliday would go for his shoulder gun, if it came to that. His dagger was another option. After all, he had promised Chancey no gunplay. Holliday stacked the cards neatly on the table between himself and Bailey. "Cut," he said softly, "unless you trust me."

Grabbing the stack of pasteboards with his pulpy paw, Bailey eased the top half of the deck away, then dropped it from about six inches off the table, the cards hitting the green felt and fanning out into a messy stack.

Holliday nodded at Bailey. "Cocky, aren't you. Fifty dollar ante! See how long that stack of bills lasts." Holliday tossed his chips out in the middle of the table, but Bailey tarried. Holliday gathered the cards, then snapped the top one from the deck. "You'll not get another card until the pot is right, Bailey. You do understand how the game is played, don't you?"

Bailey drew his arm across his mouth, wiping the droplets of sweat on his coat sleeve. "What's your hurry, Doc," Bailey said, throwing bills on top of Holliday's chips. "This game'll last until one of us is finished. Let's enjoy it. All right if I smoke?" Bailey pulled his silver-inlaid pipe from his coat pocket and clenched it between his teeth.

"As long as you're not dealing." Alternately, Holliday tossed cards between himself and Bailey.

Bailey toyed with his cards, viewed them, then placed them on the table. Under Holliday's suspicious eye, he eased his hand into his coat pocket and slowly drew out a packet of tobacco. He fingered tobacco from the pouch, sniffed at the weed, then stuffed it in the pipe. His hand retreated to his coat pocket, trading the pouch for a box of matches.

His eyes never leaving Bailey until the match flared, Holliday saved a pair of nines from his hand and prepared to throw the others away after Bailey adjusted his cards. The delay in play was having its intended effect. Holliday could feel the anger rising explosively in him. And, he enjoyed it.

Sucking his pipe to life as he shook the match out, Bailey glanced at Holliday. "Two cards. Honest cards. Raise you a hundred dollars." He tossed his money into the pot.

"Separate your throwaways from your hand, Bailey, if you want new cards." Holliday matched his raise and discarded three.

On his pipe Bailey drew deep, then emitted the smoke in short shots from between his puffy lips. Picking up his cards, he casually tossed the discards between himself and Holliday, who then pitched two cards in front him.

"Dealer takes three." Holliday dropped a trio in a stack by his keepers, then mingled the replacements with them. Holliday played square with Bailey. In this game, cheating did not seem so important. As long as Bailey lost.

Bailey was slow and precise with every move, his hand going again inside his coat, reappearing with a pocket watch. He stared at the time. "It's getting late, Holliday."

"Rate you're playing, it'll be late tomorrow night before we finish this hand."

Bailey responded with a puff of smoke toward Holliday. "I'll go another fifty dollars."

"I'll match you and go fifty more. You still in?"

Bailey smiled. "I'm not taking down my tent this hand, no matter how much you bet."

"Then raise me, if it's so good."

"I'm fine."

"Then show your cards."

Fanning his hand out in an exaggerated arc, Bailey revealed them as slowly as a banker okays a loan. "Full house. Deuces over jacks."

Collapsing his cards, Holliday tossed them on the deadwood.

Bailey laughed heartily. He reached out to rake in the money with his hands like he would pull a woman to him, then retreated to the deadwood, picking up the top five cards before Holliday could stop him. "Two pairs, fours and nines," he grinned. "My three little deuces would've beaten that."

A river of rage flowed through Holliday. "You don't monkey with the deadwood, Bailey, or see my discards unless I show you."

Bailey leaned back in his chair and laughed. "Worried I'll break you? I've got your woman, and now I'll get your money, Doc." He slurred the nickname with disgust. "Deal!"

Nodding, Holliday tossed a hundred dollars out in the pot. "The ante's going up, Bailey. A hundred dollars to start."

Bailey laughed and counted out enough from the last hand's winnings to match Holliday's bet. "I'm in and staying in." Bailey laughed again and announced to spectators. "You're about to see Doc Holliday eat his cards."

A smile with the wicked curve of a bowie knife flicked across Holliday's face as he corralled the cards and remixed them. He shuffled without watching the cards, staring intently at Bailey, glancing once at the crowd. Chancey was there, cradling his shotgun in the crook of his arm. Holliday gave Bailey the cut, then dealt the cards. Slipping the deck on the table, Holliday picked up his hand and fanned the cards apart. It was miserable—a pair of sixes and junk—but enough to teach Bailey a lesson with this hand.

"The bid's to you, Bailey."

"I'll up it fifty dollars, Doc."

Holliday smiled. "I'll see your fifty and raise you two hundred." Spectators whistled.

Bailey fidgeted with his cards, stared at them doubly hard, then reluctantly pushed the money into the pot. "I'll take three cards," he said.

Lottie's Luck

Three cards, Holliday thought. Indeed he would teach Bailey a lesson this time. Best he could have was a pair. When Bailey started a stack of deadwood, Holliday passed him a trio and gauged Bailey's reaction to the new cards. There was little pleasure in his eyes. Holliday laughed to himself.

"The dealer takes," then Holliday paused until Bailey gazed behind bloodshot eyes at him, "one card." Without picking up his hand from the table, Holliday shoved the top card to the deadwood. He dropped the new card atop his other four, picked up his refurbished hand and spread the cards apart. Knowing Bailey was watching, he arched his eyebrow for a brief instant. "You good, Bailey?"

The gambler pondered for a moment, started to nod his head, then seemed lost control of his fingers, which put another fifty dollars in the pot. "I'm upping you fifty."

"I'll see that and I'll raise you five hundred dollars." Spectators moved closer to the table."

Bailey squirmed in his seat, looking from his hand to the spectators, as if waiting advice. None came. He collapsed the cards in his hand and tossed them atop the deadwood.

Holliday grinned. "Shame to win that much money on a little pair of sixes."

Bailey clenched his fist until it whitened.

Holliday drew in the deadwood and picked up the top five cards, Bailey's hand. One at a time, he turned them over. A pair of jacks and three discards. "What do you have to say for yourself, Bailey, letting my sixes scare your jacks?"

"Leave the deadwood alone, Doc. That's what you told me."

"You saw my last discarded hand. We're square, now that I've seen yours."

Bailey's fingers edged toward the table edge.

"Don't try it, Bailey," Holliday ordered. "Keep your hands in sight." Holliday started shuffling the deck.

Bailey's hand returned to his stack of money.

"That's better," Holliday chided. "Now it'll cost you a hundred dollars to start this hand. Can you manage that, Bailey, or do you need a loan?"

"I'll manage." He shoved the money to the middle of the table. "Deal straight."

"You accusing me of cheating?"

"I'm just making sure you understand me."

"You'd do better, Bailey, if you played a little smarter." Holliday shuffled, then passed the cards to Bailey for the cut.

Bailey sliced but a dozen cards from the top. "Cut thin and win, I always say."

"Just cut without all the blabbering, Bailey."

Bailey clenched his teeth against his pipe stem, sucking on it until the tobacco glowed and smoke balls rose in the air.

Holliday pitched cards to Bailey and himself. Bailey drew hard on his pipe as he eased his cards apart. Holliday squared his cards between his fingers, staring intently at Bailey. As Bailey's demeanor grew accustomed to the cards in his hand, Holliday looked at his own. Three clubs. A chance at a flush, but little else. This wasn't a good start for a heavy betting hand. He watched Bailey pull one from his hand and drop it on the table. Holliday was playing him for two pair. That would be a winner, Holliday guessed, looking at his own hand and figuring the odds of drawing into a flush.

"I'm raising you two hundred dollars, Doc, and taking one card." Bailey picked up the money and held it over the pot, letting the money drop as his fingers loosened.

It was as Holliday feared; Bailey thought he had a good hand. Maybe he could bluff Bailey again. "I'll see your two hundred and raise you three hundred more, Bailey."

"You bluffed me once, Holliday. Not again. I'll see you and add fifty more to that."

Holliday matched him.

"Now give me my card, Doc."

Holliday obliged. "Hope it was worth the extra fifty dollars, Bailey." Holliday looked at his cards once more, then tossed two atop the deadwood. By keeping three, he could go for his flush and perhaps mislead Bailey that he had three of a kind. That would beat two pair, if that was indeed what Bailey had. It was worth a try. "I'll take two." Holliday dropped two new cards atop his keepers. He fought to hide the disappointment when he spread them apart. He had lucked into a single pair, a new card matching his jack of clubs, but nothing more. Bailey would win this hand sure as the devil, but he couldn't back down, not now.

Holliday looked up at Bailey. "Now show me how valuable those cards are."

"Three hundred," Bailey said, throwing money onto the table like it was worthless.

"I'll see your three hundred, Bailey, and match you two hundred more."

Bailey paused, working the pipe from one side of his mouth to the other, clamping it tight between his teeth at its new destination. His cards he folded, then fanned out again, looking from them to Doc and back. As his hand dropped toward his money, he stared at the pile, then back at Doc.

"You in, Bailey?"

"I'm thinking."

"Make it quick."

With his free hand, Bailey reached for the deadwood.

"Leave them alone, Bailey."

Disregarding the warning, Bailey bent up the corners of the top two, Holliday's discards. "This doesn't tell what you have."

Holliday dropped his cards on the table. "But you know what I don't have."

As Bailey eased his hand away from the deadwood, Holliday reached with his left for the pot.

"What goes, Holliday?" Bailey's voice was high with fright.

"You lose, Bailey!"

"Not without seeing your cards, I don't," he shouted.

Bailey jerked his hand away from table top and to his side. He was going for his revolver. His mouth flew ajar and the pipe dropped in his lap, scalding ash burning into his britches and leg. He screamed as his free hand slapped at his lap.

Holliday jammed his hand inside his coat. His fingers slipped between the gun under his shoulder and the knife sheathed in his coat pocket. His instinct said gun, but his fingers wrapped around the dagger. In Bailey's eyes Holliday saw a glaze of terror magnified by a cloud of doubt. Bailey's arm was rising. Holliday jerked at the dagger, but the leather sheath seemed to come with it. He pressed his left arm against his ribs and pulled. The knife cleared the sheath, then his coat lapel.

As Bailey lifted his gun, the barrel struck the edge of the table. A gunshot exploded into the floor, a cloud of white smoke engulfing both men. Bailey regained control of his gun and twisted his arm toward Holliday.

In a deadly arc the dagger flashed toward Bailey. Their weapons came together with a clang. Bailey screamed. His revolver fell on the table. So did his thumb.

The dagger, bloodied, could not be stopped. It sank into Bailey's chest. Bailey's eyes bulged out, and his uncomprehending mouth widened farther at the knife. His face turned suddenly ashen, the ghostly paleness heightened by the cloud of smoke around him. His lips parted for him to speak, but nothing came out—except blood. And from his nose, a pink foam bubbled. A gurgling in his throat preceded the quietness of death. Then Bailey tumbled sideways onto the floor.

With the knife, Holliday brushed Bailey's thumb from atop the cards and onto the floor. He gathered the pot, taking Bailey's stake as well. Looking up toward Chancey, Holliday snarled. "I didn't shoot him, Chancey."

Leaning over in his chair, Holliday wiped the bloody blade on Bailey's pants leg then re-sheathed the knife and sat up to count his money.

"You went too far this time, Doc," Chancey said.

Doc stared at Chancey and the gaping black eyes of the shotgun pointing at his neck. "Bailey was cheating. Put your gun away, Chancey, it makes me nervous."

"Don't lift a hand off the table or I'll shoot. Somebody fetch the sheriff. I can't have killings in my saloon. It's bad for business."

Chapter 25

"You gotta help him, Chancey."

The breathless voice surprising and angering him, Chancey jerked around in his chair. "How in the hell did you get in here, Kate?" Chancey gauged the distance between himself and the shotgun propped in the corner. He eased up from his chair.

"You gotta help him, Chancey."

"Kate, you fool, Bailey's dead."

"I never cared for Bailey. Doc's the one I wanted."

"Fine way of showing him your affection," Chancey answered, inching toward the corner, "but that's to be expected of a wag-tail." He took a bold step to the shotgun, stopping cold at the sound of a metallic click. He turned to Kate, his eyes focusing on the cocked revolver in her hand.

"Step an inch closer to that shotgun, and I'll kill you, Chancey." Kate waved the revolver as her witness.

Chancey retreated to his desk. "What do you want, Kate?"

"To free Doc."

Chancey laughed, then slid into his chair, stroking his chin and propping his feet on the desk. "Free Doc? The law's got him now, and I'm not interfering with the law."

"The law," Kate screamed. "You know where they took him? The Southern Hotel! Last time they had someone under guard there, the vigilantes treated him to a necktie party."

"Ain't it a shame, Kate." Chancey calmly built a cigarette. "I warned Doc. Now, he deserves what he gets."

"He thought you were his friend. I ought to kill you."

"Then maybe they'll hang you two together."

Kate spat at Chancey. "You made money off both Doc and me, and now you're turning against us."

"Doc was stewing for trouble 'cause Lottie left."

"Noooo!" Kate's voice turned deep and menacing. "He never liked her. He was jealous of Bailey having me. Doc killed him for me. It was me Doc did it for."

Chancey smiled behind a veil of cigarette smoke. "Believe what you like, Kate, but it was her."

"He did it for me, Chancey. He loves me. You wouldn't know about love, would you? It might be bad for business."

Again Chancey smiled. Then the door creaked, and Kate spun around. Instantly, Chancey bolted from his chair and grabbed her arm before she could shoot the entering bartender. His massive hands strangled her gun wrist, the revolver falling to the floor.

Kate screamed, "Let go of me," and pummeled Chancey's broad chest with her free fist before the bartender finally muzzled her flailing hand.

"What are we gonna do with her, boss?" he asked, a grimace blooming on his face from a shoe point planted on his shin.

"We'll escort her out. If she ever returns, kill her." Her wrists clamped in one hand, Chancey bent over to pick up her gun. Then he and the bartender herded Kate out of the office, through the saloon, and beyond the swinging doors. At the edge of the plank walk, they shoved her into the street.

"You ingrates," Kate shouted as she tumbled into the dirt.

Chancey yelled, "Remember my warning, Kate. Come back, you'll die." He pitched the gun over her head into the street. "You're bad for business."

Kate scrambled for the revolver as Chancey scurried back inside. "I hope your business withers away first. Then your manhood."

****

"Where you been, sheriff?" Holliday spoke before Jay Larn could shut the door. "Meeting with the vigilantes?"

Larn flexed his arm and slammed the door. "Shut up, Holliday."

"Take me up to the fort. They've got a stockade." Holliday struggled feebly against the ropes binding his legs and arms to a chair.

Turning to his two deputies, Larn motioned toward Holliday. "Check the rope and tighten it."

"Your record for protecting prisoners in the hotel isn't too good, sheriff."

"And gag him, if he doesn't shut up." The deputies moved cautiously about Holliday, as if he might suddenly wrench free.

Larn strode about the room, stopping on each revolution by the window, holding the curtains back and staring into the darkness. As the deputies finished checking Holliday's bindings, the tall one plopped on the bed.

"Get your butt up and stay on guard," Larn ordered.

"But he can't get loose," the deputy answered.

"His type is slippery as an eel."

The deputy snickered, dropped his feet to the floor, and stood. "We won't have to watch him much longer, though."

Larn averted his eyes from Holliday's. Then Holliday stared at the window, the thought of what awaited beyond the darkness stabbing deep into his brain.

"No sense in delaying justice with a judge and jury, is there, sheriff? Even if I killed in self-defense."

"Bailey was a popular man," Larn answered.

"Bailey was a pig."

"I've been out trying to calm down some of the men that called Bailey a friend."

"That shouldn't have taken long."

"Holliday, shut your mouth." Larn spun around and marched by the washstand, stopping to inspect the two guns, the dagger and a weather-beaten faro dealing box beside the wash basin. "Which one of you left his weapons here?"

The tall deputy nodded. "Me."

"I tell you, don't leave nothing around he could grab. Stick them in your gunbelt."

"You're sure jumpy," the tall deputy said as he joined Larn. He shoved both revolvers in his belt and slipped the dagger in his boot. "I'll be glad when this night is over."

"Me, too," Larn said, sitting on the bed and facing Holliday.

Though Holliday stared in Larn's direction, his eyes focused behind him on the window. For an instant, he saw a specter pass before the pane, his body tensing as if he had seen the face of death. Then, between the parted curtain, he caught a brief glimpse of a familiar face, disappearing the moment Larn twitched his head around.

It was Kate. What could she want?

****

Kate saw him bound behind the sheriff, then jerked herself away from the window as Larn turned her way. She wasn't sure how many deputies were with him, and she didn't have the time to check again. Down the street a crowd of men gathered quietly in the deep darkness between buildings where no light from illuminated windows could seep. And toward that black chasm, Kate had seen one man carrying a rope.

Kate had tied the horses by the Cattle Exchange. She carried in one hand Doc's valise, half filled with his clothes and half with her own, and in the other his medical bag bulging with his dental tools, his marked cards and her favorite book, *Tom Sawyer*. Next she needed coal oil. She should have thought of it before. Without a distraction, she had no hope of springing Doc. She didn't have much time to improvise, not with those men smoldering for his neck.

She stepped around the corner and onto the plank walk in front of the hotel. Catching her breath, she pushed open the door and struggled her way inside. A spindly clerk with jerky motions and nervous eyes stood up suddenly from a chair behind the desk. He watched Kate carry her bags across the room. It was the same room where the puppet show had been held, but now it seemed too small for such a crowd. Two couches, squeezed between mismatched end tables, bordered the threadbare carpet leading from door to desk. And on each table, sat an unlit lamp.

Kate dropped the valise and medical bag at her feet as she leaned over the counter. A head taller than the clerk, she peered down on him. "A gentleman would've given a lady a hand!"

The clerk sniffed his upturned nose. "A lady wouldn't be out on the street this time of night!" He backed away from the counter as Kate lifted her hand.

"The pen." She smiled at the inkwell and writing instrument by the register. "I'd like a room."

"We don't do business with your type, madam."

Kate scowled. She didn't have time to waste arranging a room with this puny specimen of manhood. Again she smiled, but her voice was a deep, dark whisper. "Mister, a lot of men of been treated to the inside of my blouse. But besides my womanly charms, I hide a pistol there." She paused, then yelled. "Now give me a room or I'll put a bullet hole between your eyes."

The clerk froze as Kate's hand flashed toward her blouse. Down the back hall, a door banged open.

"Everything okay up there?"

Kate recognized Larn's voice. She turned her head away from the hall in case the sheriff came to investigate. With the gun in her hand, she whispered to the clerk. "Tell him nothing's wrong."

"Everything's fine, sheriff," the clerk called, "some drunk woman stuck her head inside 'fore I shooed her out."

Kate heard the door slam. She sighed.

"A room'll be four dollars for the night."

"That's more like it, fellow." She stuck her gun back in her blouse and exchanged it for four dollars. "Cash in advance. I know you wouldn't trust me to pay in the morning."

The clerk grabbed the money, held it up to the lamp.

"It ain't tainted."

He put the money in his pocket, then shoved the register and a pen toward Kate. "Last room on the left," he said as she signed.

"What about a key?"

"Only the Planters House has keyed rooms. You should've started there."

"The least you can do is carry my bags, light the lamp, and open a window."

Muttering beneath his breath, the clerk shook his head. "What's a woman like you got to fear from the dark?"

"Men like you. Now move, so I can get a good night's sleep."

"Alone, I suggest." The clerk primly straightened his shoulders.

"As always." Kate curtsied as the clerk fished for a tin of matches beneath the counter and marched down the hall. "You forgot my bags."

"Bring them yourself," he called without looking over his shoulder. "You coming."

"Soon as I get my bags." When he disappeared, Kate ran across the room. At the end table nearest the door, she choked the lamp between her hands, then jerked them away. The lamp was still hot; it must have been blown out only minutes earlier. The clerk's footsteps stopped, and she heard him fumbling with the door, which swung open on oil-starved hinges. She didn't have much time. She wrapped her hands in the folds of her skirt and gingerly picked up the lamp, only then noticing the emptiness of the glass bowl that should hold the coal oil. She cursed. The lamp had burned itself dry. She slid it brusquely back on the table. Jarring the chimney off, she caught it with her bare hand, then clenched her teeth as the hot glass seared her palm. Hearing the clerk opening the window, she realized she had too little time to worry about the pain. Twisting around to look at the other three table lamps, she cursed at the sound of the approaching clerk. She grabbed another lamp, scurried to the door and wrestled it open. The footfalls sounded closer. She leaned out the door, half placing, half dropping the lamp on the rough plank porch. She straightened up to close the door just as the footsteps turned silent behind her.

"What the devil are you doing?"

"Wind blew the door open." She lied and closed the door softly.

Folding his arms across his chest, the clerk stopped at the lampless table, lowered his arms, and placed the tin of matches there, as if he realized something were amiss but couldn't quite figure it out. "Likely story," he said, moving to her side.

Kate held her breath and rubbed her hands together, the friction aggravating the pain in her palms.

Staring at Kate, the clerk nodded, a smile spreading across his face like sunshine breaking through a cloud. "You're trying to slip a fellow in here." He lunged for the entry, pushed Kate aside, and wrenched the door open. He stuck his head out, looking around. "He's gone."

Kate eased away from the door, stationing herself between the clerk and the table minus the lamp. Backing up, she slipped one hand behind her and groped for the tin of matches. Feeling it, her hand closed tightly around the tin.

"Woman," the clerk said, shutting the door, then glaring at Kate, "you'll not conduct yourself as a harlot in this hotel."

Kate harrumphed, then nodded compliantly. "This is not what you think." Her lying lips smiled.

The clerk stepped past Kate, and she moved closely on his heels, the clerk heading for the counter, Kate grabbing her bags and going down the hall.

"Sleep soundly," he called in her wake.

Kate struggled against her feet to keep from running. Reaching her room, she stepped inside, kicked the door to and tossed the bags on the bed, taking in the space as she did. It was a corner room with two windows, both open. She flew to the side window and stuck her head out long enough to see the mob of men crawling out of the dark holes of night into the street. Quickly, she pulled the window down and jerked the curtains together. Racing to the back window, she raised it as high as it would go, then shoved a leg outside, worked her head and torso out and pulled the other leg out behind her as she landed on the ground.

Kate crouched low as her eyes adjusted to the dark. Gradually, buildings took shape and not forty paces from the hotel was a small stable. It would do. As she stood up, the match tin slipped from her hand. She caught a glimmer of it from light coming out her window, but as she stepped forward to pick it up, her foot kicked it into the darkness. She fell to her knees groping madly for the tin, slapping the ground with her burned hands. The noise of the mob grew louder and closer. Time was growing shorter, Kate thought. Then she felt the tin, and her fingers closed around it. For a moment she clutched it to her breast, then she shoved it in her blouse and ran around the front of the hotel.

She stuck her head around the front corner of the hotel. The mob, with two angry torches lighting the way like malevolent eyes, was coming. The lamp. She must fetch it before they got here. She raced down the porch, grabbed the lamp, and dashed off the walk, stumbling as she turned the corner of the hotel, the lamp chimney tumbling to the ground, shattering like a crystal explosion. Startled by the breaking glass, a stray dog growled, then chased her, nipping at her heels until she spun around and kicked at the dark form behind her. The cur yelped and receded deeper into the darkness that was night.

What the hell else could go wrong? She wondered as she reached the shed. Surely, it would burn, she thought as she flung the door open, the clatter seeming to thunder across the Flat. She caught a glimpse of the mob as it advanced on the hotel. The vigilantes came like a giant growling bear, emboldened by its own noise. She hurried inside the stable, the sweet smell of hay tickling her nose. The lamp tucked under her arm, she pulled the tin of matches from her blouse and struck a match against the wormwood walls. It flamed just long enough for her to see the bed of hay scattered across the entrance, then died. This building would make a good fire.

Lifting the lamp over her head, she flung it to the ground. As the lamp splattered glass and coal oil against the hay, Kate was startled by a kicking and nickering in the back of the stall. A horse! Kate jumped deeper into the stable and followed the noise to the animal. The horse flinched at her touch, but she patted him long enough to find the halter that bound him. Undoing it, she slapped his flank and the animal bolted for the door, darting outside and away from the advancing terror of the mob.

Kate hoped she wasn't too late. Moving to the shattered lamp, she scratched another match against the wall, a small flame erupting. She threw the match too quickly at the hay, and it died before striking the ground. She stuck her fingers in the tin for another match, and nurtured it to life against the wormwood wall. She bent over and held the flame to the hay. Slowly the match licked the hay, taking hold and beginning to assume a life beyond control. As the flames grew, she fed them more hay, then picked up a burning pile and tossed it deeper into the barn. She jumped back at the swoosh of flames taking to the coal oil. The hay seemed to explode, and Kate laughed as she dashed for the corner hotel room with the open window and the burning lamp.

At the window, she could hear around the side of the building the shouts of the vigilantes, screwing up their courage by their noise. She jerked up her skirt and shoved her leg through the window, following it with her torso. Before she could bring her other leg in, she was petrified by a voice.

"I knew it."

Her head twisted instantly toward the sound of the clerk's voice. "Don't you give your customers any privacy?" She pulled her leg in.

"Not," he gloated, "when they use this hotel as a brothel."

Kate stuck her head outside. "Run, cowboy," she yelled.

The clerk pushed Kate away from the window and stared into the night. "So I was right," he said, turning to Kate and folding his arms across his chest. "The sheriff's just down the hall. I'll get him to take care of you."

Kate pulled her revolver from her blouse and stepped toward the clerk. "We'll settle this without the sheriff."

"Oh my god," the clerk answered, his hands dropping to his side as he took a step toward Kate.

Cocking the revolver, she pointed it at his nose. "Another step, and you're a dead man."

He pointed out the window, his skin turning pale. His lips mouthed a word twice before he mumbled, "Fire."

"Don't move."

"Fire. The barn. My horse." He lunged for the door and out into the hall. "Fire," he screamed. "Fire out back. Everybody out to save the town."

Kate ran to the door and watched as adjacent rooms emptied of half-dressed men. Toward the front of the hall, a door opened slowly, and a man stepped out with a drawn gun. It was Larn. Kate ducked inside, closing the door except for the inch-wide crack through which she spied. For a moment the sheriff surveyed the hall, then called for a deputy. Together, they bolted toward the front of the hotel. It had worked. She forced herself to count to fifty, then picked up the medical bag and the valise.

****

At the sound of a knock on the door, the deputy twisted his face to the door. He eased his gun out of his holster and slipped toward the noise. His hand reaching for the knob, the deputy called, "Who is it?"

"Aaaaghh," a woman screamed.

Holliday recognized Kate's voice.

"Who is it?" the deputy repeated.

"Wilma Plunkett. You're in my room."

The deputy twisted the knob and cracked the door, which flew open, Kate barging in behind it, her head downturned, away from the deputy. She dropped the valise and the medical bag on the floor. "Aaaaghh," she screamed at the deputy's gun aimed at her chest. "Don't shoot me just because I got the wrong room, sir. I—I feel faint." She lunged for a chair and plopped down, burying her face in her hands. Her mumbled voice muttered through the palm mask. "I'd paid for the room, and the clerk was going to show me to it, and then he started yelling fire, and everybody started running out, and I thought the building was on fire, and I was going to burn to death, and now you're in my room, and pointing a gun at me to kill me." She sobbed.

Holliday watched the deputy holster his pistol and then shut the door. As the deputy turned his back, Holliday caught Kate observing him through her fingers as she mumbled incoherently.

"There's nothing to fear ma'am," the deputy began. "Been a lot of excitement outside here the last few minutes."

Kate sobbed louder. "And, there's a mob of men outside, and I thought they were going to kill me. Some of them were carrying a rope, and a couple was wearing hoods over their heads, and I don't know what's to become of me. I shouldn't have been out on the street, but I thought we had brave lawmen in town that would stop that mob. Guess I was wrong."

"You've made two mistakes, ma'am," the deputy coughed. "This isn't your room, and the law will take care of you." The deputy sidled toward Kate and placed his hand upon her left wrist. "Just calm down and we'll get this straightened out. It's a simple mistake."

Kate nodded and leaned forward to stand up. She stumbled into the deputy. In one fluid motion her left hand jerked his pistol from its holster, and her uplifted knee caught the deputy in the groin. He groaned. "No mistake, deputy."

"What the hell," the deputy gasped through the pain, looking full into Kate's face for the first time. "Why, Kate you bitch!"

His hand flinched toward his empty holster.

Kate cocked his revolver. "Raise your hands or you're dead." The deputy complied.

"In his belt, Kate," Holliday warned, "he's got my revolvers and in his boot my dagger."

Kate smiled coyly at Holliday. "Aren't you gonna say you're glad to see me, Doc?"

"Kate, we don't have time to argue."

Kate motioned with the revolver for the deputy to move toward the bed. "Let me correct you, Doc. You don't have time for this. If I hadn't fired that barn, the vigilantes would already've hoisted you from a cottonwood. Now, are you glad to see me?"

"More than ever. Untie me before your little fire burns out, and we're both hung."

"Fall on the bed, deputy." He tumbled forward and she placed the gun at his temple. "If you so much as break wind, I'll blow your brains out." She removed Holliday's guns from his belt.

"The knife in his boot," Holliday said, rocking toward the bed in his chair. "Get it and cut me free."

"Shut up, Doc. I'm in charge now." With Doc's guns under her arm, she backed away from the bed and turned the deputy's gun on Holliday. "Now, Doc, you tell me something. Did you kill Bailey 'cause you were mad about Lottie leaving? Or, were you jealous Bailey'd been sleeping with me?"

"Why do you think I killed him, Kate?"

"You were jealous, Doc. That was it, wasn't it?"

"Sure, Kate, sure. Now untie me before the sheriff returns."

"Deputy," Kate called. "You get up easy off that bed and cut the ropes. If you so much as draw a drop of his blood, I'll spill yours all over this floor."

The deputy slid off the bed and drew the knife from his boot as he eased toward Holliday. For a moment, he held it menacingly over Holliday's spine.

"Do something foolish, you'll die, deputy. You're dealing with his wife-to-be."

His lips twitching, the deputy lowered the knife to the bindings and freed Holliday's arms, then his feet.

Holliday flexed his arms and rubbed the circulation back into them. As the deputy finished slicing the rope around his boots, Holliday spoke. "Put the knife on the floor by my feet." As he obeyed, Holliday raised his boot and stomped the deputy's hand into the floor.

The deputy screamed and jerked his injured hand free, massaging it with his other.

"Now," Holliday said, "you'll feel the rope burn." He leaned forward and picked up the knife, then stood, his knees wobbly as a newly dropped calf. He staggered toward the bed. Kate steadied him and slipped Doc's sidearm back in its holster. She kissed him on the cheek, but he shrugged her off. "Not until I get him tied." He shoved his knife back in its sheath and took the shoulder gun from Kate. Then he stepped behind the deputy, grabbed him by the hair, and jerked him against the chair back. "Sit straight while I tie you. Kill him, if he moves," he commanded Kate. Holliday held his pistol by the barrel and slammed it with all his might into the deputy's head. The deputy sat motionless for a moment, his only movement the upward roll of his eyes. Then Doc crashed the pistol butt against his head again, and the deputy toppled over like a sack of flour onto the floor.

"We've gotta steal horses and get out of town, Kate."

"I've taken care of that. I've tied horses the other side of the Cattle Exchange." Kate grabbed Holliday's medical satchel.

Holliday motioned Kate to the door with his gun, but he lingered a moment by the washstand, fingering the corroded dealing box and shoving it in his coat.

"What's that, Doc?"

"You're asking too many questions, Kate," he answered, picking up his valise. "Just lead the way to the horses."

Easing the door open, Kate surveyed the hall. It was vacant. Holliday cocked his pistol as he followed her down the hall, through the deserted lobby, and cautiously out on the walk. Everywhere men ran, as if the city might not survive. Kate and Doc moved against the stream, conspicuous by their cautious pace, but no one took time to watch. Nearby, men were directing a water wagon to the fire and sending another to the creek for refilling. As Doc and Kate passed the deserted Cattle Exchange, she pointed to two mounts at an adjacent hitching post.

Holliday eyed the horses. "Damn, Kate, not Haverty's pinto and that damn Golden's chestnut?"

"Nothing can outrun them, Doc." She stopped on the walk. "You never approve a thing I do for you."

"Haverty will have the sheriff out looking for them."

She pitched Doc's medical bag on the walk. "You don't like it, you get your own horses and get the hell out of my sight." She folded her arms across her chest and tapped her foot on the plank walk. "Burn the stinking town down, get the drop on a deputy so you won't hang, I do, and all you do is complain."

Footsteps on the plank walk behind them interrupted Holliday's response. Turning, he saw a bulky figure step from the shadows toward them. For a moment, Holliday paused as mutual recognition washed over himself and Chancey.

"Doc Holliday," Chancey called, "what are—" Then as he inched close enough to confirm Holliday's identity, Chancey broke toward the main street. His husky voice seemed to carry over the noise of the fire. "Holliday's escaped! Holliday's escaped!"

Kate laughed. "Now, are my horses good enough for you?"

"Plenty, Kate, let's get out of here." He pitched his valise over the saddle and mounted the chestnut. Kate hesitated. "You can't back out now," he shouted.

Kate picked up the medical bag and jumped toward the pinto, untying it from the hitching post and climbing unladylike aboard.

Holliday jerked his mount around and rode off toward the river, not by the main road but by a trail among the buffalo ricks. Cautiously, they wended their way through the obstacles, then clearing them, raced toward the line of trees, dimly visible three quarters of a mile ahead. Quickly, they were among the cottonwoods. Holliday drew up his horse and ordered Kate to stop.

"Maybe no one's taken up the chase." His voice was sharp, despite his breathlessness.

The seconds seemed to draw past as slowly as years, and then, after an interminable time, it seemed that no one was giving chase.

Holliday spent the time tying his valise to his saddle, and Kate doing likewise with the medical bag. And when nothing emerged following them, Doc spoke, "I'm surprised Chancey turned against me."

"He'd never was with you, Doc. I'm the only one who's for you." She nudged her horse closer to his, just as Holliday heard the noise of pounding hooves.

"Damn, Kate," Holliday muttered. "They're after us."

Maybe twenty riders just coming into view from behind the huge buffalo ricks were aimed straight at them.

"Let's go, Doc," Kate implored, "but where can we hide?"

For a moment, Doc was silent. "The baseball field, the giant cottonwood."

"What?"

"Listen, Kate, just follow me. We'll make a wide circle away from the creek and head back into it upstream where they play baseball. Let's go."

He slapped the flank of the chestnut and splashed through the creek shallows, Kate behind him. And, in a few moments, the posse was, too. Over the thundering hoofbeats of their mounts, Holliday thought he heard the shouts of riders and then the retort of their guns. Thank goodness, Kate had stolen the best horses. "We've got to put as much distance between them and us as fast as we can, Kate," Holliday yelled. "Don't save your horse for later. Just stay with me."

The two animals sensed the urgency. Their clean even strides gave Holliday a sense of confidence his plan would work, if only their speed bought enough time to hide when they struck the river again.

Whipping their horses forward, Kate and Holliday made for the ridge leading out of the valley, then turned sharply heading the direction the stream flowed. For maybe two miles they paralleled it, then swung back toward the Clear Fork. They had stretched the distance between themselves and the posse, but would the distance be enough? Holliday wondered.

Nearing the watercourse, Holliday shouted at Kate. "Hit the creek, then head back for town."

"Back to town?" Kate drew up on the reins, then slapped the pinto on the flank, the horse stumbling from the indecision. "You're a fool, Doc," he heard her yell.

The chestnut hit the water hard, then struggled to regain its stride as Holliday jerked the reins. Holliday cursed as the animal faltered, then dashed upstream, almost jarring Holliday from the saddle. Ahead, Holliday could see the bend in the creek that cradled the baseball diamond in its elbow. The huge tree at the stream's edge suddenly loomed ahead of him like a giant fortress. He twisted his head over his shoulder to see Kate approaching. The posse had yet to come into sight. If only Kate made it in time. In the darkness, he could gradually make out the somber bank. The giant hole gouged out from under the tree's roots by last summer's floods had not caved in.

Holliday aimed the chestnut for the space beneath the bank and between the gnarled roots. Reaching the hole, the animal shied away. Holliday jerked the reins taut, then beat the animal's chest with the slack. The horse eased cautiously forward, and Holliday dismounted to lead the animal into the chasm as the splashing pinto neared. Holding tight the reins of the spooked chestnut, he leaped from his hiding place to stop Kate.

She screamed, then recognized Holliday. "You scared me. I thought I'd lost you, Doc."

"No time for that," Holliday called. "Take cover." He grabbed the pinto's bridle, jerking it toward the undercut bank.

Kate slapped the pinto, and he moved skittishly into the hiding place, which smelled of moist earth and rotten wood. She jumped off the horse and maneuvered it as deeply into the cut as she could. "Some damn spot you picked to hide, Doc Holliday."

"You got any better ideas? They may spot us if they come down the creek, but if they ride up the bank, we may get away with it."

Kate wrapped the reins around her hand. "This place gives me the creeps. If there are any snakes in here, I may scream."

"You do, you may hang the both of us." Holliday caught Kate's arm and squeezed it tight. "Quiet." He poked his head out from a tangle of roots and stared down the creek. "They've stopped in the creek," he whispered. He could barely make out milling forms in the distance.

Kate peeked toward the riders. Then the pinto spooked and bolted for the stream. Kate yelped as the horse jerked the reins tied around her arm. Holliday lunged for the saddle horn of the animal, missing it, then grabbing for the stirrup. He shoved his hand in the stirrup and pulled. For a moment, as the pinto broke for the open and the chestnut backed away, Holliday thought he would be torn in half, between the hand caught in the stirrup and the other wrapped in the chestnut's reins. But Kate jerked savagely at the pinto's reins, then slapped it hard on the nose. The horse whinnied, then retreated into the little cave.

Both horses under control, Holliday glanced downstream. The posse was coming toward them, moving at a canter.

"They're coming, Kate, stay quiet. Our lives depend on it."

Kate grunted. Holliday pulled his gun from his holster. "If there's shooting, Kate, you break for freedom. I'll cover you as long as I can."

"What about you, Doc?" She reached for his arm, squeezed it tightly. "You'll get killed."

"I owe you one, Kate. There's little future for a gambler with consumption."

"Nor for me without you, Doc. I can use a gun."

"Not this time, Kate. For once, you'll do as I say."

She released his Doc's arm and patted the pinto to calm him.

From down the river, they could hear the muffled sound of voices, words made indecipherable by distance and the splash of horses' hooves. The riders drew within fifty yards. Holliday cocked his pistol. "If I shoot, you mount and ride, Kate."

The distance between the quarry and the hunters halved. Holliday heard Kate's breathing between his own labored gasps for air, and it seemed that even the posse would hear them, too. Then the voices of the pursuers carried to the hiding place.

"They'd be fools to head back to town."

Holliday recognized Larn's voice, but not the reply that answered him.

"But I know I heard a woman scream and maybe a horse."

Larn spoke again. "Sound travels far at night. Probably a whore in the Flat. Let's head downstream."

They came within ten yards, and Holliday felt himself backing against his horse, pressing it against the pinto. He grabbed for the horse's nostrils and covered them with his gun hand. Finally, the riders turned from the stream and went up the bank. Holliday exhaled a heavy breath of relief. There was more conversation, which he could not make out, then Larn's voice.

"Okay, you two ride on toward town. We'll follow the stream until after dawn to see if we spot them or any trace."

Then the pinto kicked at the chestnut. Kate and Holliday shoved the nervous horses apart, but the noise was lost in the sound of the posse galloping away from the cottonwood tree. Slowly, Holliday twisted from his horse and looked downstream, raising his revolver. At least now, he and Kate would have a better chance against a pair of men instead of a whole posse, but had the other two ridden away at the same time?

"Kate," Holliday whispered. "Did they all leave?"

"I couldn't hear for my pounding heart," she answered.

For several minutes the man, woman, and animals huddled together beneath the great cottonwood tree as rivulets of dirt shook loose upon them from the earthen roof, the seconds dragging by like minutes, the minutes like hours until Doc had no perception of actual time. His urge to flee battled his need for caution. Finally, he dared to ease his head out between a tangle of roots. He held his breath and looked both directions along the stream. As he lifted his hand to motion for Kate to emerge from hiding, his eyes spotted a silent pinpoint of light arc from the bank overhead into the creek. Someone had tossed a cigarette into the creek. He slammed his hand against Kate. Two mounted men lingered on the bank above them. Holliday caught a whiff of cigarette smoke and knew the wait must be longer. His heart seemed to pound as loud as a drum on the Fourth of July. He weighed the merits of killing the pair and making a dash for freedom until he heard one of them speak.

"Maybe the sheriff was right, but I swear I heard something."

"Like the sheriff said," the other answered, "sound can play tricks on you at night. Let's let the sheriff catch up with this fellow. That's his job, not ours."

In a moment the hoofbeats of their mounts trailed away into the distance, and all was silent, except for Holliday's and Kate's breathing and the pounding of their hearts.

Kate whispered. "What'll we do now, Doc?"

"We'll stay a while." He eased the hammer down on his revolver and stuck it back in its holster.

And they waited. Gradually, they allowed their mounts a little more freedom and themselves chances to work the cramps out of their muscles. Painfully slow, the night continued until a hint of dawn rimmed the sky. "Get ready to ride. We'll have to make good time."

She smiled back. "I'll go anywhere with you, Doc."

He nodded, brushing the dirt from his coat. "I'll look around. You wait here." Holliday emerged fully from the dirty den. Slipping cautiously upstream, he crouched his way up the bank, lifting his head eye-level against the flatness that stretched to town. Like a prairie dog emerging from his den, he looked all around, then climbed out into the open. Nothing he saw ahead or in the surrounding country frightened him, but he bent over and ran to the cottonwood tree. Finding the lowest branch, he lifted himself aboard and climbed as high as he dared. As if he were in the crow's nest of a sailing vessel, he scanned all around the country. The Flat was awakening, but nothing seemed amiss there, and the posse was nowhere to be seen.

Quickly, he descended to the low branch, then dropped himself to the ground. He pitched forward as he fell and landed on all fours. Shaking his head, he stared at the ground. In the dimness his eyes slowly focused on a bed of Indian blankets strewn among the grass. The flowers were mostly dried up, having lost most petals to the summer sun, but Doc broke eight off anyway and formed an awkward bouquet. Standing, he felt his coat fall heavily against his hip, and he remembered the corroded dealing box Lottie had saved for him. He pulled it from his pocket, shaking his head as he studied it. Then he turned toward the embankment and slipped down to the horses and Kate.

"Things seem calm, Kate," he called softly. A frail light reached the edge of the hiding spot, enough for Holliday to see Kate's features, as she emerged. She wasn't a bad looking woman, he thought, even with a dirt-smudged face and eyelids drooping with tired. He smiled at her. As she moved beside the horses, Holliday tossed the dealing box into the creek. Then he slipped his hand in his coat pocket, extracting the tintype image of Lottie. Without looking at it, he tossed it in the water by the dealing box.

"What was that?" she asked with a start.

Holliday looked from the water up at her. "Something I don't need anymore." Stepping beside her, Doc lifted his hand and extended the pathetic flowers to Kate.

"For me?"

"No, for your pinto," Holliday shrugged. "Sure, they're for you."

Gently, she took them from him and leaned against him, kissing his cheek.

"From now on, Kate, I'm your Huckleberry."

She hugged him. "I knew you'd come around, Doc."

"Save it for later, Kate. We've got to ride."

"But where to, Doc?" She handed him his reins, and they both mounted.

"Kansas, Kate. I've got a friend named Wyatt Earp in Dodge City."

Epilogue

Doc Holliday rode from Fort Griffin to Dodge City and into legend. His acquaintance with Wyatt Earp became the single enduring male friendship of his life. Together Earp and Holliday would become myth and survive—at Tombstone's O.K. Corral—the most famous gunfight in the history of the Old West. A tumbleweed of a man, Holliday drifted among the boom towns of the 1870s, winning money and enemies.

Big Nose Kate Elder considered the following years in Dodge City as the happiest of her life and herself as the wife of Doc Holliday. Their tempestuous relationship was never sanctified by marriage vows, though Kate followed him from Dodge City to Tombstone. And when consumption finally caught up with Doc Holliday in Glenwood Springs, Colo., in 1887, she was with him.

Keeping his promise, Jack Jacobs never revealed Lottie Deno's true identity. Lottie disappeared from history the day she carried her money-laden trunk aboard the stagecoach outside Fort Griffin. However, in 1934 Charlotte Thurmond, the widow of a one-time gambler Frank Thurmond, died in Deming, N.M. Among the possessions of the devout 89-year-old Episcopalian was a leather trunk with Jack Jacobs' initials over the latch.

About the Author

Preston Lewis is the award-winning author of more than 50 western, historical and juvenile novels. In 2021 he was inducted into the Texas Institute of Letters for his literary accomplishments.

Western Writers of America (WWA) has honored Lewis with two Spur Awards, one for best article and the second for best western novel. He has received three Will Rogers Gold Medallion Awards for written western humor, two more for western short stories and one for traditional Western.

Lewis is a past president of WWA and the West Texas Historical Association, which has named him a fellow. He holds a bachelor's degree from Baylor University and a master's degree from Ohio State University, both in journalism. Additionally, he has a second master's degree in history from Angelo State University.

He lives in San Angelo, Texas, with wife Harriet Kocher Lewis.

E-mail: prestonlewisauthor@gmail.com
Facebook: prestonlewisauthor
Website: prestonlewisauthor.com

www.ingramcontent.com/pod-product-compliance
Lightning Source LLC
Chambersburg PA
CBHW030546310726
48979CB00010B/2049/J

* 9 7 8 1 9 6 4 8 3 0 0 1 8 *

To watchmakers
who spend their days in a postcard-sized world
creating technologically amazing pieces of art

Prologue

The dog licked his human's face, trying to stem the ongoing trickle. His human did not respond. It nuzzled the hood covering his human's head, still no response.

With the leash wrapped so tightly around his human's arm, the French bulldog could barely move. As if resigned to his fate, he sat and panted as he looked around.

The scent of an acquaintance came on the wind. He pointed his nose to the sky and sniffed the air. Yes, he knew the golden retriever heading his way. Shortly, he spied an approaching light bouncing up and down. As the light grew larger and brighter, he could hear the rhythmic panting of the other dog straining at her leash.

The Frenchie let out a soft whine, and within moments, the golden retriever was upon him. The flashlight briefly shone into the Frenchie's eyes and then traveled down his body over to the face of the human lying next to him.

A scream broke the evening's calm.

Eight weeks earlier

Chapter 1

John Harrison concentrated on his notecards as he spoke. He wasn't reading from them. Having practiced his pitch numerous times at home and having already delivered the same presentation to two other groups, he knew his talk verbatim. The cards were one of the strategies his companion, Suzanne, had helped him develop. She was well aware of both the limited amount of time he had to create audience interest in his development and the degree of anxiety that public speaking caused him. The cards kept him on track and helped regulate his anxiety, allowing him to start and finish his presentation.

Standing at the end of a conference table to the left of a large screen displaying his presentation, he spoke in a monotone drone and made no eye contact with anyone in the audience. Wearing a dark blue jacket over a white collarless shirt (collars bothered him), a pullover, and no tie (ties were another source of discomfort), he looked like a typical corporate employee. A closer look would reveal that all the labels had been removed from his clothing, and his brown shoes had textured rubber soles to prevent any possibility of squeaking when he walked. Despite those attempts to ease his unease, he stood at the podium, his right foot in front of his left, perceptibly rocking back and forth. His curly, dark, unintentionally stylish brown hair and his slight stature gave him a quite unassuming appearance. There was no chance a casual observer would mistake him for a gym rat or an athlete of any kind. And he gave no outward indication of the sharp intelligence he possessed.

Even though the conference room was large enough to hold thirty, he had an audience of only five. Of the three companies he came to Switzerland to address, this organization seemed the most eager to meet with him, so he was advised to leave this presentation for last. That way, he would be better prepared.

When he first began teaching at the college, someone had recommended that he make eye contact with his students. But that was just not possible. This room was no different. When not studying his cards, John stared at a point in space somewhere in the middle of the conference table, his light brown eyes behind tortoise shell frames seemingly unfocused. Periodically, he'd awkwardly point to images on the screen. On the rare occasion, he'd lift his eyes to look through the windows. Outside, he could see a pastoral scene in the Vallée de Joux: cows grazing on deep green grass, a corona of pine trees in the background, and fluffy white clouds floating in the deep blue sky.

Coffee cups, a scattering of chocolate wrappers, and plates sprinkled with leftover pastry crumbs rested on the table. Three members of the company's executive team appeared to listen carefully, taking notes from the slides. From what John could tell, they were making rough renditions of what they saw. Another man sat midway down the table, staring out the windows. His blank face gave him the demeanor of someone more senior than those scribbling away on their pads.

John was unconcerned about the attempts to copy his presentation. The diagrams and data on the screen were incomplete; he'd omitted essential details for the sake of secrecy. And the notes he'd scrawled on his cards were like hieroglyphics, mysterious ciphers that prevented unwanted eyes from discovering the secrets behind his invention. Reliance on promises to respect the confidentiality of information only went so far. While technically an outsider in this industry, John had studied it well. He knew how revolutionary his development was and that, conceivably, it could set the entire industry on its collective ears.

At the head of the table, opposite him, sat the only woman in the room. Her long blond hair was stylishly draped over the shoulders of her blue pinstriped suit. Under her jacket, a chartreuse blouse was open at the neck, exposing an emerald and diamond necklace. A sixth attendee was present via a telephone placed on *speaker* mode. Whether the unidentified person was really on the other end of the line, John couldn't tell, as there was only silence coming from the phone.

His talk lasted twenty minutes. When finished, he braced himself for the time he hated most: question time. Unlike the students in his classroom, he couldn't predict what the people facing him might ask.

The team members of the Frédérique Zeller Watch Company took a collective breath when John finished. All heads—except for the blond woman's—turned toward the man gazing out the window. He, in turn, sat straighter in his chair and slowly shifted his eyes from the windows to stare at John. His white lab coat, pink sports shirt, and well-worn jeans completed the hipster look he seemed to be embracing with his blond ponytail that extended beyond his collar. "You believe that it will work?"

"No, Mister…" John paused to look at the list of printed names and titles resting on the table in front of him and found that of the head watchmaker addressing him. "Rousseau. I do not think this will work. I know it works." John gazed at the loupe connected to Rousseau's clear eyeglasses. It was tipped up against the man's forehead.

"How so?"

"I currently have a movement I modified to contain the system, and it has been running flawlessly, gaining only one second, over the past six weeks."

Rousseau's right eyebrow twitched upwards; otherwise, his face remained impassive.

From the end of the table, the woman, Charice Bonet, co-CEO of the company, spoke without taking her eyes from her cell phone. "If we were to move ahead with this, we would require exclusivity rights."

For the first time, John looked directly at her. "No. I own the patent."

Charice's head shot up. She stared so hard at him, John averted his eyes to his cards.

"I intend that it will be open-sourced," he said. "So that anyone will be able to use it. The information will be in the public domain, and I will always be available by email to provide details in addition to the specifications that I will publish for reference."

"If so," Charice spoke slowly. "Then why all the secrecy?"

Beads of moisture formed on John's upper lip. He closed his eyes and took a deep breath. "The movement is working, but it is not ready for production. It still needs further testing."

"Then why are you here talking to us?"

John had been asked this question at each meeting. Despite expecting it now, he was still nervous to answer. "Because I am looking for a company to help me with the final adjustments before we put it into production. Once the initial production run has been successful, it will then be presented to the watch community so others can use it." He paused again to check his notes. "The company that helps me will have the advantage of being in front of the rest of the market. They will be a leader in the field and will benefit financially."

"Maybe initially," Rousseau muttered in a stage whisper loud enough for the others around the table to hear.

"Thank you, Monsieur Harrison." Charice rose and left the room.

John looked up as she made her exit. Rousseau gave him a quick nod, stood, and followed in her wake. The others chatted amongst themselves for a few minutes before mumbling their goodbyes and leaving the conference room. No handshakes were exchanged, as John had made it clear at the outset of the meeting that he wasn't comfortable with that sort of physical contact.

Standing at the head of the table in a now-empty room, John emitted a brief sigh of relief. Only a couple of questions, much fewer than at his other presentations, and that was glorious. At the last presentation, he'd been peppered with questions for fifteen minutes before he could escape. He gathered his few things and removed his thumb drive from the computer. The receptionist who had guided him to the conference room appeared in the doorway and beckoned him to follow her back to the lobby of the building.

It was only as he walked down a flight of stairs that John started to wonder whether the limited number of questions indicated a lack of interest. Did they get it? Did they understand the revolutionary nature of his development?

The first group he spoke to showed no appreciation for the significance of what he was offering them. Based on their questions, the second seemed very interested. John considered for a moment that maybe all those questions at the last presentation were meant to squeeze as much information out of him as possible so that they could steal his invention.

Stepping from the staircase into the lobby, John saw Suzanne relaxing on a couch, reading a magazine. As if sensing his approach, she glanced up, saw him, and immediately rose to greet him.

Smiling, she punched something on her phone.

"I just arranged for a car for us," she said. "Our flight out of Geneva leaves in four and a half hours, so we'll have plenty of time to get to the airport from here." She nodded toward the two roller bags near the receptionist's desk, and in step, they retrieved their luggage and headed for the lobby's exit.

"What do you think?" Charice's voice had a nasal twang coming through her brother's cell phone.

Jean-Louis wasn't sure what he thought as he stood before a window of his chalet near the Gstaad ski slopes. His mind was consumed by his latest conquest, who was busying herself in the bathroom in preparation for facing the luncheon crowd at the Hotel Alpenland. "What would Father think?" he asked.

"He's dead," Charice shot back. "It's up to *you*. You're the head of watches. This time, you had better be right."

Jean-Louis glared at his phone, wishing he could shoot darts at his sister via the cellular connection. Before he could respond, a female form floated out of the bathroom. Long chestnut hair framed her beautiful face, and the semi-sheer pink blouse and black yoga pants left little to the imagination about her magnificent attributes that he'd been exploring an hour earlier. At the sight of her, he forgot all else. She skirted around his outstretched hand, leaving only the wisp of her perfume for him to savor.

"Jean, did you hear what Harrison said?" Charice's voice brought him back to the topic at hand, though his hands sought to feel another topic.

"Yeah. For the most part. I think we should go after it."

"Are you sure? You were positive that we couldn't lose with the Elegante line, and you know how that turned out." Charice's voice had that edge her brother was all too familiar with—that edge that said she was trying to modulate it to keep him from knowing how pissed she was. But he always knew. "We are teetering on a financial cliff here. And we're going to fall off if we make another bad move."

After their father died six years earlier, Charice and Jean-Louis were appointed co-CEOs of the Frédérique Zeller Watch Company. Their father had inherited the company after the untimely death of his father, who had been killed in a car accident on a mountain pass in the Italian Alps. Left with a Geneva-based storefront that housed four watchmakers and two technicians, their father had succeeded in growing the company to employ more than 300 people, producing over 4,000 watches per year. Before his death, Zeller was consistently making a handsome profit for the family.

With Charice and Jean-Louis at the helm, profits plummeted, and she was right, the company was now teetering on the edge of insolvency. Bad decisions, unsuccessful campaigns, and a lavish lifestyle had all but decimated the company's bank accounts. To date, they'd been able to hide that truth from the other members of the leadership team as well as from the investors they'd been courting to bolster their sagging financial state of affairs. No one would take kindly to the knowledge that the promised healthy return on their investment was but a figment of Jean-Louis's and Charice's imaginations. At this point, a significant cash infusion was essential; it was the difference between survival and bankruptcy. If Harrison's invention was as innovative as he claimed, it could be quite the carrot to dangle before potential investors, promising a lucrative return.

"Are you sure?" Charice repeated before Jean-Louis could respond.

"I am. This is a game-changer. Not only for the company but also for the whole industry. Once we get an exclusive agreement, we will be able to market the shit out of it."

"Yeah, but what about his open-source bullshit?"

"I'll take care of it. Don't worry about it."

"How?" Charice snapped.

Jean-Louis watched the brunette slip into knee-high boots. "I just will."

"Right." An exasperated sigh came through the speaker. "Meanwhile, I'll get with Rousseau to get his take on the presentation."

Chapter 2

When John's cell rang, Suzanne wasn't sure what to do. First, he was in his workroom, which meant he didn't want to be disturbed. And second, she couldn't remember the last time he had a telephone conversation. He did most of his communication by email and occasionally by text. However, after realizing the call was from Switzerland, she chose to answer.

"Good evening, I'm sorry, good morning." The voice on the other end had a strong French accent. "May I speak to Monsieur Harrison?"

"Who is calling, please?"

"*Excusez-moi.* This is Jean-Louis Bonet. I am president and CEO of the Frédérique Zeller Watch Company. My team met with Monsieur Harrison a couple of weeks ago."

"Ah, yes. This is Suzanne Lang, John's, um, assistant. How can I help you?" She figured Bonet wasn't calling just to say hello, but her protective instincts kicked in. She wasn't going to pass him on to John until she knew the man's intentions.

"I am here with our head watchmaker, Michel Rousseau," Jean-Louis replied. "We would like to discuss moving forward with a collaboration with Monsieur Harrison."

Delighted, Suzanne quietly did a quick, happy two-step dance. She cleared her voice before responding. "Let me see if I can get him. And please call him John."

"*Oui*. I'm sorry, yes, of course. I'll wait."

Suzanne muted the phone and hurried to the workroom. She paused to listen at the door. No noise from the other side. Lightly, she tapped on the doorframe, unsure if he had his headphones on. If so, she'd have to knock louder, but it was better to start softly and not take the chance of startling him. Typically, when engrossed in his work, John listened to heavy metal or some other…music or whatever you could call that discordant screaming she'd hear through his headphones. Even Louis had learned that if he wanted attention from John, he had to gently paw at one of his human's legs rather than yip or bark.

After several forceful knocks, John opened the door by no more than a crack. Suzanne tapped her ear to remind him to remove the headphones. "It's someone from the Zeller watch company." She handed him the phone.

John's eyebrows twitched upwards, which, for him, was a sign of excitement, equivalent to anyone else shouting in joy or giving an exuberant fist pump.

He stepped out of the room, and to Suzanne's relief, he unmuted the phone before hitting the *speaker* icon.

As he said, "Hello," Suzanne put a hand on his back to help him keep calm and focused.

"Hello John, this is Jean-Louis Bonet from Frédérique Zeller. I am here with Michel Rousseau, our head watchmaker. You met him and my sister when you were kind enough to visit us in the Vallée de Joux at the Manufacturer. Unfortunately, I had a conflicting meeting I was forced to attend when you were there. Nonetheless, I was able to listen to part of it over the telephone. I heard enough to get an idea of your innovative concept."

John made a quiet grunt as if in acknowledgement.

"To say the least, we are very interested, no, excited, to learn more about your development. We would like to discuss moving forward with a collaboration. But first, we do have several issues to work out."

"Okay."

There was a pause. Suzanne assumed Jean-Louis was waiting for a further response from John. After a moment of silence, he began speaking again. "Michel and his team have done some preliminary investigations into what you propose and believe that you are on to something. If this pans out, what you presented could revolutionize the watch industry almost overnight. We believe partnering with you to move this project forward to completion would be a wonderful opportunity. However, doing so would, of course, require a fair amount of upfront investment for the development and retooling of machines. As such, we feel that it would be in both of our interests to proceed with the usual confidentiality and exclusivity agreements."

Suzanne understood that John was at a potential inflection point. When he glanced at her, all she could do was raise her eyebrows in interest and subtly nod her head to encourage him.

Before he could respond, another voice came on the line. "John, this is Michel. My team is excited about this possibility. And you would have the advantage of working with one of the best design and technical teams in Switzerland."

"I will think about it."

"Sure, sure, John," Jean-louis replied. There was something about his voice that set Suzanne on edge—it reminded her of when her son was a little boy, dragging her through the mall, worried they'd miss Santa before he'd have a chance to sit on his lap and tell him what he wanted for Christmas. "How about we call you in two days?"

"Okay. Goodbye." John disconnected. Wordlessly, he disappeared into his workroom and shut the door.

"I'm proud of you, John," Suzanne called after him.

John remained in his workroom until it was time to take Louis for his midday walk. Upon returning, he sat at the dining table, slowly working his way through the sandwich Suzanne had prepared for his lunch. Engrossed in something on his cellphone, he took small bites from his smooth peanut butter and orange blossom honey sandwich on white bread, which she had precisely cut into quarters, the crusts neatly removed. She stood just outside the kitchen, looking at him.

Over the four years since his sister, Jacqueline, had hired her, Suzanne had developed a motherly attachment to him. She knew her emotional connection was unlikely ever to be reciprocated. His autism limited his ability to understand and communicate human emotions. The only being he demonstrated any affection for was his dog, Louis. Similarly, John wasn't capable of an outward display of emotion except when distressed or anxious. At those times, his stimming would amplify or, worse, he'd scream or attempt to harm himself. Fortunately, those eruptions had become much less frequent since Suzanne began working with him, but she always feared upsetting him.

She took a deep breath. "John."

He did not divert his eyes from the screen.

Unsure if he was listening, she continued. "I need to leave a bit early today." She realized that not telling him before was potentially a tactical error. John needed time to adjust, if possible, to any change in his routine. She wanted to head out within the next half hour, so she had no choice but to break the news to him and hope for the best.

"You see, I have a date tonight." She giggled to herself. "It's my first date in a long time. Really, it's the first since I met my husband. His name is Matthew. We met at our grief counseling group. He's a real nice guy."

Although it had been five years since her husband died, she still felt the need to attend the grief counseling group. It was more of a social gathering at this point, but she wondered whether somewhere deep inside of her, the group had become an emotional crutch. Regardless, that was where she met Matthew Daniels a couple of years prior. They'd built a friendship that had been limited to the meetings until the week prior. They'd struck up a conversation that lasted over an hour and decided to continue it at a local Italian restaurant. Nothing fancy, just reliably good food in a setting that allowed them to talk undisturbed.

"He is a retired police officer from New York City, a detective, I think," she continued her narrative, unsure if John understood the significance of this momentous event. "He moved out here a couple of years ago after the death of his wife."

John remained quiet. She explained that she had prepared his dinner, which was in the usual place in the refrigerator. Instructions to reheat the meal in the microwave, again as usual, were written out on an index card for him to follow at 6 o'clock.

She was relieved to see no negative reaction. It would have been nice to have a sign of affirmation from him, but that was never going to happen. She found it interesting that she'd told John about the date before she told her son, Stephen. She knew she could tell Stephen anything, and he would be supportive, but she chose not to make a big deal about the possibility of a blossoming relationship at this point. Besides, it was just two adults with some mutual interests going out to have dinner. Nothing special.

John and Jean-Louis Bonet communicated via email to set up a call two days later for 8:00 a.m., John's time. Suzanne arrived at his house at 7:45. Although he was capable, she volunteered to dial the Swiss mobile number he'd been given. She knew he was nervous about it. John spent most of his time squirreled away in his workroom. He left only to teach his course at the college or to walk Louis to the park and back. When he was stressed or nervous, he'd pace in the living room, which is what she found him doing when she arrived that morning. Pacing circles, muttering. Suzanne had been sure he was practicing what he intended to say.

Jean-Louis Bonet answered on the second ring.

"Good morning, Mr. Bonet, this is John Harrison." John's voice came out in his usual monotone.

"Good morning, John, it is good to speak with you once again," Jean-Louis's voice boomed through the phone's speaker. Suzanne thought it sounded too cheerful, as if he was putting on an act. "Have you had an opportunity to think about our proposal?"

"Yes, Mr. Bonet. As I said during my presentation, I plan to release my work to the public and make it open-sourced. I want anyone who wants to use it to do so freely. When I met with your team, I was looking for one or more partners in Switzerland to assist me in producing a completed watch. Once we have a proof-of-concept prototype, other companies will want it in their watches as well."

"But John, if we were to work together exclusively, I am sure the financial benefits would be very robust for many years to come for you and our company. You will get all the recognition you rightfully deserve. If you give your work away for free, you will not see monetary gain for all the time and effort you put into its development. I am willing to guarantee that someone else will take the credit for what you achieved, and you will be relegated to the deep, dark recesses of horological history. I know you are not interested in the ego factor. Still, you must understand that the cost of development, production, and bringing the product to market will require a significant capital investment. How many watch brands would be willing to make that kind of investment in unproven technology? I'm telling you, Zeller is in an excellent position to commit to you immediately to expedite its release, once we confirm it works."

"It works."

On the other side of the pond, Charice watched her brother struggle to come up with a convincing response to Harrison during a long moment of uncomfortable silence. Jean-Louis's eyes darted from her to Rousseau, who scribbled notes on a pad neither of them could read, and back to his sister. She fingered her emerald-and-diamond necklace as she only partially listened. Her attention was split between Jean-Louis's struggle to make his case to the American and the tennis bracelet she had on hold at her favorite jewelry store in Geneva.

Though the line was silent on the other end, Harrison hadn't ended the call. Jean-Louis resumed his pleading. "I know you've spent a lot of time in development, and I'm sure you have other ideas. I guarantee that our team can assist you with whatever you need, even the tiniest of details, related to producing such an innovative creation, and, for that matter, any other innovations you may come up with in the future. We can supply everything it takes: CAD designs, computer programming, production facilities, and, importantly, marketing. Our partnership will free you to do what you truly enjoy: work on innovative ideas. Believe me, you will be involved in every step of our development and manufacturing process. You will enjoy working with our watchmakers, who are the best in the industry. I am sure you know that."

Still silence on the other end.

"I am positive we can come up with a very generous compensation package for you, too. That will give you financial security and, again, allow you to continue your development work without concern. I have spoken to our Board and to several of our major investors. They are all very excited at the prospect of us working together."

The hyperbole coming from Jean-Louis's mouth was inventive to say the least. Charice's eyes popped as it caught her attention. A wry smile formed on her lips, and she appreciated Rousseau's ability to control his reaction to the fiction; not a snicker nor disparaging guffaw escaped him.

"I do not want to sign an exclusivity agreement with anyone," Harrison replied after another short pause. Charice could see her brother's hands start to tremble, a sure sign that he was nearing desperation. "I want this to be available to anyone who wants it. I already have the detailed manufacturing plans and have done cost estimates for its production. I will work with any company to develop modifications that can be incorporated into their watch movements. After the initial release, other companies will want the information. They will not want to be left behind."

Charice was surprised by what Harrison seemed to have achieved, not just the creation of his innovation, as surmised by Rousseau, but to have gone so far as to construct a business and production plan. Still, this invention was the key to their company's survival. Neither she nor her brother had any other opportunity to explore that had such upside potential.

Behind closed doors, Jean-Louis had promised her that they would be able to develop, put into production, and market Harrison's invention within eight months, if not sooner. With proper marketing, it would set the watch world on its ears. They would own the patent for the movement, which would surely secure their place in the history of watchmaking. With exclusivity, millions of Swiss Francs were destined to flow into their coffers, and their current problems would melt away. As for the patent Harrison claimed to have filed, their lawyers would simply have him sign over the rights to Zeller when the deal was finalized. If he refused, a slight modification that Rousseau was certain he could engineer would allow them to file for a new patent.

This project would avert the financial crisis looming ahead. The debts were crushing. Without Harrison's creation, she was unsure they would be able to bring the company back from the precipice of ruin, much less develop any profitability. More importantly, their plan would assure their ongoing extravagant existence.

Charice knew that Harrison was the white knight they desperately needed. Rousseau finally lifted his eyes and met hers when she looked at him. "Shit." Charice didn't know who said it, but the sentiment was shared by the three of them.

Chapter 3

Carlton Sommers gazed down Park Avenue through the rain-streaked floor-to-ceiling windows of his seventh-story office. He never tired of looking at the MetLife building to the south or the landscaped islands to the north. Even though his company had tentacles spanning the globe, and despite multiple invitations, he would never move his corporate headquarters from its current abode. He was a born-and-bred New Yorker. No tax haven or rent-free space could replace the view he loved and the vibrancy that is New York City.

According to the Patek Philippe watch on his wrist, he had ten minutes before his next meeting three floors below, yet still no phone call with an update. His company, the CharS Investment Group, named after his mother, already had a diverse portfolio, but he, as president and CEO, wanted to expand its breadth. In particular, he wanted to expand into the watch industry. Ever since his grandfather gave him a TAG Heuer for his eighth-grade graduation, he'd been fascinated by watches, obsessed even, which made gift-giving easy for his family. He'd received an Omega Speedmaster Moonwatch Professional upon his high school graduation, then an Audemars Piguet Royal Oak Chronograph when he finished college—a selection, made after much deliberation by Sommers himself. It was only after he completed graduate school, when he started earning an income, that he made his first watch purchase, a Breguet Marine chronometer. Subsequently, as his investment portfolio expanded, so did his watch collection.

Now he was in a position to take his avocation to the next level: a division of his corporation. At first, his preference was to acquire a controlling interest in one of the blue-chip brands. However, after a discreet investigation revealed that none of the major brands were interested in selling a share large enough to suit him, he decided that a mid-level brand might serve his needs better anyway. He'd have a freer hand to bring it to premier status. Of course, that meant the price had to be right. The less he had to pay upfront, the more funds he'd have to allocate toward the development of *his* brand. Unlike his other divisions, his watch company would be his personal project. Certainly, he knew no one more qualified to lead a watch brand to the heights of the horological world than himself.

Several months ago, associates in Switzerland had recommended he look into the Frédérique Zeller Watch Company. Rumor had it that the company's financial foothold was on shaky ground. It didn't take him long to find an insider over there willing to keep him informed of any developments. Even better, for the right price, that person was close enough to the inept siblings in charge to influence them to go in a direction that furthered Sommers' plans.

Generally not a patient man, Sommers was willing to wait while the siblings rapidly drained the company of money and resources. The further into the red Zeller went, the less capital Sommers would need to acquire his controlling share. That number had already decreased substantially from when he first considered the purchase, and he was getting antsy. But now someone named John Harrison had recently put a kink in his plans. He may have to speed things up.

With five minutes left before his meeting, Sommers turned back to his desk to get ready to leave. The anticipated update must not be happening.

But then his cell rang. The sight of the Swiss number on the screen brought a twinge of excitement.

"What have you learned?" Sommers asked his source.

"Well, nothing, really. Not yet."

"Then why have you called?" Nothing irritated Sommers more than someone wasting his time.

"I've spoken to everyone I know at the other companies that Harrison approached. None of them has more information than I do," the source replied. "I have to be very circumspect when I talk about him. I don't want to reveal our level of interest. We don't need to get into a bidding war with anyone."

"*We* wouldn't be getting into a bidding war. *I* am the only one making a purchase. *You* are responsible for keeping me abreast of the situation. Once *I'm* firmly in control of the company, *I* will have control of Harrison and his discovery one way or the other." Sommers's reputation for letting no one stand in the way of him achieving his aspirations was well earned.

"Maybe. That's one thing I did confirm." The source sounded dubious. "He has already said no one company will have exclusive ownership. He is emphatic in that regard."

"He will change his mind; I am quite sure of that. He just needs a little persuasion. *If* he resists, I will be sure he does not present an impediment." Sommers moved to the office door and rested his hand on the doorknob. "I'll do whatever it takes."

He hung up, and despite knowing he'd be late to his meeting, he paused to relish this moment. Granted, it wasn't quite the update he'd been hoping for. He would have rather discovered Harrison was in talks with a Zeller rival so that the siblings would be even more desperate. He could swoop in to "save" the company, then convince Harrison to come on board. Regardless, it wasn't the first time he had to switch up his strategy.

He gazed across his office at a small Monet painting of water lilies as he considered the possible scenarios in front of him. If Harrison's invention were truly earth-shattering, it could substantially increase the company's value. Sommers was convinced that even if the Bonets succeeded in contracting with Harrison, their ruinous behaviors would not save Zeller's financial future. If they were to come to an agreement with Harrison, it might take some time for the price to settle back to an acceptable range. However, if Harrison could be dissuaded from coming to an agreement with the Bonets or anyone else, then nothing would change, and the purchase price would continue to slide. After the acquisition was completed, engaging with Harrison and retooling Zeller leadership, the value of the watch company would provide a healthy return on investment in short order.

Harrison was the wild card. From what Sommers was led to believe, the man wasn't to be counted upon to do what seemed most logical. That being the case, it was good to know that Sommers' assets had arrived on the scene in Costa Mar and were now monitoring the situation. They were professionals trained to take any action he deemed necessary.

Chapter 4

When John's sister, Jacqueline, hired Suzanne, the job was billed as no more than a babysitting service with a bit of housekeeping. Suzanne had been out of the workforce for quite some time at that point, having spent the previous decade helping to take care of her husband, who had leukemia and required full-time assistance. Prior to that, she had put her degree in psychology to use working in a center that provided services to young adults with autism. Once she started working with John, it didn't take long for Suzanne to realize that Jacqueline had greatly underestimated her brother's abilities.

Frankly, Suzanne was often in awe of the young man's brilliance, but she wasn't sure if he understood what was at stake by insisting on the open-source nature of his invention.

"John," she started as she drove him and Louis to the college campus where he taught. "What happens if no one wants your invention because they don't like the idea of the technology being open-source?"

"Then I will have to release the information myself."

"Okay." She drove in silence, trying to reframe her thoughts. "But, then how will...well, who...How will people find out about it?"

John remained quiet until they turned onto the campus. She knew better than to prod him. If he was quiet, that meant he was thinking through his answer.

"I guess I will have to find a way," he said as he and Louis exited the car.

Because he had a faculty meeting of an unknown duration after class, he was going to take a car service home, which meant Suzanne could meet Matthew for coffee before returning to John's house for the rest of the day.

Coffee with Matthew! Yes, she enjoyed his company. And he obviously enjoyed hers. She decided she'd tell Stephen about him.

Suzanne returned to John's house a little after two o'clock that day. She entered through the back door, as she often did when coming in with groceries, and was puzzled to find it unlocked.

That was unusual. They had left the house that morning by going out the front door. John must have had a reason to open it before she arrived. She would have to start checking it more frequently, she thought, as she put away the groceries.

The kitchen was in its usual state of disorderliness. Two empty containers were left in the sink for cleaning. One from the meatloaf, the other the mashed potatoes that she'd prepared for John's dinner from the night before. She had left them in the refrigerator as an alternative to one of the frozen dinners she always kept stocked in the freezer. Stacked haphazardly next to the containers were two plates, a bowl, silverware, and two glasses. She chuckled to herself. Kitchen cleanliness wasn't in John's wheelhouse, but still, with just a little effort, they might avoid some of the ant invasions that periodically occurred.

In the living spaces and his bedroom, John was neat and orderly but certainly far from fastidious. He showed no genuine interest or willingness to do anything but the most superficial cleaning. In contrast, on the rare occasions she was permitted to enter the workroom, it was meticulously organized and spotless. If she didn't know any better, she'd think Louis never went in there. His small bed sat wrinkle-free with dog toys neatly piled on one side, and the room was completely devoid of any wayward dog hair. Frequently, she heard the whirling whine of the handheld vacuum, and three times per week at a minimum, John would roll in the full-sized vacuum for a half hour of deeper cleaning. He would spend even more time on the room after using one of his strange machines.

Close to three o'clock, as expected, she heard a car door slam shut outside. Assuming John and Louis had come home, she continued cleaning. After several minutes, she grew curious about what could be holding them up and approached the front door. Looking through one of its small windows, she saw John on the other side, staring with a perplexed look on his face, and could hear Louis panting anxiously.

Suzanne opened the door, and without a greeting, John and Louis entered the house, with John pausing to inspect the door latch. He dropped his computer bag on the couch and returned his empty lunch box to the kitchen. Suzanne followed him and was glad to see that the box was empty; at least he had eaten a good lunch. He then, as was his habit, took Louis for his afternoon walk.

Upon their return, Louis emptied his water bowl, then followed John to the workroom door as if ready for a long, overdue nap. John reached into his pocket for the key to unlock it, then froze before he inserted it into the deadbolt.

"John, are you okay?" Suzanne asked.

John continued to study the door.

"John, is something wrong?" She walked toward him.

"Someone has been in the house and broke into my workroom."

A woman appeared to be waiting for Officers Kristin Sanchez and Marc Leitner when they arrived at the house where a potential break-in had been reported.

"I'm Suzanne Lang," she said. "I'm John's caretaker. He—"

"Who's John?" Leitner asked.

"He's the young man who lives here. He has autism, so I wanted to set some ground rules before you go in."

"Um, ma'am," Sanchez said in a polite tone. "We are usually the ones responsible for setting those."

"I realize that, but John is, well, it can be hard for him to adjust to new people and changes in his life. And having two police officers enter his home is quite a change from the normal course of the day."

"Were you here when the break-in happened?" Sanchez asked her.

"No." Suzanne explained what had transpired that led her to call the police.

"So, you didn't see anyone?" Sanchez asked.

"No."

"And nothing was taken?"

"I don't believe so."

"Any damage done?"

"Again, I don't believe so."

"What do you believe happened?"

"I—we—believe someone entered the house while neither of us was here and left."

Sanchez glanced at Leitner. As expected, he looked as if he were trying to hold back his laughter.

"Why do you believe someone entered the house and left?" Sanchez asked the woman.

"Well, first, the back door had been unlocked. Neither John nor I had gone out of it. And second…" Suzanne paused. "Well, John noticed scratches on the locks."

"Scratches?"

"Yes, I personally didn't see them, but he is meticulous. I trust his judgment."

"Okay. May we speak to him?"

"Yes, but please keep your voice calm and don't push too hard. We don't want to upset him."

"Okay." Sanchez waited for the woman to open the door and let them in.

"Please promise me you'll tread lightly."

"I promise."

With that, they were let inside the small house. The living room looked neat and tidy, and toward one side stood a man in front of a closed door.

"John, the police are here," Suzanne called. Then, lowered her voice as she spoke to Sanchez. "I told him not to move until you arrived."

Sanchez blinked at the woman. If he hadn't moved since she'd called the police, he'd been standing still for about forty-five minutes.

"Hello, John," Sanchez said in a quiet voice as he turned and sat on the sofa. She briefly looked at Suzanne, who gave a nod of approval. "I need to ask you some questions."

He didn't respond. A dog jumped up on the sofa next to him and lay across his lap.

"Can you tell me what happened when you came home today?"

John stared at her mouth as he spoke. "When I came to the front door. I noticed there are scratches on the lock that were not there before."

"Leitner," she looked at her partner. "Can you check out the door?"

"On it."

"OK. And then what happened?"

"Suzanne opened the door. I came inside and put my computer bag on the sofa. Then I went into the kitchen and put my lunch bag in the sink. Then I went to my workroom and noticed there are scratches on that lock."

"Can you show me?"

John nudged the dog, who jumped to the floor. He stood up and went to what was apparently the workroom. "Look." He pointed to a deadbolt on the door.

Sanchez examined it. "These are ordinary scratches. They could have happened at any time."

"They were not here before." John's voice was a little louder than earlier.

"Officer," Suzanne interjected. "As I mentioned, John is very detail oriented. I have complete faith that if he says someone was in the house, then someone was, indeed, in the house. His extreme attention to detail is typical of someone with autism. And he works in micromechanics, so he's used to noticing things you and I wouldn't."

Sanchez wasn't sure what micromechanics were, but made notes on her pad. "Have you been upstairs?"

John shook his head.

"Can my partner go up?"

John nodded.

"Can we go into this room?"

"Why?" John asked.

"We should check to see if anything has been disturbed.

John stood still for several minutes. Sanchez opened her mouth to repeat the request, but Suzanne tapped her arm. She stuck her forefinger up in the universal sign for "wait a minute." Eventually, John nodded and began unlocking the door, while Leitner headed upstairs.

His hands trembled ever so slightly as he worked his key into the lock.

Suzanne followed them into the room with a hand pressed against her mouth as if fearing the worst. But the room seemed immaculate to Sanchez. On the left wall was a workbench with a closed laptop, tools carefully arranged and stored, and several pieces of paper, with neat, handwritten notes. Above the workbench were three bookshelves crammed with watch company catalogs and books about watches and watchmaking. They were carefully organized by height, tallest to shortest, from left to right. Opposite the door, against the back wall, was the dog's bed with some neatly stacked toys. Next to the bed was an air purifier unit emitting a gentle hum. Along the center of that wall, extending to the right toward what looked to have been a closet at one time, were three cabinets, each individually locked. There were no labels on any of the drawers.

"Is that a safe?" Sanchez pointed to a small cabinet resting on the floor that appeared to be much more robust than the others. It had a dial mounted on its front door.

"Yes." John stared at her feet.

"Can it be moved?"

"It is bolted to the floor."

Sanchez walked around the room. Approaching the windows, she saw they were covered with an opaque film. After inspecting them, she stood before the right-hand wall. Up close, she could definitely tell it once housed a full-length closet. The sliding doors had been removed, and now the space housed a reinforced table supporting a machine enclosed on all sides by thick, clear plastic panels. She had no idea what its purpose was. There were two other smaller machines adjacent to the table. One she thought was a small lathe, and the other, she couldn't even make a guess about.

"John, do you see anything missing?" Sanchez asked, making notes in her notebook as she spoke.

John did not respond right away. He slowly walked to his desk, stopped, then, while touching nothing, he methodically inspected the room with his eyes. "Someone was in this room," he eventually said. "He was looking for something, but nothing was taken."

"Are you sure? Looks pretty clean to me."

John looked at Suzanne and then looked back at his workbench, not sparing even a glance at the officer.

Suzanne kept her eyes focused on John when she responded. "Officer, if John says the room was searched, believe me, the room was searched."

Sanchez raised her eyebrows in what she hoped was a questioning, not a sarcastic, look.

"He is that meticulous," Suzanne said. "If anything was moved even by a hair's breadth, he'd know."

"Okay, John, but how do you know it was a guy? You said 'he' when I asked." It was hard for Sanchez to maintain a polite voice.

He again failed to answer.

Sanchez shrugged. There really wasn't much anyone could do here. She left the workroom and met Leitner at the bottom of the stairs.

"Doesn't look like anyone was up there." He pointed his thumb over his shoulder.

"Doesn't look like anyone was anywhere," she replied.

Sanchez gave a business card to Suzanne, asking to be notified if either of them found anything missing or if they came upon something that might shed light on the identity of the intruder.

"Will you find who was here?" John asked.

Sanchez blew out a puff of air before responding.

"Right now, all I can do is file a report. We don't have anything else to go on."

Chapter 5

The next morning, John sat at the dining table with two quarters of a piece of white bread, its crusts neatly removed, covered with smooth peanut butter, remaining on a plate beside a half-empty glass of milk. In front of him, precisely laid out and organized by company and job title, were the business cards he'd gotten from the meetings he'd had in Switzerland.

Rays of early morning sun shone through the living room window. He had slept very little. After Suzanne had left the night before, he carefully cleaned the workroom again and ensured everything was in its proper position. When he tried to sleep, images of a masked person picking locks, rummaging through his papers and books, and rearranging his carefully arranged tools flashed in front of him whenever he closed his eyes.

His watch told him it was 5:45 in the morning. He had already made several unsuccessful phone calls to Switzerland. Neither of the Bonets was available. As a last effort to contact someone at the Frédérique Zeller Manufacturer, John punched in the number for the head watchmaker, Michel Rousseau.

Rousseau answered on the second ring.

"This is John Harrison," he said. "Do you know if Mr. or Miss Bonet are available? I cannot reach them, and I want to speak to them."

"I don't think I can find them if they are not answering their phone," Rousseau said. "I know Jean-Louis is at his chalet near Gstaad. Sometimes the reception is a bit spotty there. I believe Charice is in Geneva. She has several meetings scheduled for today and may not be in a position to answer her phone. Can I help you?"

"I want to tell them I will not change my proposal. Do they want to be part of this project? If not, I will call the other companies to discuss their interest. Your company called me first, so you have the first right to develop the innovation with me." Glancing at the notepad on the table in front of him that contained neatly typed out talking points, he read his next line. "Either way, I plan to announce my project to the public shortly."

"Hold on! There's no need to be that hasty, John. When were you thinking about making the announcement?"

John glanced at his notes again. He had anticipated a few questions he might be asked and had written answers. This was one of the first questions he expected to get. "Within the next several weeks."

"John, I know both Jean-Louis and Charice are very interested and absolutely want to partner with you. We have had a number of meetings regarding your project. Plans are being drawn up to present to you. Please give us three weeks to finalize the company's proposal and contracts. I am sure everything will meet with your approval. It's a big deal, and we want to manage it correctly. I know you have been working on this project for a long time, but you don't want to rush into anything, even at this late date."

John thought for a few moments as he looked over the business cards in front of him. The break-in had sped up his plans. He had no intention of telling Rousseau or anyone else about the recent events, nor of sharing his concerns with them. The longer he waited to finalize his plans, the longer he would have to worry about someone trying to get to his invention. As a result, the longer he would have to stand guard, limiting his ability to leave the house. "I will wait for two more weeks and no more."

"Thank you, John. We'll be in touch soon," Rousseau replied to a dead phone connection.

Glancing at his watch, not a Zeller product, he weighed whom he should call first. Contrary to what he'd told Harrison, he knew cell reception at the chalet was fine. If Jean-Louis was there, which he most likely was, and not answering his phone, that meant there was a very beautiful and curvaceous reason for him being incommunicado. He could only imagine Jean-Louis and his flame-of-the-moment, sitting on a deck overlooking ski slopes, sipping champagne, staring into each other's eyes.

As far as Charice, he couldn't hazard a guess where she might be. Not one for the luxurious mountains of Switzerland, her tastes ran more to the Mediterranean climate. It was quite conceivable she had flown off to an Italian or Spanish beach for an interlude or was on some shopping spree in Paris or Milan. Such was the corporate dedication of the co-CEOs.

In the meantime, while the company Rousseau had been part of for fourteen years was careening toward insolvency, he was taking steps to preserve his job. Instead of calling either of his bosses, he retrieved his burner mobile from his pocket and punched in Sommers' number.

"This is a rather unexpected time for a call," Sommers answered.

"It's an important time." Rousseau cleared his throat. "Harrison has us on a deadline."

"What does that mean?"

"He's expecting the children running this zoo to bring him a contract within two weeks."

"I see."

Rousseau let silence sit between them, wanting Sommers to be the next to say something, as he had no idea what to do next.

"Well," Sommers eventually came to the rescue. "I appreciate the update. I'll handle the situation."

They clicked off without Rousseau asking what that meant; he preferred not knowing.

Now seemed to be a good time for some coffee and a pastry to fortify him before meeting with one of the few remaining senior watchmakers in the company regarding the latest problem with a specific production model. He would try calling the "kids" when he got a chance.

Two phone calls and a couple of passing words in the hallway with either Bonet was the sum total of the conversations he'd had with them about Harrison's movement, so he wasn't technically lying when he'd told the American they'd been discussing it. He had also done some preliminary work with a fellow watchmaker to evaluate the feasibility of Harrison's proposal, even though they possessed minimal technical details. Meanwhile, aside from Jean-Louis speaking with Harrison on the phone, the siblings had spent little effort on the project to date. Regardless, Rousseau was sure both would launch into panic mode when he informed them about the call he'd just received from John. He wasn't in the mood to hear any of their whining.

Chapter 6

It took quite a bit of time for John to recover from the anxiety induced by the break-in he continued to insist had occurred. For the first few days after the incursion, he spoke very little, and when he did, that was the sole topic of discussion. Suzanne felt as though she was caught in a continuous loop, constantly reassuring him that nothing bad had happened and they were perfectly safe. To help ease his anxiety, she came to the house every day. He left only to teach or take Louis for his walks, while Suzanne stood guard. She had to promise not to go anywhere, not even to run a quick errand when he was not there.

When she was able to break away, Suzanne made sure to keep the house fully stocked with provisions, more so than usual. She paid close attention to whether John was eating and taking care of himself. Before she left in the evenings, she had to perform what she termed "a perimeter inspection" to check and double-check the doors and windows to be sure they were locked shut before she'd leave through the front door. Then, she'd remain on the front steps until she heard John secure the deadbolt. At that point, while John watched from a window, she was required to survey the house from the outside to ensure there was no one hiding in the bushes, waiting to make entry upon her departure.

Despite his recurrent requests, Suzanne resisted calling the police to check if any headway had been made toward solving the mystery of the break-in. She knew the police officers who took the initial report were dubious, as was she now, about whether anything had actually occurred. The only hard fact was the unlocked back door, but that didn't mean someone had entered the house. Mistakes do happen, even when dealing with someone so compulsive as John. The police had given her a report number, which she had kept from him. Instead, she worked to distract him as best as possible from obsessing further about what might have occurred.

When the two weeks went by with no return call from Zeller, she found a positive: John had something else to focus on. He took their silence as a "no," and, since it had been a full eight weeks since their trip to Switzerland, he'd given up on them, too. That meant he wouldn't wait any longer. He would release the information.

Their conversations shifted in topic to *how* he would release it.

They spent several days hashing over his options. He would need to craft an announcement, a press release of sorts, and a full presentation. Because Suzanne wanted to help him, he gave her a rudimentary lesson in watchmaking. He explained the core concepts of his development as simply as possible, its significance to the industry, and how it would change the course of watchmaking.

He also accumulated a list of names, journalists from watch-focused and luxury goods publications, websites, and podcasts. They would be the first to reach out to. He and Suzanne also discussed whether to approach influencers on social media, but John decided against it. If he had to speak with anyone, he preferred talking to journalists, people better versed in the technical aspects of watchmaking. Those were the people most likely to grasp the significance of what he had accomplished.

Suzanne got busy on the phone and computer, trying to arrange the first meetings for John's announcement. They sat on opposite ends of the dining room table, working primarily in silence. When Suzanne made a telephone call, she would go to the kitchen so as not to disturb

John, even though his headphones were firmly in place. From across the room, she could hear the screeching and screams that comprised the music John preferred.

Working her way down the list he'd created, she was able to entice three journalists to meet with him, promising them an explosive story. All John really needed was just one of them to hear the whole presentation and report on it. He was a compulsive reader of watch-related websites and magazines and knew that once his innovation was reported by one outlet, the news would spread like wildfire. Within no time, other journalists of all stripes would be lining up to get the story, which would be misery for him.

"I will be here for you," Suzanne promised. "I'm new to watches and public relations, but I think I can handle this."

He nodded and returned to focusing on the presentation. He was obsessed with making it just right. Unlike the ones he'd given in Switzerland, what he'd provide the journalists would be a much more detailed description of his discovery. Suzanne had several copies made of the key drawings and data to support his claims. Two meetings were scheduled, one with one of the journalists and the second with the other two. They would occur at a local coffee shop that Suzanne had inspected with John. The selected times for the two meetings would be when the shop was relatively quiet. The first was scheduled to occur in the morning between the breakfast and lunch rushes. The other would happen later that same afternoon, once the lunchtime crowd subsided and before the end of the school day, when the shop teemed with teenagers. The one thing John refused to bring to either meeting was the prototype. It would remain in the workroom, hidden on a shelf behind a false book binding.

Closing her notepad after sending an email to confirm the last journalist, Suzanne sat back in her chair and looked at John. Oblivious to her gaze, he remained immersed in whatever was on his computer monitor. If the next few days proceeded as she anticipated, they would be the most disruptive he had faced in years, if not ever, and she was truly worried about him.

The third time she called his name, John pulled his headphones down. He did not take his eyes off the computer screen, but clearly was listening to her.

"Are you absolutely sure this is the path you want to take? I still think you might want to consider working with a watch company, at least for a while. That way, you will be sure to maintain control of your invention because you'll work more efficiently with their engineers and designers. If you let anyone have it, anything can happen, and you will have no say about how or where it is used. It is even conceivable that it could be taken and buried, never to see the light of day, because of costs or competition between companies. I know the money means nothing to you, but for all the time and effort you have expended on this, it would be a shame to see its creation credited to someone else. Think of the satisfaction you will achieve watching your design come to fruition."

John sat in his chair staring at the computer screen. "We decided this was the right thing to do. Let the watch companies decide how to use it." He replaced his headphones and returned to his presentation.

Suzanne was puzzled about who the "we" was. John never spoke in the third person, but who might he have discussed this with? Granted, she didn't know everything about his watches. It took a year and a half of helping him before Suzanne even got an inkling about what took place in the workroom, and that occurred only because his handheld vacuum needed to be replaced. Although that's when he told her the equipment and tools were required to create a watch movement, John didn't seem interested in explaining anything else.

Now, after four years of being his companion, she finally understood he had developed something revolutionary for watches. When he'd told her his invention would change the mechanics of timekeeping forever, he was undoubtedly right. Now he had a working model of his concept, and it was time to introduce it to the world. He had hoped a watch company would incorporate it into their watches before its formal introduction. However, since no one seemed willing to take the leap of faith, he was left to send it out to the world on his own. She was so proud of him, but she was also worried about how he'd handle what was to come.

She glanced at her watch, surprised at how the time had flown by. She had stayed much later than usual. John remained consumed by his presentation. Although he claimed he was looking forward to the next day, she could tell his anxiety was approaching overdrive, but she couldn't stay any longer.

She reached across the table and tapped his hand. In response, he pulled down his headphones once again. "John, I have to leave," she said to the crown of his head as he continued to study one of the drawings for the umpteenth time. "My son, Stephen, and his fiancée are coming to visit tomorrow evening. I need to stop at the supermarket before it closes. I'll be here as early as I can tomorrow."

All she received was a grunt. She collected her purse and headed toward the front door, waiting for John to stand and watch her do the outside perimeter inspection. She paused with her hand on the knob and turned to see what he was doing. He was still focused on his computer.

Louis seemed to realize she was leaving and approached her, panting—a clear signal of his need for a walk.

Glancing back at John, she judged that he wouldn't be ready to take the dog out for a while. "I'll take Louis for his walk before I leave, so you don't have to worry about it," she said more to herself. There was no response to her offer.

She put down her purse and grabbed Louis' leash. When she opened the door, a cool breeze met her. "It's chilly. I'm going to borrow one of your sweatshirts." A slight nod was the only indication that he heard her.

Chapter 7

The police were able to trace Louis to John's house from the address engraved on the back of his name tag. When the first responding police officers arrived at the murder scene, they found him unable to move. His leash was wrapped tightly around the victim's arm. To release him, the officer had to approach cautiously, calm him, and relieve him from his bondage while being careful not to contaminate the crime scene.

Sanchez and Leitner were on patrol when they heard the call regarding a homicide in the park within their sector. At first, they headed toward the park, but when dispatch reported the dog's address, they recognized it immediately and drove directly to the house. Sanchez uttered a quiet prayer that John wasn't the victim. But she knew that if he wasn't, someone would have to interview him, and they'd need advice on how to approach him. Understanding how to question John would increase the likelihood of obtaining useful information about what happened in the park while minimizing the risk of him becoming defensive or shutting down.

They arrived just as Detective Colin Brown, the assigned investigating officer, pulled up. Before he could climb the steps to the front door, Sanchez pulled him aside to give him a rundown on John.

Inside the house, they found John sitting on the couch in the living room, cradling Louis. Head down, he slowly rocked side to side, making eye contact with no one. The officer who'd brought the dog home shrugged at Brown. Sanchez waved her hand at him, indicating he should leave.

"Hi, John," she said as she approached him.

John continued to rock.

"Do you remember me?"

Still rocking and petting the dog.

"This is Detective Brown. I know this might be tough for you, but Detective Brown will need to ask you some questions."

Brown pulled a chair from the dining table and sat on the other side of the coffee table, across from John.

"Hello, John." Brown ducked his head, as if trying to make eye contact with the young man. Sanchez tapped him on the shoulder and shook her head when he looked up. "Okay." He let out a long breath. "Um, I'm sorry, John, but can you tell me who was walking your dog?"

John rocked faster. "Suzanne."

"Suzanne? What was her last name?"

John mumbled something.

"I'm sorry. What was that?"

While Brown was trying to interview John, Sanchez saw a purse on a table by the front door. From inside, she pulled out a wallet and found a driver's license. "This is the woman who was here with John the first time we received a call."

Brown gently asked John if Suzanne had taken the dog for a walk. After repeating the question twice, John confirmed that Suzanne Lang had taken his dog, Louis, for a walk in the park. No, she had not returned. Detective Brown, as carefully as he could, informed John that Suzanne might be the victim found in the park with Louis's leash wrapped around her arm. He then asked Sanchez to report Suzanne's address so another unit could be sent there to notify the next of kin.

Not sure how to proceed, Brown turned back to John, who was now staring at his fingernails, still rocking but at a higher velocity than before. There was no sign of any other emotional response.

Sanchez continued searching through the purse. She found a cell phone and looked for the health app, which emergency personnel can access without a passcode.

"Detective Brown," she said. "There's an emergency contact here." She tapped on the phone. "Stephen Lang. That's the same last name. He is up in Santa Barbara."

"Can you see what you can get from him?" Brown nodded toward John as he stood up. "I'll make this call."

Sanchez handed him the phone and took his seat while Brown went outside.

"Hello, John," she said softly. "Do you remember me? I was here the other day?"

John emitted a quiet grunt.

"I know this is a tough time." Sanchez wanted to reach out to touch his arm but was afraid he'd recoil. "So, I'm here to help you. It's probably not a good idea for you to be alone tonight. Is there someone I can call for you?"

John rocked in silence.

"Do you have any family members I could call?"

He paused rocking. "I have a half-sister. Jacqueline."

"Would you like to call her?"

John shook his head.

"Is it okay if I call her?"

He nodded.

"What is her number?"

John rattled off a number that Sanchez dialed.

Jacqueline burst into the house twenty minutes later with Brown following in her wake. Dressed in a rumpled T-shirt, shorts, and sandals, she appeared as if she had intended to spend the evening at home, certainly not with her brother or the police.

She fell onto the couch, as far away from John as possible.

"Do you know the victim, Suzanne Lang?" Brown asked Jacqueline.

Jacqueline's eyes bugged out as she nodded.

"How well did you know her?"

"Um, well, I hired her to be with John."

"How long ago was that?"

"Like, four years."

Sanchez thought the woman's answers sounded as if they were spat out with disdain. Where was her sympathy for her brother?

"John, can you tell me why Suzanne was out with Louis?" Brown asked.

John's response came as an unintelligible mumble.

"Did she typically take Louis for walks?" Brown pressed.

John's rocking speed increased still more. Jacqueline watched him. At first, she made no effort to calm her brother despite his obvious distress. Eventually, as if sensing she was being judged, she hesitantly reached out toward him.

In response, he flinched and then recoiled. It was as if he were trying to avoid any contact with his sister.

"I know you're upset," Sanchez said in a calm tone. "But these questions are important. They might help us find out who did this to Suzanne."

Finally, John spoke to no one in particular. "Suzanne took Louis for a walk because it was late, and I was busy." He paused for a moment as if girding himself. "She wanted to leave but offered to walk Louis first. Her son is visiting tomorrow, and she wanted to get ready."

Brown repeated his question in a quieter voice than he'd been using when he first arrived. "Did she usually take Louis for his walks?"

John shook his head.

"Who did? You?"

John nodded.

Brown paused. "John, do you have any idea who might have wanted to hurt Suzanne?"

For the first time, John raised his eyes and looked blankly at Brown. "No."

"Had she said anything to you to indicate that she was worried about anything or if anyone was angry with her?"

Once again, John's head dropped. He shook his head. His rocking had diminished. His attention was now focused on his dog lying in his lap. Mechanically, he stroked the dog's back.

Brown glanced at Jacqueline before meeting Sanchez's eyes. Sanchez shrugged. She guessed at what Brown was noticing. There seemed to be no indication of warmth or evidence of consolation emanating from Jacqueline, especially in a time of what appeared to be a significant loss for John. She seemed not to know how to comfort John. Sanchez wanted to yell at his sister for not even trying to provide consolation. Surely, she must know how to relate to him.

Meanwhile, it was clear that John couldn't offer much help. Brown stood again. "Let's chat," he said to Sanchez and headed out to the front porch.

"Give me a rundown on what happened here two weeks ago," he asked as soon as she shut the door behind her.

"Leitner and I responded to a call about a potential break-in. The thing is, only John saw any evidence that someone had been here. He claimed to have found scratches on the deadbolt on the front door, indicating that someone tried to pick the lock. He said they were not there before. He also found similar marks on the lock to his workroom. I guess he makes watches or something like that."

"What did you see?"

"Honestly, we saw no evidence of any tampering on either of the locks." She pointed to the lock on the front door. In the porch light, neither could see any signs of scratches. "The victim did mention that she'd found the back door unlocked earlier in the day, but, again, if someone came in, there was no evidence that anything in the house had been disturbed, much less taken. Do you think that has something to do with her being killed?"

"Slim chance if you ask me," Brown smirked. "That lock looks good as new, and who hasn't left a back door unlocked by accident? Especially in a nice neighborhood like this."

"So, what do we do?"

"The emergency contact was her son. He's on his way from Santa Barbara." Brown glanced at his cellphone. "I'd like you and Leitner to stay and wait for him. Interview him immediately. See if he can give us anything to go on."

"Sure." This would be a new experience for Sanchez. Murders didn't happen regularly on her beat. But she was up for the task. Although she knew she had to maintain a professional demeanor, it broke her heart that someone took the life of a person John obviously needed in his life.

She went back inside to let John and Jacqueline know she and Leitner would be in their cruiser waiting for Suzanne's son to arrive. The siblings looked as if they hadn't moved or said a word to each other the entire time she was outside with Brown.

Chapter 8

The conversation with the bank director, Pierre Martin, couldn't be going any worse for Jean-Louis. He politely listened to the request for a short-term bridge loan, but Zeller's financial situation was well known to *Monsieur Directeur* as well as to the members of the bank's board.

"You must understand," Jean-Louis emphasized to Martin. "Future riches lie just around the corner. We are on the verge of finalizing a major deal involving a revolutionary development in the watchmaking industry. Once it's released to the public, money will pour into the company's coffers in a torrential flow." Jean-Louis waved his hand through the air as if casually shooing a fly. "Of course, before that can happen, we need preparation time; therefore, the request for the bridge loan."

Martin stared at him, deadpan.

"You, this bank will benefit. As will all the other investors." Jean-Louis sat up straight in his chair.

Still, not even the slightest of nods from Martin.

"I will offer my estate as collateral for the loan." He pressed a hand over his heart.

"Your estate has already been maximally mortgaged."

"But..." Jean-Louis ran out of ideas. Deflated, he fell back in the brown leather chair, wishing the floor would open up, swallow him whole.

Apparently, the pathetic look worked a little magic. "I will, as a personal courtesy to you, and with respect for all the business your father has done with us—"

"Yes?" Jean-Louis straightened again.

"I will scan the proposal and supporting documents once more to see if there is any possible way to construct a secured loan, but I'm doubting there will be any wiggle room."

"How can you say that?"

"I'm fairly positive, Jean-Louis, that there is not enough equity left in the Zeller company, nor the Bonet's private accounts, to fund a chestnut stand, much less support the loan application."

Jean-Louis furiously hurried out of the bank. For all the money the bank had made over the last forty-two years from Zeller, this was their thanks? He headed toward the garage where he'd parked his car, but a men's bespoke clothing store caught his eye, one he patronized with some degree of regularity. Without a second thought, he entered and set about inspecting several samples of cashmere that the proprietor was happy to show him. After some discussion and very little consideration, he selected a lighter blue sample with black stripes. The fabric would be perfect for the coat he'd been eyeing for several weeks.

After a quick inventory check confirmed that a bolt of the fabric was already in stock, the proprietor promised to have the coat finished within a couple of days, for an additional fee. Jean-Louis eagerly agreed to the supplemental charge.

Trying on a sport jacket to complement the coat, Jean-Louis stared at himself in the mirror. The jacket looked nice, but thoughts of Pierre Martin clouded his appreciation of it. He never liked the man and was sure the disdain was returned equally. Jean-Louis had several high-powered friends in the world of finance. Actually, they were more like social contacts, but he was sure they would back his loan request without a second thought. Certainly, they could influence the bank's board of directors to see things his way, if not for Martin's interference.

After ordering the jacket, two pairs of slacks, as well as the coat, he continued on his way, ducking into the first bar he came upon. In a quiet booth, he left his scotch untouched while he called his sister.

"Did you take care of matters on your end?" he asked after quickly updating Charice on the happenings at the bank.

"Everything is in process," she responded. "If we don't get it, no one will. But, if we don't get it, I hope you can pull a miracle out of your ass for us to keep the company solvent."

Jean-Louis chose not to tell her about the idea percolating in his brain. Better to wait until it is more formalized before bringing her into the plan. They were his contacts anyway.

She interrupted his thoughts. "Just find us money."

Sommers didn't like being kept on hold longer than necessary, and this wasn't necessary. A simple "yes" or "no" was all he needed. There was little doubt in his mind that the bank manager would fulfill his request, straightforward as it was. Besides, it wasn't a stretch to convince Martin of the risk posed should he conduct further business with the Bonet kids.

"Monsieur Sommers, I am so sorry to have kept you waiting," Martin offered once he picked up the phone. "We are quite busy, and I was on the phone with several of our branches in Zurich and Neuchâtel. I am sure you have had plenty of..."

"Listen, Martin, I am not interested in your excuses. Did Bonet come in today?" Sommers could smell victory coming his way and did not have the time or patience for the pleasantries often required when dealing with the Swiss.

"Much apologies, monsieur. Yes, Monsieur Bonet was here. He left about an hour ago, very unhappy."

"Wonderful. Thank you for your assistance. Your accommodation will make its way to you in short order." Sommers smiled. There was no way this ass was going to get any "accommodation" but let him continue to think he was. He was a cog in the system, to be sure. His long-term utility was limited for Sommers' future enterprise, so why the hell be nice to the guy? Denying the Bonet loan request meant the ticking clock for the end of Zeller had sped up.

Stephen woke up feeling Siobhan's naked body next to his in the bed in his mother's guestroom. Did the previous evening actually happen? He'd rather it be a nightmare, but as his mind became more alert, he was gradually forced to acknowledge the grim reality of his situation. His mother was dead.

Immediately, the memories from the night before flooded his brain. The surreal phone call. The drive down from Santa Barbara with Siobhan, which seemed to take forever, though when he arrived at the house where his mother used to work, that same drive felt as if it lasted only minutes. The police officers. Their strange questions. Did he know of anyone who would want to hurt his mother? What the hell? No one wanted to hurt his mother.

He reached for his phone on the nightstand next to him, and *damn!* He'd neglected to set the alarm. He was supposed to be at the police station at ten. He had less than an hour to shower, dress, and get there.

He let Siobhan sleep. While he appreciated her being by his side for the drive down, and what felt like an interrogation by the police officers last night, he wanted to spare her from the trauma that was ahead of him. He had an appointment to meet Detective Brown to identify the body of his mother.

Identify her body. It was just too unreal.

He arrived at the police station only five minutes late. Unshaven, Detective Brown had heavy bags under his bloodshot eyes. Stephen assumed he also must be operating on only a few hours of sleep. Together they proceeded from the lobby of the police station to the hospital morgue, mostly in silence.

Twenty minutes later, he stood in the small waiting room outside the morgue. It was her. It was definitely his mother. Who could do such a thing?

"It just doesn't make sense," he told Brown as they walked out of the cold room. "Everyone liked my mother."

"We're doing our best to find out who was responsible," Brown assured him. "Let's get some coffee."

The last thing Stephen thought he could do was eat, but he figured the detective really wanted to ask him more questions. As soon as they'd taken their place in a booth at a nearby diner, he discovered he was right.

Brown peppered him with the same questions that Officer Sanchez had asked the night before.

"Had your mother mentioned anything unusual happening in her life lately?"

"No."

"Had she seemed upset? Worried?"

"No."

"Did she ever mention anything about someone being upset with her? Or she with them?"

"No! Everyone liked my mother. She got along with everyone."

Stephen couldn't touch his food. He knew his answers were beginning to sound defensive, but he needed time to process what had happened. He understood the police wanted to get this case wrapped up, but he needed to deal with whatever it was he was feeling—the anger, the grief, the realization that he'd never see his mother again.

"I hate to say this," Brown eventually said. "But we don't really have much to go on at this juncture."

Stephen stared at him, waiting for the detective to voice the words he knew were probably coming but didn't want to hear: they'll never know who killed his mother or why.

Brown just shrugged and stood up.

Stephen was outraged but powerless. The man was right; they had little to go on.

Back at the station, Brown handed him a bag with his mother's effects. Effects! Not her wallet, watch, phone, and keys, but effects. What was he supposed to do now?

On his way back to the condo, he realized he would have to organize his mother's funeral. He was the last relative she had. But she did have friends; her closest ones were part of the support group she attended regularly. He should notify them; maybe they'd help with the arrangements? And there was that man she'd mentioned.

She was almost embarrassed to tell him she'd started seeing a man from the group. Only after Stephen assured her he understood and was happy for her, did she tell him his name, Matthew Daniels. Stephen never pressed his mother for more details, but it was clear to him they were seeing more of each other than she let on.

She'd seemed so happy lately. The last time Stephen spoke to his mother, he could hear a change in the tone of her voice when she mentioned Matthew. It made Stephen happy to hear that his mother was enjoying life once again. And then someone cut that short!

Something needed to be done.

At the condo, Siobhan handed him a plate of cut-up fruit. "What happens next?" she asked as she sat next to him in the kitchen.

"Thanks, but I'm nauseous." He pushed the fruit plate aside and leaned back in the chair. "I guess I need to figure out a memorial or something. But..." he pulled his mother's phone from the bag containing her effects. The previous night, he had been truthful when he said he didn't know the password for it, but it didn't take him long to figure it out: his birth date. He went to her contacts and found the phone number for Matthew Daniels. "I think I should probably call that man she'd started seeing and tell him, well, you know."

He punched Matthew's phone number into his own mobile, and, giving little thought about how to hold the conversation, he hit the call button. As he listened to the phone ring on the other end, a knot formed in his stomach. On the third ring, the phone was answered in a hushed voice.

"Mr. Daniels? This is Stephen Lang, Suzanne's son."

"Hi, Stephen," Matthew maintaining his hushed voice "Give me a minute."

Stephen waited a few beats as he heard a door close in the background. "Sorry, my granddaughter just fell asleep, and I didn't want to disturb her. What's up?" His voice dropped an octave with concern. "Is Suzanne OK?"

How was Stephen going to say the words he needed to say about his own mother? He clamped his eyes closed and plodded on.

"My, uh, my mom…"

"Yes?"

"She was killed last night." Tears spilled down Stephen's face, his voice caught. He felt a gentle pressure on his shoulder and leaned his head against Siobhan, unable to go on.

Matthew was quiet on the other end.

"I'm sorry." Stephen eventually pulled himself together.

"I am too." Mathew's voice was still soft, but the tone had changed. "What happened?"

Stephen blundered through the story, providing as much detail as he could, which felt woefully insufficient. "I didn't know who else to call. I know you were close to her…"

Matthew was silent for what seemed to be hours, but it was really only seconds. "Listen, I'm watching my grandchildren this morning. I'll call their mom. I'm sure she can get here in an hour or so. I'll get to you as soon as I can."

"I'm at my mom's place."

"Good. Stay there and don't talk to anyone else."

Chapter 9

Matthew sat on a chair in Suzanne's living room that felt too small for his frame. He had gained more weight than he wished to admit to since Muriel died; his dietary choices were not as balanced as when she was preparing his meals, nor was he as active as he had been before retiring. He wore a blue polo shirt under a New York Athletic Club sweatshirt and jeans, knowing full well the club's logo on the sweatshirt probably sent the wrong message. It was false advertising, as the bulge of his midsection would testify to. Not that he cared. He always chose comfort over fashion.

His life choices were not doing much to improve the image he saw reflected in the mirror every morning, nor probably the image Stephen was getting of him. He knew his hooded eyes, drooping cheeks, and a penchant for not shaving regularly probably gave an initial impression of him being slow-witted, which was anything but the case. Miraculously, Suzanne had not been disturbed by his appearance, although she had hinted that he would feel better if he regularly joined her at the gym.

He listened as Stephen explained what little he knew about Suzanne's death. When Stephen finished, he took a deep breath and stared at Matthew's face as if expecting answers.

"Why call me?" Matthew asked.

"Well, I know you were seeing each other."

"Right. Did she also tell you I'm a former cop?"

"She mentioned something to the effect."

"New York City Police, retired, homicide division." He paused to watch Stephen's reaction. Seeing the young man's eyes widen, Matthew continued. "So, forgive me if I sound a little cold and calculating when I ask you some questions. I don't know what the police are doing to find out what happened to your mother, but I intend to make sure they leave no stone unturned."

"I'm so relieved to hear you say that." Stephen's eyes glistened as if he were about to cry. "I spent the morning with a detective, Brown is his last name. Don't remember the first. He didn't seem to have much experience in these kinds of things. Please, find out who did this."

Like an old fire horse responding to an alarm, Matthew reverted to detective mode borne of thirty-one years' experience. Another homicide to investigate, one more to add to a long list of cases he'd worked on during his career. His ingrained role as an experienced investigator would work in his favor. He could compartmentalize his emotional connection to Suzanne for now, but he knew the reality of the situation would deliver its emotional punch later.

Methodically, he had questioned Stephen and Siobhan about Suzanne's history, going as far back as they could remember, regardless of whether or not they thought it was relevant to the current situation. After about an hour of probing, he finally got to the events of the prior night. Despite forays down multiple paths, Stephen and Siobhan provided nothing that, for the moment, could be considered useful. Matthew skirted around the particulars of the murder except to ask about the cause of death.

"Shot twice in the head," was all Stephen was able to get out.

Forty minutes later, they were at John's house. On the way over, Stephen had given him a brief preview of John's challenges through the lens of what his mother had explained to him. Matthew admitted to having a limited understanding of autism. However, he felt confident that, with his experience conducting interviews, he would be able to get something useful from John.

"Does he drive?" Matthew asked as he parked behind a car in the driveway.

"I don't believe so," Stephen said. "My mother mentioned a few times how she'd take him places."

"That's probably Jacqueline's car," Siobhan noted. "She ran out while we were here last night to get clothes to stay over."

"Who's Jacqueline?" Matthew asked.

"John's sister, *half*-sister, as she made sure we all knew." Stephen shook his head. "Clearly, my mother's death was an inconvenience to her."

"Really?"

"Yeah. I guess she hired my mom to help with John. She seemed pretty resentful she'd have to take time off from her job until she found a replacement."

Inside the house, Stephen introduced Matthew as a friend of his mother to Jacqueline and John. John sat quietly at the dining table, eating a sandwich. A dog was curled up on the floor near his water bowl in the kitchen, his eyes locked onto John.

"I'd like to ask you a few questions," Matthew said to Jacqueline.

"What? Why me?" Jacqueline wrinkled her nose at him."

"I'm under the impression you hired Suzanne." He glanced at Stephen and Siobhan standing in the living room. Jacqueline was sitting on the sofa and hadn't invited anyone else to take a seat.

"Well, yeah, like four years ago." Jacqueline glanced at John before answering.

"Who had her job before her?"

"Nobody."

"Did you take care of him?"

"No, it's um, it's complicated. Does it matter?"

"Everything matters right now."

"Who are you again? Like, a police officer or something?"

"I am 'like' a police officer," Matthew used his hands to make air quotes. "And I'm a family friend. I'm not resting until I figure out what happened to Suzanne." He knew how to put a commanding tone in his voice when necessary, and it was obviously necessary here. "Who had Suzanne's job before she did?"

"Oh, um, no one."

"He lived by himself?"

"Well, no. He lived with his mother."

"*His* mother, not yours?"

"Um, so, like, John and I have the same father, but different mothers."

"Where's his mother now?"

Jacqueline looked at John again, then lowered her voice as she met Matthew's eyes. "So, when John graduated from college, his mom just kind of disappeared. I was contacted by an attorney in charge of a trust that'd been set up for him. He told me if the mother wasn't around, I was to be the executrix."

"Who set up the trust?"

"I dunno."

"Who is your father?"

"That's the million-dollar question." Jacqueline rolled her eyes. "Apparently, he's some dude who likes to get women pregnant and abandon them. My mom was so totally pissed at him that she refused to list his name on my birth certificate. As far as I can remember, she never mentioned him, nor did she allow me to ask about him."

While the information was interesting, Matthew wasn't there to learn about family drama. "So there's just you and John in your family now?" he tried to redirect her.

"Yes."

"And John has a trust that some attorney said was set up for him."

"Yes."

"I'm not understanding where Suzanne fits into this."

"The trust says that someone needs to be hired to take care of John in case his mother can't. So I had to hire someone."

"I see. Who is the attorney managing the trust?"

"Why does that matter?" She snarled at him.

"When there's a homicide, you have to look at every angle. Suzanne was close to John. Maybe someone thought she was in the way of his trust. What is the name of the attorney?"

"Michael Livingston." Jacqueline wrinkled her brow.

"Thanks." Matthew realized he'd forgotten his favorite accessory, a notepad, and looked around the house. "Do you have any paper or anything I can write a note on?"

"Maybe in the kitchen." Jacqueline stood and went into the kitchen.

Matthew sat at the dining table across from John. The young man kept his eyes glued to his plate. "OK, so you hired Suzanne with funds from the trust," he said to Jacqueline as she handed him a notepad and a pen. "And no one had the job before Suzanne?"

"So, I think I said that already."

"And you don't have any idea where his mother might be?"

"I seriously don't know."

"John," Matthew said as he tapped the young man's arm.

John leaned away from him but lifted his eyes to stare at Matthew's chest.

"Suzanne would go on and on about how brilliant you are," Matthew continued. John raised his eyes for a hint of a second to meet Matthew's, then glanced at Stephen and Siobhan, who had sat on the sofa, before dropping his gaze back to the table.

"I know this is hard," Matthew said. "But we need to talk about last night if I'm going to be able to help the police find the person who did such a terrible thing." Again, Matthew paused to let John absorb his words. "Did she seem to be worried about anything?"

"No." John's voice was flat.

"John has problems reading people's cues," Jacqueline interjected. "He might not be the most reliable source of information regarding other's feelings."

Matthew nodded at Jacqueline. "John, did Suzanne mention anything about having any issues with someone?"

John shook his head. "No." He looked over Matthew's shoulder at Stephen. "She said Stephen was coming and wanted to leave to get ready."

"But she took your dog out instead?"

"I was late getting home from class and was behind schedule. I had work to do. She offered to take Louis for his walk before she left." Suddenly, John sat straight up. He stared at his watch. "I have to go to the appointment." He pushed back from the table and started to stand, but Matthew put out his hand. Jacqueline, in turn, touched John's arm briefly as if to hold him back.

"John, I need you here," Matthew said. "This is very important. What appointment do you have?"

John cryptically explained that Suzanne had set up a meeting with journalists at a nearby coffee shop. He avoided describing any details, just referring to "a project." His eyes widened. "I missed the one scheduled for this morning. There's fifteen minutes before the afternoon appointment."

"I'm sure we can reschedule the meetings with the journalists once things settle down," Matthew said.

Siobhan stood. "I can go to the coffee shop, find the journalists, and explain the situation."

It took John a few minutes, but eventually he agreed. He gave her the address and the names of the journalists. "But do not disclose any information about my project."

"I have no idea what your project is even about," she said gently. "I'll confirm their contact information so the meeting can be rescheduled."

"What about the one from earlier today?" he asked.

"Find their name for me. I'll take care of it."

John seemed pacified, but his wringing hands and wide-eyed expression gave evidence to a heightened level of agitation. Despite seeing that, Matthew wanted to ease back into talking about Suzanne.

"Was that what was happening last night? You were preparing for today's meetings, so Suzanne took the dog for his walk?"

John refocused on Matthew's words and nodded.

"Louis goes out three times per day," he explained.

"Where do you take him?"

"The park and then return home."

"The same path each time?"

"Yes."

Matthew glanced at a clock on the wall opposite where he sat. It was twenty-five past one. "John, what time does Louis go for his walk?"

"Between eleven thirty and two o'clock. Depends on whether I have a class."

John previously mentioned something about a class, and Matthew did not question what he meant. This time, he glanced at Stephen, who shrugged.

"He teaches at a local college." Jacqueline piped in.

"Really? Suzanne never mentioned that to me. Did you know?" he asked Stephen.

"Yeah. I think I remember her mentioning it. Is it important?"

"I don't know. But it's a point to explore." He faced John again. "Let's take Louis for his walk. I want to see the path you take with him." What Matthew did not say was the actual reason for the walk. He wanted to see the murder scene, but he had no idea how John would react if he knew.

"It's not time for his next walk. He went on his walk at eleven forty-two."

"I know dogs well. I had one for eleven years when I lived in New York. I will never say I was able to read his mind," Matthew looked at the others and then back at John, remembering how there were several reasons his dog's name was Damn It. "But I do know, he'd never refuse the opportunity to go for a walk and explore the sights, sounds, and, most importantly, the smells of his territory. I bet Louis is similar. And he's been through a lot. I'm sure he'd like to get out of the house and go for a walk."

Perhaps he heard the word because Louis looked up. John stood and headed toward the front door with Matthew close behind. As soon as John reached for the dog's leash hanging on a hook, Louis jumped to his feet and ran to him, panting excitedly.

With Louis straining at the leash, Matthew, Stephen, and John followed the route he took three times per day, every day. After walking three blocks, they crossed into a park and followed the main pathway, pausing only to let Louis investigate a smell or relieve himself.

Matthew noted the placement of light poles, trying to imagine how well lit up—or not—the area would be in the evening. Eventually, they turned onto a smaller path and rounded a corner. After several turns in the path, they came upon a solitary, uniformed police officer sitting in a camp chair in front of an area cordoned off by yellow crime scene tape. Tall bushes and several pine and maple trees ringed the area adjacent to the pathway. The stand of trees obstructed the nearest light pole. Matthew judged that this part of the path would be poorly lit at night. At the insistence of the police officer, they were forced to backtrack twenty-five yards to find an alternative way around the murder scene. Matthew tried to survey the area from a permitted vantage point, resisting the urge to ask the uniform for permission to get closer to the actual scene; he already knew what the answer should be and would be.

As they headed back toward the house, Matthew was lost in thought until he pulled Stephen aside after they exited the park.

"Dark area. No lighting," he said under his breath.

Reflexively, Stephen turned around to look even though they were well out of sight of the crime scene.

"She was on the cement when it happened." Matthew looked at Stephen to make sure his narrative wasn't too much for him.

After a momentary pause to consider whether to ask the next question, he decided to forge ahead. “Stephen, I’m sorry, but this is important. Where was she shot?”

“In the head.”

“Yes, but where?”

Stephen pointed to the left side of his head, behind his ear. His hand shook visibly.

“I’m sorry.” Matthew touched his arm. “I know this is tough.”

Stephen nodded. “Yeah. Just do me a favor, will you?”

“Anything?”

“Get the fucker who killed my mom.”

Chapter 10

Siobhan met them back at the house.

"I apologized to the reporters and said an emergency came up, but that you'd get back to them soon," she said to John.

"Did you tell them anything about my project?" John asked as he rehung Louis' leash on the hook.

"Of course not," she assured him. "Again, I don't even know what you are working on."

John took in the information, nodded once, then sat down at the dining table again. Jacqueline was in the kitchen, rummaging through the refrigerator.

"I just need a minute," Matthew said to Stephen and Siobhan, who returned to their seats on the sofa. Stephen was visibly shaken. His face looked taut and pale. Siobhan gripped his hand. Matthew knew she wanted to say something, but really, at times like this, there were no words. He was glad Suzanne's son had somebody to lean on.

He sketched out a rough drawing of the crime scene on the notepad Jacqueline had given him, indicating the area where the murder occurred. As he reviewed what he was doing, he spoke out loud, not caring who heard him. "Definitely in the shadows. The perp was either waiting for her there or was following her. Whoever did this must have been familiar with the path John and Louis routinely follow." Matthew looked at John. For the first time, Matthew saw that John was looking straight at him, listening intently.

"Weird!" Jacqueline said. At first, Matthew thought she was responding to him, but when he looked up, he realized she was holding a glass of water and staring at her brother.

"Is there something wrong, Jacqueline?" he asked.

"No." She shook her head. "I just, well, John doesn't usually look at anyone so attentively. He seems to be making a connection with you." She shrugged and took a seat at the dining table with them.

Matthew didn't want to indulge her tendency to talk about her brother as if he weren't in the room, so he ignored her and addressed John directly. "You're sure you always take the same route?"

"Yes."

"At any time on your walks with Louis, did you notice anyone following you, or did you ever pass someone who looked even remotely unfamiliar to you?"

"No," he replied after a pause.

Matthew wondered about the reliability of his answer. He acted as though he were wrapped up in his own universe, oblivious to the world and the people around him. He figured he would have to accompany John on their evening walk so he could look at the lighting at the approximate time of the shooting to confirm his suspicions. Also, he wanted to survey the landscape for potential hiding spots the killer could have used.

So far, Matthew was trying to tread lightly while questioning John. Since he was starting to respond willingly, Matthew decided to press ahead. There was no one else able to give him the answers he needed. Still, he wanted to maintain a balanced approach to avoid overwhelming John by pushing too aggressively—a delicate balance. It was difficult to understand how deeply John was affected by Suzanne's death. The blank look in his eyes gave no clue to his innermost thought processes. Delving into the depths of his and Suzanne's relationship, and how it might relate to the murder, would have to proceed at a deliberate pace.

"Think hard on this, John," he started. "Over the past couple of weeks, had Suzanne ever mentioned anything that was troubling her?"

John sat staring blankly for a while and then slowly shook his head.

"No. She was happy. She was happy that Stephen was coming home with his girlfriend."

"I believe that's her bag," Matthew pointed to the pocketbook resting on the table by the front door. "Stephen, are you OK if I look through it?"

"Of course." Stephen retrieved the bag. On a cursory inspection, nothing seemed out of the ordinary. Her checkbook showed there were several thousand dollars in the account. No checks were unaccounted for. Her wallet had two credit cards, a bank debit card, her driver's license, and several pictures. Thirty-seven dollars in cash and a couple of receipts rounded out the contents of the wallet.

There was no indication that she was targeted for a specific reason. Her purse, like the bag of personal effects Stephen had shown him earlier, held no clues. That bag held a Victorinox quartz watch, a sapphire and ruby ring, a delicate gold necklace with a charm featuring two hearts intertwined, and two thin bangle bracelets that pained him to see. He'd given her the bracelets on a whim. They'd been out walking around a craft fair, having spent time together nearly every day since they finally decided to go on a real date. He wasn't sure if it was too early in the relationship for gifts, but they'd bonded so much that he felt comfortable with her, and...

That twinge of pain returned to his chest as a recurring suspicion had entered his head. "She was still wearing her jewelry when she was shot," he said. "This wasn't a random event. This was targeted. Why? I don't know."

Everyone in the room, including John, stared at Matthew. After a brief moment of silence, John spoke to no one in particular but seemed to be directing his words toward Matthew. "When can I get my sweatshirt back?"

Collectively, all eyes fell on John.

"What sweatshirt, John?" Stephen asked.

"The one Suzanne borrowed to walk Louis."

Matthew looked up from his scribbled notes. Already, he was referring to the notepad as his "murder book"—the notebook where he'd compile information about what happened to Suzanne. He used to keep such books during his days on the NYPD. So far, all he had was what he'd gleaned from the murder scene and the interviews of the people currently sitting around him, but still, it was a beginning. He'd have to get a real notebook and translate all these from the tear-off pad from Jacqueline onto it. "Suzanne was wearing your sweatshirt?"

"She asked to borrow it when she left to walk Louis. It is my favorite. When can I get it back?"

Matthew leaned back on his chair and intently appraised John. He wasn't a tall person, maybe 5 feet 7 inches, and about one hundred thirty-five pounds. Closing his eyes, Matthew pictured Suzanne and realized that she was about the same size as John. Maybe she was an inch or two shorter. Matthew pictured embracing her and being able to kiss her forehead without bending down.

Matthew's lungs collapsed. He felt as if a ton of bricks had crushed his chest. He was used to death, particularly violent death, but not when it came to someone he cared about. This was a new experience for him. Muriel's passing wasn't unexpected. As her cancer progressed, so had her suffering. Watching her wither away, he accepted the inevitability of her passing. Nonetheless, he still missed her terribly. The sudden and unexpected loss of Suzzane was a totally different situation. Friends for a few years, they had bonded into something that meant so much more to him than he realized would be possible after Muriel. Countless times in his career, he'd witnessed the pain and suffering brought on by the cruelty of man upon man. Never in his wildest imagination did he ever think he would be the one to suffer such an incalculable loss.

The only way to deal with the newfound pain was to revert to the professional role he had assumed for decades on the job: divorce himself from the emotional impact of the violence, become engrossed in the investigation, use all his energy and psychic capital dispassionately to uncover the identity of the perpetrator. That way, he avoided facing the psychological toll the crimes took on his colleagues. Eventually, another body was just that, another body, no matter what state it was found in at a crime scene. Developing the hard exterior and being outwardly unaffected by such examples of the inhumanity of man, he knew, was a necessary defense mechanism.

By returning to that hard detective mode, it was easy to conceive that Suzanne would comfortably fit into John's sweatshirt. And, Matthew realized, if she put the hood up, someone might easily mistake Suzanne for John, especially in the shadows of a poorly lit section of the park. "Did Suzanne often walk Louis?"

"No."

"A couple times per week? Once a week? How often?"

"Rarely. It is my responsibility to take Louis for his walks. Last night she was being nice because I had a lot to do to prepare for the meetings with the journalists."

"Maybe we've been looking at this all wrong," Matthew said out loud, although he meant to speak to himself. He stared into John's eyes. Within seconds, the young man averted his gaze to look at Louis. Was this situation too much for him to process?

"John," Matthew wanted a way to approach the subject without frightening him, but without direction, his only option was a full-frontal assault. "If what you say is true, and Suzanne had the hood up, there's the possibility that the killer wasn't after her, but rather you."

"Shit!" Charice's preference to curse in English rather than her native French or Swiss-German amused Michel Rousseau. Spitting out the word in English just seemed to be more satisfying, according to her. "Do you know how many times I've called over the last six hours and no damn answer?" She stood up at her desk, then sat back down. "Even worse, no return call. Not even a text to say we could talk later."

Rousseau raised his eyebrows as he looked at her over the magazine he'd been pretending to read. "I'm not sure I understand what you are referring to."

"Time!" She waved a hand in the air. "Time is pressing. We are running out of time to move the seemingly immovable force that is John Harrison." She stood and paced in a figure eight behind her desk. "Jean-Louis's lack of success at the bank makes my job ever more urgent. The walls are closing in on us, I can feel it."

"I still do not understand." Rousseau set his magazine aside. "Have you done something?"

"Arrangements! I made arrangements to ensure that Harrison would not have the opportunity to offer his work to anyone else. Despite his resistance." Charice closed her eyes and pinched the bridge of her nose. Rousseau squinted as he looked at the light refracted through the enormous diamond on her finger.

"What have you done?" he asked.

"Frankly, I don't know at the moment." She slammed her hand on her desk. "I'm waiting on a phone call that refuses to come!"

She stood and began pacing. "The fiscal viability of Zeller depends on my success, on me getting what I want, no, what I need. I have a plan in place to ensure Harrison cooperates or...well, I'll be left with no other option. My path is clear. No one besides me will have access to him, his ideas, or his creation. No matter what it takes."

Rousseau nodded in agreement. His plan was diametrically opposite to that of his bosses. The one he'd worked out with Sommers was proceeding precisely as they had mapped out. The vultures were circling overhead—over the Zeller Manufacturer, more accurately. In short order, he would have a part ownership in a watch company, something he had been dreaming about for years. As the on-site director of watches, he would have complete creative freedom in the new company's future product lines. He judged that it would take some time to retool the factory. However, they would start producing technically and creatively wonderful, unique watches in a relatively short timeframe. His concepts and designs would take the company to unrealized heights within the industry. In the end, the investment of his time and Sommers' money would be paid back multiple times over. Sure, Harrison's movement would make things even more interesting, but they weren't needed. Still, what did Charice do?

"Who is to call you?"

"No one of your concern." She waved her hand in front of her face and made a growling sound, a decidedly unbecoming sound from such a beautiful woman, Rousseau thought.

"Well, I think it is time I head home," he said, standing. His wife hated it when he worked late, and it was very late indeed, almost bedtime. His attempt to learn anything Sommers would be interested in had been all for naught this evening as he babysat the co-CEO. "It is well past the dinner hour."

"Go!" Charice threw herself back into her desk chair. "Time is wasting, and we are in the business of time measurement, not creation. Why not distract ourselves for the night? Which reminds me, there's a beautiful pair of earrings up for bid on my favorite auction site." She shook her mouse to wake up her computer.

Chapter 11

John stared at the ground. After a pause that seemed to last for hours rather than the seconds after Matthew's question, he rose and walked stiffly to his workroom with Louis following at his heels. He entered the room, shut the door, and everyone could hear the loud click of the deadbolt.

Initially, no one said anything, but as soon as the door closed behind him, Stephen, Siobhan, and Jacqueline started peppering Matthew almost simultaneously.

"Why would anyone want to go after John?"

"What does John have that anyone could possibly want?"

"John has no friends or enemies. He barely socializes. What makes you think he was the target?"

"You've got to be kidding me."

Matthew raised his right hand, signaling silence. "We have to look at all angles. There is a possibility the killer mistook Suzanne for John. They have, or had, I should say, a similar physical build. In a hoodie and in low light, it is quite possible that the mistake could have happened."

"But why?" Siobhan stood up and approached the table. She gripped the back of a dining chair. "He seems so…so…well, harmless."

"I don't know." Looking at the others, Matthew's demeanor softened. He realized that they collectively, which included Jacqueline, did not understand much about John, including his interests and what he was up to in his private life. If he were right, he'd need to get a better understanding of the young man himself. He turned to Jacqueline and motioned to the workroom door. "Is that his bedroom?"

Jacqueline smirked. "That's where the magic happens, I guess. You must know about John's obsession with watches. He spends hours in there working on them. What exactly he is up to, I don't have a clue. I have never been graced with an explanation, much less given the opportunity to enter the inner sanctum." She entered the living room area and began opening and shutting the drawers of a small side table. "Anyone seen the TV remote?"

"My mom never really knew, either," Stephen said, as everyone watched Jacqueline search the very spare living room. "Actually, it wasn't until just before they went to Switzerland that she learned he was making a prototype of a watch or something. She didn't really understand."

"John and Suzanne went to Switzerland?" Matthew furrowed his brow, trying to think back to when that could have been. Glancing at the closed door separating them from John, it was hard to fathom the concept of him traveling to Switzerland. People like John have difficulty managing to go to the supermarket, let alone travel eleven hours on an airplane to a foreign country. How was that possible? "Right, I remember now." He found himself nodding as it came back to him. Suzanne had mentioned something about a short trip to Switzerland. It was shortly before they started dating, and he never gave it much thought. "About two months ago, right?"

"I think so," Stephen said.

It was an interesting development. Now, with a sense of who John is and his challenges, the fact that John saw the need to travel to Switzerland raised numerous questions. Matthew jotted down a few notes. "Did your mom tell you why they were going?"

Stephen shook his head. "You know, she was kind of vague about it." He paused and pressed the heels of his hands against his eyes. "I can't believe I didn't ask more questions. I mean, why didn't I talk to her more often anyway?" He crumpled back into his chair, letting his head hang down. Siobhan reached out to comfort him.

"I know this is tough," Matthew said. "But it's important we don't leave any stone unturned. Most likely the trip has nothing to do with her death, but if there is anything you can remember..."

"I remember that trip. I had to approve the funds to pay for it." Jacqueline apparently gave up on looking for the remote and was scrolling on her phone. She sat at the end of a sofa, her feet tucked up under her.

"Why did they go?"

"That, I don't know."

"Why..." Matthew started to ask why Jacqueline took care of making sure the trip was paid for without asking anything about it, but realized there was no true love between the siblings. She probably never cared why her brother was traveling halfway around the world.

After a few minutes, Stephen sniffed and looked up. "I didn't really press her on why. After they got back, I asked what they'd done, and all she'd talk about was how proud she was of John, given his issues. She raved about how he was able to tolerate the stresses and strains of traveling and, more so, meeting strangers."

The pressure in Matthew's chest did not let up. That sounded just like Suzanne—so compassionate. The concept that she could have been an unintended victim was devastating. He tried to take some cleansing breaths. The air hunger persisted no matter how deep a breath he took. But, if not Suzanne, why John? It was clear to him that John's world was very limited. "Tell me about your brother, Jacqueline."

Jacqueline replied to Matthew's questions methodically, with little emotion. As best as she knew, John had no friends except for Suzanne. Teaching was his only touchstone to the outside world. She knew of no one on the faculty who socialized with him. Jacqueline was his only known relative, and they were not close. Once Suzanne was hired and grew more comfortable in her role, Jacqueline visited John at most once every one or two months. There was little for her to do in her role as executrix of the trust, except sign quarterly bank statements and approve the rare request for an extraordinary expenditure, such as the trip to Switzerland or a costly piece of equipment John wanted. His needs were modest and well covered by the monthly allowance provided by the trust.

As for the neighborhood, Jacqueline never heard John or Suzanne mention anyone by name with whom he might have socialized.

"Why then would John be a target for anyone, much less a killer?"

Matthew let Jacqueline know he was driving Stephen and Siobhan back to Suzanne's condo and that he'd return later. She barely acknowledged what he'd said.

Before dropping him off, he assured Stephen that it would be okay to inform everyone in Suzanne's contact list about her passing, suggesting he let them know what had transpired in very general terms and that a memorial was being planned. He then bought a "real" notebook to use as his murder book and decided to spend the afternoon at his son's house, under the guise of giving his daughter-in-law a break. He really just wanted the innocence and sweetness of his grandchildren around him to balance out the anger and angst he felt as he transcribed the notes from the notepad into his notebook.

A quick internet search confirmed that John's house, located in a middle-class neighborhood, was situated in a portion of the city classified by the police department as a low-crime area. The homeless and drug crises rampant in many of the surrounding communities hadn't affected the area, and definitely not that particular park. It was one of the reasons his son, Sean, and his wife chose to live in this section of Costa Mar.

He made sure to return to John's house a few minutes before it was time for Louis's walk. Jacqueline let him in and returned to focusing on the laptop she had open on the dining table. Precisely at 6:00 pm, the workroom door opened. Glancing out the living room window, Matthew saw that dusk was making way for nighttime. As John bent down to clip Louis's leash to his collar, he stood up. "John, can I come with you and Louis?"

John gave a curt nod. Grabbing a sweatshirt from the coat closet, off he went with Louis leading the way. Matthew hurried to follow in their wake.

As expected, they followed the same route they'd taken earlier. It seemed to Matthew that Louis left his markings on the same patches of grass and bushes as before. At first, they walked in silence. Matthew marveled that John did not need to talk to or interact with Louis, yet the dog was clearly very attuned to his human's routine. From the limited time he spent with them, Matthew was able to tell the dog had an intuitive understanding of John; he was typically found at or around John's feet but never under them. When John was stressed, the dog would either draw close or even, when possible, leap onto John's lap to provide comfort. And now, Louis needed no direction. The dog knew to wait when they came to a driveway or to a street corner. Besides the hum of distant traffic, the only sound to be heard was that of Louis's coarse breathing brought on by his incessant straining at the leash.

After several minutes, Matthew broke the ice. "You doing okay?" He gave a subtle shrug of the shoulders.

"John, I know it is very disturbing to think that somehow you may have been the target. We don't know if that's true, but I have to look at all possibilities." Another shrug.

"Is there anyone you can think of that may want to hurt you?"

At that, John immediately stopped and stared off. Fortunately, Louis was occupied by a scent on a nearby bush, leaving John undisturbed for the moment. Slowly, John turned to face Matthew. Deliberately, he shook his head. "No, I can't."

"Nothing going on at school?"

"No."

"No issues with any students?"

Again, a rapid no. "Only have a few students. No complaints."

At this point, it seemed like a dead end. They resumed their walk with Louis's approval.

They proceeded in silence until they reached the section of the park that had previously been cordoned off. The yellow tape that had been strung from tree to tree was gone, as was the policeman who stood over the scene. The area was indeed in the shadows as Matthew figured. Looking around, he had difficulty making out the bushes he knew ringed the patch of grass. He took out his cellphone and used the flashlight to inspect the area as best as possible. From what he could see, there was nothing out of the ordinary. That was no surprise. The crime scene technicians would have thoroughly swept the area. Taking the time to do a proper inspection would be a waste of his effort at this juncture. Nonetheless, it was useful to see the section of the park at the same time frame as when the shooting occurred. Pausing for a moment, Matthew listened to the ambient sounds. There was the hum of traffic from a nearby freeway; otherwise, silence. The surrounding dense bushes and trees probably muted the sound of the gunshots. From where he stood, he could see no one else around. If that were the case, the other night, there'd be no one to hear the reports of gunfire anyway. He surmised the park wasn't a place where people tended to hang around in the evening, especially at this time of year, now that the air had turned chilly after the sun set.

Matthew clapped his hands together loudly. The sudden noise startled Louis, but the sound was otherwise muted, as he had suspected.

Matthew continued to stand in the middle of what had been the crime scene, lost in thought, when he realized that John and Louis had resumed walking. Coming up behind them, he heard John softly mumbling. As they passed under a street lamp, Matthew could see that John's free hand was shaking. The young man seemed to be struggling to maintain control. Matthew sensed that John was caught between the need to follow the same path with Louis and the grim reality of passing the patch of grass where someone had taken Suzanne's life.

Seeking to distract him from thoughts about Suzanne, Matthew asked the first question that came to his mind as they emerged from the darkened area. "John, what happened to your mother?"

"Who?"

"Your mother," Matthew repeated.

"Don't know," John said over his shoulder. "She left without saying goodbye. I don't know where she went. I haven't heard from her since."

They were now in a well-lit, open area of the park. As they walked toward the street, they came upon a bench. Matthew suggested they pause there. He thought that the change in environment would make John more comfortable talking. John accepted the invitation to sit, ensuring he was seated on the opposite end of the bench from Matthew. Louis walked behind John to check out an interesting group of weeds.

"You're a smart guy, John. What do you think happened to your mom? By the way, what's your mom's name?"

"Brenda. I don't know. She just left me."

"And there's been no word from her? How long has it been?"

"Four years, three months, and six days."

"How do you feel about it?"

He responded with his standard answer, a shrug.

Chapter 12

Detective Colin Brown glanced at the clock hanging above his office door. It was much too late to be at his desk. There were plenty of other places he'd rather be. Still, the interminable paperwork required by any police department during an investigation, especially one involving a murder, had him tied to his chair. His only choice was to manage his fatigue with cups of coffee, a Red Bull, and several coffee candies.

After parting ways with Stephen Lang around noon, Brown revisited the park to examine the crime scene in daylight, then met with the crime scene technicians to review their initial findings. Despite careful inspection of the area, nothing useful was discovered; they even extended the search into the street. No footprints, shell casings, or even a broken branch were found.

He spent the afternoon canvassing the neighborhood again, to no avail. No one in or near the park had seen or heard anything around the time of the murder.

He was still waiting for the crime lab or the autopsy reports, but Brown didn't hold out a candle of hope for any earth-shattering revelations from either.

He rubbed his eyes, trying not to think about what lay ahead of him: reinterviewing the victim's son and John Harrison. He didn't relish the concept of either, but he knew it had to be completed soon.

The odds of making significant headway in a case and, ideally, catching the perpetrator were highest within the first forty-eight hours after the crime was committed. Distraction and delay were counterproductive. Much as he wanted to be sensitive to the needs of the family and friends of the victim at such a traumatic time, he was well aware of the need to press ahead with the requirements of the job.

He realized he was staring at his computer but absorbing nothing. As he tried to refocus on the screen, his phone rang with a local number.

"Detective Brown." He prayed it was a wrong number. He just wanted to go home and go to bed.

"Matthew Daniels," the voice at the other end of the phone said. "I was hoping I could talk to you about the murder of Suzanne Lang."

"I'm sorry. This is an open investigation. I cannot—"

"I understand, detective. I'm retired from the New York City Police. I've got more than thirty years of experience working homicide and could be an asset to you on this case."

Brown's curiosity was piqued. A homicide didn't occur very often in his city, a seasoned vet could be helpful, but... "And you'd be willing to do this because?"

"I, I was in a relationship with Suz—with the victim." Matthew said after a beat.

"Look, I appreciate the offer of help, Mr. uh—"

"Matthew. Matthew Daniels. Check out my record with the City. I know what I'm doing."

But, and it was a big *but,* if you asked Brown, there were two things he didn't want to find out after the fact. One was that Daniels was the murderer. And two, that Daniels retired because he'd lost his touch. Besides, what guaranteed he would be able to maintain objectivity given his admitted relationship with the victim?

"I know the young man she was working with," Mathew continued. "I've spent some time with him. And yes, I'm personally invested in the case, but I can stuff my feelings down and be the consummate professional."

"OK, even if I take you at your word, I'd need to get clearance to permit civilian assistance with any official investigation. Particularly something as sensitive as one involving a homicide."

"I would expect nothing less. Let's at least meet for coffee."

A touch of heartburn lit up Brown's chest. The last thing he needed right now was more caffeine, but it would come in handy tomorrow. He agreed to an eight o'clock meeting at a diner not far from the department's headquarters.

Hanging up, Brown uttered a long sigh and turned back to his computer to make some final entries. He'd had little experience in homicides, which only made having minimal to work on seem that much worse. His initial search of the computer databases yielded no results regarding the victim, Suzanne Lang. Her story was unremarkable, and everything her son, Stephen, told him checked out. At this point, he had a victim, a mode of exit, but no weapon, prints, or motive. Why not talk with her boyfriend?

An ex-cop with nothing to do but get in the way. Fantastic.

Although he was exhausted, he stayed at his desk a short while longer to dig into Matthew Daniels' history. It didn't take long to discover that the man had been a homicide detective with an exemplary record, including several meritorious service medals, even a Medal of Honor, the highest honor awarded by the NYPD.

Brown had been on the force long enough to know or hear tales about cops who retired and all but lost their minds with boredom. Within months, some went the security guard route, while others found a mind-numbing low-wage job. More recently, there had been a tendency toward gig jobs, which many also found unfulfilling. The fortunate ones, especially those coming out of the LAPD or Sheriff's Department, got connected to the movie industry or private security consulting firms as contractors or hired on for personal protection of celebrities. Those "lucky" ones were more likely to be content with their lot in life. Since this Matthew guy hadn't spent his career in Southern California, he wouldn't have those kinds of connections.

Despite some emotional involvement with the victim, Matthew's years of experience might give him the ability to maintain his objectivity, as he said. In the end, for no good reason, Brown trusted that Matthew was genuinely interested in providing the benefit of his experience and not just looking to interfere for the sake of something to do. Besides, maybe he needed Matthew. Brown wasn't aware of anyone in the Costa Mar Police Department with sufficient experience in homicide investigations to provide the required guidance. Of course, although he had come to the decision that Matthew could be a helpful resource, he was well aware that he'd have to make a convincing argument to the Chief.

Why on Earth did people have children? The idea had never sounded appealing to Jean-Louis and was being reinforced for him now as the tour boat left the Quai du Mont-Blanc on Lake Geneva. There were too many of the short humans around him. They were like ants scrambling around. Where was Phillipe?

Jean-Louis had met Phillipe at a charity event eight months previously. Bored with the ceremony, they had each chosen to get a drink at the hotel's lobby bar rather than suffer through interminable self-congratulatory speeches. Jean-Louis couldn't care less about the charity. His interest was focused on the statuesque blond who had invited him. His plans for the evening were exclusively concentrated on what he dubbed the after-party in her room.

Phillipe, a stranger to him at the time, had been distracted by something on his phone and suddenly let out a rather loud and harsh guffaw that drew Jean-Louis' attention. Apologizing for the disturbance, the man explained that a business associate was having difficulties that could only be considered comical. Jean-Louis said he understood, even though he had no idea what the stranger was referring to. But before long, the two men had ordered another round and were engaged in quiet conversation about life and politics.

The man, who introduced himself only as Philippe, owned a private firm that handled all facets of personal security. Enticed, Jean-Louis was intrigued by his emphasis on the words "all facets." Philippe explained that his company had branches worldwide and employed "executives" who were experts with an assortment of skills acquired during their time with various special forces and covert services. No job, he proudly said, was beyond his company's capabilities. Jean-Louis attempted to probe the man discreetly for more details but only received vague answers.

Before they had parted, Philippe handed Jean-Louis a card with only an embossed phone number on it and invited him to call if he should ever have a need, any need, for the company's services, locally or anywhere in the world. The message wasn't explicitly stated, but Jean-Louis was quite sure of its intent.

With his back pressed against a financial wall and seeing no other option, Jean-Louis decided the time for extreme measures was upon him. Phillipe's was the second number he dialed after the disastrous meeting with Martine. And now, at too-early-in-the-morning, he had an appointment with the mysterious man on a very public tour boat.

Phillipe managed to find Jean-Louis among the tourists and somehow steered him to a discreet spot, away from the eyes of the onlookers, who were oohing and aahing at the enchanted scenery. There, with the wind blowing their voices behind them, Jean-Louis provided Philippe with the name and address of his "problem." His request was straightforward. Philippe's terms were equally simple and to the point. To his surprise, Philippe was confident the job could be promptly executed, chuckling as he apologized for the pun.

Jean-Louis was at the end of his rope and saw no other option but to accede to the man's proposal. With nowhere else to turn and the matter of utmost urgency, there was nothing to negotiate. He even agreed to an exorbitant surcharge due to the contract's expedited nature.

When they parted ways, Jean-Louis's thoughts flashed between relief at having set in motion a plan that would assure him the financial support he required and the ambivalence about the finality of what he was forced to arrange. That said, doing away with a problem in such an efficient and permanent fashion gave him a bit of a thrill. He gave brief thought as to whether, once this mission was completed, he might consider a similar contract to handle Harrison, especially if he continued to refuse to cooperate. Charice, he was sure, would resist this suggestion initially, but, in the end, he was also sure he could convince her of its propriety, should the need arise. As he walked away from the pier, he made plans to make the required down payment on the contract the next day; it would simply be a matter of finding the right buyer for an heirloom he didn't see much use for anyway.

Chapter 13

"Sorry, buddy. You're a bit too old to apply for a position with the Department. Maybe you should go for a PI license. Might keep you engaged and use some of your experience for the betterment of society *and* your pocketbook." Brown sat back in the booth.

Matthew figured he was kidding but applying for a PI license might not be a crazy idea. The benefits were numerous, and at the moment, no downsides came to mind.

Age difference aside, over pancakes and coffee, the two men had made an instant connection.

"I mean, for sure," Brown continued. "You could be an asset to this investigation, but the bigwigs are going to need some heavy-duty convincing."

"I'd expect nothing less." Matt didn't expect things to be different in California from New York. Permission from any police supervisor to permit a civilian's participation in an ongoing investigation, even someone with as much experience as he had, is extraordinarily hard to come by. "I'll think about the PI thing, though." He nodded. "Actually, I kind of like the idea, but before I hang out a shingle, I'd like to get to the bottom of this case." He'd been more impressed with Brown's approach to the investigation than he'd expected. Brown wasn't the small-town rube Matthew initially figured him to be.

Within the limitations of departmental policies, Brown shared what information he could, repeating frequently that he'd need to check with his lieutenant before giving Matthew unfettered access to the case notes. However, what he could share was essentially all they had, and it was mostly nothing of any consequence. Brown figured the likely reason no shell casings were found was because the murder weapon was a revolver and not an automatic weapon. Which made sense: in the evening's dim light, it was doubtful the perpetrator would want to take time searching for spent casings. Besides, they'd need a flashlight, and that could draw unwanted attention and risk discovery. Do the deed, don't leave a trace, and beat it, seemed to be the most logical operating theory. If so, then the killer had to have been deliberate in the planning of the ambush. They agreed this wasn't a random act of senseless violence.

"There were no powder burns on the entrance wounds or the sweatshirt," Brown said. "So the shooter was a distance away from the victim. Unfortunately, no shoe prints were found."

"Which lends support to my theory that this may have been a case of mistaken identity." Matthew sipped his coffee, then stared at the brown liquid at the bottom of the cup. He appreciated that Brown hadn't provided a detailed description of the body. Still, he found it hard not to create a mental image of Suzanne splayed out on the grass. "If the killer was in close proximity to Suzanne, he or she most likely would have realized he was targeting the wrong person."

"That is, if John was the intended target." Brown pointed his fork at him before scooping up the last bite of his pancakes. "At this point, we have no reason to believe that was or wasn't the case."

"Given the poor lighting in that section of the park, and with Suzanne and John having similar physiques, it's a definite possibility." Matthew leaned back while a waitress refilled his coffee. The breakfast meeting that was only supposed to take as long as it took to drink a cup of coffee was now well into its second hour.

"But if not Suzanne, why John?" Brown asked the obvious question.

"I don't know." He filled Brown in on what he knew about John.

"Not much to go on, eh?" Brown said. "I came up with nothing on Suzanne's background check. A big fat zero. I'll run one on John, too, for completeness' sake."

"Appreciate it. I mean, I'm pretty sure you'll find John's record is squeaky clean, but you never know. While you're at it, check his school records. Maybe something'll turn up from his youth. He's still in his twenties. Anything's possible."

"You got it."

"And I'll keep working on him. He's not exactly forthcoming with information. Maybe as he gets used to me, he'll open up."

"Good luck with that." Brown looked at his watch. "While you work John's angle, I can take the lead on Suzanne since she was the victim, after all. That should ease departmental regulatory concerns. What do you think of the sister?"

Matthew told him about the trust. "The money angle is difficult to take seriously, but it could be a long shot. You never know. Maybe someone thought Suzanne had something to do with guarding the trust." He threw his napkin onto his plate. "I got the attorney's name. I think I'll pay him a visit."

Once they parted, as Matthew walked away, he pulled out his phone and typed into the Google search window: *How to become a private investigator in California*. He clicked on the website for the Bureau of Security and Investigative Services and read the requirements.

The BMW effortlessly ate up the curves and switchbacks on the drive from Geneva to the Vallée de Joux. The pleasing growl of the engine was music to Jean-Louis's ears. He attacked the curves as he would if he were driving his high-performance car through the turns of the Le Mans racetrack.

About six miles outside of Le Brassus, he turned onto a side road and, after several hundred meters, pulled into a parking area for the trail ahead. He got out of his car and, as directed, followed a path to a crop of tall bushes behind which was a bench. Hidden from the view of any passing vehicles, Phillipe sat with a flask propped next to him, eating a baguette filled with ham and cheese. Appearing at peace, the man stared at the distant hills as he chewed. Jean-Louis could hear the faint clanging of cowbells in the distance, which seemed to accent the pastoral atmosphere of the setting.

At the sound of Jean-Louis's approach, Philippe took a drink from his flask and tossed the remnants of his baguette onto the grass and the wrappings into a nearby trash can.

Jean-Louis sat close to him on the bench, but before he could say anything, Philippe rose and brushed the breadcrumbs off his jacket. Wordlessly, he started to walk down a path toward a more secluded area. Jean-Louis hurried to catch up. Casting a glance behind him, he saw no one around and withdrew a package from the inside pocket of his new cashmere coat. He went to hand the package to the man. Subtly, the man shook his hand and slightly nodded toward the ground. After a moment, Jean-Louis understood and dropped the package behind a bush as they passed.

They continued to stroll wordlessly for about fifty meters and then, without hesitation, Philippe turned around, approached the bush, and picked up the package. He returned to Jean-Louis and handed it to him. Confused, Jean-Louis put the package back into his pocket. Several meters further, they came to a fork in the path. As instructed, Jean-Louis took the right fork and headed back to his car. The man continued along the left branch without any acknowledgement.

Not clear about what had just transpired, once back in his car, Jean-Louis peeled open a corner of the envelope and found it contained a bound stack of blank copy paper cut in the exact dimensions of two hundred Swiss Franc notes. Jean-Louis's down payment was fulfilled. The second payment was due upon completion of the contract.

Chapter 14

Instead of going to his son Sean's house, as he did most days, Matthew went home after the diner. Not that he didn't enjoy spending time with his preschooler grandkids while their parents worked undisturbed for a little bit, but he had to admit the idea of becoming a PI was lighting up something within him. He loved his son and his family. As wonderful as it was to spend time with them, Matthew felt unfulfilled and, to a certain extent, bored. When he'd expressed those thoughts to Suzanne, she understood. That was why she'd taken the gig with John after all. He just hadn't figured out what to do with himself. Maybe becoming a PI was just what he needed. That Suzanne's murder could be his first case was a horrible irony. He knew it was totally magical thinking to fantasize that, from the grave, Suzanne was trying to give him a purpose in life, but his imagination drifted that way anyway.

Matthew spread out all the notes he'd taken the previous day onto his dining table. With the midday news broadcasting on TV as background noise, he organized the scribbles into the notebook he'd purchased. Thoughts of Suzanne, the woman he knew so well and had grown so fond of, periodically interrupted his concentration on the victim Suzanne in his notes. He hadn't realized the depth of his feelings until she was gone. Ethically, if a similar situation had occurred when he was with the NYPD, he would never have been assigned to, nor would he have accepted, the case. Nor would he offer any assistance to the investigators without a specific request. Maintaining objectivity was always at risk when family ties and emotional attachments were involved. In this situation, he rationalized to himself that he was helping the authorities at Stephen's request, the next of kin, and hoped to maintain his neutrality.

While staring at the last page of notes, his phone rang: Colin Brown's mobile.

"That didn't take very long," he answered.

"I thought about what you said regarding the possibility of mistaken identity at play," Brown replied.

'Yeah, and?" Matthew sat straighter in his chair.

"I dug up what I could on Harrison. So, get this: there are 237 John Harrisons in Southern California. When I limited the search to those aged twenty to thirty, the number was cut to thirty-eight. When I limited *that* to Orange County, the number went down to twelve, of whom two live in Costa Mar. To be sure, I searched the twelve as a start. I found the John Harrison at the address in question. Here's the kicker: I was able to trace the other John Harrisons to prior addresses, schools, or other points of reference, but when I looked into *our* John Harrison, there was no information on him before five years ago, when he was twenty. Absolutely nothing. It's as if he didn't exist. I called a friend who has access to juvenile records, and he found nothing. I called the Board of Education. They have no record of our John Harrison. He did grow up in Orange County, didn't he?"

"As far as I know. Maybe he went to a private school because of his autism."

"Thought of that, but no go. Regardless of where the kid went to school, the local school district would have a record of him. And there is nothing, absolutely nothing."

Matthew stood and arched his back in a stretch. The cracks and pops reminded him that he really needed to move more often. "Did you have them search by his birthday?"

"Yeah, his birthday, address, anything I could think of, nothing. Did find his sister. Working from her records, still a big fat zero on him."

"Wouldn't think there'd be anything there, John didn't live with his sister. What about his mother? John told me her name is Brenda."

"I'll see what I can find about Brenda Harrison."

"There's got to be some records of her. She bought his house, I think." Matthew made a note to check whether he was correct about that. "Regardless, she must be listed with the DMV or on tax rolls or a voter registration list or something." He returned to his chair and tried to make sense of this twist. He knew very little about John and was only assuming John grew up in Costa Mar, but maybe he didn't? Did this have anything to do with what had happened last night? Was there something in his history that made him a target? "So, I think I need to talk to John and his sister again."

"I do too," Brown agreed. "Let me get with my Lieutenant to see what we can do about you."

Brown's lieutenant gave a hesitating nod of approval. Matthew could serve as an unofficial observer of the investigation due to John's interpersonal challenges and Matthew's relationship with the young man. The caveat was that if Matthew wanted to question any family or potential witnesses, it could only be done in Brown's presence. When Brown spoke to his lieutenant, he "conveniently" left out any mention of Matthew's relationship with the victim. Why complicate matters with details? At this point, the lieutenant was on a need-to-know basis, and he did *not* need to know about Matthew and Suzanne.

"Hello, Jacqueline," Brown said when the sister answered the door. "Glad you're here, we'd like to talk to you and John." He nodded to Matthew.

"Sure." She stepped aside to let them in.

Brown pointed to a large shopping bag filled to the brim with clothes and a toiletries bag next to the sofa. "Is someone else here?"

"Oh, no. That's my stuff. I'm gonna have to stay here for a while, I guess, until I can find another person for John."

"Where is he?" Matthew asked.

"I'll see if I can get him to come out of his workroom."

While she knocked repeatedly on the door, Matthew dragged a chair into the living room from the dining area and motioned for Brown to follow suit. "You won't get an invitation to sit," he said.

A few minutes later, John and Jacqueline sat on either end of the couch facing them.

"You holding up OK, John?" Matthew asked.

John nodded.

"Great. We'll try not to take too much of your time. Just a few questions. Let's start with where did you go to high school?"

John did not hesitate. "Costa Mar High School."

"How many years did you attend that school?"

"All four years."

Brown was surprised. Not only was John answering immediately, but he was also looking directly at Matthew. He seemed calm and engaged in the conversation. It was as if a light switch had been flicked on. Maybe the kid had been in shock the night before.

Matthew cast a questioning look at Brown before continuing. "What about before high school? What school did you attend?"

"Saint Theresa's Learning Academy. Was there from second grade until high school."

Matthew waited as Brown wrote down the name.

"Never heard of it," Brown said. "Where is that school located, John?"

John paused, keeping his eyes directly on Matthew. "Santa Adela."

Brown pulled up a map on his phone. "Santa Adela is about twenty-three miles south of here. Why did you go there?"

"My mother thought it was the best school in the area for kids like me, with autism."

"Who paid for it?" Matthew resumed the questioning.

John shrugged.

"Probably his mother," Jacqueline said after a beat. She'd been sitting quietly, seemingly disinterested in the questioning, focused instead on her phone. Brown wasn't even sure she was listening to the exchange. "I mean, she was in charge of all of his finances as he grew up."

Things still didn't make sense. "John," Brown tried to modulate his voice to keep it on the softer side. "If you went to a private school and then Costa Mar High School, the Costa Mar School District would have a record of you."

John stared at the floor.

"But when I called the school district office, they told me there is no such record."

"You're investigating John?" Jacqueline sat forward on the couch, the corners of her mouth twitched upwards, as if on the verge of breaking out in laughter. "Do you think he is the one who shot Suzanne? Are you serious?"

John moved as far away from his sister as the couch would allow.

Brown cleared his throat and, while trying to keep his voice soft, wanted to let Jacqueline know she was out of line. "No one said he is under suspicion. This is all for background. It's standard procedure." He almost ended by saying "ma'am" but caught himself. Jacqueline seemed on the edge of either anger or bursting out in laughter, and he wasn't sure what any perception of condescension would cause her to do.

He made eye contact with Matthew again before they both looked at John, who was intently studying a thread protruding from the couch cushion.

"Wait!" A small laugh escaped Jacqueline's lips. "Of course, the school district did not have a record of John. He changed his name."

"What?"

"When?"

"Why?" Brown and Matthew asked the questions over each other.

"John's watch obsession."

"Why John Harrison?" Matthew asked.

"I don't know." Jacqueline looked at her brother. "Some watch guy. Like how he named his dog after a French guy who made watches a couple of hundred years ago."

"Breguet. Abraham Louis Breguet," John interjected, although he still seemed to be lost in his own world. At the sound of his name, Louis's head bobbed up to survey the humans. Seeing no one moving toward the front door or the closet where his food and treats were stored, he rearranged himself at John's feet and resumed his nap.

"Who is that, John?" Matthew asked.

"He is considered the greatest watchmaker of his time." John looked directly at him. "Possibly of all time. He was responsible for significant horological innovations that are still valued today."

Brown wasn't sure how innovative a watch could be, but he thought that with a name like that, the dog had an awful lot to live up to. He scribbled *Barton Alves* on his pad. "Same date of birth?"

"I didn't change that," John said.

"How come we weren't told this before?"

John shrugged and resumed staring at the loose thread.

"I guess it never occurred to us to say anything," Jacqueline offered.

Brown used his phone to do a quick Google search for Barton Alves in California. Nothing came up. Not even for the country. He'd have to make some calls.

Matthew sat back in his chair and regarded John for a quiet moment while Brown scribbled notes. "John, what is your mother's name?"

"Brenda," he immediately responded while staring at his fingernails.

"Brenda Alves?" Matthew asked.

John nodded. "Hmm."

"Where is she, John?"

John shrugged. "She left. June 17. Right after I graduated from college."

"Where did she go?"

Turning his attention to his fingernails, John shrugged again. "Don't know. She never told me."

"Do you know anything about her, Jacqueline?" Matthew asked.

"Like, what do you mean?" Jacqueline blinked at him, her mouth hung slack.

"I mean, do you know anything about what happened to her?"

"Oh, um, no. Just that she went missing."

"Who filed the official notice?" Brown asked.

"Um..." She continued to blink. "You know, I'm not really sure."

"You weren't close to them?" Matthew asked.

"Um, not really. I mean, John and I never met until I was in high school. At some point, his mother contacted mine for some reason. I don't remember why she did it." Jacqueline shook her hair out of her face. "Maybe she thought John could benefit from having more of a family. He's two years older than I am, and at the time, I was more interested in my friends than suddenly having a weird brother. After a while, we kind of got to know each other. Or, at least, I sort of got to know John. He's not one to communicate if you haven't noticed."

"So how did you find out about the trust and needing to get a companion for him?"

"The attorney told me."

"Michael Livingston?"

Jacqueline nodded.

"And you didn't ask questions about his mother?"

"Look, I was nineteen, OK? And I had my own crap I was dealing with. I could barely keep my own life together, and suddenly I found out I was responsible for making sure John was all right. I didn't ask a lot of questions."

Brown made a note to see if a missing person report had been filed on Brenda Alves when he returned to his desk. From Jacqueline and, to a lesser extent, John, he was able to cobble together a vague description of her. John, for his part, was able to provide her date of birth.

"What about your father? Do you have any information about him?" Brown asked. The question elicited a less-than-subtle snicker from Jacqueline.

"That asshole disappeared without a word from both of our lives," she responded before John had a chance to answer. "Not even a goodbye note. My mother never spoke one word about him. She wouldn't let me speak of him. I don't even know his name. My mother said the name he told her, some German name, may or may not have been his real one. The guy was a total slime bucket." As she spoke, her cheeks reddened.

"I'd like to talk to your mother," Brown said. "Maybe she can tell us about your father since he was also John's."

A dark shadow fell over Jacqueline's face. Her eyes moistened. "That's not going to happen. My mom is dead."

"I'm sorry for your loss. When was that?"

"About five years ago," she replied. "When I was still in college."

"If you don't mind, tell us what happened to your mother. Her name was?" Brown resumed taking notes.

"Why?" Jacqueline asked.

"We can't leave any stone unturned. Maybe this is related to John's father."

"Oh. Um, her name is, was, Angela Henderson."

"What happened to her?"

This time, Jacqueline stared at her hands. "I was in college, Santa Barbara City College. She came to visit me for the weekend. That Saturday night, my friends and I were invited to a party in Isla Vista, the town next to the UC Santa Barbara campus. I wasn't going to go because my mom was visiting, but she insisted we all go. She never went to college and liked to think she was one of the girls when she came up. So, we went to the party. It was on Del Playa. That's the primo street in Isla Vista. The houses on the ocean side sit on a cliff overlooking the beach. I guess she had too much to drink and went for a walk...at some point...as best as anyone could figure, somehow she slipped or fell over the edge. Landed on the rocks below. The police told me that it happens every few years. Someone, typically a drunk college kid, dies after falling off the cliff. They ought to do something about that."

"That must've been tough," Matthew said.

"You have no idea." She dabbed her eyes with the sleeve of her shirt. "Never finished school. Couldn't face going back. Between my mom and then having to deal with John, it was too much."

Chapter 15

It had been a long day for the bank director; one filled with back-to-back meetings. There had even been a long and arduous one during his usually sacrosanct lunch time. The board of directors had requested an urgent report on the bank's holdings in the South of France. Hotels in the region had been hit by various work stoppages, and the ongoing French railway strike doubled the threat to the tourist trade. Subsequently, the significant decline in the bottom line of a vital hotel client in the region was hurting the bank's quarterly ledger. So, Pierre Martin had to work well into the evening with his senior staff to finalize the report and prepare it for presentation to the chairman of the board by ten the following morning.

Although he managed to have all but the final touches completed by the time he finally left the bank, he remained frustrated by the unrealistic demands of his superiors. The bank was in excellent fiscal shape, much of which was the result of his expert stewardship. It was so Swiss that the board should panic whenever there was even the slightest possibility of a downturn in one of the sectors of their investment portfolio.

Born in Lyon, France, Martin became a naturalized Swiss citizen sixteen years earlier. Even though he now considered himself more Swiss than French, he still had limited tolerance for what he considered the Swiss penchant for obsessive attention to the smallest of details, especially by the bank's board. His tolerance for the micromanaging that occurred on a routine basis had its limits, and it was rapidly approaching the breaking point. Even though the rest of the bank's portfolio was outperforming its competitors, it was impossible for the chairman of the board not to worry about every centime. The bank had been in existence for over one hundred and twenty-seven years, and although it was positioned to last well into the next century, he wasn't.

The director left the bank through the underground garage. Straight home, have a whiskey, and go to bed, that was all he wanted for what was left of the evening. Sadly, that meant the morning would come all too soon, and he would have to be back at his desk by eight at the latest, preparing for what, no doubt, would be a contentious meeting. Hopefully, the whiskey would settle the anticipatory butterflies already churning in his stomach.

In the lateness of the hour, the streets of Geneva were empty. Despite the proliferation of traffic cameras throughout, his Mercedes sped along the route with him paying no heed to posted speed limits. Music blared in the car, keeping him awake and alert as he headed along Lake Geneva and passed the estates of some of the wealthiest citizens in the Canton, if not the country. When he pulled up to the front of his estate, he impatiently waited while the gate slowly opened. As he entered his house through the garage, he was welcomed by his Bernese mountain dog, who, as usual, was generally the only being that was truly happy to see him over the course of the day. Two weeks ago, his wife had been called away to Bern to attend to her mother, whose dementia had recently taken a turn for the worse, leaving him to his own devices in the big house. He selected a bottle of Glenfarclas 25 from a shelf containing a selection of Scotch and Irish whiskeys, and glass in hand, made his way to his favorite chair in the living room.

The first sip of the scotch gave a comforting combination of sweetness, from the sherry overtones borne from the years spent aging in a cask, and the faint burn of the alcohol. Before he could completely relax, the dog started barking. Martin saw him standing by the side door. He had been cooped up in the house longer than usual. With the combination of the early departure of the housekeeper and the late return of his human, the dog was probably in need of a patch of grass to relieve himself. The director was in no mood to take the dog for his usual evening walk. Instead, he opened the side door. Without hesitation, the dog bolted to the spacious yard.

Turning back to his drink, he took a long sip, then glanced through the day's mail piled on a side table while waiting for his dog to return.

Suddenly, gloved hands surrounded his head and occluded his mouth and nose. At first confused, a sudden and clear realization hit him. The crash of his glass tumbler onto the stone floor accented the urgency of the moment. Being slight in build, Martin felt himself lifted by a larger man pressing into him from behind. Barely able to support himself on his toes, he panicked as the need for air became desperate. Within moments, his vision blurred. Desperate efforts to peel away the hands and arms surrounding him proved ineffectual. Soon, everything went dark.

Matthew was a little envious of Brown having an office to go to after meeting with John and Jacqueline. He didn't want to go back to his condo, as the memory of Suzanne's presence had been too much of a distraction earlier. Instead, he went for a walk in the local state park, a source of pride for Costa Mar. A tourist attraction with a restaurant directly on the sand and a dozen cottages that a lucky few could rent, the park also had a series of paths along the bluffs that overlooked the beach and ocean.

He passed several access points leading down to the beach, preferring instead to stay on the path above. He enjoyed the soothing sound of the rhythmic pounding of the surf. At an isolated point, he found an unoccupied bench overlooking the beach and decided to make it his office for the moment. Growing up in Queens, he never developed an appreciation for the beach. The ones near where he lived in New York were crowded, dirty, and noisy. The color of the water tended toward a sickly brown rather than the clear green-blue of the Pacific in Southern California. Beautiful though the water might be, he wasn't tempted to go for a swim as the Pacific Ocean was colder than the Atlantic. He much preferred the heated swimming pool at his condo complex over the cold reality of the ocean, even on hot summer days. Actually, he had become quite enamored with the hot tub and found it to be a luxuriant pleasure he knew nothing about back East. However, although the pool was a good place to cool off on a hot day or entertain the grandkids, it was not a conducive place for thinking about a murder case.

Sitting back on the bench, he enjoyed the sounds of the waves and the calls of the seagulls as they surfed the wind and scanned the water and beach for their next meal. Yeah, he could get used to this being his office. This is where he could sit, relax, and give free rein to his thoughts.

He had a victim but no suspects. Even the victim was in question; was she the intended target? Could it have possibly been a case of mistaken identity, and John was the actual target? Was it a random event or was it premeditated? The overarching question, especially if this was planned, was why? Establishing a motive had to be the first order of business. He rejected the possibility of a random attack. His gut told him otherwise. And yet everything he knew about Suzanne did not lead him to believe he was missing something dark or sinister in her background, but one could never be totally sure. On the other hand, John, an autistic kid with no social skills and very few contacts with the outside world, was even less likely to involve himself in anything that would attract the wrong type of attention. That said, one possibility to consider was whether one of John's students was seeking revenge for not receiving an "A" as a course grade.

Being able to clear the detritus of useless thoughts gave him some clarity. But without any hard evidence or true path to follow, he felt the need to talk to someone. Someone who could help him parse out what he knew and plan his next steps.

He pulled his phone from his pocket, went to the list of his recent calls, and selected the name three down from the top, Bernie Hopkins.

Of the few people he still kept in contact with from the department in New York City, he missed his closest friend, Bernie, the most. They'd met at the Police Academy, and although their professional careers took different paths—Matthew in the Detective Division and Bernie in the Property Department—they had remained close. Bernie had no experience as an investigator, but despite his, at times, self-deprecatory description of himself, he provided Matthew with a reliable sounding board. Matthew had learned to appreciate the occasional cogent question Bernie asked seemingly out of the blue. In fact, it was with Bernie's help that Matthew was able to solve his most significant case while he was part of the NYPD—one involving Russian spies, multiple murders, and several high-profile arrests. It was a story straight out of a classic spy thriller.

After three rings, Bernie answered with his usual "So, what's up, Sherlock?" In the background, Matthew could hear the clamor of Bernie's obsession: model trains. After a year searching for a hobby to occupy his post-retirement days, he somehow became passionate about model trains. Now, whenever they spoke, Matthew had to endure prolonged and detailed discussions about the intricacies of train engines and layouts. Whenever Bernie waxed poetic, Matthew realized a twinge of emptiness. He suspected he was jealous of not having such a passion. He now wondered if the private investigator gig could fulfill that void.

The wind started to pick up. The rhythmic crashing of the waves below and the sound of Bernie's trains made it difficult for Matthew to hear about Bernie's latest additions to his collection. Before he could proceed with the reason for his phone call, Matthew retreated from the overlook to a sheltered area.

Bernie was the only one Matthew had felt comfortable expressing his burgeoning feelings for Suzanne. Not having spoken for three days, his friend was shocked at the news of Suzanne's death.

As he'd done when Matthew's wife Muriel passed away, Bernie put aside his usual sarcastic nature and penchant for snarky comments while Matthew relayed the events of the past couple of days. Not one to mince words, Bernie asked pointed questions throughout. However, by the time Matthew finished his summary of the case as he understood it to date, they had made no headway toward new or constructive ideas.

Chapter 16

Brown didn't stay long at his desk. His contact at the school district was able to email him the face sheet of Barton's, or John's, school file. Brown now had the address where Barton had lived with his mom when he was in elementary and high school. Interestingly, there was an empty space where the father's name was to be entered.

Next up, he pulled a report on Brenda Alves. Her current whereabouts remained unknown. The only entry in the system he could find was a speeding ticket issued to her eight years prior. The address on the summons matched the one on the school form, not John's current address. A quick phone call revealed that the listed address was for an apartment not far from John. The current resident had been in the space for the last two and a half years.

He was surprised no one had filed a missing person report on Brenda Alves, so he entered one into the national database system. He expected little to come of it. An absent mother for several years seemed to have nothing to do with the murder of Suzanne Lang, yet a nagging feeling encouraged him to at least try to look for her. If they could find her, maybe she'd fill in John's early history, even though the likelihood of there being anything actionable from so long ago was minuscule. Next up was a visit with Dr. Joanne Friedberg, a recently appointed deputy coroner, in the Orange County sheriff's department headquarters.

Even though Dr. Friedberg had only been on the job for three months, her desk was cluttered with piles of files and loose articles, either torn from various medical and legal journals or printed out from online resources. Despite the apparent lack of a system in the office, she was able to quickly locate the file containing all the case material about the deceased, Suzanne Lang.

"So, looking at the preliminary crime scene report," she handed Brown a piece of paper. "The technicians who processed the scene agreed with my assessment regarding the lack of a struggle. The grass had not been trampled or dirt kicked up. They didn't find any broken branches in the surrounding bushes. The dirt was dry at the time of the attack, but soon after, the sprinkler system turned on. Unfortunately, the pooled water muddied the area before the investigators could process it. Before they could get anyone to shut off the sprinklers, any chance of recovering footprints or potentially useful physical evidence from the scene was impaired at best or otherwise made impossible."

She passed a manila folder with photographs to him.

Brown took his time opening it. He hated seeing photos of dead people. For reasons he couldn't explain, seeing a murder victim frozen in time, captured in the two dimensions of a photograph, was more disturbing than seeing the actual body. To make matters worse, she included copies of pictures taken during the autopsy. Brown had not yet gotten used to seeing such graphic images of the human body's internal parts. They did not prepare for this kind of ugliness in detective school. A brief wave of nausea passed after several deep breaths.

"So, you can see," Dr. Friedberg continued after giving him a chance to review the pictures. "The assailant shot the victim from behind on her left side. The autopsy won't be finalized for several days, and it will be even longer before the toxicology tests are completed."

"Judging by these," Brown handed the file back to her. "They're not really needed."

"That's my assumption as well, but I want to be complete."

"Anything else?"

"There were no bruises or defensive wounds. As best as I can tell." The doctor slowed her words. "The shooter stood at a distance from the victim. The two shots were fired in rapid succession as the entry wounds are close to each other."

"How far?"

"There was no gunpowder residue found on the hood of the sweatshirt or around the entry wounds, so not close. I'm estimating the shooter was seven to ten feet from the victim."

"The bullets?"

"I was able to recover bullet fragments and small threads from the sweatshirt from her brain. Neither I nor the crime scene team found remnants of the second bullet. The exit wound above her right eye is evidence that the unrecovered round was a through-and-through shot."

"So there's another bullet somewhere."

Friedberg shrugged. "Yes. But I doubt it will ever be recovered. For what it's worth, my assessment is the killer was lying in wait, hidden until the victim walked by, and then they took a couple of steps into the open, fired twice, and left. The report states the bushes started about eleven feet from where the body was found, so everything fits."

Brown would need to revisit the crime scene to be certain, but from his memory, he recalled there were bushes in the vicinity. Suzanne would have been caught totally unaware. This had the appearance of a planned assassination attempt.

Having the advantage of a badge, Brown was granted access to various official agencies, which he visited as soon as he left the coroner's office. Flashing his credentials in the face of a young clerk at the county health department upstairs from the coroner's office, he was able to obtain a copy of Barton Alves s birth certificate. Notably, as indicated on the school forms, the father's name wasn't listed.

When he pointed out the empty space on the document, the clerk shrugged.

"There's no law mandating the father be named."

"It's late there. I thought you Swiss were up and at it early in the morning, crunching away at the bench after a coffee and croissant," Sommers said as soon as he answered his cell.

"Something's not right," Rousseau replied. He sat in his apartment not far from the Zeller Manufacturer. The money Sommers had already transferred to him, plus what remained of his less-than-generous Zeller salary after his meager living expenses, sat in a bank account waiting for the next infusion of cash. Once Sommers transferred that installment, he would have sufficient funds to purchase a house on the French side of the border. The one he had his eye on befitted the co-principal of a watch company. Living in France, thirty minutes from the factory, had definite tax benefits for Rousseau, a French citizen. If he were to purchase a house in Switzerland, the taxes would deeply chew into his nest egg. He'd be left with enough to purchase a modest home, not one suitable for someone with his future position. Many workers in the Vallée de Joux commuted across the border from nearby French towns for similar tax reasons, as well as to avoid the higher cost of living in Switzerland. Finally, he'd be one among them.

"What do you mean?" Sommers sounded annoyed.

"I just got off the phone with Bonet. He sounded different."

"Oh? How so?"

"He was almost giddy. He sounded relieved."

"Why is that so upsetting? Maybe he just got laid. Why should I care about that?"

"No. It's something else." Rousseau stood and stared out the windows of his apartment. Pressing his forehead against the glass, he took his time trying to keep his calm. How to convince Sommers that something was off? "Over the past week or two, whenever I talked to him, he seemed preoccupied, stressed. Clearly, he was worried about the viability of the brand despite all his machinations. But tonight, it was as if he didn't have a care in the world. He acted as if he had the money he needed already in his pocket."

"Interesting. Hmm." Sommers snickered. "Let's remind him how much shit he is in. I'll make a call to Martin tomorrow and have them call the loan. That will put the squeeze on Bonet. We'll just move up the schedule. No worries. I have done this before and can easily do it again. I'll squeeze his nuts until his eyes are bulging out of his skull."

"You can do that?"

Sommers outright laughed. "Watch me."

As he waited in front of John's house for the third time that day, Matthew could hear the sounds of traffic from the freeway that bordered Costa Mar. The din was nothing like New York. He missed the adrenaline rush that came with living and working in the City. The ever-present sounds of sirens and blaring car horns, the press of crowds on the sidewalks, the crush on the subway were all part of the City's character. Here in Costa Mar, such frenetic activity was nowhere to be found.

In contrast, the echoing sound of Brown's hurried footsteps as he approached was nothing that could ever be heard in the City, unless it was in the middle of the night, at the end of a dead-end alley.

"Good work," Matthew said to Brown after the detective gave him a rundown of what he'd discovered. He rang the bell, then glanced at his watch. "And it's 6:30 now, so John should be back from his evening walk. Maybe he'll remember something new."

Jacqueline answered and, to Matthew's and Brown's surprise, Stephen was standing in the kitchen.

"Siobhan had to run some errands," he explained. "I didn't want to be in my mom's condo alone." He paused and looked around. "I really didn't know where else to go. Thought I'd see if John needed something."

Matthew felt bad for the boy. No one is ever prepared to handle such a situation. "You holding up okay?"

"I don't know." Stephen appeared ill at ease, searching for something to say. After a pause long enough for Jacqueline to sit at the table and open a laptop, he found his tongue. "Just know, I'm more than willing to reimburse you for any and all expenses related to solving who...who killed my mom." The catch in his voice was indescribably painful to hear.

Matthew was taken aback by the open-ended offer of money to work the case. He had not even begun to complete the application process for a PI license, and here he was being offered pay to investigate a murder as if he'd been hired to do just that.

"Seriously." Stephen visibly swallowed. "Whatever comes from her insurance policy or estate or whatever. I don't want it. But I do want to know who killed her."

"I appreciate the vote of confidence," Matthew said. "But I'll have to think about the offer. At the moment, I don't feel comfortable taking any money from you."

The young man's face fell. Matthew wondered if the offer of money from Suzanne's life insurance policy or whatever savings she might have had was what Stephen was hoping would assuage his guilt over something related to his relationship with his mother. Suzanne never spoke of a problem between her and her son. But then again, the dark secrets held onto by family members were not typically the subject of conversations had during the blossoming of a new relationship. "We can work that out later." Matthew looked at Brown, hoping he'd shift the conversation.

But it was Jacqueline who cut the silence.

Jacqueline looked up from her work and twisted around in her chair to look at them. "You asked why John chose John Harrison when he legally changed his name. I don't know if it means anything, but I asked John about that, and he showed me a book about a man named John Harrison. He was an English carpenter in the eighteenth century who invented the first successful marine chronometer. I don't know what that is, really. Some kind of clock. It was supposedly this big thing because it helped sailors know where they were at sea."

Matthew had also looked up John Harrison and found the same information on Wikipedia. During the eighteenth century, errors in navigation due to the inability to measure longitude correctly at sea led to the foundering of many ships. The damaged and sunken vessels were responsible for the death of sailors in numbers far greater than those killed in combat. So desperate was the problem that the king offered a prize of 20,000 pounds sterling to the first person to develop a marine chronometer that would allow for the accurate calculation of longitude at sea. Harrison made four attempts to create a portable one. Despite the politics of the time, Harrison's H4, his last attempt, allowed a British warship to cross the Atlantic Ocean from Portsmouth, England, accurately, to Jamaica, a significant triumph of navigation at the time. Unfortunately, although he dedicated much of his life to the invention, and the trans-Atlantic crossing proved successful, he never received his full and deserved prize money.

The boy certainly is possessed by watches, Matthew thought.

Meanwhile, he was nowhere in sight. Matthew figured John was holed up in his workroom. He nodded toward the closed door. "Is he in there?"

"Yeah. You might have to knock a lot. Sometimes he wears headphones."

Matthew tried softly, at first. "John?" he called. No answer.

He rapped with greater force. "John?" After several moments, he could hear the thud of a heavy door closing from inside the room. Eventually, the dead bolt slid free, and the door cracked open.

"John, can we come in?" Matthew asked.

After a momentary pause, the door slowly opened wide enough for Matthew and Brown to enter. Once they were inside, John shut the door and relocked it with the deadbolt. The workbench, where Matthew assumed John spent his time, looked undisturbed. It was an unusual piece of furniture with a wide, protruding arm on either side. Each could be independently moved in and out and adjusted up and down. Interestingly, the working surface of the desk was at chin level, and the edge had a shallow semicircular cutout. The odd desk must be necessary to allow John to work in his miniature world without bending over. Screw drivers with different colored heads jutted from a circular holder on the right side of the bench. To the left sat three magnifying loupes, the kind Matthew had seen jewelers use. High-intensity lamps extended over the surface from the two back corners. In the center of the white desk pad sat two inverted stemless wine glasses. Matthew suspected their purpose was to cover something, but at the moment, there was nothing under either of them. Resting behind the glasses was a probe and a closed pocketknife. On a small extension on the left side of the desk sat a closed laptop. Hanging off the back of the stool pushed away from the bench was a pair of noise-canceling headphones.

To the left of the workbench stood a small but substantial safe. That must have been the source of the noise they heard while waiting to be allowed entry. The soft hum of an air purifier standing nearby was the only ambient sound. Judging by the two handheld vacuums mounted on the wall, John had a thing about dirt or dust. There was also an upright vacuum cleaner standing in the far corner of the room. Meanwhile, there was no attempt at decoration. The room was purely functional in nature.

The only seat was a stool adjusted, Matthew assumed, to give John the right perch to do his work. That work, however, remained a mystery. John stood by the door, hands shoved in his pockets, staring at the space in front of Matthew and Brown. No one made a move for the chair.

"John," Matthew started. "You understand Detective Brown and I are trying to establish exactly what happened in the park and whether

Suzanne was the intended target or if she was mistaken for someone else?"

John barely acknowledged the question.

"Have you thought about what we asked you already? Is there any reason you can think of that would lead someone to want to harm Suzanne, or you, for that matter?"

John's facial expression did not change. A flicker of his eyes suggested to Matthew that he registered the question and its significance. Silence was his only response.

Matthew tried a different tactic. "John, has anyone threatened you in any way? Maybe a student or someone you know or knew?"

Silence continued.

Brown stepped closer to John. "John, we have got to get some answers, please. Every minute we delay makes it harder to find the person who did this to Suzanne. Please, why would anyone want to hurt her or you?"

Slowly, not diverting his eyes from the spot he was focused upon, John shook his head. "Don't know."

"Can you remember anyone being angry with you?" Brown pressed. "Anyone threaten you now or in your past? Maybe a friend or an acquaintance?"

Matthew shot a disapproving look at Brown, who immediately backed down. He was showing his inexperience by using too aggressive a tone. He worried John would totally shut down if he perceived a threat. Trying to defuse the situation, Matthew interjected more softly. "Listen, John. We need to find answers. Maybe the answers are in your past." He paused before continuing. "Where's your mom? Do you know?" Rephrasing the question might lead to a different answer, he reasoned, especially if John had time to think about it.

For the first time, there seemed to be a slight crack in John's expression. He walked to his workbench and sat down heavily in his chair. Staring at the orderly desk, John found that one of the screwdrivers in the holder was turned out of alignment with the others. He carefully corrected the anomaly. "I don't know. She left. I have not heard from her since then."

"Do you know why?"

Slowly, he shook his head. "Maybe she was angry at me."

Matthew was unsure but thought he saw John's eyes get watery. If so, it was the first sign of an emotional response to any question.

"What about your father? Do you know anything about him?"

John studied his workspace as if looking for an errant speck of dirt or another misplaced tool. He slowly shook his head. His gaze rose to the bookshelves and, from his chair, he reached up to adjust a volume, putting the spine of the book in perfect alignment with its neighbors.

"Anything. Maybe his name?"

No response.

"No friends." John said after a pause.

Initially confused, Matthew realized that John was responding to the prior question about friends possibly being a threat to John.

"John," Matthew decided to switch gears. "Tell me, who set up the trust?"

"I don't know."

Matthew spent his career interviewing suspects, witnesses, and victims. He had learned to separate the wheat from the chaff. To identify the bullshit from the truth. It defied logic that John had spent so many years living off a trust and not have the least bit of knowledge regarding any of its details. For all his brilliance, John's lack of interest or knowledge about certain particulars regarding his situation was surprising.

"How did you know your mother was missing?"

"She did not come home."

"How did the attorney find out?"

"Jacqueline must have told him."

"How did Jacqueline know about your mother?"

"I needed to go to the college. My mom would take me. She wasn't home, so I called Jacqueline."

"And then she told the attorney?"

John shrugged.

"Is there anyone else in your family?"

No response.

They seemed to be at an impasse. John simply stared at the floor in front of Matthew's feet. Matthew looked at Brown and nodded toward the door. Wordlessly, the two left the room. No sooner had they closed the door than they heard the dead bolt slide back into place.

Chapter 17

In the kitchen, Jacqueline leaned against the counter, punching away at the screen of her phone, as if in a heated texted discussion with someone. Stephen was nowhere in sight, which Matthew found odd. He'd expected the guy to wait to find out if John provided anything new.

Looking up, Jacqueline tucked her phone into the back pocket of her jeans. "So did John shed any light?"

Brown shook his head. "I'm gonna head out. Be in touch with you early tomorrow," he said over his shoulder to Matthew. "Good night."

Jacqueline didn't bother seeing him out. After the door shut, Matthew rubbed at his two-day-old stubble and approached her. "So, what can you tell me about the trust?"

As if caught unaware, Jacqueline's eyes bulged, and her head jerked back. "Not much," she said when she seemed to have recovered. "It was established a long time ago. When John's mother went missing the lawyer contacted me. He said there was something written into the trust, a proviso or something like that. It made me the executrix in case something happened to his mother, and she couldn't do whatever for him."

"The lawyer contacted you or you contacted him?"

"What do you mean?"

Matthew thought he was clear, but he didn't want to come off as sarcastic. "John said that after his mother hadn't come home, he called you. He believes you called the attorney."

"Yeah."

"But you said the lawyer contacted you."

"Yeah." She scratched her head. "So, like, John called me. He needed a ride to the college. I got here, and the place was a wreck. It's like he never thought to wash a dish. Weird, though, 'cause Louis's dish was clean. But like, it was pretty disgusting in here."

"Okay." Matthew sat at the dining table.

"So, like I took him to college and came back here to straighten up the place. I kept trying to call his mom, but no answer. I didn't know what to do. I snooped through the mail and found a letter from an attorney talking about stuff John needed. So I called him."

"Got it. So you called him."

"At first. A couple days later, he called me to say that until his mother came back, I had to administer the trust for John."

"And what does that entail?"

"Just making sure his needs are met. That he has food, a home, clothes, whatever."

"And you don't know who set up the trust?"

"I've asked countless times." She crossed her arms over her chest. "Livingston kind of hinted it was our father who'd set it up. He always says the same thing, 'per specific instructions in the documents,' he can't disclose anything. I was given instructions about how the money is to be used for John's care."

"How much is in the trust?"

"I don't know that either. I'm sure it is quite the sum. I don't have a trust but have to watch him live high off the hog while I get a small stipend for all my trouble. My job is to sign papers the lawyer puts in front of me every quarter."

"You don't have a trust?"

This time her shrug was accompanied by a raised left eyebrow and a snort. "I suppose the rationale is that I have a job and am employable. I mean, John has a job, too, but he, well, obviously he can't take care of himself."

Matthew took a moment to scrawl notes on his pad. Money, sex, and power were the primary motivators for the majority of crimes he'd investigated. A brother with a comfortable lifestyle funded by a mysterious father who, in turn, essentially snubbed the sibling is a good motive to consider.

"That sucks. John gets a nice nest egg, and you get a few pieces of straw." As he spoke the words, Matthew watched for any reaction, dilating pupils, flushing of the cheeks, or sweat on the brow, but saw nothing. Biometric monitoring was better than any lie detector created.

Jacqueline smirked. "You're telling me. I can't tell you how many times I talked to the lawyer about it. The asshole is rock-solid stubborn. According to him, the trust is written in stone." As if anticipating the next question, she continued. "It even has specific instructions on what to do with the money if anything happens to John, and they don't include me. Livingston has told me his hands are legally and ethically tied. I tried to get a raise in my stipend. Inflation, you know? But he refused even that."

The next day, Matthew sipped hours-old coffee from a Styrofoam cup Michael Livingston's secretary had given him to "enjoy" while he waited for the attorney. No amount of sugar could mask the burned, sour taste of the brew.

It was all he could do not to shuffle through the papers on the giant antique oak desk in front of him. Sitting on the edge of his chair, he craned his neck trying to read the upside-down words. He didn't expect to find anything about John but was merely scratching the itch of his inquisitive mind.

The office was well-organized and decorated in a manner that was intended to convey to visitors that the occupant was a serious and important individual. Lots of antique oak furniture filled the room: the desk and credenza behind it, and a bookcase filling one of the walls, were colored with the same honey oak stain. Dark green velvet upholstery covered two chairs facing the desk. The requisite ego wall behind the attorney's desk had an impressive display of diplomas and certificates, along with pictures of the attorney standing next to people Matthew didn't recognize but assumed to be significant to those who might care.

A quick online search of "Michael Livingston, Esq.," revealed that he specialized in estate planning as well as tax law. The few reviews online were positive. He was given four stars by each of three anonymous reviewers.

While Matthew appreciated the lawyer's agreement to an impromptu visit, he would have liked the man to be on time. As he was getting frustrated, the door to the office was flung open, and Livingston entered quite unceremoniously. After a cursory handshake, he sat behind his desk and got straight to the point. "Mr. Daniels, what can I do for you?"

"As I mentioned to your secretary this morning, I'm a former detective with the New York Police Department, and I was asked to look into the murder of Suzanne Lang. I'm sure you know who she is, or was, I should say. John Harrison's companion." Matthew leaned forward and placed his Styrofoam cup on the edge of Livingston's desk. It was a power move to assure the attorney that he wouldn't be easy to dismiss.

"I'm aware of Mrs. Lang. But I'm not sure how I can be of assistance." Livingston eyed the cup before meeting Matthew's eyes.

"I was hoping to get a better idea of John's legal and financial situation."

"I am not at liberty to discuss the matter. Besides, I don't understand what it has to do with the unfortunate passing of Mrs. Lang." Livingston paused as he leaned back in his chair. "I can't imagine it has anything to do with Mr. Harrison's affairs. It seems like it was just another random tragedy, all too common these days. How is Mr. Harrison handling it?"

"We can't really be sure, but it seems he's holding his own at the present."

Livingston nodded. "Well, I am sorry for what has happened, but as you are here in an unofficial capacity, I am limited by the law and professional ethics as to what I can disclose to you about John's trust or anything else that might have to do with my role as trustor of his account."

Matthew understood the legal limitations he faced. If needed, he was sure he could persuade Colin Brown to intercede with the appropriate subpoena. Still, even then, the law was quite strict. Matthew was willing to bet that the trust was ironclad and that no court in the land would grant him or Brown access to the secrets it held.

"Perhaps you could help me understand its history. Did you draw it up?"

"No, I was only asked to administer it."

"Who asked you?"

"A colleague in San Francisco, Samuel Chang, was the originator of the document."

"Have you had any contact with the person, I believe it was the father, who established the trust?"

Livingston shook his head. "Ethically, I am not permitted to discuss any of the details. That said, I will say I have had no contact with anyone associated with the creation of the trust since I took over its administration. Really, there is no need to meet with anyone except for the executrix periodically. The document is one of the most detailed trusts I have ever seen. The instructions are specific and written in stone. My role was specified, well, not mine exactly, but the role of the trustor. This trust will be in effect in perpetuity."

"In perpetuity?" That raised Matthews' eyebrows.

"Yes. For as long as John walks this planet, he will be cared for."

"And after the money is gone?"

Livingston chuckled. "Believe me, the fund is very healthy. There are no worries that the money will run out. It was established more than twenty years ago, so it has had plenty of time to grow into a tidy sum."

Matthew was too tempted. "How big a sum?"

Livingston shook his head.

"What happens when, as you put it, John stops walking on the planet?" Matthew recalled Jacqueline's bitterness when she discussed how the trust was set up. He wondered if even her stipend would disappear.

Livingston pursed his lips and, once again, shook his head. "The trust is very detailed and specific about that possibility. All I can say is the arrangements are iron-clad regarding the distribution of funds, without any possibility of modification."

Trying to eke out anything of use, Matthew attempted for more. "Who gets the money? Does it go to the family?"

Livingston stared across the desk, his face blank—the true definition of a poker face. "Since the young man has only his mother and his sister as family members, I assume your question is asking whether they would benefit if he died. Again, sir, I am not at liberty to answer, but I will tell you this, no."

"Well, I appreciate your time." Matthew stood. "May I contact you later if I have further questions?"

"I'm still not quite sure what John's trust has to do with the murder of his companion."

"To be honest, nor am I. I just don't believe in leaving any stone unturned."

Matthew left the office. Passing the secretary, he nodded goodbye to her and recalled he'd left his half-finished cup of coffee on the attorney's desk. "Screw it."

In his car, Matthew used his cell to search for the phone number for attorney Samuel Chang in San Francisco. He held out little hope

Chang would remember much about a trust he drew up more than twenty years ago, but it was another stone to look under.

A stone that would have to wait for later, as Chang's secretary said he was in a meeting and would return the call.

Chapter 18

I am sorry, the director is not here." The secretary's voice sounded oddly unsteady to Sommers. Whenever he'd called Martin, the secretary was *always* curt and officious. Now she seemed unprofessionally distracted, a trait very uncharacteristic of someone in such a position.

"When do you expect him to return? It is quite urgent that I speak with him."

"I am sorry, sir, but I cannot say." There was a catch in the secretary's voice, which almost sounded like a sob followed by a sniffle. "Perhaps the deputy director, Monsieur Golay, may be of assistance."

Sommers was now officially annoyed. He was used to people jumping to his will and immediately making themselves available at the sound of his voice. He replied with a gruff "Fine."

In an instant, George Golay came on the line speaking slowly and deliberately. "Hello, Monsieur Sommers. How may I help you?"

Sommers had no time for gofers. When he called, he expected to speak to the boss exclusively. They, in turn, were expected to jump to Sommers' every whim. "Where's Martin? I need to speak to him immediately."

Golay cleared his throat and seemed to be taking a long, deep breath. "I am sorry, but *Monsieur Directeur* is not available."

"Where the hell is he? Get him."

Golay seemed to be breathing heavily into the phone. There was a definite rhythmic whooshing sound for a few seconds before he finally mumbled an answer. "*Monsieur Directeur* is dead."

"What?"

"Sadly, Monsieur Martin died last night."

Damn Swiss, Sommers flared to himself. Can't get a straight answer from these assholes. "What the hell does that mean?"

"*Il est mort. Er ist tot.* He is dead!" Golay cleared his throat. "That is all we know at this moment. The authorities have told us nothing more regarding the circumstances of his passing. As far as I know, he was in good health, but one never knows the hidden truth."

Sommers stared out the window. His beloved view of his even more beloved city did nothing to stop the roaring thoughts going through his head. How the hell could this have happened?

"I want to assure you," Golay eventually continued. "All the projects Monsieur Martin was involved in are being handled by the appropriate department manager. They, in turn, will be reporting to me when necessary. We expect the board will meet to name an interim director within the next one or two days. In the meantime, sir, is there anything I can address at this moment?"

Sommers punched his phone to disconnect. "Shit."

After a fitful night of no sleep, Matthew arrived once more at John's house. He could see the young man coming up the sidewalk, returning from a walk with Louis. He glanced at his watch; it was late for a morning walk. Inside, he found Jacqueline sitting at the table, punching away at her phone as she ate a slice of toast.

"John and Louis went out late today," he said.

"He had to do some prep work for class. Lost track of time, I guess." Jacqueline didn't look up from her screen.

It was Thursday, and John was due to teach. Apparently, he had no intention of missing his class despite the events of the last few days. Matthew was surprised that John wasn't aware of the time. Perhaps it was an indication that Suzanne's murder had affected him.

Entering the house, John shed the black hooded sweatshirt he was wearing.

"John," Matthew said. "Is that the sweatshirt Suzanne was wearing? You got it back?"

John shook his head. "No. The police would not return my sweatshirt."

Matthew nodded. As a piece of evidence for a murder investigation, the sweatshirt would be kept in the property department or a storage facility at least until the case was solved and the killer convicted and sentenced. Even then, it would typically remain in police custody for quite some time thereafter, along with Suzanne's other belongings relevant to the case. Besides, would John want a sweatshirt with two bullet holes in the hood and coated with Suzanne's blood? This wasn't a celebrity's murder where such a gruesome artifact might have some financial or historical significance. Plus, John wasn't the kind of person who would want it for sentimental purposes. Of the last point, Matthew was certain.

With no further comment, John opened the door to his workroom. As he entered the room, Matthew followed closely behind. John immediately turned around with an uncomfortable look on his face, obviously not pleased with the invasion. Over John's shoulder, Matthew saw an open laptop displaying a schematic drawing of two gears with several measurements noted on the side. The drawings looked to be an attachment to an email. John was the addressee, but from the distance, Matthew was only able to make out a portion of the sender's address.

John followed Matthew's line of sight and turned to slam shut the laptop.

After a brief pause, Matthew took a chance. "Hey John, someone sent you those drawings? They were some kind of gears?"

His questions were met with silence as John stared at the now closed laptop. It was as if he were having an internal debate while his fingers tapped the closed lid.

Matthew waited patiently, making no further move into the room.

"From someone," John ultimately responded vaguely.

"Something to do with watches, I suppose?"

"Hmmm."

Matthew decided not to quiz John about the sender's identity for the moment. He saw that one of the stemless wine goblets was covering something. A cloth was draped over the top so he couldn't see what was being protected. Given his penchant for secrecy and security, Matthew was surprised that the mysterious object lying under the glass remained on the workbench rather than squirreled away in its hiding spot while John had taken Louis for his walk. John surely must be distracted.

Stacked on top of the filing cabinet nearest the workbench were several books, including two textbooks. One was titled *Introduction to Engineering*. Matthew figured the title was about the only thing in the book he would be able to understand.

"Do you have to leave for school soon?"

John nodded yes and returned to his workbench. After putting the tweezers away, everything else seemed in order except for the upside-down glass. John went to lift it, but seemed to think better of it and withdrew his hand. He turned back to face Matthew, who realized John was waiting for him to leave the room before exposing the hidden treasure.

"How about I drive you to school today?" Matthew offered. He wanted to get a look at the class. As preposterous as he knew it seemed, he wanted to see if any of the students gave him a "feeling" of not being right. The old instincts, the special "feeling" he sometimes got, were part of his sixth sense—something not to be ignored during an investigation. When Matthew's sons were in college, they'd regale their parents with stories of students who were so obsessed with grades that they'd make idle threats toward professors when they didn't receive an A in a course. For sure, there were a lot of crazy reasons for someone to contemplate murder; maybe one of them was the difference between a B and an A on a college transcript. He'd never heard of a student acting on such an impulse, but one never knew these days, as the pressure for academic achievement was ratcheted to ever-increasing heights.

John agreed but still waited for Matthew to leave the workroom. Standing outside the room, Matthew could hear the faint sound of tapping on a keyboard.

Charice's fury grew by the minute. She had a plan. She had set it into motion. And...silence! When will she receive confirmation that things are going the way she wants them to?

"Yes!" she yelled when her cell rang. But it was not her contact. It was her brother. Surprisingly, he sounded jubilant. As far as she knew, Jean-Louis was somewhere in Geneva. Odd for him to be so happy. It was late in the afternoon, and that wasn't the time he typically entertained any of his lady friends.

"You sound quite pleased," Charice said. His voice added more to her dark mood. "What the hell have you got to be so chipper about?"

"Sister, sister, sister. Did I not promise you all will work out?"

Charice was taken aback. "What? Did you get it?"

"No, darling sister," Jean-Louis was laying it on thick. "That is *your* part of this play. I am to keep the company afloat until you have successfully concluded the acquisition of the movement, remember?"

"Well then, what has happened to make you so cheery?"

"Let's just say the situation has turned in our favor."

Charice frowned as she looked out the office window. The sky was dark, shrouded by heavy clouds. Several rivulets of rainwater ran down the window, a precursor to the upcoming storm the weather report predicted. "What have you done?"

"*Moi*? Nothing. But circumstances seem to be bending our way."

"You got the bridge loan?" Charice's mood lightened ever so slightly. She had long been convinced that the only thing Jean-Louis would succeed at was getting the clap from one of his conquests.

Jean-Louis paused. "Well, not quite yet, but let's just say that a major impediment has been removed and the path to the ongoing successful existence of our company is brighter." After another pause, he continued. "Have you listened to the news?"

Chapter 19

Matthew caught a glimpse of the workroom before John shut and locked the door: the glass that had been on the workbench was gone, and everything was neat and orderly. John had his laptop, several notebooks, and the two textbooks in a bookbag slung over his shoulder.

The short car ride was made in silence. Louis stood on John's lap, propping his front paws on the armrest of the door so he could look out the window. Matthew wondered if the dog feared he was heading to the dreaded veterinarian's office. His old dog seemed to know as soon as they left for the vet's. He'd start drooling and shaking, which would stop only after they safely returned to the confines of his home.

Louis must have felt similarly. Once Matthew drove onto the college campus, he settled and laid down until they reached their building's parking lot.

Louis led the way to the classroom. They walked across the quad with a pond in the center of the green space. A sign was posted to inform anyone who cared that the ducks, named Heckle and Jeckle, were college mascots, and please do not feed them. Inside the classroom, five rows of chairs with attached writing desks sat empty. Louis walked to a small pillow under the whiteboard in the front of the room and made himself comfortable.

John put the books and his laptop on a table before booting up the computer and connecting it to the screen behind him. In the meantime, Matthew took a seat in the back row of the classroom.

Five minutes before the hour, a dozen students straggled in and took their seats. By the start of the class, sixteen desks were occupied. Matthew spotted a camera pointing toward the front of the room. He couldn't tell whether it was on, but John wore a wireless microphone, so he supposed several students were attending the class remotely.

Matthew studied each of the students as best as possible. All had laptops open and were in various stages of taking notes, playing games, or engaged in a kind of computer-based version of doodling. Several students seated in the first row seemed bent on recording every word John spoke, while the majority of the others were, at best, very passive. None of them posed an obvious threat, except if the occasional cough or snore could be considered disruptive. Of course, Matthew had no idea about those online. On his computer screen, John could probably see their faces. Matthew debated sidling down the perimeter of the room to get a glimpse, but decided not to, fearing it would raise unwanted questions.

As if reading Matthew's thoughts, John hit a key on his computer keyboard. The image on John's computer screen was projected for the whole class to see. Now visible to all were the diagrams John was referring to. On the right side of the screen were thumbnail images of three students. From what Matthew could see, none of the faces showed evidence of evil intent.

There was nothing to be gained by remaining in the class for the next hour and a half, so Matthew quietly exited to take in the sights and sounds of college life. After high school, he had served in the Army for four years before getting accepted into the police academy. A number of his colleagues had suffered through college with the hope that a degree would give them a greater chance for rapid promotion. For most, it turned out to be an expensive, unfulfilled gamble; in the department, academic achievement took a back seat to adeptly playing the political games necessary to climb the command ladder.

Although college courses were required for promotion to certain ranks, the departmental exams were given a higher priority than any college exam. He'd taken several courses in night school, primarily in psychology and sociology, to earn the necessary credits for his detective first grade rank, but he never had a college experience. What he needed to learn, he did on the streets of New York City. Promotion came because of his dogged attention to detail and determination to close cases expediently, and not from studying words in a textbook.

Walking around the campus, he noticed the bevy of girls heading to and from class or lounging on grassy patches and benches. Of course, he looked at the girls. When chided by Muriel for being lecherous, he would defend himself, saying that it was only natural. It was a sign that he was still alive. He insisted he would stop looking at pretty girls only when he was dead. And now the years were mounting up, as was the girth of his waistline. Surrounded by so many twenty-year-olds, he couldn't help but feel young and vibrant. Yet, when he walked past a window, he caught sight of his reflection and was brought back to the harsh reality of his age.

Eventually, he settled on a bench in a quiet section of the campus, removed the spiral notebook from his pocket, and figured he'd call Brown to update him on what little he learned from Livingston. But his cell rang with an unknown number. However, it wasn't classified as "spam." He answered, and a voice identified the caller as attorney Samuel Chang.

"Thank you for returning my call," Matthew said. "I truly appreciate the courtesy. I realize you've probably authored hundreds of trusts since Barton Alves's"

"Thousands, actually," Chang laughed. "But this one I'll never forget."

"Oh?" Matthew grinned. Maybe his luck was changing.

"In the thirty-two years I've been doing this, that one was one of the most peculiar due to how extraordinarily detailed it was."

"Meaning?"

"Meaning it was very detailed."

"Can you tell me who wanted the trust created?"

"I'm sorry. That is a matter of attorney-client privilege."

"Mr. Chang, I know I'm putting you in an awkward position. The reason I'm asking is I've been asked to investigate a homicide." Matthew liked the sound of that. Somehow, the word "homicide" had a more official ring to it than did the word "murder."

"Not of the child?"

"He's a grown man now, and no. But of his companion. We have reason to believe someone was trying to..." he hesitated. If this were part of an official investigation he was leading on behalf of the police department, he'd be limited by what he could say. But in his role as private investigator, perhaps he had a little more creative leeway. "...get to John. Perhaps because of his trust."

"Who is John?"

"Oh, sorry, sir. Barton Alves legally changed his name to John Harrison a few years back. That probably gave the attorney administering the trust a bit of a challenge in making the necessary changes in the document."

"Ah, I see. Interesting. I am sure it was a bit of a complication, but in my experience, it is not an uncommon situation and is relatively easy to handle. Think about what happens when a woman gets married and changes her name. As far as providing you with any information about the trust, I am afraid I am unable to give you any of the details."

"I understand his father was the one to initiate the trust—"

"Again, attorney-client confidentiality—"

"Can you tell me if his father was German?"

"I cannot ethically confirm that," came Chang's curt response. "But, it is possible the person had a German accent. That is all I will say, sir." He ended the interview and clicked off.

Matthew grinned at the answer. Seemed as if Chang had possibly, unethically, confirmed it.

As a soft breeze rustled the leaves on the nearby eucalyptus trees, Matthew dialed Brown's cell.

"You got ESP now?" Brown asked.

"What?"

"I was just about to call you. I filed a missing person report on John's mother, Brenda Alves. I also filed under the name of Brenda Harrison for completeness. The description I had for them wasn't very detailed. John was useless, and his sister more so. We'll see what pops."

"Great." Matthew was very familiar with the process of entering a missing person's report into the national database system and the low likelihood of a successful result. "You think a DNA analysis from John would help with the search?"

"Possibly. You wanna talk him into swabbing his cheek?"

"Not right now," Matthew grinned. "But let's keep the idea simmering on the back burner. Meanwhile, I'm sitting on campus waiting for John to finish teaching his class."

"Yeah?"

"Thought I'd check out his class for signs of a disgruntled student."

"Interesting..."

"Most likely a waste of time. None of them seems to be exuding murderous intent."

"So, what else do you got?"

Matthew looked at the time on his phone before answering. "I just spoke to the attorney who created the trust."

"Get anything out of him?"

"Only that the person who filed it was probably German."

"And that helps us how?"

"I'm still working on it."

"Anything else?"

"Not really. He confirmed the trust is iron-clad and pretty substantial."

"But you don't think it has anything to do with this case?"

"No idea. My sense from him is that the trust makes no provision for any person to benefit upon John's death."

"Are we gonna solve this?"

"God, I hope so."

They clicked off. Matthew strolled in the direction of the classroom, quietly reentered the room, and was surprised to see students engaged in a vigorous dialogue with John. The topic was indecipherable to Matthew, but what fascinated him was how John interacted with them. Questions and answers flew back and forth between students and the instructor. John was transformed into a social and communicative person. Whatever they were talking about clearly brought John out of his shell. More so, the students were totally engaged. There was no question that they had a fair degree of respect for John. Looking around the room, everyone was caught up in the discussion. Studying the faces of those in the room, there was nothing to suggest the slightest hint of disdain for their instructor, much less a violent agenda.

Chapter 20

The ride home was in silence except for Louis's panting. Back at the house, there was no sign of Jacqueline. John immediately headed for his workroom. Before he could unlock the door, Matthew stopped him. "John, we have got to talk."

John turned and stared at Matthew with a curious expression. Matthew was surprised to see the change from his usual deadpan appearance.

"What goes on in there? What are you working on? I assume it has something to do with watches. True?"

John looked over his shoulder at the closed door and then back at Matthew. He turned, unlocked the door, and went into the room. Unlike any other time, he left the door open.

Matthew took the gesture as an invitation and followed.

John connected his laptop to a power cord and opened the lid. Once he signed in, Matthew saw the schematic that had been projected onto the screen in the classroom at the end of John's lecture. Wordlessly, John minimized the screen to reveal another drawing. It was a coil. On either side of the image were notations typed out in a font so small that Matthew couldn't discern what they said.

John stared straight at Matthew, making direct eye contact. "I am working on something that has never been done before," he started.

"It is a perpetual power system for a watch movement. Do you know anything about watches?"

Matthew furrowed his brow and shook his head. He bared his left wrist to reveal a Seiko chronograph watch that Muriel had given him on a distant birthday. "I know how to set it and how to operate the stopwatch function. Every two or three years, it needs a new battery. That's all I know about watches."

John nodded, once.

"So when you say 'a new source of power,' I'm assuming you mean a new type of battery. But that doesn't look like it has anything to do with electronics." He pointed to the screen.

John took a deep breath. He appeared to transform back into the role he'd assumed in his classroom. Once again, he was the kind and patient instructor. "First, I'm not talking about a battery-powered watch. The earliest clocks, dating back to ancient Egypt, utilized the sun, water, or candle flames to mark the passage of time. Beginning in the thirteenth to fourteenth century, clocks were built with mechanically supplied power sources. Many of the early clocks used hanging weights to drive the mechanisms. In the fifteenth century, the mainspring—a tightly coiled strip of metal—was invented as a means of storing energy to run clocks and, ultimately, watches. Until the development of the quartz watch in the 1970s, virtually all watches were similarly mechanically driven."

"A spring?" Matthew asked.

"Spring coil. By winding the watch with a key or the crown, the metal coil tightens. As spring unwinds, it gradually releases tension and, in turn, energy. The released power causes the components of the watch to function."

"Got it."

"In the 1770s, Abraham-Louis Perrelet, not the watchmaker that Louis was named after, invented a mechanism that automatically wound the mainspring. The rotor's rotation was designed to respond to the movement of the watch during daily wear. Over time, the winding mechanism has undergone numerous modifications in an effort to enhance its efficiency. With similar goals in mind and improvements in metallurgy and creative experimentation, the composition of the mainspring has been modified to enhance energy storage and subsequent release. In present-day watchmaking, the composition of the mainspring is constructed out of a metal alloy. Regardless of the inventiveness of watchmakers, the mainspring is only able to keep the watch functioning so long as it is kept wound."

Matthew put up a hand to pause the lecture. He was trying as best he could to follow along but needed a moment to digest what John was saying. It was all new, the technology, the terms, and the concepts. He had no basic knowledge to make sense of the information and make the concepts understandable.

John waited patiently until Matthew was ready for the next installment.

Besides needing to incorporate what he was being told, Matthew was fascinated by the transformation that had come over John. He was a different person, calm and confident, freely speaking about something he had spent years studying. There was no awkwardness. He was in full control of the subject and able to communicate the concepts clearly and understandably. When Matthew nodded, John resumed where he left off.

"The problem with mechanical watches and clocks continued to be the need for the mainspring to be kept wound sufficiently for the watch to function. Watches that are manually wound require hand winding of the mainspring by way of the watch's crown, the knob on the side of the watch case. Depending on the size and composition of the mainspring, the watches have a power reserve of a specific number of hours before they will need to be rewound."

Matthew nodded again.

"Watches we call 'automatic' can be wound either by hand or by the movement of the wearer's wrist. The rotation of the weighted rotor contained within the movement would keep the mainspring wound, as originally conceived by Perrelet. In either case, watches work only as long as the mainspring remains wound. If left unattended for a period of time, the mainspring would unwind, and the watch would stop working, an unfortunate reality when dealing with mechanical timepieces."

John continued his lecture, explaining that the accuracy of time measurement in watches had to do in part with the consistent release of power from the mainspring. In most watches and clocks, time measurement was negatively affected when the mainspring was either fully or almost completely unwound. "At those particular instances," he explained. "The power release is not steady and as a result the amplitude of the escapement deteriorates, which, in turn, negatively affects timekeeping."

Matthew stared at John, barely comprehending. He hadn't bothered to take notes, as he wouldn't be quizzed. He was just trying to get a vague idea of what John was talking about, rather than grasp every detail and parrot it back to him. Besides, the amplitude of what? He was over his head.

"It's all a matter of torque of the mainspring," John continued, apparently unaware of Matthew's confusion. "What I have created is a watch movement that does not need to be wound either by hand or by an automatic system. It can and does work continuously to keep the mainspring wound sufficiently, providing a steady release of power. I have successfully made such a movement work flawlessly. However, before it is ready to be put into production, it still requires a few adjustments and further monitoring, but it's close to its final form."

Matthew never gave much thought about the watch he slipped on his left wrist every morning. Even with John's explanation, he still couldn't fathom why anyone would care about John's invention. The battery took care of powering the watch, and there was always the ubiquitous cellphone to accurately tell time. John was so engrossed in the topic that Matthew did not want to interrupt the lecture with the obvious question: "Who cares?" He just wanted a basic understanding of what John was up to here in the confines of his secretive workroom. Now, with an inkling about John's project, he still couldn't understand the need for all the secrecy. Besides, he was no closer to an understanding of how any of this could be related to Suzanne's death, if at all.

"A Swiss watch company, Jaeger-LeCoultre, produces a clock," John continued. "It's called the Atmos clock. It is self-winding and functions through the expansion and contraction of a specific gas, ethyl chloride. The gas expands and contracts due to changes in ambient temperature. As it does, it affects a metal bellows within the clock, which in turn winds the clock's mainspring. I have applied the same principle to a wristwatch. Not by using gas, but rather by using the properties of two metals that expand and contract at different temperatures." John paused to see if Matthew was comprehending his words.

Mathew responded with a soft chuckle. "Interesting, I guess."

"It is revolutionary."

Knowing no better, Matthew took John's words as gospel truth.

"How did you get into this?" Matthew was unsure if he was more fascinated by the complexity of watches, something he had previously taken for granted, or by the transformation he was witnessing in how John was relating to him. He wondered whether he would need to take a crash course on watches and watchmaking to continue conversing with the young man. It might be the only way to unlock history and delve into his innermost thoughts. Equally, Matthew wondered why he was so fascinated by him.

John nodded toward the book-crammed shelves above his workbench. "I've always been interested. I read any book I can find about watchmaking. Some I've read two or three times. The most important one was the book by George Daniels, *Watchmaking*. It's considered to be the bible for watchmakers."

Matthew looked at the shelves and located the book John was referring to. That and most of the others had well-worn covers.

"I also got help from a friend."

This caught Matthew's attention. "A friend? Who? Anyone around here?"

John shook his head. "He lives in Europe somewhere. Have known him for a long time. He helps me solve problems."

"But he is a friend?" Matthew's curiosity was piqued. John had never previously spoken of a friend, and to hear that the relationship had been ongoing for years was even more curious.

"Yes." Suddenly, John looked less confident and seemed to be reverting to the old John.

Hurrying to change the subject, Matthew tried to think of something to do with watches separate from the last line of questioning. "What fascinates you most about watches, John?"

John shrugged and moved toward his workbench. "Need to get back to work."

With that, he pulled his laptop closer to him and focused on an email that had been minimized. Assuming it was from the person John had just alluded to, Matthew moved a step closer and tried to read the sender's address. His vision wasn't as sharp as it once had been. The optometrist suggested glasses during his last check-up. Maybe it was time to give in and accept the realities of his age. From what he could see, the address was comprised of a random series of numbers and letters, some capitalized, others not. At the end of the string, he was able to make out ".uk", indicating that the email originated somewhere in the United Kingdom.

Understanding that the conversation was over, Matthew turned and left John to his work. After he took three steps out of the room, the door closed, and there was the ever-familiar sound of the deadbolt sliding into place.

What was it that turned John's switch off? Was it the question about the mysterious person in Britain? Or had John just reached his limit? Once again, more questions than answers.

"Your mom told me you were a computer whiz." Matthew's voice boomed through Stephen's phone speaker. The loud noise made Stephen genuinely smile for the first time in a couple of days. His mother had never been sure how loudly she had to speak to be clearly heard when she called from her car. Frequently, Stephen had teased her that drivers two lanes over could probably hear her. It sounded like Matthew had the same inclination, given the background road noise coming through the phone. "Hypothetically, if I gave you an email address, could you find out where it came from and who it belonged to? That's the kind of computer stuff you know about, right?"

Stephen sat back in the chair by the kitchen table in Suzanne's condo. He had spent the morning catching up on a couple of urgent matters at work. At first, he felt uncomfortable working so soon after having to identify his mother's remains, but it served as a helpful distraction. Siobhan sweetly remained by his side at the table, tapping away on her computer as she worked.

"Sure, it can be done," Stephen replied, though mystified by the question. "But I'm not the one to talk to. My beautiful associate is much more knowledgeable about such things."

Siobhan glanced up at him with a smirk.

Stephen continued. "I work for a gaming company, and although I know my way around computers, she has a much better handle on cybersecurity. In that field, she is the bomb. Why do you want to know?"

"Let's just leave it at that for now. What would she need to do the tracking?"

Stephen looked at Siobhan, who was now staring at him, trying to figure out what the conversation was about. After he winked at her, she blew him a kiss and went back to studying her laptop's screen.

"How about we start with the email address in question, and we'll see where that goes?"

Chapter 21

These late-night phone calls are getting old, thought Rousseau. "I'm sorry, but this'll have to be a short conversation. I don't have much battery life on this burner and haven't had an opportunity to get another one."

"What the hell is going on over there?" Sommers roared.

Rousseau sat at his kitchen counter, where he was briefly distracted by his wife walking by, dressed in one of her more revealing nightgowns. Only after she was out of his line of sight could he refocus on the phone call. He emitted a soft groan. He didn't give a shit how powerful the billionaire was; his wife's wiggle was much more enticing. Sommers was an arrogant ass, but he was a means to an end for Rousseau. "What do you mean?"

"Have you heard anything about Pierre Martin? I found out he died last night or whenever the hell it was."

"I have not listened to the news since I got home today. Who is Monsieur Martin? Never heard of him."

"Christ. No one seems to know anything. Nobody I've called in Geneva knows shit from Shinola."

Rousseau didn't have a clue what Sommers was talking about. "I am very sorry, sir. Is there anything I can do?"

Sommers' mumble was barely discernible. "Need to come up with another plan to put pressure on Bonet. Time is of the essence."

Running out of time wasn't new news. They talked about this very subject *ad nauseam*. The Americans always seemed to be in an unnecessary rush. Sommers was so confident the other day that he had the Bonets over a barrel and was ready to strike. What had changed? "What do you want me to do that I am not already doing?"

"I don't care," Sommers sounded so furious, as if he was ready to commit murder. "Whatever it takes. Whatever this kid from California has up his sleeve and is offering the Bonets, kill the deal. They are to have no lifeline for survival. I want them on their knees begging for help."

Before he had a chance to reply, the phone died. Rousseau looked at the blank screen and shrugged. He would get a new phone first thing in the morning, but for now, his attention turned to the bedroom and the faint whiff of his wife's perfume still lingering in the air.

"Guess what?"

Matthew was surprised at the sound of Brown's excitement. He imagined him literally jumping for joy. But he wasn't in the mood for games.

"Not a clue," Matthew replied curtly.

"I just got a call regarding the missing person report I filed. You know, John's mother."

Sitting in Sean's backyard, Matthew's attention was divided between the phone call and watching his grandson, Ben, go through his karate routine. Simple though it was, the boy punctuated his moves with aggressive grunts and shouts. Matthew waved at Ben to keep the decibels down. "Really? That's impressive. I figured it was a shot in the dark at best with no chance of success."

"Yeah, I held out little hope that we'd get any kind of response, much less one this fast."

"So, let's hear it."

"A call came from a detective Raul Chin, with the San Bernardino County Sheriff's Department. He has a file on a Jane Doe from about four years ago. He says the general description of Brenda Alves, though not exact, was close enough to prompt him to call."

"San Bernardino County's pretty big, right?"

"Huge. Over 20,000 square miles. Chin was and still is assigned to the Big Bear Sheriff's station in the mountains. His Jane Doe is a woman whose body was found by a couple of hikers near a stream off a remote hiking trail. According to the coroner, she'd been dead for a few days. No identification was found on her except for a tattoo of a heart surrounding a letter B on her left wrist. With nothing to identify her, the body was listed as a Jane Doe, and so she has remained."

"So far, this isn't helping much."

"Keep listening, my impatient friend!" Brown laughed. "The conclusion at the time was she slipped and fell, striking her head on a rock as she went down the fifteen-foot embankment next to the stream. Her death was determined to be due to accidental blunt force trauma to her head. But Chin said he was never satisfied with the coroner's conclusion."

"Why's that?" Matthew gave his grandson a big, open-mouthed grin and a thumbs-up for a great kick.

"Well, first of all, he said she wasn't dressed for hiking, especially that kind of challenging remote trail. She was wearing street clothes and shoes. He did say she might have been another confused flatlander who had taken the wrong trail at the wrong time."

"A confused what?"

"Big Bear is one of those hot spots where the locals see the folks from LA and other coastal areas as interlopers. They call them 'flatlanders.' Sometimes, the flatlanders don't realize how remote the trails are and try to conquer the great outdoors completely unprepared."

"Gotcha."

"It didn't make sense to Chin that she'd go out alone on that kind of trail dressed as though she was headed to the mall. More so, she got a fair distance into the trail, including having to manage her way around some tricky sections. You'd think she'd have gotten wise long before where she was found and turned around once she realized how poorly prepared she was. And why had she not been reported missing? When he checked, he found no report of a missing hiker filed around the time they discovered the body. There were too many unanswered questions."

Brown paused as if letting Matthew digest the information. "From the outset, Chin believed the department closed the case too fast. He was suspicious that it was given short shrift. He wasn't sure if it was because the department was short-staffed, or so that their statistics, and hence the Sheriff, looked good for his re-election campaign. Unsatisfied, Chin decided to keep her in his cold case file. He made an entry in the national computer system to alert him should a missing person be posted in the appropriate time period, roughly fitting her description.

"Definitely interesting," Matthew agreed. "Don't jump to conclusions, but definitely something to pursue."

"Right," Brown continued. "I called Jacqueline to see if she knew whether John's mother had a tattoo. She said she had no idea. Said she hadn't seen much of Brenda Alves, much less her left wrist. The presence of a 'B' certainly is very suggestive. Maybe you can get something from John?"

"Yeah. I'll do my best." Matthew stared in the direction of Ben, but wasn't focusing on the child. "Chin get DNA?"

"He's gonna look and see. But you know how that can be…" Brown didn't have to say anymore. If the department still had her belongings, and if there was anything free from contamination, maybe they could get a DNA sample, but those were a couple of big ifs, very long shots in a four-year-old cold case.

"If he can get some of her DNA—" Matthew cut himself off. He realized he might be insulting Brown's intelligence by stating the obvious, but decided to press on nevertheless. "We will need a court order to get a specimen for DNA from John."

"Working on it as we speak."

Across the yard, there came a blood-curdling yell as Ben kicked a small punching bag, a noteworthy exclamation point to Matthew's just concluded conversation.

Chapter 22

Matthew pulled into John's driveway and stopped behind Jacqueline's car. Hoisting himself from behind the steering wheel, he was reminded of his five-month-old plan to join the gym at the senior center. He stretched out the kink in his back and then headed up the steps to the front door.

He didn't bother to knock or try the doorbell. Instead, to his surprise, he found the front door unlocked, so he entered.

He heard Jacqueline before he saw her. She was loudly talking on the phone as she paced in the living room. Without pausing, she waved him to a chair. After several minutes, she suggested a meeting time for the following morning. Apparently, the person on the other end agreed.

"I think I found a companion for John!" She looked relieved. "Going to interview her tomorrow, and hopefully she can start immediately. I need to get back to work. My boss is being a complete ass. Won't accept that I can do most of my job remotely. He wants me in the office so he can crack the whip."

Matthew nodded his understanding. "John in?" He cast a glance at the closed door leading to the workroom.

"Of course."

Matthew approached the door and knocked. "John, it's Matt. I need to talk to you."

"Any news?" Jacqueline asked.

"Do you know if John's mom had any tattoos?" Matthew asked, ignoring her question.

Jacqueline rolled her eyes. "I told you, or that other guy. I wouldn't know. It's not like we were BFFs. Why?"

Matthew disregarded her question again. There is a time when it is appropriate to be a fountain of information and another time when it is best to be a locked repository. Through experience and training, he knew this was a time to be the latter.

"John," he knocked again with added force. The door opened. John stood back to allow Matthew entrance, immediately shutting the door after he cleared the door jam.

A pair of headphones lying on the workbench emitted faint, discordant electric guitar licks and a heavy drumbeat. John must not have initially responded to Matthew's knocks because he'd been wearing noise-canceling headphones blaring very aggressive noise, or was that music?

Louis remained in his bed, curled up; he expended just enough energy to raise his head to sniff the air and register the presence of the intruder. Once he identified Matthew, he returned to his napping position. In short order, he was gently snoring.

"What are you listening to?" Matthew searched for a way to reestablish a line of communication with John before getting down to business.

He figured John's two-word response was the name of the band whose "music" was utterly foreign to him.

The laptop was open on the workbench, but the device was turned away from Matthew, so he couldn't read the screen. Other than the computer, the workspace was bare. "I'd like to learn more about what you're working on." Matthew quickly understood that anything to do with music wasn't the key to opening communication with John. Asking about engineering principles, which he knew nothing about, or watches, of which he knew even less, stood the best chance of getting John to feel comfortable enough to reengage.

John shot a glance behind him and seemed relieved to see nothing on the surface of his bench. He turned back and stared through Matthew. What seemed like an internal debate took several seconds to resolve. Standing up and reaching for the third shelf above his workbench, he pulled down a thick, well-worn book. The title printed on the spine was barely legible. Careful to keep it upright, he set the book on the workbench and opened the cover. From inside, he slowly extracted a short cylindrical object—a clear tubular plastic case, about two inches in diameter and an inch tall. Within the cylinder, there was a metal device, something Matthew had never seen before.

Unceremoniously, John tossed the empty book aside. Carefully holding the plastic case vertically, he rose from his chair and took a step closer to Matthew but remained at arm's length. John held the case up for Matthew to examine but refused to relinquish it to his open hand. Inside appeared to be a small machine. Matthew wanted to get a closer look but stood back, choosing instead to respect John's personal space.

"This is the watch movement I developed," John said.

Matthew leaned his face closer to the case. Inside were several shiny brass plates with gears turning. In the six o'clock position, a spiral wire curled and uncurled as the ring of metal encircling it rotated back and forth, never completing a full circle. There was no dial, nor were there hands to indicate the time. Matthew was stunned.

"This is it? This is the big secret?" Matthew controlled the tenor of his voice, not wanting to put John on the defensive. "I thought you were working on a watch."

"This is it," John calmly said. With his free hand, he picked up a screwdriver whose head was barely visible to Matthew and pointed to the metal spiral moving forward and back. As if speaking to his class, he took on a professorial role. "This is the movement I have been perfecting. It has been working non-stop for the past four months. I still need to verify the accuracy of the timekeeping; however, the amplitude of the escapement has been consistent, so the timekeeping should be accurate. I have made the hands and will be attaching them to the central pinion within the next couple of days. Once I have tested it, I will case the movement and do final testing over the next several weeks."

Matthew shook his head slowly. The short description was full of words he did not understand. "So, if I'm remembering right, the movement, if that's what it's called, runs without being wound. Something about two metals expanding and contracting at different temperatures?"

John didn't take his eyes off his handiwork. Ever so slightly, he nodded.

"Okay, so explain to me again what is so revolutionary about this?" Matthew's crash course in watchmaking was clearly insufficient for him to grasp the significance of what John claimed to have developed.

"With this winding system, once the escapement is put into action, it will never stop. The movement will never need to be wound, whether the watch is being worn or sitting on a counter. As long as the ambient temperature varies over the course of the day, even small changes, the mainspring will be kept sufficiently wound to power the escapement."

Matthew stared at the device in John's hand. Slowly, the explanation started to make sense.

"That is why I call it the perpetual winding system," John continued.

"Impressive, a watch to work for eternity." Matthew stood straight. "You said there is a piece that has two different metals attached. Where is that?"

Maybe the corners of John's mouth twitched up in what could be interpreted as a smile. Brief though it was, Matthew had not seen such an expression light John's face previously. John turned the plastic case around, then used the fine-tipped screwdriver to point to a coiled piece of wire that was attached at each end of another component. "That wire is comprised of two strips of metal fused together, forming a bimetallic coil. The metal components have different temperature sensitivities. They expand and contract at slightly different temperatures. As a result, even when there is a minimal temperature change, the spring coils and uncoils, causing the arms to extend to a ratchet wheel, which in turn winds the mainspring. The mainspring stores the generated energy, which, in turn, provides power to the timekeeping components of the watch movement."

John reached for a magnifying loupe and handed it to Matthew. Matthew wasn't sure which end of the loupe to put up to his eye and selected the one that flared. He must have chosen the right end since John didn't correct him. The first thing he noticed was how steady the head of the screwdriver was in John's hand. If he were the one holding the screwdriver, Matthew was sure the tool would be shaking like a leaf.

Carefully looking where the screwdriver was pointing, he saw several gears that were not turning; meanwhile, below them, three tiny gears turned in a coordinated fashion. He had no idea what he was supposed to be looking at. Handing back the loupe, Matthew shrugged.

Realizing his student wasn't appreciating the mechanics of the movement, John gently placed the plastic case containing it on the workbench and turned to the laptop. Opening the screen, Matthew saw there was an email open.

"How long did it take you to make the components?" Matthew asked, not caring for a minute what the answer was. Instead, he stared at the email address, which was a series of numbers and letters, similar to the one he had previously seen with the .uk suffix. It was a Hotmail account. Assuming this was the address for the "friend" John had spoken about, Matthew concentrated on memorizing the email address, as John mentioned something about years and ordering parts from somewhere. Before John could finish his very detailed narrative, Matthew interrupted to say he needed to use the bathroom and made a hasty exit from the workroom. Once inside the bathroom, he did his best to recall the email address and record it in his notebook.

Returning to the workroom, John quickly unlocked the door at Matthew's first knock.

"Sorry, an old man's bladder has to be attended to when the need strikes." Matthew smiled, but there was no reaction from John.

The email was gone from John's laptop screen and was replaced with a drawing of the watch movement. John explained his creation in exquisite detail, which meant very little to Matthew. Although he eventually got the general concepts, he wasn't going to waste what precious time he had trying to understand the intricacies of a watch movement, metallurgy, and time measurement. At the moment, he had other fish to fry. Anything that did not move the investigation forward had to be left for another time.

When John paused, Matthew cut in. "Remind me, how did you get so involved with watches and watchmaking?" Matthew knew he had asked the question previously and hoped that John wouldn't be bothered by the repetitive query. Posing a question more than once was a technique he used during interviews to ensure consistent answers. Any difference in an answer, no matter how small, might open another avenue to explore in the investigation.

Not bothered by the repetitive question, something he probably dealt with frequently from his students, John nodded toward the bookshelves. "Read several books, some two or three times."

"Did you take any classes?"

John shook his head, thought a moment, and then answered. "There are some online courses, but I didn't think that they were valuable. I got the help I needed from my friend."

Matthew tried to keep his face emotionless. Once again, the mention of the unnamed person. "Friend?"

John shook his head in a way that made Matthew wonder if John knew the friend's identity.

"How?" Matthew asked.

"We have been emailing for a long time."

Whoever this person was, he seemed to have made a durable connection with John. What the friend had to do with the investigation, if anything, was an unknown. As far as Matthew knew, besides what happened at the college, this friend seemed to be John's most reliable contact to the outside world, and, Matthew suspected, was the person who had the email address scrawled on the pad in his pocket. This friend also seemed to be a key to a better understanding of John, past and present, something that was becoming increasingly necessary to the investigation as he delved deeper into the case.

Matthew looked at his watch. "I guess I gotta get going." He headed toward the door. "Thanks for the watch education. I really enjoyed it." At the door, he turned to face John. "Oh, by the way, did your mom have a tattoo?"

John's face flinched. He nodded and pointed to the inside of his left wrist.

"What was it?"

Matthew must have gone too far. John immediately shut down. Instead of answering, he returned to his workbench and gently replaced the plastic case containing the watch movement into the cutout in the book.

"Take care, John. I'll check in on you soon," Matthew tried.

John didn't even shrug.

Chapter 23

Jean-Louis comfortably lounged in one of the cushioned armchairs facing the director's desk. It was the same chair he'd sat in only a couple of days earlier. Much had transpired since he was last in this office, certainly so for the late Pierre Martin.

He'd been surprised the previous day when he received a call requesting his presence at the bank first thing in the morning for a meeting with the interim director. He figured it was just a formality to fill out the necessary paperwork to secure the loan funding. Most likely, the interim director was cleaning up the outstanding projects cluttering up Martin's desk so he could transition to his new position smoothly and unencumbered.

Gratefully, he accepted a coffee from the secretary as he waited for George Golay's arrival. Hopefully, the caffeine from the espresso will help speed the effects of the aspirin he'd taken earlier. With the approval of the loan, the company's survival was guaranteed. At the bar last night, his relief was measured in the number of rounds of whiskey he'd ordered for himself, his date, and her friends. He sat back in his chair and smiled. A headache was a small price to pay for such a joyous celebration. The removal of the main obstacle to the loan had gone without a hitch. The cost of the contract was a drop in the bucket compared to what he stood to gain moving forward.

Jean-Louis rose with a big smile on his face when Golay entered the room. He was met with a dour expression. Golay walked around the desk and sat down heavily in the high-backed leather chair. He indicated for Jean-Louis to resume his seat with a wave of his hand.

Golay and Jean-Louis met during their last year of secondary school. By coincidence, two years later, while attending the same university, Jean-Louis dated Genevieve, the woman who eventually became Golay's wife. He never slept with her, much to his regret, given the beauty she was and still is. Over time, they socialized on occasion. In fact, Jean-Louis had been a dinner guest at Golay's house or a hiking companion once or twice a year. The last time they saw each other was about three months previously at a soirée that Genevieve hosted as a fundraiser for a children's charity.

Anxious to be done with the formalities, Jean-Louis was a bit surprised by the absence of the usual stack of papers required for such a sizable loan. He'd been through these measures enough times to expect such a hefty pile to be at the ready. Perhaps a secretary would bring it in due course.

"How are you, Jean-Louis?" Golay broke the silence. He was impeccably dressed, as expected for a person in his newly ascended position. However, his face had deep stress lines, and his eyes darted around the room, perching anywhere except on Jean-Louis' face.

"It has been a bit of time since we last spoke. I am very well, George, and you? How is the family?"

"Genevieve and the kids are quite well. We just got back from a short trip to Provence for the school break. Little did I know what I'd be walking into several days later." Clearing his throat, Golay continued. "Jean-Louis, I figured it would be best if we met in person rather than discussing matters over the phone."

Jean-Louis nodded his agreement. For a loan of this size, this is what he expected. They may be friends, and this was merely a formality, but processes had to be respected and followed.

"Last night, I met with senior members of the board of directors. They instructed me to inform you that your loan application has been denied."

Jean-Louis suddenly felt as though he were swimming in slow motion upstream through murky water, weighed down by a lead vest. A wave of nausea overcame him. His stomach plummeted into his groin. No doubt the color in his face disappeared as beads of sweat burst onto his forehead. He stared at the person he was convinced would be able to grease the wheels for the loan without a problem and not be the impediment Martin had been.

"George. What?" At least he had enough breath left to expel those few words. "But...we're friends. We've known each other for decades. I've known your kids since they were born. What happened? Martin was working against me and had not yet approved the loan, I know, but he's no longer in charge. You're in charge now. I was counting on you."

"The board decided your company and its officers lack sufficient equity to secure the loan. You are quite leveraged, Jean-Louis, and the corporate finances are deep in the red. There was nothing I could do. The board of directors has the final word."

"But you're the bank director. You have the power to influence the board. They usually listen to the recommendations of the director."

Golay shook his head. "With the passing of Monsieur Martin, I am the *interim* director. The board made that quite clear. I have no authority to approve anything. They are looking to name a new permanent director in the next week or two. They want to appoint someone with more experience. And, frankly, Jean-Louis, looking at the application and the due diligence report, I have to agree with the board's decision."

Matthew and Brown sat in a small interview room at the Big Bear Sheriff's Department to go over the Jane Doe file. It was a two-hour trip from Costa Mar—one way. Both felt it better be worthwhile.

Jane Doe's body had been found partially submerged in a stream, down a slope from a secluded hiking trail. She seemed to approximate the physical description listed on Brenda Alves' driver's license, which surprised Brown. Everybody lies on their driver's license; he hadn't put much credence into her details, except for eye color, but even that could be fudged by contact lenses. However, according to the coroner's report, this woman's height, weight, hair, and eye color were a match. Comparing the postmortem photographs of Jane Doe to those on Brenda's license wasn't conclusive, but with a bit of imagination, they could appreciate a similarity.

"As I told you," Raul Chin said as he sat down with them. "Where she was found was remote. Certainly, not a trail frequented by weekend warriors from the flatland. I mean, several times a year, we're called to rescue a lost or injured hiker who wasn't prepared for the rigors of hiking, especially at Big Bear's altitude of 6,700 feet. But not from this kind of trail. Anyone with an ounce of smarts would have realized the dangers of that trail within a hundred feet of the trailhead and turned back. She was found a quarter of a mile up that trail."

"And you're the only one who thought that odd?" Matthew asked. "I mean no disrespect or anything to your department, just wondering what I'm working with here."

"Who are you again?" Chin asked.

"He's a consultant to my department," Brown interjected. Matthew bit his tongue.

Matthew realized he may have overstepped the boundaries, but he truly wanted to know what kind of outfit this sheriff's department was. Had they missed anything else during their investigation?

"To be honest, the coroner had some doubts too." Chin looked at the closed door before continuing. "Look, I'm sure you've experienced similar problems. The coroner told me he'd been pressured from the higher-ups to clear as many cases as possible before the election. Without evidence to pursue and nothing more than a feeling, he caved."

Matthew scanned the autopsy report. Nothing suggested the victim had been assaulted. Her arms and legs had several superficial bruises and abrasions attributed to the fall. Under her nails, there was dirt, but there was no evidence of human tissue to indicate she'd put up a fight. Sexual crime had been ruled out. The victim had detectable traces of THC in her blood; otherwise, the toxicology tests were negative.

"You mentioned a few times she wasn't dressed for the terrain." Matthew tried to make amends with Chin. "What was she wearing?"

"Yeah, she certainly wasn't dressed for hiking in the mountains. Had on a thin, button-down blouse over a tank top, shorts, and well-worn tennis shoes. This is the kind of place where, if you don't like the weather, you wait an hour, and it'll change. Any sensible person would have dressed in layers. The cheap sneakers she had on were not made for hiking on trails such as these, especially ones with any degree of difficulty. I don't think anyone with an iota of common sense would have gone as far as she did in those shoes. It was March, which means the rainy season. It was probably slippery as all heck out there."

"That's a good point. Is there any way you can get us a weather report for that time frame?" Matthews asked.

"Probably on Google." Chin pulled out his phone and started tapping, confirming the love side of Matthew's love-hate relationship with technology. At times like these, the ability to obtain information with such rapidity was a definite plus. At other times...

Within a minute, Chin had an answer. Sure enough, it had rained off and on for three days before the body was discovered.

"And no one filed a report of a missing hiker in that time frame?" Brown reconfirmed.

"Nope."

They covered the table with the photographs taken at the scene and methodically matched them to the details of the investigators' reports. The stream's flow was above average due to the rain. Several boulders and large rocks were near the body. Any of them could have caused the fatal head injury if she'd landed on one at the right angle with sufficient force. Blood was found on a rock near the body. The typing of the blood recovered from that rock matched the victim's.

Matthew peered closer at a photograph. "Of course, the rock could have been used as a weapon, and then intentionally placed where it was discovered to make it look like the landing spot for her head."

"Anything's possible," Chin admitted.

A partial footprint in the semi-soft dirt near the body was identified as coming from a very common hiking boot. It was only a partial imprint; the shoe size couldn't be definitively determined, but it seemed small enough to be a woman's boot. Investigators were not convinced of its relevance to the case, as one of the hikers who discovered the body wore a similar boot.

A small backpack was recovered near the body. It was empty except for a hairbrush, a tube of lip balm, and a pack of tissues. No car keys, wallet, or other means of identification were found. Neither was there a bottle of water nor any snacks typically carried by a hiker.

"How could she have gotten to the trail?" Brown asked

"Good question," Chin nodded. "Like I said, the trail is remote, well outside of town. You can't just walk to it. There should have been a car or truck nearby, but a search of the area at the time near the two trail heads failed to reveal an abandoned vehicle."

An autopsy photograph was particularly intriguing: a close-up of the tattoo on the victim's left wrist showing a heart, the approximate size of a half-dollar coin, with a capital B in the middle. Even though it was simple in design, it appeared to have been professionally done. The edges of the design were clean and solid. The font was unique, and hearts formed the negative space in each loop. It took some artistic talent to accomplish the design. Brown asked Chin for a copy of the picture.

"It's suggestive," Matthew nodded. "But not enough."

"What do you mean?" Brown dropped the photo back on the table.

"The tattoo. It's suggestive, but we need more evidence to confirm her identity as John s mother." He turned to Chin and explained who John was and his possible relationship to Jane Doe. "Any chance of getting in that box to see if there's something we could send to the lab for DNA analysis?"

"The evidence box is stored in the sheriff's repository down the mountain in San Bernardino. It should still have all her clothing, the backpack, and whatever personal effects there were." Chin grinned. "I can go down the hill tomorrow and see what they have."

Chapter 24

Jean-Louis couldn't face the drive back to his office. Instead, he headed to the bar in the Four Seasons Hotel on the Quai des Bergues. Currently, he was staring at his third scotch. Everything had been perfectly planned until he was cut down at the knees by the one person in whom he had confidence. He used to believe Martin was the major impediment. He had always been an obstacle to Zeller s growth. With Golay in charge, he was positive he'd be approved!

After all the years he and Golay knew each other, how could he not be relied upon to push this small loan through such a huge bank? Golay had always been a pushover. Who knew he could grow a spine? The loan he requested was nothing more than pocket lint when compared to the bank's assets. Besides, he never defaulted on any loan. Well, except for the one three years ago when he used the business to purchase a Ferrari, which was now gone. And there was that issue of the loan for the apartment in Paris, which he eventually signed over to the bank, but it was a small apartment. Golay putting the onus on the Board was sheer crap. Friends do not treat friends like this.

His hand shook to such a degree when he tried to take another sip that he looked around the bar to make sure no one was looking at him. His stomach continued its circus performance, and his head ached more than ever. He dreaded talking to his sister, but that was a task for later.

Glancing at his watch, not a Zeller, he saw it was time to head to the next meeting. Leaving his car at the hotel, he walked north along the walkway adjacent to Lake Geneva to the Parc du Château-Banquet.

By the time he reached the park, he had sobered up sufficiently, though the quivering in his legs and arms continued. These were not people to take on cavalierly. As instructed, he entered the park along a tree-lined path. He passed several couples, but none spared him a glance. Walking along, he suddenly felt a slight brush of someone's arm against his. He looked to his left quickly and recognized Philippe.

Without breaking stride, looking straight ahead, Jean-Louis cleared his throat. Barely moving his lips, he spoke in a whisper. "I, ahem, I don't have anything for you. I am not in a position to make the payment."

"That is not acceptable. We had an agreement, and it is our expectation that it will be honored unquestionably." The response was quiet and devoid of emotion.

An icy current ricocheted up and down Jean-Louis' spine. He took several quick steps forward and turned to face Philippe. "The end result wasn't as desired. The benefits did not justify the full cost." Panic zapped his chest. It was all he could do not to bolt from the scene.

The man simply walked around him. Jean-Louis ran to catch up.

"The agreement was fulfilled on our part, sir," Phillippe said in a passionless voice. "What you define as 'end result' is not our concern. You have until this hour in two days to make the final payment, in full. We will meet at the same time in the Parc Mon Repos. There will be no further extension. Do not be late and do not think you can hide from us."

There would be consequences for a failure to abide by the instruction, and there was no doubt in Jean-Louis's mind that they would be dire. His stomach spasmed. He could barely keep upright.

At the next fork in the path, Phillipe strolled down one branch leading out of the park, leaving Jean-Louis staring after him. His forehead was covered with sweat. The armpits of his shirt darkened from a torrent of perspiration.

After his long day driving to and from Big Bear, Matthew headed to his "office"—the bench overlooking the ocean to collect his thoughts and give Bernie an update call.

"Money as a motive to kill either Suzanne or John seems ruled out," Matthew told him. "Stephen point-blank offered me everything he'd get from his mother's life insurance policy. Meanwhile, Livingston confirmed no one stood to benefit in the event of John's death. So, we're looking into John's past to see if there is a clue to his present situation. As a start, I'm hoping to connect John to this Jane Doe and see where that leads."

"All you need is a tiny bit of something from her clothes to get a DNA sample. Anything's possible." Bernie laughed. "But hey. You could always get a court order and exhume the body."

"I'll put that at the bottom of my list of ideas." Judges didn't issue court orders based solely on hunches. Besides, the idea of watching a backhoe dig up a four-year-old casket and the remains within wasn't something he had a stomach for.

"So what's next?" Bernie asked.

A text from Siobhan dinged in. "I have no idea," Matthew told his old friend. "But keep noodling this. I'll call ya back."

Siobhan sounded rushed when she answered his call. "Sorry, in the middle of two projects. I just wanted to check in with you. I had a bit of free time and was able to run some analytics on that email address you gave me."

"Great. Who is it from?"

"I have no idea."

Matthew bit his tongue from asking why the hell she called him. "Did you learn anything?" he said after a pause.

"Well, I was able to confirm that, despite ending with a .uk, it did *not* originate in the United Kingdom."

"That's possible?"

"Yeah. That address is a link to another email address, which probably links to another and another. So, even though it's a UK address, the message could have originated anywhere in the world. It's an old-fashioned strategy to mask the sender's identity."

"So it's not really telling us anything new."

"Not yet. I sent a message to see if I'd get a bite. Nothing yet, but I'm going to play with it more as soon as I have a little more time. I think there's a better app to trace it." Matthew could hear her tapping on a keyboard as she spoke and wondered how anyone could do that.

"If I said it may be coming from Germany, would that help?"

"Huh? Why?" Siobhan stopped typing for a moment. "I'm not sure that helps, but why Germany?"

Matthew wasn't convinced he was correct, but it was a thought. "I wonder if this person is John's father. According to Jacqueline's mother, her father, and therefore John's, had a German name. The attorney for John's trust suggested that the person who set it up had a German accent. Maybe he's using emails to maintain some kind of relationship with his son. It's just a hunch."

"Interesting. Well, I'll let you know. I just wanted to give you an update."

An update that provided nothing, Matthew left unsaid. He wasn't mad at Siobhan. She seemed like a nice young woman, and she was willingly helping him. But he was getting annoyed at all the dead ends. What was it going to take to crack this case? Would he ever know who killed Suzanne?

Despite being after midnight, Charice couldn't sleep. She paced around the study, her father's old favorite room. The shelves were lined with leather-bound volumes, what was left of his treasured collection. Many of the valuable first editions he'd lovingly acquired over his lifetime had already been sold to cover her and Jean-Louis' lifestyle.

When he was alive, her father could be found in this room most evenings, enjoying a favorite book and a brandy. Long ago, her mother forbade smoking cigars in the house. Nonetheless, a faint, sweet, residual scent lingered in the fabric covering the sofa and plush chairs. Neither his memory nor the aroma could calm Charice, though. This estate, like the company, was mortgaged to the maximum extent possible, if not beyond. Their options to keep the company viable had been whittled to a very few, the best of which rested in the hands of some oddball kid in California.

Since she last spoke to Jean-Louis, she'd been unable to sit still. There was no possibility of sleep any time soon. Her brother had devolved into a puddle of fear and panic. What was clear to her was that she needed to act very soon. Her tactics, usually slow and deliberate, now needed to be accelerated. If only she would get that damn call!

As if willed by her psychic powers, her phone did, indeed, ring. Charice didn't answer right away, fearing she was imagining it. She looked at the screen, sure enough, the men she'd recently hired, two Italian Special Forces Operatives, were finally checking in.

"Where have you been?" she hissed into the phone.

"Oh, bella! We have been here, in California, just as you asked."

"I sent you two weeks ago, and you're just now calling me?" She'd met them on the Italian island of Isola del Gilio eight months earlier. What started as a weekend getaway for sun, food, and sex evolved into a week with all that and more. One does not easily forget such a time or the men who made it possible. While together, she learned of their talents beyond the bedroom. It was for these special skills that she had hired them and sent them to California. The contract was costing the company a pretty penny, but they were a necessary backup option given her near certainty that her brother would fail to deliver on his end of the bargain. And apparently, he'd failed.

"We have been waiting and watching."

"And?"

"And, when you give the word, we know exactly what to do."

Charice breathed in the scent of her father's cigars long and deep. She felt her body soften, and a small smile form on her face as she exhaled. "Word."

Chapter 25

The evenings were the worst. Without any distraction, Matthew was left at the mercy of his own thoughts. In such a short period of time, Suzanne had become more a part of his life than he realized. The emptiness was difficult to endure. When Muriel died, there had been time to try to prepare for her absence. Her passing was still difficult; no amount of time to prepare would have been enough. With the advice of the hospice chaplain, he was able to arrange a support structure for himself that embraced him during his period of transition. The pain of loneliness was tempered by those who rallied around him.

This situation was different. Although they had been together for just a couple of months, they'd been good friends for much longer. The suddenness of Suzanne's death and the lack of a support structure left him feeling empty, adrift. The concept of going through a second course of group therapy to deal with this loss was overwhelming. True, the grief counseling for Muriel had helped and led to meeting Suzanne. But he wasn't ready for any part of that again. Certainly, no time soon. How many times can a guy go through this kind of trauma?

He knew he was spiraling into a vortex of self-pity and wondered what he could do to distract himself. He picked up his phone and texted Stephen: "You doing OK?"

Within minutes, Stephen called.

"Hi Matthew." Actually, it was Siobhan on the other end. Judging by the ambient sound of a television in the background, she was on speaker. "I just spent the last hour and a half tracing that email address." She sounded more relaxed than on the prior call. "I still don't have a response to my email query, but they haven't bounced back, so that means it's a valid address. I reconfirmed that the emails don't originate in the United Kingdom. Even better, I was able to trace them to an area in Switzerland, specifically in or around the capital city of Bern.

"Who the hell does John know in Switzerland?" Matthew was quiet for several moments.

"Didn't Suzanne take him there?"

"Yes, but..." Was it possible that John had met someone and they became friends in such a short interval of time? That did not make sense. John intimated that his friend had made significant contributions to his knowledge of watches and watchmaking. He had traveled to Switzerland to present his movement to watch companies, so the work with the friend had to have taken place over months, if not years, before the trip. More so, it was extremely unlikely that John would grow such a strong attachment to a stranger in such a relatively short time period.

"I guess you'd have to ask John," Siobhan answered, jarring him out of his thoughts.

"I'm sorry. My sense is that John has been communicating with this person he calls his friend for quite some time. I'll bet anything that trip to Switzerland was the first and only trip outside of this zip code, much less out of the country."

"I get it, but the world is much smaller these days," Siobhan replied. "There are so many ways to meet people from all over the world now. Maybe a chat group?"

"Have you met John? He won't carry on a conversation if you're sitting across the room from him, much less halfway around the world."

Matthew sat back in his chair. Something wasn't adding up. He pulled up a map of Europe on his computer. "Okay, is it possible the email originated from somewhere close to Switzerland, like Germany?"

"If the sender lives in Germany, he would have to travel to Switzerland anytime he wanted to send an email. I don't see how that would be feasible."

Matthew wasn't going to be dissuaded. "Let's assume for the moment my hunch is right, and the friend is John's father, and John's father is German..." He paused as he looked at the map. "Maybe he lives in southern Germany and crosses the border to send emails in order to cover his identity. Aren't there internet cafes or Starbucks in Bern? Maybe he works somewhere in Switzerland?"

"I guess it's possible. Doesn't seem practical, especially if John is communicating with this person at different times of the day and night. But if someone is motivated enough to hide his identity and location, I suppose anything is possible."

"Is there anything else you can do to get a more precise location of the sender?"

Matthew could hear her and Stephen talking. After a minute, Stephen spoke. "We were just looking at a map of the area. Bern is quite a distance from the German border; it would be a long trip every time they wanted to send an email."

"Damn."

"As far as I am concerned," Siobhand said. "The email is originating somewhere in the vicinity of Bern. If John's father had a German accent, it's possible he's from Austria or even Liechtenstein. Both share a border with Switzerland. Maybe he's moved around. Born in one country and now living in Switzerland. In Europe, people move from country to country like we move from state to state, especially in the EU."

This is getting us nowhere, Matthew thought.

When Matthew arrived at John's house the following morning, he found Jacqueline in the living room with a short, stocky middle-aged woman whose cheerful, confident demeanor contrasted sharply with Jacqueline's dour appearance.

"Oh, hey," Jacqueline said to him when he walked in the front door. "Just make yourself at home, like usual." She turned back to the woman, waving a dismissive hand toward Matthew. "He's a family friend."

Matthew could quickly tell the woman was a potential replacement for Suzanne, and that John's opinion didn't seem to matter. He sat at the dining table, staring at his phone.

Brown was on his way to the house with a DNA kit. Matthew figured John wouldn't object to a cotton swab rubbed gently on the inside of his cheek. However, neither he nor Brown was certain whether he'd be willing to give informed consent for the testing. To play it safe, Brown had obtained a court order.

"Hi, John." Matthew sat at the table.

"Hi." When John briefly looked up, his face was devoid of any visible emotion.

"So, uh—" Matthew started.

"Great!" Jacquline almost shouted. "Hey, John. Dahlia's gonna stay with you for the rest of the day. It's just a trial basis." She picked up her purse and headed toward the door. "I'm outta here."

Within moments, they could hear the engine of Jacqueline's car turn over, and she was gone. Good thing Matthew parked on the street today.

John stood and wordlessly retreated to his workroom, of course locking the door behind him.

"I'm going to make some coffee, would you like some?" Dahlia asked.

"No, thanks. I'm gonna chat with John for a few minutes."

"OK." Dahlia headed to the kitchen and started rummaging through the cabinets.

"Oh, um, a friend of ours will be stopping by soon." Mathew pulled out his cell phone to text Brown an update. "He'll be asking for me and John. Please let us know when he's here."

"Of course." She continued hunting for coffee-making supplies.

He finished his note to Brown, instructing him not to identify himself to Dahlia as a police officer, and knocked on John's workroom door. After several knocks, John unlocked the door and cautiously opened it. Before letting Matthew into the inner sanctum, John made sure the new interloper wasn't close by or a risk to enter uninvited.

John returned to his bench where his watch movement rested, uncased from the plastic container. As Matthew approached, he could hear its soft ticking. John adjusted the light fixtures, placed a magnifying loupe over one eye, and then leaned over the movement. With a fine screwdriver, he adjusted an almost imperceptible screw. Near the movement stood a small device with a digital readout. A cable connected it to John's computer.

Matthew pointed to it. "What is that?"

John took his time answering. "A timegrapher."

"What do you use it for?"

"To measure the timing accuracy of the watch."

Once more, Matthew was confused.

John straightened up and returned to teacher mode as he pointed to a small wheel on the movement rapidly moving back and forth. "That's the escapement." A pause. "The heartbeat of the watch. This device provides information about the precision of its function, which translates into the accuracy of its timekeeping."

Still far from understanding what he was looking at, Matthew admitted to a certain fascination with the sight of the watch movement's inner workings in action.

John explained how the watch measured time, while Matthew interrupted with questions. They spoke in a natural, give-and-take fashion. They were once again teacher and student. Taking on the role of an instructor was very comfortable for John, especially when the topic of discussion was something he understood backwards and forwards. Fascinated by John's metamorphosis, Matthew's attention alternated between what was being said and who was saying it until a series of soft knocks on the door interrupted them.

Matthew stepped toward the door but then thought the better of it and stopped. John passed him, unlocked the door, and opened it slightly.

In the opening, blocking most of the light shining from the window in the living room, Dahlia stood, hand raised, poised to knock again. "There is a gentleman at the front door asking for the two of you." Message delivered, Dahlia rapidly retreated.

John looked over his shoulder at Matthew, who nodded. "I'm expecting Detective Brown."

Quickly, John returned to his workbench and covered the movement with the bowl of the wine glass and then covered it with a cloth. Together, they exited the room. Of course, John engaged the deadbolt once the door clicked shut.

Brown handed Matthew a small white envelope with indecipherable writing on one side. Inside was a vial containing a cotton swab. A paper clipped to the envelope gave specific instructions on how to properly obtain a specimen for DNA analysis.

John watched the exchange with a blank expression, turning toward his workroom as Matthew read the instructions.

"Let's take a seat," Matthew suggested as he approached the dining table. John turned back and sat in a chair as directed.

"John." Matthew withdrew a pair of latex gloves from another package Brown handed him. Peering over his shoulder, he saw that Dahlia was standing inside the kitchen watching them. "We need to swab the inside of your cheek with this Q-tip. It's for Colin. No big deal."

John stared wide-eyed at Matthew's gloved hands and then at the withdrawn cotton swab.

Matthew moved closer to him. "John, please open your mouth. All I have to do is put this swab against the inside of your cheek. It's going to take a second, and then we'll be done."

John vigorously shook his head. He emitted a shriek and shot out of the chair. Wordlessly, he headed for his workroom and disappeared inside, shutting and locking the door behind him.

Matthew shook his head. "I guess that's not going to happen."

"Can you imagine if we needed blood?" Brown responded. "That would have been a cluster."

"So, what are our options?" Matthew blew out a stream of air. "I guess hair?"

"We should have thought of that to begin with."

Matthew walked to the door and knocked. Speaking loud enough to be heard through the door. "John, I need to speak to you. No swab, I promise. I've taken off my gloves. I am not going to touch you. Please, this is important."

The door cracked open. Matthew brought both hands up for John to see that the gloves were gone. Not wanting Dahlia to hear, he spoke softly. "Detective Brown and I spoke. We don't want to hurt you. All we want is to take a few strands of your hair."

Before any further discussion, John's eyes shot wide open again, and he pulled back from the doorway but did not shut it.

Cursing to himself, Matthew quickly recovered. In a reassuring voice, he replied. "Not from you. I told you we weren't going to touch you, and definitely not hurt you. We want to look at your hairbrush and see if we can get a few strands of your hair."

Fortunately, John again did not ask why this was being done. He pointed toward the ceiling of the workroom. Matthew took that to indicate that the brush was upstairs.

"Can I go get your brush?"

"No. I will." John exited the workroom and locked the door.

Brown and Matthew spent a few minutes in uncomfortable silence, occasionally smiling benignly at Dahlia while they waited.

John returned with a hairbrush in hand and silently gave it to Matthew. In renewed horror, he stared at the new set of gloves Matthew had donned in his absence.

"I'm not going to touch you, I promise." Matthew returned to the table where Brown was still sitting with the open vial. He carefully removed strands of hair from the brush and placed them in the vial. Brown put it in the envelope, then sealed and signed it. Matthew removed the gloves.

"Thank you, John." He was thanking him for more than the hair sample. He was greatly relieved they didn't have to answer any questions that could send John further into a tailspin.

Chapter 26

Rousseau was getting tired of playing the game with Sommers. The ultimate objective of throwing off the yoke of the Bonet siblings seemed no closer. He was losing his patience with the billionaire and the endeavor as a whole. Despite his frustrations, in his spare time, he'd been making progress on the design for the first watch to be released by the company he'd soon be running. Sommers might think he would be the guiding force and creator of the renamed company, but he was just the money. Michel Rousseau was going to be in operational control, and to hell with whatever "brilliant" ideas Sommers might have. He wasn't going to work for another rich guy who thought, just because he had a bank full of money, he understood what it took to design and build a perfect watch.

He dialed the number for Sommers' phone from a new burner.

Sommers answered on the third ring.

As was their custom, no names were used. Much to his annoyance, Rousseau was asked to utter the short code phrase, as instructed by Sommers, to confirm his identity. Stupid games these damn Americans play, he thought. He was able to adopt a polite pitch to his voice. "It was not my plan to call, but something's up with him."

"How so?"

"Not sure. Yesterday, he was flying around high as a kite and may in fact have been. It seemed like he didn't have a care in the world. But today, when he stopped by the office, he looked as if the world had fallen in on his head. He was a mess."

"Any idea why the 180?" Rousseau thought Sommers sounded happy with this news. His voice was light, almost joyful.

"Well, we know that he is having money issues. Maybe he thought it had been handled and now not?"

"Ha! Good guess!"

"What does that mean?"

"It means nothing. Don't worry about it." Sommers laughed. "Meanwhile, we continue as planned. I'll check my sources, make sure they know to ratchet up the pressure."

"That will be enough?"

"I have more than one trick up my sleeve. Trust me, there are other...um...options that are moving along quite nicely."

Brown had requested that the lab expedite the hair sample due to an ongoing homicide investigation. Simultaneously, Chin in Big Bear had asked the same for the samples he obtained from the clothes and hairbrush in Jane Doe's evidence box. The box also held a rock collected from the scene that had several blood splatters on it. For good measure, Chin sent it in for analysis, as well.

Meanwhile, Matthew felt guilty and wanted to undo the damage he may have caused in his relationship with John. He was flying blind, trying to deal with someone with autism. Already, he had triggered John several times, making him clam up and retreat into his private world. The resultant backslides limited John's willingness to communicate, and rebuilding his trust took time away from the investigation. He needed to stop making those blunders.

He returned to the house in time to join John and Louis for their afternoon walk. They started in silence. This time, Louis did not seem particularly interested in the bushes, trees, or fences they passed.

Previously, he had spent an inordinate amount of time checking for strangers in his territory. For whatever reason, not today. The dog seemed to be going on the walk as pro forma, intuitively mirroring the stress he sensed John was feeling.

Once they entered the park along their usual path, Matthew broke the silence. "John, I want to apologize for what happened before. We needed a sample of your DNA as part of the investigation into Suzanne's murder. I should have explained things before I asked for a sample."

John made no response but kept walking, studying the cement path immediately in front of him. Matthew noted that John made a conscious effort to avoid stepping on any crack in the sidewalk.

Without a response, positive or negative, Matthew changed the subject.

"With all the changes going on in your life, I'm glad you have your friend," Matthew said. "A steady friend is a rare find."

John said nothing.

"How long have you known your friend?"

John shrugged.

"I guess since you've been into watches. How long has that been?"

"A while."

He quit asking questions as they approached the scene of Suzanne's murder. Even Louis seemed to understand the solemnity of the site and ceased his tugging on the leash and harsh panting. As they walked past the patch of grass, Matthew spied a small piece of yellow tape hanging from a tree branch, a vestige of the barrier placed during the processing of the scene.

After passing the area, Matthew gently tried again. "So, about your friend..."

John gave no indication of any interest in continuing the conversation.

"Is it a him or a her?" Matthew plowed ahead.

John shrugged one shoulder, then answered while watching the sidewalk. "Him."

"How did you meet him, again?"

Again, John gave his patented shrug. "He contacted me."

"How did he find out about you and your interest in watches?" Matthew figured he would keep probing until he got a sign from John to back off.

"Don't know."

"Do you know his name?"

All Matthew got was a brief shake of the head of unclear meaning, which he caught out of the corner of his eye. Keeping the tenor of his voice detached, Matthew repeated himself. "What's his name?"

"Don't know."

Matthew turned to look at John, who continued to watch the pavement. His face was expressionless. Matthew spent his career interviewing thousands of people and felt comfortable reading faces to discern truth from fiction. There was nothing in John's face to give a hint of the validity of the answers. However, knowing John and his intricacies, Matthew was sure John was being totally honest and not hiding the truth. Besides, what motivation would John have to lie? Was John even capable of lying?

"Do you know where he lives?"

Finally, John answered with a full sentence. "His email address is dot UK. So I guess he lives in England."

Matthew saw no point in correcting him. "What do you talk about? Do you discuss topics other than watches?"

Again, John shrugged. "Mostly watches. Occasionally, something to do with engineering. Nothing special."

"Has he had anything to do with the development of your watch movement?"

"Hmm." Matthew took that as a positive response.

"How so?"

John frowned in thought. He did not immediately answer. It was as if he were having an internal debate about how much to reveal of his most important secret project. "He helped me."

It was a cryptic answer, but Matthew sensed that was all John was going to reveal at this point in time. He figured he would have to work on repairing his relationship some more before they could have a free exchange of ideas again.

"Dealing with an adult with autism can be very challenging, and especially so when you're questioning them on a potentially emotionally charged subject." Dr. Sharon Diaz leaned back in her office chair and regarded Brown and Matthew. Brown had set up the meeting with the department's psychologist so they, especially Matthew, could get tips on how to communicate with John.

"Yeah, I kind of noticed that already. In fact, I just came from spending time with him. I feel like he trusts me, but that I keep messing up and challenging that trust." Matthew tried to ignore the tinkling sound of a small fountain resting on a table next to the sofa where he sat. The sound of running water often gave him the urge to use the restroom.

"Symptoms of autism are not generally something checked off as a person having versus not having. They can manifest variably, in ways that some people would deem quirky on one end, to being seen as severely impaired on the other. For instance, their communicative abilities can range from those of a neurotypical person to total aphasia. The degree of involvement extends across a wide spectrum, which is why the condition is labeled autism spectrum disorder."

Matthew nodded.

"From your description," she continued. "It sounds as if he requires Level 1 support structures. For people like him, one of their main challenges involves socialization. They often struggle to form meaningful connections with others. Typically, the autistic person is unaware of the subtle and, often, the not-so-subtle social cues that we commonly attend to when interacting with others. They can appear standoffish or lost in their own world, but this is usually due to their difficulties with interpersonal relations and communication. Oftentimes, their isolation is also related to their intolerance to what they perceive as over-stimulation. They tend to be very concrete in their thinking and follow rigorous, regimented patterns of behavior. Sensory stimulation, such as loud noise, strong smells, flashing lights, or even certain textures of clothing or food, can be triggering. They lack the ability to modulate their reactivity to perceived noxious stimuli. They are often faced with fight-or-flight reactivity when confronted with a trigger. What those triggers might be can be very individualized."

At the last sentence, Matthew looked at Brown. "Explains why he reacted the way he did this morning."

Brown nodded.

"Their reaction to a negative stimulus can be out of proportion to the type or level of threat they perceive," Dr. Diaz raised her eyebrows. "I mean, they can regress or totally shut down. They can start stimming, such as making repetitive gestures of an extremity or vocalizations. Some can have self-abusive or aggressive behaviors when significantly stressed. Reaction patterns vary from person to person but tend to remain relatively consistent for each individual. However, even in the face of these issues and other challenges, these people can be extremely bright. Some of the greatest minds in history may have belonged to people on the autism spectrum. You'll find them to be more prevalent in engineering and the sciences rather than in the liberal arts. They can relate to numbers and the physical sciences much better than to the subtleties and nuances inherent in the study of social sciences and humanities."

"That makes sense. Our subject is an engineering teacher and a watchmaker." Matthew found himself nodding again.

"Another thing to understand is how they process information," Dr. Diaz said. "Many tend to perseverate both in thought and communication."

"What does that mean?" Brown asked.

"It can be quite the challenge to get them off a particular subject once they get going."

Matthew and Brown peppered the psychologist with questions about how to approach John, referring to him not by name but rather as their "subject." Diaz repeated several times the suggestion to let the subject come to them and do their best to avoid any hint of antagonism or aggressive questioning. Working with him, she advised, in a very non-threatening, consistent fashion takes practice and patience.

They also needed to respect his personal space, she instructed. Should they trespass too close, they risked shutting them down or even fleeing. Diaz emphasized again that if they were able to identify his triggers, whatever they might be, sensory, social, or the like, there was a better chance of avoiding regression or worse and obtaining the information they sought.

"One of the things you must always remember is that your subject will be prone to being very concrete. Start with yes-and-no questions. Once he is answering without stress, gradually increase the complexity of the questions you're asking. Always be on the lookout for symptoms or signs of activation. At the first sign of any stress reaction, retreat, pause, and then try a different tactic."

"Appreciate this, Dr. Diaz," Matthew said. "Thanks for taking the time to talk with us, too. I just have one more question."

"Sure."

"How is it I am able to have two-way conversations with our subject, and no one else can?"

"Who else has tried?"

"Well, his sister, Suzanne, I mean his former companion, and the new companion."

"Is it possible that it's because they are women?"

Her response surprised Matthew. As he reflected on Diaz's observation. From what he knew of John's history, his world was populated mainly by women: his mother, sister, Suzanne, and now Dahlia. If it is true that John relates better with men, he wondered if that added credence to his idea that John's friend was a man. If that is true, might that add further weight to his supposition that John's friend was, in fact, his father?

Chapter 27

The morning sun shone through the windows of Jean-Louis' study in Geneva. Somehow, he felt wide awake despite having slept only an hour or two. Perhaps it was due to the multiple cups of espresso he'd had in the past couple of hours.

Hell bent on securing funds to, firstly, pay off the killers, and secondly, make up for the bridge loan he'd been denied, he'd come up with a new plan. Already, he'd called several people, two in China and one in Dubai, each of whom had extensive watch collections and access to a significant amount of capital. He invited them to join Zeller in a new venture destined to bring excellent returns on their investment. When asked for details, conspiratorially, he expressed that he wasn't at liberty to discuss the specifics, except to say it was a guaranteed gold mine. Each conversation lasted only minutes. None expressed any interest in what Jean-Louis had to say or offer. Sales was never Jean-Louis' strong suit. In fact, he wasn't sure what his strong suit was, aside from bedding beautiful women.

Undaunted, he moved across the globe with the sun. It was now time to call New York City.

"I would like to speak with Carlton Sommers, please," he told the officious secretary in as friendly a tone as he could muster, given his current state of distress. "This is Jean-Louis Bonet of the Frederique Zeller Watch company."

He must have impressed her, as she passed the call through immediately.

They had never met in person nor spoken on the telephone, but Jean-Louis knew Sommers was an avid watch collector who, according to the grapevine, was actively looking to invest in a watch brand. Searching the internet, Jean-Louis discovered Sommers had a vast investment portfolio centered on real estate, finance, and energy sectors—no luxury goods. He found several articles geared toward watch enthusiasts that mentioned his extensive personal collection, and two fluff pieces containing interviews with him. While he expressed an interest in horology, he didn't seem to know much about the business of watchmaking. In other words, he was a perfect target for Jean-Louis to entice.

"I'm a busy man. Why are you calling?" Sommers answered.

A typical New Yorker, Jean-Louis thought, brusque and straight to the point. Though, Jean-Louis granted, that the billionaire had plenty of people trying to blow smoke up his ass in order to get into his wallet. Sommers wasn't the kind of person to be won over with unnecessary and unwanted adulation.

"Very well," Jean-Louis cleared his throat. "As a watch collector, I'm sure you're well-aware of the Zeller watch company."

"I am. I've owned a few of your very special pieces."

His use of the past tense wasn't lost on Jean-Louis. But at the moment, he couldn't care less if Sommers owned every one of their watches or just a branded coffee cup. "Very good. We are currently introducing a new product line that features groundbreaking technology, never before seen in the history of watchmaking. To achieve this, we are seeking a forward-thinking investor to help accelerate the company's transition into the future. In consideration of this investment, I am authorized to offer a stake in the company. With a modest investment and Zeller's technological prowess, the company is well-positioned to solidify its deserved place in the top echelon of watch companies." Jean-Louis paused.

"Go on."

Go on with what? Jean-Louis had thought his vague hints were very clear. "You are being offered something very special, a generous 20 percent stake in the company for a price that would typically purchase only about 10. Not only would you have this stake, but you are also being offered the unique opportunity for creative input and exclusive distribution rights within the Americas." Jean-Louis paused again.

"And what number would be required for this 20 percent?"

Jean-Louis's hand holding the telephone shook. He knew what he needed. He knew this guy had a huge cash reserve, and he wanted to squeeze as much as he could from Sommers. Yet, his father had taught him that in business negotiations, the person who said the first number was the loser. He demurred.

"I'm sure we can come up with a reasonable number to cover the offer on a subsequent call. For now, I'm just asking for a modest sum to serve as good-faith money to hold the offer." Jean-Louis dropped his voice to barely a hush to hide his intent from anyone listening, although he was the only one in his house. "I know this out of the blue, but Zeller has a once-in-a-lifetime opportunity that requires the company to act immediately. To bring this project to fruition, we require a modest amount of additional capital to be added to our reserve fund. We prefer not to go to our bank because they are conservative and lack the vision to understand the incredible opportunity we have been presented. Also, the bank wasn't interested in an ownership stake. Besides, it would take too long for them to arrange the financing. I am told we are not the only ones the inventor has spoken with. He has expressly said we are his first choice, but you never know, things can change at a moment's notice."

"It's an interesting offer," Sommers' voice was, at best, neutral. "I appreciate it, but I would need to see the details. While it appears to be quite generous, it may not be something that will fit into the strategic plan of my company."

Jean-Louis noted Sommers did not express any interest in the technological breakthrough that was the key to the promised riches.

Of course, had he asked, in typical Swiss fashion, Jean-Louis would have been, at best, vague about the details anyway. Swiss or not, the fact was that he did not have very many details about what the American had accomplished.

"Again, interesting," Sommers said before Jean-Louis could devise a response. "Thank you for the call." Sommers hung up without suggesting a follow-up meeting. Jean-Louis thought he heard the man raucously laughing before the phone went dead.

Matthew offered to accompany John to his class once more. In part, because he wasn't sure how else the young man would get there. Did Dahlia's trial day work out? If he didn't take John, would Jacqueline? He knew Suzanne had developed motherly feelings toward John and was beginning to suspect maybe he was developing fatherly ones. Was that another gift from Suzanne?

Since when was he so sentimental?

Doing his best to follow Dr. Diaz's recommendations, he kept the conversation light on the ride over, discovering John was willing to listen to Matthew discuss the latest trends in jazz. In response, John mentioned several of his favorite heavy metal bands.

Walking across campus, John allowed Matthew to hold Louis's leash. Louis, after a moment of confusion, accepted the reality of the situation and trotted along, consumed by passing smells. Glancing at him, Matthew thought John seemed unusually relaxed.

Hoping the time was right, he cautiously repeated his earlier question. "This friend we talked about, you said you've spoken to him about your discovery."

In typical fashion, John kept his eyes directed toward the sidewalk, careful to avoid stepping on any cracks as they approached John's building. "Yes." He responded without hesitation. "He helped me problem solve at different stages of its development."

Matthew now knew better than to react to the revelation. "He must have some knowledge about watches, don't you think?"

John stopped and looked at Matthew, not quite making eye contact, but instead staring at a spot somewhere between his lips and throat. "I suppose so," he said, after thinking for several minutes.

It was as though John had not thought of this fact previously. Matthew was willing to bet John had taken for granted the degree of assistance the friend had provided over the course of time. He doubted John even gave a moment's thought to the kind of training or experience the friend might have that made his input so helpful. Given that John had a working prototype, Matthew assumed the advice provided was on point. Matthew couldn't comprehend the complexity of the interplay of metallurgy, engineering, and watchmaking required to create John's movement. Could John have figured it all out? He was sure John was smart, if not brilliant, but did he have the knowledge base to achieve what he had? He believed the likelihood of John succeeding would have been doubtful had it not been for the assistance of someone with the necessary expertise. The mysterious friend must have some formal training in one or more of those disciplines. Matthew was willing to wager that the friend was a watchmaker with an engineering background, if such a person existed. Regardless, why, if he was not John's father, would he be so willing to help John?

"How do you suppose he got that knowledge? You think he's a watchmaker?"

John took his time answering again. Matthew looked carefully at his face and saw no evidence of an impending stress reaction. "Maybe."

Matthew decided to retry a line of questioning from before, since things were going okay. "And you don't remember how you met him online?"

John pursed his lips and shook his head.

Trying to avoid compound or complex questions, Matthew continued cautiously. "And you never met him in person?"

Another shake of the head, this time a bit more vigorous. "He never came to my house."

An interesting answer, Matthew thought. He was unsure why John specified his house. The question had not been so specific. Was John implying that the friend had been in California at some point? Not sure, Matthew made a mental note to consider exploring the question further at a later date.

"So, he knows about your invention?"

"Of course."

The two Italian men entered John's home through the back door with little difficulty. After three previous surreptitious visits to the house, they knew exactly how to get in and where to look.

Opening the interior locked door was no challenge, either. They took more time than usual to avoid any chance of leaving even the smallest scratch on the lock. Once inside the workroom, they took photographs with their phones to be sure that, upon leaving, everything was exactly as it was when they entered. Charice had reminded them ad nauseam that this Harrison man was exceedingly particular.

As before, their search was fruitless. Expecting the lack of results from this foray, they came prepared to set up video and audio surveillance. They installed a tiny camera in the upper corner of the closet, securing it to a metal bracket that once held a sliding door. Mounting the transmitter, small though it was, presented a challenge to avoid detection by a fastidious person. Once that was successfully accomplished, they attached a microphone, the size of a tiny button, to one of the lamps on the side of the workbench. A second one was placed in the binding of one of the books on the first shelf above the workbench.

While the monitoring devices would take the guesswork out of their mission, it would be even more helpful if they had a complete description of what they were looking for, besides a rough drawing and Charice's vague "it's so small, it could be hidden almost anywhere."

Back in their car two blocks away from the house, they tapped into the camera and microphones when they saw the young man return to the house with his dog and the older guy. All they could hear were very distant murmurings. The men looked at each other; perhaps they had made a mistake by not placing a couple of listening devices elsewhere in the house. They may need to make another visit to install additional equipment.

"Should we hook up the computer to start recording?" the one in the passenger seat asked.

"We can do it later. Sounds like we need to move the microphones."

"Good, the movie starts soon."

They headed toward the cinema where they'd become regulars. En route, the driver called New York.

"We have installed the surveillance equipment," he said.

"It's about time!" the response was barked. "Keep in mind, time is a factor. You are being paid handsomely. I expected this to be done in a matter of days, not weeks. How often do you need to be reminded?"

The Italians looked at each other and rolled their eyes. How often did they need to be reminded of the terms of their contract? Highly trained contractors such as themselves only needed to be told the details of their mission once. Micromanagement never sat well with them. Give them the task and get out of the way; that was their modus operandi.

They were not cowed by the American's arrogant attitude. The pair were getting paid handsomely by two different clients for the same job. They knew who the winners of this game were.

Chapter 28

After class concluded and the students' questions answered, Matthew, John, and Louis returned to Matthew's car in silence. Louis hopped into the back seat without hesitation, as if he were getting used to his new routine.

"So, no one else knows about what you have accomplished," Matthew resumed his questioning once they left the parking lot. It was a statement and not a question. John was so secretive that Matthew felt comfortable making the statement. He left it up to John to correct him if he was wrong.

"The three watch companies know something about it."

John might have been commenting about the weather or about the contents of his refrigerator. There was no sense that he had any appreciation of the significance of his revelation.

"Come again?"

"I said, three watch companies know about the development. Well, they know something about it, not the details."

Matthew was so stunned by the revelation that he stared at John, but then he had to slam on the brakes when he almost plowed into the rear of a car stopped at a light.

"John, how did they find out about it?"

"I told them."

Up to that moment, John seemed to be obsessed with the need for total and complete secrecy regarding his project. Yet, he had willingly told others, presumably complete strangers, about his invention?

"Who did you tell?" Not that Matthew expected to know anyone in the watch industry, as he didn't even know any company names.

"Three companies in Switzerland."

Trying to concentrate on his driving, Matthew was incredulous. "You met with three Swiss companies? How?"

"I went there and talked to them," John replied nonchalantly.

The trip to Switzerland! Matthew knew he had some notes about it, but had yet to follow up on them. He'd make that a priority.

Back at John's house, they sat in the small living room. As best as Matthew could remember, this was the first time they had a conversation of substance within the confines of the house outside of John's workroom. On the coffee table in front of them, John placed the business cards he'd been given by the various attendees at his three meetings in Switzerland and described, in broad strokes, how Suzanne helped to orchestrate the trip.

Since John's revelation, Matthew's brain functioned at warp speed. He did not need to know much about watches to estimate the potential financial implications for a watch company to incorporate John's creation into their product lines. Even more so, having sole rights to the invention might be an added benefit should it prove as impactful as he claimed.

John gave an overview of the presentation he had made to the three companies, which, for the most part, was a rehash of what he'd previously explained to Matthew. Much of the other material was techno-speak that jetted over his head. Matthew knew it wouldn't serve the investigation's purpose to gain a complete understanding; he was more interested in the financial implications of John's system to a watch company's bottom line. John clarified Matthew's question by saying that his intention was for his development to be open-sourced. He wasn't interested in an exclusive arrangement with a single company as the sole proprietor of the invention. Rather, he wanted anyone with a desire to utilize his movement to be able to do so.

As if struck by a lightning bolt, Matthew had clarity. There it was: the motive. He could not be certain, but he sensed that the invention had the potential to revolutionize the watch industry. It was reasonable to assume that millions of dollars were at stake. The potential demand for such a revolutionary watch movement could be intense. What he did not know was whether the competition between watch companies could rise to the point of murder. He was surprised when John said that only three companies had expressed any interest in his project.

"But why so little interest?"

John shrugged his shoulders. "I don't know. Suzanne thought it was because they didn't know me. Maybe they were not convinced enough to spend any of their time with me. She tried to contact several other watch companies, but they wouldn't take her call."

Matthew was amazed. Suzanne never discussed anything about their trip to Switzerland. He suspected she chose to respect John's overwhelming desire for secrecy, a reasonable decision as Matthew and her relationship had nothing to do with watchmaking.

Given what he knew about John, he thought it would be fascinating to ask about the details of the trip. How had Suzanne managed to get John to fly to Europe in the first place? Once there, how did she manage the journey in view of his numerous restrictions? Those kinds of questions would be for another time; Matthew needed to stay on task.

"So no one was interested?" he asked.

"One was." John pointed to the business cards emblazoned with the logo of the Zeller watch company.

Again, Matthew was surprised by the lack of enthusiasm. Could the watch companies be so shortsighted as not to see what even someone with no knowledge about watches whatsoever could clearly visualize? This had to be a gold mine. Or so he thought. Except that making it open source would mean anyone could replicate it. As far as motive, if there was only one company in the running to bid on the movement, what would be the reason to threaten John, much less do away with him?

"Someone from the Zeller company called me. Two times I received calls," John continued. "They seemed like they were interested, but I haven't heard from them since."

"Who were they?"

"It was two different men. This was one of them." John picked up the card for the head watchmaker, Michel Rousseau.

"And the other one?"

"He wasn't in the meeting."

As Matthew reviewed the cards, he noted that a woman was listed as a co-CEO. That meant there was another person in a leadership position. "Could I use your laptop?"

No sooner had the words left his lips than Matthew realized he may have crossed a line. John suddenly looked unsure and seemed to disengage from the conversation. Clearly, his computer held secrets precious to John. Asking to use it wasn't the approach he should have taken.

"Actually," Matthew back-pedaled. "I can do this on my phone." He pulled out his phone and googled the Zeller company. Matthew's thick fingers made typing on the phone challenging; a computer keyboard was so much easier, but not at the expense of causing a meltdown. After several attempts, Matthew was finally able to access the Zeller company's website. There was no information available about the company's corporate structure. With a bit more searching, he found pictures of two of the people whose cards John had on the table. After a little more time, he found an article about the brand's co-CEOs, Charice Bonet and her brother Jean-Louis. Matthew showed John pictures of the sister and brother. He recognized the sister but had no memory of Jean-Louis.

John permitted Matthew to borrow the business cards only after he promised to return them first thing the following morning. After a quick search on the computer back at his apartment, Matthew saw that the three companies they'd visited were close to each other within the city of La Chaux-de-Fonds, the watchmaking capital of the world, he soon discovered.

Since Switzerland was nine hours ahead of California, he sent an email to each person he had a card for. Stretching the truth, he claimed to be a private investigator seeking information about a matter involving their watch brand. Well, he submitted his PI application to the State, so the statement wasn't that far from the truth. Besides, who's going to check on him from halfway around the world?

While his leftover lasagna heated in the microwave, he received a text from Siobhan: "Nothing new to report. Used different software. Got the same result—email from Bern or the immediate vicinity."

While he appreciated that she didn't use emojis or abbreviations, he would have preferred better news. As he struggled to type a question, another text from her appeared: "No response to my email."

Thankfully, she answered the question he was struggling to ask. Against his better judgment, and only because it was easier, he gave a thumbs-up emoji.

Matthew tossed around his options while eating dinner. John's friend seemed to be a missing puzzle piece; it was just too coincidental that this person who emailed from Switzerland was helping John create a monumental, potentially world-shaking timepiece. However, if so, why hadn't he made it and presented it to the local watch companies? Why use John as an intermediary? He'd need to communicate with this person to gather any information that would fit the puzzle he was trying to assemble. As important as it was to question this friend, though, it was equally critical, at least for the time being, that John not discover this avenue of investigation. He had no idea how John would react to the concept of Matthew deeply delving into his past.

Well aware of the volume of emails that choke every inbox daily, most of which were unwanted trash, he decided to set up an email address that would grab attention and have a better chance of being read—his email would come from MDAInvestigativeServices. The MDA was Matthew Daniels and Associates. He wasn't clear who his associates were, but at least it looked impressive.

He did not have a name to go with the .uk email address, but he couldn't go with "to whom it may concern" for a salutation. That was already a problem. Anyone reading those first words would immediately delete his email. Instead, he typed into the subject line: "To be read by the friend of John Harrison." That should grab the addressee's attention. In the body of the email, he wrote:

> *I am a private investigator hired to do a background check on a young man by the name of John Harrison. As part of this investigation, I was made aware that you have known Mr. Harrison for a period of time. It is, therefore, my hope that you will be willing to provide some vital information to assist us. Unfortunately, I am not at liberty to disclose the details of the investigation, but a prompt response would be greatly appreciated. As an addendum, I strongly request that Mr. Harrison not be informed of this communication. The needed information is only for background purposes. Rest assured, he is not the target of a criminal investigation nor in any jeopardy. We have no desire to cause any distress to Mr. Harrison in any fashion and ask for understanding and cooperation.*

Chapter 29

His brain was on fire. Back when he was on the Force, he could rely on the quiet of the night to free him from distraction. He'd wake up with a revelation in a case he was investigating, jot a note down on the pad he kept on his nightstand, and fall back to sleep. In the morning, he'd feel clear about what to do next, what lead to follow up on, and what direction to pivot an investigation.

That wasn't happening with Suzanne's murder. His brain was on fire, but clear thoughts eluded him. Despite the churning in his head, nothing came to him, neither ideas nor sleep.

The first item of business for Matthew the next morning was to check his new email account. Nothing. To be sure, he checked the sent box to reconfirm that the message to John's friend had successfully transmitted. It had.

Disappointed but still hopeful, he called Brown.

"You know," Brown said after Matthew updated him. "It's all interesting. And, yeah, I get it that John's invention could potentially be valuable for someone. But I'm having trouble connecting the dots between the Swiss watch industry and this homicide. Why and how could anyone overseas be a threat to the victim?"

Matthew winced at the word "victim." He had to remind himself that's what Suzanne was to Brown. "I don't know. But my gut is telling me if we look deeper in that direction, we'll find the connection. What do you think about contacting the people on John's business cards?"

"No can do on my end, buddy." Brown laughed. "I'm not looking to walk into an administrative buzzsaw if anyone complained. Could you New York cops just call citizens of other countries without approval from the higher-ups?"

"Of course, not." Matthew sighed. He knew better, but he hoped that maybe things would be different out here.

"Of course, you, Matthew, as a private citizen, can contact anyone you choose."

"Which, I have. Just waiting for a response." Matthew decided to forego, for the moment, mentioning anything about the fictitious Matthew Daniels and Associates Investigative Services and his liberal claim of being licensed in the email sent to John's friend.

After hanging up, Mathew checked the time in Geneva. It was early evening. He knew nothing about the Swiss work ethic but decided to make a few calls and see if he got lucky. At random, he selected two of John's business cards.

Swiss phone numbers had more digits than those in the US, and there was a + sign he didn't understand. With the help of a Google search and after a couple of failed attempts, he successfully completed a call and, after several rings, was greeted by a recorded message—in French. Supposing the message was asking for a name and return number, he waited for the predictable beep, then left a message in English, identifying himself as an investigator who needed to speak to someone "regarding a matter of importance."

Wondering if the recipient would understand his message, he dialed the number from the second card. It was to a team member at a different watch company. This time, he successfully completed the call on the first attempt, but the result was the same as with the first one. He left the same message. The two tries were enough to convince Matthew that the employees in the Swiss watch industry were very obedient to the dictates of the workday clock. Five o'clock and out, he assumed.

He headed out to return the cards to John, as promised.

Jacqueline and Dahlia were sitting on the sofa when Matthew let himself into the house. Several sheets of paper were laid out on the coffee table in front of them. Matthew glanced at them as he stepped over to say *hello* and realized the papers were an employment agreement. Dahlia's trial run was apparently successful, and she had passed muster. Jacqueline was hiring her as John's companion. Matthew wondered whose muster she had passed. There was no evidence that John cared for Dahlia. Had they spent any time together to get to know each other? He couldn't imagine it. Dahlia simply represented a warm body that met the need, leaving Jacqueline free to go about her life without the added stress of having to deal with her brother any more than the trust required.

As usual, Matthew had to knock on the workroom door several times to get a response.

John unlocked and cracked open the door just enough to peer out, as he had the first time Matthew interacted with him. Once seeing who it was, he let Matthew in. Obviously, John's reticence was directed toward the unwanted visitor in the house, Dahlia. Matthew wondered how John would fare without a companion. As far as he knew, John had never lived alone nor been allowed to fend for himself. That might be an interesting experiment or a terrible idea. Either way, it wasn't for him to suggest.

John quickly shut and locked the door behind them. He immediately returned to his chair by the workbench, leaving Matthew to sit in the only other option available in the room, an adjustable steel stool on wheels.

John had been working on the computer. There was a CAD drawing on the screen, which Matthew guessed represented some component of the watch John was building.

"Were these all of the ones given to you?" Matthew asked as he handed back the business cards.

John, not making eye contact but rather looking at the cards and putting them back in order, nodded. He seemed nervous. Was Dahlia's presence in the house causing his agitated state?

"I received cards from everyone who attended the meetings," John said.

"And there were three meetings, correct?"

"Yes." John gave a brief overview of the meeting schedule Suzanne arranged for him.

If Suzanne made the contacts and arranged the meetings for John, that meant people in Switzerland knew who she was. People in the Swiss watch industry. "So she spoke to the people there? Or just through email?"

"Both."

"And did she attend the meetings with you?"

"Not in the rooms with me. I spoke alone. But she would come with me to the companies and would wait in the lobby."

Matthew nodded. "Did she meet, in person, any of the people you spoke to?"

John shook his head. "I don't think so."

"OK. So, Zeller was the company that expressed interest. Did either of the other companies give you any indication why they were not interested?"

John shook his head again.

"I know I asked this yesterday. Two men called you from Zeller. One was the head watchmaker. Are you sure you don't remember who the other one was?"

John stared straight at the business cards. "He said he was the person on the phone during my presentation. Someone couldn't attend, so he called in and listened to me." He crinkled his eyes, as if he was trying to focus on something in the distance. "Maybe the same last name as this one." He pointed to Charice Bonet, the co-CEO.

"Could it have been Jean-Louis?" Matthew remembered the co-CEO's name from the website.

Again, John looked at a point in space, then squeezed his eyes shut. After several seconds, John's head slowly bobbed up and down. "Yes. I believe that was him."

"Do you remember when he called you?"

"Twenty days after the meeting."

Matthew had no doubt regarding the accuracy of John's response.

"The meeting in Switzerland took place about eight weeks before Suzanne passed?" Matthew needed to confirm the information while being gentle with his choice of words. He was still unsure how John would react to the brutal details of Suzanne's murder. "And this call was about three weeks later? What was the purpose of the call?"

"They said they were interested in my project and were going to draw up a contract. They said they wanted exclusive rights to the movement. I told them I wanted it to be open-sourced. We called them back a few weeks later, and they said they were still interested and were working on a contract. I haven't heard from them since."

"What about the other two companies?"

"No word."

"Did you try to call them?"

John shook his head. "I decided to make the news of the project public. She helped me arrange meetings with three reporters to share the news with them. I was to meet them the day after..." His voice seemed to catch. He looked down at his hands, not finishing the sentence.

By "she," Matthew surmised Suzanne. He was surprised by the inflection in John's voice. It was the first sign of a definite emotional response regarding Suzanne's death. Now he knew what John meant by the meetings and the reporters Siobhan had connected with.

He would need to try contacting someone at Zeller as the next step. Though not today. No one was likely to be at work at this time of the evening in Geneva.

"John, hypothetically, is it possible that someone is trying to steal your movement?"

"Why would they? I intend to make it available to anyone who wants it."

"I know, but maybe someone has other ideas, and they want to keep the technology to themselves. Do you think the movement is safe here?"

John cast a glance at the bookshelf and then turned back to face Matthew. He waited a beat before answering. "It's fine where it is."

Jacqueline had already left when Matthew came out of the workroom. Dahlia was in the kitchen preparing, he assumed, a meal for John. Had she made any effort to befriend John? Would she? Did she understand the challenges she faced trying to establish a relationship with him? If so, did she have a plan for breaking the ice with him? He highly doubted Jacqueline provided much in the way of suggestions.

He was tempted to share some of the insights he'd gained from Dr. Diaz but changed his mind. Really, it wasn't his place to interject, so he nodded goodbye to the woman and headed over to a café to give Stephen an update.

The place was about half full with customers occupying tables both inside and out. The majority were hunched over computers. A coffee drink of some sort and, for most, a plate with a half-eaten sandwich or pastry sat on their tables. Headphones or earbuds were de rigueur, Matthew assumed, to blot out the mind-numbing soft rock music emanating from overhead speakers.

He ordered a black coffee and approached Stephen. The table for two was strewn with notes and the obligatory laptop. Stephen looked up and nodded a greeting. Once he finished whatever he was in the middle of typing, he removed his headphones.

"So, what do you think?" Stephen asked. "Was my mom the target, or was it supposed to be John?"

"My sense is your mom was in the wrong place at the wrong time, wearing the wrong sweatshirt. I can't be sure it wasn't a random act, but I believe it was a targeted hit," Matthew paused. "Tragically, the wrong person was shot. The question remains, if the intention was to shoot John, why?"

After a pause to let that sink in, Matthew continued. "I'm sorry for being so blunt, but there was no way to soften the reality of the situation."

Stephen nodded. "So, what's next?"

"Well, if we think that John was the target, then we need to think about who could do such a thing. For sure, John's isolated existence doesn't lend credence to him having done anything to cause such animus. I mean, most homicides are committed by someone known to the victim. That seems highly unlikely with John. However, there is one factor that could be at play." As best as he could, Matthew explained the watch movement John had developed. He figured the details were not relevant to the conversation except to say that it probably had the potential of a big-time financial windfall for whoever controlled it.

"So, you think someone would want to take a potshot at John because of whatever it is that he's working on?" Stephen asked.

"If there's big money involved, it wouldn't be a stretch to think it a possibility. A big wad of money can be a strong motivation for murder. People have been killed for a lot less than what we're talking about."

"Man!" Stephen leaned back in his chair. "Now what?"

"I'm going to contact someone at the Zeller watch company. The one that expressed interest in John's work. The challenge is actually getting somebody in the know on the phone."

"Well," Stephen did not hesitate. "Maybe you need to go there."

"What do you mean?"

"I told you. I am covering the costs of the investigation with the insurance money. If you need to go to Switzerland to talk to someone, then go."

Matthew took his time answering. He wasn't used to hopping on a plane for an eleven-hour flight to Europe just to have a meeting.

Besides, he wasn't completely sold on the idea that he needed to go. "Let me try by phone."

Chapter 30

Charice was about to leave her house when her phone rang. Recognizing the number as belonging to one of the Italians, she returned to the library and closed the door.

"We just watched your guy have a conversation with another man."

"Who?"

"I don't know. He's been there a couple of times. That's not what I'm calling—"

"Then why are you calling me?"

Charice thought she heard a sigh on the other end before her goon continued. "We're pretty sure what you want is hidden in the house. When he spoke about it, he looked in a specific direction in his workroom."

"Which direction?"

"To the west, maybe? I don't know. That—"

"That's not what I meant! What was he looking at?" Once again, Charice fumed over having to do everything and think for everyone.

"Towards his bookshelves. Not sure at what. There was nothing there when we were in the room, but I guess we'll focus on that area of the room the next time we go in."

"You guess?" She clenched her phone in one hand and balled the other into a fist. "Find out who he was speaking to."

"Will do our best. He just showed up a couple of days ago. We think he's a cop. Doesn't dress like one but sure acts like one."

"When are you going to get back in there?"

"In two days. That's when—"

"Two *days!?* You can't get in any sooner?"

"Probably not. The guy will be teaching then. It's our best shot to get in there for an extended period of time. It will work, *mia bela*."

The term of endearment instantly lightened Charice's mood. She relaxed her hand and admired her manicure. "I have complete faith in you," she purred into the phone. "And I look forward to celebrating your success upon your return."

The thrill of imminent victory would be best if she could share the news, but the only one she dared speak to about it was her brother. She'd left several messages on his cell over the last two days to no avail. She still had no idea what had happened during his meeting with Golay and could only assume that no news was certainly *not* good news. If he had secured the loan, he would have taken time from his celebrations to call her.

She had a bit of time before her tardiness would upset her date with a German movie star. The evening had all the hallmarks of a delightful distraction from the stresses of the last several days. But making him wait just a little longer might make for an even more joyous reception from him.

She remained at the desk and, after trying her brother's cell one more time, only to be told his voicemail was full, she logged into the company credit card account. She knew Jean-Louis had personal credit cards but preferred using the corporate card for most of his expenses, especially those amounting to more than a slice of pizza. She reviewed the recent transactions and was surprised by the latest one. After another few mouse clicks, she had all the information she needed. She didn't have to be Hercule Poirot to know where her brother was and where he was headed. Currently, he was in a place with no cell reception. He was obviously on the run.

"Shit."

Matthew did a quick calculation. Despite meeting John early and having a short talk with Stephen, he still wasn't able to call anyone during standard business hours in Switzerland. It was early evening in there, but, with nothing to lose, he figured he'd go ahead and try Rousseau. There were two phone numbers on his card, which John had agreed to lend him for one more night. Perhaps one was to a cell phone. The first went to a voicemail where he heard the word "Zeller," which made him assume it was an office number. He hung up without leaving a message and dialed the second number.

Doubtful, he was surprised when Rousseau answered on the first ring.

"Hello, I hope you speak English," Matthew started.

"I do."

"I am a friend of John Harrison. I believe you met him a few months ago."

"Yes?"

"I'm assisting Mr. Harrison with a personal matter, and I was hoping you could supply some information regarding his trip to Switzerland."

Rousseau paused for a moment. "I will try."

"I understand your company was interested in what he presented to you."

Rousseau cleared his throat. "Mr. Daniels, I am not in a position to comment on such matters. I refer you to our CEO, Monsieur Bonet. He is the one to speak to."

Matthew expected that answer. Undeterred, he asked for Mr. Bonet's mobile phone number or the direct line to his office.

"I am sorry. Monsieur Bonet is currently unavailable. I suggest you call back, the main office number, maybe in several days."

"Is there anyone else I could speak to regarding Mr. Harrison's meeting with your company? The matter is quite time sensitive."

"I am sorry, but no." With that, the phone went dead.

Throughout his career, many people attempted to obstruct Matthew during his investigations. They were usually unsuccessful. Rather, their attempts led to him developing what he called his bullshit sensor. At the moment, it was blaring, and Matthew realized Stephen was probably right. The only way to get his questions answered with actionable information was to make a quick trip to Switzerland. There, he could interview the Bonets, Rousseau, and anyone else who attended the meeting with John. Listening to words spoken over the phone was one thing, but listening to them while studying the face of someone trying to hide the truth was a whole different ballgame.

The Italians had a few minutes before their movie started, so they stayed in their car to make another call.

"I guess this means you have news?" Sommers answered.

They passed on the same information as they'd just given to Charice, with one difference.

"We'll return tomorrow to search the house. We have the man's patterns down. We know how to get in and precisely where to look."

"Very good news, indeed." Sommers became uncharacteristically chatty in his jubilation. "You will bring it directly to me here in New York. I'll get it sent to the right people in Switzerland and then put it into production by the Sommers Watch Company."

"Yes, sure, all right." The Italians did not care about the watch movement, nor did Sommers' machinations mean anything to them. As long as the money was good, they were satisfied. Their contract with Sommers was much more lucrative than what Charice was paying them. The side benefits that Charice provided in the bedroom were nice, but they never had difficulty procuring female companionship. And, should the need arise, they could always purchase those kinds of services. Besides, it was Sommers who had arranged for them to meet Charice on Giglio, granted it was to get close enough to keep an eye on her and not take the extra side gig. But it had all worked out just fine. Soon they'd be back on their home turf, going to their favorite cinema.

With nowhere to turn, Jean-Louis had decided to fly to California to demand Harrison's invention. He had no other option. All attempts to find the funds to not only keep the company afloat but to fulfill his debt to the organization that handled the bank manager had catastrophically failed. Friends and colleagues uniformly turned their backs on him. No one wanted anything he had to offer, not even a forty-nine percent stake in the company, in exchange for a loan with a very attractive interest rate.

He was either going to force the man to give it to him, or he would steal it. No matter what, he would return to Switzerland within twenty-four hours with the movement in hand. They would immediately announce the breakthrough to the world. Once the news hit the press, investors, he was positive, would flock to his door with open checkbooks, demanding shares in the company. He promised himself he would be forgiving of those who previously slammed a door in his face. Of course, there was no way they'd get a deal anywhere close to the one he had offered previously. With the movement in hand, the promise of a flood of money was his for the asking, so he was positive Philippe would grant more time to make the final payment. Whether the movement was ready for production was irrelevant. He was sure Rousseau could handle any remaining technical issues in short order.

After a meal of three glasses of wine and one brandy on the flight, he'd been able to drift into a fitful sleep as he flew westward. In what seemed to be an instant, he was awoken by the announcement of the plane's initial approach to Los Angeles International Airport. Jean-Louis adjusted the hour hand on his watch to the local time.

As soon as he turned his phone from airplane mode, it dinged multiple times. He had twenty-seven missed calls. Most were from his sister, which he promptly deleted. He had nothing to talk to her about. The other calls were equally unimportant at this juncture. He would return them when the opportunity presented itself.

Exiting into the arrivals hall, passage through passport control and customs took longer than expected. Every time he flew to the United States, he was stunned by American inefficiency. While in line, he pulled up a GPS app on his phone and entered Harrison's address. It would take close to two hours to get to Costa Mar, once he got a rental car. It was late afternoon now. Certainly, the man would be home by then.

Chapter 31

True to his word, Stephen insisted that everything for Matthew's trip be charged on his credit card, and without second thought, he agreed to pay for Bernie to accompany him. Bernie was happy about the idea, too, but not as much as his wife seemed to be. She seemed rather eager for him to get out of the house.

Matthew was glad that Bernie was coming with him. He knew his old pal would be beneficial on several fronts. Bernie's eyes and ears would see things Matthew might not.

He flew from the Orange County airport to Newark, where Bernie joined him for the flight to Geneva. They had reservations for two nights at the Ambassador Hotel in Geneva, though Stephen assured them there would be no problem should they need to stay an extra day or two.

Before heading out, he'd managed to reach a representative from one of the other watch companies who had attended John's talk. She agreed to meet Matthew, and, surprisingly, said she'd send a car to transport him and Bernie to the manufacturer from their hotel the following morning. As welcome as that news was, even better was a response from John's friend that had suddenly appeared in his inbox when he took a break from packing.

The note was brief and to the point: *I'd be willing to meet with you should you ever come to Switzerland. Otherwise, I'm afraid it could be quite difficult to answer your questions.* Obviously, the man didn't realize Matthew would be willing to travel. As rapidly as possible, given his inefficient typing capabilities, Matthew let him know that he was, in fact, imminently flying to Geneva. He suggested they meet the day after his arrival. Not knowing anything about Geneva, he requested that the meeting be at his hotel.

He checked his email upon landing in Newark and found a response from John's friend. He agreed to come to Geneva and meet at Matthew's hotel at nine in the morning on the day after his arrival. That was almost too easy.

And now, there they were, flying across the Atlantic. Bernie was fast asleep in the typical "O" position: head tilted back against the headrest, mouth open, lips forming an O. His snoring could be heard above the hum of the plane's engines. Matthew was glad that at least his friend was able to get some sleep. The last eight to twelve hours, he had no idea how long it had been, were a whirlwind. Coordinating with Bernie, emails, updates, packing, and getting to the airport left him little time for sleep the previous night. He was exhausted, but sleep still eluded him.

With the use of GPS, Jean-Louis was able to find Harrison's house after only two wrong turns. It was evening by the time he parked the rental car in front of it, and two maple trees blocked the streetlight, casting shadows on the front of the house. After fifteen minutes of no sign of activity from within the home, he couldn't make himself get out of the car. Although desperate to lay his hands on the movement, he was still subject to the rules of Swiss etiquette. It was impolite to barge in on someone unannounced at night. Should he wait until the morning?

However, perhaps this was not a time for politeness. The cover of darkness might be what he'd need to mask his entry, should he need to break into the house or force his will upon the man. This time, the guy wasn't going to say no to him. Of course, he'd start out politely, but if Harrison continued to be obstructive, he'd do whatever it took to get a hold of the movement.

Jean-Louis left the rental car unlocked and walked alongside the house. Didn't seem to be any cameras on the property. Harrison had never met Jean-Louis, so even if there were a camera system, the man wouldn't recognize him.

Approaching the front, he glanced at the neighboring houses; their windows were dark as well. Did everyone in this neighborhood go to bed early? Or were they out? Regardless, it was his understanding that Americans didn't care much about their neighbors. He figured he could use a sledgehammer on the front door, and no one would pay attention. Not that he had a sledgehammer.

On the porch, he tried to peer in through one of the windows. He could see nothing. Out of habit, he tried the door handle, but to no surprise, the door was locked. About to turn around to return to his car, he felt something poke his back.

Before hearing the voice, he smelled the faint stench of body odor. A sickening sweetness mixed with cigarette fumes.

"Do not turn around," a deep, soft, but matter-of-fact voice said in his ear. As if to emphasize the point, Jean-Louis felt the jab of the object push further against his lower back. Surprise rapidly morphed into panic; he found no words to respond. He began sweating and shaking. His thoughts were a jumble. There was no chance his assailant was Harrison. From his descriptions, the man was probably afraid of his own shadow. Confused, he tried to turn around, but instead was pushed against the door, his head crushed into the doorjamb.

"I said, don't turn around," the matter-of-fact tone turned bone chilling. The object pressed into him hard enough to hurt. The man had a knife!

He knew America was a dangerous place with rampant crime, but why him, why now, why here? Clearly, this was a matter of mistaken identity!

"My associates are very upset with you, Mr. Bonet. You have an obligation that has not been fulfilled, and you were informed of the consequences of such inaction."

"Who?" Jean-Louis croaked.

"You thought you could run and hide from us? The organization has a reputation to maintain. Debts must be paid as agreed upon. You were warned there would be consequences. You were granted a stay of sentence, but you decided to try to disappear."

Jean-Louis was stunned. It couldn't be. How did they find him? "I...I...I wasn't running. I'll have the money for them in a couple of days."

"Not—"

Jean-Louis heard two thuds, and the sharp poking in his back fell off. Too frightened to move, he stood, breathing in harsh spurts. Barely able to keep his knees from buckling, he waited, but nothing happened.

"Go!" a man's voice said.

Jean-Louis slowly turned and saw a man lying on the ground. Beside him lay a knife with a long, shiny blade glinting in the low light. There was no sign of movement. Beyond him, another man stood on the sidewalk holding a pistol with a long protrusion extending from the barrel. Jean-Louis knew very little about guns but had seen enough movies to figure out he was staring down the barrel of a handgun with a noise suppressor. He immediately raised his hands. His brain was so overwhelmed with terror that he couldn't fathom what was happening.

The man looked around, nodded to someone in the darkness on his left, and then turned back to face Jean-Louis. "Leave, now." The order was spoken in an accented voice that emphasized the two words. Killing someone, if that is what happened, seemed not to disturb the stranger's demeanor.

Recovered enough to start processing what had just transpired, Jean-Louis realized this man had just saved his life. "Who are you? Who is, was he? What are you doing here?"

"Not important. Just go, now, and don't look back." The man spoke with what Jean-Louis recognized as an Italian accent.

Without a further word, Jean-Louis stumbled back to the rental, trying to organize his thoughts. Barely able to see clearly, he fell into the car and headed in the general direction of the hotel he had located earlier.

Chapter 32

They had to dispose of the body and his car quickly. There was no time to deal with Charice's sniveling brother. That would be for later.

They still couldn't believe how well their luck was holding out. They had just left the movie theater when Charice called, saying she believed her brother was on his way to see Harrison in person. She'd texted photos of him and asked if they'd be willing to protect him if need be.

Of course, they would be delighted to provide the service. Of course, they didn't mean it, but fortune fell in their favor, and there he was at the right place at the right time. Since this wasn't in their original agreement, they would add the fee for this courtesy to their final bill.

What was unexpected was the man with the knife. Being professionals, they efficiently took care of the threat. They did not care who the assailant was, and his elimination was the most logical and efficient option.

As promised, the car parked in front of the hotel was waiting to take Matthew and Bernie to the watch company. Too early to check into

their room, they left their bags with the bellman and identified themselves to the driver.

Within fifteen minutes, they were surrounded by the Swiss countryside, as picturesque as seen in any of the thousands of travel brochures, advertisements, and postcards. They passed rolling hills carpeted by emerald green grass and houses with window boxes overflowing with dark red geraniums. Cows populated the pasturelands, each equipped with a bell. Even with the car windows shut, they could hear the musical clanging of their bells as the beasts grazed.

There was little traffic, yet it took an hour to reach the factory located within the Vallée de Joux. The scenery was no match for the effects of the long flight, and Matthew fell into a deep sleep for most of the drive.

Upon arrival at the watch manufacturer, a receptionist welcomed and escorted them to a small conference room on the first floor. Placed on the table was a platter of croissants, pastries, and coffees. Not one to demure, Bernie asked for a coffee and helped himself to a chocolate croissant. Matthew accepted the offer of an espresso and waited for whoever was going to meet with them.

Ten minutes after the appointment was scheduled, so much for Swiss promptness, they were joined by a young lady from the company's design department who introduced herself as Renée. Matthew and Bernie identified themselves as investigators working on a matter involving Mr. John Harrison and were relieved that Renée did not request to see their credentials.

"Due to the sensitive nature of the case," Matthew added. "We are not at liberty to disclose the details of our investigation. Rest assured, our inquiries do not involve any direct involvement of your company." Without allowing Renée the opportunity to ask questions, Matthew pressed on with the interview. "Were you in the meeting with Mr. Harrison? Are you familiar with his presentation?"

"I was."

"Was your company interested in the movement?"

"Oh, absolutely interested." After a brief pause, she continued. "However, the team decided we couldn't pursue it."

"Why?"

Renée smiled and knit her brows together at the same time, as if she thought the question was odd. "The expense!" She laughed. Matthew and Bernie exchanged glances, which apparently told her they hadn't a clue what she meant. "Creating a new movement and putting it into production requires a significant investment of time and money. Even though Monsieur Harrison's description was devoid of details, it was evident that the company would have to spend a considerable amount of time on engineering and design to study his proposal. We would need to do a step-by-step analysis to evaluate the accuracy of his claims and the marketability. Once that was done, if we found it warranted further development, the next step would be to build several prototypes. Then and only then, if the prototype passed rigorous evaluation, we would consider entering the production phase."

"That's a lot of ifs." Bernie chose another croissant.

"Exactly," she nodded. "And, before the production schedule could be developed, the marketing department would have to assess customer demand. Meanwhile, the finance department would have to conduct a cost analysis, create a budget, and ultimately calculate an initial unit price. After all of that, we would need to consider how and when to produce the components of this new model, which would require either creating new machines or retooling current ones, and this, in turn, would affect the production of other models. Only after all the departments had given their input, the leadership would make a final decision as to whether or not to produce the watch."

Matthew and Bernie sat speechless. Matthew was stunned by her description of what it took to introduce a new watch to the market. He assumed Bernie was equally impressed, or maybe he was quiet because he was eating his second croissant.

"My apologies," Matthew said. "We must appear as rubes. I had no idea what goes into making a watch."

"Yes, it is quite the time *and* financial investment. And, unfortunately, our group did not feel that the return on investment penciled out in a positive fashion for the company."

"Why is that?" Matthew asked.

Renée set her coffee cup on the table. "I just explained—"

"I get that. It's a risky move, but..." Matthew pressed his fingertips together and recalled his conversations with John. Could it be his invention wasn't as significant as he portrayed it to be? He had to tiptoe around the question he wanted to ask for fear of exposing one of John's secrets. "If a watch movement was truly revolutionary, wouldn't that make it worthwhile to pursue?"

"Ah, yes." Renée nodded. "There was that, too. If it worked, why yes, it could be a huge revolution in the watch world. However, our director was concerned whether it would work as described. It would have been a huge gamble, one we were not willing to accept, particularly due to the fact that Monsieur Harrison insisted on making the technology open source. Even if it worked, we would lose the ability to be competitive enough for the watch to earn back what it cost us to put it on the market. Therefore, we could not recommend it to upper-level management."

Bernie wiped off crumbs from his shirt. "Is there any possibility someone in the company disagreed with that decision?"

Matthew appreciated the question. Maybe someone went rogue and took matters into their own hands.

Renée shook her head. "We're a relatively small company. We all agreed with the decision."

"Could you imagine," Bernie persisted. "Someone else finding out about John's work and deciding to steal it or otherwise gain access to the movement even if it meant doing so without John's agreement?"

Renée sat straighter in her chair as she mulled over her answer. "I can guarantee no one in *our* group broke our promise of secrecy. We have been working together for several years and frequently learn information not destined for general consumption. We are quite adept at keeping secrets."

Seeing nothing more to gain, Matthew and Bernie quickly reassured her that they had no suspicion of foul play involving her company. They thanked Renée for her time. She offered to have the company car drive them to their next stop, which was only ten minutes away.

At the next watch manufacturer, Bernie and Matthew found themselves in a similar conference room, accepting a coffee and Bernie helping himself to another croissant. The result of this interview was the same as the first. While not unexpected, it irritated Matthew that it took traveling twenty hours to accomplish what a video call could have achieved if he had been able to get someone on the line.

It was lunchtime. They exited the administrative offices and watched the building empty around them as people made their way to the company's cafeteria in an adjoining building. Most likely, the same thing was happening at Zeller, so going there now would be fruitless.

"When in Switzerland," Matthew said as he turned around. "Do as the Swiss do."

Back inside the building, they asked the administrative secretary for a recommendation for lunch. Courteously, she made a suggestion and arranged for a car to take them there.

"I could get used to this VIP treatment," Bernie snickered.

Chapter 33

The Zeller watch company was an eight-minute drive from the restaurant. The entrance to the building had glass walls on three sides. The reception area housed several display cases containing what Matthew assumed to be old watchmaking tools. This was confirmed by the receptionist perched behind a marble desk. She said the cases used to contain examples of the company's watches, but for security purposes, they were removed and replaced with the tools, considered much less valuable and less likely to tempt a burglar.

Matthew turned around to look out the entrance. Cement barriers placed two feet in front of the windows guarded it. Before he had a chance to ask why all the security measures were in place, the door leading out of the reception area opened, and a tall man in his early forties, blond hair pulled back in a ponytail, dressed in a T-shirt and jeans under a white lab coat, walked in and approached them.

Hand outstretched, he introduced himself as Michel Rousseau, head watchmaker. "We spoke previously. If I'm not mistaken, you are friends with Monsieur Harrison."

The handshake was perfunctory. Matthew thought he read suspicion in Rousseau's eyes. He confirmed their identity with equal brevity.

"It is a pleasure to welcome you to our manufacturer," Rousseau said. "Too few people who claim to be interested in watches make the trip to Switzerland to see how we go about building them. I wish more would do so. If they did, there would be a greater appreciation for mechanical watches.

Matthew decided not to disavow Rousseau's idea of the depth of his and Bernie's interest in the world that the watchmaker had dedicated his career to. Rousseau suggested they take a quick tour of the factory before sitting down to discuss the issue that brought Matthew and Bernie to Zeller.

They started on the first floor, where large machines, the size of SUVs, were grinding away. These CNC machines, they were told, produced cases for the watches as well as components for the movements, from base plates to the smallest gears, which were sculpted automatically by computer-driven programs. The metal blanks were sprayed with oil to minimize friction and heat during the multiple, precise grinding and drilling processes. Trays of raw and completed parts stood next to the machines.

Smaller machines were used to manufacture smaller and more specialized components. They watched one machine cough out tiny screws produced from rods of steel. In a separate room, technicians sat cleaning and polishing an endless stream of components, working with the help of loupes, microscopes, and drills that could have come from a dentist's office.

On the second floor of the three-story building, in airy rooms filled with plenty of natural light, employees sat in white lab coats, attaching small parts to what were called base plates—the foundations of the watch movement. Trays of forming watches were at each station, where several components were added and then replaced in the tray, which was then passed to the next technician in the production line. Technology, Matthew and Bernie were told, could only go so far in the production of a watch. Ultimately, a certain percentage of the watch assembly had to be done by trained staff members. The production line atmosphere belied the image that watch companies often projected of a solitary watchmaker huddled over a bench building each watch by hand, one at a time.

In the decorating department, steady-handed workers decorated the larger components and the dials. Off in one corner of the second floor was the enameling and art department, where three artists created miniature copies of paintings or photographs onto watch dials or cases. The tour solidified the validity of Renee's reasons for her company not partnering with John. Clearly, a significant expense was involved in producing a watch. An innovation such as John's would only pay out if it were successful, desired by consumers, and no one else could replicate it.

After twenty minutes, they were ushered to the third floor, which housed the design and engineering departments as well as administrative offices. Before heading to a conference room, they peeked into what Michel Rousseau called the "high horology department." Here, very complicated and higher-priced pieces were built one or, at most, two at a time by a master watchmaker. Rousseau described what constituted high complications in watchmaking, but the explanation flew way over their heads.

As was true on the second floor, the watchmakers and technicians sat in front of expansive windows with views of pastoral scenes of fields and forests. Seemingly typical for most employees, the staff sported various headphones and earbuds affording them musical isolation even though the ambient noise was barely above a whisper. The design department, on the other hand, was in the central core of the floor. The designers and engineers sat in front of large double-screened computer monitors using advanced programs to design and study each component of watch movements. There too, the quiet was impressive. Those talking did so in hushed tones.

Interesting though it was, Matthew noted that there seemed to be more empty desks and benches than occupied ones in the departments they visited. It was after the lunch hour, something everyone seemed to take at the same time. He figured the employees assigned to the empty workstations were on a break or attending to other duties in another part of the building. But what was odd was how uncluttered, almost sterile, those unoccupied areas were; it was as if no one worked there at all. When he pointed out his observation to Rousseau, the watchmaker dismissed the question without explaining.

Finally, they were escorted into a conference room that was similar to, but smaller than, the ones at the other two factories. Again, there was a tray, this time with several chocolates on it. As was apparently customary, they were offered a variety of drinks, now including wine and beer. Matthew accepted a bottle of sparkling water while Bernie selected a local beer.

Rousseau excused himself, saying he had to attend to a brief bit of business. Not hungry after their substantial lunch, even Bernie wasn't tempted by the offerings sitting in front of him. In hushed tones, they discussed what they saw on their tour. Neither had any concept of what it took to build a watch. Both knew watches could be ridiculously expensive. Neither could rationalize the price for even what they now realized to be a low-end Swiss watch. After getting a glimpse of the production process, the price tag attached to these timepieces became somewhat more understandable, although still unjustifiable, in their minds. Separately, Matthew had a better understanding of what consumed John Harrison and took up so much of his time. He appreciated the delicate nature of the work John was trying to master behind the locked door of his workroom.

It seemed that they were kept waiting an inordinate amount of time. Finally, Rousseau returned, apologizing for his absence as he sat down next to them at the conference room table. "We will be joined by Charice Bonet, the CEO of the company.

No sooner did he finish his sentence than the door to the conference room swung open and in hurried a quite attractive blond woman in a blue suit. She nodded to Rousseau as she took a seat across the table from Matthew and Bernie.

"Good afternoon, I'm Charice Bonet. Sorry for keeping you waiting, but something came up that needed immediate attention."

Matthew took the lead. "We're not inconvenienced at all. In fact, we enjoyed the break as we are starting to feel the effects of our long flight."

She gave one, curt nod. Apparently, her time was limited.

"Ms. Bonet, it is our understanding that your company is interested in a movement designed by John Harrison," Matthew began after identifying himself and Bernie as investigators from California, here at the request of a private party. They each had their New York Police Department shields in their pockets, but preferred not to display them unless absolutely necessary. Matthew's detective shield was stamped with "Retired," while Bernie somehow avoided the branding of his Sergeant's shield. If, for some reason, they needed to show their credentials, they could flash their badges, but it would be difficult to explain why two New York City policemen were investigating a private matter in California. Charice didn't come off as someone easily bullshitted.

She cast a quick look at Rousseau and then nodded at the two men. "Yes, we expressed an interest in what Mr. Harrison described. We had some preliminary discussions with him about a future partnership."

"I see," Matthew replied. "Have you drawn up any papers to formalize a contract?"

"Not as of this time. We are still looking into his project and its feasibility."

"You mean if it works?"

"That would be part of the discussion." She seemed to be making an effort to keep her face expressionless, but her eyes darted back and forth between Rousseau and the investigators.

"I was led to believe you were more than interested in Mr. Harrison's work but were quite determined to have an exclusive agreement with him. He, on the other hand, was interested in working with your company on development but expected the end-product to be open-sourced, available to anyone who wanted to use it."

Charice reached for a bottle of water on the tray in front of her and took a long drink. "I am not sure who gave you this information. As I told you, we are still in the evaluation stage. We have had some preliminary discussions with Monsieur Harrison and have found that both sides have some minor differences to iron out before we might consider drafting a working agreement. That is, once we decide on its feasibility."

"Minor differences?" Matthew repeated.

She did not respond. Instead, she glanced at her mobile phone to check the time.

Matthew wasn't going to let her go until he was ready. "Is it possible someone may have made a more direct attempt to obtain the movement?"

Her brow instantly furrowed. "I don't know what you mean."

"Ms. Bonet, I have not been completely forthright with you."

Charice cocked her head in a questioning manner.

"We believe that there was an attempt on the life of John Harrison," Matthew continued. "And, by accident, a different person was murdered."

Matthew let the news sink in as he observed Charice and Rousseau's reaction to the news. Charice's lips paled; she grimaced. It was brief, and she recovered quickly. He noticed her pupils dilated, a definite sign of anxiety. Rousseau sat impassively, but soon his right leg started pumping. What was it about the news that caused such reactions?

"Murdered?" Charice whispered. "Who? And why do you think Monsieur Harrison was the intended target?"

"I am not at liberty to disclose those details," Matthew paused for effect. "I can tell you that the victim worked with Mr. Harrison, and it is the family of that person who asked us to look into the matter."

Charice's whole face had now paled. Her carefully applied makeup couldn't mask the shock. She tried to probe for more specifics, but Matthew refused to budge, emphatically stating he was under no obligation to reveal any details to her.

"At any time did you speak to John since the meeting?" he asked.

Charice shook her head, staring at her watch. She was distracted by something, he thought. There was no need for her to stare so long at the timepiece just to read the time, especially since she had her phone on the table in front of her. Clearly, he was in control of the situation and not Charice. And clearly, she wasn't comfortable with the current arrangement. At the moment, she wasn't a suspect. Not yet. He was well aware he had no jurisdiction anywhere and certainly not in Switzerland, but he figured he could turn to the local authorities for assistance should it be necessary.

Unceremoniously, Charice rose from her chair, her hand on its back to support her. She explained she was late for her next appointment.

Matthew wanted to proceed with further questioning, but decided to let Charice stew on the matter overnight and suggested they meet the next day. He knew he was taking a chance. The delay would give Charice an opportunity to create a backstory, but he was starting to feel a bit woozy from the overnight flight and the wine at lunch. He wanted to take on Charice when he was clear of mind.

Definitely shaken, she agreed to meet them at their hotel in Geneva late the next morning. While deciding on the time, Matthew suggested she come alone. Rousseau wouldn't be needed.

"Oh, one more thing," Matthew said before anyone left the conference room. "Could I get a list of everyone who attended the meeting with John?"

Chapter 34

The following morning, Matthew and Bernie woke much earlier than planned, a result of the havoc wreaked on their body clocks by crossing so many time zones. They took a walk along Lake Geneva, admiring the cloudless blue sky and enjoying the gentle crisp breeze. Matthew had to laugh at Bernie. He was strangely entranced by the Jet d'Eau, an iconic fountain blasting water up over 450 feet above Lake Geneva. He wondered if Suzanne and John had taken the time to enjoy their trip and was saddened by the realization that there probably wasn't much time for it. How wrong it was for someone to take her life! She had so much more to experience.

When it was time to meet John's friend, they chose a table in the small plaza in front of their hotel. A waiter brought coffee, the ubiquitous croissants, and sparkling water for them. Precisely at nine o'clock, a man approached them.

"Excuse me," he said. "Are either of you Matthew Daniels?" He appeared to be in his mid-sixties, trim and fit. There was no evidence of the middle-aged bulge so familiar in similarly aged men in the States. Well-coiffed with a neatly sculpted beard, both hair and beard were brown, dusted with gray, giving him a very distinguished visage. He was dressed in a stylish gray suit with purple pin stripes. A purple tie with red highlights complemented his light blue shirt.

"Yes." Matthew stood and offered his hand. "My partner, Bernard Hopkins."

As they shook hands, Christian Schmidt introduced himself.

"I appreciate you taking the time to meet with us," Matthew started. "I hope, as a friend of John Harrison, you will be willing to assist us."

"As the father of John Harrison," Schmidt corrected, confirming Matthew's suspicion.

Matthew tried to keep his face expressionless. "We've been hired to investigate a private matter that involves John. We're at a bit of an impasse and need a better understanding of his background."

"Some context would be appreciated here." Schmidt furrowed his brows. "Why are you so interested in John and, especially, his background"?

Matthew didn't immediately answer. The fact that Schmidt had basically abandoned his son, except for anonymous email correspondences, made him unwilling to trust him. However, regardless of his opinion, as a father talking to a father, Matthew decided Schmidt should know what was happening to his son.

"Sir, it is our suspicion," Matthew leaned forward and spoke in a quiet voice. "John may have been the intended target of an assailant. We believe an innocent woman, someone who worked with John, was attacked in a case of mistaken identity. Assuming we are correct, we are trying to find out why he might have been the intended target. To do that, we need to know more about his background. He is not very forthcoming, either intentionally or because he is unaware of the details of his past. I am sure you understand the barriers we face when trying to extract information from him."

Schmidt looked irritated. "An assailant? What does that mean? Coming all the way to Switzerland, you must have more to investigate than a simple mugging."

Matthew nodded. "You are quite right. Actually, the woman was murdered. However, we believe John was the intended target. It was dark, and she was dressed similarly to him."

Schmidt sat back in his chair and pulled at his chin, clearly stunned.

Matthew and Bernie, with notepad in hand, waited and watched as a somewhat pained expression crossed Schmidt's face. His posture softened.

"What do you want to know?"

"Anything you can tell us."

"I suppose from the beginning then?" Schmidt smirked. "I was born in East Berlin in the late fifties, but my father moved our family to Bern in 1960 to escape the Communists. He founded an industrial design company on the outskirts of the city; it is still in business. Much larger now, it is an international supplier of machine components for various industries." He waved a hand through the air. "Including the watch industry."

"Are you part of the company?" Matthew asked.

"Now. Of course, my father wanted me to follow in his footsteps, but I wanted to find my own way. I went to California with some vague notion of using my newly minted engineering degree to create my own business. California in those days was a wild and glamorous place. I guess you could say I got caught up in the lifestyle. I spent most of my time going from party to party. At one of which, I met a woman named Brenda Alves." His voice softened. "In short order, we were seeing each other regularly, and soon, Brenda became pregnant with our son."

"Go on." Matthew really wanted to learn about John. However, the man seemed to need time to set the scene that had played out over twenty-seven years ago.

"I had fallen in love with her. We moved in together. I rented a small apartment south of Los Angeles, in Manhattan Beach."

"Did you work?"

"Soon, Barton, as we named him, was born." Schmidt ignored the question. "It didn't take long to realize he had some developmental problems. He didn't make eye contact with either of us. He was able to nurse but had trouble accepting solid foods. He made high-pitched noises whenever he got upset and never made the cooing sounds typical of newborns. The pediatrician shared our concerns but was unable or unwilling to make a conclusive diagnosis because of Barton's young age. Only later did he confirm a diagnosis, autism spectrum disorder."

Schmidt picked up his glass of sparkling water.

"So, when you found out that there was something wrong with Barton, is that when you left Brenda?" Matthew asked.

Schmidt almost choked on his drink. "God no." After recovering, he continued. "No, I wanted to stay and help. I was in love with Brenda *and* Barton. I would have done anything for the two of them." Sitting back in his chair, Schmidt almost whispered. "I never wanted to leave."

Matthew wasn't following. "But you did."

"Yes, I did. I had to come back to Switzerland."

"Why? For work or your father's company?" Matthew remained perplexed.

Schmidt once again ignored Matthew's question. Thoughts of a distant past clearly enveloped him. "When I realized I had to return to Switzerland, I was an emotional wreck, and Brenda was crushed. She moved out before I left."

Bernie scribbled rapidly, trying to get everything down.

"But why did you have to go back to Switzerland?" Matthew pressed.

Schmidt inhaled long and deep. Matthew could tell, hard as it may be, that Schmidt was telling the truth. "Brenda is an incredible woman. So sweet. So giving. She is such an amazing woman, I would have given anything to stay in California."

Matthew noted how Schmidt was speaking about John's mother in the present tense. If Jane Doe were John's mother, clearly Schmidt had no knowledge of her fate.

Now it was Bernie who jumped in. "Then why didn't you?"

"I had to come back. I had no other option. You see, I was already married."

Jean-Louis could tell Charice wanted to reach through the phone and throttle him.

"What the hell are you doing in California?" she yelled.

Still shaken, he managed to control his tears, but he was teetering on the edge of sheer panic. The hotel room was small, and it lacked the usual luxury amenities he was accustomed to. He glanced at the room door to reassure himself that the desk chair he had propped under the doorknob was still in place. Unfortunately, the hotel did not have any rooms without a balcony. The sliding door was locked, and a security rod that he felt was too flimsy was in the track to prevent it from being pried open from the outside.

He huddled fully clothed under the covers. Four bottles from the minibar stood empty on the nightstand. Two had contained whiskey, and the other two gin. He gripped one still half-filled with vodka, waiting for a pause in the conversation to down the remaining contents. Weakly, he answered. "We need that movement. No one will lend us money. I offered a large stake in the company, but no one took the offer. We can't wait any longer if we're going to survive."

He took a gulp. After hearing no response from his sister, he pleaded. "If I get the movement, we can market it right away and get credibility. I guarantee that with that thing we will attract investments and our problems will melt away in no time."

He could hear Charice breathing—strong, long inhales and exhales. "We don't even know if that thing works. I spoke to Michel, and he was cautious about committing to it until he could examine it and test it."

"Right now," Jean-Louis shot back. "I don't give a damn if the thing works or not. Get the news out there, and it will create enough of a buzz that people will be falling over each other to get a piece of the action. But it's got to be now. We have no time to wait."

"Oh," there was a shift in Charice's voice. Possibly, she could see the logic of his argument, he thought. "Jean-Louis, get on the next flight and come back." It didn't sound like a request, but an order. "Do not go near Harrison again. Showing up at his house risks all sorts of questions we are not prepared to answer. Besides, I have a few tricks of my own up my sleeve."

Jean-Louis remained paralyzed. If he flew back to Geneva, what was to prevent the contract killers from coming after him there? If they could follow him to Southern California, he was positive they were still watching him and knew his every move. He was convinced they would make another attempt on his life at the next opportunity. He needed to get the balance of the money he owed them *now*. It was either get the cash by any means or face a horrible end. To hell with his sister, Zeller, or Harrison, survival was his only objective now.

"Did you hear me?" Charice asked.

"Yes."

Chapter 35

"Did you ever tell Brenda about your marriage?" Bernie asked Schmidt.

"I couldn't." Schmidt shook his head. He stared at his fisted hands. "I wasn't in love with my wife. To me, our marriage was a product of youthful indiscretion. I met her when I was in college; she was a waitress at a local restaurant. I married her to piss off my father. I was worried that telling Brenda about the marriage would end any chance of us having a life together. Had she been willing to come to Switzerland, I would have figured something out."

A sad smile came to Schmidt's lips, but he couldn't mask the pain in his eyes. "She is so beautiful." Schmidt paused to collect himself and then continued his narrative. "I kept renewing my visa to stay in the States, but eventually, I had to return to Switzerland. With no other employment options, I agreed to work for my father, who instructed me to meet with some business associates in San Francisco before returning to Bern. While there, I decided to set up a trust for Barton. I desperately wanted to help Brenda in any way I could. She refused any money from me, but I knew she wasn't in a position to provide for everything I figured Barton had to have, certainly not for the long haul."

"I see." Something didn't sit right with Matthew. "Why didn't Brenda want to come?"

"She was in the process of arranging the services she was told Barton needed to manage his condition. I had no idea about the availability of such therapies at home. She was determined to provide whatever Barton required as soon as possible and was unwilling to risk any gap in that care. Besides, why uproot her life to move halfway across the world to a place where she didn't speak the language with a man who had, so far, refused to talk marriage?"

"Got it." Matthew nodded. "So, you had a trust executed."

"Yes. An acquaintance recommended an attorney. I met with him, and he drew up the paperwork. Brenda never knew what I did. Once that was done, I felt a bit better, I guess. But not really."

Matthew squinted his eyes at him, intentionally letting the man know he was being evaluated. He glanced at Bernie, wondering if his friend was thinking what he was thinking.

"So, just curious," Matthew said. "Why nothing for Jacqueline?"

"Excuse me?"

"Your daughter?"

"I don't have a daughter."

"Jacqueline Henderson isn't your daughter?"

Schmidt blinked at Matthew a few times before the expression on his face changed, as if he suddenly remembered something. "Angela's daughter?"

"Yes, you and Angela—"

"Were a mistake. I had met Angela before I knew Brenda. I ran into her again after Brenda moved out. She was a shoulder for me to cry on. Foolishly, I spent a night with her, something I regret to this day." He stopped talking. It was apparent that all these years later, the pain of those memories remained evident. As if he still felt the need to justify his actions of so long ago, he continued. "I was in such a state of depression, I guess you could say I used her for comfort. Maybe she took pity on me. I don't know why, but it happened."

"She became pregnant?" Matthew prodded.

"The day before I returned to Switzerland, I got a call from Angela informing me she was pregnant."

Bernie looked up from his scribbling. "That must have been quite a shock. Is that when you modified the trust?"

Slowly, Schmidt shook his head. "I was stunned by the news because I didn't think it was a possibility. I didn't believe her. I thought she was trying to pull something. You know, a woman scorned kind of thing."

Bernie knitted his brow slightly. "Why do you say that? It's not a rarity, one and done. Happens a lot, one fling and then you're on diaper patrol."

Matthew bit his lip to prevent himself from grinning at Bernie.

"Yes, I know that, now," Schmidt said softly. "But, I am not supposed to be able to have children. That was one of the issues between my wife and me. Not the only reason by far. She was constantly pissed off at me. My wife wanted children in the worst way. When we couldn't conceive, I had tests. When I was a kid, I had the mumps. The doctor told me the illness left me with an extremely low sperm count, to the point of virtual sterility. Nothing I could do about it."

"But you say John is your son?" Matthew questioned. The story was getting quite convoluted. He hoped Bernie was keeping up.

Schmidt's jaw jutted out as he answered. "Barton, or John, *is* my son. I am sure of it. Miracles do happen. Brenda swore to me she hadn't been with another man for at least a year before me. Besides, Barton looks like I did at his age when I last saw a picture of him. We never had him genetically tested, but I'm sure of it and so is Brenda."

"And you're sure lightning didn't strike twice with Angela?" Bernie asked.

"I'm sure. Aside from my condition, it was too soon after we'd been together. When Angela told me she was pregnant, I was hours from leaving the country. I was stunned. Again, I was certain the child wasn't mine."

"So, if you didn't change the trust once you found out Angela was pregnant, how did Jacqueline get to be executrix of it?" Matthew asked.

Schmidt stared at Matthew. It was his turn to be confused. "I don't know what you mean. Over the years, I received several calls from Angela. She told me about the child, a girl, and had asked for financial support. At first, she asked, but over time it became a demand. Ultimately, I stopped answering her calls, and eventually, she must have gotten the message because she stopped calling. So, I knew about the girl, but I still don't believe she was mine, and I absolutely did not make any modifications to the trust. In fact, I have not spoken to the lawyer since I originally signed the document."

Although primarily relying on Bernie's scribbles, Matthew had been making a few notes of his own, but now put down his pad and pen. He fixed his eyes on Schmidt's. "Jacqueline is, theoretically, your daughter or at least Angela's daughter. She became executrix of John's trust when his mother disappeared. I was told that was per the instructions in the trust."

The tables turned; Schmidt looked shocked. He grabbed at the edge of the table as if to steady himself. "What do you mean, Brenda disappeared?"

"She went missing four years ago." Matthew thought it best not to discuss anything related to Jane Doe in San Bernardino. "To date, we've been unable to find out why she left or where she is currently."

Slowly, Schmidt recovered his composure.

"I have no idea who Jacqueline's father might be, and I certainly did not amend the trust." Schmidt repeated slowly and definitively, emphasizing each word. "When I returned to Bern, I tried to keep in touch with Brenda. She was so dedicated to the boy. She even got a tattoo of a heart with the letter B in the middle."

Matthew sat back in his chair. He was still trying to process the revelations about Jacqueline.

"So you stayed in touch with Brenda after moving back home?" Bernie stepped in.

"Yes. I spoke to Brenda every few months and offered to help in any way I could. I sent her money, but she didn't want it. She is an amazing woman, so independent. I kept trying to convince her to come with Barton to Switzerland, but she refused. By then, she had connected him with various therapy services and felt he was making progress. She didn't know how such a move would affect him, whether he would regress, and what it would take to obtain similar services here, especially since he wasn't a Swiss citizen. Although I understood her position, I was and still am miserable."

Watching Schmidt unload his story, Matthew had the sense this was the first time he had recounted the complete story of his relationship with Brenda and John. He needed minimal prompting to continue.

"About four years ago, my wife and I finally divorced. As soon as the paperwork was signed, I tried to contact Brenda but couldn't reach her. I was finally free to marry the woman I loved, but still, I had to deal with my businesses. I couldn't understand why she didn't answer." He pressed his hand against his forehead. "But now I know. Who is looking for her?"

"I guess, I am." Matthew felt for the man; there was no doubt his story was entirely true. He could see the pain in Schmidt's eyes and hear it in his voice. "But what about John? How long have you been in contact with him? Does he know who you are?"

"I guess he was in what you call middle school when I first contacted him, and we have been in email contact intermittently ever since. No, he does not know who I am. That's why I mask my email address. When Brenda found out I was communicating directly with him, she begged me not to tell him who I was. She told me that he had accepted the reality of life without a father at home. She worried about how he might react if faced with such an earth-shattering change in his world. It hurt, but I had no choice but to follow Brenda's request, even to the present day.

"When I learned that he had developed a fascination with watches, I realized we shared a common interest, something to build a relationship around. I have been fascinated by timepieces since I was very young. At one point, I considered returning to school to become certified as a watchmaker. He and I developed a relationship through watches to the extent that I was able to help with the development of his revolutionary movement. It is quite extraordinary, you know."

Matthew was curious to know if Schmidt thought the invention worked but figured he would leave that question for another time. Before he could ask anything else, Schmidt continued, still focused on Brenda.

"I can't believe she disappeared without a word. She loved John. She would never leave him willingly. What do you think happened?" Schmidt's eyes pleaded for answers.

Matthew could see that the reality of the situation was overwhelming Schmidt. He paused to give the man time to collect himself, then, after a suitable interval, he steeled himself. "Mr. Schmidt, unfortunately, I have terrible news. We believe there is a possibility, a definite possibility, Brenda is dead."

Schmidt stared at Matthew, mouth ajar. Had he not been sitting, Matthew was sure he would have collapsed. He described the Jane Doe situation and mentioned they were awaiting confirmatory testing. Then, doing his best to avoid specifics, he gave an overview of what was known about the circumstances of her death.

Over the course of his career, Matthew was required to deliver news of the death of a loved one too many times to count. Even an experienced homicide detective never grew immune to the crushing blow such news had on the survivors. Such was the case with Schmidt. Matthew could see a mask of deep grief cover his face. His sophisticated, urbane façade crumbled, leaving an old and lonely man.

Schmidt sat staring out at the lake. When he reached for his glass of water, his hand was notably shaking. The cool and collected demeanor he projected had been shattered. "Does my son know?" he eventually uttered, almost in a whisper.

Matthew shook his head. "No. He still believes she left him but doesn't know why. In fact, he blames himself for her disappearance. We thought it best not to tell him the truth yet. We want to confirm her identity before we even think about telling him."

Schmidt nodded in agreement. "But what was she doing in the mountains?"

"We believe she was hiking."

"She hated hiking. She never went to the mountains, especially not to go on a hike. In her way of thinking, a hike was a four-letter word." Schmidt's weak attempt at humor wasn't lost on Matthew. "Any time I suggested we go to a park or the local mountains for a walk, she would find a museum or theater production instead."

With so much to digest, the three men sat at the table, looking off into the distance, each lost in his own thoughts. Matthew figured Schmidt needed some time to process what he had relived over the last forty-five minutes and, worse, the news of the death of the woman he still deeply loved. But this couldn't last forever. Charice would soon be there.

"Well, um," Matthew broke the silence. "I guess you've told me everything you can."

Without a moment's consideration, Schmidt shot out of his chair as if he wanted to escape from his current reality. "How can I reach you if I need to?"

Chapter 36

The body count was starting to add up. But Sommers didn't get to where he was by being concerned about shedding some blood, figuratively or literally, of those standing in his way. The desire for the betterment of others didn't consume his social consciousness. However, despite his callous nature, he knew it was always best to avoid unwanted attention, hence drama, involving anyone even remotely connected with his business activities.

A puppet master, ultimately, is responsible for the actions of the puppets suspended on their strings. His preference was to brief subordinates regarding his objectives and goals and leave them to their own devices to fulfill his instructions. Sommers prided himself on his ability to find well-suited hirelings for the tasks at hand. Such was the current situation. He completely agreed with the Italians that micromanagement benefited no one. Rather, it tended to be a barrier to the efficient completion of a mission.

"I agree," he assured them after they reported what had happened the previous evening. "You acted appropriately given the set of circumstances."

"*Grazie.* What about Bonet?"

"Again, you did the correct thing by removing the threat." Sommers gazed at his reflection in the window. Killing Bonet may have provided a certain satisfaction, but it would undoubtedly delay his acquisition of the company for an indeterminate period. Though both Bonets were easily manipulated, Charice was, for sure, the more challenging sibling. Killing the brother might risk empowering her and perhaps making her a more formidable adversary.

"When will you return to the house?"

"Within the next twenty-four hours."

"Perfect." Sommers clicked off.

All was going well except for Rousseau getting squirrelly. Sommers had been surprised to hear about the two Americans dropping in on Rousseau and Charice. He had to assure his soon-to-be head watchmaker that he had nothing to do with the caretaker's death. Why Rousseau was so concerned, Sommers wasn't certain. He hoped it wasn't a sign of weakness in the man, or worse: that his resolve to bring the plan to fruition was cracking.

Once the Italians took possession of Harrison's creation, the Bonets would have nowhere to turn. The axe would fall, and Zeller with it, making it wonderfully ripe for the picking. The financial and associated legal documents for a bargain basement purchase price were drawn up and resting in his attorney's digital cloud, ready for action at the appropriate moment. Rousseau was confident that everything was in place for the takeover and the subsequent relaunch of the new brand. All that was left was to decide the name for the new company. Not one to shy away from broadcasting the completion of a long-held dream, Sommers Watch Company was the leading contender or something with a similar ring. He still had some time to make a final decision.

Matthew and Bernie sat quietly for several minutes after Schmidt left them. Neither noticed the clouds moving in, bringing a slight chill to the air. Bernie sorted through the pages of notes he'd taken on Schmidt's narrative. Matthew stared off at the lake, watching the water shoot from the fountain. He was able to fill in a number of the gaps in John's history, but he was far from having a complete story. Adding to the confusion was Jacqueline's back story. Her relationship with her brother, if in fact he was her brother, now came into question, not to mention her involvement with John's trust.

A gurgling noise from Bernie's stomach, audible from across the table, brought him back to the present. It had been a long time since their somewhat limited breakfast. Matthew glanced at his watch. They had about forty-five minutes before they met with Charice Bonet. "How about lunch?"

"I'm about to eat my arm. So yeah, feed me."

They ordered baguette sandwiches and Fanta orange sodas. Bernie added a piece of chocolate cake to compensate for missing a mid-morning snack.

While waiting for the food, Matthew called Brown. As the phone rang, Matthew realized he may have miscalculated the time in California. Colin was probably fast asleep.

"Am I glad to hear from you!" Brown answered. At first groggy, his voice rapidly perked up. "I was trying to figure out the time difference to call you."

Matthew snickered. Brown should be able to figure out the correct time by consulting the app on his phone. Before making a snarky remark to that effect, he realized he should have done the same. He apologized for the hour of his call. "How's it going? Any news?"

"I heard back from the lab. They are very confident that Jane Doe is closely related to John Harrison. Their confidence level is in the ninety-five percent range that she was his mother."

"Great!" Matthew was happy for the young detective; having a hunch confirmed was a way to build confidence. His idea to file the missing person's report, four years after the fact, seemed like a long shot, but as it turned out, it was bearing fruit.

"Also, I showed Dr. Friedberg the lab results, and she agreed with the interpretation."

"That's good news." Matthew nodded to the waiter, motioning to set his food down on the table.

"What's going on over there?"

"Well, I'm not sure how any of this is going to help us." Matthew set his phone down and put it on speaker. "By the way, meet Bernie, my partner."

"Hi, Bernie," Brown said. "But, uh, we may need to talk about this partner thing. I only got permission to let you consult on the case."

"Nothing to worry about. He's working on *my* case. Remember, I'm working for the deceased's son."

"Gotcha."

Matthew gave Brown a rundown of the most pertinent facts he had gleaned from the meetings at the watch companies and from Schmidt.

"I thought it was interesting that Schmidt emphasized how much Brenda hated hiking," Bernie chimed in. "Schmidt was emphatic, she would never voluntarily put her feet on a hiking trail."

"If what Schmidt said is true—"

"There's no reason to think otherwise," Matthew interrupted.

"Then what was she doing on a hiking trail hours from her house, and why so ill-prepared? Did someone else persuade her to go when Schmidt never could?"

"Both are good questions."

"Hm. Leaving the case open was an excellent bit of police work by Chin!" Brown said. "I'll get with him soon. I'm pretty sure we have enough intel now to heat up this cold case and turn it into an active homicide investigation. What do you think?"

"Agreed."

With a four-year gap and minimal evidence to work with, their realistic chances of making credible headway on the case were something neither could answer, but one could never know without trying. Brenda, John, and Christian Schmidt deserved their best efforts, of that they were certain.

"One more thing." Another glance at his watch told Matthew he was running out of time before Charice Bonet arrived. "Schmidt made matters even more interesting. He is certain Jacqueline is not his child. He found out about her long after she was born and claims he has no idea how she was designated executrix of the trust."

"That's a twist."

Shortly after they hung up, a clock outside a nearby watch retailer struck the hour. As the last chime sounded, Charice's arrival was heralded by the clicking of her heels on the pavement. Rounding the corner, she walked to where Matthew and Bernie sat. Matthew chided himself for appreciating the curves of her body.

Charice appeared calmer than when they had parted the previous day. Taking the offered chair, she flagged a waiter and ordered a glass of wine and a ham and cheese croissant.

"I hope you had a pleasant evening last night." Gone was the edge in her voice, at least for the moment.

"The pizza was fair. Better than I expected but not as good as home," Bernie told her.

Charice nodded as if she agreed. She reached for her purse, removed a sheet of paper, and slid it across the table to Matthew. "As requested, the list of the people who attended Mr. Harrison's presentation."

With a quick scan of the paper, Matthew recognized the five names listed as those on the business cards John showed him. He passed the paper to Bernie, who slid it into his notebook for safekeeping.

"I would like to know more about the investigation," Charice immediately insisted.

"What would you want to know?" Matthew asked her

"Why do you believe there is a connection to Monsieur Harrison's business here with a murder in the United States. Who was killed?"

Matthew decided there was nothing to be gained by withholding the information any longer. "The woman who was John's companion, Suzanne Lang."

Charice's right eyebrow twitched upwards for a brief second. She reached for the glass in front of her and took a long drink of wine. "I still do not understand what that would have to do with Monsieur Harrison meeting with us."

Matthew watched her eyes for the least hint of emotion. "That is what we were hoping you could help us understand. As I indicated yesterday, there is the possibility that it was a case of mistaken identity. So far, our investigation has led us to suspect the actual target was Mr. Harrison."

"Interesting."

"As far as the phone calls Mr. Harrison received from people associated with your company, you're sure you had no part in any of them?" John told Matthew the callers were men, but maybe she was a silent attendee.

"Absolutely not."

"Could Mr. Bonet have been a participant?"

Charice remained stoic. "I don't know. You'd have to ask him. Maybe you can speak with Michel Rousseau. As the head watchmaker for the company, he might have participated in any phone call with Monsieur Harrison."

"How come your brother wasn't in the first meeting with John?"

"He was out of town, so he couldn't physically be there, but he listened to the presentation over the phone." Anticipating the next question, she added: "We share leadership of our company. Jean-Louis and I have had several discussions regarding Monsieur Harrison's proposal. We remain quite intrigued, although at the same time, we continue to have a healthy degree of skepticism since it is so revolutionary."

Matthew could tell she was holding her cards very close to her chest. He was learning how tight-lipped the Swiss could be, particularly when it came to matters of business. As with any investigation, and seemingly more so with this one, he needed to find the weak link within Zeller to obtain pertinent answers. Charice wasn't that link.

"Why is Zeller interested in Mr. Harrison's discovery when no one else is in the watch industry?" Matthew asked.

Charice sat back in her chair and assumed a look of superiority. "By nature, we Swiss are generally conservative. In our industry, one that has been in existence for hundreds of years, change occurs at a very slow pace. Traditions are strong and cemented into the foundation of most watch companies. Very few people in this industry have the guts, or balls, to consider innovative changes. Witness what happened during the quartz crisis. We are the ones who developed the quartz movement but failed to appreciate its significance. Rather, it was left to the Japanese and Chinese to market the hell out of it. Our industry was nearly destroyed by our own arrogance and lack of foresight. Fortunately, there were several of us who were able to lead the way and rebuild our now robust market."

Matthew had no idea what Charice was talking about. While reading about the Swiss watch industry on the flight, he came across several references to the quartz crisis of the 1970s and early 1980s. The article confirmed it had almost wiped out the multi-billion-dollar Swiss watch industry. He did not appreciate the significance of the event until now. "So, could John's development be similar to that situation?"

Charice was noncommittal. "I don't think it will have the same kind of impact. That said, it has the potential to be a significant development. The first to bring it to market would have a major strategic advantage. The publicity it will generate will bring huge, invaluable attention to the company, not to mention a significant financial boost to the company's bottom line."

"Is your brother available to speak to?"

"He is on vacation and purposely had gone off the grid for a few days." She paused and gave him a closed-lipped smile. "I'm sure he'd be willing to make himself available to you once he reemerges."

Charice motioned to the waiter for a refill of her wine glass. She fished around in her Louis Vuitton pocketbook and produced a cigarette and lighter. Choosing tobacco over the croissant, without thought of the others at the table, she lit the cigarette and blew a long stream of smoke over Matthew's head.

Ignoring the aggressive gesture, Matthew moved on. "What will happen if Zeller does not get a contract with John, or if he decides to go in a different direction?"

Charice shrugged. "Then we move on. We believe we are the right company to work with Monsieur Harrison, but if he chooses otherwise, then so be it. Good luck to him."

Bernie looked up from his notes and studied her. Matthew's bullshit meter sounded the alarm. Her cavalier response wasn't landing with authenticity. Before Matthew could move on, he felt his cellphone vibrate. A glance at the phone revealed that the incoming call was from an unrecognized number, starting with +33. The vibration ended, and Matthew expected the phone to chime, signaling that a voicemail had been recorded, but it did not. A couple of minutes later, his phone emitted the sound of an old-fashioned typewriter, indicating an incoming text message. Matthew resisted the urge to look at his phone and returned to the conversation with Charice.

"Well, if there's anything else you can think of—" he started.

"I'll be sure to reach out." She put out her cigarette on her plate.

"We appreciate you taking the time to come to Geneva."

"It was no trouble at all. I live on the outskirts of the city." With that, she rose, turned, and strode off. Her second glass of wine stood empty while her sandwich remained untouched.

Once out of earshot, she reached inside her pocketbook and retrieved her cellphone, then disappeared around the bend of the walkway along the lake, talking into her phone. Matthew stared after her. She had worked hard to disguise her determination to acquire John's invention. He was convinced she was the sort who would go to any lengths to get what she wanted. He wondered if that included arranging a murder to either get access to the development or to prevent anyone else from benefiting from it.

He pulled out his cell to see who was trying to connect with him and read a text.

"This is Rousseau from Zeller. Please call me as soon as you can."

Chapter 37

Now what?" Bernie asked.

"That was Michel Rousseau on the phone," Matthew told him after clicking off the call. "We're having dinner with him tonight."

"Okay. But I meant, now what do we do?"

"Right. Well, I think it's time we visit the local police. Who knows? Maybe they'll have some info on the Zeller company."

"I like it." Bernie stood up. "Besides, if I remember correctly, back in the day, wasn't that what we were expected to do as a professional courtesy? Weren't we supposed to present ourselves to the local authorities?"

"Yeah, you remember correctly, if we were visiting on official business. None of this is official. We're not officers of the law any longer, so we are not under any obligation to do shit. I just hope they don't have a problem with us popping in off the street."

They used the map app on Matthew's phone to find the nearest police station, then headed out for what was promised to be a seven-minute walk.

Inside the station, they approached a uniformed officer sitting behind the reception desk. Bernie presented his NYPD shield and asked to speak to a supervisor. The officer carefully inspected it while Matthew held his breath, hoping he wouldn't have to show his. Thankfully, it must have passed muster because after a quick phone call, a man in civilian clothes entered the reception area through a side door and motioned for Matthew and Bernie to accompany him. He escorted them to his office located at the end of a quiet hallway.

Lieutenant Patrice Gauthier, the shift commander, sat down and regarded the two men from New York. Dressed in a blue suit, a pink shirt, and a blue and red striped tie, neatly coiffed and smelling of a manly fragrance, he did not portray the image of a prototypical policeman, certainly not one Matthew or Bernie knew in the States. Uniformed or plainclothes, American police officers had no sense of couture, at least not when on the job. Even the Feds they knew didn't dress so fashionably.

"When did you arrive in Geneva?" Gauthier asked.

Matthew was happy to let Bernie take the lead, since it was his shield they used to gain access. "Yesterday."

Lieutenant Gauthier scowled. "You are aware, are you not, that when arriving in a foreign city on official business, it is customary to register yourself with the local authorities before embarking on any police investigative work."

"Um, no, sir," Bernie admitted. He looked at Matthew.

"I wasn't aware either," Matthew said. "You have our apologies. We meant no disrespect." He couldn't afford for Gauthier to get angry and pick up the phone to call their "command" in New York. That was guaranteed not to go well for them.

"Sir, we are very sorry," Bernie nodded. "We are on a tight schedule and neglected the formalities. Please accept our deepest apologies."

"Such courtesies typically take minutes," Gauthier continued to scowl. "Surely, you could have spared the time. Now, how might we be of assistance?"

Bernie looked at Matthew again, then back at the Swiss police officer. "We are investigating the murder of a citizen in our jurisdiction. We have information to suggest that the victim wasn't the intended target but rather a case of mistaken identity. We have evidence that the person who was the actual target traveled to

Switzerland before the murder. During the trip, the target met with representatives of several Swiss companies. We are looking into the possibility of a connection between any of those meetings and what subsequently transpired."

"Are you suggesting a Swiss citizen was involved in a homicide in the United States?" Gauthier sounded as if he was starting to get agitated once again.

Quickly, Bernie jumped in. "No, sir. We have no evidence to suggest any Swiss citizen is directly involved, but they might have information useful to our case."

Gauthier frowned again. "You mean you flew all this way from New York just to ask some questions. I am sorry, my friends, but that seems to be a considerable waste of taxpayers' money."

Bernie shrugged. "The victim has, or had, an international profile. We are under orders to maintain a very low one as we go about our investigation. Our boss told us to do this the old-fashioned way, you know, minimal technology. Pound the pavement was our instructions." Matthew avoided looking at Bernie for fear of bursting out in laughter at his friend's creative fiction. "And besides, if you saw the tight budget we are on, you wouldn't be concerned whether the taxpayers are getting their money's worth." He smiled at his own joke.

Gauthier's face softened, and he chuckled. "If you insist. Can you tell me the names of the people you are looking to speak to? If I may?"

Matthew figured it was his turn to jump into the fray. "We have several names, but the ones we are currently most interested in speaking to are Jean-Louis and Charice Bonet."

"Ah, the brother and sister, I know of them," Gauthier replied without hesitation.

"How so?"

"The brother is a big spender and quite the playboy. Living very well off his father's money. The sister, Charice, is a cold bitch. She is the brains of the two. The word on the street is they have burned through their father's fortune and are trying to raise capital to save their watch company."

Matthew pulled out his notepad and flipped through several pages as if he were looking for the name of the company. "Zeller?" Matthew made as if he were reading from a page. He wanted to be sure the Lieutenant was playing straight with them.

"Yes. That is the one. The father built the company into quite a successful watch manufacturer, but now, its survival is hanging by a thread." Gauthier pulled a pack of cigarettes from his inside jacket pocket and lit one. Taking a deep drag, he slowly let out the smoke. Matthew and Bernie looked at each other. Smoking had been banned from station houses in New York several years ago, way before they retired. The assumption from command was that cigarette smoke was much more dangerous to the welfare of the staff than the drug dealers, murderers, gangbangers, and the like that the police dealt with daily.

Compounding the surprise of the cigarettes was the information regarding Zeller's fortunes, or lack thereof. Gauthier painted a picture diametrically opposite to the one Charice described.

"As far as you know," Matthew probed. "Have there been any reports of either of the Bonets being involved in any 'off-the-books' activity?" He curled his fingers to make air quotes even though he did not think Gauthier needed an explanation.

Gauthier thought a moment before responding. "Nothing I have heard or read about." He paused again, took another drag on his cigarette, and emitted a slight grunt. "Actually, several nights ago, the director of a prominent private bank here in Geneva was murdered in his home. We deal a lot with financial crimes, but not so much with violent ones. I'm sure you know we have a very low homicide rate in Switzerland."

Matthew and Bernie nodded.

"The Canton government is very concerned that the murder of such a high-profile member of the banking community could adversely affect the banking sector. They are putting huge pressure on the department to solve the case. Staff are being reassigned to it from across the canton. My office was asked to lend several detectives to assist with the investigation. My people have been sifting through the projects the director was handling at the time of his murder to look for any irregularities or for anything of interest. This morning, my senior detective told me the director was in the process of evaluating a number of loan applications, several personal ones and three from businesses; one to a real estate developer in Lausanne, another to a Saudi prince for hotel development in Provence, and an unsecured one to the Zeller Watch Company."

"That's interesting," Matthew said, though really, he was losing interest.

The corners of Gauthier's mouth crept up. "I am not sure how it might help your investigation, but my man went on to tell me that of all the loan applications on the director's desk, Zeller's was the only one he rejected."

Matthew and Bernie simultaneously sat back in their chairs as if they had both been blown by the same gust of wind.

"Let me tell you a little more about what brought us here," Matthew started, then went on, in very broad generalities, to explain John's innovation and its potential impact on the industry. He then added that Zeller had more than a passing interest in acquiring it.

Gauthier impressed Matthew as a bright guy with the ability to think outside the box. He took it all in, then crushed out his cigarette. He scrawled a note on a pad. "The evidence suggests it was a professional job and not a random hit. If so, the question is, was this a contract hit? If so, by whom and why? Money is often a very strong motivator for such a scenario. As I said, we have a low homicide rate here in Geneva, but financially driven murderous intent knows no geographic boundaries."

That got the ball rolling. What was supposed to be a brief meeting turned into two and a half hours as the men discussed the possibility of a potential link between the Bonets and the death of the bank director, Pierre Martin. Once they left the police station, Matthew and Bernie had only an hour to get to the restaurant to meet Rousseau.

"Good thing you still have your New York cell number," Bernie grinned. "Might have been hard to explain why a New York City cop had a California phone number."

"Right. And good thing they didn't ask for business cards." If he really was going to become the head of Matthew Daniels and associates, he should start thinking about those kinds of things.

Chapter 38

Matthew and Bernie showed up on time at the restaurant Rousseau had recommended, Le Relais de L Entrecôte, and were surprised to find themselves in a long line to get in. Matthew called Rousseau's cell, as they took their places at the end of it.

"Did you make reservations?" he asked as soon as Rousseau picked up. "We're here, but there's a line."

"Always a line. I'll be there soon."

"This better be worth it," Bernie grumbled.

"It always is," said someone who had joined the line behind them.

Rousseau still hadn't shown up by the time they were shown to a small table in a, thankfully, quiet corner.

They scanned the limited menu and listened as the waitress informed them that the restaurant was known for *entrecôte*, a specific cut of meat, covered with a special sauce, accompanied by frites.

"Special sauce?" Bernie smirked. "We have McDonald's."

"No, monsieur. Our sauce is nothing like that one."

With the main course came a salad and a bread basket. The only choice to be made when ordering was how they wanted their steak prepared and whether they wanted wine with their meal.

"Don't know why it's so hard to get a burger around here," Bernie mumbled as she walked away.

"It's not like you've gone hungry while we've been here." Matthew chided. "You've managed just fine without one."

"True, but you know what?" Bernie padded his pockets. "I forgot my notebook. You gotta pen?"

Matthew gave it to him. "Want my little notebook? Just write legibly."

"Nah. I can use this." Bernie padded the white paper covering the table.

"Yet another reason I'm glad you're here. You're resourceful."

Rousseau rushed into the restaurant, refusing the hostess's assistance, and headed to where Matthew and Bernie were seated. As soon as he took the unoccupied chair, the waitress appeared. They ordered their steak and let Rousseau handle the wine.

The second the waitress turned away, he leaned in toward the two Americans. When they had met the previous day, Rousseau seemed reserved, almost aloof. As he started to speak in a hushed tone barely audible above the din of the restaurant, he seemed to be on the verge of panic. His eyes did not rest. They jumped around, as if on alert for an imminent threat.

"You must help me," Rousseau pleaded. "He may come for me."

Matthew looked questioningly at Bernie, then turned back to Rousseau and asked: "Who?"

It was as if Rousseau did not hear Matthew. "If he killed that American woman, he could very well be arranging to have me killed, too."

"Who?" Matthew repeated.

The waitress returned with the bottle of wine. No one said a word as she filled the three glasses. Rousseau grabbed his glass and swallowed half the serving. Before he could continue, the waitress returned with salad and bread. Bernie immediately dove into the food. Rousseau paid no attention to it, swallowing the rest of the wine and pouring himself another glassful.

"Who is threatening you?" Matthew repeated.

Rousseau refused to raise the volume of his voice. "Sommers."

Matthew and Bernie blankly stared at him. "Who is Sommers?"

Rousseau ignored the question. "He hasn't directly threatened me, but if he is the one behind the woman's murder, he has every reason to come after me as well."

"Hang on." Matthew tilted his head over the table. "What woman are you talking about?"

"The one who accompanied Harrison when he came here to make his presentation."

"How'd you find out about her?"

"Charice."

Matthew frowned. Rousseau must have been whom Charice called after their meeting. He couldn't help but wonder why she felt the need to inform him so quickly.

The waitress returned yet again, this time carrying a platter of sliced steak and a mound of frites. Having had lunch ages ago and no afternoon snack, Bernie dug into the portion on his plate. Matthew cut a few pieces to sample the perfectly cooked beef. He was more interested in what Rousseau had to say than in the meal.

Rousseau continued to ignore the food in front of him, preferring to swallow down more wine. "Sommers, Carlton Sommers, is a money man. He has a company in New York called CharS Investment Group."

"What's his connection with this?" Bernie was able to get out through a mouthful of steak and frites.

"He wants to buy Zeller." Rousseau's voice was barely audible. "He has a significant watch collection, I am told, but he sees owning a watch company as the ultimate status symbol in his billionaires' boys club. Somehow, he got wind that the Bonets are in financial difficulty and approached me about six or seven months ago to work with him. My job was to keep him apprised of the Bonets and their attempts to dig themselves out of the hole they were in. I told Sommers about Harrison's invention. If the thing works and the Bonets can get the sole rights to it, they could conceivably rescue the company."

"And in so doing make his deal a lot more expensive," Matthew realized.

"That or even give them enough reason not to sell."

"So, you were a mole working to sabotage their deal with Harrison?" asked Bernie.

Rousseau nodded and grimaced. "In a sense."

"What did you expect to get out of it?" Matthew asked between bites. The first couple of mouthfuls of food made him realize how hungry he was.

"I am, or was going to be, the operational control of the new watch company. Essentially, I would serve as the Chief Operating Officer. That kind of position doesn't come around very often in this industry, especially for watchmakers. Usually, that goes to those who won the genetic lottery, you know, family members. But these days, some financial or marketing people with an MBA can be considered for a leadership position." Rousseau momentarily had a wistful expression, which passed within a blink and returned to the panic that consumed him. "It's an opportunity of a lifetime. I have so many ideas and plans for a new watch company. The offer was too much to pass up."

"But what makes you think Sommers would want you out of the way?" Bernie asked as he sucked on a piece of sauce-soaked bread.

"He figures Harrison's invention could be a gold mine. It could either save the Bonets or, at the very least, drive the company's price through the roof. Removing Harrison from the equation would be the final bullet to send the price for the Zeller company into the basement. The Bonet's situation is so tenuous that even a sufficient delay in releasing the invention, assuming it even works, would bury their ability to keep their company afloat. For all I know, he may have other ideas in play as well. I don't trust him. He's toxic. I am willing to bet he is no stranger to doing whatever it takes to get what he wants."

Matthew sat back in his chair. Somehow over the course of the conversation, he managed to finish most of the food on his plate but wasn't satiated. As he regarded Rousseau, the waitress returned with the second half of their order of steak and frites, which she wordlessly portioned onto their plates except for Rousseau's, who hadn't touched his first course. Bernie was delighted to see that the skimpy portion he finished wasn't the total of his meal. Once served, he again turned his attention to his food and dug into his steak. On either side of his plate, aside from several drippings of sauce, the paper serving as a table covering was filled with the notes he'd taken as he relentlessly chewed.

"If he is indeed behind the attempt on Harrison," Rousseau continued without prompting. "He might come after me. I know enough to get him into deep water with the authorities here and in the States. I can't stand the Bonets for sure, and I want to see them gone. But I didn't think anyone was going to get hurt, much less killed. I didn't bargain for this shit."

This was enough to confirm that Suzanne wasn't the target, but rather it was almost certainly John. It was a bit of a relief to hear that Suzanne wasn't caught up in a web of intrigue. That said, John was probably still in the crosshairs of Sommers, if Rousseau was correct. Without much to offer at the moment, Matthew emphatically suggested Rousseau get out of town for a few days. When he was on the job in New York, he could promise protection in similar situations, but there was very little he could offer to comfort the man when he was six thousand miles away. He considered giving Lieutenant Gauthier a call but had no proof of the validity of Rousseau's allegations. The one thing he knew for sure was that he did not want to create an international incident, especially when the accused was an internationally known billionaire. That was the kind of situation that could only end badly for them, at least at this stage.

Rousseau wasted no time; he said he would leave with his family immediately, then stood and left the restaurant without a further word. His plate remained full of cold food. Bernie ripped off the portions of the paper table covering with his scribbled notes and folded them up before shoving them into his jacket pocket.

"Think that's too cold to eat?" he pointed to Rousseau's untouched plate.

"Get some dessert," Matthew suggested, wondering how much weight Bernie was going to gain on this short trip.

Bernie settled for creme brûlée.

Chapter 39

Before going to bed, Bernie compiled their notes into one document. Then, on separate index cards, Matthew transcribed salient points, which he would use to establish relationships between the various players.

"You know, there's probably an app for this paperwork," Bernie smirked.

"I'm not even tempted to look for one." As Matthew reached to turn out his light, Brown called.

"Chin just called," Brown reported. Matthew could hear the excitement in his voice. "The lab tested blood samples from the rock in the evidence box, and they definitely confirmed one of the specimens of the blood matched our Jane Doe. Maybe we should start calling her by her name, Brenda Alves?"

Not wanting to crush the young detective's enthusiasm, Matthew's only reaction was: "Okay."

"Not a big deal, I know. Kinda old news." The enthusiasm grew. "But they also tested a second sample of blood from the rock. We never saw pictures of the rock, but Chin says it is a decent-sized one, about a foot in diameter at its largest point. One of the spots had several strands of hair stuck in the blood, which have been confirmed to belong to the victim. The other blood stain was about a third of the way around the rock, separate from the first. That's the one that had not been previously tested. Up 'til now, no one thought much of it. At Chin's insistence, the second sample was tested. The lab confirmed it was human blood. But, get this, the DNA isolated from that second specimen was from someone else, totally unrelated to the victim. Again, it's definitely human. No doubt. But, whoever it was from, it wasn't the deceased, nor was the person in any way related to the victim."

Matthew scratched his chin through his two-day-old stubble. Before he could say anything, Brown continued. "Chin is reopening the case officially and has convinced his boss to list it as a homicide."

"That is interesting," Matthew acknowledged. He was always dubious about coincidences. But a mother possibly murdered, and her son targeted four years later, that was odd to say the least. "Stay on it. Follow up with Chin and see what develops. I'll check in with you when I land tomorrow."

Dahlia paused before putting detergent into the washing machine. She thought she heard the front door open and looked at her watch, confused. John was supposed to be at the college now, and the car service wasn't due to bring him home for another hour or so. She hoped there wasn't a problem with him.

She left the laundry and went through the kitchen toward the front of the house. Turning the corner into the living room, she almost ran into a tall, broad-shouldered man. From his build, she figured bumping into him would be tantamount to slamming into a brick wall. He was dressed in a button-down shirt and jeans. Wearing wrap-around sunglasses, a knit cap, and a several-day-old beard, his features were hard to make out. The two stood staring at each other. Eyes bulging, mouth open, Dahlia found no air with which to utter a sound.

The intruder recovered first. He put a gloved hand up and spoke in heavily accented English. "Please remain calm. We're not here to hurt you."

Behind him, beyond the open front door, another man softly called in a foreign language that Dahlia thought sounded similar to Spanish.

Without another word, the intruder turned and casually walked out the front door, closing it on his way out.

Jean-Louis stared at the ceiling of his hotel room. He couldn't take staying here any longer. For one thing, he was starving. He'd eaten and drunk everything the minibar had to offer. All that was left was one small bottle of rum and a third of a bottle of red wine, one step above the boxed variety, vintage yesterday.

He'd been paralyzed by fear, unable to leave the room. All the alcohol the room had to offer had done very little to overcome the terror induced by the point of a blade in his back. Now, if he was going to make the afternoon return flight to Geneva, he was going to have to brave the outside world.

It was one thing to pay for someone to be killed. That was very transactional. His hands were clean, well, sort of. He was confident the organization he contracted to do the job would never disclose his association with them, but—his stomach suddenly seized—they'd have no reason to protect him if he didn't pay them in full. He was used to seeing his name in newspapers, usually in the society gossip columns. If he did not handle his current situation soon, he would again be in the papers, but in a different section, the obituary page.

Of course, he had fully intended to meet his obligation when the contract was agreed upon. And of course, their agreement wasn't documented anywhere; that would have been foolish and unnecessary. But the assailant definitely drove home, almost literally, his employer's message. He highly doubted that Philippe's organization would give up on him and write off his debt. They were going to collect the balance due either in cash or blood.

Downing the rest of the rum, he again thought of the stranger holding a silenced pistol. If not for that guy, Jean-Louis would have been the huddled mass by Harrison's front door. Of course, if neither he nor the assailant had been there at the time, he'd have the movement and been well on his way back to Geneva by now.

To overcome the growling in his stomach, he reached for the bottle of wine and downed the remaining liquid before checking for flights to Geneva. He ignored the flight out at one o'clock. There was a seat in business class on the plane departing at five, which meant he had plenty of time to get to Harrison's house. A quick visit there and he would leave with what he needed to keep his company and, more importantly, himself alive. To hell with what his sister ordered.

Quickly and as silently as possible, he took the back stairs to his car. The hotel had his credit card information, so there was no need to check out. After a moment's hesitation, he programmed the GPS to Harrison's house. There was no way he could find his way back there, even in the daylight. Although numb from the alcohol and exceedingly hungry, he was sure he was alert enough to drive the car and willed himself not to speed but to obey all the traffic rules. The last thing he needed at this point was to be pulled over by a police officer for some ridiculous infraction.

Driving the streets of Costa Mar took him longer to go the three miles than it had in the middle of the night. The daytime traffic was unyielding.

Eventually, he turned off a major thoroughfare and shortly found himself driving down Harrison's street. Unable to find parking, he passed the house, turned the corner, and tucked his car into a spot on the side street.

He tried to get his thoughts to congeal enough to create a plan of action as he walked up the road. He wasn't planning on having tea with the man or engaging in an in-depth conversation. He just needed to use his natural charm and persuade Harrison to do the smart thing. Frankly, at this point, if the guy wouldn't give it to him willingly, he'd just grab the damn thing and beat it back to his car before the kid could call for help.

He took a deep, calming breath and reminded himself he was intelligent, suave, debonair, and—he stopped cold in his tracks at the sight of a police cruiser parked in Harrison's driveway. Was it there when he'd just driven by, looking for a parking spot?

The police car shocked him into some semblance of sobriety. Instinctively, so as not to draw attention to himself, Jean-Louis casually crossed to the opposite side of the street and continued in the same direction. As he passed the house, he couldn't detect any movement from within. The front door was closed, and the windows blocked by drawn blinds.

Although he briefly fantasized about it, he was sober enough to know it would be a terrible idea to walk up to the house, bang on the door, and ask the police if they had any clues about the identity of the guy who almost stabbed him. And, oh by the way, could he have the movement he was seeking? He walked around the block and returned to his car. He waited twenty minutes, then took another walk to see if the police were still there. They were. While he was en route, a car drew up to the house and discharged a man and a dog. Jean-Louis took a few quick steps back and watched from behind a tall bush. The young man approached the house and let himself in. He guessed the man was Harrison.

Once more, Jean-Louis returned to his rental car. He sat staring straight ahead, his mind a thoughtless cavern. The squeak of a passing car's brakes startled him back to reality. With no other option coming to mind, he programmed the GPS for LAX. He saw he still had some time before he had to be at the airport. Leaving might very well doom the company and, more importantly, him. However, staying carried no guarantee of success, and he couldn't take a chance of running into the police, who showed no sign of leaving the house.

Returning to Geneva empty-handed wasn't ideal, but maybe he could find a friend willing to help him. A momentary smile lit Jean-Louis' face when he thought of a lovely someone he could call to pick him up in Geneva and take him to a remote village above Bern. There, he would be able to stay in her apartment, where he could plan his next move.

Chapter 40

Sanchez looked up from the dining table when she heard John come in. "Hello, John," she called. "It's good to see you again, although I am not happy that it is in our official capacity."

John gave her a curious look, then turned his eyes to Dahlia, who sat across from the police officer. Her face was tear-stained, and her hands gripped the edge of the table. A mound of used tissues lay in front of her. Louis seemed to sense something was up because he pressed himself against John's leg.

Sanchez motioned for him to take one of the empty chairs at the table. "Please, sit down. We need to talk with you for a minute."

Before taking a step, he looked at the closed door to his workroom. Sanchez feared he would go lock himself in there, but instead, he did as she'd instructed. Louis sat next to him, looking from one face to the other with the same lack of understanding as his human.

Dahlia began sobbing again. She blew her nose in a tissue Leitner offered her, making it flap like a flag in a stiff breeze. She tried to speak, but Sanchez couldn't understand the occasional syllables she got out between snivels.

"John." Sanchez dragged her chair closer to Dahlia and patted her hands. "Mrs. Herrera reported that an intruder in your house confronted her. Mrs. Herrera is certain that all the doors and windows were locked. Somehow, he must have gotten in the front door, which he had left open. There was no sign of forced entry, so we're thinking he picked the lock. He was in the living room when she came out of the kitchen."

John looked from Dahlia to the two police officers and back again at Dahlia before training his eyes again on his workroom door.

Dahlia sniffed. "No, he didn't get into the room. He saw me, turned around, and left."

"Fortunately, no one was hurt, although Mrs. Herrera is quite shaken up," Sanchez said. "We've called Detective Brown and asked him to come. He already ordered a crime scene technician to come as well. That person will dust for fingerprints, but I doubt they'll find anything. While we wait, John, please remain at the table and don't touch anything." Dahlia's renewed sobbing punctuated the officer's instructions.

Sanchez and Leitner had been skeptical regarding John's previous report of a break-in. This time, there was no cause for doubt, and the police officers were reassessing their opinions of the first one. Maybe there was something to John's prior assertion.

John remained sitting as instructed, staring at a spot on the table. Sanchez wasn't sure if he was listening or if he understood what had happened or what its significance might be. She resumed asking Dahlia questions while Leitner leaned against the kitchen door.

"So, you were about to describe the intruder," Sanchez said to Dahlia. "Do you remember what he looked like?"

Dahlia took a deep breath before speaking. "He was a big man, not fat but looked full of muscles. He wore a hat, one that you pull down over your head, and dark sunglasses. He was hairy with a dark beard. He spoke a foreign language when he called to someone outside. I think maybe Italian. I think I surprised him, too. He...He just kind of looked at me, then said he wasn't going to hurt me, and turned around and left."

"Do you remember anything else he was wearing?" Leitner asked.

Dahlia shook her head. "I think the shirt was dark. I really don't remember. I was so scared." Tears poured down her cheeks again.

"Think it's the same guy?" Leitner asked Sanchez.

"Anything's possible." Sanchez scribbled a note.

"What do you mean, 'same guy'?" Dahlia asked. "Same as who?"

Sanchez met Leitner's eyes before they both looked at Dahlia. "We're wondering if this guy was the same person John thought broke into the house previously."

"What are you talking about?" Dahlia's eyes widened.

"John reported a break-in a couple of weeks ago," Leitner said. "Didn't you know about that?"

Dahlia slowly shook her head. "No! What happened?"

"At the time, there was little to go on other than John finding a few scratches on the locks. Also, Suzanne mentioned finding the back door unlocked when she returned to the house. But we—"

"Who's Suzanne?" Dahlia's eyes remained wide open, clearly confused.

Once again, Sanchez looked at her partner before answering. "You don't know?"

"Know what?"

How could Dahlia not know about the fate of the person she replaced, Sanchez wondered. The murder had received press coverage; certainly, she must have read or heard something about it in the news.

Realizing she may have inadvertently opened a proverbial can of worms, Sanchez glanced at John, who continued to appear disconnected from the conversation, and proceeded to give a brief sketch of the events surrounding Suzanne Lang. Despite the intentional lack of any details, as she listened, Dahlia's eyes managed to get wider, and tears, once again, flowed down her cheeks. If she hadn't been sitting, she probably would have wound up prostrate on the floor.

"Do you think this man could have been the one?" Dahlia's knuckles were white as she gripped the edge of the table.

"The one?"

Dahlia's whole body seemed to shake. "The one who murdered her?"

John seemed unfazed by the conversation. Wordlessly, he stood, as did Louis, and despite Sanchez's request, headed to the workroom.

John examined the door's lock. He saw no evidence of tampering. As soon as he and Louis were inside the workroom, he shut and relocked it.

He stood still as he methodically inspected the room. The bookshelf did not look disturbed. The workbench was as he had left it. Along the wall, nothing had been touched. Louis's bed didn't have a crease in the pillow. The safe was where it was supposed to be. In the far corner of what used to be the closet, above the metal track that once held the sliding doors, something was different. There was a glint from a reflective surface. It was something, he was sure, that had not been there before.

He left the room, being sure to close but not lock the door behind him, and, ignoring Dahlia and Sanchez, grabbed the step stool from the kitchen. Back in his workroom, he placed the ladder by the closet opening. When he climbed the three steps, he was able to rise to just below eye level with the corner of the track. Using the flashlight from his phone, he saw a reflection of what appeared to be a small circular piece of glass.

With a screwdriver from his bench, he carefully removed a thin cylindrical object with an attached wire. He traced the wire to a small device that appeared to be some sort of transmitter.

Once he removed what he now guessed to be a camera, he took it to his workbench, sat on his stool, and returned to studying the room. Nothing else was out of the ordinary until he examined his desk. Inspecting his work area, he saw something attached to the underside of the light fixture to his left. It was behind the lip of the lampshade. He used a pair of tweezers to remove the device and placed it next to the camera on his workbench. That done, he sat back in his chair. Glancing up at the bookshelf, he noticed that one of the books was slightly out of alignment with the others. He went to push the volume back into its proper position, but on a hunch, first took it down. The bottom of the spine looked slightly bent. On further inspection, he found another button-sized device.

At first unsure, he decided that the buttons were likely microphones.

For the next fifty-five minutes, he carefully searched the workroom but found nothing else out of the ordinary. When he was satisfied, he sat back in his chair and stared at the devices. With the use of his loupe, he could find no identifying serial numbers or manufacturer logos on them. They showed no evidence of wear. He surmised they were relatively new. Someone had placed them in his room recently, confirming his assertion that an unwelcomed visitor had been in there.

He cut the wire connecting the camera to the transmitter. Inspecting the buttons, he couldn't figure out how to deactivate them, so he submerged them in a glass of water. That done, he returned to the door, but instead of exiting, he took a flashlight and started inspecting the door frames surrounding the closet and the entry door again.

Fifteen minutes later, satisfied that he had checked every millimeter of the workroom, he emerged from the room.

Charice sat at her desk in her home study, trying to concentrate on whatever it was she was supposed to be doing as part of her daily management responsibilities for the Zeller Watch Company. The papers strewn across the desk were of little interest to her. She was repeatedly distracted by thoughts of her brother's antics and the visit from the American investigators.

A knock on her door startled her. The staff knew this was her private time. They were under strict orders not to disturb her. Recovering her composure, she rose and answered the door.

"Sorry to bother you," her housekeeper said. "There are two police officers at the front door asking to speak with you."

That now all-too-familiar sinking feeling in her stomach returned. She was glad she had hold of the doorknob; her weakened knees might have given way. "I guess you can send them in."

She returned to her desk, leaving the door open.

Soon, she heard the approach of multiple footsteps on the stone floor. After a soft tap on the door, two men entered the room.

"Good evening, mademoiselle." One of them took off his hat. "I am Lieutenant Patrice Gauthier, and this is my associate Detective Rochat from the Geneva Police Department."

The buzzing in her head distracted her from hearing the name of the second police officer. After a few deep breaths, she was able to find her voice. "How, um, how can I help you?"

"We are looking for your brother," Gauthier said. "We would like to speak to him about an urgent matter."

Charice recovered her composure. She felt a modicum of relief when she understood they were not here for her, at least not at this juncture. "May I ask what this is in reference to?"

Gauthier politely smiled before continuing. "We would like to ask him some questions regarding your company, Zeller. If we understand correctly, you are responsible for the day-to-day operations, while he oversees the finances. True?"

Charice's head felt as if it were suddenly full of cotton. She could barely understand what the police officer was asking. She wasn't sure where the questioning was headed, but it wasn't in a good direction. "Yes," she replied without thinking clearly. "We share most responsibilities, but we tend to lean into our strengths."

"We would like to know his whereabouts, if you please. We know he left the country two days ago and flew to the United States, specifically to California. There is no record of his return. Could you tell us where he is and when he is scheduled to return?"

"I'm sorry, but I don't know where he is. He had some vacation time, so he took it. He usually doesn't check in with me when he is going on vacation, and I don't ask. You could try him on his mobile."

"Believe me, we have, but to no avail."

Charice wasn't surprised. She hoped he got her message about not coming home. "The best I can do for you, sir, is to give him a message to contact you if he calls me. Please be so kind as to give me your contact information." She held out her hand, expecting a business card.

Gauthier's friendly demeanor darkened. "Mademoiselle Bonet, we are investigating a serious matter. It would be most helpful if you and your brother fully cooperate with us."

Gauthier placed a card on Charice's desk, turned, and the two men left.

She wasn't sure how long she sat in silence. After hearing the front door close, she rose and reached behind her to pour a glass of brandy. The burning sensation of the liquid provided no comfort. Grabbing for her phone, she texted the Italians, ordering them to call her as soon as possible.

Within minutes, their familiar number shone on her cellphone screen.

"What, ahem, is the status of our project?" she asked, hoping her voice sounded stronger than she felt.

"We have a problem. As planned, we entered the target when the subject was out. Unfortunately, the house wasn't empty. The new companion was there. We made contact and had to withdraw. Shortly after the subject returned, our surveillance equipment was deactivated. We've decided it's best to call off any further attempt to reenter, at least for the time being. The subject and others will be on high alert, so the likelihood of success of this project does not outweigh the risks. Maybe at a later date, we can try again once things settle down?"

"I see." Charice sipped her brandy. Anger percolated but didn't bubble over.

"We feel the funds you've already paid have been earned. We're willing to call the rest of the deal off."

Charice took a long enough sip to drain her glass.

"Are you there?" the Italian asked.

She coughed to clear her throat. "Fine."

She clicked off the call.

Yes, this was fine indeed. With the police literally knocking on her door and the insinuations by American investigators, dispensing with the added stress of the Italians on the loose wasn't a bad idea. She was sure they would keep their mouths shut and not throw her under the proverbial bus. To hell with her brother and the company.

Chapter 41

The Italians suspected Charice was drunk. Hopefully, she wasn't so far gone that she wouldn't remember what was said. Regardless, it was time to call the New Yorker.

After several rings, they heard a gruff "Hello."

The report the Italians gave to Sommers was less cryptic and more detailed. Their conclusion remained the same, however. "We have to assume our identity was blown. We have concluded that attempting another entry would be unwise, to say the least."

Sommers listened until the report was completed. "Why didn't you take care of the obstacle?" he asked. "You had no problem last night."

The Italian knew better than to respond with bravado or sarcasm. "Sir, we do have professional ethics. We have no problem eliminating threats; that is what we are trained and very comfortable doing, but taking out innocents is not something we will do when it is avoidable."

"What about the monitoring equipment?"

The Italians had discussed how to handle this question before the call. They didn't care what Charice thought, but Sommers was different. The last thing they wanted to tell him was that their equipment had been disabled. There was no need to give Sommers an opportunity to accuse them of incompetence. He paid very well, so they wanted to stay in his good graces, figuring they would get more job opportunities from him in the future.

"It's still in place."

Liz greeted Bernie with a cup of coffee and a kiss. At their kitchen table, he gave a quick run-through of his time in Geneva.

"That's what you were up to?" Liz wasn't impressed or intrigued by his story. In fact, she seemed angry.

Bernie took his time answering. He realized she wasn't used to hearing tales of intrigue from her husband. Life manning a property room for the NYPD had been mundane. There, Bernie wasn't subjected to unwanted excitement or potential danger, something she much appreciated. Sending her husband to work every day was never accompanied by the fear that he might not return that evening. This was something else.

"Maybe I'm making it sound more dangerous than it was," he tried to placate her.

"As if dealing with murderers and thieves has less dangerous levels?" She stood, then sat back down again, as if unsure what to do with herself. "Even worse, you're treading in foreign territory! This isn't the life we're supposed to be living right now, Bern. The trains are filling the basement! Aren't they enough?"

"Matthew will protect me at all costs—"

"Matthew isn't here right now, is he?"

"No, but—"

"This is Matthew's world, Bernie. Not yours."

"Liz..." Bernie hated that she was so worried. "I promise, all I need to do now is make a few calls, and that will be it. I promise."

She folded her arms across her chest and stared at him.

"Have I ever lied to you?"

"I wouldn't know, would I?

"C'mon, Liz. It's me! During my career, when did I ever do anything to put myself in anything close to danger?"

Liz stared wide-eyed at him.

"Okay, besides that one time."

Shaking her head, her expression softened. "Promise it's just a few phone calls?"

"Promise." Bernie hoped he was telling her the truth. As soon as they finished breakfast, he went down to his basement but didn't tend to his trains. Instead, he retrieved the piece of paper from his jacket pocket and ran through the lines Matthew had coached him to say on the plane ride home. When he felt ready, he dialed CharS Investment Group.

Chapter 42

Within seconds of Matthew turning on his phone after his plane touched down in Santa Ana, it buzzed and dinged with so many messages, the explosive sounds turned heads. Apparently, there were things going on, but no one provided details in the abundance of texts and voicemails, just requests for a callback.

After a seemingly endless disembarking process, Matthew was rewarded for having only a carry-on by getting to avoid the interminable wait at baggage claim. He breezed past the baggage carousel and, once outside, called Brown first.

"Matthew!" Brown's voice was a mixture of relief and concern. "There was another incident at John Harrison's house."

Any jet lag he may have been feeling instantly left him.

"What happened?"

"First, know that John is fine."

Matthew was relieved at that, but as Brown continued to describe what had happened to Dahlia, he tensed up again.

"And she was definite the front door was locked?" he asked.

"Yes. John agreed with that, as well."

"How did he handle the situation?"

"He wasn't there when the intruder made his entrance. The officers on scene were the same uniforms that responded the first time John reported a break-in and when Suzanne was shot. So, they were able to work with him when he got home from teaching. As best as I can tell, he's fine."

Matthew realized he'd been holding his breath and let it out in a sigh of relief.

"Third time's a charm," Brown said. "John must have been onto something when he reported that first break-in. I'm sure we were wrong to doubt him."

"Meet me at John's. I'm heading over now." It was late, but sleep would have to be left for the dead.

On his way, he called Stephen. "Nothing definitive right now," Matthew told him. "But I think we have a few new directions to look. Right now, I'm on my way to John."

"This late?"

"Yes. I don't know if you've heard, but there was an attempted break-in—"

"I'll meet you over there."

"You don't have to."

"I want to." Stephen clicked off.

Bernie's voicemail summarized his call with Sommers: "Not bad results for a first-time kid like me. Baiting billionaires could be my new gig. I got talent, if I say so myself. He's willing to meet me—us, with you on FaceTime—tomorrow afternoon. So, I guess Daniels and Associates Investigative Services is now a thing." He ended the message, chuckling.

The rest of the drive was spent trying to figure out how he would break the news to John about his mother's demise, his father's existence, and the questions he now had about his "sister." It would be good to have others in the house when he spoke to John to provide what little support they could. He considered calling Dr. Diaz despite the lateness of the hour and asking her to come over, but she had no relationship with him to build upon. The person best suited to handle the situation would have been Suzanne, but…

At that thought, another wave of sadness hit him. The distraction of the last few days had occupied his thoughts and minimized the painful memories. Now, as he tried to concentrate on his driving, his fatigue lowered his guard, and he found his mind drifting to memories of time spent with her. Desperately, he tried to avoid picturing her lying on the coroner's table. The nakedness, the cold metal table, the sterility of the autopsy room, the tag on her big toe, all the bodies he's seen over the course of his career were framed in the same settings. But none of them were someone he cared about.

All the lights were ablaze inside and outside John's house when he arrived. Brown's car was parked in the driveway; there was no sign of Jacqueline. He almost found it odd that no neighbors were huddling in front of the house, curious about the comings and goings of police officers.

Inside, Matthew found Brown coming from the workroom with something in his hands. Close behind, John followed, pausing to close the workroom door behind him. Interestingly, he did not lock it. When John looked up and saw him, Matthew saw a flicker of light in his eyes, and the corners of his mouth turned ever so slightly upwards in what could be interpreted as the slightest of smiles, a first from John. His response surprised and pleased Matthew.

Brown placed whatever was in his hands on the coffee table. Matthew sat on the sofa and bent over to inspect the items: a small tube, two buttons, and a cube the size of a die with a wire protruding from it. Brown dragged a chair from the dining table.

"A video camera," John said from the other end of the sofa without prompting, another first. "Found similar types online, but nothing that matches it. May be higher resolution than what's commercially available." He pointed to the cube with the wire sticking out of it. "Transmitter. Also not commercially available." He went on to tell Matthew and Brown where he had found them.

Matthew picked up the small, circular devices, which were no more than a third of an inch in diameter. He marveled at how John was able to find any of them. But, thinking about it, if anyone could, it would be John.

"Microphones," John confirmed, as if knowing what Matthew was thinking. "I put them in a glass of water to short them out."

"Good job," Matthew grinned at him. There was no mystery regarding the purpose of the devices, but who planted them was the question. The intruder must have concealed them at an earlier time, possibly during the first suspected break-in, to determine where the movement was hidden. Had it not been for Dahlia's presence, they probably would have found it.

"My best guess is, whoever was here is connected to what I just learned in Switzerland," Matthew started. "But we still need to figure out how to connect the dots."

The front door opened. Reflexively, Brown reached for his belt holster but relaxed when he saw Siobhan and Stephen enter the room. The couple pulled over more chairs from the dining table.

"Do you know who killed my mother? Was this break-in related to that?" Stephen asked.

"There's no way to answer that for sure right now," Brown said. "We haven't identified the intruder or his partner. The crime scene technicians found nothing useful when they swept the house. They conducted a careful inspection of the first floor of the house, including, much to John's dismay, the workroom."

Matthew was willing to bet they were not as diligent as John was when it came to looking for any evidence of the intruder's presence.

"Unfortunately," Brown continued. "The woman who was here was in such a state of shock that she couldn't describe the man beyond generalities. She's supposed to come to the station tomorrow morning to work on a composite drawing and to look at some mug shots. Hopefully, she'll be in a better frame of mind and will be able to give us something to work with. Right now, if we put out an APB for a big, brawny, bearded guy with an accent and a knitted cap, it is not going to be very fruitful."

"Another dead end!" Stephen threw his hands in the air, then turned toward Matthew. "Did you find out anything in Switzerland?"

Matthew gave them a rundown of the conversations with Michel Rousseau and Charice Bonet. For the moment, he chose not to mention anything about Christian Schmidt. "Someone, or a number of people, are after your movement," he said, looking directly at John. "Clearly, this stuff," indicating the camera and microphone, "was put in place to try to locate its hiding place in your workroom." Matthew paused but continued to study John's face, remaining alert for any sign of an adverse response. Convinced John was doing OK handling the news, he shifted his focus to Stephen. "No one seemed to have any interest or connection to your mom. That brings us back around to the logical conclusion that John was the intended target. However, even if the motive had something to do with his invention, the question remains: why take such extreme measures? Steal the damn thing and be done with it. That would be less messy and easier."

Matthew continued to modulate his words, not wanting to cause undue fear or anxiety in John. "We plan to talk to Carlton Sommers tomorrow."

"Who's 'we'?" Siobhan asked.

"My, uh, partner, Bernie. He'll be there in person. I'm tagging along by phone. Rousseau seems to think the man would go to extremes to get what he wants." Matthew found himself shrugging. "So that's one loose end we can tie up. And we have yet to find Jean-Louis Bonet and see what he has to say."

Chapter 43

Stephen and Siobhan left. Matthew wasn't sure if that was better for what he was about to tell John, or worse. He was so damned tired he wasn't even sure if now was the best time to go into things.

"Do you have any questions, John?" he asked.

John gave a slow and deliberate shake of his head, not moving his eyes from the devices on the tabletop.

It was late. The adrenaline rush started to wane, and all Matthew wanted to do was climb into his bed and sleep for a decade. But Matthew realized he should tell John about his conversation with Schmidt before Schmidt told him. Otherwise, he'd risk ruining the young man's trust in him, which he had to admit was important that he maintain.

Since John wasn't in a hurry to escape to his workroom, and he seemed to be handling the conversation fairly well, Matthew plugged on.

"John," he started cautiously. "We have news about your parents. I know hearing this might be upsetting, but you need to know the truth. I am not sure of its relevance to what's been happening recently, but I am not going to keep any secrets from you."

John gave no encouragement to continue. He did raise his eyes to look in Matthew's general direction.

Matthew began by explaining what he and Brown had discovered about his mother, specifically that Brenda had died at the time of her disappearance. Because there was nothing to be gained now, if ever, by telling John how his mother had died or that a homicide investigation into her death had been reopened, he left out the information regarding the two sets of DNA on the rock.

There was no identifiable reaction from John. He nodded when Matthew asked if he understood what he was being told, and no, he didn't have any questions, which surprised Matthew. After years of thinking he was responsible for his mother's disappearance, to find out that this wasn't the case, but rather she had died, must be an earth-shattering piece of information.

He took a deep breath and moved on to Schmidt. "John, also, we found your father and spoke with him." He thought that would stimulate a response, but again, nothing.

As Matthew gave an overview of meeting Christian Schmidt, he realized that John and his father had similar facial features. Their eyes were the same shade of blue. The two had the same nose, hairline, and cheek structure. He abbreviated the story, leaving out the more lurid details and the fact that he was married at the time. He also didn't bring up Jacqueline or the trust; those parts he wanted to discuss with Brown first. "John, he loved your mother deeply," Matthew emphasized. "Leaving her when you were two years old had nothing to do with you or her. He very much wanted to stay but couldn't."

John furrowed his brow. "My sister says she is younger than me by two years."

Matthew looked at Brown and wordlessly cocked his head to the side. She said the same to him. "I know, John." He cleared his throat. "Your father maintained contact with your mom until about four years ago, when she stopped responding to him. We believe that's when your mom died."

Matthew had no way to soften the news and yet remain honest. He wanted to protect John, but it seemed John did not need any protection. He appeared to be handling the news without a hint of distress. This shocking information would be too much for almost anyone to handle. Anyone, that is, except for John.

"Mr. Schmidt went on to describe how he got in touch with you, John, and how he has been communicating with you over the years. He is your friend from the UK, except he doesn't live in England but rather in Switzerland. He is the one who has been helping you with your work and the development of your movement."

For the first time, John's eyes widened ever so slightly, and there was a slight snicker. An odd response from someone whose world was being turned upside down. John looked directly at Matthew. "I know."

"Excuse me?" Matthew blurted.

"I have suspected for a long time that he is my father."

"But how? He went to great lengths to hide his identity from you. He cares for you, but didn't know how you would relate to him if you knew the truth. He said even your mother didn't want him to tell you. She was also afraid of how you would respond."

John shrugged. "I wasn't sure. But I decided if he was my father and wanted to remain anonymous, I wasn't going to disrespect him."

The combination of direct eye contact and compassionate, insightful answers left Matthew speechless.

The sum total of the evening's revelations wasn't what Matthew predicted. He was the one left surprised and a bit shaken. John was indeed an incredible young man. He had shown a side of himself not previously revealed. It was amazing, over so many years, John had been so perceptive and sensitive to his father's desires. This was not what Matthew had been led to believe was in John's character.

Matthew didn't want to leave John by himself for the night. Brown agreed to have a patrol car parked outside to keep watch over the house, an arrangement which seemed to be acceptable to John as well.

Outside, after Stephen and Siobhan left, Matthew tapped Brown's arm. "One more thing."

Brown turned to look at him in the porch light. "There's more?"

"Hard to believe, but yes." Matthew glanced at John's house to be sure the front door was shut before continuing. "Schmidt doesn't for a second believe Jacqueline is his daughter."

"Interesting. So why is she in charge of the trust?"

"That's a good question. He claimed he never amended the trust or added her name to it."

Chapter 44

The late-afternoon sun had just descended below the Park Avenue skyscrapers. Bernie stood on the sidewalk outside of Sommers' building as he spoke to Matthew. "Gotta admit, you sound good for a guy running on fumes."

"Guess I'm faking it well enough," Matthew said. "I'm thinking international travel is not for me. This crossing time zones thing sucks. I was up at 3 AM this morning and couldn't go back to sleep. Anyway, I'm ready to log into FaceTime."

"Great. I'm going in." At the appointed time, Bernie was ushered into the office and invited to sit at the conference table opposite Sommers' mahogany desk.

"Good afternoon, Mr. Hopkins," Sommers spoke cordially as he entered through a door hidden in a wall. "I thought we would be more comfortable at the table since you have your associate on the telephone." He pointed to a stand where Bernie could prop his phone.

Sommers remained standing at the head of the table as two other men entered through the same door. They sat down in chairs opposite Bernie without the courtesy of an introduction. One was a very distinguished white-haired gentleman, dressed in a blue pinstriped suit, a white shirt, and a purple tie. Next to him, clearly the underling, was a younger man similarly attired, who opened a laptop on the table.

Sommers settled into the chair at the head of the table and nodded to the senior man.

"Good afternoon, Mr. Hopkins. My name is Frederick Whiteside. I am Mr. Sommers' personal attorney. To my left is my associate J.P. Vartanian."

Bernie introduced himself and informed them that the face on the phone screen belonged to Mr. Daniels, the lead investigator at Daniels and Associates Investigative Services.

Whiteside gave a courteous grunt in the direction of the phone and then continued. "Mr. Hopkins, before you get started, I have one issue to discuss. We attempted to research your company but were unable to find any evidence of licensure or incorporation for you, Mr. Daniels, or your named company. Would you be so kind as to explain this to us?"

"I am sure you looked in New York state, but our company is based out of state. We are a very private concern, and our services are provided only on a referral basis. Now, if you don't mind, we would like to get on to our questions."

When Matthew and Bernie had prepared for that question, they agreed to answer as vaguely as possible. What they hadn't expected was someone in the room tapping away on a computer. With enough time, Mr. Vartanian would, no doubt, expose their fictitious story. Of course, they didn't have a website or any internet presence. To look for licensure state by state would take more than a bit of time. They figured they'd have enough opportunity to ask the more important questions before Bernie would be escorted out the door in a less-than-friendly manner.

"We have established that Mr. Sommers is planning a takeover of the Zeller Watch Company." Bernie pulled several sheets of paper from an inside jacket pocket and laid them out in front of him.

Whiteside nodded.

"A Mr. John Harrison is currently in the process of discussing a revolutionary innovation he's developed with the leadership of Zeller. Are you aware of that?"

Again, Whiteside nodded.

"Are you aware of the status of his negotiations with the Bonets?"

Whiteside reclined slightly in his chair. "It is our understanding they are coming close to completion."

Bernie made a show of putting check marks on the papers as he asked his questions. He could be as officious as this pompous lawyer.

"Have you, Mr. Sommers, had any discussion regarding Mr. Harrison's development and how it would affect the purchase of the company?"

"Obviously, it is something we are tracking," Whiteside replied. Sommers sat quietly, glowering at Bernie, shooting an occasional glance at Matthew's image on the phone. "Our plans regarding our future with Zeller have remained on track."

"And that track would be what? A hostile takeover, a purchase? I'm not sure how you would describe it."

Neither the attorneys nor Sommers made an effort to answer the question. After a moment of silence, Whiteside leaned forward. "Mr. Hopkins, that is proprietary information, and we will not disclose any discussions or plans this organization may be considering."

Bernie returned his gaze directly at Sommers. "Mr. Harrison had an associate by the name of Suzanne Lang. Are you aware of her?"

"No," Whiteside sternly responded.

"Sir," Bernie immediately shot back. "I asked Mr. Sommers the question. I know full well Mr. Sommers can speak for himself."

Sommers raised his right hand as if signaling Whiteside to back off. Bernie was reminded of how trained dogs are taught to respond to hand signals instead of verbal commands. "As you were just told, the answer is a definitive no," Sommers said.

"Are you aware," Matthew piped in. "That Ms. Lang accompanied Mr. Harrison to Switzerland when he presented his development to several watch companies, one of which was Zeller?"

Sommers seemed bored. "I may have heard something about the presentation by the young man. Who accompanied him was of no interest to me and of no relevance to our interests."

Matthew pursued. "From whom did you get the information?"

Sommers thought a moment before replying. "I don't remember. It wasn't important to make note of."

Bernie looked down at his notes. "Was it important enough to kill someone and threaten another?" he asked without looking up.

Whiteside sat up straighter. "That is absolutely preposterous. How dare you make even the slightest insinuation that Mr. Sommers, or anyone in this company, would have anything to do with such despicable actions? Mr. Hopkins, you are bordering on libel."

It was as if Whiteside and Sommers had read their portion of the script Matthew prepared. Bernie was well rehearsed and not shaken. "Sir, we are just having a friendly conversation. Nothing is going to leave this room. We are here at the behest of our client to follow up on the information provided to us.

Whiteside visibly calmed himself. "Who is the person who claims to have been threatened by Mr. Sommers?"

"We're not in a position to reveal our sources at this time."

"Well," Whiteside cleared his throat. "Mr. Sommers will not be answering any further questions at this time. If you have more, you may submit them through my office." With that, he placed one of his business cards in front of Bernie. The two lawyers and Sommers stood up and turned to leave. Magically, the office door opened, and the secretary entered to usher Bernie out of the room.

Matthew's eyelids felt as though lead weights weighed them down. Physically, he was exhausted, but his brain was racing. Once the phone call with Sommers ended, he pounded down another cup of coffee to keep himself awake while he waited for Bernie to get somewhere private.

"How long are you going to be?" He texted Bernie.

"Not sure. Gotta take care of something for Liz," was the reply.

Matthew interpreted that to mean he had time to check on John. He poured more java into a to-go cup and headed out.

Jacqueline's car was in his driveway. Inside the house, he found her sitting on the couch next to Dahlia, engaged in a deep conversation. They each had a cup of coffee in front of them. Several cookies were laid out on the coffee table.

Matthew waved as he headed toward the workroom, overhearing Jacqueline say something about some strange goings on in a house a couple of doors down the street.

"But the police said *this* house had been broken into," Dahlia insisted. She must have been on the verge of quitting.

He knocked on the workroom door.

"In this neighborhood," Jacqueline rolled her eyes, "a lot of the houses look the same. Mistakes like that happen."

"But I know that front door was locked! That man picked the lock." Dahlia picked her purse up from the floor. "I'm lucky to be alive." She started sobbing as she stood.

"Please." Jacqueline pulled her by the arm to get the woman to sit back down. "If you feel you can't stay, give me a few days to find a replacement."

"I don't know. I need to make a phone call." Dahlia wiped her face with the tissue before heading to the kitchen.

"Where's John?" Matthew asked.

"Keep knocking." Jacqueline tilted her head toward the workroom.

"Have you spoken to him? Is he ok?" Matthew pounded harder.

"I have no idea. How can you tell with him?" She flipped her hair over her shoulder.

"You could ask."

"I don't need a lecture from you." She stood and placed her hands on her hips.

Dahlia returned to the living room. "My husband does not want me to stay. But I told him I will finish the rest of the week." She cast her eyes at Matthew. "But no longer."

"Thank you!" Jacqueline ran toward the woman and gave her an awkward hug. "OK, I'm outta here. Wait! Are you parked behind me?" She glared at Matthew.

He moved his car and then re-entered the house. Dahlia had tucked herself out of sight in the kitchen.

After the typical repeated knocks on the workroom door, John opened it, apparently in his usual state, unaffected by the events of the previous day. What seemed to have been an opening to a more communicative and conversational John last night had closed. He was back to his earlier self, quiet and consumed by his own world.

His computer was open. "Were you emailing with your father?"

John nodded.

"Please send my best to Mr. Schmidt."

John typed a message and closed his laptop.

"Just thought I'd check in with you, make sure you're OK," Matthew started.

John nodded.

"Do you have any questions or comments about what I said last night? Or anything else, for that matter?"

John's only response was to shake his head.

"John," Matthew began cautiously. "Your sister, or your half-sister to be more precise, is two years younger than you, right?"

"Yes," John said in a virtual monotone. "She said our father was with her mother after he left mine."

"Did you ever ask your mother, or your father, for that matter, if that was true?"

John shook his head again. "No. My mother told me about my sister a year or two before she went away. I don't know how she found out about her."

Went away was an interesting choice of words. Having been told the police believed her to be dead, was he not willing to accept the truth?

Matthew stared at John's back. Schmidt was definitive when he told his story to him and Bernie. Schmidt oozed honesty and heartbreak when he spoke of Brenda and Barton, or John. The only way Brenda could have found out about Jacqueline's existence was if Schmidt told her or, as he insisted, Jacqueline's mother, Angela, contacted her directly. Why would Angela want to find Brenda? Because John accepts Jacqueline as his sister, that rather suggested Brenda believed Schmidt was Jacqueline's father, even though Schmidt claimed otherwise. Perhaps Angela had attempted to allocate some of the money to be set aside for Jacqueline in the trust. And possibly Brenda had begun to consider what would happen to John if something were to happen to her, so she had the trust amended in a way that could also appease Angela. Why else would she have told John of Jacqueline's existence? But she was long gone, as was Angela. Would those maybes ever be confirmed?

Jean-Louis was bleary-eyed as he exited the jetway in Geneva. If he could get through passport control quickly, which was usually the case, there was a train to Bern leaving in twenty-two minutes. The next train was scheduled in one hour and forty-three minutes. He was in no mood to hang around the airport for the duration, even if it was in the first-class lounge. He had enough common sense to know he needed to be as far away as possible from public areas where he might be spotted.

The line at passport control for Swiss citizens was unusually long, but in typical Swiss efficiency, it moved smoothly, and Jean-Louis was through in nine minutes. He moved away from the border guard and started for the escalator that would take him to the arrivals concourse. The sign overhead indicated that the train platform was an eight-minute walk away. Plenty of time as long as he didn't dally.

As he approached the escalator, two police officers blocked his way while a third came up behind him. They escorted him to one side of the hall, where another officer, neatly attired in a fashionable suit and tie, approached and presented his credentials.

"Lieutenant Gauthier of the Geneva Police Department. We would like you to accompany us, if you please."

Jean-Louis dropped the handle of his roll-away bag and stared wide-eyed at the police officers. A hand reached out and grabbed his left arm, redirecting him. In the distance, he saw a sign for a Police sub-station.

All Jean-Louis could do was stammer and sweat. None of the officers seemed to hear or care about his protestations.

Chapter 45

Matthew stretched out on his couch. The meeting with Sommers went as well as he could have expected. Cool though he was, Matthew was sure Sommers and his lawyers were, at this moment, huddled together trying to figure out what Daniels and Associates Investigative Services was and what they knew. Their next order of business, he had no doubt, was to assess the threat posed by Matthew, Bernie, and their client to Charlton Sommers and CharS. How it affected the Zeller acquisition was now of secondary concern for them, at best.

Attempting to jump the gun and get set up as a legitimate business concern before Sommers' team found out otherwise, Matthew reached out to Brown for help. As with any organization, it wasn't what one knows, but who one knows, that can grease the administrative wheels. In this case, Brown had spoken to his chief and asked if the chief could call his friends in Sacramento to expedite Matthew's PI license application. Trying to include a firearms license would prolong the application process, so Matthew deferred that portion of the application to a later time. Colin agreed to "forget" to inform his chief about Matthew's "company" and his recent activities, which were performed under questionable pretenses, especially those involving a certain billionaire and citizens of a foreign country. It did help that the billionaire was far from California, as were the

Swiss. It would be very beneficial if the license could be issued before that particular billionaire's minions had a chance to locate Matthew. Most likely, they were also looking for Bernie in California, a search that would be fruitless.

Matthew realized he was asking for a significant number of favors that he might have to repay eventually. He hoped to bank on an element of professional courtesy.

A call from a blocked number interrupted his train of thought.

"Detective Brown told me you had a bit of an adventure." Raul Chin greeted Matthew.

Matthew yawned. "Indeed."

"Sounds like you're beat, so I'll get right to it. Detective Brown let you know about the second blood sample on the rock and that it wasn't the victim's, yeah?"

Matthew listened with his eyes closed. His body was drained from the aftereffects of jet lag. "Hmmm." He smiled at the sound of his response. Terse as it was, he wondered if John's penchant for answers in the form of grunts was rubbing off on him.

"After we reopened the case, my partner and I went through everything in the box of personal effects, as well as the case file with a fine-tooth comb. On the back of her shirt, we found a couple of blood stains not accounted for in any of the notes or lab tests. We sent them to the lab for analysis."

Matthew fought to open his eyes. "Glad you opened the case!" Sitting up, he shook his head to clear out some of the cobwebs, then briefed Chin on his discussion with Schmidt. "He was genuinely surprised to hear about the circumstances of her accident. He claimed he'd tried to convince her to go hiking numerous times, and she'd refuse. The idea she would go on a moderately difficult trail on her own, not to mention be so poorly equipped, made no sense to him, to the point he insisted it was impossible fiction."

"For sure, this is pointing more directly to a homicide," Chin said. "If the blood stain from the victim's shirt reveals DNA that matches the second one from the rock, that would be sufficient evidence to pursue the assailant."

"Only if we identify the perpetrator and match the DNA," Matthew grumbled.

"Well, there are only thirty-nine million people in California to start with." Chin laughed.

"That's some haystack." Matthew didn't add in the rest of his thoughts: they were talking about finding someone four years after the fact. This wasn't a cold case; this was an iceberg.

"Whether or not we can officially call Alves' death a homicide," Chin said. "I'm not waiting for the lab report. I'm entering the DNA findings into the National Crime Information Center database as soon as I can to see what, if anything, might pop up."

Despite having several hours of uninterrupted sleep, Matthew's exhaustion was no better when he woke up before sunrise the next morning. Figuring it was at least an hour before his alarm was set to ring, he refused to look at the clock and fell back asleep until his phone rang.

Brown told him to get out of bed, shower, and get to the airport. Convinced he was suffering a sleep hangover, Matthew was confused by the urgency in Brown's voice.

"Why the rush and why the airport?"

"So, my chief pulled more favors than expected," Brown said. "He got you an interview with the director of the Bureau of Security and Investigative Services."

"The what?" Matthew thought the name of the department was vaguely familiar, but his brain wasn't clear enough yet to fully comprehend what he heard.

Colin repeated the instructions. "Your appointment with the director is scheduled for this afternoon. It's to get your private investigator license," he added.

Matthew's appointment was scheduled for 3:00 p.m. in Sacramento, but it was already 9:15. For reasons unknown to him, due to the urgency of the matter, the director was unwilling to conduct a virtual interview. There was a flight leaving in just under two hours from the Orange County airport. It would get him there in plenty of time.

Matthew shot out of bed, showered, shaved, dressed, and was out the door in twenty-five minutes, grabbing his notebook on the way to give himself something to read on the plane. Over the course of his career, he'd learned to re-read his case notes on a regular basis, especially when he had new information to add. Often, a note or something once thought insignificant could take on a completely different meaning when seen in the context of new evidence.

Fortunately, his jaunt to Sacramento went well, as did the interview. There was no question, given his years of experience as an NYPD detective, that he was qualified. The director of the bureau handed him a flimsy piece of cardboard with his signature under an embossed seal of the State of California. That would serve as his temporary license until all the official paperwork was completed and his official credentials were sent to him.

Matthew debated asking if his credentials could be backdated by a few days to cover the meeting with Sommers. On balance, he figured that would be a bad idea as the director was already doing him a huge favor. Besides, the flight up and the chance to review his notes with a clearer head were exactly what he needed.

He returned to Southern California with renewed vigor.

Chapter 46

Refreshed and clear-eyed, the next day after breakfast, he headed to the station house to meet Brown, stopping, of course, for coffee and a box of donuts. Despite the common perception, not all police officers like donuts, but he did, and wasn't ashamed to admit it. These, however, would be a thank-you gift for the Police Chief.

With donuts delivered, Brown led him to his own desk, where they compared notes.

"If one lie is exposed in the course of an interview, there are usually others waiting to be uncovered," Matthew said as the evidence before them began to fit together like a jigsaw puzzle. "As they are exposed, the path to the truth begins to be unveiled."

With the picture coming into focus, it was left to Brown to take care of the necessary paperwork before they could proceed with the next steps. Brown got right on it.

Matthew rang the doorbell of the townhome and then stood aside to let an active-duty police officer handle the official procedures. Just like old times, as they had approached the front door, Matthew snickered at the thought that they were about to ruin someone's day. It was a joke, maybe a bad one, but one most police officers in similar circumstances would understand and appreciate.

Jokes aside, they were approaching a high-risk situation. There was no way to know whether the person on the other side of the door posed a potential threat to the officers' well-being. This was not a time for jokes but rather for heightened vigilance.

When the door opened, Brown stepped forward to block it from being slammed shut. "Hi, Jacqueline."

Jacqueline pinched her forehead together and looked first at Matthew, then stared at Brown. "Yes?"

"We would like to speak with you. May we come in?"

The furrows deepened, but she stood aside to allow them entry. They entered a small living room with bare, stark white walls, a utilitarian couch, which appeared to be anything but comfortable, two mismatched straight-back chairs, and a glass-topped coffee table. Nothing in the room softened the coldness of the decor. Wordlessly, Jacqueline shut the door and headed for the couch. On the coffee table sat an open laptop and her cellphone. A half-eaten sandwich and a plastic container of coleslaw sat on a paper plate next to her computer.

"Working from home?" Matthew asked.

"Huh?" She blinked at him. "Oh, yeah."

"That surprises me. I thought I remembered you telling us your boss insisted you come into the office."

"Oh, yeah, well, I guess he realized how productive I can be from home."

Judging by what Matthew could see, the place was neat and uncluttered, though devoid of anything decorative. Had she recently moved in? Or was this a reflection of her taste in décor or the state of her finances?

"Well, sorry to interrupt your workday, but we need to clarify some facts related to our investigation." Matthew took a soft and non-confrontational tone. Why get her hackles up at this point?

"How well did you know Brenda Alves?" Brown asked.

At the name Jacqueline's eyes perceptually widened. "Why do you ask?"

Brown did not respond but waited for a reply.

"As I told him before," she pointed at Matthew. "I barely knew her. About five or six years ago, she began calling my mother and me, trying to create a relationship where there wasn't one. At first, she was a pain in the ass. I guess she figured just because she and my mother fucked the same guy, they should be friends. Eventually, she said it was for John to know his sibling."

"How did your mother react?"

"My mother wanted nothing to do with her, but after she died, Brenda started reaching out to me. She was quite persistent and actually," Jacqueline rubbed her eyes with the heels of her hands. "I actually started to like her."

As Matthew watched her, he didn't see a flicker of nervousness as she told the story. "You said Brenda reached out five or six years ago? Why do you think it took her almost twenty years to contact you?"

Jacqueline shrugged her shoulders as she leaned back on the couch. "No idea. She might have told my mother, but no one ever told me. After a while, I didn't care. It didn't seem to be important."

Matthew made a quick lane change. "Your mother died, correct?"

Jacqueline seemed to relax a bit at the question. "Yeah. After her accident, Brenda started reaching out to me."

"When did she die? Remind me."

Jacqueline flashed a look of annoyance at Matthew. "She died a little over five years ago. A freak accident in Santa Barbara." Suddenly, Jacqueline became solemn, and her cheeks flushed. Her hands were knotted together, knuckles white. "I was in college there."

"Right," Matthew nodded. "You said she came up for a visit and went to a party with you."

"Uh-huh." Jacqueline nodded. "She got wasted and went out for a walk. I don't know how it happened, but she fell off a cliff."

She reached for a tissue from a box on the floor near her feet and dabbed her eyes.

"How come you didn't go with her?" Brown asked.

Jacqueline paused and looked at the detective as if she were trying to decide whether to answer the question. Eventually, she relented. "I was in one of the bedrooms with a guy. One of the biggest mistakes of my life."

"Who was the guy?"

Jacqueline snickered. "Don't remember. My mom wasn't the only one partying. Never saw him again after that night."

Matthew allowed her a moment to recover her composure. "Remind me, what school did you attend at the time?"

"Santa Barbara City College."

"Sorry for your loss," Brown said, although Matthew didn't think there was much sorrow in his voice. "So, it was after your mother's accident that you developed a relationship with her, Brenda?" Brown took out his phone and started typing notes.

"Eventually, yeah. We started spending time together. Occasionally, we'd go to the movies or go for walks together."

Colin looked up from his phone. "Where'd you go for your walks?"

Jacqueline shrugged. "Around. Nowhere in specific, a park, the mall, the beach, wherever."

Matthew cut in. "You ever go on any hikes, like in the mountains?"

Jacqueline looked quizzically at Matthew and then nodded. "Yeah, several times. As John would lock himself in his room for the whole day, she felt comfortable on occasion being away from him for several hours." Jacqueline seemed to have forgotten her previous descriptions of the relationship she had with John's mother as she continued talking.

"Who drove?"

"What?"

"Who would drive you to the mountains?"

"What's that got to do with anything?" Jacqueline's shoulders hunched up toward her ears.

"Just curious. How long would Brenda be comfortable being away from John? Ever go for overnight trips?"

"No. We'd drive to the local mountains, go for a hike for an hour or two, and then get back before it was time for John to have dinner."

"How often?" Brown asked.

"A couple of times. I think she went to the San Bernardino's on her own at other times. I tagged along when I could get away from work. I guess she saw hiking as a way to clear her head after dealing day in and day out with John."

"So, it was her idea?" Colin asked neutrally.

"I'm not one for nature! But I guess I started looking at her as my substitute mom. When I think about it, I was searching for a parental figure. I mean, I didn't have a mother or father then."

"By chance, do you remember when you last went for any kind of a hike with her?" Brown continued typing on his phone without looking up at Jacqueline. Matthew marveled at how fast he could finger-type.

Jacqueline shook her head. "Well, it had to be more than four years ago. Sometime before she took off."

"Was it possible that was one of the times you went to the local mountains?"

Again, Jacqueline shook her head. "Sorry, I just don't remember. I don't think so, but it's so long ago."

"And you don't know anything about the circumstances of her disappearance?"

She stared back, suddenly, her face turned a shade paler, and her eyes narrowed. There was a slight tremor in her hands in her lap. "Why do you ask?"

Colin and Matthew sat stoically, staring at her. The time for her to ask questions was over.

The last time you remember going on a hike with her, whose idea was it?"

Jacqueline looked to Matthew as if searching for the correct answer. Finding nothing in his blank stare, she shrugged her shoulders.

"Was it your idea?"

Another shrug. "Like I said, it was always her idea. So, I'm sure it was her idea. I'd much rather have gone to the mall."

"On that hike, do you recall anything happening to Brenda? Did she trip or fall?"

"What do you mean?" There were several beads of sweat forming on her brow. She ignored them as she knitted her hands.

Brown paced his questions to avoid overwhelming Jacqueline and risking her shutting down. "Did she fall?"

Jacqueline stood and raised her voice at the two men who calmly watched the brewing meltdown. "What are you suggesting?"

Matthew looked at Jacqueline impassively. "We're not suggesting anything. We're just trying to fill in John's history, and since you are very much a part of that history, it is important for the sake of the investigation that we get the whole backstory."

She seemed to be mollified for the moment and sat back down. Matthew calmly resumed his questioning. "When did you first find out about the trust? I know you made some mention of it, but I want to get the timing right."

Jacqueline closed her eyes for a moment, seemingly trying to calm herself. "I don't remember. Brenda may have mentioned something about it, but I don't know. It was only after she disappeared that I realized what I had been saddled with. A while after she disappeared, I can't remember exactly when, the lawyer called me and told me I was responsible for John until she returned. What could I say? I went to his house. It was a total mess."

It took Brown a couple of minutes to finish his typing. When he was done, he stood up and stretched. Looking around, he asked to use the bathroom. Jacqueline indicated where it was. After Brown left the room, Matthew turned to Jacqueline and asked for a glass of water.

Visibly annoyed, she disappeared into the back of the townhouse to fetch a bottle of water. In her absence, Matthew cautiously picked up the used napkin from the coffee table with his pen and placed it inside a plastic specimen bag he'd pulled from a pocket. Quickly, he sealed the bag and put it back into the same pocket.

When Brown returned, he headed toward the door. Matthew rose to join him. Having barely touched his water, he asked if he could take the water bottle with him. Jacqueline shrugged. She seemed to relax again. Her shoulders dropped, and her tightened face softened. Whatever was concerning her was no longer an issue.

Standing by the front door, Brown's phone rang. He excused himself and headed outside, leaving Matthew and Jacqueline standing in an uncomfortable silence. Jacqueline seemed puzzled as to why Matthew remained. He stood there holding his bottle of water, occasionally smiling at her.

After what seemed to be an interminable amount of time, there was a knock on the door. Matthew stood back to allow Jacqueline to open it. Brown, standing on the threshold, nodded ever so slightly at Matthew. In return, Matthew retrieved the bagged napkin that would have Jacqueline's DNA on it and gave it to him in case it was needed.

Brown put the baggie in his pocket, cleared his throat, and turned to face Jacqueline.

"Jacqueline Herrera," Brown spoke in a very officious voice as he pulled a folded piece of paper from an inside jacket pocket. "I have a warrant for your arrest on the charge of murder of Brenda Alves."

Jacqueline collapsed, bursting into tears as she fell back against the door.

Matthew knew it could take a few hours to process Jacqueline before she'd be formally questioned. He'd gotten permission to watch the proceedings, so he wanted to get to the police station soon. However, he first wanted to check in on John and let him know what was happening.

On the way to John's house, he called Stephen and suggested that he and Siobhan meet him there. He wanted one or two familiar faces to support John when he relayed the news.

It was déja vu: the four of them sitting in John's living room, with Stephen and Siobhan once again on either side of John on the couch, maximizing the degree of physical separation as much as possible. Matthew heard the clinking of dishes in the kitchen and assumed it was Dahlia going about her business. He was happy she had decided not to leave after all, but rather to continue in her position with John.

He looked straight into John's eyes. John immediately dropped his to stare at his hands.

"John," Matthew started. "Detective Brown and I have concluded that your mother's death wasn't accidental."

He paused, wanting to mete out the information in small portions to allow John to absorb and process what he was being told.

"We believe she did not slip off the hiking trail but was intentionally struck on the head, causing her to fall down the embankment. The blow to her head was the cause of her death. We have the rock that was used as the weapon."

John barely moved. Siobhan let out a soft gasp.

"How could you possibly know that?" Stephen asked. "It was so long ago."

Matthew filled them in on the most pertinent details before leading up to the recent events, including Detective Chin's handling of reopening the case in Big Bear. "The rock your mom supposedly fell upon had a couple of blood spots, separate and distinct from each other. The lab was able to identify several strands of hair incorporated with one of the blood spots. Analysis of the two spots showed completely different DNA profiles. One of the blood spots and strands of hair we recovered from a hairbrush in the victim's backpack had matching DNA profiles. We now believe they belonged to your mother, Brenda Alves. The other spot was from someone, a woman, totally unrelated. The detective we are working with also noticed a couple of blood spots on the back of Brenda's shirt, near one of her shoulders. The lab analysis matched those to the second blood spot on the rock, the one that wasn't Brenda's.

"Recently, Detective Chin asked a pathologist he knows to review the autopsy pictures and report. The pathologist firmly disagreed with the conclusions of the deputy coroner who did the original autopsy. He was adamant that Brenda's death was the result of an intentional blow to the head with an object similar to the rock they have."

Stephen blinked several times as if to clear his vision. "Whose blood was on the rock and shirt?"

Matthew paused, looked at John again. "Jacqueline's."

"John's sister? How's that possible?"

Matthew sat back in his chair and took a breath before continuing. "When I spoke to Christian Schmidt, John's father, he was adamant Jacqueline wasn't his daughter."

Suddenly, John rose from where he was seated and wordlessly walked from the living room to the workroom. When he disappeared into the room and locked the door, Matthew stared after him. He thought of Dr. Diaz's conversation. Upon her advice, Matthew was trying to be thoughtful and avoid agitating John. He wondered if his efforts may not have been necessary. He realized John was possibly, in effect, monitoring himself. Breaking away from the conversation was likely how John removed himself from the stressful situation. John must have sufficient self-awareness to avoid, or at least minimize, the risk of not being able to handle his emotions.

Choosing not to pursue John, Matthew turned back to Stephen and Siobhan. He explained Schmidt's condition that led to his assertion.

"Bernie and I discussed Schmidt's revelations with Brown. Adding that information to what we realized were inconsistencies and gaps in Jacqueline's story, we agreed we needed to look at her as a potential suspect."

Matthew was interrupted by a text message on his phone. Brown was letting him know Jacqueline's interview wouldn't start for another hour or so. Her lawyer was on the way and wanted to have some time with his client before she was interviewed. Matthew stared at the phone for a moment. It was interesting that she already had a lawyer. Typically, someone in her position in life did not have a criminal defense lawyer immediately at hand. Matthew replied with a thumbs-up emoji and went back to his story.

"We got lucky the other day when I came over to check on John. Jacqueline was here talking with Dahlia."

"Uh-huh." Dahlia made her presence in the kitchen known.

"Detective Brown, by chance, also stopped by. I asked him to take the coffee cup Jacqueline used and see if we could collect any DNA from it. He took it to the lab, and indeed, they were able to analyze some sputum. The DNA matched the specimen recovered from Brenda Alves' clothes and the second one on the rock. As a backup, I took a napkin she was using when I was just at the house. Brown will get that run to double-check."

Siobhan sat bolt upright. "Wait a minute," she started. "You said the DNA from the second person did not match Brenda's, correct?"

Matthew nodded in the affirmative.

"Did it match John's?"

Matthew smiled. Someone was sharp. "No, it did not."

"Then how could she be his sister? That corroborates what Schmidt said. True?"

Stephen looked from Matthew to Siobhan and back again, unclear what she was saying.

"They should have fifty percent," Siobhan explained. "Or at least a significant proportion of the same genetic make-up, if one of their parents was the same person."

Matthew smiled. "Exactly. We are going to have a nice chat with Jacqueline and get to the bottom of this. The question you didn't ask is why? What was the motive, if indeed she murdered Brenda? It's going to be quite the afternoon and evening with Miss Henderson."

He also pointed out that they still needed to understand how Jacqueline became part of the trust, given that Schmidt denied making any changes to the document. The attorney in San Francisco would have to clarify that.

Stephen had listened intently. "That's all well and good, but what does that have to do with mom's case?" he asked. "I don't get it."

"Honestly," Matthew said. "I don't know. What I do know is there is more to the story than we ever thought." He added that Brown was still working to find the men Dahlia encountered. At the moment, they were the best and most logical lead. "In the meantime, to understand the present, we still need a better understanding of the past, especially as it applies to John. That said, we're making progress."

Chapter 47

On the drive to the station, Matthew placed a call to the San Francisco attorney, Samuel Chang. According to his secretary, he was out of the office and would return shortly. The man must go out a lot, Matthew thought before pressing for his cell number. She refused but did promise to have him return the call ASAP.

At the station, Jacqueline sat in a stark room that contained three unmatched straight-back metal chairs and a metal table bolted to the floor. A video camera was mounted on a tripod in a corner, focused on the side of the table closest to her. The feed from the camera was sent to a recording unit and a video monitor positioned on a desk outside the room. From Matthew's vantage point, standing near the monitor, the image was a bit grainy. A civilian employee informed him that the audiovisual feed typically worked, although it occasionally cut out for several seconds without apparent reason. Fortunately, the peculiarities of the system were not known to interviewees or their attorneys. Budgets being what they were, the Costa Mar Police Department had to prioritize use of its funding, and upgrading this system wasn't high on the list.

On the monitor, Matthew watched Brown and Chin enter the interview room. The lack of clarity of the screen's image didn't allow him to watch Jacqueline for any unconscious reaction to the upcoming battery of questions. Matthew hoped Brown understood what to look for as he questioned Jacqueline. A component of the human nervous system is called the autonomic nervous system. It regulates certain body functions, such as the heart rate, blood pressure, flushing of the cheeks, sweating, and pupillary size. None of those biological reactions is under voluntary control. Monitoring changes in biometric parameters is useful when assessing someone's stress level.

Sitting slumped in the chair, Jacqueline appeared deflated but oddly calm. Perhaps even more odd, sitting next to her, was the man serving as her attorney, Michael Livingston. The same attorney Michael had spoken to about John's trust fund. Livingston dealt only with trusts and estates. What was he doing there representing a murder suspect? Perhaps he was the only attorney she knew, but it would have made more sense for him to refer her to someone who specialized in such matters.

The detectives started the interview by formally introducing themselves. Livingston returned the favor by passing a business card to each of them.

Brown looked at the card. "Trusts and estates? Interesting. You do understand why we're here, don't you, Mr. Livingston? Your client is here on a murder charge, quite a different set of circumstances than, I would assume, you are used to."

Livingston nodded. "Detective, I fully understand why we are here. I did some criminal work in the past and am capable of representing my client."

Brown looked down at his notes. "As you wish."

The questioning began. Jacqueline admitted to knowing Brenda Alves, though only vaguely, until after her mother's death. She repeated the narrative of her relationship with Brenda, virtually verbatim to her earlier explanation to Matthew and Brown. Yes, of course, she knew John, her brother, confirming she was now responsible for John's welfare. Interestingly, during that answer, she glanced at Livingston, who nodded ever so slightly.

Jacqueline replied succinctly, without explaining any of her answers. Matthew could tell Livingston had coached her. She was either a quick study or was practiced at answering such questions. What would be her motivation to practice before today?

Brown and Chin took turns asking questions in rapid-fire succession for forty-five minutes. Jacqueline maintained her calm. On several occasions, she asked why she was here because she had done nothing wrong. Matthew was struck by the emotional disconnect between the cruelty of the crime she was accused of committing and the tone of her answers. He wondered if she truly appreciated the severity of her current situation. The emotional breakdown she displayed when they were at her townhome was diametrically opposite from what she now manifested.

At Livingston's request, the detectives took a break and left the room to confer. When the detectives joined Matthew and Brown's lieutenant, they watched on the monitor as Jacqueline and Livingston took sips of water but otherwise remained silent. They did not even look at each other. The audio feed had been turned off at the break per regulations. At one point, they thought they could see Livingston's lips moving slightly as if in hushed conversation. After several seconds, he placed his hand over his mouth so even a talented lip reader would be ineffective.

Brown and Chin agreed they had gotten as much as possible from Jacqueline voluntarily. She continued to insist John was her younger brother despite the evidence in their possession to the contrary. She steadfastly insisted she did not know the name of her father, insisting he was German and wanted nothing to do with him.

Matthew stepped away from the group. He'd left his trusty notepad behind, so he was forced to pull a blank piece of paper from a nearby printer to scribble some notes. Brown and Chin were doing a good job, but there were other inconsistencies in Jacqueline's version of history that needed to be resolved. His cellphone buzzed while he jotted down those issues.

Samuel Chang was returning his call. Matthew thanked the attorney for his quick response. "Do you remember making any amendments to John's, I mean, Barton's trust documents without the trustor's knowledge?"

"I would never!" Chang's voice became curt. "Once the trust is signed, it is locked in stone."

"I'm not implying you did anything untoward or illegal, but is it possible someone else could have?"

"Possibly." Chang's voice softened ever so slightly. "Someone could make changes with proper instructions from the trustor."

"Would it be possible to get a copy of the trust?"

"Absolutely, not. That would go against client privacy concerns."

"I get that. But in general, could changes be made to the trust without the trustor's knowledge?"

"Legally, no." The two-word answer was phrased in an interesting manner. Although anything was possible, Chang indicated that any change without the trustor's approval would be illegal, regardless of who made the change.

Matthew thanked the attorney for his assistance. But before he disconnected, it occurred to him to ask another question.

"I'm sorry, sir. If I may, by any chance, do you remember the name of the attorney down here you asked to administrate the trust?"

Chang paused. Matthew could hear him mumbling to himself. "You realize it was more than twenty years ago, but I'm pretty sure I referred it to Jack Renfro. I was using him in SoCal around that time."

Matthew clicked out of his call and stood as the lieutenant walked by.

"Is there a quiet place I could use for a few minutes?"

"Quiet is a relative term around this place. The closest would be my office. Have at it!"

Inside, the lieutenant's computer was locked, of course, so Matthew had to use his clumsy thumbs to do a couple of Google searches on his phone.

Thankfully, it didn't take long to find what he needed. The first article to come up in the search results when he looked for an attorney named Jack Renfro in Southern California was an obituary. Mr. Renfro, an attorney who specialized in estates, died a year ago. He found three other Jack Renfros, none in California, and the one attorney still living was too young to be considered. The second search was equally fast. He found the phone number he sought without difficulty.

He picked up the lieutenant's desk phone and dialed the Sheriff's Department in Isla Vista, the town adjacent to the University of California, Santa Barbara. Matthew felt somewhat awkward identifying himself as a private investigator before asking to speak to a detective regarding an old case. During his time on the job with the NYPD, he, like most of his colleagues, looked askance at civilians calling themselves private investigators. He and his fellow sworn officers of the law considered them bottom feeders, running after insurance cheats and adulterous spouses. Now here he was, lumped in the same category.

His call was transferred to a detective who sounded as if he had just graduated from high school. Matthew explained what information he needed and why.

Sitting quietly and ignoring the constant din outside of the lieutenant's office while he waited for the younger detective to call back, he opened his email on his phone and sent a note to Christian Schmid, choosing not to go through the UK address.

Fifteen minutes later, the detective in Isla Vista called back. As Matthew suspected, Jacqueline Henderson never attended Santa Barbara City College.

"Just for certainty," the detective said. "I did a quick survey of the colleges in the Santa Barbara vicinity. None have records of a Jacqueline Henderson enrolled as a student in the approximate time frame you asked about. But yes, a woman by the name of Angela Henderson died after falling off a cliff on Del Playa about five years ago. According to the case file, witness statements placed her at a party in a house a block and a half from where she fell. The report indicated she had been there with a much younger woman. Witnesses were able to positively identify Angela Henderson as the victim, but no one was sure who her companion was. Alcohol was thought to have been the contributory factor in what was labeled an accidental death."

Matthew thanked the officer for the information. He wasn't one to believe in coincidence, especially when it came to murder investigations. He had reason to suspect who the younger woman was and the role she played in escorting her mother into oblivion. There was the operant question of motivation, but they would get there in time.

Brown knocked on the lieutenant's door. "Show time, part two about to commence!"

Matthew returned to the monitor as Brown and Chin walked back into the interview room to resume their questioning.

Chin put a laboratory report in front of Jacqueline. "That is the DNA analysis of a blood specimen taken from the rock discovered at the scene of Brenda's death."

As Jacqueline and Livingston studied the sheet of paper, Chin presented other laboratory reports indicating where each specimen came from. He pointed to the results. "Here are the similarities, and that's where you'll find differences."

As he watched the proceedings, a thought struck Matthew. He wrote a note on a piece of paper and handed it to the civilian employee who had explained to him about the poor quality of the video feed. He asked her to pass the note to Brown.

"Jacqueline," Chin said. "We have the victim's DNA. On the next report, we have the DNA report for John Harrison. The lab is convinced that the victim was John's mother, Brenda Alves. We next have lab reports from three other samples, each containing the same DNA profile. That DNA was found to be completely different from Brenda's or John's. The first specimen came from a blood spot obtained from the rock we now believe was used as the murder weapon. The second came from a blood stain on Brenda's shirt. The last one is from a test of your saliva. All three are identical. They all contain your DNA. What's more, your DNA has no similarity whatsoever with John's."

Chin paused while Jacqueline and Livingston studied the results.

Suddenly, Jacqueline's face collapsed. As if a switch was flipped, she started crying. "It was an accident. I swear. I told her to put on better shoes, but she wouldn't listen. The trail was damp and slippery. She slipped, and before I could grab her, she fell down the embankment. When I got to her, she wasn't moving. I saw the rock she hit her head on."

Pleadingly, she looked at the two police officers and then at Livingston.

Chin looked on impassively. "You didn't hit her with the rock?"

Viciously, Jacqueline shook her head. "I should have gone for help, but I panicked. Plain and simple. I've had to live with the guilt for the last four years."

Brown stepped forward. "How did you convince her to go hiking?"

"Like I said, she loved hiking. I was the one who didn't like hiking. She wanted to go to the mountains. She was stressed out about something. We never had the chance to discuss what was bothering her."

"Yet she was wearing cheap street shoes."

Glancing down at the paper with Matthew's note, Brown made a sudden change of course. "Where were you the night Suzanne was murdered?"

It was as if she had received a gut punch. She gasped, trying to catch her breath. Livingston asked for water for his client. After taking a sip, she looked up at Brown. "What are you saying? Now you're accusing me of Suzanne's murder? Really? I was home that night until I got the call to come to John's house."

"Can anyone confirm your presence at home?"

"No, I was alone watching a movie. Wait a minute. I ordered pizza, and the delivery guy was the one who usually brings my orders. We talked for a while since he was done for the evening. His name is Tito something." She mentioned the name of the pizza joint. "Hey, I paid with a credit card. I can look up the account and show you the time stamp for the charge. That'll prove where I was."

Brown made a note before continuing. "Do you own a gun?"

Jacqueline shot back. "No! What's going on? I had nothing to do with Suzanne! I swear it." Jacqueline shoved her attorney's shoulder. "Do something. They can't accuse me of every murder in the past four years. Say something."

Livingston, again, patted her hand and murmured in her ear something neither detective could hear. He asked if they could take a break.

"Just give me a few more questions," Brown replied. "Jacqueline, we know you are not John's sister or any blood relative. That being the case, how can you be the executor of the trust when we have evidence to the contrary? John's father, who arranged for the trust, denied ever having you designated as executrix or beneficiary. In fact, he insisted you are not his daughter."

In an odd twist, Jacqueline jabbed a finger at Livingston. "Ask him. He's the lawyer."

Watching the drama play out, Matthew smiled. It was as he suspected.

Brown looked at a second piece of paper that had been given to him. It contained Matthew's handwriting. He passed it to Chin while the others watched. When Chin finished reading, he nodded at Brown, and they turned to face Livingston.

"Sir, do you happen to know an attorney by the name of Jack Renfro?"

Four years earlier

Chapter 48

Jacqueline stooped next to her car to remove the hiking boots and slip on a pair of sneakers. She retrieved a towel from the trunk to clean her hands with water from a bottle. Once done, she threw the towel into a large plastic bag filled with clothes. On the way home, she planned to parcel out the contents of the bag into several dumpsters. She was relieved to see no one else had parked at the trailhead. They had selected this trail because of its combination of difficulty and rarity of use. Pulling out onto the main road, she dialed the number on her cellphone.

When the call was answered, without a greeting, she said: "Done. All went well."

"Any issues?"

"None. It was steeper than I remembered and more slippery from the rain. There were a lot of thorny bushes. My hands got chewed up when I went to check her."

"Any problems getting her there?"

"Not when she was staring down the barrel of your gun. That thing is enough to scare anyone and make them very compliant." She chuckled. "I sat in the back of the car, and she drove. It was like she was my chauffeur; it was fun. When we got to the trail, a poke in the back, and she was on her way. I found a nice-sized rock. She didn't see it coming. It was easy to shove her down the muddy embankment. When I got down to her, I heard a gasp or two, and that really was it. I removed all her ID and was able to cut out the labels from her shirt and jacket as you instructed. Once I was done, I didn't hang around, but I'm sure mission accomplished. We can check her off our list. No one's going to find her for quite a while. The whole thing really was easier than with my mother; that bitch put up quite a fight, drunk as she was."

"Whatever it took, it's done. Now we wait."

Jacqueline pouted, though for no one's benefit. "When can we get the money?"

"Patience. This is a marathon and not a sprint. I have a meeting with Renfro in a week. I've pretty much convinced him to give the documents to me. It will take some time to transfer the trusteeship to me, but I'm not concerned. We need to move slowly. Once I am made trustee, I will need some more time before I can work on the changes necessary to make you executrix of the trust."

Jacqueline groaned.

"We're right where we need to be. We've one last step, but it's going to take a while. We don't want to raise any concerns. I'll take care of John when the time is right. We can't be too hasty. If we are too fast to pull the trigger, literally, someone may get curious, his mother disappears, and then him? That's too much of a coincidence. I don't like it. Time. That's what we need.

"Meanwhile, you're going to need to find someone to be his companion. Find someone who doesn't give a shit and doesn't care what happens to John. Someone whose only interest is a paycheck."

Jacqueline paused to consider how far they had come over the course of several years. Her mother did her part, claiming Jacqueline was that German's kid, so she could get a piece of the trust. When that didn't work out, it was left to her to get close to Brenda Alves, convincing her their children were half-siblings. Unfortunately, Brenda wouldn't talk to the German about amending the trust. Jacqueline cursed under her breath at the thought of Brenda not willing to part with a few bucks out of her moron son's largesse. When her mother started to get close to Brenda, she somehow had a change of heart and refused to participate any further in their plans. Steadfast in her decision, the die was cast, and it was left to Jacqueline to remove her from the equation.

Now with Barton or John, or whatever the hell he wanted to be called, left in the way, the course was clear. Take him out, and all the money would be hers, or theirs.

"Believe me, I am sick and tired of the day-to-day grind."

Jacqueline wasn't bemused by his statement. The only thing that would make her happy was to finish the project and have the kid taken care of. They had been working on this for years. She had to be old enough to be eligible to take control of the trust legally. Then they had to space out the interventions that needed to be made. Finally, she could see the light at the end of the tunnel. It was frustrating as hell, but she knew giving it a bit more time before the final act was taken was the smartest decision. "I know what you said, but the sooner you take him out, the happier we'll both be. Then you can throw away your 'Michael Livingston, Attorney at Law' shingle and never look back."

Jacqueline heard a deep sigh over the phone.

She was coming to what she knew was a dead zone for her phone. "Listen, I've got to hang up 'cause I'm going to lose you. Speak to you later, Dad."

Epilogue

Matthew sat at his dining table, thinking of Suzanne. The Celebration of Life was lovely, if such an event could ever be lovely, especially for someone so near and dear. He set his cup of coffee to one side and stared at the case notes spread out in front of him.

Stephen was grateful for the work Matthew, Brown, and Bernie did to bring Livingston and Jacqueline to justice. Over the last six weeks, Livingston and Jacqueline continued to point fingers at each other, but the truth had become apparent.

The drama began when Angela Henderson first laid eyes on Schmidt shortly after he arrived in Southern California. When she found out about Schmidt's family fortune in Switzerland, she had devised a plan to ensnare him. Before she had a chance to put her plan into action, he met Brenda and moved in with her. Angela kept tabs on Schmidt from afar so that when he left Brenda, she was suddenly by his side, offering a shoulder to cry on and more.

Already pregnant by her boyfriend, Michael Livingston, they arranged for her to seduce Schmidt to trap him into an arrangement to generously support "his" child. But he left for San Francisco before they could put their plan into action. Although never married, Livingston lived with Angela intermittently. Only later, after Angela managed to befriend Brenda, did they discover the existence of a trust created by Schmidt exclusively for the boy to cover his special needs, while providing nothing for his "daughter."

Through his legal channels, Livingston was able to track down the trust and pry it from Renfro's hands by concocting a story about being a friend of the family and close with the boy. It made sense for him to administer the trust since he understood the challenges the boy faced.

Livingston creatively altered critical words and amended the trust over the signature of Christian Schmidt, which he expertly forged. Once that was done, they only had to remove one last impediment: the boy's mother, who ruled Barton's, now John's, world. Matthew figured Angela Henderson must have had second thoughts about the plot and probably stood in the way of Michael Livingston's and Jacqueline's plans. Whether she knew about the plans to kill John to access the trust or not, Matthew didn't know, but he was willing to bet she said something to one or both of the plotters to seal her fate, and off a cliff she went.

With the passage of time, their patience was to be rewarded. Matthew remained puzzled by the length of time between the murders of Brenda and Angela and the attempt on John. Leafing through his notes, he could find nothing to explain their delay. He sat back in his chair and stared off.

Suddenly, it came to him; the answer was obvious. Suzanne was hired to fill the gap created after the removal of John's mother, Brenda. What neither Livingston nor Jacqueline anticipated was how strongly Suzanne cared for John. Matthew was willing to bet that her presence interfered with whatever plot the killers had concocted to remove John. In fact, over the course of time, they probably created several scenarios, all of which she had somehow foiled, unknowingly.

Another pang of sadness clutched at Matthew's chest. Unbeknownst to her, Suzanne no doubt saved John's life on any one of several occasions.

Ultimately, they were forced to choose the sloppiest option, using a gun in a park in a setting where their intent would be obvious and detection highly risky.

With no other option available to them, Michael Livingston took it upon himself to lie in wait for John. In his pocket was a thirty-five-year-old revolver, the one found hidden in his bedroom closet with two spent cartridges in its chambers.

The chime of the doorbell brought Matthew back to the present. He opened the front door of his condo, and John unceremoniously entered with Louis close behind. Looking past John to the street, Matthew saw the Uber driver pulling away from the curb. Over the six weeks since losing Suzanne, John had become more comfortable using the car service to take him to places other than the college.

As he watched, John proceeded directly to the kitchen to help himself to a glass of water. Matthew remained fascinated by how unfazed the young man was by what had transpired over the last couple of months. The fate of his mother, being the target of a killer who mistakenly murdered his companion, the betrayal by his "sister" and her father, any one of which would be a devastating revelation. And yet, John seemed to move on with his life. Already, he was considering his next project, another one he and his father would work on collaboratively.

While John poured some water from a container in the refrigerator, his dog inspected various crevices in the kitchen. Once John had what he needed, Matthew got a bowl to give Louis some water. Even though their familiarity was growing, Matthew was careful not to crowd John, respecting his continued discomfort with the proximity of others. But if their visits were to become routine, Matthew was going to have to buy a proper water bowl and maybe a couple of toys for Louis.

John must have had a session with Dr. Diaz today. The psychologist had agreed to meet with him weekly and recently instructed John to visit Matthew after each of their sessions to encourage him to leave his house and socialize.

"I heard from Michel Rousseau," Matthew said once man and dog were served.

"Did he test the movement?" John asked.

The Zeller Watch company had recently declared bankruptcy after the Geneva news services reported that the company was deeply in debt. Jean-Louis was in prison, charged with arranging a murder-for-hire scheme involving the death of the bank manager, Pierre Martin. His sister, Charice, was the subject of an ongoing police investigation into various illegal activities, business-related and otherwise, that she conducted, most of which were associated with her brother.

Rousseau parted ways with the company shortly after Matthew and Bernie met with him in Geneva. Currently, he was doing some consulting work from home, spending most of his time designing his first independently developed watch. He was still debating whether to start his own brand or join a friend who already had his own company. He expressly had no interest in working with a snake like Carlton Sommers, who, it was rumored, had given up his quest for Zeller. Sommers was said to have set his sights on another watch company he thought ripe for the picking.

Bernie and Matthew felt that there was nothing more to gain by pursuing Sommers, at least for the time being. They had the perpetrators, and they had no evidence, hard or soft, of Sommers' involvement in any of the criminal matters they investigated. The fear Sommers incited was nothing more than scare tactics geared to giving him a financial advantage as he worked toward acquiring Zeller. Maybe what he did was less than ethical, but not illegal, sadly. The only loose thread to the investigation was the identity of the man whom Dahlia found in John's living room. No one was ever able to hypothesize the role he or his possible companion played in the drama. Neither Matthew nor the police was able to get a lead on his whereabouts. After several weeks, the interest in pursuing the man waned and was finally shelved, except as far as Dahlia was concerned.

"Rousseau said he put your movement in a case," Matthew told him. "On the bench, when open to the environment, the movement worked as designed, but once he cased it and strapped the watch on his wrist, the mainspring did not wind. He tried it several times, and each time the mainspring ran out of power after about forty hours. Even going from hot to cold environments and back again, the mainspring would not wind."

John stared straight ahead.

"I'm sorry, John." Matthew was sad for him. He had invested a great deal of time in creating the movement. John looked blankly at Matthew. It was as if Matthew was telling him about the latest fashion trends in Paris. There was no sign of emotion. Clearly, he was listening but did not seem to be affected by the news.

"Rousseau told me his theory is that when the movement is exposed to the ambient environment, the temperature variation is sufficient to create differences in the expansion and contraction of the two metals, causing the mainspring to wind. But, when the movement is in a case, the temperature within the watch doesn't change much, if at all. And certainly not enough to take advantage of the two metals' different expansion points. Then, because the critical components are on the back of the movement, closer to a person's skin, there's even less of a fluctuation. We are warm-blooded, so our body's temperature is maintained except in extreme situations."

Matthew had a passing thought: would the watch movement work better for a cold-blooded animal such as a lizard? But do they need watches? Highly unlikely.

John remained undisturbed by the bad news. Matthew expected him to be crushed. All that work over numerous years had been for naught.

"Again, I'm sorry," Matthew repeated.

"For what?"

"For the time and effort spent on a failed project."

John shook his head and replied. "I met my father and you."

Matthew nodded and smiled. "And I'm glad you did."

John finished his water.

"I hate to cut this short." Matthew stood up. "But I have to go. I have a grief support group meeting starting in half an hour. I'll call you later when I get home."

John looked up in Matthew's general direction. "Can I come?"

Acknowledgments

In 2002, Stephen Phillips, a Hungarian-born watchmaker and founder of the Budapest Watch Company, announced the creation of the Eternal Watch System, or EWS, to the watch world. Using a bi-metallic coil, he claimed that with temperature variations of as little as two degrees, the differences in expansion and contraction of the two metals caused the coil to wind the mainspring of a watch. The revolutionary winding system was granted a US patent in October 2002. He claimed to have built a functional prototype and was planning on marketing the movement. Sadly, Mr. Phillips died of natural causes in 2004. After his passing, the EWS disappeared and was never seen in a commercially produced watch.

While the concepts of John Harrison's creation are similar to the EWS, there was no subterfuge or criminal activity ever associated with the EWS. The rest of the story is entirely fictional, as are all the characters.

Watch companies, large and small, whether corporate or family-owned, present us with machines every year that are mechanical marvels, built to work flawlessly for decades, if not centuries. What is also true is the amazing and innovative watches that a growing number of independent watchmakers, working in their homes, garages, or leased spaces, are creating.

I want to extend my deepest gratitude to those who provided incredibly valuable input as I developed this first-in-a-series novel. Thanks go to my kind readers, Paula Fell, Tim Rhone, Tim and Sheryl Brown, Rich Haier, and Mike Roeder. Also, I appreciate Rick Rabin for his legal-eagle advice.

To Lisa Shiroff of Tasfil Publishing, thank you for just about everything. Your patient guidance has been invaluable. This book would never have existed were it not for your teaching and encouragement. Who would have thought any of this would have been possible when I sat down and wrote the first few pages? Writing this book has been fun, to be sure. Editing could be a headache, but you made it educational and, in so doing, helped me learn how to put my thoughts and ideas onto the page.

Lastly, and always, to my wife, who, through patience, partnership, and love, read the book at least four times during its course of creation. I have enjoyed our "process" as the book developed, and together we formed an editing team. I promise never to leave you wondering what's next in the stories to come, at least not for too terribly long.

Keep reading for an excerpt from Mitch Katz's memoir, *Time on My Hands*

A Family Affair

I am part of a family of collectors.

My father was the first to manifest the collector gene. Stamp collecting was his passion. He devoted a lot of his free time to the pursuit of working with and furthering his collection. My mother collected pieces of china and teaspoons as souvenirs from their travels but never developed a consuming interest or desire to create a collection in the truest sense of the word. Products of the Depression, with modest resources, my parents were cautious when it came to spending money on non-essentials. However, that did not prevent my father from building his collection.

My sister collects in a different fashion. She frequents antique shops, yard sales, and second-hand stores. Possessing an uncanny ability to see the beauty and uniqueness of things that, to others, would be nothing more than pieces of bric-a-brac, she is able to take odd pieces of china, dolls, or fabric structures and create an admirable antique collection. She is an excellent practitioner of the saying that one man's trash is another's treasure.

Over the course of our years together, my wife, an avid tea drinker, has developed a collection of teapots. She does freely admit to being a collector of teapots. Some of the teapots are utilitarian while others are pure works of art. Building her collection has been a family affair. Whenever my father came for a visit during the summer, we would visit a gallery for their yearly exhibit of teapots. Traditionally, he bought her one handcrafted teapot on each visit. To repay his generosity, we gave him the invitation to the show. The postage used on the invitation was composed of stamps from the 1950s and 1960s. A win for both collectors.

Although my wife denies it, she also collects scarves. Wherever we might be, should she come upon a display of scarves, she is unable pass by without stopping and carefully inspecting the wares. Color, design, and texture are all variables that can tempt her. She shares this passion with our daughter-in-law, who has already benefited from my wife's collection. My wife insists that she is not a collector. But when someone has over a hundred scarves and shows no ability to walk away from a scarf that catches her eye, she definitely qualifies as a collector. She insists that since the collective monetary value of her scarves is less than one of my watches, she is not a collector. Sorry, my dear. No, that is not how it works. Being a collector is not defined by the inherent value of the items being collected.

From an early age, both of our sons have been collectors. Our older son started by collecting rocks. He, together with his brother, also began collecting what they labeled as "odds and ends." What exactly defined an "odd" versus an "end" my wife and I never could discern, but they knew.

Starting in second grade, our older son has had a love for baseball. For years he collected baseball cards and related paraphernalia. That passion served us, his parents, quite well as a tool to reward good behavior or as consolation for having teeth extracted. His collection remains in our house. We will not commit the same "crime" of discarding his cards and memorabilia as my mother did with mine.

In time, his collecting gene changed focus. He has always had a love of music and now has an ever-growing collection of guitars, amplifiers, and electronic gear. The "collecting gene" is strong in him, and we are seeing signs of passage to his son, who desires all things having to do with trains.

In high school, our younger son developed a deep interest in cars. The more exotic the better. Model cars became his passion throughout his high school years. In college, his collecting interests turned to denim. He, by his own admission, joined a collective of "denim nerds," people interested in the history of denim and who buy and trade samples of vintage denim. They also actively support artisans who currently work with denim. Recently, he has developed an appreciation of fine art (something shared with his parents). Time will tell if and to what he will turn his collecting eye. The collecting gene is strong in him, though he might not realize it at this time.

When speaking of collectors and collecting, it is necessary to define terms. What defines a collection can be debated, but it is reasonable to state that to be considered a collector there is the requirement that there be an element of ownership of the item of interest. The number of items possessed is not a part of the definition, but it is assumed that the collector will possess at least several of the particular category.

When trying to define who a collector is, there needs to be differentiation from the enthusiast and the "flipper." There are, of course, those who work on the commercial side of the business, but they are not part of this discussion. The definition of these categories—and there may be others to include, but for simplicity I am keeping it to these three general categories—can also be debated.

The "flipper" is someone who will purchase a collectible with the expectation of selling it in short order for a profit. This might be for financial gain, much like trading stocks, or to fund another purchase that will then be sold as well. This group is composed of people who see collectibles only as commodities, a source of income generation. There may be an appreciation for the objects that pass through their hands, but they have no strong desire for ownership. They may own a few of the collectibles, but their motivation is primarily financial. This group serves as a source of information for collectors when there is a desire to place a valuation on one's collection. Unfortunately, this group often detracts from the beauty of the collectibles by treating them merely as chattel and putting the monetary value far ahead of the appreciation of the artistry or intricacy of the particular piece. The interest regarding the workmanship is only in how it affects the financial return for the piece. For the purists, those who appreciate the work for what it is, this can be very distressing. Flippers can contribute to the creation of a false buzz and at times unwarranted inflated valuations and excess demand for particular models. Sadly, for the collectors, the insertion of the discussion of financial gains in collecting can put a cloud over the joys of collecting and diminish appreciation for other, more skillfully produced products. It is a constant challenge for collectors to try to counter the financial and hype-based discussion with education regarding what separates something of quality from others, emphasizing workmanship, artistry, technology, or the like.

The enthusiast is someone who has a true passion for a particular category of collectibles but does not extend their interest toward ownership. These are the people who read extensively, post on social media frequently, and at times develop a reputation for expertise. They might possess an encyclopedic knowledge of the subject and be an excellent reference source. Some may own a few of the particular category of collectibles, but for them the greater pleasure of the hobby is the ability to accumulate deep funds of knowledge rather than possession either because of personal preference or financial considerations.

The collector extends knowledge to actual possession. Some say that the collector is possessed by passion and obtains the collectibles with the goal of long-term ownership. At some level, the collector is someone who identifies one or more classes of objects that stimulate an interest and the desire for possession. Some collectors are of the belief that in order to be considered a collector, one must have a focus and go deep into one subset of a particular collectible category (with regard to watches, developing a single brand collection or a certain type of watch such as dive watches, military watches, or chronographs). Others consider a collector to be one who acquires pieces based on one's own criteria, no matter how eclectic the choices may be. (Special note: words in bold are defined in the glossary.)

When collecting something like stamps, coins, or baseball cards, there are a finite number of varieties produced, and it is easy to say what is owned and what is needed to complete a particular collection. Building such a collection is a process of acquisition of pieces that fill the empty slots in an album or allow checkboxes to be filled in (it is the old game of "need 'em, got 'em"). With regards to other collectibles, such as watches, there is a huge diversity to choose from. Millions of pieces are produced yearly, with different sizes, shapes, varieties, and price points. Building a collection takes a dedication to whatever principle fits a collector's objectives or passion. A watch collector may "need" a certain model or complication to fill out their collection, but more often the desire is more of a "want" when the particular piece speaks to the collector for a reason known to themselves: aesthetics, emotional, financial, technical, or the like. For me, my collection is dictated by my own guiding principles; I obtain what I like. I collect what appeals to me, whether it is based on uniqueness, technical innovation, artistry, story, or just fun. For whatever reason, a timepiece must resonate with me. Essential is the emotional response I experience whenever I put on the particular watch.

On the Importance of Making Connections with Your Collections

My wife and I collect art and have for decades. A number of years ago, we decided to look for a painting by a particular artist. We already owned several small pieces by her, but we wanted a larger one for a specific spot in our house. The owner of a gallery we frequent told us he had a painting by the artist that was an excellent representation of her genre. When we saw the piece in the gallery, we were interested.

We thought that it would go well in our collection, and the gallerist allowed us to take it home so we could "live" with it for a couple of weeks.

We brought it home, and for the next two weeks the painting sat on the floor propped up against my desk, in front of the space we were looking to fill. We never hung it on the wall. After two weeks we realized that for some unexplained reason, we could not make an emotional connection with the painting even though it was exactly what we thought we wanted. Ultimately, we returned it to the gallery. The owner was fine with the return and accepted the painting back without question. As we were talking to him, he flipped through some transparencies of other artworks (yes, it was quite a while ago, when transparencies of artworks were still a thing). I spied a piece that I instantly recognized as one created by a different artist, whose work we also knew. I asked about it, and he told me it was in his bedroom in the back of the gallery. With his permission, I went to his bedroom, saw the piece, and immediately had to sit down on the floor as I was emotionally overcome by it. Within minutes my wife and I agreed to buy that piece of art, and it has been hanging in our study ever since. The emotional connection was instantaneous. I cannot express in words why one was right for us while the other was not. However, I have learned that if I trust my eye *and* my heart, I will not be led astray.

It is my opinion that many people do not have that trust in themselves. Too many want the "right" piece and worry too much about what others may think (made worse by the advent of "influencers" on social media telling us what to think, feel, and be). I believe that one must kiss a lot of frogs before one finds the prince. After frequent exposure to many possibilities, one slowly develops a sense of what appeals to them and what does not. With that, it will then be easier to start building one's own collection, if the trust and confidence is there.

About the Author

Mitch Katz lives in Southern California with his wife and his two rottweilers, Blood and Jaws. You can connect with Mitch at Mitch@Tasfil.com.

www.ingramcontent.com/pod-product-compliance
Lightning Source LLC
Chambersburg PA
CBHW030548310726
48979CB00010B/2079/J